Dudes and Demons. An Unauthorized And Unofficial Guide to Supernatural

Mila Hasan

Published in 2009 by New Generation Publishing

First Edition

British Library C.I.P.
A CIP catalogue record for this title is available from the British Library

Published by New Generation Publishing

Contents

For those we love…for those we have lost…

I Love Supernatural and after watching the show, I had to write about it, from a fan perspective and beyond... I've included lots of background and all those 'quotey' bits. So hopefully it's almost like we're virtually there with our beloved Sam (Jared) and Dean (Jensen) and the rest of the cast and crew!

Background to *Supernatural*

Many people would say that, first of all *Supernatural* is a show that has been done before if you look at all those that have gone before: - *X-Files* all about the paranormal, aliens, government conspiracies, unsolved cases, mysteries. *Charmed* all about magic, witches, covens, demonic folklore, and monsters. *Buffy the Vampire Slayer* about vampires, monster, teen angst and *Angel*. I'm not one of them.

Supernatural is more darker than this and delves more into lore and the occult lore. There's a more adult tone of content.

The appeal of *Supernatural* is many-fold as opposed to two. Not only is it based on urban legends, hence there's a sense of reality or actuality as opposed to just plain fiction and what might be – (as the *X-Files* said it best "The truth is out there!") Even if to the average viewer the stories still seem far-fetched. Maybe from a purely entertainment standpoint that could be said about this show. However, that's just the tip of the iceberg. Scratch the surface and step inside there's a lot going on here than the simple battle of good versus evil, or just finding a mystery every week and running with it until it's solved - with a joke and a song or two thrown in for fun! Eric Kripke says, "The idea is that we took a heroic structure, the Joseph Campbell hero structure and crossed it with *An American Werewolf in London* and that's the closest way to describe the tone of the show."

There's a real family struggle too: brothers, father and sons – finding each other through the emotional turmoil that claimed their childhood and their innocence – family deaths, lost friends and lovers. Once estranged, attempting to be a family loosely tethered together like fine strands of silk. The burden to carry on, fighting for good, protecting the unsuspecting populace from the unknown – everything people would find absurd and irrational if they ever knew what was happening right under their noses. It's within our realm and understanding to still believe in the unexplainable and impossible.

So it's not *Charmed* though it's charming! It still entails the family dynamic. It's not meant to be seen as a replacement for any of the aforementioned shows, nor for any other para-psychological, 'normal', teen angst drama. Thank goodness it's past that, though we get adolescent behaviour from the duo at times and the jokes and teasing by Dean of Sam, it's all good natured. It's unique and has its own personality and presence.

Originally Eric Kripke had envisioned Sam and Dean being reporters investigating legends in a newspaper column, rather than two brothers on a 'road trip'. Well, just as well it didn't turn out that way since that's been done several times.

In Canada *Supernatural* is advertised as *Hot Guys. Hot Show.* In the UK ITV advertises it as *Scary Just Got Sexy.* Though it's not hard to understand why. *Supernatural* aired on the *WB Network* in the US on September 13th 2005 which is why creator, writer, Eric Kripke was ecstatic about being on that Network. He said, "On The WB you can be a modest success but still be a success. The WB is excellent at nurturing shows they believe in and letting them grow. On some of the other networks we might have gotten lost in the shuffle." Also in the title to season 2 watch out for the first 'A' forming a pentagram.

The show is successful since it filled the void left by other shows with similar themes. He continues, "How confident was I that the show would catch on? I passionately believed in the show itself. Did I know it would catch on? I look at those things as out of my control: all I can do is make the best show possible. We had produced a couple of episodes before we started airing and I knew that what we had on our hands was pretty great, and all I could hope for was that an audience found us. They keep coming and hopefully we'll keep growing." Eric describes the show as "the bastard step-child of the *X Files.*

AOL.com's vote to find peoples' *Guilty Pleasures* placed *Supernatural* at number 14. Why, since it's not a guilty pleasure! It's an outright pleasure and where's the shame in admitting that.

Kripke hands all the success of the show over to its two charismatic and gorgeous stars: Jared Padalecki and Jensen Ackles. Kripke says, "The boys are so wildly charismatic and so believable as brothers. It's a real grounding influence on the show and people respond to them." They do respond to the stories, the dark atmosphere and the scary horrors. But continues Kripke, "They're responding to the scares and the humour because they're responding to Jared and Jensen, to the relationship between their characters. Nothing would work if you didn't have these two guys." So incredibly generous a comment since some credit should be given to the writers too and the rest of the crew, but we don't mind Jared and Jensen being the centre of attention! As I say, sometimes a show is only as good as its cast but with this you get a great cast and a brilliant show too!

Eric gave Jensen and Jared books and DVDs on urban legends to help them focus on the premise of the show. In fact, did you know when Jensen and Jared auditioned formally for their roles; it was a done deal since no one else was up against them for the parts. They read the parts for the Network and got their roles there and then!

The cast and crew have varying comments and thoughts about the show. Jared says, "It's truly scary and not just one of those shows that they call a scary show when it's not. Eric Kripke is bringing some great dialogue to the screen and we just have talented people working around us. We put on a fun show, we have a good time doing it and we're working hard to give people a show that they will enjoy. I think it's one of those shows that's going to last for years. Everybody who has seen it has been pleasantly surprised with the quality."

As does Jensen, what's scary is how they both think alike, no, actually portraying brothers on screen, it's amazing how they do think alike. Jensen continues, "We're scaring the hell out of everyone with a small horror movie each week…you can look it all up on the net and there's a story about everything. The fact that we're dealing with the stuff of legends separates us from a lot of other shows!"

Sam and Dean remind Kripke of *The Defiant Ones* (the Sidney Poitier and Tony Curtis movie about two convicts chained together who escape from prison and go on the run.) Kripke: "When either one of them goes too far ahead of the other one, the other one starts dragging behind." Sam went through anger over Jess's death and Dean was reassuring – that it would take time to find the demon, exact revenge. He continues, "Sam started to settle into his new life on the road, so now Sam is starting to exhibit a certain amount of impatience again because of the hunt for Dad had been going [slowly.]"

As season 1 progressed, Kripke wanted to get more into the story behind the brothers, having their father turn up a lot more, what killed their mother and Jess. He says, "We fleshed out Missouri [the psychic fortuneteller in **1.10 Home**] with her good side and we'll start fleshing out the evil demonic side." With their respective adversaries coming into the picture and getting in the way. Kripke also wants to put in a mythology episode about every few episodes into the show; but wants the rest to be fun for first time viewers.

One aspect of the introductory Pilot episode was the events that happened to an ordinary family in humdrum Kansas. Something so unexpected and shocking that the event would resonate throughout the entire first season and onto season 2 and indeed the entire series. Thus establishing a recurring theme or arc: that of a mother waking to find an eerie dark figure hovering over her baby's crib, whom she mistakenly believes is her husband. This is repeated again in episode **1.21** and subsequently as Sam and Dean discover, this happened to many other children all over the country.

Sam's girlfriend, Jessica also suffers the same fate as Mom but that was more so as to draw Sam into the demon hunt with Dean. Also not only do they lose their mother – but coincidentally Dean shows up looking for Sam to search for Dad who has gone missing whilst "hunting." (One of main themes throughout this show.) So significantly, it not only turns out to be what they do best: hunt demons and the like, but also a hunt for Dad. Following up on a lead, or, directing them to a hunt, or case, that of a dead woman, could she be classed as a zombie. (See **2.4 Children Shouldn't Play With Dead Things.**)

For John Shiban, writer and executive producer on the show, the pilot "had two important things for me because obviously a lot of *X-Files* type shows have been tried and failed. This had a good franchise in having a great engine, the two brothers on the road seeking monsters and demons. The other thing is it had chemistry between the two stars, which is something you can't make happen. David Duchovny and Gillian Anderson had it on the *X-Files*. It was a happy accident and so is this. Speaking of; will either David or Gillian guest star on the show as it's made it to a third season. Thank you. For getting us to season 3 and even seasons 4 and 5, someone must have been listening to us, the fans. Wonder if anyone read the unofficial online petition which, thus far, over a thousand number of fans signed to *SOS: Save Our Supernatural*. Though some of us were a bit too passionate (like Moi and also wrote a personal letter to the network! Well I guess someone had to tell them about what a great show they'd be losing out on so soon!) Okay digression and rant over!

John Shiban: "The clangers when you have characters with this much back story and baggage is they become selfish and you don't want that. You still want them to be heroes so we try to keep the balance of the personal and what they are doing for all of us. You don't always want 'me, me, me' because that gets tiresome. We also want to keep the big/little brother dynamic going without it getting too comical or too heavy. The show is fun or it can be dark sometimes but we want to keep it *Butch and Sundance.* We want those fun bickering moments [as they're easy to relate to] among brothers rather than the darker ones. To tell you the truth those are the scenes Eric and I both beat on. You want all the emotions too and the deaths of Jessica and Mom are big stuff!"

As *Butch and Sundance* are mentioned, it would be great to have Jensen and Jared play the leads in a remake of this, even if it was only a TV movie.

Shiban's shocked at how much violence and images in the show were allowed to be included by the Network. "They are not being irresponsible. The viewer-ship has changed and there are so many more options compared to even when I was on *X Files*. There is stuff we've done on *Supernatural* that they would never let us do." Well that's the Fox Network for you. They either cancel a show when it's a great premise [such as *Dark Angel, Tru Calling, Killer Instinct*] or don't bother with it.

He continues, "We want to answer a few questions and ask a lot more. We want to expand on the mythology and not make it smaller so Meg will come back and we learn more about her. She's the mysterious girl Sam met in **1.11Scarecrow** and we see again in **1.16Shadow**. We're just bringing our very last story and it is big, exciting and opens the door to so many possibilities. The Dad comes back and we see a dynamic we've been dangling out there, which is the family working together [not for very long!] They do manage to get close to their goals!"

Hey even some of the *CSI* shows are getting in on the *Supernatural* bandwagon. In *CSI:Miami,* Calleigh mentions urban legends, i.e. this one about having mines on beaches at the time of the Cuban missile crisis in a season 5 episode. Also Five (in the UK) which airs all three *CSI* shows advertised a weekend of *CSI* episodes as *Death By CSI* and in the trailer said, 'Unnatural facts, Supernatural evidence'. Hey, Sam and Dean are kind of *CSIs* for spirits and all things supernatural aren't they: finding evidence of their existence, who or what is behind the killings; unexplained events…especially **2.14 Born Under a Bad Sign** when Sam is possessed. See how they "process the evidence." If the show is ever cancelled (not anytime within the next three years at least! We hope) it can come back with a new title: *Supernatural: CS* (i.e. crime scene.)

We learn about the brothers, their relationship, volatile at times, in the past and today. How Sam wanted something better for himself, went to university to become a lawyer and how Dean stayed behind, to carry on the family tradition or as he calls it, "the family business." This appears to be belittled and seems trivial in nature to Sam's achievements. Though this alters as the series progresses. Also they have changes of heart. Sam wants to go back to school and this is what Dad wants for him too. Dean wants them to stay together and this isn't what Sam wants to hear. (Dean would've probably become the manager of an all chick rock band or something. What do you think?)

Jared likes the mythology part of the show too, "For me it is totally more interesting. What I originally loved about the show is that there was that element, that mythology. In school, you study Joseph Campbell and archetypes you recognize in movies like *Star Wars* and *The Matrix*. You see good v evil, the trusted companion and the friendly demon, the unfriendly family member…there is a whole list and that is what got me interested in the show. One of the reasons we're still keeping the monsters of the week is because it is just fun. Especially when trying to get new viewers, as opposed to having them tune in [to see us] talking about if Sam's a demon, and if he has demon blood, or if his Dad or Mom was a demon."

The reason season 2 was commissioned according to Jensen is because of the underlying story of the relationship of Sam and Dean as brothers and their feelings towards one another. It's also very family orientated in its approach, 'whereas other shows concentrated on the lone crusader' or roving reporter; or partners. This one has the fraternal element which makes it stand out. Jensen: "One of the things we pride ourselves on is the brother's banter. You see then bicker and get in fights and get upset."

In season 2 it's all change, to a degree. Dean no longer wants to hunt but Sam does. As for accusing Sam of carrying on Dad's tradition out of guilt, me thinks Dean only stayed around, not only because he was the eldest son so more responsibility fell on his shoulders, but something to do with a little matter of letting the shtriga (the witch in **1.17 Something Wicked**) get away when it came for Sam. He had to redeem himself in Dad's eyes for that.

Season 2 of *Supernatural* found itself on the newly created CW Network and débuted in September 2006. Dad had made it to **2.1 In the Hour of** My **Dying** but only for the first episode. Kripke: "Everyone who was pissed that Denny [Jeffrey Dean Morgan's character in *Grey's Anatomy* which is scheduled against *Supernatural* in the US on Thursdays at 8/9pm Central] was dead. Come over and watch *Supernatural*. But he was only in the season 2 opener! Coincidentally, season 2 of *Grey's Anatomy* shown in the UK on Five is scheduled against season 2 of *Supernatural* on ITV2 on Sunday nights at 9pm. Throughout February 2007 and onwards.

Though *Grey's Anatomy* got double episodes so ran from 8-10pm.

About season 2, Jared comments Sam and Dean also fought a lot. "We're keeping it interesting. We definitely have found our niche this year. The writers, actors and everyone involved with the show, we're all trying new things. I definitely feel like here in the second season we've had lots of strong showings and I'm very proud of a lot of our episodes. The pro and con of being up in Vancouver is that while I don't get the benefit of seeing how successful *Supernatural* is. I also am not subject to how successful *CSI* and *Grey's Anatomy* are. I get to focus on my work without having these other shows thrown in my face, so to speak."

However, Dad was never meant to feature so extensively in the new show, primarily as it's about the brothers and their journey of self-discovery, bonding and demon hunting. Said Kripke, "We didn't want the search for John Winchester to be endless and we were always interested in what happens to the dynamic of these brothers, who we've come to know very well, once John comes in as a way to really mix things up. We've never pictured and still never picture John to be a continuous part of the show. It's never going to be the Winchester family show, it's always the show about the brothers, but we think bringing John in to mix things up and then to have him leave and then to have him come back…is a way to handle this because we didn't want it to be endless. We knew the demon mythology was going to be for multiple seasons, but we didn't want the search for Dad to go on."

So what better way than to write out Dad by having him sacrifice himself in order to save Dean; leaving the dilemma, for some, of whether he would've done the same if it was Sam who needed saving. Although Dean says to Sam that Sam dislikes Dad, when they find out for sure what Dad really did, would Sam pose that question to himself: 'what if he had been in Dean's position?'

Urban legends are also a particular favourite of Kripke. "Now that we've burned through the greatest hits of urban legends [or urbane as I like to say] we can get into the ones I really love which are really obscure ones that maybe fifteen people know about. So there's a great scarecrow skinning people legend…phantom automobiles which are just spirits of people. There are stories and legends of actual spirits of trucks! So we're doing a *Duel* episode, we're doing our version of *The Texas Chainsaw Massacre* which I'm excited about, based on a real family from folklore…back wood sadists and we have a witch coming up that I'm really excited about."

Eric comments, "We have the best fans in the world. I want to get the message out to the fans that we want to mobilize that army of 'Tell your friends'. {Already done that and I didn't even need any prompting!}. We want to come back for season 4 [and they did] but that's far more in the audience's hands, the fans hands than it is in ours. So, uh, tell your friends! Have parties." Perhaps *Supernatural* should've done something similar to the marketing for *The Blair Witch Project* when they came up with the whole Blair witch legend, but also it probably wouldn't work for a TV series. But the premise is there, only maybe that can still happen now for season 5. Although many people would be weary of the device now. However, if done right it could give some weight to season 5. I would've thought of something, but at this point, not sure where season 5 is heading. Okay, I haven't had any psychic moments or thoughts, as I seem to have had for certain episodes and storylines!!

Eric says the show does have an arc, but you don't need to know it – which is true because mostly the episodes stand out on their own, i.e. stand alone. On the other hand, if you don't understand everything happening, you'll enjoy what you've seen nonetheless, so much so, that you'll be jumping for the DVDs and catching up in no time to our 'hunks with weapons in their trunks', hey that sounds rude!! Oops. I guarantee it, or I'll eat Jensen's cowboy hat when I get my hands on it, or another piece of pie!!

The show looks set to run and Kripke likes the idea of this too. "I walked into the season with a list of seventy five ideas of viable urban legend stories and those were just my favourites. It's a subject, urban legends that I've been passionate about and obsessed with my whole life. It's kind of my hobby which I've done whether I was getting paid for it or not. So there's a limitless, endless supply of these stories all across the country and more regionalized ones are the most fascinating because they speak to a particular place and time." There are hundreds of them he says, and he has hundreds in his bookcase..."We have a very full gas tank."

Eric also got his wish to have Mitch Pileggi on the show, he played Mom's father in **4.3 In the Beginning**. He wants Bruce Campbell on the show. (That's a tribute to Bruce there, when the name Campbell was given to Mary's side of the family.) Eric originally wanted Bruce to play Dad; the role played by Jeffrey Dean Morgan, but was pleased Jeffrey did get the part. Bruce did guest in a season 5 episode of *X Files* entitled, **Daemonicus** where he played a demon who wanted a normal family.

Eric considers Sam and Dean to be "the descendants" of Ash from *Evil Dead 2*. That's whom Ash was named for in season 2. He considers this to be one of the greatest movies ever made and attributes *Supernatural* to being inspired by the *Evil Dead*.

Jared clearly enjoys the show, but it is hard going and tough at times. "Supernatural is super physical. They had us working out with a physical trainer and kickboxers. It has been very physical which is exciting to me. That was actually one of the huge draws about this – you get to be a little action hero. You get to do a couple of your own stunts, fight, learn about that sword/gun and how to use a whip properly. I've been bruised up. I think we did a fight scene and I got knocked. Here and there you get knocked around a bit but you're too busy playing tough to realize how it hurts. Then you wake up the next morning and you're 'oww that hurts'. What did I do? Oh yes!"

Jared's had girls screaming at him and made top hunk lists. He feels, "That is funny. Anytime I read some flattery fan mail or have this girl screaming or proposing, it really doesn't compute with me. It is like I am standing outside of myself and looking at what is going on. That is interesting but I can't really explain it. It is a weird feeling and ultimately it comes down to it, is flattering. If it will get two more people to watch the series then great. I would love to be a heart throb because we are putting together a good show."

Referring to the 'hot show'. He continues, "Urban legends are fun but I hope the family dynamic and the relationship between the brothers is why they tune into the show. All the other stuff can come and go, the fighting, the action, the cars and demons – that stuff is neither here nor there at the end of the day. It is just whether you care about these two guys and whether you can relate. [Of course we can and do!] Even though they are going through these problems in a crisis situation, can you say, 'Oh yeah, I've had a horrible argument with my brother, sister, the person I'm closest to and that is how I screamed at them or how I felt when they screamed at me."

Think everyone can do that – me and my sis we argue all the time, make jokes and fun of each other – that's just what siblings do. Also share in the grief of losing a loved one, just as Sam and Dean lost their father – at a moment when we were going through the grief; the emotions; of losing our Dad too. So it's not that difficult to relate at all and part of the appeal is knowing we all go through this in real life, what they've been through in screen life. Maybe appeal isn't the right word, maybe draw upon sounds better, as we draw upon their experiences of life.

Kim Manners directed 53 out of 201 episodes of the *X Files;* was semi-retired after the *X Files*, when David Nutter sent him the pilot episode tape of *Supernatural*. "I loved Jensen Ackles and Jared Padalecki and thought they had great chemistry and it seemed an interesting premise so I came out to do an episode, **Dead In The Water**," which was liked by everyone so it shunted further up the schedules than originally planned to be shown.

He was then asked to become co-executive producer and join the rest of the team. After taking time out to think about it, he decided he'd do the show; as Jensen and Jared are great to work with and he also liked the show. "It's a funny show – it's a spooky show and the guys are just great." He found the whole premise of the show interesting, "The story centres round two boys that have lost several years of their lives together. Sam went to college and Dean was hunting evil with his Dad so there's four years of each of their lives that they have not shared, so there's a certain discovery between the two boys that we are trying to capture and just making a good healthy brother to brother relationship is the key. I think if we can capture that then we're halfway there."

He also says you have to put a lot of detail into making the supernatural element work, as in the *X Files*. "If you don't stretch the moment before the scare, it's lost. You've gotta build the tension and that involves shooting more film so directors have got to come in and be very prepared, and that is really the approach to this series." The important thing is to make it believable which is the exceptional challenge for any director.

On January 25th 2009, Kim Manners sadly lost his battle with lung cancer and passed away at Cedars Sinai Medical Center. He was 59. He made his directorial debut in a 1979 episode of *Charlie's Angels,* **Angels Remembered**. Kim was raised in Hollywood and worked with his father, as well as his brother, Kelly. He had a varied and successful career, being associated with such hit shows as *X Files, Baywatch, Mission: Impossible, Buffy The Vampire Slayer, Angel, 21 Jump Street.*

Familiarity and Similarity to Other Shows

Kripke comments *Supernatural* has got similarities to the *X-Files* and yes, it's got similarities to *Buffy*, but it's also its own animal. "It's a new kind of show where it's a version of a genre show that people hadn't seen before, with our balance of humour we hope, and legitimate scares. Just doing a scary movie each week and also makes it feel unique. All these factors added up." Not surprisingly since people like executive producers, John Shiban, Kim Manners and director David Nutter all worked on the *X-Files* too.

Jensen Ackles doesn't seem to think the show is similar to *Buffy* "as they're two ordinary guys with non super-human powers, just old shot guns." More of an in-yer-face scary horror. Kripke wanted to keep it away from stuff that's a little more flashy and sleek. He wanted "two good ol' boys, kind of like *The Dukes of Hazzard*. Good old muscle car with shotguns coming out of the back of the trunk." Well, *Dukes of Hazzard* minus the shotguns – they may have used them but they didn't keep any in the trunk. Oh and the squeaky doors on the Impala, are just sound effects courtesy of the sound editing crew! Since on the DVD of the show, the blooper reel doesn't have any such sounds. So that's another reason why the squeaking didn't disappear when Dean fixed the car in season 2 and I take it no amount of oil will make it disappear either. Still it's all good, as they say, like another characteristic trademark of the show. An urban legend all of its own, the car doors squeaking, that is!

Some people have likened the show to the 2002 film *Frailty* starring Bill Paxton about two brothers who were brought up by their father to fight demons.

Supernatural has also been likened to *Nightstalker* the remake of the 1970's series Kolchak. The executive producer of this was Frank Spotnitz (also of *X-Files* fame) that didn't excel in the ratings. John Shiban commented after reading the pilot Frank had written for this show and doesn't believe they wanted the same audience as *Supernatural*: "because our show is meant to be a popcorn movie and *Nightstalker* was trying to tackle bigger themes and darker fears of the day. I don't mean to demean the other show but that was a little more adult than us. We want to have fun and rock'n'roll a little. I never thought we were in competition but if we were on the same night I feel I might have felt differently. It is inevitable because everyone is trying to find the next *X-Files* but *Supernatural* really is a different beast." Something some critics still find hard to understand and need to have it hammered home to them. As they can't do without forever comparing this show with others!

As Season two progressed and concluded, Eric was nothing short of enthusiastic for the shows continuation, which we're all relieved about since it was facing an uncertain future at the time. He said, "We're working hard to make a show we can be proud of, we all really care about it, so it's gratifying that it's getting the response that it is. I have to be shameless and say to the fans, 'If you love the show, please spread the word. Let your friends know there's a smart genre show on the CW – a show for people who dig *Buffy* and *X Files*. Drag 'em in front of the TV and make 'em watch.' We don't get a lot of marketing and word of mouth is the only way we're gonna get a long, healthy series run. We need your help." Hey no need to ask twice, I've already converted my friends to the show, so that should make a hefty audience for you. Especially since we do nothing but eat, sleep, breathe, and even dream *Supernatural* (now work out the latter!)

On the Mulder and Scully question, Jensen would want to be Mulder which we already know from the show! (Specifically **2.7 The Usual suspects**.) Jared wouldn't mind wearing a wig! Would that include the obligatory skirt and heels too? Jensen: "I'm not sure about the wig but if we taste a little bit of their success and longevity, that'd be awesome."

Jared wanted the show in season 2, to maintain its scare factor. "I'll have to watch it from behind my hands!" Jared enjoyed the final run of episodes in season 2. "The episode after Tricia's [**2.16 Roadkill**] which is one of my favourites – is the one where Sam gets some 'special lovin' so to speak [and does a lot of cryin' too]. We have a great time when Sam and Dean go visit a haunted movie set. It gets better from there…I can see being more proud of season 2 than any of the other work I've done."

Jensen and Jared don't get to see any of the episodes as they're aired since they're still filming when the episodes are aired on US TV.

Jared says he's been watching some season 2 ones to see what Jensen was doing with his character. "I thought it might be neat to play off that. So that was really the thought behind it. That was a decision of mine." Referring to his decision to play Sam on a darker note in season 3.

As for coming up with the show's storylines, we love it! So when Eric says, "Because of the show I wonder if I had a disturbed childhood, or tortured puppies, stuff like that. But I'm a normal Ohio boy from a tight-knit family. Though my friends and family do seem surprised that I'm coming up with such twisted crap. About twice a month my sister calls me and says, 'what the hell's wrong with you?" Never mind, we all share the passion too! For the show.

Jensen says, "I have become more aware of the fan base in the past couple of weeks than I had been the last couple of seasons. It's neat. It's neat to have that base of fans out there that are truly fighting and going to bat for us because that's what we need. I think that this show has survived because of these people, because of their word of mouth, much more than anything else."

Jared pleads to tell family and friends about the show and that they all love to hear online and through other forums, fan mail etc, that everyone's loving the show. "If you know anybody who might be interested in the show but hasn't watched it yet, try to convince them to sit down with you. We'll buy you pizza!" {Jared laughs.] Hey where's my pizza then, considering the number of friends and family I've converted to the show?!? Oh and I also demand to eat it in good company! So Jared and Jensen you better be listening!..

Robert Singer says season 2 will have the same formula as season 1: some mythology and some stand alone episodes. Kripke says they had very few serialized stories in the first half of season 1as they were still finding their feet but believes the self-enclosed [stand alone] episodes "are our bread and butter and almost make us unique in this heavily serialized world we live in now. So I think we're going to continue with self-enclosed episodes in a row and then a serialized mythology episode. We're bringing more characters into the show that will thread in and out every four or five episodes."

They hoped to bring back Loretta Devine (Missouri) but she didn't return, which was a shame since there was real potential in storylines with her, such as the questions posed in the end of **1.10 Home**. Jim Beaver (Bobby) returned. "This was *Star wars* in truck-stop America – that there was always a universe out there and by the end of last season we met Bobby, Pastor Jim and Caleb – who both died. There's this loose affiliation of people who are tapped into the truth of supernatural America and we want to see more of those hunters, characters, more.

We want to get to know their world a little bit more. The road trip element will never go away. The fact that it's about two brothers primarily will never go away but again every three or four episodes a new character swings in and out." Kripke wants to do a *28 Days Later*, *Night of the Living Dead*, zombie episode. "We need to spend more time worrying about zombies. Therefore my joke, that if possession is nine tenths of the law then why aren't we all walking around like zombies! (Feel free to groan loudly!)

This was Jensen's first leading role in a US TV series. He commented, "There's more longevity in a show that finds its audience in its second or third season and I think that's the major problem that we have today in television: the Networks are looking for a quick fix. But when you give a show time to grow and find itself, that's when you get some really good quality programming. There's 86% chance of failure for a show in its first season. So we've already overcome that. The vote of confidence for a full next season is definitely what we needed to come in guns blazing for season 2"

Peter Johnson, producer , said Sam and Dean are set to have a romantic story arc in season 2, or at least one of them, luckily this didn't materialize as planned, we don't need no love interests! He comments, "The model for the first season and this one too is season 1 of *The X Files*, where mythology was kept in the background and then it accelerated into arcs more towards the end of the season. We are picking up exactly where we left off at the end of the last season [1] in very continuous action, in terms of what happened at the end of the season finale."

Looking at what happens to the duo, as well as their father, including stand alone episodes and a bit of mythology as in season 1. This includes the wider universe – other hunters out there at the roadhouse, where the two do tend to stick out like sore thumbs.

On returning for a third season Jared said: "We're all worried too. We're doing the only thing we can do, which is work on the quality of the show. It's just one of those unfortunate things since we're in this ridiculous night of television, [with *CSI, Grey's Anatomy,* scheduled at the same time on other networks]. I don't remember ever in my life the number 1 and 2 [scripted] shows being on in the same hour." Like being in the ring with Muhammad Ali and George Foreman, he says, "It is a little like we were thrown to the wolves. From what I know, the powers-that-be are happy with what's going on, but unfortunately I think coming back has to do with how many people are watching."

Supernatural is going great guns in the ratings against *Grey's Anatomy* and *CSI.* Also with the *Save Supernatural* campaign online which was started in response to the near cancellation of the show after season 1 and has been going ever since, does to a small extent make people aware of those important this show is and should remain on air.

As for *Supernatural*'s time slot up against *CSI* and *Grey's Anatomy* with the Network saying those shows cater to an older audience. You can't really use "age" demographics since *Supernatural* is a show watched by all age groups. As Jensen says, "The same audience as these shows watch *Supernatural* and buy the DVDs too. They had little or no promotion for the show. "Take a little time with this show", Jensen declares, "You've gotten us to this level, why not put the extra energy into it and get us to an even bigger level?" And so say all of us, especially since it's the best show on the CW Network (aside form *Smallville* but that's into its eighth year now so doesn't need any help in promotion.) In fact, it's the best show on any Network at the present time!

Eric Kripke says, "The show has always existed in a real cool world of these supernatural evils that are in the dark corners of America and there is this select very scruffy, blue collar group of people who know about it." In reference to some new additions in the form of Ellen, Jo, her daughter and Gordon, another hunter. Also opened up are the realms of a whole different universe out there – as the brothers learn they are not the only ones who hunt and know of the demonic existences. Eric: "We've always been interested in expanding the universe and will continue to do so. I'm interested in Ellen because **(2.2)** having that fiercely maternal energy in the boys' lives is something they've never really had before. I love the character Gordon **(2.3)** and the idea of a dangerous hunter who takes the attitudes the boys have and doesn't take much to nudge them into something anti-social and dangerous."

True to a certain extent, but Dean is the one who's most susceptible to Gordon's way of thinking and...killing. He sees a lot of himself in Dean and vice versa – both having to, or needing to kill before finding out the bigger picture and when Sam objects to his blatant actions, Dean reacts with anger and lashes out at Sam in a way unimaginable – he punches him. Something we couldn't perceive of him doing before – obviously one reaction to their loss but also to how he really feels about the situation he finds himself in and how his life has really turned out. The loss of Dad affects him, obviously more than Sam, because he was the loyal son – the staunch supporter of Dad and the "family business". So when Sam takes the side of the vampires – the evil ones in the eyes of Dean and Gordon, Dean feels he has no choice but to take Gordon's side. The man whose life he's just saved and who he's opened up to more than even Sam after the past events. A special affinity develops with Dean for Gordon.

Eric: "We've never leaned heavily into this but Gordon is a rabid racist. He's a racist against creatures. He is in an upcoming episode and talks about pure humans versus tainted humans. He has this master race thing going on but it just happens to be for humanity." Also not reading much into this but Gordon also happens to be black which kind of adds more to this racist element.

Also coming to light in season 2 is why Sam has psychic powers. "I can speak to why emotionally we made the choice and we explain in terms of plot later on and it's a mythology secret. It allows us to eliminate aspects of the brothers. If they both had abilities there wouldn't be much conflict, but for Sam's side, it makes him feel like a freak and separated emotionally from his brother at a time he wants to feel closer...it is a metaphor for how everybody has something that makes them feel weird or embarrassed. From Dean's side everything has been in terms of doing the job, his duties and he is suddenly looking at his brother and saying 'Well, technically my brother is something I should be hunting'. By the same respect, there is nothing more important to Dean than protecting Sam. That dichotomy is pretty substantial, yet you couldn't play that if they both had abilities."

Eric didn't much like the psychic children storyline in season 2. As a matter of fact, he got fed up with it, which is why it came to an early conclusion. Probably explains why he killed off all the psychics, putting them and us out of misery. Says Eric, "Now it's war. Time to choose a side and pick up arms and fight." Would've been good to see Sam becoming closer to his dark side.

Season 3 is meant to ask questions posed at the end of season 2 and provide some answers and where Sam is concerned, more specifically whether he came back as Sam or something more sinister possessing him possibly; or being changed when brought back by Dean. Jared: "This season it's certainly delivering a lot more into Sam's past…it's sort of asking, 'is he completely normal, is he not?' So it's definitely got darker and in my opinion more exciting, because I'm really into that and going there." Season 3 deals with Dean's decision to save Sam. Eric: "Dean is trying to have as much sex and eat as many cheeseburgers and it's sort of like the rollicking, red-blooded *Supernatural* where it's fun and it's scary and it's emotional and think we're actually in a much cleaner, more exciting place than we were last year." Later changing his mind on the outcome of season 3 after it ended. But hey that's a creator, writer and occasional director's prerogative.

Sam's character is meant to change and going from past episodes, he is meant to become more like Dean in his approach to hunting. More specifically instead of asking questions; he shoots first, questions later or not at all. Jared: "Sam starts to be rude where he wouldn't have been rude before and acting out of instinct instead of saying, 'Wait a second, we have to make sure that they're evil and maybe they can be helped and there's a way to save them instead of killing them'. Now he's just going – 'They're bad, kill'…so we're seeing the dark side of him come out for sure."

Jared continues, "Sam's almost been scared himself that he's not all human and we find this season what Sam's relationship was like with his Dad beyond what we know and if his Dad really was his Dad and if Dean really was his brother." Which is something I've been saying since season 1. However, all this didn't materialize in this third season, which is a shame. Hate it when questions are posed and hinted at and then the show veers away from answering them. Either because they forget they asked the questions to begin with, or since they take the series into a completely different direction. Jared: "Sam has to kind of go evil to save his brother and he finds he fares very well." It's not evil, evil, more like ruthless to a point.

Jensen: "We're seeing them fight for each other but also fight with each other, and they almost both seem irrational but also passionate about whatever it is they are irrational about, so we see their relationship develop like that." This we were seeing all the way through the seasons: season 1 they were looking out for each other, again mostly Dean for Sam; especially when he got abducted for the umpteenth time). Season 2 was more about Dean's spiralling into guilt and Sam had to look out for him, whilst Dean also had to do the same for Sam in case he becomes evil. In Season 3 was Sam looking out for Dean, trying to get his one year life sentence expunged; with Dean wondering if Sam was wholly Sam? So there was a nice thread of continuity running through the seasons.

Also in season 3 everyone keeps telling Dean that Sam's changed especially the demons. Jared: "A lot of demons are going, 'Look, you don't know who your brother is' and Dean's like; 'He's my brother' and some demons are saying, 'He's supposed to be our leader and we're going to follow him' and others are saying,' I follow someone else'. And they want his head. So Jensen's character is thinking, 'Oh crap. I'm in a lot more trouble than I thought. I'm not just a demon hunter, I'm the brother of somebody who is a legend in the demon world' and this is so much bigger than he ever realized'." Yes, but why exactly was Sam chosen, what was so special about him that nobody else had. Even if Yellow Eyes did reveal he was special to him – why didn't he explain this fully. Azazel (Yellow Eye's name revealed in season 3 episode 4 - Sounds like an angel of sorts, oh there I go being right again even before watching the episode and since the name sounds so close to Azizil in Arabic.)

Eric "I have mixed feelings about season 3. I think we had some great episodes, but I feel it was probably my least favourite season. I think that's because it's the middle and it's that weird transition point." I have to add, the episodes which were a big disappointment in season 3 were the Ghostfacers one especially as that didn't really add anything to the show. (Alright Ghostfacers fans don't throw things at me all at once, it's just my opinion!) As well as the addition of Bela, again doing nothing for the show. Her story and character were both as dull as dishwater, if I may be so bold to say, write! But the rest of it was just as great except for the writers' strike. That was a bummer as we were shortchanged 6 episodes!! Hey, Deano's life was shortened by 6 episodes too!!

Jensen: "Once you get past the freshman season, and you get that season 2, and you get to that sophomore slump which a lot of shows have to get through, getting to season 3 is a massive battle in itself. Once you've won that battle and you get to season 3, I think you can really start exploring the ideas that you have held back because you're just trying to do everything you can to get the support of the Network and the studio and stuff like that."

Eric says, "I think we'll be cancelled long before we run out of story ideas." In season 3 there were a lot of stories to portray and that's hard for a show; not forgetting what made things worse was the fact season 3 was SHORT! As for being cancelled before running out of ideas, that's not a nice thing to say, not for all the loyal fans out there who expect to be given their money's worth, er, if we were paying for it that is! You have to do justice to a show once you begin it, and not leave it hanging in midair or finish it quickly without resolving any of the outstanding storylines or issues. We've had that sort of treatment from too many shows in the past already.

Eric also says we were meant to find out why Mom recognized Yellow Eyes' face at the end of this season 3 and there's more mystery about Mary promised too. But didn't get any of that at all, aside from Ruby telling Sam all of Mom's friends, everyone she knew had all been killed, again for reasons not mentioned or dealt with at all. Also not addressed, well not in so many words, is why Sam was given Yellow Eyes' blood, other than the fact Sam was meant to be the new 'demonic' army leader, in opposition to Lilith, but this was already dealt with in **2.21**. Again no discussion or mention of how Mary and Yellow Eyes relate to each other, if they do and no more about Sam.

Reaching season 3 (and season 4) is a milestone for any show to achieve, but for *Supernatural* is more than just an achievement since it faced so many hurdles to reach this peak. Facing cancellation, amongst other problems. Including Warner Bros, where the show premiered, becoming the newly launched C W Network and having to go up against other shows in terms of competition. Happily it stood its ground, much to the delight of relieved fans and avid followers. Jensen: "There's a lot of politics that play into the first two seasons, and Eric did a very nice job in doing that, but also walking the fine line of staying true to his creativity...Getting to season 3, I'm very excited about, because now it's like we can really sink our teeth into it and figure out what's going to happen with these two guys, where they're going to go, who they're going to meet, how that's going to affect them, what storylines are going to pick up."

Jensen also comments on how great season 3 will be, "It's another thrill ride this season. We're really hitting our stride. If the audience likes what they've seen in the last two seasons, it's a little more intensified version of the same. I'm real proud of it." As for the season 3 finale, which was so sad, Jensen adds, "Please write to Kripke. Tell him not to kill me." As if Dean would be removed from our screens permanently, so soon!!

On season 4, Jim Beaver said, "Drama is about giving characters goals and then throwing obstacles at them. Eric and his troupe of writers have done that wonderfully this season. I like that they've continued to tighten Bobby's relationship with Sam and Dean. Made more of the growing familial aspect."

As for Katie Cassidy not being in season 4, cited as budgetary reasons, Eric: "She's great but this was unfortunately a financial decision. I have nothing but great affection for Katie, and she was great for the show. It was a very difficult business decision. Even so, how can you justify replacing her with another actress – a cheaper version of her! Which still means paying someone else. Seems like female characters (especially the ones you like, don't mean much in the show. They're only there for 'quick' love interests.) Nah, won't be the same as having Katie around playing our Ruby! Liked her!

On the subject of romance seems I'm not the only one with such feelings on the show. Jensen comments that romance was tried with Jo – but none of the audience wanted it. No. Jensen and Jared are possessive of the characters and so are we, the fans. Romance is all fine and proper but at the right time and place. If it's added unnecessarily, it'll just ruin a show, and with this show, not having serious love interests is fine at the moment because otherwise it'll detract from the main story arc. From their family business, world, their road trip, it's a lonely affair and as for closeness, they're close to each other. We want to see their own relationship with each other grow and drift apart at the same time too, not anyone else.

Also, maybe and maybe, sticking my neck out, you know, believe it's to do with fans being a tad jealous too – some can't bear to see their fave guys in the arms of another – even if it's just acting!

On how long the show will run, Eric Kripke: "No one believes me, but I really feel like that would be a favour to the fans. Better to have, 'Now that was great and what a satisfying ending' rather than literally jumping sharks... I feel Buffy did it pretty well. You know it ended and that was a great finale episode. [Was that season 5 or 7?] Never say never, I guess, but at this point, Jensen and Jared and my contracts are all up at year 5 and I'd rather just go out bold. That's my plan. Beginnings are easy because you're launching everything. Endings are easy..." Hey that's not what Eric said before!

Eric: "We're on the right track for the overall series arc. Some things were accelerated and other stories took longer to tell than I thought they would. I've always thought that we could tell this story properly in five years. That's what I'm currently aiming and hoping for [so are we!]. But I love the show and if it turns into a monster hit that goes on for eight years, I guess I'll adjust accordingly. You know. Weddings, Raven Symone! Maybe we'll literally have Dean jump the shark like Fonzie did." We wouldn't mind eight years or even just seven will do, for the purposes of numerology!! That's a significant number in itself!

The cast seems to concur, Jared: "I love my character and I love exploring it, but I know Eric wants to keep the quality up. He doesn't want it to be 39 seasons of *Bonanza* or something, where it's like, shotgun in a wheelchair, 'C'mon, Dean!' With our sons running around fighting for us. If Eric says four is good, then four is good. If he says five is good, then five is good. He hasn't steered us wrong yet." Yes but wouldn't you miss it just a little bit when it ends? A little….just…

Jensen agrees: "I think five would be good. If I was on *Lost* then maybe it would be a different story – it's 30 characters and I'm living in Hawaii with five days off an episode. Putting the work aside, as far as the story goes, I would never want people to get tired of it. I would never want people to be like, 'Okay, they're phoning it in now'. I'd rather go out strong and leave them wanting more." When the show ends (rumoured after five still, come let's make it to an uneven seven!) Jensen doesn't want to continue if Eric doesn't want it. "I'm passionate about the stories Eric writes and if he stops writing them then I'm afraid the passion I have for the show would end."

Well true, but here's one fan and avid viewer who'll never tire of the show! Some shows I feel can go on and on and drag but this isn't one of them in my, well, maybe not so humble opinion, since it's great in every category, casting, crew, storylines! So let's hope long may it continue. Or if not, I'll be one disappointed fan! But then perhaps we can have a few movies, especially if questions are left hanging in mid air, so as we get a superb ending and most of all closure, even if the ending isn't a happy one!

Eric says he has an ending planned for the show – for Sam and Dean but in true Eric Kripke style, won't give it away!!

Characters

Eric also says he based Sam partly on himself, since he has an older brother like Dean. Eric left to pursue a career in California, like Sam. Dean is based on his big brother, Matt and some of his best friends.

To Jensen, "The undercurrent of the show, the common denominator for the brothers is that they're looking for their father [at least in season 1.] That's the reason the two of them get together in the first place and then hit the road. You've got the reluctant hero with Sam and I'm Dean, the crazy cowboy. There's a nice balance between them. The brothers are very much yin and yang. They balance each other out. I like to think that they're two individual characters when they're separate, but that when they're together they're a third character. That's what we're trying to do."

Eric Kripke comments; "Sam wonders why he and Dean so blindly follow Dad's orders no matter what, and Dean has always been the good little soldier, dedicated to carrying out those orders. In terms of Dean's evolution, Jensen is doing such an unbelievable job because this character started out very brash and Han Solo like, still has that Devil-may-care attitude, but as the series goes on, you're catching those careful, quiet glimpses of the absolutely screwed –to-hell psyche that'd create a personality like that. That's what's been intriguing about Dean: the feelings of abandonment but also fierce loyalty he has for his father. Dean has an incredibly troubled childhood and didn't adjust nearly as well to the outside world as Sam.

Is this why he finds it impossible, at times, to virtually trust people – or is there a wider purpose behind his character adjustment, or maladjustment, shown by his constant jokes, his usually one night stands, displaying an inability to maintain a long-term relationship. The only one he had for a while was with Cassie in **1.13 Route 666**, where we discover he was ready to give his all, maybe even commit, only to be dumped by, a chick, as Dean would say, when she couldn't handle what he did, let alone believe him.

On his character Jensen says, "Dean loves it, he got a kick out of the whole weapons and the hunting and it is really something he enjoys and takes pride in and loves to do. Jensen says Dean is always the good guy – no matter how much of a cocky SOB (in Dean's words) he is! As well as a womanizer. Whereas Sam is the opposite. Jensen: "It's a very ebb and flow, yin and yang sort of relationship. Sam and Dean really balance each other out. Dean can get out there and be really wild and crazy and lie and get stuff done that way and Sam can come in and be truthful and honest and compassionate and have sympathy for the victims and get things done this way. It's a nice mix and we have a lot of fun playing them." Oh and he also claims to get the chick in the end! Well, Deano when there's one to get, but not always!

As for having a little of Deano inside him, Jensen adds, "There are a lot of aspects of myself that I elaborate on to make Dean. It's like that with every role I do. It's may be a little portion of yourself mixed with what you observe from other people. You take all that and magnify it and you have a character. I'd say with Dean – he is a lot more confident and cocky and more brash than me. He's a lot more prideful. He's not the first guy to admit that he's wrong about something and those are qualities that aren't me. As far as the characteristics that are most like mine I'd say, his passion. He's got a huge sense of passion

20

for what he does and towards his brother and his cause. That passion for what we do is something a lot of actors share."

He thinks it's much cooler to believe in the supernatural and maybe he'll start re-thinking his whole on-the-fence stance.

Jensen On Dean: "[Dean's] a modern day ghost hunter who has spent his life on the road with his Dad hunting down urban legends. He's a bit of a loose canon and he's got a little crazy in him." Certain parts of his character are reminiscent of his character Alec, in *Dark Angel*. Yes, I said that too but no one listened and now you have it straight from the cowboy's mouth! "That devil-may-care, going-out there, no –fear thing. He's just doing what he does and he loves it." Alec also having to be rescued by Max so many times and here, Sam gets him out of trouble too. Though more times than not, it's Dean who needs to save Sam. He's still surprised at finally landing a leading role in a hit show.

Not playing favourites between characters (and actors) that'd be too difficult, because they're both unique, wild and lovable in their own ways. On the one hand Dean would be our favourite because of what he's been through – loss of childhood, constantly on the road, knowing what happened to Mom even before Sam did, or could have known about it. Still wanting to protect Sam from the creatures of the night and give him back his innocence. Bearing the brunt of Dad's anger; guilt, always directed at Dean and never at Sam, the baby. Having been through so much, we feel sad for him not being able to live his dreams, leave like Sam to follow his heart and all he could do was to follow orders. Another reason why anyone else would've gone off the rails and be a little envious of Sam.

Executive producer, Robert singer wasn't really surprised at the show, but the first year did go smoothly. Eric Kripke: What surprised was how psychologically complex Sam and Dean turned out to be because I think the actors inspired us, the writers and vice versa, those characters really took on a life of their own." Last year Eric's first thought was wanting the show to be scary and was moved by the depth of the characters he'd created; "How touching they could be , how poignant and how bittersweet and how poignant their relationship could be and that the show really became just grounded in these boys and their sense of family and their dysfunction." Eric doesn't credit himself as that great or "classy" a writer and owes much of that to their writing staff and Rob Singer and was surprised at the quality of the scripts he'd read and comment on how he came to be attached to excellent writing, "They elevated my game."

Commenting on Dean since the first season, Jensen says, "He's [Dean's] definitely changed quite a bit since the first season. There's been a lot happening, from losing his father at the beginning of season [2]. It was almost a role reversal for Sam and Dean. In the first season, Dean was really gung ho and he was like, 'Just accept this. This is our destiny. This is what we do.' I love it. I love it and he was just trying to convince Sam to come along, to be a family and to be this family of hunters. By the end of the season you saw that Dean was finally getting what he wished for – he's got his brother and his Dad and they're altogether and they're fighting. That was a big moment for him.

Then, at the beginning of season 2, when Dad trades his life to save Dean's life essentially, it really put Dean on his heels and he started to take a step back and analyze everything he's gotten himself into. And he just wasn't convinced anymore and that this was what he wanted to be doing. He felt as though he'd paid too much and now that his father is gone he felt like he was the only person left to look after Sam; that the weight of the world had come down on his shoulders.

On Sam: Jared says, "..he is definitely the more introverted and thoughtful. He loves the puzzle and it is, 'Here is the problem and let's figure out the best way to solve it'. Sam's a classic, reluctant hero. [Again Jensen described him as this too]. He's Luke Skywalker. He's like Neo from *The Matrix*, an innocent. He doesn't know why he has to do what he does. He's not got any magical supernatural abilities himself – but he has a big heart and this understanding and ability to help others. [Though Sam does have some psychic kinetic powers revealed in season 1.] With Dean, it is more like 'Here's the problem, let's grab the guns and go get them'. He's more of the Han Solo, both guns blazing. With Sam – it is, 'Well, maybe he's just a pawn in the guy's plan'. Another thing is he's very independent. He wants his dad to know, 'I know you have a great boy in Dean that will just listen to whatever you say, but I need to know why'. I don't want to just do something like Dean does… 'There is a demon so let's kill it.'"

"I want to know why, what has it done and what will it do'. I can figure it out myself and then I'll listen. I am not going to take your word for it'. [Like in **2.13**, when Sam wanted to believe so much that it was an angel – with Dean telling him it's just a spirit and Dean had to be right in the end! Well, because he almost always is.] That is also part of the deal of being the oldest son. You sort of do what your daddy says and don't ask questions. I am actually the second son myself, just like Sam is and I remember my brother, who is great, and I was like 'He's doing what my Dad says but I want to cause a ruckus.'"

Jared comments that at the beginning of a show; "You're trying things out with the characters and it takes a while to see what works. At first, we thought that Sam and Dean were going to be on the road with their Dad. We all figured it was going to be about the boys finding their father and then teaming up with him. But we didn't know where it would go from there. You see how things unfold and you see what the audience connects with and likes and you do more of that. You also see what they don't like and so that isn't concentrated on." In the pilot, Sam and Dean were butting heads and not in the 'Oh I love you, you're my brother. I've got to watch out for you' way. It was more, 'I don't want to be a part of your life. I tried to leave you behind years ago, and you're getting in the way'. Now Sam is doing whatever he can to save his brother's life."

Jensen on killing Sam: "It's something that he's had to battle with and he deals with that in almost every episode. To tell you the truth, from my standpoint I don't think Dean could do it because Dean relies too much on his family, even though he likes to think that he doesn't. Sam is basically his lifeline and I think that if you cut Sam out he wouldn't last much longer." (As I said too before. The show wouldn't last much longer either.)

Wouldn't Dad warrant some criticism or blame in their upbringing too: being on the road, no stable home, or make shift home; leaving them on their own, sometimes with others like Pastor Jim, not even leaving them with proper food at times. So when Dean needs a break and plays the arcade machine, he's doing what every boy his age should be, instead he's told off for almost getting Sam killed as if he didn't feel blameworthy enough already. Something the demon in **2.8 Crossroad Blues** tries to point out to him. On the other hand, as a single father, going through the pain and loss, he did the best he could or knew how to.

The anguish the brothers go through has been captured tremendously and is a real joy to watch in that you can relate and feel for them. As explained by Jared, "Sam sees his brother falling apart and he has to be the strong one. He finds himself doing things for Dad or doing what he thinks his Dad would have wanted. But at the same time he's lost his father, lost his mother and he lost his girlfriend and it seems like bad luck is following him and he starts to wonder if some demon has a beef with him."

Sam would also be our favourite – the baby – not knowing Mom at all and perhaps never fully understanding why they didn't have a normal childhood and couldn't be the ordinary, average family. Looking up to big brother, could Sam do half of the things Dean had to, hunting, killing without blinking an eye? He was protected for most of his life, sheltered from the evil and hate in the world, until it caught up with him again when he lost Jess. Dean is Sam's hero. They probably don't need heroes when they have each other and their heroic quest…but they are our heroes!

Says Kripke: Dean is "so damaged on the one hand and so charming on the other and putting these two actors and these two characters together, is a potent combination."

So let me put this to you: who's your favourite: Sam or Dean, Jared or Jensen?

The question has been posed as to why Dean has no abilities like Sam. John Shiban replies; "I'll have to say 'Stay tuned'. It is a big mystery and there are reasons for everything but I don't want to give it away." Well, no signs yet of why, though in season 2 – we get glimpses: because Sam was born in a certain year. Others like him were also born in that year too, but certain weather or freak weather conditions, storms have been known to affect the activities of the yellow-eyed demon and the time it surfaces. Then there are others like Sam who doesn't exhibit the same trademarks, i.e. their moms dying in a nursery fire; yellow-eyed demon appearing to them in dreams telling them it has plans for them, urging them to kill. The yellow-eyed demon didn't appear to Sam in his dreams/nightmares/premonitions, but Sam only has them when the same demon is involved.

Another reason could be Dean wasn't meant to have abilities, he's meant to be Sam's protector; looking out for him so he doesn't turn evil – a sort of guardian angel, however not a true angel in the same sense of the word. Though it would be interesting if he turned out to be an angel after all, or have angelic qualities, say a fallen angel. This is something I've pondered over. Dean could be "fallen", or lost his religion and Sam could still pray (as he said he did in **2.13 Houses of the Holy**.) I also said Sam was more religious (and more moral) than Dean so one of them being religious was a good thing considering what they hunt.

Maybe Sam and Dean could have spiritual angels or have guardian angels, 'placed' there by their mother to protect them. It's said guardian angels are meant to be connected to the four elements:- earth, air, water and fire, especially fire, hence a reason why fire doesn't kill Sam in the opening episode, why it killed Mom and Jess and why it appears a lot in episodes. Also since the yellow-eyed demon seems to be immune to it. Sam could be more demonic, as it was revealed that's the plan for him, and Dean could be more angelic (especially since he doesn't believe in angels.) A nice twist for them would be to save each other and not just Dean needing to save Sam.

Oops sorry, but I wrote this before season 4 was even written, filmed and aired so maybe if it sounds familiar it's because I had all these ideas about the show and so I put them to paper. Hey why am I apologizing anyway?!

One other perhaps not so obvious reason is that they're only half brothers. Perhaps Dad isn't really Sam's Dad; questioned this lot in season 1 especially since Mom hardly said a word to Dean when she appeared to them in **1.10 Home**, but said "Sorry" to Sam. Of course there could be many interpretations to this as well. Sorry for not being there for him, seeing him all grown up, for what happened to her, or to Jess and so on. So we haven't had any definitive answers thus far and even further into seasons 2 and 3. However, turns out Sam is Dad's son after all and is Dean's brother too, but apparently there is another Winchester sibling on the horizon, so let's see how that story develops if it comes to fruition at all. (See season 4.)

Jensen on season 2: "Now there's this role reversal where it's Sam saying, 'No, now this is set in motion and we've got to do this and we've got to hunt this thing down'. And Dean is like, 'Look why do we have to do that? Why do we have to be heroes? Let's just let somebody else do it.' So what, that was a near transition'." Thank you Jensen – once again – for reinforcing my views and line of thinking, or should I say adding credibility to it. As you'll recall, I said season 2 leads onto a great character change-over or reversal for Sam and Dean – whereas Sam now wants to carry on the family business – Dean feels like he'd rather have a life now because up to now he hasn't had one and just wants to give up on the life he's seen or known. Which I said a few times through the episodes summary.

Also he says in his interview – about being heroes – is what I mentioned in the season 2 opener where the reaper wants Dean – she says he's a warrior and would have such a celebrated death – and I added, Dean would say or substitute heroes in place of warriors. It's great when I come up with something to write about the show – and then Jensen came up with the same exposition, it's almost spooky. Okay, great minds thinking alike!!

Continues Jensen, "I was concerned that it would throw me off a little bit as an actor because I really loved the guns blazing aspect that Dean had the first season. I thought that was kind of going to be taken away and in a way, I guess it was emotionally, but still, physically and in all the stand alones, you still get that sense of the crazy cowboy that Dean is." It's good to see the guys have oodles to say about their characters and each other, as well as being on par with what's happening in the show, considering some actors can hardly string together two words, let alone two sentences about their character and what's happening in the show and out of the show.

Jared says he was upset over the writers' strike. "I was extremely pleased with season 3, [because of the strike] I thought we were going somewhere and that we were doing some great stuff…I thought everyone was doing their best work. The writers were coming up with fantastic episodes and as actors Jensen and I had really started to vibe with the characters." The episodes were good in season 3 and there was a nice mythology building up with Lilith which could have been explored in more detail.

Not to mention the fact we could have seen Katie play Ruby for a lot longer and who knows, if the show had gone to 22 episodes, then may be she might have been back in season 4 too. Jared continues, "Some of my favourite shows are from this past year [season 3]. Usually after season 2, the third one is going to be better. The writers now know what we feel comfortable with, and we know a little bit more about what to expect from them. *Supernatural* has more of a direction. We were feeling things out in season 1, and we had to do certain episodes to realize that we didn't want to make those sort of episodes anymore. We tried certain things with the characters…so it's a collaboration that only gets better with time."

Jared comments he'd like to become evil but his parents and family wouldn't like to see that happen. Jared thinks it would be interesting to see Sam go weak and succumb to the darkness within him. "See if Dean, through love or affection or just stubbornness, pulls his brother out. I think it would make for some interesting brother moments."

Is Sam human? Perhaps it took him to die for his powers to get stronger and return. Lilith is powerful and there seems to be a demon hierarchy relating to eye colour. Black eyes being the lower tier with demons being the usual sort, and what Dean saw himself as becoming. Yellow eyes are powerful, like Yellow Eyes himself and what Sam appears to be becoming, if he does turn. Only we have only seen one demon with Yellow Eyes, so perhaps he was unique in being one of a kind. Since he did have a name after all, Azazel. Red eyes are the crossroads demons but they're all inter-related anyway. Lilith has white eyes and is a-lined with Satan. Lilith had white eyes when she made the deal with Bela in season 3.

Jared thanked everyone, especially fans, for ensuring the show returned for a fourth season after the writers' strike in 2008. They thought it may have meant saying their goodbyes permanently but they were back. Jensen found it hard to get back into playing Dean after the strike, and had to watch some episodes of the show to help him get back into character. They didn't see each other during the strike as they were off doing other things. Jensen says "I think one of the great things about the show is how these characters are ever-evolving and ever-changing."

He loves the way Dean changes in each episode and isn't left the same character. Some of the stand-alone episodes were lost due to the strike and much of the storylines had to be shortened or squeezed into an episode. Jensen has learnt to, "Never to try to predict Eric – tried to make predictions when I first started shooting the show and he would always prove me wrong. Eric likes to twist things up all the time." It's probably since everyone does second guess him and figure out plots, that Eric has to go back and undo them and come up with something different, well it's a thought!

Jensen believes everyone's very passionate about the show and the characters to the point of protection, of which he does the same. "I get protective of the characters. If I read something on the pages that I don't agree with, I'll call Eric Kripke and say, 'Eric what are you doing here, buddy?' We're lucky enough to be able to do that...the Network always talks about how we skew to a younger audience, but at the events we go to, the ones who show up at the set are usually women ages 30-50. It's actually pretty cool". That's me covered then! And no, I'm not 50! Or even close!

Jensen also hates how certain characters are only on the show for a brief moment. "It's like, 'Hi, how you doing? I'll be making out with you today and then they're gone and it's like, 'Okay – who's next?' But he prefers this to having long term relationships on the show.

Eric says many characters were killed off since the actors who played them were busy elsewhere. Jeffrey Dean Morgan had a busy schedule. Sterling K Brown is a series regular on *Army Wives*. Charles Malik Whitfield has a series regular role on other shows.

One person he regrets killing off is Meg, as she brought energy and humour to the show. As for other female, lead characters, he says, they're introduced abut didn't work out. Kim Manners begged him not to lose Meg. However, being *Supernatural* she could've been brought back (she was in **4.2**.) They could've had her being possessed by Ruby, I should say, Ruby could've taken over her body.

Kim Manners said about Jensen and Jared, they're great fun to work with; "They both have to take direction and they work really hard to make a scene come off especially in the exposition scenes. We work hard to make those scenes conversationals so we're not boring the audience to death. They're eager. They want this thing to be right and want it to be well-mounted. Jensen and Jared are going to be breakout stars with this. They are very directable. They genuinely like each other which really makes the chemistry work. So that's the easy part. And why I came back to join the staff as executive producer is because of these two kids. They're sweet, they work hard and it makes it a very nice working environment to work. It's a creature environment which is a treat for a director."

Jensen believes the show is doing a much better job of being scary and spooking everyone than most others around and that wouldn't be too far fetched from the truth either. There's a certain atmosphere, part gothic, in some episodes; part 'don't look behind you' which has you on the edge of your seat every episode. He says, "You have shows like *Lost* which deal with the unexplained [no that show is just lost!] but that's more mysterious and then you also had shows like *Invasion* and *Nightstalker* where it kind of leaves you hanging with the mysteriousness. Whereas I think the difference is the fact our show is an all-out raw horror movie each week. We show you the monster or demon straight up and we deal with it and it is scary. We are going to scare you as opposed to leaving you hanging for the next episode."

More people are watching such shows, me in particular, was not only because of the show itself but because Jensen and Jared were in it and I knew them from other things they had done and to escape the hell of reality based shows and mundane so-called celebrities! Jensen comments, "The horror genre has taken off in the film industry and I think now it is starting to translate to television. You always had television shows like the *X Files*, and even going back to the *Twilight Zone*; that have always been very, very successful but I think with the recent interest in horror movies the executives are trying to mould it into television."

Jensen also attributes the show's success to horror films of late, "That separates us from the other shows that are in that kind of genre and that's why we encourage people to watch it with the lights off." (Which we do anyway! But thanks for the encouragement! The darkness gives the show a much darker (ha!) atmosphere sooo as you feel you're actually there too. Though the wonders of modern TV haven't evolved to that stage yet!)

As for the paranormal, Jared says he believes in the supernatural. "I think it's a pretty big world and it would be hard to imagine there not being something else." Whereas Jensen's a bit of a skeptic and a realist. Everyone told him their own weird tales – he's on the fence since he's found they do carry a lot of weight. "I haven't been haunted or spooked out or anything like that but I'm not ruling it out now."

Jensen also likes to believe there is a logical explanation for everything so in that sense he calls himself more of a realist. However, due to *Supernatural* he's able to know paranormal signs (should we be worried?) "The flickering of lights or the cold rooms or certain noises." Next time your light bulb flickers before it gives out, think there may be a more sinister reason behind it! (Or just invest in some energy saving ones, you won't need to change those in a hurry.) "I would definitely say I'm much more attuned to that than I ever was before." He isn't quite sure after season 1 and has a lot of questions in his mind on the supernatural and paranormal. Jared also feels the same way – that said, he has a Texan friend who knocked at his door one night asking to stay over as his place was haunted.

Jared: "I was actually sitting in my house with my mother and my father in Texas and there was a big thunderstorm outside and we were inside and the lights flickered for a second and I found myself, and this is really embarrassing, I found myself going, 'The demon' and of course they watch the show and they looked at me and I went, 'Oh no, I need a vacation or something to clear my head'. It's way too ingrained in my head." To which Jensen adds, "Yeah you need a break man."

Jensen: "I think just working with the show; learning what all this stuff means – like cold spots or certain electromagnetic waves or crackling noises, the dimming lights and stuff like that we do on a daily basis. This is stuff that's researched by the writers so now, when you're in a hotel room and it gets really cold and the light starts flickering it's like 'Aw rightie, where's my salt gun when I need it?'"

Jared claims he doesn't like "unexplained noises in the middle of the night. When you wake up and you have an uneasy feeling and you just don't know what it was. That's scary sometimes. But big boogedy monsters don't get me." Jared says the show isn't just about ghosts and demons… "It plays on all our fears of the unknown. We just did an episode called **Blood Lust** where we've run into vampires but they're actually not vampires and that sort of touched on racial issues. You can't just look at somebody and assume, 'I think we've done pretty well at exploring issues and not throwing them in your face'. But at the end of the day we are not making *The West Wing* or a Michael Moore movie, we're making a show about demons and ghosts."

Jensen on Jared: (not literally of course!) "We've worked on it but working with Jared is like working with a buddy. We are both pretty laid back guys who enjoy music, movies and going out for beer and a steak at the end of a long day." Yeah and that translates nicely into the show too. Jensen jokes, "I can't stand the kid. [No – that's one of the most fortunate things about the show, the relationship between Jensen and Jared.] We get along like brothers and best friends on set and I think that only has helped the show. He's a good kid. I'm proud to be working with him. I think that as an actor he has come miles from where he was. Not to say that he wasn't any good in the beginning because he's definitely been putting in a great performance from the get-go, but just watching him grow as an actor and seeing him where he is now, I'm proud of him."

Hey spoken in true Deano fashion! It's amazing and heart warming how these two guys have nothing but praise for each other and kind words compared to the on and off set bickering of some shows and their cast. It's truly great to see that real gentlemen still exist in the world of showbiz! "Jared is great. He is special. We had similar backgrounds growing up. He reminds me of some of my buddies back home so we're having a good time, it's a good situation."

Jared: "I think I would rather hang with Dean because Sam is smarter than I am, so I think I would be intimidated by that. I could kick Dean's ass, but if Sam went berserk he could mess me up pretty good. You have to print that so I can show it to Jensen." Hey, Dean always whoops Sam's ass!

Jared: "It would be more comforting to hang out with Dean and know he wasn't possessed by a demon or have weird headaches and see people dying. It is always a buzz kill when you argue with your buddy and he gets a headache and says, 'We've got to go three states over and save someone before they die'." Yeah, but the visions are all for the greater good. Probably he'd like to transfer his psychic powers to Dean for a while and see how he handles it. Take on the whole visions gig. Don't they see people dying all the time anyway in their line of work. Ooh, well suppose we'd all like to hang out with Dean – hey?!

Commenting on Sam and Deans' relationship Jared likens it to *Star wars*. "People enjoy the Ewoks and the Storm Troopers and all the characters but it's the mythology and heroes journey that binds people to the story. Luke Skywalker finding his identity and the relationship he has with Han Solo and Princess Leia. We deal with something very similar. I think that Sam is much like Luke and Dean is much like Han Solo as far as this is a hero's journey."

Jared has always been a fan of horror. After reading the script he felt *Supernatural* was on a par with the *X Files*. He thinks, "Sam is a fun character. I'm very quick to question what I'm doing and why I'm doing it – whereas Dean is more 'I've been told to do this and this is what I'm doing'. I always question things. What purpose does this serve? Who is going to help? [That's the lawyer in Sam's character, as you recall he was studying law at Stanford, or as we'd say in the UK,

Reading law.] I always try and think about the repercussions of something before I do it. Much like Sam. I'm really interested in the purpose of things and try to learn everything I can about a subject before I tackle it."

He had met McG since he had tested for the *Superman* movie and knew David Nutter and was excited about the show.

Jared on Jensen (Now that'd be a sight to see, um, no, er,) "When Jensen and I met each other, we immediately got long. He's a laid back Texas guy and I'm a pretty {yes! Ha!} laid back Texas guy. So we just clicked and I think that shows on screen." They both have lots of fun on set and have brothers too so the relationship in the show isn't new to them, i.e. "Where you love somebody but you want to give them a hard time."

Jensen on that " Yin and yang relationship. [again]. They can hold their own but when you put them together they complete each other."

Jensen points to Jared as the success behind *Supernatural* and why it's such a big hit. Jared agrees. It's fun for them.

Kim Manners: "It'd be fun to bring in somebody like Jaclyn [Smith], or Farrah Fawcett or Kate Jackson, but that's probably not going to happen." Hey, my friends and I mentioned it'd be fantastic to see Jaclyn turn up in the show a while ago. (To those of you who don't know, the three actresses mentioned were the original *Charlie's Angels* from the 1970's-1980's hit TV show.) Sadly, it won't happen with Farrah Fawcett either, as she lost her fight against cancer and passed away on 25th June 2009. RIP. Kim Manners passed away 5 months ago to the day.

Writing *Supernatural*

John Shiban has written three episodes in season 1 – **Skin, Hook Man** and **The Benders**. He says "We have a white board in the writers' room and we just brainstormed about things that scared us and ideas for stories. We started a master list we could look at. Once you begin shooting, you need a script every eight days. So I'll go in, sit down with Eric Kripke and say, 'Listen I have this notion about what would be good for an episode' and we'll kick it around a bit. When we're happy with it, it is, 'Ok, go do an outline' and essentially break the story. For example, we tried to break **The Benders** [season 1] with a different writer and it just wasn't clicking. It was basically – let's do our own *Texas Chainsaw [Massacre]*. How can we do that in our world?' The original version sort of fell apart, so we went with a different idea for that episode. I still remember Eric walking in and saying 'Hey, why don't you take another crack at this Texas *Chainsaw* thing? It could be really scary.' That was an assignment I was glad to get because it turned into one of my favourites!"

He also states they used to "fret over that [the best storylines being used in season 1] every year at the *X-Files* and somehow manage to have faith that when you bring together talented people and are open to new ideas, you will find them. We'll always find things to scare people with. I'm not worried about that."

The real worrying thing is how long people will continue to watch the show without getting any real answers as people usually give up thinking the show won't reveal anything new. Hopefully that won't be the case with this, as you can't really expect to have anything answered straightaway.

Eric Kripke doesn't like the episodes, **Bugs, Hook, Route 666, No Exit, Red Sky At Morning.** Have to agree with him about **Route 666, Red Sky At Morning** and **No Exit**, Sam was absent for the most part in the latter. He likes **Faith, crossroad Blues** because of the legend and **Nightshifter**. These are some of the better ones too and especially since most of these could be called 'Dean episodes'. Far be it for me to play favourites between characters, but they were for the most part. **Faith** was about Dean coming to terms with being saved when he didn't want to, but Sam wanted him saved. About Sam having faith in finding a cure to Dean's failing heart and about Dean maybe reaching inside and finding some of the faith that he lacks in God, in miracles and himself, and possibly having some faith in Sam saving him. **Crossroads Blues** about Dean seriously thinking of bringing back Dad and realizing the sacrifice he made for him. **Nightshifter**, since they finally get the FBI on their radar.

Jared would've liked for Ellen to return in season 4. As for his favourite episodes, "I love the shapeshifters and the sort of cat and mouse game of 'Who is it now?' The riddle to it." He says it's a fun episode for the viewers, in trying to work out who the shapeshifter really is. Whereas Jensen seems to be in tune with the Ghostfacers lot for the pure comedic side. Their storylines are dark, so Jensen likes to play Dean with as much added comedy as possible, enabling a balanced tone to the show.

Eric also comments Dean and Jessica being born on the same day, was because "January 24 is my wife's birthday, and it's kinda my Valentine to her."

The comics *Hellblazer and Sandman* inspired *Supernatural*. DC/Wildstorm focus on John Winchester. Says, Eric Kripke, "We decided to tell the John Winchester story so it's much more of a

Supernatural prequel. The issues begin with Mary dying on the ceiling, but instead of jumping forward 22 years we stay with John. It is the John Winchester Chronicles, we learn about how he became a demon hunter, we see him meet misery for the first time, and find the roadhouse. We see the story of this man becoming this hunter and he still has these two young kids he has to take care of while he searches for the thing that killed his wife."

So we probably won't get any questions answered about the show itself in the comics, until perhaps the series is over.

Jensen takes an active role in developing Dean. He has meetings with directors, writers about where Dean is going and how a scene should play out. Luckily it's something encouraged by *Supernatural*. He thinks taking part in such areas is "kind of a mesh of creativity now starting to form between the writers and actors and directors. We're really starting to hit out stride and go like, 'Okay, now we know how to do this and the writers', I can trust them even more now, because they're [known]. 'He wouldn't do this or he wouldn't say this'. So the perfection of knowing who he is and what he would do and where he's going is something that really gets explored in season 3, 4 and 5...I like playing the guy. Anytime you enjoy doing something you don't want somebody to ruin that for you."

Jared takes a different view to all this than Jensen and doesn't like to say much, if at all over creative matters or differences. Jared: "I don't want to interfere. If I were to say to Eric, 'Hey, let's maybe do this with the character' – I'm sure he would be open to my input. But I get paid to act the words they put on the page, not to write the script. So that's what I do. It's a 24-hour job trying to act properly so I'm not even going to try to write." It's not about writing, you're not going to change a script if you give some input into your character or if you don't like where it's heading. Jensen likes to have his voice heard which I think is a good thing since you can get some insight and thoughts from the actor playing the part of the character, like if you want him to inject a certain emotion into the scene or the role itself. It's not a bad thing to do. Especially since the show gives the actor the freedom to actually have personal discussions with the writers and producers, whereas other shows are so closed-off and standoffish and wouldn't even let you have any say on where or how your character is going. Which in my opinion, makes *Supernatural* more refreshing and constantly improving, if something is approached with fresh eyes.

At the 2007 San Diego Comicon, Eric and some of the other writers and cast gave their input about season 3. Jared couldn't attend this convention since he missed his flight from Vancouver to San Diego.

Eric comments on season 3: "It's a world about war. It's this secret war that's going on and we actually draw as many modern day parallels as possible because the demons operate in a very terrorist-cell mode." Ben Edlund says the show isn't political but they share their thoughts together... Nor should the show be political, a perspective should be kept on things after all it's demons we're dealing with here and not anything else. We don't want *Supernatural* honing in on terrorist storylines in that sense since such subjects are best covered by other shows. Unless it's demon terrorists and demons acting like that.

Although the analogy is there and can be made about the subject *Supernatural* covers and how closely it resembles real life events, the fantasy element needs to be maintained at all times to set it apart from such events. It is meant to be a piece of escapism after all and should not be bogged down in too much political realism; if at all.

Eric: "For us, the best episodes are the ones about shades of grey. In Gordon Walker, we had that hunter who was taking it to that level of being a Fascist, or in a way, like we sometimes like to call him, a 'human supremacist'. Sometimes the demons in our show, since they always possess other people, raise those moral questions of how much collateral damage are you willing to take in the battle to fight evil? – should continuously be running across hunters whose moral line is much further down the mine than our own boys."

Eric calls Bela a supernatural mercenary – created by Ben Edlund. She's in it for the money. All these talisman and amulets these guys are always using to stop their monsters are all very valuable and so she's interested in the buying and selling of these objects since she's in it for herself."

Ben concurs when he says, "Bela is a pretty cool character. She brings in a different point of view, a very selfish, end of the world point of view. All the characters we've been dealing with, if they're not bad, most of them, are really good. The idea that this person is causeless gives us something to play with."

On the mythology aspect of the show, since it is mostly based on mythology, Eric says the writers attempt to use actual myths as far as they can. "The mandate to all the writers which we've continued is the show has to be *Google-worthy* [other search engines are available!] A majority of the time, the references in the show are accurate; that the legends they deal with do exist out there somewhere. Even the throw-away references that the boys are always just saying as part of their dialogue."

As for accuracy and mythology on the show, Eric's son was born on Sam's birthday, November 2nd, and the Winchesters lost Mom when

Sam was six months old. Eric says "We're going to a very, very cautious exactly six months. November 2nd's going to be a very nervous day in our home. Sometimes we worry that we're Satan's writer room. Every so often we'll come up with something then it'll happen in reality." Yeah, know the feeling, like my storyline I penned for the show. About a Dr Frankenstein-type doctor who uses people's organs in a very nasty and supernatural way. Which **3.15** turned out to be like. That was a case of déjà vu for me, since I penned it back in 2006. Hey, I have proof! Maybe I'll publish is as fan fiction.) Actually my mum, whenever she says something will happen, it does happen. It's like she has an uncanny knack of predicting or foretelling the future, or a sixth sense about such things.

Eric continues, "Killer bees were happening just as we were doing **1.8 Bugs**. We have the troubling theory that we're coming up with ideas for Satan. I hope not. I hope we're working for the forces of good."

Sera Gamble who has been a writer on the show since season 1 and is now a producer, said, "For a long time I had been pitching stories about making deals with the devil – throughout season 1 and through the beginning of season 2 and it wasn't until mid-season 2 that the mythology sort of caught up with the idea and we were able to do **Crossroads Blues** and it made sense to do it at that time because Dad had just made this really horrible deal…we are in some ways, thinking and synthesizing and trying to incorporate what we see around us into what we do and in that way, I think I have the best job on the planet…it's the best fans in the world. My friends who are writers who don't primarily write genre shows, they counselled me before I took this job that generally these shows will never be hits on the level of *Grey's Anatomy*, but to me, the fans are so much more invested in the show like this and it's for the good."

Who wants to watch *Grey's Anatomy* anyway – well fine if you do, but you can say that doctor shows are a dime a dozen and are seen as good investments without taking risks by Studios and Networks. Hasn't anyone tired of these medical 'dramas' yet? Then they add in all this personal stuff about love triangles and it all becomes a soap in the guise of drama. It's never ending. No, be sticking with *Supernatural* thank you! *Supernatural* reigns supreme!!

Filming

The show is filmed in Vancouver, along with many other shows not necessarily in this genre, such as *X-Files,* Stargate SG-1, *Stargate*

Atlantis, Tru Calling, but Shiban enjoyed filming there as he found the light there is very different. "It was fun to go up there and prep an episode or two…it gives an instant creepy feeling if you shoot there. It also affords you so many different locations and *Supernatural* is a road show. We promise a different city every week. It could be impossible to do it in LA. You can make Vancouver look like 80% of the US very easily."

Kripke is amazed at the team, producer Cyrus Yavna; executive producer Kim Manners. They don't have any standing sets and always have new stories, in new towns with new monsters. They have eight days of prep and a low budget to get it right first time. He says, "It's a great looking show. Some of our scripts are no better than others and sometimes we nailed it and quite frankly I think we learned a few things in season 1 and there's some episodes that in season 1 that I kind of say, 'Oh well, that didn't work out as well as we'd hoped.'"

On shooting on location in Vancouver, Jared says, "It has been a great way to see the city and it is a nice change of pace, but I'm a dude from Texas so I like to establish a home of some sort. It is weird not knowing where you are going to work or how far you are going to be away from set. When you are on stage and you need to go to the bathroom, it takes 30 seconds to go. Sometimes when you are outside it is snowing, you really have to go pee and it takes 5 minutes to get anywhere to go to the bathroom." Ah, yes, there's a bit of 'potty' background for you.

"Honestly I hope our schedules get less grueling because I am so interested in this character of Sam and passionate about *Supernatural* that I'd really like to put my best foot forward each and everyday. That comes with getting some rest and having time to work on your script or character instead of filming and filming, waking up next and not even knowing what you are filming because you're too busy the day before memorizing the stuff you were filming for that day. I would like all the questions answered about our father and if he's gonna be with us. Sam and his father have had issues in the past and I'd like to see them resolved. [But they weren't because Dad was killed off adding only more issues to the mix and even more questions!] and I'd like to see some more witty banter between Sam and Dean." Explains Jared.

Jensen commented; "I think it's definitely a big plus for this show, the fact that we can have a long, inter-twining storyline and then also have the stand-alone episodes. I know coming from my standpoint, filming the mythology episodes is emotionally draining. They're much more draining than shooting the stand-alones. The stand-alones are nice, fun episodes to mix in with the heavy ones. So I think you need that balance of drama and …not necessarily comedy – but definitely the light-heartedness that those stand-alones bring."

(Should come up with a game and call it, *What Sam and Dean Would Do.*)

Jared stated they shoot 80-90 hours a week. "I lose track of the fact that people are enjoying a show and what we do. [Filming in Vancouver.] . Jensen and I went out to eat and I was talking about the show, how the hours are starting to get to me. (9 days for each episode, Monday to Friday. 12-16 hours a day, 5 days a week) and how I wish we could just be shooting back in LA."

Jensen concurs about the tough schedule, "I was coming off of *Smallville* and I knew how much he [Tom Welling] worked in the first few seasons before they started. Surrounding him with people to really give him some time off. I did *Dark Angel* where they did the same thing with Jessica Alba and she was working out of her mind. So I kind of had some what of a grasp on what to expect."

So he was all for getting in new actors on the show. "I at least thought by now we'd have some help and we're getting some help, so I'm looking forward to having somebody, not just to look at, because God knows I'm sick of looking at Jared – but also someone to come share the workload a little bit because after 22 episodes and nine months doing that everyday, all day, you just burn out because it's a great job, and it's a great gig and I love playing this role and I love this show and I don't want to ever get tired of it. I hope it helps the show in kind of mixing things up, where not only the actors are still getting refreshed and still showing up and doing their best everyday, but the audience is getting something new and refreshing, but still staying true to what the show is and what it always was and what it will continue to be." That was a mouthful.

Jensen definitely is tired of staring at Jared, Aww how could you. He says, "We're begging for new characters. I look at a show like *Heroes* and I laugh. Those characters are probably working two or three days a week, whereas Jared and I are in every single scene of each episode. If we get a scene off, we're laughing." At least they can boast, yes boast, they've given their all to the show and really put in the effort, make it their own and get to portray a range of emotions all across the board!

Eric commented on the presence of Ruby and Bela in season 3 that, "These girls organically move in and out of the story just like the other hunters and other characters in our show." On the role of Bela played by Lauren Cohan, Jensen says "I read with her for her audition. It was neat because Dean is this motorhead, blue-collar, Southern gun slinging cowboy guy and Lauren is this refined English person and it was like two totally [different] ends of the spectrum, in that opposites attract – or they may not [thank goodness]. I don't know – it definitely lends itself to possibly having some interesting dynamics."

Jensen however, still had his doubts about how they would fit into the show which focuses solely on the two brothers. "After reading the scripts and meeting the actresses, 'You look at *X Files* and it was always about David [Duchovny] and Gillian's [Anderson] characters, but they had characters surrounding them that supplied critical points of the story'. Hopefully this will keep the show very much about what it's always been about and just add more dynamic to the show."

Sera Gamble: "I think these women are really cool and unexpected and I've been having a great time writing both of them."

Eric says Ruby is a hunter "whose moral line is a lot further down than our boys. She's pretty ruthless, a little unhinged and very controlling and manipulative and as early as in episode 2 [of season 3] there'll be a big twist on Ruby and she isn't going to be who we thought she was, which will spin her story off in a different direction."

Well some people did think Ruby and Bela would be love interests for the boys, but that wouldn't really have worked (though Sam did have a 'fling' with Ruby in season 4, not our Ruby from season 3 mind you, so in that sense she wasn't really a love interest.) Eric: "There's a misconception that it's going to be two girls in the back seat of the Impala [As if! That made me laugh, 'Who's driving now Dean? So I can have a bit of nookie with one of them! Agh!] and it's not going be the Scooby gang – that's not the case."

We're in our own reality up here, which isn't really reality." In Jared's interview with TVGuide.com, TV Guide commented;"The fans are analyzing every detail." To which Jared responded, "[In a girly voice] he looked uglier in this episode than he did in the last episode." [Clearly he must've been referring to Jensen! Joke!]. Jared also explains it takes 8 filming days to do one episode. 15 hours a day, 120 hours an episode. {See above.} So it's tiring, especially with the fight scenes, running around, being chased by monsters. "With Jensen and I as the only series regulars there's a lot of responsibility put on our shoulders which we both love and we're trying to knock it out of the park!"

They get hurt during fight scenes, attempting to act like the cocky Texans that they are; tall tough and macho, but that's all part of the show and the appeal. The fight scenes also look professional as Dad trained them all their lives. He's suggested some monsters like Jack

Frost, but admits Jared; he's not a good writer, only an actor. He hates getting up in the morning.

His stuntman is really good to him. Jared on stunt work: "I do a lot until I broke my hand. Then they thought that maybe we shouldn't have him doing that. But I have a stunt guy who is a great match for me and he's a lot tougher than I am. He does all the hard stuff and I just look pretty." So did he work out for his scene in **1.17 Hell House**, with his towel on! Ha – his shower scene – because he still looked buff in that too – didn't he – in the buff! Well, almost!

Jared enjoyed the fight training as that's the skills their characters have on the show. "It was fun to work out this summer and have to box, work in martial arts and do some of the fight scenes."

As mentioned Jensen also enjoys the same stuff, it's uncanny their line of thinking, once again, Jensen, "All the cool things I get to do. This includes practicing a scene in which he took apart a shot gun and a pistol and put them back together. Also liked driving a tractor in the snow which he hasn't done since he was little and driving trucks on a farm. Jensen: "We get to do a lot of cool and unique stuff as obviously we're dealing with the supernatural every week. It's all the stuff you dream of doing as a little boy."

He's actually likened some of the episodes they've filmed to being chilly. Jared: "When we are filming the demons are pink tape's' on the walls that we have to look at and be scared of. It's definitely the hardest part to act scared."

On filming the episodes and especially the monster of the week, Robert Singer commented, "I think one thing we've found is that if something was just kind of a purely supernatural entity; it was a little hard for us to pull off and that less was more. For credibility's sake if it was corporeal, and walked and talked and looked like a human, it gave us more latitude in our storytelling."

Eric was more concerned with how they'd be able to transfer the real scares and horror onto the screen due to a limited budget and time. "Our first creature, you never see the thing in the episode, and that's because we made this monster and it was terrible-looking, it was like a 1950's sci-fi movie" which was cut because of the above.

Episode **1.8 Bugs**, said, Eric, "I think the CG guys did a valiant job, but it looked CG because I think we over-reached. I always aim for less is more and I always aim to put more and more in the shadows but even when you see what the thing is, you have to be really smart about what the thing is, you have to be really smart about what it's going to be and you have to tell effective stories.

Acting against a backdrop of what isn't really there. Jared said, "In the pilot I see Jess on the ceiling, on fire. Obviously she's not actually on the ceiling burning but still I had to lay down and look up, start yelling and screaming. They set fire around me and had me run out of the room."

Jared would be terrified of anything from *Supernatural* in real life – except for the bugs. Jensen says everything on the show isn't real, it's CGI, except for the bugs. Where they were in a small room filled with 60,000 live bees. "…camera and sound guys were like,' Okay, Jensen and Jared, it's time for you guys to come in and we walked in, in just street clothes. There was no make believe in that."

Jared continues, "The beekeeper told me the bees were drones and not aggressive – so they swat the bees and he didn't want to wave his arms around like a ballet dancer, so he swat and hit them. It was funny how the bee wrangler's story changed from when we were rehearsing up to the point of filming because on the actual day of filming he was like, 'Oh they're getting angry – they're being vacuumed too much because they'd shoot and then the guy would vacuum them back into their little box." The bees apparently were placed on tarpaulin in boxes and they'd fall onto the tarp, the wranglers would shake the tarp allowing the bees to fly up and hit them.

Our scariest adversaries of the [first] season were the backwards cannibal family [**1.15 The Benders**]; or the little girl ghost in **1.18 Provenance**. Where she came out of the painting and it was just a little girl [but a scary one]. It took us a while to really learn that to conceptualize our creatures as human; they're scarier than inhuman things, which are very difficult to mount anyway."

Robert Singer, "**Dead In the Water** was really hard due to the shooting schedule; working with water, trying to make this thing in the water, this little boy, be scary."

Kim Manners said, "I like my show [episode] called **Dead in The Water**, but **Home** which goes back to the home that the boy's mother was killed in when Sam was a baby and Dean was about 4 years old and it's a great script so I'd look out for that one for sure."

Of course Jensen and Jared joke they don't get paid enough for what they have to go through, but Jared says they were hired because they could take the physical "beating" that accompanies the show. Jensen adds they spent six weeks in the gym before season 1 began filming. Had kick boxing lessons and boxing lessons. "It paid off we're still walking fine after season 1." They notice bruises, like in the shower, that weren't there before, but they played sports as youngsters and so are used to it. Jared disagrees, "Me, personally I thought I was going to be a pretty actor boy and not get beat up anymore!"

On the subject of fan mail, Jared and Jensen get some odd letters. Not to mention some from prisoners. Well, it's hardly surprising since the show caters to all tastes and the guys did look particularly cute in their prison issue glowing orange suits; as they did in their priest outfits! Jensen: "I got one letter from someone who said they'd actually quoted Sam and Dean at their father's funeral and that watching the show had helped them get through it. That made me feel good inside. I got a note from a paranormal investigator telling me that in his travels he's come across some interesting demons, so if I'd like to know about any of them I should call him. But we get some funny ones in block capitals and you look at the return address and it will be like 'Cell 345.'"

Casting

A show comes along only once in a blue moon, where you can say the cast is truly gifted and brings so much into the show, giving it their all. Can you imagine *Supernatural* without Jensen and Jared? Neither can I.

Eric Kripke on his two leads: "I had high expectations and they met them and exceeded them. Each one brings his own distinctive personality to the character. They both are the guys in so many ways as real people. As the season progressed we all got to know each other better, we as the writers shared writing things the guys would say naturally into their parts, and the parts just evolved and became more and more the boys and the boys became more and more the parts. It just all melded together. Jared is so relatable and sympathetic, Jensen is so funny and sharp – they've inhabited those boys and they brought depth to it and they really do love each other, they really did become brothers. I watch them at parties all the time. They're like, 'Hey man' watching each other and watching each other's back. You can't fake the camaraderie they have."

Also Warner Bros selected Jensen and Jared for the prospective roles of Dean and Sam without either of them screen testing together for the parts, which makes it doubly more convincing since the chemistry was there without them having met and playing their roles before filming. Jensen: "It is extremely unusual, but it is also a vote of confidence. They wanted us from the get go. With the shows we had been a part of, *Dawson's Creek, Smallville, Gilmore Girls*, those were all somebody else's shows and we were kind of not background, but we were definitely window dressing. I think with this show it is ours and we feel that and every week it is he and I, we are at the heart of it. But at the same time I think we both knew that now it was ours to lose; its success lay on our shoulders."

The studios confidence paid off since their brilliance at portraying their characters had a significant impact on the show; making it real and believable. Everytime you watch a sad scene; happy or funny, you feel as if you're right there with them sharing every moment; every single facet of their lives; their fights and their heartaches!

Jensen came aboard immediately, I said 'Yes' when I heard who was attached to it, when I heard who was going to do it. I got a call from David Nutter and that's definitely a very convincing call. When he told me that he was attached [to direct the pilot] and Co-executive producer, and that Peter Johnson was attached as Executive Producer, I was interested immediately. I knew these guys. I knew their work. When David Nutter directs a pilot you pretty much know it's a sure thing. He gets the pick of the litter. As soon as I read the script I wanted to read more. That's what you want from any script. From any series. When I was doing *Still Life* it was such a great pilot script, but at the end everything got tied up nice and neat. I don't think the show had any idea where it was going to go and with *Supernatural* the possibilities are endless. I couldn't wait to see another script."

On Dean, Jensen also comments, "I was originally supposed to go for the part of Sam and then I read the script and just really liked the humour of Dean. I like his sarcasm, his crass way of talking to people and his cockiness. I thought I could have a lot more fun with that. There are bits of me in there – he's a more exaggerated version of parts of my character, a more over the top version of myself."

Eric Kripke scripted *Bogeyman* in 2005, which also starred Lucy Lawless (from Eric's other shortlived show *Tarzan*) and Emily Deschanel (*Bones*) which grossed almost $70 million globally.

Maybe a good time to interject with my *six degrees of separation*: *Eric Kripke created Tarzan; the title song of which, Try, was sung by Palo Alto; the location of Stanford University; where Sam from Supernatural was studying law; Supernatural also created by Eric Kripke.*

Kim Manners had worked in Vancouver since 1986 on shows like the pilot of *21 Jump Street*. Everyone made him feel at home on the set, like a family. His father told him, 'If you can't enjoy the working environment in the motion picture industry get out of it'. It's advice you have to follow because I'm with these people more than I'm with my wife and kids."

He hopes the series remains scary (like Jared) and "stylish and the relationship between the brothers stays honest and real. I think they are going to have a show here that lasts at least 5 years. Or long as the chemistry works and they keep ratching up tension I think they'll have a big hit on their hands!"

Veteran's Day, Chicago, Jensen and Jared were presented with Special Forces Coins and letters of Congratulations by Army Master Sergeant Kevin Wise of the First Special Forces out of Baghdad. *Supernatural* was the most requested DVD, helping the soldiers based over there escape the reality of their own situation and escape into a show about family. The duo were clearly moved by this.

Locations

The weather is always a factor in Vancouver. During the penultimate episode they had snow.

Asylum says Jensen "was actually filmed in an abandoned mental institution and it was so spooky the art department didn't have to do anything to it. It was a huge five storey building completely deserted and not used. We were filming on the third floor and when they called 'lunch' the whole crew started walking towards the stairwell. So I took a shortcut down the back stairs. I went down it was just completely dark and there was this long, long hallway with a little light at the end of it, it was really freaky. So I walked a little faster and then I was running past all these rooms. So that was a little freaky. It made all the hairs on the back of my neck stand up."

Season 4

Eric Kripke thought it was great to end season 3 by sending Dean to hell, well being practically skewered in hell. "Sort of MC Esherr meets *Hellraiser*." Dean ended up in hell because he wanted the show to go into a new direction. Also since he says everyone thought Dean would be saved in the end. Now, whatever made him think that, considering no one's <u>ever</u> safe in *Supernatural* territory. You can come and go and just go for good. Mom went, Dad went. Sam bit the dust and was brought back, so why not the last of the Winchesters, so to speak, in Dean. Having him experience the phrase, he always said in the show was something to be expected. Raising the bar, since not many characters in shows actually get to hell, then return. *Angel* aside. *Buffy* died, but she didn't get to hell, she was in a better place. Not that I'm making any similarities or differences here between the three shows.

Sometimes you wonder the point of interviews when everyone says, 'I can't give too much away'. Remember if you're an avid follower of a show, you'll come back to it over and over irrespective of what is revealed or not. Seeing something on the screen is completely different to how you perceive a scene or show from when you read about it. Besides not many people take on board and remember what they've read (well I do, but I'm probably just one of a few exceptions). Eric continues, "I can give this away. Dean spends a lot more time in hell than anyone's probably thinking. Dean could spend – in human time, six months. In hell time, who knows how many years or decades that might be. He will emerge to a different landscape."

However Dean won't be a demon; but he'll be shrouded in mystery. (So no demon black eyes as shown in **3.10**.) "We'll slowly unfold Dean remembering what happened in hell and that will drastically affect their relationship. Dean is a POW coming home from the worst hellhole literally, ever. That becomes one of his issues." Dean is still the same as before though.

Season 4 was meant to have some great plot twists for us though, do they come about, I won't know at time of writing about season 4, since we are halfway through the season and all of it won't be covered by me, yet as I have a deadline to submit this book! Unfortunately, but if you like it let me know, and anyway I will be continuing writing since I have to finish season 4 in my own words and write about season 5 too and anything else that comes along! So I will be back in some form or another to finish off my *Supernatural* obsession (but in a good way!)

Interviews at San Diego ComicCon 2008

Upcoming season episodes include Sam and Dean heading back to high school when they were teens. Eric Kripke: "We're just starting to talk about it, but I think we'll do it this season 4 (see **4.13**). An episode where the boys investigate a haunting at one of the high schools they used to go to and their flashbacks to what the boys' high school lives were like. We'll sort of see them played by 18 year olds and giving people swirlies…we haven't worked it out." (Is Sam really the type to give swirlies to anyone, even as a teen, though Dean would revel at it.) No, they didn't give them swirlies, but Dean was older and Sam wasn't 18 either!

On hell, Eric comments: "We're not really going to see hell except in quick flashes and those types of moments. There isn't going to be like, fade in hell, Dean being poked with a pitchfork. It's going to be more about his return to earth, and what that does to you psychologically. He's still Dean, but deep in his soul he's been in the worst POW camp ever." Another mention of POW. "By the time Dean returns, four months will've passed in Sam's life. The boys have never been able to keep secrets from each other before. Not since season 1, when they were separate. So to have a period of time where they were separate, and then can surprise each other again, has been refreshing and fun to write."

Actually Sam and Dean did keep secrets from each other. Sam never told Dean in season 1 that he actually dreamt about Jessica being killed, but wasn't able to tell her. That was his secret in **1.5** causing his eyes to bleed. We never found out Dean's dirty, little secret – which caused his eyes also to bleed. Then Dad made Dean promise to kill Sam if he ever turned bad in season 2. Dean also kept his belief Dad sacrificed himself to save him to himself for quite a while, until **2.9** and **2.8** respectively. Then Sam being given demon blood in **2.21**, he also doesn't tell Dean until it comes out in a roundabout way in **4.4**, where Dean almost forces him to confess by what he says to him about Mom and Dad. So yes, they have kept secrets before, for a while, before actually revealing them.

Jared carries on in his part of the interview; "I think Sam and Dean are both more individual. They've both done things in the last four months [four months for Sam] that they're kind of worried about...I think as we get into the meat of the season, episodes **8-15**, we're really going to delve into what Sam did for those four months which Dean was gone and the pain that he's gone through. His brother was dead...probably did some things he wasn't necessarily sure about and proud of [like sleeping with Ruby]. He's definitely more hard-edged."

Eric: "For the first time there's a lot of story mythology centred around Dean. A lot of it was about Sam being psychic, <u>now</u> there's mysteries about each of them." What I said for awhile too, that there must be more to big brother Dean than just being Sam's brother and guardian. He must have more of a role to play in all this, otherwise his character and the show would get boring if no one evolved, changed and developed into something different; stronger in momentum, reserve. Dean is the chosen one and it will be interesting to discover the impact this has on both their lives and the journey they travel together in this season as they face the possible Apocalypse.

Jensen: "I always figured Dean would come back, otherwise it's the *Sam Winchester* show (he jests.) I didn't know how, why. It would be that they find away to get me out, and that I would go back to just being Dean and trying to save Sam from whatever the demons had in store for him. But now that I've come back and I can't figure out how or why, it's really starting to play into the psyche of Dean and what he's going to go through, how that's going to involve himself into the mythology of not just Sam, but the entire show."

Dean was chosen to be the one to help save the world and maybe even to stop Sam from evolving, or more like devolving into the darkness. Eric: "I'm really excited about this one. We're giggling like schoolgirls in the writers' room. We think we're onto something this year. I think we have some really, really, cool stuff in store."

In August 2008 the author of the book, *The Outsiders* and *Rumblefish*, SE Hinton visited the *Supernatural* set, as a huge fan she asked Eric Kripke if she could visit. Would that we all could have such privileges?!! Quick I'll put on my begging face!!

Jared believes the audience doesn't want Sam turning dark (actually some of us do.)

Used to say you know a show has come so far when the leads get their own covers on magazines of which our guys have had plenty!

In the *CW Awards Winners Gallery, Supernatural* was Best Series with 38.4% of the votes. Best Actor Jensen Ackles 31.3%. Best Writer/producer/auteur Eric Kripke 38.8%. (*Watch With Kristen CW Awards*.)

Jensen Ackles took 5th place in *AfterElton's Hot 100 of 2009*, desirable male celebrities in TV and movies. Jared Padalecki took 12th place, whereas Misha Collins peeked into the 100 in 93rd place.

Season 4 of *Supernatural* gained 3.96 million in the US. For the second episode of the season, then this dropped to 3.2 million, so it has gained more viewers this season than season 3.

Heroes season 3, episodes, **3.10 & 11 Eclipse Parts 1 & 11**, when Matt, Hiro and Ando travel to Lawrence, Kansas in search of Daphne; they come across a comic book store run by a character called Sam!

The Coventry Telegraph reports Jensen saying that he and Jared both have six year contracts for the show. Meaning both Sam and Dean should be back if the show is picked up by the CW Network for a sixth year. Jensen said he has to return. "I have a six year contract." Whilst Jared says, "My best guess is that *Supernatural* will go beyond season 5. Season 4 had the best viewing figures we've ever seen and it just seems to be on an upward curve. So the studio's really keen to see more."

They were speaking at *Asylum 3* at the Birmingham Hilton Metropole, in June 2009. Jared also added if he feels the show will 'jump the shark', then he doesn't want to be involved in a season 6. Great news for us, even though at the time of writing, season 5 hasn't started filming yet. But there's a downside, Eric Kripke's contract expires after season 5. So either he's offered a lucrative new contract to stay with the show, or it will continue without him – that just wouldn't be the same!

However, in an interview in *Entertainment Weekly*, Eric Kripke commented on season 6 by saying, "Despite what the networks and studio may or may not want, I don't have more than five seasons of a story." The CW network are not looking to lose a ratings winner. Says Eric, "I certainly would be willing to make sure there are enough villains and heroes around to continue a new storyline and I would be around to answer a few questions – that's it. I'm outta here. There's no way I'm doing season 6."

Jensen Ackles reportedly feels the same way, as does Jared Padalecki. Jensen: "We don't live at home. We don't sleep in our own beds. Our families aren't here…to do it for another five years or whatever, I don't know if I could handle it."

Jared doesn't like the publicity involved. He comments, "I enjoy working but what's the point? Do I just want to keep on doing more photo shoots and work so I can get more famous so I can do even more photo shoots…and I get sick of talking about myself." Well, that's an actor's lot. Besides fame, press etc, whatever else comes with it, will always follow him around – and the same for anything he does as an actor. That's the nature of the beast – whether it be for a TV show, stage play or movie.

So it's too early to tell on a season after 5, since there have been conflicting reports. Maybe it can have a movie or two instead.

Eric did tell *TV Guide Magazine* that Meg will return in season 5, but not in the guise of Nicki Aycox, who played her originally. She is filming *Dark Blue* and so will be unavailable. Meg will be played by Rachel Miner, from the US Daytime soap, *Guiding Light.*

Also Adrienne Palicki is reportedly to resume her role of Jessica from season 1. Mark Pellegrino will play Lucifer. He has appeared on *Lost, Dexter.* Jensen said he's going to rent his own place when season 5 gets underway, as they just do too much stuff together and so stay up nearly all night, when they have early starts.

Misha commented on Castiel's character in season 5: "I'd like to see him operate according to his own moral compass. To see him stop looking to others for answers. If he stopped taking orders and really stuck to his own more. I think it would be much more interesting for Castiel and maybe – maybe he should get, like a girlfriend or something. Castiel deserves his scene with a girl in back of the Impala."

The expected return date for season 5 in the US is 10th September 2009.

Biographies

JARED PADALECKI

Jared Tristan Padalecki was born in San Antonio, Texas on 19 July 1982. He is of Polish descent, as you can guess from his surname. 6'4" tall. He attended James Madison High School in San Antonio. He was the Presidential Scholars Program Candidate in 2000, his senior year. He and fellow classmate, Chris Cardeans won the National Forensics League National Championship in Duo Interpretation in 1998. Jared graduated May 2000 Magna Cum Laude and intended to study Engineering at the University of Texas.

Jared attended acting classes in Texas when he was 12. On the first day of Drivers Ed he believed he was on a one way street and drove on the left side (the correct side of the road to drive on of course, okay in the UK it is!)

He is has an older brother, Jeff and a younger sister, Megan. His Mom is Sherri and Dad is Jerry. He was a 'Claim to Fame' Contest winner on *Teen Choice Awards Fox*, where he met his present manager who saw him and signed him up straightaway. Presented the 1999 teen Choice awards.

He filmed a Pilot for NBC which wasn't picked up, then joined the cast of *Gilmore Girls*. Jared was the third actor to be cast in the role of Dean in *Gilmore Girls*. A lucky name for him, as Jensen originally auditioned for the role of Sam, this means perhaps Jared may have played another Dean! Jared had to wear hair extensions for the season 5 premiere of *Gilmore Girls* as he'd cut his hair after the season 4 finale. Jared was the second tallest cast member of *Gilmore Girls*, 3" taller than Scott Patterson. 1-2" shorter than Edward Hermann. Jared on *Gilmore Girls*: "It was a great time. I started when I was 17 and finished when I was 22 and they nurtured me. If I even have any free time, which I don't, I would feel comfortable popping in to say, 'Hi' to everybody."

He still wanted to attend university, but changed his mind after he got the role of Dean in the show.

During the filming *House of Wax,* he locked himself out of his house on numerous occasions and had to call, then co-star and roommate, Chad Michael Murray to let him in.

Michelle Branch wanted Jared on her video for the song, *Everywhere* but he was busy filming.

On 2 December 2006, he won the Celebrity Poker Tournament in Canada. His prize, a Giantto watch, and was entered into the 2007 World Series of Poker main event. But it wasn't Texas Hold 'Em though!

Jared's favourite foods are cheeseburgers with lettuce, tomatoes and mustard. (A fave of Dean's in *Supernatural*!) Chocolate chip cookie dough ice cream. White chocolate Macadamia nut cookies and he eats lots of sweets (candy.) His fave ice cream' Cold Stone Creamery, "..could eat it all day everyday. I'm actually a little lactose intolerant so it kind of makes me feel sick, but I can't stop myself, I'd be about 400 pounds if I didn't."

The March 2003 issue of *YM* listed him as one of *The Hottest Guys on TV*. He used to make home videos with his friends in Texas.

In 2007, he was number 37 on *TV Guides 50 Sexiest Men.* Sandy (his former girlfriend) gave him a PSP for his birthday in 2006. On 18 September 2006 he appeared at the CW launch party.

In 2000 he was the Grand Marshal for a parade in San Antonio.

Jared is interested in making a movie from the book *Back Roads* by Tawni O'Dell.

In 2000-2002 season, he played on the Hollywood Knights Baseball team.

He owns a Toshiba laptop (snap so do I!) His favourite video game is *James Bond 007: Nightfire.* He owns a sprint PCS Touchpoint. Has a German Shepherd and a pit-bull dingo named, Sadie and Harley.

Jared wants to make the most of every moment; to work hard and be grateful for what he's received. Both Jared and Jensen would prefer to have Bobby on the show more often and they both love Jim Beaver to bits. Jared also likes having guest stars on the show and set, but then ultimately they get killed off – like Meg (Nicki Aycox), Jeffrey Dean Morgan, Sterling K Brown, for who Jared has nothing but praise and hated it when his character of Gordon was killed off. He likes how the show has guests who should be movie stars in their own right. Jensen agrees with this too. When filming begins, Jared and Jensen are both 100% committed to the show and most of it's for us fans and followers, so Jared doesn't watch any TV or reads when he's filming.

A favourite music is any Pearl Jam CD. Listens to the band: *Our Lady Peace*.

He wears T-shirts, jeans, tennis shoes or anything comfortable. His favourite novel is The Great Gatsby by F Scott Fitzgerald.

49

After presenting the *Teen Choice Awards*, Jared was cast in his first movie, *New York Minute.* When he was a *Teen Choice awards* presenter, he didn't think he'd be an adored actor with his own TV show. In the *New York Minute* DVD, Jared appears in the Extras talking of the Olson twins and his name is spelt 'Paladecki'. He didn't notice this and neither did any one else until an observant fan mentioned it.

He didn't want to be covered with wax in the *House of Wax* movie and complained, eventually having to give in and found it wasn't as bad as he thought.

Jared filmed **1.3 Dead in the Water** with a broken hand as he injured it defending himself and Jensen in a fight.

His celebrity crush is Jennifer Love Hewitt (no wonder Dean mentions her a lot in seasons 1 and 2.)

He plays for Orlando Magic on BAE League.

He got a Starbond at the Hollywood Stock Exchange. He was a bit red faced at *TV Guide* when it misquoted him joking to co-star Alexis Bledel that, "the dork store called and they're out of you." in between shots.

He changed his basketball jersey from number 24 to 32. He was considered for the role of Clark Kent/Superman in the new *Superman* film franchise. He also auditioned for the part of Anakin Skywalker in *Star wars*.

Nominated for two Teen Choice Awards for *Gilmore Girls* and *House of Wax*

He and Jensen play street hockey between takes on the *Supernatural* set.

In 2005, Jensen and Jared were voted *People Magazine's Sexiest Ghostbusters.* Jared wanted to be a teacher if he wasn't an actor, just like his mother. He hates it when he gets blamed for things he didn't do as he's seen as an "easy target". Jensen and Jared enjoy playing practical jokes and pranks (just like their on-screen personas, Sam and Dean.)

His fave car is the *Firebird.* Is that the *Trans Am Pontiac Firebird* because that was mine too when I was younger! Fave show: *The Simpsons.* (Wonder if Jensen and Jared will get to do a voiceover for the show?)

One of his character flaws is procrastination.

Originally considered for Clark Kent in *Smallville,* which went to Tom Welling. Jensen also auditioned for this, so that's another thing they also have in common.

His eye colour is blue-green and not brown as described in **1.15 The Benders**. His fave colour is blue; he had a penchant for blue shirts on *Supernatural*. Jared and Jensen also watch football and drink beer together. Carpool to work and share a place together in Vancouver, whilst filming the show. Jared sold his house in LA.

Fave movie: *Good Will Hunting* and enjoys horror movies, his favourite is *The Shining*, also mentioned oft times in the show.

Jared was best man at his brother's wedding. His idol is Johnny Depp. Jared says, "Obviously I daydreamed as a kid [like Jensen sporting his *Superman* pajamas in his modelling days, then ending up on *Smallville*.] and always hoped and prayed for this to happen. I've been super-lucky and had talented people working for me. I've just been in the right place at the right time [some of Jensen's advice to his best friends there!] I am on this great rollercoaster ride and I'm going to ride it. I'm going to enjoy myself and try and soak it up for as long as I can!"

He likes to move around the *Supernatural* set on a scooter. His friends, as well as Chad Michael, include, Derek Lee Nixon, Andrew Pozza. He was cast in the lead of the WB production of the new *MacGyver* as a relative of the original, but the Pilot wasn't picked up.

Jared on Jensen: "I have an older brother and a younger sister and Jensen does as well, so he and I just kicked it off pretty quickly. He's Texan, I'm Texan. You hear these horror stories about *Desperate Housewives* and stuff where everybody's arguing about trailers, but we just want to work hard and make sure our crew is happy."

He loves baking cookies. In the winter they have cookie smelling candles and he buys them by the truckload.

On girls: there has to be more than a physical attraction. Must be someone he can talk to, have fun with doing any stuff. Who he can enjoy and vice versa. With a good sense of humour.

He says: "I can rest when I'm older, now's the time to work hard and try to make a name for myself...I'm so happy with my family, my career and my friends and I'd like for them to be here forever so I guess loss is what scares me the most."

Jared believes in the supernatural: "I've never had any personal experiences, but it's a big world and it's hard to believe we're the only things around. I'm sure there are other people like us, or a bizzarro earth. I'm sure a lot of it is scary."

He doesn't like to party, "I have a house with two big Plasma screens, two dogs, a grill, chessboard. I like to keep it low key, invite friends over, order some 'Papa John's pizzas and Coors light; play poker and ping-pong and chill. I'm pretty private." Oh and Jared can rhyme too, "I'd much rather play guitar and go to a bar."

In his opinion, *Supernatural* fans are more intense, they can say how a demon was killed and they know their *Supernatural*.

On meeting former girlfriend Sandy McCoy, on the set of *Cry Wolf*, "We met and flirted and all we went out as a group, but she and I didn't go to on a date or anything. When we started dating a couple of months later people were like, 'What took you guys so long?' I thought, 'Was it that obvious?' She's a really great, generous person. She has a huge heart and makes people laugh and smile. She's a lot of fun and very genuine. We make each other laugh which is important. Looks only last so long and passion is fleeting."

He's the opposite of Sandra, "If you asked if she'd rather have a deranged murderer break in or a ghost, she'd say a deranged murderer."

Director Jeff Wadlow, of *Cry Wolf* said of Jared, "...came in and he nailed the jock blueblood that we wanted but he also added a goofyness and humour that was very endearing."

People said he looked like Matt Damon. "Now I get Brad Pitt." Well, we don't thinks so, you're great just the way you are Jared, as Jared!!!!!

Whilst filming the *Flight of the Phoenix* he was involved in a minor car accident and believed he was dead. He continued to think this until a passer-by asked why he was standing at the roadside. "We were on sand roads that were just sort of - you follow the tracks of the car in front of you and I wasn't used to driving in sand. I grew up in Texas where its asphalt and gravel if anything, but the car started to swerve a little so I started to try to get it straight and just turned and it ended up flipping and I'm on the side of the road and it does a whole roll and it lands upright and you're sort of at the second like, 'Am I okay, what's going on?' and you sort of quirk your neck and you move your back and then I remembered seeing movies where you know a car crashes into something and everybody's okay and then it explodes!

So I'm like, 'Oh no!' So I open my door and run across the street and I'm like 50 feet away and I'm like 'Thank God I'm not gonna be in there when it explodes!' I'm looking at the car and it's not exploding and it doesn't really look damaged and I realize that I just ran outta the car after flipping it and I start looking around and I'm like, 'There's no sounds, no wind, no birds or trees, I'm dead.' I thought, I was sure I was dead. I just heard some story about a guy who sees a car accident and goes up to help and sees himself inside and I was like, 'That is me. I am dead.' [Like an episode of *the Dead* Zone.] I better call the set and tell them I'm dead. So I run back to the car to get my phone and I turn the car upside down, which it's now used to because it just flipped and I look for the phone and I can't find the phone and I'm like 'Of course I can't find the phone I'm dead and I don't need the phone, why would I need the phone." This is Jared's "goofy story" as he calls it.

On being so well loved, he comments, "You know since Jensen and [Jared] are so hot – it's very flattering and so cute and a girl will come up and a guy will, and say, 'Hey you're so cute'. You know blah, blah, blah whatever.' [**In 2.15 Tall Tales**, that's what Dean says about Sam in his version of the story, that Sam, "blah, blah, blahs" a lot!] It's just, 'No' I'm here to film a TV show. It's flattering and it's fun to tease each other about that. I don't think we take ourselves very seriously. Growing up I used to see these people who were called cuties or hotties or sex symbols and they'd be like, 'You know I'm sexy [Jared 'striking a pose' – that'd be something to see!] – 'Look how sexy and hot I am' and I think it's just disgusting and I think you gotta kinda be able to make fun of yourself you know. However you look is just a shell of who you are – it's really nothing to do with you."

He's from Texas but doesn't have an accent – when he's tired or drunk (so you get drunk then d'ya.) it sneaked out. 'Hey y'all!'

As to love, Jared says, "Don't place expectations on someone. Enjoy the time you have together and let it go where it goes. Be yourself and the right guy [or gal] will come along. Whether it be today, tomorrow or next year. It'll happen." His drama coach gave him self-confidence when he wasn't sure of himself.

"I'm a little self conscious about my body. I love to wear hoodies because you can get cozy and eat some food and your belly doesn't show."

"On Dean: "It's pretty funny – every now and then someone will say, 'Okay Dean is over there' and I'll take a little stutter step, then think, 'Oh wait –I'm not Dean anymore'.

He's not "Mr. Tough but I can't name any specific fear I have…I don't know if this qualifies as a superstition, but everytime I step on a plane, I kiss my finger and touch the top of the doorjamb. I started doing that in high school when someone would run a red or yellow light. I don't know what that means."

It's definitely the people that I love – my parents, brother, my sister. We're a close family. We're also good friends and for that, we are very blessed."

Jared comments, "I have seen an unidentified flying object. I couldn't identify it, nor could anyone I was with. But no, I haven't been abducted just yet." Always did acting a as child, in school plays etc.

"Australia is gorgeous. It's green and the Great Barrier Reef is a wonder of the world. I had a great time. I flew Sandy out she and I flew out and we went scuba diving. It was so beautiful. Everybody is like, 'It's the Outback. It's going to be sand'. It's gorgeous.

They were together almost 2 years at the time. Jared says, "That's been my limit so far so I've got to break up with her. That's my cut-off point. I can take a hint. But seriously I hope we can do another movie together. That would be fun." Alas, no movie and they did break up, sadly, but Sandra did appear in an episode of season 3 with Jared as the crossroads demon and Jared shot her with the colt. Make of that what you will.

It was reported that Jared called off his engagement to Sandra; they were engaged in March 2008. A source said: "Now that Jared is starring in *Friday 13th* he's starting to see that his career could really take off and he doesn't want a wife to hold him back from becoming a major star. He's really ambitious and he wants to be very successful. He's been telling everyone, 'There's more to life than relationships and I want to be single'." Sandra was devastated, " She really didn't see it coming." But this really doesn't sound like Jared at all; he doesn't come across as being so callous and uncaring. Some people just want to get in and spread rumours don't they. They take pleasure in it.

In actual fact, Jared announced their break-up at the Dallas Convention in 2008. A source of mine, who was actually at the Con when Jared announced this stated, that Jared never said he didn't want the burden of a wife. They both just decided on parting, on friendly terms. They both wanted different things from their lives. Jared didn't say Sandy would get in his way or would hold him back in his movie career. She's so sweet. It's just common sense when you think about it. Since it'd be his choice as to what he'd want to do and where he'd want to take his own career. How would a wife hold him back? Duh. Perhaps Jensen should take him under his wing and incidentally, Jensen would be a good role model for anyone, not just for Jared. No, I'm not being condescending, but Jensen has been around a few years longer so he knows the score.

On *Supernatural* preparation, "I just watched a lot of scary stuff. *The X Files, Twilight Zone, The Ring.* I also researched mythology. My Mom she studies Greek Mythology. There's so much literary value to the show, so I wanted to know the deeper sides to the stories and Jensen and I got the fight training. We boxed and did martial arts because both of our characters are supposed to be pretty well-versed."

Jensen and Jared, "We clicked pretty much off the bat. We have similar interests in sports. We're both laid back. We like to eat food, have a good beer, hang out and have a good time. We leave each other when we need to need to, jazz each other up too." Jensen wins Jared at golf and he beats him at basket ball and *Guitar Hero*.

"I had a nightmare about being on a cruise ship and the ship going down. It was an arduous process of the ship going down and we knew it was going down. There was everyone I know and love on the ship. Anywhere I can be with my family is the happiest place on earth."

More recently Jared will be seen in the remake to *The Texas Chainsaw Massacre* where he plays Clay and in a remake of *Friday the 13th*. Let's not have typecasting now! He filmed this from 30th April 2008 in Austin, Texas and was filming *Supernatural* in Vancouver too. "The last thing I wanted to do was to watch a movie where some skinny, pretty boy was fighting...I drank my protein shakes. I like to work out and keep in shape anyway." That's why he looks more muscular in season 4 of the show. He also says he can still watch a movie and still be frightened by it. "One of the great things about horror movies in general, it's total escapism." He was glad to be in Austin. He says, "Austin is my favourite city in the nation. It's about an hour away from where I grew up." He was a fan of the *Friday the 13th movies* and now revels in the chance of having being involved in it. "This movie is a reimagining, it isn't a remake. Even though Jason is still there, the characters are completely different. I decided to sign on for *Friday the 13th* after reading the script, because it tells a different story and strives to do something other than simply scare kids."

Jared doesn't mind making horror films and being associated with such a genre, (hey, I just mentioned typecasting). He says, "Talented and hardworking actors don't get pigeonholed no matter how many TV shows, movies or projects they do in the same genre. I'm just grateful for the projects that come my way. So I'm just going to keep working hard and whatever genre I'm in, well, that's the genre I'm in."

He also made the movie, *Home for Christmas* about the artist Thomas Kincaid, the early part of his life. Whose main reason for painting was to save his mother's home. The movie also stars Peter O'Toole – a legend in his own right. Jared was in awe of him. "He's very wise, confident and passionate and he's still very funny and sharp. It was amazing. I mean. He was *Lawrence of Arabia*."

TV SHOWS:

A Ring Of Endless Light Zachery Gray
Gilmore Girls Dean Forester (episodes 22-65 and recurring.)
Movie Life House of Wax Himself

Supernatural Sam Winchester
ER Paul Harris
The Ellen Degeneres Show Himself

MOVIES
Cry Wolf (Tom) *(2005)*
House of Wax *(Wade) (2005)*
Flight of the Phoenix *(Davis) (2004)*
New York Minute (Trey) (2004)
A Ring Of Endless Light (Zachery) (2002)
Young MacGyver (Clay MacGyver) (2003)
Cheaper By the Dozen (High School bully) (2003)
A Little Inside (Matt Nelson) (2001)
*Close to Home (*2001).
Silent Witness (Sam) (2000)

Jared played *Guitar Hero* the video game against Justin Hartley
*(*Oliver from *Smallville*) "So I owe it to myself to work this year. I do
like video games. I have a *Nintendo* in my trailer – the original one
with *SuperMario Bros* – it's old school, 8 bit or whatever you call it."
(Snap number 2, so do we, my sis and me, and one of our fave games is
SuperMario Cart.) Jared: "You know what I do, I cough on them and
then if you push it up and down a bunch of times it will work [yes and
blow on it too, a lot!] We're playing *Contra* Jensen and I. Sometimes
I'm in my trailer and he comes in and we spend 25 minutes and beat
Contra. Now we can move on with the day now that we've saved the
world from the *Contra*. I got a PS3 for Christmas and it has been in
Texas so I just called my Mom and Dad and asked if they could ship it
out to me." He'd like a *Wii*, a *Nintendo Wii*, he'll play one of his
friends and get too addictive and he won't walk his dogs or feed them,
they'll poop in the house. Okay Jared, I challenge you to a game of
SuperMario Cart! We have a *Wii* and the *DS Lite* is good too!
    Jared on *Supernatural*: I had never read anything like it. The talent
of the people behind it preceded them. I was familiar with David Nutter
and McG's work and Eric Kripke is obviously a very talented,
intelligent writer. The first thing I thought it was going to be another
Buffy the Vampire Slayer or *Charmed* which are great shows but not a
show I was interested in doing at this point in my career. I was like, 'It
is great but I don't think it's my style. I want to do something more real
and raw'. I then had a meeting with everybody and they were like, 'It is
going to be as campy'. I like love campy horror and thrillers but I
wanted to do something real (what about *Cry Wolf*]. They explained it

was going to be serious and scary. It piqued my interest, I signed on and here I am a year later."

House of Wax and **Cry** *Wolf*, he didn't want to do those again but were different kinds of horror. *Supernatural* is television instead of movies which makes it a different beast in itself. Then it is based on American folklore so it wasn't 'Let's just make up something scary. It is based on cool lore, urban legends and myths. I remember I studied a little of this in high school and my mother actually teaches *Heroes, Myths and Legends* at a high school in San Antonio, Texas. I was like, 'This is really cool and interesting so I'd like to be a part of it'. I'm really happy I did." As are we!

Jared on Jensen: "We didn't do anything. Jensen and I just hung out. I really lucked out. Jensen is a good, down-to-earth guy. He's friendly and he'll rib you. If you make fun of him, he'll make fun of you right back which I really like." (Much as their characters, Sam and Dean do in the show.)

Jared comments the viewers/fans are those who like himself and Jensen, since the show isn't as huge as its rivals on the same night: *CSI* and *Grey's Anatomy*. "That means a lot because I know some people who can't tell you a single actor on *CSI* {I can! On all three CSIs and then some!} Even though they watch it every week. When you're thinking about building a career – maybe these people will go and see a movie I do, or another TV show, if I do one. I hope so." Yes, as the case with Jensen, we saw him in everything before he starred in *Supernatural*.

Jared only has time to watch DVDs not TV. "I learned a long time ago that if I make any other plans while I'm filming, I'll only end up resenting the show." He doesn't like to watch a show as he doesn't have much time, then he'll miss a new episode – he was desperate to catch, he'll be working and his mind will think, 'Man, I wish I was in my trailer watching that show.'"

Jared likes to work in the Summer hiatus sometimes. He took off 2006. "I didn't even do a one day cameo on a movie or show. I went on vacation with my [then girlfriend], my brother and my sister-in-law. I spent time with my sister as she turned 21; another one of my buddies got married. The first season was really tough for me. Even though it was only Canada, everytime I wanted to go home I had to go through customs and Immigration. It was so weird. The first season was crazy hours, I missed my girlfriend and home. This year, [2007], not that I don't miss them, but I knew what to expect, and the benefits are a little better this season. I have a bigger trailer, I have wireless Internet, I'm all spoiled now. My girlfriend and I have the little camera things on our computer [webcam] so if she's in LA, I get to 'see' her. It's been easier so I think I am rested and ready to work this Summer. Hopefully a good project comes up."

In 2008, Jared came to London during the writers' strike, then France and Spain. He saw family in Texas and friends in California. Then says he grew fat! After season 3 was filmed and *Friday 13*th before season 4, thus he had time to turn the fat he grew (ha) into muscle. Whilst filming for *Friday 13*th, Jared's sister graduated UT-Austin (University of Texas – Austin) with an Architecture degree and he was there for that. The film was shot mostly at night. There were rain towers so they could be covered with mud and hosed down during filming of the fights between Jason and Clay. One of Jared's favourite scenes from the movie was when Jason kills the policeman; he thinks this scene sets up the entire movie. The horror films he's made slotted into his filming schedule for *Supernatural*, so he was happy to do them. He likes *The Shining* as it's a pretty scary movie and if he wants a good fright this is the one he'll tune into.

Jared loved Stone Henge, Wiltshire, England, when he came over, but thought it was rather small – but eerie nevertheless. Hey, everything's small here compared to the US.

Jensen Ackles

Jensen is of Irish, Scots and English ancestry.

Jensen graduated from Dartmouth Elementary, Richardson, Texas in 1990. Apollo Jnr High, Richardson, Texas in 1993. Lloyd V Berkner High School, Richardson, Texas in 1996. He was into baseball and lacrosse and had ambitions of studying sports medicine at Texas Tech University in the hopes of becoming a physical therapist.

He first began modelling at the age of two and appeared in TV commercials at the age of four, these were for *Radio Shack, Nabisco* and *Wal-Mart*. Jensen quit modelling at four and began again at the age of ten, (Hey he changed his mind aged only 4, when most four year olds would be thinking about, er, toys! Well, it's the way it was written in the article!)

Jensen gave up modelling out of embarrassment when his school friends found a picture of him modelling *Superman* pajamas. Hey nothing to be embarrassed about – just a case of life imitating art or is that the other way round. I sometimes get them mixed up! He after all, auditioned for the part of Clarkie in *Smallville*, good 'ol' *Superman* himself. How many of his school friends, or even any of us, can say that we got to live our dream or have it come true. Not that he got the role, but it opened up so many other avenues for him and for us. Just think we'd probably never even have heard of him – and that's a lot to be missing out on!

Jensen was spotted by a talent scout at a theatre group, "He approached me and said, 'Hey, I think you ought to come out to LA'. At first I thought he was full of crap but I decided to try. I was enrolled in college and about three weeks before I was supposed to start, I went out to LA, and started working right away. I have friends that have gone to Julliard one of the most prestigious art schools in the States and have a degree and are still struggling to find jobs in LA. I get asked for advice a lot on how to become an actor but there's no formula. I think you have to be prepared, you have to be talented and you have to be in the right place at the right time." Also being modest, (unlike Dean) he wouldn't really say another crucial factor is you have to be good looking too! That's always an added incentive – after all – isn't your face one of the first things talent scouts and studio bosses see about you, besides your acting, but that comes second!

Jensen's parents were going to name him Justin, but decided on Jensen as it wasn't that common a name.

In 1996, his first acting role was in *Wishbone*, in the episode *Viva Wishbone* as Mic Duss. *Seventh Heaven* in the Hallowe'en episode where he was credited as *Hallowe'en Kid #9*.

Sweet Valley High (1996) episode *All Along the Watchtower*. Brad.

Mr Rhodes Malcolm in seven episodes (1996/1997).

Cybil episode *The Wedding* David.

Days of Our Lives Eric Brady (1997- 31 July 2000).

Jensen was nominated for a Daytime Emmy in 1998, 1999, 2000, for Outstanding Younger Actor in a Drama Series. In 1998, he won *Soap Opera's Digest Award* for Best Male Newcomer. He appeared for three years in *Salem*. As well as the mini-series *Blonde* about the life of Marilyn Monroe where he played Eddie G: a boyfriend of Marilyn's. After *Dark Angel* he went on to the sixth season of *Dawson's Creek* where he played CJ, Jen's boyfriend peer counseller. As well as the never aired series for Fox, entitled *Still Life*. (I thought this was aired but cancelled, oh well, we didn't get it here anyway. As we usually get all the US cancelled shows, or most of them.)

When Jensen guest starred on *Dark Angel*. He says, "I died. I went out for a Pilot that didn't get picked up and I went off to Europe where I got an e-mail that they wanted me back full-time. Then I auditioned for the part of Clark Kent." The cast was narrowed down to Jensen and Tom Welling for the lead and they decided on Tom which Jensen agrees was the right choice. "Two seasons later they called and said, 'We've been thinking about you' and pitched me the role of Lana's boyfriend. I said, 'Yeah that sounds cool'. When I got the call from *Supernatural* I had a whole other year on *Smallville*, so that drastically changed my storyline. I ended up turning evil a little ahead of the plan."

Hang on, *Smallville* has been around since 2000, so if it's two seasons later Jensen was wanted for the part of Jason Teague, that' would've been in 2002 and not 2004, when he actually came in the show. Unless his part had been written already as early as that.

Jensen loves action and wanted to do some of his own stunts on the *Supernatural*, which they are allowed up to a certain extent. He'd much prefer to film an action scene on the show, than sitting around doing emotion! Aww – but they do emotion so well. You can feel the vibes coming through the TV! Ha! Seriously, they are great at pouring their hearts out, as well as the big fight scenes. But you know what they say, boys will be boys. To which Jensen comments, "This is true…it's a necessary evil we like to say."

Jensen sees Tom Welling up in Vancouver too and plays golf with him. He also used to see Michael Rosenbaum (Lex Luthor, *Smallville)* now and again, when he was in the show. As well as Jeffrey Dean Morgan when he's in Vancouver. He doesn't have any free time though. He also plays more golf than Jared, who he started up on golf. Jared lost all the balls Jensen had got (Jensen in Dean mode would've probably thought this funny if the word was applied to something else.) But he admits Jared would win him at hoops because he's taller. It's all about being fast too, not just tall and Jensen stop selling yourself short! (Pun not intended!) Jensen: "He makes me look like a midget! Dean's such a short-tempered hot-head and he's not nearly as big as Sam is."

Jensen and Jared got their own place together up in Vancouver and carpool together, wonder who gets to drive the most?! They joke about who is the most laziest. They also have their own favourite gum flavour and it's readily available for them on the set too. Well chewing gum is better than smoking! Comments Jensen, "If Jared and I didn't work as much as we did, we might be able to keep somewhat of a life going in LA. We literally put our lives on hold for nine months out of the year. I spent the last week of my hiatus just dusting my house. It's a sacrifice but it's a good problem to have. We got off at 3 in the morning and we don't work until 4 in the afternoon. Our schedule is much different than anybody else. So we do hang out quite a bit, especially with the crew guys too. It's become a pretty tight knit family."

Jensen also says he has similar qualities to Dean, including sarcasm. Only Jensen's not as short-tempered, though he can become Dean when pushed too far. Agh, beware Jared! (joke).

Jensen also recalls the bar fight when they were up in Vancouver. "There had been this fight at a bar and these guys got kicked out. They were pretty terrified. This one girl sees me walking by and says, 'That's the guy'. Meaning she knew me from the show, but they thought I was some guy she had been fighting with. They started swinging at me and it was an all-out brawl." Two of them ended up in hospital. "I turned around and saw three or four guys teaming up on Jared. I was like, 'Oh man.' I ran back in and I was fly-kicking at some kid, hit another guy, grabbed Jared's shirt – of course I ripped his favourite shirt." The guys are even more closer now after this experience.

Jensen declares he's a fan of Jared and he's proud of him like an older brother would be.

Jensen acted in a film in 2006 Summer hiatus called, *Ten Luck Hero*, released in 2007, at Film Festivals including Santa Cruz Film Festival and Newport Beach Film Festival and has earned great festival reviews in his portrayal of comedic Priestly. Did you like Jensen with a Mohawk and tattoo in this?

Jared went travelling that year. Jensen went to Japan to promote *Supernatural* and then Europe before heading to Texas to be with his family.

He admits he's not into all of the red carpet "paparazzi stuff and 'I'm like, really – do I have to?' I like to work and I know that's part of the job. But you kind of take it in your stride…it's been fun to get dressed up and take your girlfriend to a big event somewhere. But for the most part I work so hard that I want to spend my off time just for me. I think that people are very much in control of how much they are in the public eye. You see the pictures of guys with their shirts off running through Malibu, but they know what they're doing. I think it's silly to think they're just getting caught by the cameras. If you put yourself out there, you're going to get your picture taken."

It's just great to see Jensen so level-headed and down to earth. That success hasn't gone to his head and he's such an approachable, sweet guy, still.

He also made *The Plight of Clownana* (2004) a film about a man who earns his living as a shop's dancing mascot: half clown, half banana (only don't tell Sam about the clown part!). Jensen played one of the men who beat up Clownana. Devour *(2005)* where he played Jake Gray, in a murderous online video game akin to *The Ring.* This was his first lead in a horror movie. It was also the first time he worked with his Dad, Alan, who played Jensen's on-screen character's father too, Jake, who has a terrible daydream which ends up becoming reality.

After *Supernatural* in 2005, he was nominated for a Teen Choice Awards Breakout Star and lost to Zac Efron of *High Street Musical.* Recently, Jensen will be seen in *My Bloody Valentine 3D*, a remake where he returns home 10 years following the Valentine's Day Massacre. This was filmed at *Tarentum's Tour-ed Coal Mine* which is part of a museum. Jensen enjoys things being directed at the audience in 3D, that's what they intended to do and therefore he feels it's more exciting and cool. As for filming in the mine, they were surrounded by bats; lots of cold and there was only one entrance which was also the exit. This movie earned $24 million at the box office making Jensen into a very bankable movie star.

June 5-10 2007 Jensen made his theatre debut in *A Few Good Men*, where he played Daniel Cassidy at the Casa Manana Theatre in Fort Worth Texas. He hasn't been on stage for 11 years since he was in musicals in High school. Says Jensen: "It was back in Dallas, so I got to go home and put on a show for my whole family and friends." It was hard work and he had to put to memory 125 pages of the play. But he looked awesome in his uniform! (judging from the photos.)

He doesn't believe in ghosts per se, but does say he's superstitious; like wearing his lucky hat when he used to play basketball. Also he'll "knock on wood" (like the song!). After *Supernatural* I've got this false sense of confidence that I know how to handle strange phenomena – [which] probably isn't a good thing."

He's interested in four-wheel cars and sold a 1973 Bronco. He loves the Impala. "I'm going to write into my contract to get one of these Impalas; so when the show's over, maybe I'll scoop it on up and get it shifted."

Jensen is dating an actress from Louisiana, but he won't reveal her name.

His first on –screen kiss was for *Days of Our Lives* in his screen test. He had to kiss Christie Clark, and ended up playing the role of her brother, Eric, on the show.

His first real kiss was in the seventh grade (there's that numerological seven again!) he kissed her at the last song playing and she dumped him the next day. Wonder if she regrets that now – to ponder what could have been. What am I saying, only shallow people would say that – that's like saying you only like someone for their fame, or money, or both; not because of their personality or the sort of person they are! As for on –screen kissing, Jensen comments: "Go for the mints and minty gum, which they have available before such a scene. [No the garlic and onion, something you'd expect Jared to do!] The feelings that you get when you actually kiss somebody are totally different than what you put on the screen."

His Texan accent comes and goes and when he's back home, it does come back, but not as strong.

He aims to remain focused and carrying on with his career, with life.

40 Things You Should Know About Jensen

1. Jensen wants to make a western film – he's a cowboy after all.
2. Loves a girl in small tight-fitting boxers + blue jeans + tank top = one sexy hottie.
3. Jensen wears contact lenses.
4. Loves *Gummis* but eat too many and you get 'Gummi tummy'.
5. One of his fave episodes was season 1's **Home**.
6. Loves travelling and meeting people – one of life's great experiences.
7. He says *Supernatural* shows you all the scary bits, nothing is implied.
8. Wanted to finish High School before trying his hand at acting.
9. Sings and plays guitar.
10. He loves, "just working with the show…learning what all this stuff means – like cold spots or electromagnetic waves or crackling noises, the dimming lights and stuff like that we do on a daily basis. This is stuff researched by the writers so now when you're in a hotel room and it gets really cold and the lights start flickering, it's like, 'Alrighty! Where's my salt gun when I need it.'"
11. Sings backing vocals on his friend, Steve's album, such as on *Spot in the Corner* and *Rollin' On*.
12. During filming of **Scarecrow** he and Jared threw apples at each other.
13. He likes dark chocolate and his favourite snack's Animal Crackers.
14. Jensen is good friends with Jeffrey Dean Morgan.
15. He was number 26 on *TV Guide's 50 Sexiest Men List 2006*.
16. Teen Choice Awards presenter for *Best Grills*.
17. Loves footie.
18. Fave book *Fountainhead* by Ayn Rand.
19. Hates being late and traffic jams.
20. He's very patient.
21. Supporter of *Dallas Mavericks*.

22. First screen appearance was in *Wishbone.*

23. His father, Alan Ackles was in *Dallas* and *Walker Texas Ranger.*

24. Loves Christmas: it's cold, the lights, holidays and the good ol' Christmas spirits (that doesn't mean drink and egg nog!).

25. His grandmother sent him cards and notes every week so he didn't get homesick or too lonesome.

26. Fave show was *West Wing.*

27. Fave song; *Hallelujah* by Jeff Buckley.

28. Appeared in ads for *Nabisco* and *Wal-Mart.*

29. Offered a role on *Tru Calling* as Eliza's love interest, but opted for *Smallville* instead. The actor who played this role instead, was given the name 'Jensen' on the show.

30. Used to play on the *Hollywood Knights* basketball team, like Jared.

31. Executive producer on the movie, *The Plight of Clownana.*

32. Jensen first modelled at the age of 2.

33. His brother Josh, is three years older and his sister Mackenzie, is seven years younger.

34. Also he and Jared play street hockey between shooting the show.

35. Fave foods: pasta, root beer and chicken.

36. Fave musician is Garth Brooks.

37. Fave actors are Paul Newman and Johnny Depp (he's ace!)

38. *Dallas Cowboys* fan.

39. Another fave song is Lynyrd Skynrd's *Freebird*

40. Drew Barrymore wanted him in the movie *Never Been Kissed* in the role played by Michael Vartan, but he was busy with *Days of Our Lives.*

On 8 September 2008, Jensen and Jared took part in the *Red Bull Soap Box Derby* in Vancouver for charity. Jensen wore shirt number 13!

Personally neither of them would collect any of the 'funny' merchandise available on themselves. Jensen wore a shirt with Jared's face on it at the Chicago Convention and Jared almost had 'palpitations' ha). Jared was in a shop and saw seasons 1and 2 of the show's DVD, after thinking it was a case of déjà vu, i.e. that it somehow looked familiar, he realized, yes, it was him! Jensen's Mom would love the plate which has Jensen's and Jared's faces on it. But personally they wouldn't.

Whilst shooting, Jensen hates the scenes where he has to eat because it's just takes and more takes of eating the same food, over and over.

Think he should have a bucket handy in between takes and spit it out! Like they do at wine tastings – where you're not actually meant to swallow! (Though many people do!) Also if that happened, they'd probably end up playing pranks with the bucket, or more likely Jared would remove it completely eeww! Here's a thought, wonder if anyone's ever substituted a 'fake' burger for the real thing during takes. That plastic food looks so real these days – especially those extra large croissants. Good enough to eat! Jared boasts he can get one over Jensen in terms of pranks. They say they don't play pranks on each other on set, but I wouldn't put it past Jared, he's that cheeky, no it's just crew and guests. They'd forever be trying to outdo each other in the pranks department. Actually they do play pranks on one another.

During the writers' strike in 2008, he was sent to Australia for ten days. The perks of stardom since he also got to have a vacation whilst there! His girlfriend was also there and they've been dating for a while now. You see, he's really private about his personal life.

Katie Cassidy was born 25th November 1986. The daughter of David Cassidy of *The Patridge Family* fame and former model, Sherry Benedon. She was a cheerleader for the California Flyers and cheered as a freshman for Calabasas High School, from where she graduated in 2005. She wasn't permitted to work in acting – but only take part in auditioning, so she could pursue her career after graduating. She did modelling in high school, including ads for Abercrombie & Fitch in 2004. Dated two members of the boy band, *Dream Street*: Greg Rapuso for a year and Jesse McCartney for three years. Greg Rapuso wrote *We're In Love* for Katie's 16th. Jesse said he wrote his album Departure for his love of Katie. Leona Lewis' hit *Bleedin' Love* was also written by Jesse – who associated it with the emotions and feelings he felt when Katie broke up with him in 2007.

After graduation, Katie landed roles in *Seventh Heaven,* as Zoe, *When a Stranger Calls the remake* and the remake of *Black Christmas, Click, Live!* with Jeffrey Dean Morgan. She is in the movie version of *Dallas* as Lucy Ewing, beating contenders, Jessica Simpson and Lindsay Lohan for the role. In 2002 she released a single, *I Think I Love You* and in 2004 was in the music video of Eminem's *Just Lose* It. Recently Katie landed a role in CW remake of *Melrose* Place, playing Ella Flynn – a publicist. A part which has been described as being similar to that Of Heather Locklear's Amanda Woodward.

Originally auditioned to play Bela in *Supernatural.* Just as well she didn't get that part wouldn't have suited her at all! About Ruby she comments, "I'm supposed to be very intimidating and bad and when I walk up to him [Jared], I feel like a shrimp. But I'm 5' 7'' and they give me huge heels."

Of Ruby she says, "She definitely loves to manipulate, she's always ten steps ahead of everybody else. She knows what she wants and she knows how to get it. She's full of surprises.

She trained 6 days a week kick boxing. "It's hard coming onto a show in the third season since everybody's sort of already a family, but they really welcome you into their family. They're really, really sweet guys. Jared is a big goofball, and he and I have this banter back and forth which is funny. Jensen I actually don't see as much, but I have worked with him and he's great."

As for the fans not liking the addition of new characters to the show she said, "I know the fans are die-hard but we're not there to be love interests." [No, not until someone else gets to play your character and crops up in season 4.] She's also into fashion and just loved the outfits Ruby got to wear. "They're very Angelina Jolie inspired so I am stoked about that because she is so hot and sexy and she is one woman I look up to."

On set, if a prank is pulled on them, the whole crew sings *Happy Birthday* to them.

Katie loves the whole tough woman image and wants to portray one on screen.

Katie commented about leaving the show and her fans, "The fact that they miss me is sweet. It's heart-breaking in a way, because I loved the show. I loved the crew. I loved the boys – everyone was so welcoming." And we loved you! On leaving, she cites her choice, rather than financial reasons: "Warner Bros weren't exactly sure what they were going to be doing with my character, and I had the option to stay or leave. When *Harper's Island* came about, I was really into it, so I asked them to let me go."

Jeffrey Dean Morgan Born 22 April 1966. Raised in Seattle, Washington. He attended Ben Franklin Elementary School. Rose Hill Jnr High and was a 1984 graduate of Lake Washington High School. Height 6'1" (same as Jensen.) He wanted to play basketball but a knee injury meant this dream was put paid to. He left college without finishing, to paint and write. After helping a friend move to LA, he caught the acting bug. He has been in the TV shows, *Sliders* (Sid) (1996); *ER* (Larkin) 2001; *The Practice* (Daniel) episode *The Test* (2002); *Angel* (Sam) episode *Provider.* (2002); *JAG* (Wally) episodes: *Enemy Below, Defending His Honour* (2002); *Star Trek: Enterprise* (Xindi) episode *Carpenter Street* (2003); *Monk* (Steven) episode: *Mr*

Monk Takes Manhattan (2004); *Tru Calling (Geoffrey) episode (Two Pair);* (2004); *The Handler* (Mike) (2004); *The OC (Joe)* (2005).

He made it big when he appeared in *Grey's Anatomy, Supernatural* and *Weeds.*

Some of his movies include: *Uncaged* (1991) Sharkey. *Dillenger and Capone* (1995) (Jack). *Undercover Heat* (1995) (Ramone). *In the Blink of an Eye.* (1996) (Jessie). *Legal Deceit* (1997) (Todd). *Road Kill* (1999). (Billy). *Something More* (2003) (Daniel). *Bed and Breakfast* (2004) (Sheriff). *Six: The Mark Unleashed* (2004) (Tom). *Chasing Ghosts* (2005) (Det. Davies.) *The Accidental Husband. Days of Wrath. Watchmen. The Adventures of Beatle Bryan. The Comedian. PS I Love You.*

Some of his favourite *Supernatural* episodes were: **1.16 Shadow, 1.20 Dead Man's Blood, 2.1 In My Time of Dying** because of the deal he made. It was "bittersweet because I didn't know if I could be back on this how." He bought the *Supernatural Origins* Comics and they're still in their packaging. (As are mine.)

On the *Supernatural* Pilot, Jeffrey comments, "It was a possible recurring role, if the show got picked up. My whole thing was, 'How could I recur because I'm not going to be old enough to play their father, and I don't know how that would work'. It got picked up and I was back to work."

On Jensen and Jared, he loves them both and he felt that going to Vancouver was like going to camp. They have so many good times together and it was mostly just the three of them. They, "Act like little kids. They're both fun as heck but both so different." He refers not to the guys but to the two shows, *Supernatural and Grey's Anatomy.* "*Supernatural* is the most difficult because I could never get used to working nights. Working exterior nights in Vancouver when it's raining and snowing is a little daunting, when you haven't slept. The show is extremely hard, physically." He was exhausted between filming the two shows and "it would take a minute to get 'Winchestry' because he [John] is very intense, very ex-military and kind of gruff. The man loves his children but he's a little on the stern side. To get into that mode is hard sometimes. It's much easier for me to get into Denny [from *Grey's Anatomy*] mode than Winchester mode; especially if you're looking at Jared giggling at you from across the camera. Working in the rain, getting chucked against walls at five in the morning with those boys, as handsome as they are..."

He finds it better filming while looking at Katie Heigel in a studio! He spent his weekends working on *Supernatural*.

He can now pick and choose his own roles and he'll even work for free, if it's a well written role. His former manager let him go because she couldn't get him any roles and he wonders what she thinks now?

He is still single and was recently with Mary Louise Parker (from *Weeds*.) But some of us know him more from one of his first stints in *The Burning Zone*. Jeffrey didn't like where his character was going in *The Burning Zone* which is why we didn't see much of him on-screen after this. He says his character, Dr Edward Marcase, was "going to lose his spirituality and the show *Burning Zone* was going to lose its soul." He thinks "it is important to stand up for your beliefs. However in retrospect, I wish I had handled it differently." Show business is a bit of a fluke and a fad and he says, "As I've gotten older I have realized what a huge privilege it is to even be in this business. I more than ever love what I do."

He resides Toluca Lake, LA and the San Fernando Valley. With his dog named Bisou (meaning 'kiss' in French.) As for his relationships he likens himself to being "like Jennifer Aniston – I'm that guy."

Jim Beaver was born James Norman Beaver Jr in Laramie, Wyoming and was the eldest. He has three sisters and grew up in Irving, Texas. His father encouraged him to read, as with reading comes knowledge. After high school he served a stint in the US military, in the marines and equates it as "One of the hardest things I ever did and one of the best." He read Shakespeare when he was in Vietnam, but didn't even consider acting as a full-time occupation. He only began to like acting when he got to college. Whilst in college, he played in theatre too, such plays as written by Shakespeare, Neil Simon, Chekhov. His first paying role was in Somerset Maugham's play: *Kain* where he was paid $25 for six weeks.

Jim used to write down actors names when he was watching movies and then got into film history, but since this wasn't available as a subject at his college, he opted for drama club instead. He also writes plays, but has very little time to concentrate on this aspect more fully these days. He has directed one play he wrote. His favourite writers include, Tennessee Williams, Eugene O'Neill. He also writes books, such as writing about 1940's Hollywood actor, John Garfield, a biography entitled, *John Garfield: His Life and Films*. He thought biographies, books about film actors, were easy to write since essentially they were just rehashes of their lives and career. John

Garfield was someone he admired and wrote this book when he was studying.

He likes to surf the Net and also writes biographies for *IMDb*. He reads and watches a great number of movies. His mission is to read biographies of every American President, in the order they came to power. He's about to start reading Grover Cleveland. When he is in LA, he enjoys spending time at Theatre West Theatre Company, which is internationally acclaimed as the oldest community arts theatre, since it began in 1962. He played Henry II in a production some years ago in *The Lion In Winter*.

Look out for Jim's memoir in April 2009, entitled, *Life's That Way*; in which he openly and heart-feelingly writes about the loss of his wife, Cecily from lung cancer in October 2003 and how his daughter, Madeline was diagnosed as autistic, only two months before her mother died. The book helped him deal with his grief and how all this impacted on his daughter. She is the one who makes him laugh. Jim's late wife was an actress, casting director and acting coach. She, along with others, taught him great acting and writing lessons.

Jim loves his iPod which was in the gift bag when he was nominated for a SAG (Screen Actors Guild) Award. Music on there includes: Gilbert and Sullivan comic operas, classic movie themes, Rick Nelson, The Beatles, Yul Brynner's Russian gypsy songs.

Some of his fave shows: *The Wire, My Name is Earl, Little Britain, Rescue Me*. He wants to watch *Dexter* and *Oz*. However, he prefers movies to TV shows and some of the best ones are: *Seven Samurai, Under Fire, Farewell My Lovely, The Man Who Would Be King, Yojimbo, The Alamo, Casablanca*. (One of my favourites.) His favourite movie is *The Searchers* with JohnWayne.

Jim plays Sheriff Charlie Mills in *Harper's Island*, so he can meet up with Katie Cassidy again and share some stories.

From everything that he's starred in, Jim prefers *Thunder Alley, Deadwood, Supernatural* and *Harper's Island*. He says the cast are more like his family on these shows.

Jim Beaver can be seen in *Dark and Stormy Night*. He also guested in the season 6 **Field Trip** *X Files* episode, where he played a Medical Examiner and in *Criminal Minds* as a sheriff. Jim's movies include, *Geronimo, An American Legend, Magnolia, The Life of David Gale*. He'd like to work with Mark Harmon again (shame he hasn't been approached for a part in *NCIS*!) As well as with Ed Asner and the cast of *Deadwood* once more. He missed his chance on working with Peter O'Toole and Jared again, in the movie *Home For Christmas*. He wants to work with Peter O'Toole so badly, and here we thought it was to work with Jared again, ha!

Most actors he liked were John Wayne, Laurence Olivier, Robert Mitchum, Humphrey Bogart, Graucho Marx, Tishiro Mifune. He looks up to many actors such as, Vanessa Redgrave, Sir Ian McKellan, Clint Eastwood, Meryl Streep, Al Pacino and says, "I admire all over the business...the crews I've worked with, the guys who are there an hour before I get there at 6am, who never sit down except maybe for lunch and there an hour or two after I go home about 10 or 12 pm that night. In almost every case, these guys work rigorous jobs and do it with great spirits. The *Supernatural* crew is one of the best examples of that I've ever seen."

Jim comments you get less time off in a small cast show like *Supernatural*. "It's usually just one storyline if Bobby is a part of it he's often deeply involved. The real difference is for the leads, Jared and Jensen work virtually everyday on *Supernatural* because it's a show with two leads."

Jim auditioned for *Supernatural*, after *Deadwood*. He auditioned for his friend and the show's casting Director, Robert Ulrich, who sent his audition tape to Vancouver. Robert called Robert Singer and told him he'd sent out the tape, who asked Robert who was on the tape and then just told him to give the part of Bobby to Jim. "They never actually looked at my audition tape, maybe that's a good thing."

He describes Bobby as, "A great, colourful, rich character and that he had humour and warmth and sarcasm, which I love to play. We're just three actors who work together and enjoy it. It would never occur to me to treat them [Jensen and Jared] paternally off-camera. I'm more likely to go to them for advice, than offer my own."

The guys have pulled pranks on Jim, but haven't been that full-on, like trying to make him laugh in scenes. He hasn't pulled any pranks on them – yet. "They're great, warm, loving and fun-loving guys. They're both a lot wilder than I was at that age. They're also much more confident and self-assured than I was and they love jokes and pranks and childish stunts. He tends to just watch them pull pranks and seemed to have directed a lot at the late Kim Manners, such as stink bombs and throwing water.

Jim only has yet more kind words to say, "I love working with the JJs – they're really good guys, really hard workers and genuinely nice people." He doesn't see himself in them since they're more successful than he was at their age. "I don't look for myself in them though. I just relish the chance to work with them and hang around with them [wouldn't we all] even though I am occasionally with them, where, I feel like one of the Three Musketeers and they encourage that. Sometimes it's more like the Three Stooges – but still…"

Jim feels it would not be possible to take Jim out of Bobby on the show since they come from the same beginnings.

Jim loves his fans and meeting them at conventions. He has attended four so far and says, "I don't think that I ever had my butt pinched by a girl before I was on *Supernatural*, not that I'm complaining. I don't experience that sort of thing as typical."

However, Jim does have some advice to offer for budding actors: "Reading will open doors you never knew were there. The more literate you are, the more you understand of the world and history and how the world got the way it is. Never stop learning- there's no such thing as knowing all you need to know." That can be said for anything you want to do in life. Words of encouragement and wisdom. The motto on Jim's senior ring reads: *Esse quam videris*, i.e. *to be rather than to seem*.

Lauren Cohan (Bela) was born in Philadelphia. She moved to England and lived here until 2007 when she moved to LA. In England, she attended the University of Winchester (quite appropriately, or not, depending on your viewpoint). She co-founded the theatre group *2G4T* there. Did the play *Pygmalion* but they reversed the roles. Professor Higgins was a woman and Eliza, a man, which was also performed at the Edinburgh Fringe Festival.

She was also a model and had planned to attend drama school but got a part on *Young Alexander The Great*, filmed in Egypt. As well as in *Casanova,* filmed in Venice.

She learned archery. Her agent advised her against playing a US room mate in the BBC children's' show *Basil Brush*.

When she got the role on *Supernatural*, she had to wait eight days to see if Bela would actually be in the show or not. She describes Bela as "basically a mercenary. It's really a fun character. Eric and I decided that she was a female Humphrey Bogart because she's very much out for herself. It's about the money; it's about the goods, it's about serving higher powers who need certain results and other characters having to do with demons."

Of course she says Bela doesn't want to spill anyone's blood or hurt anyone, she shot Sam in **3.3**. But she can be violent if she needs to be. Lauren: "Both Ruby and Bela have a certain, maybe not masculinity but self-sufficiency and independence and I think that's an exciting kind of woman to bring into this."

On Jensen and Jared she comments: "They crack me up. I'm laughing all the time." Jared kept picking up mouse traps from the dingy house they were staying at, [**3.6**] in the show and threw them at people, he got his finger caught in one of them.

Her chair was moved away when she was sitting down in the episode **3.6 Red Sky** and when she went for another take; she ended up on the floor. (She told this at the Convention in England.)

Samantha Ferris started her career as a TV reporter. She says she couldn't imagine doing anything but acting; but having said that, she has had other careers. Including working in radio, and still does. As well as a marketing representative, weather reporter for a local TV station. She went into acting after her father's death. "Life is short." She thought to herself, "You had better spend it chasing what you love to do, or at least die trying." Which is exactly what she did and here she is now.

Supernatural is the closest thing to do as I get to be a sort of 'gun-toting, bar-owning, whiskey drinking, broad'." She was recently in a film with Pierce Brosnan (wow!) called *Butterfly on a Wheel* where she plays the best friend of Maria Bello. It was a small role, but since the cast wasn't so big either, she's on the cast list. It's a bit like *The Game* is how she describes it.

Samantha was no longer in season 4 of *The 4400* since they felt they were paying her too much for a few scenes. No one from the show: cast or crew, called to send their regrets at her not being brought back. "That is the part that hurt. Not a phonecall from my other casemates. Nothing. Gone and forgotten. This business can be very cruel." Well Samantha, at least you can say you were in *Supernatural* and bet not many of them (or any) can say that! Knew there was a reason why I didn't watch that show!

On playing Ellen, Samantha says she loves the boys dearly and would practically do anything for them. But whether she became a substitute mother to Sam and Dean wasn't really explored anyway. "Jared is usually the instigator [in practical jokes] and I have been on the receiving end of the pranks. Painful and gross as they can be. Canned farts, real farts, moved equipment, food and beverage fights, [seems like someone's getting a bit too much food onset! to be throwing it around.] Scenes blown purposely – they get them back. There was a scene where Jared had to climb down a manhole with a gun in one hand, cast on the other – they doused him with two full buckets of cold water."

Ellen didn't appear in season 3. She says the cast is close. "I think that comes from the boys and the producers. Jared and Jensen are two of the nicest guys you could work with. They are sweet, warm, funny and very real. I think it's the southern upbringing. There is no room for attitude on the show because the boys don't have any." Samantha would love to get her hands on Jeffrey Dean Morgan in the show, if she could, but alas no! Luckily, at one point, Samantha was the only chick on set and they all treated her great!

She believes in the inexplicable. It's her encounter with a figure she describes as a white flash when her brother came for dinner one night. She swore it was her late father. Also her mother had cleaned the windows on the very same day – something she never did at all. Her neighbour was passing by her house at the very moment, Samantha saw the flash in her house, and told her a man had his face pressed against the window.

Samantha can be seen in *Gracie,* a film about a still born baby coming back to life.

Misha Collins was born Misha Dmitri Tippens Krushnic in Boston, Massachusetts, on 22 April 1974. He attended college and did an internship at the Whitehouse. He worked on National Public Radio and also began a Summer program for teenagers, as well as being president of an internet start-up, company, producing educational software. He used to build furniture and made documentaries.

Misha wanted to attend Law School too and then thought about trying acting. He auditioned for *Liberty Heights*, which he got a part in. This lead to *Legacy*; *Girl Interrupted*. He then moved to LA for good. Though he still builds furniture for personal use. If he wasn't an actor, he would've gone into politics.

He also landed the role of serial killer, Paul Bernardo in *Karla*. When he was filming this, he says, "an incredibly violent, dark side came out in me and I was pretty shocked by it. I was dreaming Paul Bernardo's dreams...as soon as we wrapped [production] I stopped having those dreams. Misha is a great fan of Kate Winslet and would like to work with her, as well as any others, such as, Dame Judi Dench; Tommy Lee Jones; Jeff Bridges; Marlon Brando and the late Paul Newman, whom he would've liked to have worked with too. Two of his films, *Parsic* and *Moving On*, which he calls excellent, were never released, so he says, no one will see them. He has a varied taste in music, which includes, Cole Porter, Faith Hill, Electronica, Santo Gold.

On *Supernatural* he thinks, "The show works because it's not just about two guys chasing down evil monsters, it's about two very different brothers who are fighting forces of darkness in order to resolve their own personal histories and to exorcise their own inner demons. In other words, the show is compelling because the brothers are personally compelled."

Jensen and Jared haven't subjected Misha to any pranks on set and he says he feels left out! (Well that's what you get for playing an angel and having a direct line to God's ear! Joke!) Didn't think his character would be a huge hit with the fans and if he thought of it, he claims it would've made him self-conscious.

As for believing in the supernatural and life's mysteries, he comments, "I think we normally only perceive a tiny fragment of what's really going on around us and in the vast multi-dimensional soup that makes up our universe, I think there is plenty of room for angels. I think there are forces of good and presences that move amongst us that could well be angels. I have never seen anyone with wings – angel or otherwise – but stranger things have happened."

He was meant to have auditioned for a demon, Eric Kripke told him 'Castiel' was meant to be an angel – but didn't want it leaked out to the fans that an angel was being added to the cast. He quotes Eric, 'This angel hasn't been around humans for 2,000 years, so he has a curiosity about these human beings and their strange behaviour.'"

Misha is now due to appear as a series regular in season 5 of *Supernatural*, added to his part of eight episodes in season 4. He says he didn't know he would be wearing his outfit for such a long time in the show, otherwise he'd have asked for something better to wear. Then he wouldn't resemble *Columbo* anymore. Also he doesn't believe season 5 could necessarily be the end for the show. "I really don't know what the inner workings are, but I don't think that that's necessarily the final word."

Misha attended his first ever fan convention in Cherry Hill, New Jersey. (*Cherry Hill Con, New Jersey Salute to Supernatural*.) About his character he said, it's different because he's not human, so he can't be killed, shot at. He commented he has to come up with a much simpler signature with the number of autographs he had to sign. When asked which character he'd like to play, he replied, it wouldn't be *Columbo*. After everything I said about the trench coat! Darn. He would like to be George Clooney in *ER*.

Re on-set pranks, he, Jensen and Jared broke some windows at a warehouse where they filmed and were told off!

His other credits include: *Without A Trace* (2007) in the episode *Run* (Chester Lake).

CSI:NY (2007) Can *You Hear Me Now?* (Morton Brite).

Close To Home (2006) *There's Something About Martha* (Todd Monroe).

NCIS (2006) *Singles Out* (Justin Harris).

Monk (2006) *Mr. Monk and the Captain's Marriage* (Karpov).

CSI (2005) *Nesting Dolls* (Vlad).

ER (2005/2006) *B Here and There* (Bret) *If Not Now; Alone in a Crowd* (Ray's Bandmate)

24 (2002) (Alex Drazen) (seven episodes)

NYPD Blue (2000) *Welcome to New York* (Blake Dewitt).

Charmed (1999) *They're Everywhere* (Eric Bragg).

EPISODES

Season 1

Pilot
1.2   Wendigo
1.3   Dead In The Water
1.4   Phantom Traveller
1.5   Bloody Mary
1.6   Skin
1.7   Hookman
1.8   Bugs
1.9   Home
1.10 Asylum
1.11 Scarcrow
1.12 Faith
1.13 Route 666
1.14 Nightmare
1.15 The Benders
1.16 Shadow
1.17 Hell House
1.18 Something Wicked
1.19 Provenance
1.20 Dead Man's Blood
1.21 Salvation
1.22 Devil's Trap

Season 2

2.1 In My Time of Dying
2.2 Everybody Loves A Clown
2.3 Blood Lust
2.4 Children Shouldn't Play With Dead Things
2.5 Simon Says
2.6 No Exit
2.7 The Usual suspects
2.8 Crossroad Blues
2.9 Croatoan
2.10 Hunted
2.11 Playthings
2.12 Nightshifter
2.13 Houses of the Holy

Season 1

What better way to get a rundown of the legends – urban and otherwise than watching them do battle with a different spirit, monster, ghoul every week. Especially for people who have a passion for all things scary and two hot guys! Man we love this show!!

Eric Kripke quotes Neil Gaiman's *American Gods* influencing the show. "It's just two guys cruising the country with chainsaws in their trunk, battling demons that go bump in the night."

The setting for the show, at least where the brothers originate from is Lawrence, Kansas. Lawrence was one of the cities in Kansas, USA which was founded specifically for reasons of politics. October 16th 1854 saw the establishment of the first Anti-Slavery newspaper, *The Kansas Pioneer*, becoming *The Kansas Tribune* later on. Lawrence was also an important route on the underground railway which helped slaves to escape their servitude.

1985 saw investors restoring restoring the old Eldridge Hotel. The top floors were rebuilt and made into luxury suites. The fifth floor is rumoured to have a portal to the spirit world: specifically room 506. There have been reports of breath on mirrors, doors opening and closing on their own and lights turning on and off by themselves. Cold spots are also reported in the old hotel, as well as ghostly apparitions being encountered by guests on the fifth floor. One such spirit appears to open and close the doors of the lift, also on the fifth floor. The Eldridge can be found on the corner of Massachusetts and Seventh Streets in Lawrence, Kansas. A bit of a potted history of spooky Kansas. Specifically Sam and Dean's home town.

Pilot

Written By Eric Kripke. Directed By David Nutter
Original US Air Date 13 September 2005

REGULAR CAST: Jared Padalecki (Sam Winchester)
Jensen Ackles (Dean Winchester)

Guest Stars: Jeffrey Dean Morgan (John Winchester, Dad); Sarah Shahi (Constance Welch); Steve Railsback (Welch); Adrianne Palicki (Jessica Lee Moore); Samantha Smith (Mary Winchester, Mom)

Lawrence, Kansas
22 Years ago

A mother puts her baby to bed and tells him "Sweet dreams Sam." The light flickers and she hears him over the baby monitor, she reaches out to her husband, John but he's not there. Hearing, screams he rushes upstairs to find Sam's okay but there's blood dripping then he sees her suspended to the ceiling and then burst into flames. He gives Dean Sam to carry outside.

Stanford University
Present Day

Sam. Older and now at university. He comments to his friends "You know how I feel about Hallowe'en." Scoring high on his SATs he can attend any law school he wants. He has an interview here on Monday. His family doesn't know as he says, "We're not exactly *The Brady's*. Sam tells his girlfriend, Jessica he'd crash and burn without her. Sam hears a noise in his room at night and fights the intruder who turns out to be his brother, Dean. He needs to talk with Sam who wouldn't have picked the phone up if he had called. Sam tells him he's got nothing to hide from Jess and so Dean tells him Dad's not returned from his hunting trip. They talk alone and

Sam refuses to go with Dean. Sam: "He's always missing and he's always fine." Besides Sam swore he was "done hunting for good." Sam tells Dean they still haven't found the thing that killed Mom. He knows what's lurking out there but "the way we grew up after Mom died and Dad's obsession to find the thing that killed mom." Questions if Mom would've wanted this life for them, being raised like warriors. Sam doesn't want a "normal apple pie life" (in Dean's Words) he just wants to be safe...

Jericho, California

A man in a car stumbles upon a woman in white who asks him to "take me home." She lives at the end of Breckenridge Road and attempts to seduce him and asks if he thinks she's pretty? She then says, "Will you come home with me?" And he agrees. When they arrive, she tells him, "I can never go home" before she disappears. He drives away and sees her in the back of his car before she attacks him.
  ***

Jess has left cookies for Sam. When Sam lies on the bed blood drips on his face (just like when he was a baby), he looks up to see Jess burn. Dean comes back breaking the door in and has to take Sam outside again. Sam cries, and then declares, "We got work to do."

Notes

The light did flicker in the opening of this episode, as later episodes will show this is an indication that the 'thing' that killed Mom is around. (It's not called the Yellow-eyed demon yet as they don't know what it is or even that it is a demon.) The light flickers twice and again in the hallway indicating the demonic presence and from season 1 episodes this and other factors like electrical storms; freak weather conditions also show demonic activity. But they don't learn this until **2.4 Everybody Loves A Clown**.

Mom thinks it's Dad in Sam's nursery, but it's not. Dad resembles the demon from the back and in the shadows too (see 16. **Shadow**.) Either that's uncanny or he's just meant to. Since if it's Dad, you think well what's the connection – is the demon Dad, who is asleep, however with a war movie playing on TV and Dad as we know was a marine. Hence his in-built instinct, training, he gives Sam and Dean. Not only precision military training but strict discipline, such as always following his orders, which Dean obeys to the letter and Sam, chooses not to. Dean carries Sam out of the house which he later tells Lucas in 3. **Dead In The Water** but has never told Sam who will overhear Dean saying this.

Sam is at Stanford on his way to becoming a lawyer and has the same photo of his parents in their home that the camera shows us in the beginning , so where did he get that from since it doesn't appear they saved any of their possessions from the fire. (See also 11. **Home** where their possessions are found in their old house.)

It's strange how Dean chooses Hallowe'en of all days to show up to tell Sam Dad's missing. Although Sam hasn't told Jess about what he used to do with his family, i.e. hunt evil spirits and the like. He's honest when he says his family don't know about his grades, he scored 170 on his L SATs, and about his law school interview.

Sam telling Jess he'd "crash and burn" without her; ironically it's Jess who does the burning at the end. Also it seems Sam needs someone in his life that is not related to him nor does what Dad and Dean do – hunt. Funny then that when Dean has confrontations with the demon (**2.2 Devil's Trap; 2.1. In My Hour Of Dying, 2.8 Crossroad Blues**) as well as the reaper, he's told that he needs his family more than they need him. Although Sam will also need Dean more than he realizes just now when his true destiny is revealed to him in season 2.

Sam and Dean fight each other, though at first Sam doesn't know it's Dean; perhaps Dean's way of finding out if Sam hasn't lost the knack. The next time they fight again, physically, is in **2.6 Skin**, but it's not really Dean, just a shape shifter with Dean's face.

Dean is quite the ladies' man and our first indication to this is when he sees Jess and tells her she's too good for Sam!

Sam tells Dean, Dad is always missing which is a sign of things to come because Dad doesn't make his appearance until **1.10 Home**. Also he didn't come when they ask for help in **1.10 Home**, and **1.12 Faith**. Dad leaves messages on his voicemail telling people to contact Dean if they need help and the first time they hear this is in **2.4 Phantom Traveller**, but they didn't call his phone and how did Dean find out Dad was missing this time and not off hunting somewhere – to partly answer my own question – he was hunting: the demon. Also seems this voicemail message is different to the one they listen to in episode **2.4 Phantom Traveller**.

Sam mentions telling Dad he was afraid of the "thing" in his closet, was this demonic spirit just his imagination. In **1.10 Home** when Sam and Dean return to their old house for the first (and only) time, the little girl in Sam's former nursery is afraid of the 'thing' in her closet too and has her mother put a chair against the door. But as we find out, their Mom emerges from that same closet. No, she couldn't really have been keeping an eye on Sam or protecting him, though it's a nice thought. Instead Sam says Dad gave him a .45 as if that would help, unless it had rock salt in it. Dean telling Sam he's meant to be afraid of the dark because they've seen it all, practically, and knows there's evil out there. See **1.17 Something Wicked** where Dean says he wished he could protect Sam from the dark and nightmares. Dean, having said that, isn't afraid of the dark himself: they do most of their hunting at night but Dean, in particular, has to dig up remains in cemeteries during the early hours all alone.

Sam doesn't want a normal life he says, but a safe one. He doesn't say this in **1.16 Shadows**. Sam wants to return to this normal life and in **1.8 Bugs** Dean tells him normal is boring and that's not their family. Sam says they're raised like warriors (where Dean would say heroes) and that's what the reaper tells Dean in **2.1 In My Hour Of Dying** that he should be proud and face his death – like that of a warrior.

There's so much in this opening episode that sets the theme for several episodes to come as well as season 2, though maybe that wasn't the intention at the start or perhaps even the premise. But it occurs and so builds up the continuity aspect of the show superbly – as their arguments; hunts, fate, etc, all build up and overlap into more than one episode. It makes you think about what they do and more importantly as Sam and Dean can be seen as more than just two-dimensional characters. It adds depth of emotions and feelings and essentially evolves their characters rather than remaining stagnant. They make mistakes; learn from them at times; then in season 2 you feel they've come full circle when their characters' persona alter; Dean now thinks like Sam and Sam becomes a little like Dean, at least some of the time. Though throughout it all, they never lose their humanity. Until perhaps in later seasons, but it's not really humanity they forsake, or even that inside of themselves.

As far as pilots go, this was an incredibly spectacular and detailed episode, telling everything about their past in an introductory conversation between the two when they meet for the first time in two years and then in various snatches of dialogue along the way. Very intense at moments as Sam mostly pours his heart out over his family, his treatment, his life, with Dean commenting Sam sounds very ungrateful about their family. As well as hilarious moments. If Dean was so devoted to Mom telling Sam not to defile her name, not in so many words, why did he object so much in seeing her grave in **2.4 Children Shouldn't Play With Dead Things.**

From scene one when Mom puts Sam to sleep you know something ominous is lurking nearby. Within the opening minutes the scene and stage is set for what the remainder of the season is all about: the main characters, theme, background and overall demon hunt. Having done this, the story then moves to Sam, now grown up when big brother comes looking for him. Surprise, surprise Dean turns up on Hallowe'en of all days. You just know the yellow-eyed demon had his own way of drawing Sam into the scheme of things – that by killing Jess, it'd be a good motivation for revenge, forcing him back into the hunt.

Eric Kripke commented how he loves fans of the show paying attention! Saying, "We occasionally look to numerology...the yellow-eyed demon re-entered the Winchesters' life 22 years to the day after it disappeared. Sam was 22 at that time. We chose that number intentionally." Something that I mentioned too, that's how long it waited. Also in terms of real time, there must have been a reason why the show premiered on the 13th of September. Think of all the supernatural connotations of this number, not to mention the bad luck associated with it too, but for *Supernatural* it was nothing but good luck all the way!

As for Dean's "apple pie life" - well he didn't have that either, not to mention he didn't get any apple pie either in **1.11 Scarecrow** and in other episodes too!

Sam repeats what he says about going to college and Dad didn't want him back in **2.8 Bugs,** when there's yet more info on why he left and fought with Dad. As for Dad's death and Dean's comment, "Dad's in a lot of trouble right now if he's not dead already, I can feel it." That was a long time coming, also see season **1.21, 1.22** Devil's **Trap, 2.1 In The Hour Of My Dying**. Even Sam makes similar comments too.

Jess by the sound of it doesn't want Sam to go because she's surprised that he's going away with Dean now when he's never spoken of Dean and Dad.

The woman's voice on the EVP saying, "I can never go home" probably sums up everything Sam and Dean feel too and has implications for other reasons – considering they never really had a proper home to begin with, then Sam saying Dad didn't want him coming back and Dean promising to himself that he'd never go back home too (see **1.10 Home**). Of course the woman in white has her own reasons; she killed her children and herself.

Dean hasn't cottoned onto the CD, MP3, revolution yet, as his collection of music is all on cassettes, including Metallica, Motorhead, Black Sabbath. So is it any wonder he asks Sam if Myspace is a porn site in **2.8 Crossroad Blues**. We find out that Dean and Dad don't make their money in the legitimate way but use credit card fraud; poker games. As well as having an array of fake ids, the majority of which are law enforcement officials. Well, a badge does open up a multitude of doors; and hides a multitude of sins too!

There's the first mention of Dean calling Sam Sammy and him not liking it and finding out Sam was chubby at 12 and (Dean was a goofy kid in **1.10 Home**)

No TV show would be complete without the mention of the institution that is Mulder and Scully and the *X-Files*. There must be some unwritten law which states they must be referred to in most shows and rightly too!

Sam is almost like a walking font of knowledge much to Dean's dismay at having a geeky brother! As he'll call him several times and in **2.16 Road Kill** he says he's like a weird encyclopedia. Meant in the nicest possible way but they're alike too and yet are so different from each other, in that they ask the same question at the same time and again in **2.9 The Usual Suspects,** with the anagram and *Matlock* reference.

Dean finds an ample opportunity to question Sam about Jess – she doesn't know about Sam and what he's done which isn't very much, it's not like he's some killer since they only hunt the supernatural variety of deviants. (At least he's not a killer yet, see season 2). But Sam saying she's never going to know is ironic again and yet sad since she will never know. Sam's just going to become a lawyer, settle down and there's nothing wrong with that. However, it seems out dear Sammy is more into lore than the law!

Sam's resolute this is not what he's going to do forever, Sam's not a hunter. Dean tells him of his responsibility (which will later become their legacy and Sam will call it this himself in **2.8 Crossroad Blues**). However Dean then changes his responsibility angle in season 2 and at the end of season 1 episodes; when he says Sam wanting to hunt is because he feels he owes it to Dad, the gesture comes too late; whereas here he's convincing him that's exactly what he should be doing. Hypocritical much Dean? Sam finishes Dean's responsibility line by mentioning Dad and his crusade, as before, he doesn't think much of this right now – but he'll change his mind and outlook in 1.21. **1.22** and **2.2 Everybody Loves A Clown.**

This is where Sam says Mom's gone and never coming back (he's wrong she does once **1.10 Home** and **4.2** where we get to see a younger Mom) but Dean reminds him of this in 1.21, for which Sam berates him. Dean pins Sam against the bridge when he says this as if he's about to hit him and in **1.21** the position is reversed, Sam now does the pinning and Dean reiterates Sam shouldn't talk about Mom like that and which Sam also does later. So already by the close of Season 1 their outlook and perceptions, thoughts on their lives will change.

For a change Sam breaks into the hotel room. Also when Dean is arrested by the police you can see it's a sign of things to come as this happens to him a lot, about three times and less to Sam. Dean in handcuffs, we'd put him in some!

One of the best bits of the episode, Dean telling the sheriff he was three when the first victim went missing. As for Dean's chick flick moment, he's probably seen a lot, see his reference to *Beaches* in **2.4 Children Shouldn't Play with Dead Things.** Dean says he'll take Sam home, thought that was funny since the woman in white used to say "Take me home."

Sam lying on the bed and the blood dripping onto his face – a repeat of what happened to him when he was a baby in his crib, only this time it's Jess's blood. Why did Dean return when he did and know something was wrong? He didn't really sense Sam was in trouble, but breaks the door down anyway, (one of Dean's numerous trademarks, breaking, no more like kicking down doors!) He also kicked the door in before Jess was on fire, there was no smoke or flames yet so he wouldn't have seen them. Can't really say Dean had a premonition about Sam because he doesn't get those. Also Dean takes Sam out of the house again like he did when he was a baby.

When Dean comes back for Sam here, there is a deleted scene which would explain why he did this, apparently Dean's watch stops and there's static on the radio, leading Dean to believe Sam would be a target for the Thing that killed Mom. In actual fact turned out Jess was the intended victim.

The turning point where Sam's thoughts turn to revenge, he misses his interview and even now he's going on the road. But he was the one who said no amount of hunting could bring Mom back, so the same can be said about Jess. Only we don't know yet but his reasons for finding the thing or demon are different because he's he feels he's to blame as he knew what was coming for Jess and what lay in wait for her but he didn't do anything about it. (See **1.14 Nightmare.**)

Also good to see were the excellent two leads in Jared and Jensen. Uncannily you notice the way in which they seem to know in which direction their characters will go and each of their nuances. Though Jensen originally auditioned for the part of Sam, you can see he's more suited to the role of Dean: big brother, demon hunter, jockial, never serious, well not too often, always on the ball and a bit trigger happy too. It's great Dean remains consistent throughout season 1, always wanting to do everything Dad taught them, forever the loyal son.

The same can be said of Sam, more out-going, socially, able to mix with people, his peers, making friends revolving around his interests and life choices. Dean's life choices help them to survive in the outside world too, with his constant scams, fake Ids and credit cards (not that this is any form of endorsement!). Dean has friends too, but we don't meet them, aside from his ex Cassie. (**1.13 Route 666.**)

Not until season 2 do their carefully moulded characters begin to unravel and go off on different tangents. Dean, no longer that confident after Dad's death: more serious and shows his inner feelings a little more. Sam, on the other hand, now becomes more of the 'loyal' son, wanting to do everything Dad would've done.

Dean's necklace Jensen thinks is an Egyptian protection amulet. The Bull Man, Mesopotamian demon – allowing evil to be fought or *Mithras* a Roman Zoroastrian god to protect good from evil. Eric Kripke said there was no reason to go into why Dean wears it, but from **3.8** we know Sam gave it to him as Dad didn't show up for Christmas.

Sam owns a Verizon Motorola Q and got a new phone after **3.7**. There is a round blue sticker on Sam's laptop mentioning North Vancouver Mountainbike Co: *Deep Cove Bike Shop.*

The nickname for the Impala is *Metallicar* and the show uses up to five of these cars. CNK 80Q3 the number plates are for Ohio, which is Eric Kripke's home.

Dad sits on the Impala with them both, when their house burns. The number plate KAZ 2Y5 the first three letters represent Kansas and 2Y5 represents the debut year of the show, i.e. 2005. Their home is in Lawrence. Kansas which is in Douglas County. But the plates are from Sedgwick County. Kansas doesn't issue front licence plates and the county stickers are not pink.

One candle on Jessica's grave has *Virgin de Guadalupe*, known as 'the woman of the Apocalypse.'

Mom died on November 2 1983 which is All Souls Day in the Roman Catholic Church.

Sam's line of Dad being with 'Jim, Jack and Jose' refers to liquor: Jim Beam, Jack Daniels, Jose Cuervo (tequila). The others are whiskey.

Dad's death emulated Star Wars and why he'd really go on the road, revenge and to hunt.

Grand Junction is a desert in real life.

Sarah Shahi was in *Alias, Dawson's Creek* and *The L Word.*

Steve Railsbeck played Duane Barry in the 2-part X-Files episode *Duane Barry,* who abducted Scully after claiming to have been abducted by aliens himself.

Samantha Smith was Logan's ex girlfriend, Daphne in season 1 episode of *Dark Angel,* **Art Attack** and can be currently seen in *The Chosen One, Transformers: Revenge of the Fallen.* She had to audition for her role of Mom.

Quotes

Dean: "You think you're just gonna become a lawyer, marry your girl...does Jessica know the truth about you, does she know about the things you've done."
Sam: "No and she's never going to know."

Dean: "...but sooner or later you're gonna have to face up to who you really are...one of us."

Dean: "No chick flick moments."
Sam: "All right, jerk."

Dean: "Bitch."

Sam And Dean's Take On the Urban Legend/Lore

The woman in white, also known as the weeping woman phenomenon. The spirits have been seen for hundreds of years in Hawaii, Mexico, Arizona, and Indiana. They are all different women with the same story. When they were alive their husbands were unfaithful and they murdered their children in a moment of temporary insanity. They then committed suicide leaving cursed spirits. The men are never seen again.

Actual Legend

The 'woman in white' not to be confused with the book of the same name by Wilke Collins, but the woman in white is a common phenomena. This urban legend is sometimes known as The Vanishing Hitchhiker and originated in the US but occurs in numerous countries around the world. American folklorists, Rosalie Hankey and Richard Beardsley wrote of four versions of this legend; the first is where the driver is given an address by the hitchhiker and finds they are a spirit. The second is where the hitchhiker is found to be a local divinity, the third is where the hitchhiker is an old woman telling of disasters at the end of World War II and the fourth is where the hitchhiker leaves something on her grave as a form of telling evidence about who she really is and what's she's been through, usually associated with some form of an entertainment venue she's been to.

Another legend is where the driver finds something left behind by the hitchhiker he's had in the car and the driver then contacts the spirit.

A doctor returning home stopped at the traffic lights of a busy junction, looking towards the road he saw a young woman in an evening gown asking for a lift. Having his golf clubs in the passenger seat he gestures for her to get into the back. He asks what she's doing out alone at night. She replies, "It's a long story. Can you please take me home?" Even though the address she gives him is away from his route, he agrees to this. Most of the trip was in silence and when he turned back to inform her they'd reached her destination, she had vanished.

The doctor not knowing what happened knocked on the door of the house where she lived and was greeted by an old man. Telling him of his predicament, the old man replied that the woman in question was his daughter but was killed on the night of her prom. That was seven years ago and every year some man knocks on his door and tells him the same story.

In early tellings of this urban legend, the girl would ride on horseback; then the wagon and finally graduated onto the car and bears the classic hallmarks of being your average ghost story. Apparently the girl appears to be between worlds – the spiritual and the actual, real world with her appearing over and over because she wasn't able to reach home safely on that night.

Early versions of this legend date to the nineteenth century and are believed to have been the creation of European supernatural folklore legends. Spreading to the US by European immigrants. This story even has roots in the Bible- Acts 8: 26-39, New Testament: the Ethiopian who gives the apostle Philip a ride in his chariot; is baptized by Philip, who then vanishes.

The 'woman in white' is also known as the 'crying woman' or in Spanish, 'La Llorona' or even 'the weeping woman'. She is actually wailing for her dead children. There are many legends about this, as mentioned but another early telling involves the woman killing her two sons in a river. She is either named Sofia, Maria, Linda or Laura. It is claimed she walks along the riverbank at night in search of children to terrorize.

Some say the best-known account of this legend is the 'weeping woman of the south west', beginning in New Mexico. Here she was known as Maria, the daughter of a pheasant family, during the Conquistadors period. She was beautiful and adorned by men of her village; frequenting fandangos dressed in white and thought to have given birth to two sons, but it's not known how.

Maria eventually married a wealthy man and years into their marriage she bored of him and her children. He began affairs and left his family for months upon end. It is said he passed by her in his carriage one day and only acknowledged her children. This made Maria angry and she hated them, throwing them into the river. Realizing her mistake she ran into the street crying. In search of her children and refusing to eat, she roamed the riverbanks, eventually meeting her doom there.

Now La Llorona's spirit roams The Santa Fe River at night and murders any she comes across – making people afraid of going out at night. She seems to kill those who have wronged their families by way of punishment.

Robert Barakat writes La Llorona is thought to be an old tale ranging from the American south west but is said to be intermingled with another tale; demonstrating the "collision of cultures that occurred when the indigenous culture of Mexico mixed with the emergent Spanish culture in the new World". These were known as *The Legends of the Virgin of Guadalupe and la Llorona*. The story itself may be a conflation of similar tales of Spanish and indigenous origin. The unfaithful lover is a common European motif, unknown in Aztec folklore, while "such motifs as the wailing, water, knife and general appearance of the weeping woman are directly linked to Aztec mythology." But showing how the title of these can be attributed to both weeping women. "There can be little doubt that he foreigners confused their legend with a similar one of the Aztecs and consequently passed it on to the Natives. "Who in turn added their own elements.

Although close in some respects to this episode, the legend in the pilot is mostly attributed to the 'woman in white' but having references to this: she hitches a ride, appears in the back seat, wants to go home, but disappears before she arrives. In Sam and Dean's lore version: she kills men who are unfaithful because that's what her husband was and he drove her to murder and suicide. She's almost like a zombie.

There's not many scary women Dean can claim to have in his beloved Impala and the woman in white is the only spirit who's ever been in there – not that he hasn't had any women in the back seat of his car, but they weren't eerily dead, oh and he had one in 2.16 **Road Kill**, but she wasn't bad, though she was a spirit.

My dad and his friend, on separate occasions, came across a woman in white whilst returning home late at night. She got on the back of his bike and told him not to look behind. He then cycled and the bike got heavier and heavier until finally it got lighter so he knew she had gone. Turning around my dad saw a woman in white with long flowing hair running away towards some desolate buildings. This was near to a hospital too, not a sanatarium though. So who knows who or what she really was. When this happened to my dad's friend, he fell into a fever afterwards and didn't recover for days and who can say what's really out there in the dark…or in the darkest depths of our imagination…

The story of the woman killing her children then committing suicide, like oyakashinju; a sort of Japanese version where the mother would kill her children especially daughters and then herself. This was most common during World War II when they were afraid US soldiers would ravage them. Not sure if there are ghostly spirits attached to that one though and it doesn't really appear to be an urban legend either.

TV/Film References

The Brady Bunch, The Cosby Show, The X-Files, The Smurfs, Unsolved Mysteries, Casper the Friendly Ghost.

X-Files Connection

In **6.6** (notice the episode and season number) **Terms of Endearment**, Laura dreams of a demon stealing her baby, when she awakens, the baby is missing. Mulder chances upon demon baby harvesting. Another woman also dreams of her baby being stolen by a demon. Mulder stipulates the husband was a demon who wanted a normal life and family but all his children were born demons too. (See also **1.21** and **2.5** of *Supernatural*.)

9.12 Scary Monsters a boy hears scratching under his bed. Something scurries across the floor. The boy says a monster killed his grandmother. The creatures are the ones killing. Noteworthy for Sam and Dean's monsters under the bed dialogue.

In **Deep Throat**, Scully asks, "What's that?" [To loud heavy metal music playing in the car.]

Mulder: "Evidence." [She then turns it off.]

Music

Ramblin' Man by Altman Brothers Band; *Back in Black* by AC/DC; *Highway To Hell* by AC/DC; *You Shook Me All Night Long* by AC/DC

Ooh Bloops

When Constance kills in the opening scene, blood spatters on the car. When Sam and Dean are on the bridge the car is devoid of any blood.

When Sam and Dean are in Dad's motel room the article on the wall about Constance where a neighbour describes her as quiet. The neighbour's name is Deanna Kripke, named for (Eric) Kripke.

Originally Constance was meant to have killed her parents.

When Constance jumped from the bridge it was 1981, research shows the year as being 1971 in the hotel room.

Locations

The pilot was filmed at Lake Piro, California.

1.2 Wendigo

Teleplay: Eric Kripke. Story: Ron Milbauer & Terri Hughes Burton.
Director: David Nutter
Original US Airdate 13 September 2005

Guest Stars: Callum Keith Rennie (Roy); Gina Holden (Hayley). Alden
Ehreniech (Tom). Donnelly Rhodes (Mr Shaw); Roy Campbell
(Wendigo)
Blackwater Ridge
Lost Creek, Colorado.

Sam and Dean discover a wendigo is responsible for the
disappearance of some campers in the woods.

Palo Alto, California

Sam says goodbye to Jessica. *Sam: "You know you always said
roses were so lame so I brought you...Jess...I should've prepared you, I
should've told you the truth." But how would this have helped her, she
was a mere mortal and couldn't have fought off the powers of the old
yellow eyes.*

Notes

Sam is having nightmares about Jessica's death and the fact he
didn't tell her the truth: who he was and about his family. He thought it
best to keep the family secret: that they're hunters, but here we don't
yet know Sam had visions about Jessica's death even before it actually
happened, until **1.5 Bloody Mary**. Also it's not clear whether he saw
her go up in flames on the ceiling or not. So it's no wonder now he
dreams of her hand reaching out to him from beyond the grave – as if to
say "You put me here!" when he could have saved her. This is the guilt
that haunts him throughout the early Season 1 episodes (cf Season 2
when the situation is reversed and the guilt now plagues Dean about
their father's death.)

How could Sam have saved her though, knowing what his family
did; knowing about Mom and that he wouldn't always be around to
protect her.

Dean is still convinced that finding their father will lead them to
finding the 'Thing' that killed their mother and Jessica, (not yet
knowing that the 'Thing' was in fact setting its plans in motion from the

night in the nursery fire 26 years ago, until now. That killing Jessica was just a ploy to get Sam involved again into taking an active part in hunting – developing his powers and actually using them.)

Not until **1.21** do they actually find out the 'Thing' was a demon and a yellow eyed one at that, since they don't actually come across it themselves until the penultimate episode of Season 1.

Dean asking Sam when he suddenly became all gung ho, ready to pull the trigger first (trigger happy) and he replies "now"; but then changes again and goes back to his reflective: ask questions first-shoot-later mode and even tries to convince Dean he should be doing this too.

Sam mentioning 'corporeal' – meaning has a 'human' form; a solid mass, as opposed to being invisible. Corporeal penned and stated in so many shows from *Star Trek: Enterprise,* to *Buffy* where it was used more frequently.

Dean's up on his cartoon 'lore' too, re *Bambi* and *Yogi Bear*. So much time on his hands to watch TV! Dean's comment about being the most honest with a woman – ever. Well, we'll see in **1.13 Route 666,** he was even more honest to his girlfriend, who promptly returned the favour and dumped him for it. Some insight into what he really thinks of women and what they're good for and yet in **2.6** he tells Jo he's not sexist! (No only sexy! Oops sorry!)

Dean's favourite sweets are *Peanut M&Ms* also good for leaving a trail behind a la *Hansel and Gretel*. This was also alluding to *ET* where Elliott leaves *Reese's Pieces* for ET.

The Guide, Roy, comments he's been hunting since his mother kissed Sam goodnight was highly insensitive, not that he knows the circumstances behind Sam's life, but she only kissed him for 6 months. They didn't know a mother's love to its fullest extent.

Anazasi symbols – another *X- File* relic. Native American Indian folklore features a lot in the supernatural and provides many insights into beliefs prevalent even today.

Sam seems determined to find Dad and Jessica's killer now (if Dad is dead at this point), yet he didn't feel he could do this for Mom; he wanted to get away from the whole family business of hunting until now.

Dad's journal is mentioned again. Dean's ready and able to follow Dad's orders without question because Dad wants them to but also because it keeps him going.

Eric Kripke: "We learned really early, after the Wendigo episode, not to mount creatures you can't afford to produce. They're just gonna look stupid. Do it well or don't do it is the plan. That's why our werewolves have yellow eyes and fangs and are otherwise human." But

Madison in **2.17 Heart,** had blue eyes! At least in our version of the episode.

Sam is reading *The Hero With A Thousand Faces* by Joe Campbell, one influence Eric Kripke cites for his *Supernatural* show.

Jessica's gravestone date reads 2 November 2005 when she died, the same date Mom died 20 years ago.

Black Water is not a real town.

Sam owns a Dell Inspiron 6000 laptop used in this episode.

One deleted scene shows Dean, Sam, Hailey and Ben hiking in the woods. Stopping for a break, Ben wanders and Sam goes after him. Finding an Anasazi symbol on a tree, Sam ponders where he's come across it previously.

Donner Party was a group of American settlers who were caught in the snow and resorted to cannibalism.

Eric Kripke says there was more to the wendigo, but most of it ended up on the cutting room floor. "They cut around it and you never saw it, resulting in a scarier movie. He looked like Gollum's (*Lord of the Rings*) gangly big brother to me."

Callum Keith Rennie played Ray #2 in *Due South* as well as being in a number of shows, including *X-Files.*

Gina Holden was in the Thomas Kincaid movie, *Home for the Holidays* alongside Jared. As well as *Blood Ties, Smallville.* The movies: *Aliens V Predator Requiem, The Butterfly Effect 2, Final Destination 3, Travelling, Screamers 2. She also plays Dale Arden in Flash G.*

Quotes

Jessica's headstone reads: *Beloved daughter January 24 1984-November 2 2005.* Incidentally or coincidentally Dean's birthday is also the same as hers.

Dean: "Sweetheart I don't do shorts."

Dean: "This is the way, this book; this is Dad's single most valuable... Everything he knows, every evil thing is in here and he's passed it onto us. I think he wants us to pick up where he left off. You know, saving people, hunting things, family business."

Sam & Dean's Take on the Urban Legend/Lore

Sam says the creature is a Wendigo, it's in Dad's journal. Dean comments they're usually found in the Minnesota woods or North Michigan. He hasn't heard of one this far away. Dean draws Anazasi symbols around the camp for protection so evil can't cross over.

Wendigo is a Cree Indian word =evil that devours. It was once a man (I had to laugh at this point thinking of Piper in *Charmed* when she turned into a wendigo, as a man). Sometimes it's Indian, a miner, hunter. In the harsh Winter, was cut off from supplies and became a cannibal to survive, eating other member's of its tribe, hunters etc. Sam comments cultures the world over believe eating human flesh gives them the ability to be fast, strong and become immortal. Dean says if you eat enough they become less than human, but a thing and always hungry. It knows how to survive without food, hibernates and stores its victims alive to eat when it needs to. It can only be burned to be killed.

Actual Legend

Wendigos, aka, "the evil spirit that devours mankind", in other words, a cannibal. Believed to be up to 15' tall with a deformed skeleton like body made of ice; with fangs, yellow skin and glowing eyes. Found in Minnesota and parts of Canada. Perfect hunters as they know every detail of their territory. Certain Native American legends believe wendigos to control the weather by using magic.

Date back from the seventeenth century, were once human and if possessed by its spirit at night – could turn into one too; and they turn to cannibalism in a struggle for survival without food. When they return to normal life, leads to violence as they crave human flesh. Thought to eat moss and other things when human flesh can't be found.

There have been wendigo murder trials in Canada, early twentieth century. One famous one was *Jack Fiddler* – a Cree Indian saying he killed 14 wendigos. In October 1907, he and his son were tried for the murder of a Cree woman. They claimed she was possessed by the spirit of a wendigo and she was about to become one herself. They were found guilty and imprisoned. Jack died at 87.

Psychologists also used the phrase *Wendi psychosis* to talk of anyone showing symptoms of becoming a wendigo: often violent, short tempered, have nightmares and leg pains. Usually running into the woods, naked and screaming. To kill a wendigo – its heart of ice needs to be melted. Now you know why Dean used fire.

X Files Connection

5.4 Detour, Mulder and Scully investigate the disappearance of three men in the woods. Tracks are not identified as man or animal. A man claims a red-eyed creature chased him. Mulder links it to an old *X File* where a town was terrorized by a man with red eyes.

Music

Hot Blooded by Foreigner; *Down South Jukin'* by Lynyrd Skynyrd

Ooh Bloops

Dean's Ranger badge has the name 'Samuel' but he calls himself Dean'.

1.3 Dead In The Water

Written By Sera Gamble & Raelle Tucker. Directed By Kim Manners
Original US Airdate 27 September 2005

Guest Stars: Amy Acker (Andrea Barr); Daniel Hugh Kelly (Sheriff Jake Devins); Nico McEown (Lucas Barr); Amber Borycki (Sophie Carlton)

Lake Manitoc, Wisconsin

Sam and Dean investigate when a series of unexplained drownings plague a small town, opening up old wounds especially for Dean.

Notes

The first scene is right out of *Jaws*.

Dean is a right lady's' man isn't he! It's a wonder he manages to keep his mind on the job when there's all these 'fun' distractions around for him! Fun being waitresses and barmaids. Well, what's a guy to do, it's a lonely life on the road.

Sam's reference about people not just disappearing, he's preoccupied with finding Dad and if Dean hadn't come to get Sam to look for him, he would never had known he was missing – but he's determined to find him, though he says it himself in **1.8 Bugs**, that they'd probably fight again anyway like they always do and even Dean said it too.

Dean showing his resentment earlier on in the episode about Sam going away to college (or university to us!) and having his own life and fun' (!) whilst he had to stay with Dad and hunt and take all his flak! (Thought of *CSI:NY* here!) The grief, putting themselves in danger without Sam there to watch their backs and especially to watch Dean's back when Dad went missing. Though his resentment is in the form of getting angry at Sam.

Underneath you can tell he's fuming but doesn't think it's the right time to go into any details and he never misses an opportunity to tease Sam about his college education, calling him a geek.

Another film reference to *Star Wars* when Dean identifies themselves as the agents. He refers to himself as Agent Ford, the more handsome, manly character/actor. The lover and underdog Han solo in the movie (and some would say, hero who single-handedly saves the day with his Millennium Falcon – a bit like Dean with his Chevy Impala!) Incidentally Harrison Ford is one of Jensen's heroes in real life and someone he'd like to work with. Sadly he didn't get a chance to in *Indiana Jones IV The Crystal Skull.* Sam was on another planet practically (Stamford) hence he's Agent Hamill; until the two of them meet up to battle Darth Vadar (the Yellow Eyed demon) and find their Dad, who turned out to be Darth Vadar in the movie and Luke's Dad of course.

The reference to Andrea being as safe in her own bathtub is significant as that's where Andrea drowns, almost, towards the end before being saved by Sam. Also a timely reference to this scene as you just don't think this is what will eventually happen.

Dean would like to have 'fun' with Andrea who sees right through him, never mind she's got a child. Surely Dean must like children. He had to look after Sam didn't he and no matter he was only his brother. Also see **3.2** where he thinks Ben may be his son. But he does have a way with children though, knowing how to reach out to Lucas (a namesake for Luke Skywalker) telling him about his own family. How he feels about Mom's death and even carrying out Sam from the burning house. Thoughts and feelings he's never shared with anyone, not even Sam. Here's when we get to see another side to Dean. His caring, sharing side he hides less it destroys his macho, tough guy image!

Dean loved toy soldiers. Dad was a marine and Dean grew up to become a soldier too, instilled into him by Dad and he mentions taking orders and following them several times too, during various season 1 and 2 episodes.

Although Dean didn't know how much of an impact his own childhood would have for him later on in life and he probably never even dreamed he'd be doing something like hunting when he was older. Again his comments on what children can deal with and refers to himself more so than Sam; since Sam was only a baby and too young to remember the night they lost Mom and how she'd want him to be brave, which he was, taking charge of Sam, and not complaining until now.

Referring to chicks digging artists, see **1.19 Provenance** where Dean says this again.

Sam says trauma can lead to heightened psychic tendencies, prompting us to ask if what happened that night in his nursery led to his abilities becoming apparent. Though we know that Sam was born with those abilities otherwise those events when he was 6 months old would never have played out. Until the revelation in season 2 finale that Sam has demon blood in him and thus could have got his abilities in that way.

Dean's comment of having to hug, mentioned several times in **2.4 Children Shouldn't Play With Dead Things** and his "Oh god". See *Angel* episode season 2.

Dean returns to the town again as he does in **1.11 Scarecrow** episode after he's driven out of town.

They save the day, but not everybody and Dean almost gets the girl.

No bones to salt and burn in this episode, as critics love going on about having this all the time.

An episode with real insight into their past and feelings about that night.

Amy Acker was our beloved Fred in *Angel.* One of Eric Kripke's fave episodes, he said, Amy Acker was "So cool, she's a great actress."

Daniel Hugh Kelly has been in numerous films and TV shows including *Law & Order, Law & Order: Special Victims Unit* and will be best remembered for playing McCormick in the eighties show *Hardcastle & McCormick.* On You tube there's a video compilation o f the theme song from this show called *Drive* which was has clips of *Supernatural* episodes accompanying it. If you're into your six degrees of separation type thing, or perhaps 2 degrees of separation here!

Jensen comments: "A really good episode for my character specifically because there was a lot of insight into his repressed feelings about his mother and his family." One of his favourite episodes, "You get to see different shades of Dean and I get to peel a layer away for the audience to explore. I always like those kind of episodes."

Some of the guys' stunts have involved water and in this episode, Jensen was a bit frightened by having to be dragged under the water, in the scene where he rescued Lucas. Says Jensen: "I was treading water and I have this 10 year old boy limp in my arms because he's supposed to be dead. When they said 'Action' we had to hold our breath and I had two divers below me, pulling me down. I'm a fine swimmer but it was a sensation I wasn't expecting and after the first time I had to kick the divers loose and ask for a minute. But we got it on film and it looked good."

The cabin in this episode was also used in the movie *Devour* with Jensen Ackles.

There is no Lake Manitoc in Wisconsin.

Quotes

Dean: "I'm sick of this attitude. You think I don't want to find Dad as much as you do. I'm the one that's been with him every single day for the past two years. While you've been off to college, to pep rallies. We will find Dad, but until then we are going to kill everything bad between here and there."

Andrea: "Must be hard with your sense of direction, never being able to find your way to a decent pick-up line." He doesn't really need one!

Dean: "Watching one of your parents die is something you just never get over." But losing two parents…

Dean:"…oh God we're not going to have to hug or anything are we?"

Sam: "Who are you and what have you done with my brother?" That's a line he'll be asking in **1.6 Skin**.

Sam: "We're not gonna save everybody."

Sam & Dean's Take on the Urban Legend/Lore

Dean thinks it could be a water wraith or demon, something that controls water, but it turns out to be a vengeful spirit.

Actual Legend

The Loch Ness monster first sighted as far back as 565 AD. This is no legend in this episode per se.

Film/TV References

Star wars, Jerry Maguire. This episode has been likened to the Harrison Ford, Michelle Pfeiffer movie, *What Lies Beneath.*

X Files Connection

Quagmire has a series of deaths possibly connected to a lake monster.

Music

What A Way To Go by Black Toast Music; *Round and Round* by Ratt; *Too Daze Gone* by Billy Quier; *Movin' On* by Bad Company

Ooh Bloops

When Andrea fills the bath, the water rises but when the dirty water pours into the tub, the water level is much lower. When Sam rescues Andrea from the bath, her pants can be seen on the left side of the picture/shot.

Dean circles the girl's photo in the paper, when Sam looks at it, the circle is different, he circles her name, but not when Sam has the paper.

When Will drowns, the water rising up doesn't clog the sink and note the plug and chain changing positions, the plug is on the side of the sink before Will even pulls it out. When he's chopping potatoes, the sink plug is on the counter. When the sink is filling up, the plug is in the drain inside the sink.

Dean says many have drowned in the lake, however the drowned boy was only after the families who 'killed' him.

Locations

Delta, 4800 Block Delta Street. Ladner United Church. Lynwood Inn. Buntzen Lake. Claire's B&B, Ladner.

1.4 Phantom Traveller

Written By Richard Hatem. Directed By Robert Singer
Original US Airdate 4 October 2005

Guest Stars Jamie Ray Newman (Amanda Walker); Brian Markinson (Jerry).

Sam and Dean are called by an old friend of Dad's to investigate a mysterious plane crash, prompting them to find out a few home truths about Dad and each other.

Notes

In this episode we actually get to see the boys make false IDs for themselves, probably because it's Homeland Security and they haven't been around long for Dean to utilize that cover. Also as it's a plane crash they're investigating, Homeland Security are more likely to be involved too, as well as the NTSB.

Sam is having nightmares, whilst Dean appears to be in lala land, though he does keep a knife under his pillow for protection. Does he, I wonder have a name for his trusty knife?

Sam mentions Flight 401, also a film from the 1970's/1980's, called *The Ghost of Flight 401* which he obviously makes reference to here.

The cockpit recorder with 'no survivors' being heard, viewers will recognize as *Final Destination* and though there are some similarities with death not stopping until it's taken everyone who was meant to perish on the plane in that movie, that's about all there is in common with these critics endless comments on this episode swiping that movie's plot. That's where the similarities end, as it's the 'black-eyed' demon which possesses these passengers and it's all to do with demonic tendencies. Coincidentally all those possessed have black eyes and 'demon smoke' as Sam describes it later on, there's a possibility the 'Thing they're on the hunt for (Yellow eyed demon) is behind these deaths too.

Think Dean needed a bigger size suit for his *MIB* role. Homeland security also dress in black. Dean mentioning pea soup from *The Exorcist* which he'll repeat in season **2.7 The Usual Suspects** when Linda Blair guests.

We also get mentions of Biblical numerology here, for the first and only time this season and next. Like 666, here's it's the number 40. The significance of number 7 here is that 7 is a Biblical number and there were 7 survivors on the plane. Eric Kripke said, "Yes, using the number 7 was intentional. We're always trying to drop in small but significant details and we occasionally look to numerology."

The flight Sam and Dean board departs from Gate 13. Another number most commonly associated with bad luck of course. Get the feeling Dean's bad luck could've started here, when he lost Dad who sacrificed himself, then having to do the same to bring back Sam and finally going to hell for reaping the rewards. (See Seasons 2, 3 and 4.)

Dean happens to be afraid of flying, this being why he drives everywhere, but you were probably fooled into believing it was because he loves his car! Probably the only fear Dean has, aside from losing his beloved car! Also if he wasn't afraid to fly, flying would attract more attraction especially in their line of work with the 'tools' of the trade they carry. Not to mention costing a lot and faking all those passports too. Then that's where the fake credit cards come in.

Dean once more, not a believer in God, knows the Latin name, Christo, for God. But he does say "Oh God a lot..

Is the *Ritual Romano* the same one Dean uses in **2.8 Crossroad Blues** when he begins to banish the crossroads demon or is that a different ritual.

Funny no one thought it strange what the two of them were doing in the plane, making all that noise at the back and then Sam diving for the book in the aisle! Most especially with airline security being paramount these days.

The demon sees a chance to rattle Sam by telling him Jessica's death was his fault, he could've saved her and saying that she still burns. Something the possessed girl says in **2.8 Crossroad Blues** to Dean about Dad being in hell and a far worse place than he can imagine it to be. In which case what of Mom (cf **1.9 Home**. In the season 3 finale and season 4 opener, Dean won't need to imagine hell, as he ends up exactly there.) Sam telling Dean it knew of Jessica and Dean saying that's what demons do. They lie. Sam repeats the same to him in **2.4 Children shouldn't Play With Dead Things** when Dean opens up to Sam about Dad and not being able to hunt anymore. Curiously Sam only tells Dean it knew about Jessica, leading Dean to say they read minds. He doesn't tell Dean the real truth here about having nightmares about her before she dies. (See **1.5 Bloody Mary**.)

As for the comment Jessica still burns, well obviously she did burn for Sam, being in love with him. Okay maybe I shouldn't have mentioned that so lightly. Also the yellow eyed demon knew a lot about them anyway, and so too did the crossroad demons which again hint at his involvement.

Dean's hair standing on end in the plane, even though it was the wind and nothing to do with him being terrified. Also strange after the phone message on Deans' phone, not many people called them for help. They usually stumbled across their own cases, or found them in newspapers.

Dean makes his own EMF reader out of a walkman, whilst everyone else has a CD player or more likely an iPod. Hey I still have my Sony Walkman around too.

Strange also that Jerry had Dean's number for six months telling the caller to ring Dean for help, which means Dad didn't just get up or go out and disappear in the middle of the night. Dad planed to go walkabout all along in his search for the 'Thing'; deeming it easier to keep Dean out of the loop for his own good and protection. Whereas what he's really done is to bring Sam into it too.

So what are the repercussions on all of this for Jessica's death. If Dean didn't show up for Sam? Then again Sam also began having his nightmares round about that time so this was all predetermined by fate or put into motion by the 'Thing, aka Yellow Eyes.

Dean sings Metallica on the plane prompting Sam to say his distress will cause Dean to become possessed. Always travel with Holy Water wherever you go!

The plane crashed 60 miles west of Nazareth, to which Dean replies, "I'll try to ignore the irony in that!"

This episode was filmed on a real plane because of the limited budget.

Dean pulls up in the car and walks to the airport. Sam has to tell him why they're here. Dean has to put his weapons in the boot saying he's naked now.

Dean's phone number: 1-866-907-3235 was a real phone number for a time. Jensen actually left the message *This is Dean Winchester. If this is an emergency, leave a message. If you are calling about 11-2-83 page me with your co-ordinates.* This was the date of the fire in the Pilot, when Mom died.

Also when the number of Dean's mobile is called, 866-907-3255, one message reads: "Dad we really need to hear from you. Leave me a message, text me, check your jwinchester1246 email. Anything, we have new information." The other message is different, so can't tell which one or if both were actually on that number, unless you actually listened to it in the US. Which sadly, many of us couldn't!

Sam reading from the journal:

Regna terrae, cantata Deo, psallite Domino.
Qui vehitor per Caelus, caelos, antiques.
Ecce, edit vocem suam, vocem potentum.
Agnoscite potentiam Dei.
Magestas, ejus, et potential ejis in nubibus.
Ti mendus est Deus e sancto suo,
Deus Israel, Ipse potentiam dat et robur populo suo

Benedictus Deus. Gloria. Patri

Quotes

Dean: "Man I look like 2 of the *Blues Brothers.*"
Sam: "No you don't, you look more like a seventh grader at his first dance."

Dean: "Goes way beyond floating over a bed or barfing pea soup. One thing to possess, but another to use him to take down an entire airplane."

Dean: "We don't have time for the whole 'truth is out there' speech."

Dad: "This is John Winchester. I can't be reached. If this is an emergency call my son Dean. 785-555-0179. He can help."

Sam and Dean's Take on the Urban Legend/Lore

Sam states every religion and culture in the world has a concept of demons and demonic possessions, Christians, Native Americans, Hindu. Sam continues that Japanese believe certain demons are behind certain disasters, both natural and manmade: diseases or earthquakes. The plane went down exactly 40 minutes into the flight. Dean mentions Biblical numerology, for example, with Noah's Ark, it rained for 40 days. Numbers are associated with death. Sam says there were 6 plane crashes over 10 years and all of them crashed 40 minutes in.

Actual Legend

Water is powerful since it is seen as receptive. It retains energy and is used in cleansing: people and places or for consecration. It is pure and doused around the home to rid it of negative energy. Hence the numerous uses of Holy Water too.

Numerology is the occult science of numbers; encompassing science and philosophy. The mystical effect of numbers can help to look at the events in an individual's life. Science of numerology encompasses the "science of periodicity", for example, all laws of nature are grounded in certain periods of time (numbers) such as the planets, moon, sun. Hence the earth takes 365 days, 6 hours, 9 minutes and 9.7 seconds to orbit the sun once. The length of the lunar month is 29 days, 12 hours, 44 minutes and 2.9 seconds.

The Greek mathematician, Pythagoras, in 550 BC (mystic year) wrote, "The world is built upon the power of numbers." Numbers 1-9 inclusive are primary numbers, from which all the other numbers are made up. Jewish beliefs also attribute numbers as well as letters, as being fundamental to life. God used these in the creation of the universe. I.e. for example, Pythagoras and his followers say life can be interpreted using these basic numbers, 1-9. There is 1 God; 2 opposites; 3 parts to the Holy Trinity; 4 elements of life; (earth, air, fire, water); 4 seasons, 5 senses; 6 points on a pentagram (crucial for the purposes of *Supernatural* as a pentagram is considered good as opposed to evil. A pentagram is known as a symbol of "natural balance".) There are 7 colours in the spectrum (rainbow); 7 musical notes; wonders of the world; days of the week; 8 paths in Buddhism; an inverted '8' on its side is also the symbol of 'affinity'; 9 months of the development of a human foetus; the sum in a multiplication of 9 can be totalled to 9: 3x9=27 (2+7=9); 4x9=36 (3+6=9 etc.).

In the twentieth century, Correlius Agrippa wrote *Occult Philosophy in 1533* and listed these same basic numbers and their meanings.

Flight 401 the ghosts that appeared here are known as *Interactive ghosts*: those which appear since they have some sort of purpose – usually to provide some comfort to those suffering loss or bereavement. Most common was the crash of Eastern Airlines Flight 401 in the Florida Everglades. The plane crashed due to certain functions or malfunctions in the auto-pilot system.

The pilot and co-pilot on this flight were claimed to have been seen by many people, especially those on, or working on L-1011 planes. These planes strangely or coincidentally had parts salvaged from 401. The co-pilot, Don Repo on TriStar 318 had a warning of a fire. The plane was met with engine trouble. The galley of this plane was from 401. His purpose for appearing was to tell them they were watching over the L-1011 aircraft, so there'll never be another crash on such aircraft and none have been reported or recorded since.

Film/TV References

The Haunting of Flight 401. The Exorcist. The X Files, i.e. "The truth is out there."

X Files Connection

9.14 Improbable, Reyes links two cases with numerology, a form of Karmic numbers theory. The victims have marks with '666' from a ring on them. The path of the murders, when plotted on a map form the number '6'.

Music

Paranoid by Black Sabbath; *Working Man* by Rush; *Load Range* by Nichion Sounds Library

Ooh Bloops

When Sam and Dean talk, Sam chews something. In the commentary for this episode, Sam was meant to be eating a doughnut, but it never got filmed.

When the first plane crashes, the door hits the wing and part of it comes off, later the wing is back in its entirety.

Christos is Greek, i.e. *Christos*, meaning *The Anointed one*. *Deus* or *deo* is Latin for God. Not *Christos* as Sam and Dean say here.

Locations

Vancouver International Airport, South Terminal Route 10.

1.5 Bloody Mary

Teleplay Ron Milbauer & Terri Hughes Burtion; Story Eric Kripke
Directed By Peter Ellis
Original US Airdate 11 October 2005

Guest Stars: Adrienne Palicki (Jess); Marnette Patterson (Charlie)

Toledo, Ohio

Sam and Dean investigate the case of a man killed in his bathroom.

Fort Wayne, Indiana

They talk to the detective on the case pretending to be reporters. To find out about Mary.

Notes

Usually in these urban legends the spirit almost always dies in a car crash. (See Pilot episode and **2.4 Children Shouldn't Play With Dead Things**.) Nothing happened to Lily in the beginning because she didn't have any guilty secrets relating to deaths she contributed to.

Sam and Dean need to research at the library, what was wrong with Sam's laptop?

Sam's been having dreams, nightmares really about Jess in the episode as he's hiding his own secret which he feels guilt over. Coincidentally, his nightmares had to coincide with Bloody Mary appearing so he could reveal to us what his secret is, but Dean has to wait to learn it.

The in-joke in this episode was Dean's reference to Paris Hilton since Jared starred with her in the movie, *House Of Wax.* (2005). No, you certainly don't look like her Dean! Strange they gave Dean this line to say, since he's always the one teasing Sam about being the girl!

It's not really explained how Mary can punish you for seeing someone die – how can she see it? Mary was cremated so her bones can't be salted and burned (like a barbeque!) See also **2.16 Road Kill** when Molly was also cremated so she couldn't be salted and burned either.

Also see **1.4 Phantom Traveller** where the demon possessing the co-pilot on the plane tells Sam he killed Jess and what I was saying about Dean coming to take Sam away from Jess and Dean says the same thing here to Sam when he tells Sam to hit him for doing this. But Dean's right about Sam's "dirty little secret" as he puts it. Sam does believe he killed Jess.

Sam does the break'n'enter in this episode which makes a change from Dean having to kick the door in. The police seemed to be oblivious to all the mirror smashing Sam partakes in whilst they're busy questioning Dean, who happens to think he's Japanese! (See **1.15 The Benders** where he claims he has the Michael Jackson skin condition.)

The reflection, Sam's reflection in the mirror telling him he was desperate to be normal, that he was only dreaming about Jess and it wouldn't really happen, Sam did believe he was normal and didn't think he had any special powers or was gifted in any way, considering Jess's death was the first dream he had at that point in time, before he began having his premonitions about other people dying in **1.9 Home**. This line implies he already knew he had special powers. So these premonitions/dreams about Jess must have been puzzling to him since he couldn't really have known what they meant as he didn't see Mom die in the same way.

Of course then the subconscious element comes into it – that he was in his crib that night. Would he as a baby retain that sort of an horrific memory? Unless the yellow-eyed demon made him see it in some way, since later we discover Sam has these visions when the demon is involved. But he did see what happened to Mom in the penultimate episode when he has visions about the mother being killed by the yellow-eyed demon in the same way as Mom. The niggling part is that other than this, he did want to be normal in the sense of not wanting to hunt anymore.

Dean too bleeds from his eyes but he wasn't the one who said "Bloody Mary, three times – why does this happen to him, do we believe he has a "dirty little secret" of his own?

Sam's advice to Charlie of bad things just happening, that may be true for other people they come across, but it's not the case for them or their family.

So Sam chooses not to tell Dean about this secret of his, not until episode **1.9 Home** when Sam finds out his premonitions become more advanced and frequent.

Speaking of Jess, Sam then sees her on the street, was this really his imagination as we all think it so. On the other hand, his seeing her dressed in white (very angelic, like Mom, come to think of it all of the mothers were dressed in white. See also season **1.21**) her appearing to him could be a sign, telling him to forgive himself; he wasn't to blame for her death because she forgives him and like Sam said to Charlie, he couldn't have prevented her death either and bad things happen. (See also **2.16 Road Kill** where Sam tells Molly some spirits hold on too tightly and can't let go.)

Dean says he probably got 600 years bad luck for breaking all those mirrors, perhaps that's true since the bad luck begins from the next episode **1.6 Skin**. He gets wanted by the police, then it's all downhill from there, Dad dying in season 2 to save Dean and the FBI on their trail and having to promise to kill Sam if he turns evil…

Marnette Patterson guested in the final season of *Charmed* as evil Christie, Billie's sister.

Quotes

Dean: "Do I look like Paris Hilton?"

Dean: "You think that's your dirty little secret, that you killed her somehow."
Sam: "I could've warned her."

Sam: "…I'd die for you, but there are some things that I need to keep to myself."

Sam and Dean's Take on the Urban Legend/Lore

Sam says there are around fifty stories about who Mary really is. One tells of her being a witch, mutilated bride. It's always a woman named Mary who dies in front of a mirror. Sam talks of the folklore where mirrors reveal secret lives, that these are a "true reflection of the soul" so it's bad luck to break them. Dean mentions the old superstition of mirrors capturing spirits, so adds Sam, when someone dies mirrors are covered so ghosts wouldn't be trapped. Dean thus explains Mary died in front of a mirror and her spirit was drawn in.

This episode does stick to the 'real' Bloody Mary legend.

Actual Legend

The Bloody Mary research began around 1978 by the folklorist, Janet Langlois when she published her essay on the legend, aka, *The Mirror Witch*.

It's unknown when the Bloody Mary legend emerged. Girls on a sleepover (just like when camping) all tells scary stories. One of them decides to tell a story her aunt told her. Over a century ago, a lynch mob took a woman called Mary Worth from her house and accused her of being a witch. After being tortured, she was burned at the stake and as she burnt she cursed the entire village. Legend has it that if you look into a mirror in the dark and say "Bloody Mary" five times, her vengeful spirit can be summoned.

After the girl completed her story they all dare one another to go to the bathroom; turn out the lights and say it into the mirror. The girl telling the story agrees to do this because she doesn't believe in Mary Worth and besides it's only a story or legend. She says it five times and the others ask if she's okay, as they can't hear her. Later she opens the door and looks pale. She was holding her fists so tightly clenched together that they bled but she couldn't tell anyone what really occurred in the bathroom.

Mary Worth, the name of the summoned woman changes in different versions of this legend. These include: *Bloody Mary, Mary Worth, Hell Mary, Mary Worthington, Mary Whales, Mary Johnson, Mary Lou, Mary Jane, Mary Ruth, Mary Weather, Kathy, Sally, Agnes, Bloody Bones, Suarte Madame, La Llorna, The Devil.*

The name or the way it's said into the mirror also varies, sometimes it's whispered getting louder. On the thirteenth time, Mary Worth is said to appear in the mirror and slashes the summoner's face. Usually what's said is *Bloody Mary*, or "I believe in Mary Worth" or even "Kathy Come out."

There variations on the chant, some say it should be said thirteen times with the summoner turning around in circles and glancing in the mirror when turning. Another Bloody Mary tale was where the girl ended her chant with "I don't believe in Mary Worth" tripped over the doorjamb and broke her hip... Mary was also taken to be a witch, killed 100 years ago for black magic/witchcraft, or in more recent times, she was the woman dying in a car accident. (See below.)

Also Mary's grave is said to be in North Vernon, Indiana. Another legend says if you stamp on her grave at midnight and curse her, Mary will punish you by making you bleed. The vines from her grave are supposedly meant to grow around the curser's ankles and hold them prisoner, until Bloody Mary rises from her grave.

Mirrors, as Sam says, are or have been covered up after a death has occurred in the house so the dead person's spirit is unable to look at itself in the mirror, thus condemning it to haunt this world for eternity. Mirrors also reflect the soul and so it's bad luck to break them, they also reveal secrets, which is why Sam wanted to summon her: his secret being revealed in the mirror by his own reflection.

As we know it's bad luck to break a mirror which is why most people also cover them up at night and during thunderstorms, so no reflections can be seen in them in the dark and not just when someone dies in the house.

The Bloody Mary ritual was most likely performed in a bathroom since many homes had large mirrors in there and usually no windows so it was dark even during the day.

South Appalachian traditions involve husband divining rituals: such as throwing an apple peel into water, spelling out the letter of your future husband's name. If you peel the apple in one go and throw it over your shoulder, it will spell out the first letter of your husband's surname.

Also there's the Hallowe'en myth about sitting in a darkened room at midnight on this day in
front of a mirror and something or someone is meant to appear behind you, reflected in the mirror. But I personally haven't tried this!

Sometimes unmarried girls would say a certain rhyme, glancing into the mirror would see the face of their intended or future husband, similar to the Hallowe'en legend I mentioned. This rhyme goes along the lines of *On Hallowe'en by Pumpkin's light, this witch will help you choose aright. They would stand in front of the mirror and say these words whereupon the mirror would reveal the face of her future husband.*

The following rhyme could also be said, *let this design on you prevail, or try this trick (it cannot fail) back down the stairs with candle dim, and in the mirror you'll see HIM.* This was seen on a postcard from the nineteenth century which would have a picture of a woman looking into a mirror from behind the girl who holds it, she was meant to walk backwards down stairs into the cellar. This has supernatural connotations since magic involved being able to bind a spirit into a mirror and then use it for (black magic) supernatural purposes. A version of witchcraft. It's also been suggested you may see something else in the mirror, more sinister like an evil face, that of a witch, but usually seen outside of the mirror as a shadow. The explanation attached to this was that to see any image in the mirror is seen as a form of witchcraft. These were all taken to be superstitions.

Such a ritual in Sweden is known as *Black Madame.* Seen as an alternative name for Mary.

This legend is connected to the vanishing hitchhiker as another version of *Bloody Mary* has Mary Worth searching for her murdered children by the side of roads. When she's picked up, she vanishes before she gets to her intended destination. (See pilot episode.)

Another legend states Mary worth was born ugly or was in an accident so she couldn't look at herself in the mirror anymore and in a fit she cursed the mirror and broke it. Thus she fatally cut herself. Thereafter if you stare into a mirror in a dark room and chant *Mary Worth, Mary Worth come to me, come to me.* She will and will break the mirror to mar your face like hers.

Mirrors have also been seen as gateways to other worlds. In this episode *Bloody Mary* is said three times before she appears and only kills you if you're hiding a dark, secret, usually involving the death of someone which you've caused. Also, your eyes bleed before you die, just like Mary's did.

Re covering mirrors in the house after death, was done because their family would wash and dress the deceased themselves in their home and the body would be in the house for a long time. If the deceased caught a glimpse of themselves in the mirror their soul/spirit would be trapped in the mirror and consequently remain a ghost in the house.

In Africa and other countries, certain people won't let a stranger take their photo in case their soul is stolen.

Mirrors were used in the ceremonies of some ancient religions, believing evil beings didn't have a soul and because this wasn't reflected in the mirror and consequently they had no soul.

Who Mary Worth was and why she haunts mirrors has varying explanations. In an African-American Catholic school in Indianapolis it was said she was run over by a truck, appearing as a hitchhiker who vanishes from the backseat. Her 'mark' in certain rituals would appear on the person taking part in the ritual bleeding.

Others mistakenly think that Mary is Queen Mary I of England, (1516-1558) aka, *Bloody Mary*. Since it was rumoured she would murder young girls and bathe in their blood to maintain her good looks. Needless to say, Mary was not a beautiful woman. Her nickname, of course as anyone who's studied English history will know, arose from her having had countless Protestants executed. Mary wanted to dissolve the Reformation imposed by her father, King Henry VIII, re establishing the Catholic Church in England. After her coronation, she introduced the Act repealing all the religious laws passed in King Edward VI's reign (her half brother.) She arrested Protestants and tried them for heresy, burning at least 300 at the stake, hence her title, *Bloody Mary*.

Bathing in blood is credited to Elizabeth Bathroy – but her name obviously wasn't Mary!

Psychiatrists, Luis H Schwarz and Stanton P Fjeld conducted research in 1968 to see if schizophrenics saw more distorted images in mirrors and other shiny surfaces than normal people. As a control, 18 sociopaths, neurotics and normal people were taken into a dimly lit room and stared into a mirror for 30 minutes. The psychotics saw fewer images in the mirror. All 16 neurotics saw reflections alter somehow and said they felt violent, mainly sadness and fear. One woman said she saw something frightening, another a face with a vampire impression and 6 wept, 2 vomited. 12 out of the 16 normals saw changes in the reflection and experienced mood swings, women more than men.

Gail de Vos in her book wrote "children continue to summon Bloody Mary...between 9 and 12 are labeled *the Robinson Age* by psychologists. This is the period when children need to satisfy their craving for excitement by participating in ritual games and playing in the dark."

Looking in the mirror is associated with narcissistic tendencies; beautiful women see their own beauty, looking good for men. See snow white's step mother asking *who was the fairest of them all* whilst looking at herself in the mirror.

Talk about *CSI* getting in on the act, in season **7.17 Fallen Idols**, in his opening narration, Grissom talks about the camera capturing the soul and how people in olden times believed this, like the mirror being a reflection of the soul.

Mary is also a witch or mutilated bride (which explains the future husband scenario above, in a way.) In this episode she's called Mary Worthington.

This was a bit like the *Candyman* movies, though it's not mentioned in this episode, if you say his name five times he appears. In this movie, after a female grad student's death, her husband calls her name four times in the bath and she appears as a witch in the mirror and takes her 'bloody revenge.' In *Ringu* (The Ring) -) mysterious video viewers of which die after watching it. The curse can be avoided if a copy is made and passed onto someone else and they must make a copy and pass it on, etc...

In the movie, *Urban Legend* (1998) 2 students summon an evil spirit by chanting *Bloody Mary.*

Some also believe Mary Worth is the character of a comic strip with a similar name, but she isn't really.

X Files Connection

In the *X Files* season 3 episode **Syzergy** at a birthday party for Terri and Margi, Brenda, the girlfriend of the guy they both fancy, plays with a Ouija board and when asks who she'll marry, the board writes out **S-A-T-A-N**. She dashes to the bathroom where she hears Terri and Margi chanting. Brenda is found to have been impaled on the glass from the bathroom mirror (a reference to Bloody Mary).
Syzergy is an astronomical aligning of three celestial objects:- these are the earth, sun and the moon or a planet.

7.16 Chimera: claw marks and a shattered mirror at the scene. A woman is chased by a dark figure that breaks all the mirrors. Mulder believes someone is controlling an evil spirit and making it carry out the attacks.

Music

Sugar We're Going Down by Fallout Boy; *Rock of Ages* by Def Leppard. *Laugh, I Nearly Died* by Rolling Stones

Ooh Bloops!

Sam and Dean enter the house, the woman holds the coffee cup talking to a person, when the camera shows her again, she's talking to someone different.

As Sam and Dean watch Charlie go into her house, the camera reflection is visible on the Impala's window.

In the antique store, Dean holds a photo of the mirror from the policeman's house; the photo isn't a photocopy, but the exact one from the policeman's file.

Locations

George's Taverna, Mckenzie Street at Water.

1.6 Skin

Written By John Shiban. Directed By Rob Duncan McNeil
Original US Airdate 18 October 2005

Guest Stars: Amy Grabow (Rebecca); Anita Brown (Lindsay); Peter Shinkoda (Alex); Aleks Holtz (Zach)

St Louis, Missouri

Sam is called by his old college friend, Rebecca, for help when her brother is arrested for murder.

Notes

Most of the opening scenes involving Sam and Dean start with Dean talking about women (his idea of 'fun'. And if they're hot or not; even getting their phone numbers. Not forgetting Dean having a go at Sam and teasing him every opportunity he gets. This time it's saying Sam wears women's' underwear. Yeah, he'd know!

Dean says you can't get too close to people since their job is hunting. He hasn't practiced what he preaches in the past. (See **1.13 Route 666** when he told his girlfriend about what he does.) Dean's reference to the sort of people Sam hangs out with could almost be a reference to himself and their family. This time Sam lies and tells his friend Dean is a detective, reinforcing Dean's comment that Sam not telling his friends everything is nothing more than lying. He did the same to Jessica.

The dog barking because he probably recognized the killer as Dean. Sam stating cultures believing cameras can capture glimpses of the soul (how long has this myth been around, since the invention of the camera and that's not all, as we know photos can also capture spirits; and impending doom for the photographer in certain circumstances too.)

Dean's use of "Doppelganger" a German word meaning 'double.' Skin walkers were also mentioned in 1.2 **Wendigo.**

[Dean entering the sewer with Sam, reminiscent of his time in the sewer in *Dark Angel* as Alec when he went looking for prey to steal their barcodes from them in Season **2.3 Proof of Purchase**; in order to save himself.]

The method of killing a shapeshifter is the same as killing a werewolf, which is also a shapeshifter too. This time sifting from human to human, instead of human to wolf.

An episode reinforcing again that Sam and Dean aren't like normal people and telling their friends what they do wouldn't be easy since most of them just wouldn't understand and the rest of them would just be weirded out by it all.

Sam tries to catch the shifter out when he's shapeshifted into Dean by throwing the keys to him, which he catches with his injured arm and by saying Dad found a shapeshifter in San Antonio, but he doesn't gather on the shapeshifter reading minds. Incidentally, San Antonio, Texas is Jared's birthplace.

This time the shapeshifter shares some home truths with Sam – about leaving Dean alone with Dad and everyone leaving Dean. (See also **1.8 Bugs**.) This issue isn't resolved between the two of them as we keep getting to hear of Dean's jealousness at Sam having a normal life; at least for his college years. Dean, in shapeshifter form, echoing his thoughts, doesn't know how right he is about Dad leaving him (both of them) in **Pilot**. Also echoing and repeating, Dean's earlier line of the job having its perks, i.e. the weapons they get to use. Here the shapeshifter says this life has its perks, i.e. women.

(Hideous and hated until it learned to become someone else, just like *The Hunchback of Notre Dame, Frankenstein's monster*. Ben in *Dark Angel* (also played by Jensen) was called Frankenstein by Max in **1.18 Pollo Loco**.)

When Dean finds Rebecca in his lair, she's very trustworthy all of a sudden, when she doesn't know if that's the real Dean or not, since it could've been shapeshifter Dean again.

Ironically the shapeshifter was right; Dean will be hunted for the rest of his life, especially since he gets arrested again in season 2 and also has the FBI on his trail. As well as forever being hunted by the demons they hunt and kill. Also Sam will come across a werewolf of his own, when he falls in love with one in **2.17 Heart.**

There's Dean's 'freak' speech at the end – that's all they'll ever be, at least in their own eyes (not in ours!) which he says again in later episodes, as well as Sam saying this too several times, about how he hates being called a freak. In season 3, the crossroads demon will taunt him by saying he hates being called a freak too, as will Ruby.

This episode also reminded me of the *Dark Angel* season 2 episode, **Hello, Goodbye** when Alec was arrested for the murders that his clone Ben committed and he had to put up with all the aggravation for this; not only by the police, but most especially with Max who always treated him badly over her guilt at ending Ben's life. Also Alec and Max and the rest of the transgenics were all freaks, as Max mentioned several times over. Just because Sam and Dean choose to fight evil when no one else can or knows about it, doesn't make them freaks!

He's sorry he's going to miss his own funeral, how many people get to see that? Irony rings true here, since he'll miss it for real, in a way, when he ends up in hell in the season 3 finale.

The scene where the shifter sheds its skin was cut short by *ITV2*, in the UK, when the episode was aired at 9pm, after the watershed, but was left in the repeat showing.

Amy Grabow played Cheryl Ladd's younger character self in the TV Movie, *Though None Walk With Me.*

The e-mail from Rebecca has the date 5 December; the episode is set in March. Dean and Sam were going to Bisbee, Arizona on their road trip, when Sam detoured to help Zach and Rebecca.

The names on Sam's Palm Pilot, are names of actual people working on the show, such as Mary Ann Liu from the Art Department. Jerry Wanek – Production Designer. John Marcynuk the Art Director.

Rebecca's line of *Hooters* refers to a chain of restaurants in the US.

On this episode, John Shiban comments, "I was really proud of the morphing because I've certainly done a lot of shapeshifters and morphs with the bounty hunters in *X Files*. I remember Eric wanted to do it in a way that was totally supernatural. So we came up with that cool thing where his old body basically pushes its way out with the teeth and skin. It was totally cool and disgusting. And we took on vampires for the first time and do our own version of their universe... **Skin** was very much a thriller and a lot of our episodes are sometimes more melodramatic and less ticking clock so I really liked the writing it that way. The director did a wonderful job so that is my favourite."

This was one of Jared's favourite episodes. "I really enjoyed where Dean gets taken over by a shapeshifter and there was a big fight between the two brothers. It turned out to be a great episode, the music was good, and Jensen and I worked hard on the fight scene. It was a lot of fun and went by really quick…It was a time when there wasn't a really heavy, crazy workload. We had time to work on the scenes and break them down."

This episode was also one of Jensen's favorites. "I was able to play two different characters in the same episode. It was fun being the good guy and the bad guy. I think that that is one of the reasons why actors love doing what we do, is because we get to take on personalities and situations and take on storylines as people that are not us. We get to escape from the reality and kind of view it through a different set of realities and that is neat!"

Another of Eric Kripke's favourite episodes, "I loved when Jensen pulled off his own skin. I thought that was terrific…" [You mean when the shapeshifter as Dean pulled off his skin.]

Quotes

Sam: "I just don't tell them everything."
Dean: "That's lying."

Dean:"…lie to your friends because if they knew the real you, they'd be freaked – that's just easier."

Dean: "I think we're close to its lair."
Sam: "Why do you say that?"
Dean: "'Cause we're close to its puke-inducing bile next to your face!"

Dean: "…that's cos you're a freak. Well I'm a freak too. I'm right there with you all the way."

Sam and Dean's Take on the Urban Legend/Lore

Sam knows it's a shapeshifter… Dean: "Every culture in the world has one lore. Legs of creature turn into other men and other animals." Sam refers to them as shapeshifters, werewolves. When it changes, it probably sheds its skin. Any shapeshifter can be killed with a silver bullet to the heart.

Actual Legend

Shapeshifting forms are found in many old legends from the Celtic to the present.

Night animals or creatures easily able to shapeshift since they can walk the night without being seen. Therefore, shamans believed they could merge with animals and birds and see how long they perceive the world. *Skin walkers* or shapeshifters, aka, *yenaldooshi*: humans with the supernatural power to take the shape of various animals; and can take on their characteristics as well.

X Files Connection

Talk of mucus and bile in **Tooms** when Mulder and Scully were in a similar situation. Also a funny moment a la Mulder here when Dean tells Sam they're close to the shapeshifter's lair, as there's more bile behind Sam.

Glen Morgan, producer on the *X Files*, on the episodes, **Tooms (aka Squeeze 2)** wanted "To consider the scare factor of an urban myth stemming from some sort of monster living underneath an escalator." Here, the shapeshifter was living in sewer tunnels.

5.6 Post-modern Prometheus where residents claim to have seen a monster – a comic book creation. They lay a trap in the woods with a peanut butter sandwich. Mulder and Scully find the son was created by a doctor experimenting in genetic manipulation. See the shapeshifter here when he says he's the result of a genetic mutation too.

Music

All Right Now by Free; *In-A-Gadda-A-Vida* by Iron Butterfly; *Poison Whiskey* by Lynyrd Skynrd; *Hey Man, Nice Shot* by Filter

Ooh Bloops

Sam and Dean would've seen the crime scene when they drove in, but the police are still labeling it a crime scene several hours after the event.

The shapeshifter throws a tarp over Sam; he then struggles with the ropes, the tarp comes off and rests on his shoulder. When the camera returns to Sam, after showing Dean, the tarp's totally disappeared.

Rebecca wears a silver bracelet when she hugs Sam at the end, which then vanishes in the next shot.

When Dean's hit in the sewer, he holds his left arm, when they exit on the ladder, he's holding his right arm.

Locations

Gastown, 24th Ave Langley.

1.7. Hookman

Written By John Shiban. Directed By David Jackson
Original US Airdate 30 October 2005

Guest Stars: Dan Butler (Rev Sorenson); Jane McGregor (Laurie);
Christine Laing (Taylor); Brian T Skala (Rich)

Theta Society. East Iowa University.

Sam and Dean check out a mutilated body found at the side of the
road after reading about it in the paper.

Notes

Dean calls Sam an artist once more. When Dean says Dad doesn't
want to be found it's so true, though they don't know that yet; not until
they go home in **1.9 Home**, but we know this for sure.

Sam opening up to Laurie, that he saw someone get hurt once, i.e.
Jessica, similar to Dean in **1.3 Dead in the Water**, when he opened up
about Mom and you don't get over something like that. As brothers
they share very similar feelings, though they're as different as chalk and
cheese.

Dean mentions Dr Venkman, the *Ghostbusters* reference. See **1.17
Hell House** for more. Dean alludes to Sam's college days once again
and not having to be a genius. Dean also talks of *Matlock*, which crops
up in **2.7**. You'd think there weren't any other lawyers out there on TV.

There's also hazing, soriety girls, think what Dean's been missing
and because of the parties, he proceeds to do a turn around and says
college ain't all that bad. Though he still can't resist calling Sam a geek
because the whole party thing wasn't Sam's scene. Dean's line of
naked pillow fights is from *Animal House*.

Dean always has to do the dirty work, i.e. the digging and manual
labour, all alone at night...not surprising then that he doesn't notice the
hook isn't in the grave when he salts and burns the bones.

Sam knows all about Laurie and curses since he must believe he's
cursed too as everyone around him keeps dying: Mom, Jessica, the

119

people in the visions he's soon to start experiencing. Here Sam also gets his first kiss after losing Jessica.

As Laurie's alone in church, the Hookman can't be far behind her but when Sam walks in to talk to her; they don't seem to realize this, especially since she's acting all moral again. So he should've been better prepared. That was a bit annoying. Also why didn't Dean throw the cross into the fire, so it burns quicker?!

Dean watches Sam in the car mirror and tells him they could stay if he wants, which he repeats again in **1.19 Provenance**, when Sam meets another girl, much to Dean's chagrin. That's two episodes where Dean doesn't get the girl.

Re Hell week prank see **2.7 The Usual Suspects.**

This episode was akin to *I Know What You Did Last Summer*, (kind of an appropriate title where Sam and Dean are concerned!)

Says John Shiban,"That is the thing. We may be inspired but we'll do our own version. We are always conscious of making sure it is special and supernatural."

They love acting like heroes – yes – but action heroes even more, as both of them went through extensive martial arts and fights training. This came in handy when Jensen and Jared were actually involved in a real fight in a bar with a gang. Explains Jared: "During the filming [of this episode] we were out at a bar meeting our producer, Peter Johnson, It was me, Jensen and my buddy, Jordan and we got jumped by eight guys. We rocked them. I got a broken hand but a couple of them got taken to hospital.

The fight training came in useful. The producers wanted us to look like we knew what we were doing, so when we were out acting like these big, tough guys, they wanted to make sure we knew how to throw a punch and take a punch." So here's a secret form behind the scenes not many people would know of. Anyway, why start a fight with a bunch of actors anyway – did they see them as easy marks or as a couple of pretty boys who probably wouldn't be able to fight, having stuntmen to do all their fighting for them. Probably out of jealously, no doubt! Boy they must've been sorry for messing with the wrong guys!

There is no Eastern Iowa University but there is an Iowa Community College.

Spirits leave an ozone smell, so how come no one smelled the Hookman?

In a deleted scene, Sam argues on the phone after giving out his fake ID police badge number, saying "Francis is also a man's name." Then tells Dean he wants a proper man's name next time. In the actual episode, Dean calls Sam "Francis" and unless you know of the deleted scene, then this won't make sense.

FAQs: the hook was too big for just a necklace? Does the hook still exist? What was it in its entirety or its natural form, well obviously it wouldn't exist as a hook and who knows what else was made out of it.

Quotes

Dean: "Saved your ass. Talked the Sheriff down to a fine. Dude I'm *Matlock.*"

Dean: "Well you look like a dumbass pledge."

Dean: "Stay out of her underwear drawer." Dean mentioning girlie undies again as in another episode when he comments Sam wears women's undies. Not to mention, Madison throwing her undies at him in **2.17 Heart**. (Well, practically!)

Sam and Dean's Take on the Urban Legend /Lore

The events that took place in the opening, which Sam says are straight out of the legend. Dean calls it classic Hookman. Cairns spirit was laid to rest in Old North cemetery in an unmarked grave. Sam also says that a Poltergeist can haunt a person instead of a place without them knowing. Dean says the spirit latches onto Laurie's repressed emotions and feeds off them. The hook is the source of his power.

Sam immediately mentions the Hookman legend. Dean tells us it's the most common legend around. In 1862 a preacher named Jacob Cairns was arrested for murder. He was perturbed by the red light district in town and killed thirteen prostitutes. Some were found in bed, in bloodied sheets. Whereas others were suspended upside down in the branches of trees. As a warning against sins of the flesh. He lost his hand in an accident and replaced it with a silver hook. Rock salt can't kill him.

In *Supernatural's* take on the legend, Laurie appears to summon the Hookman by her moralistic stance, the way she was raised. She didn't want to be with her boyfriend in the car and so he was killed. Her friend had 'loose' morals and she was killed and her father, a reverend, was having an affair with a married woman, and was saved from the hook by Sam. The Hookman was latching onto Laurie thinking those people were immoral, just as he himself had committed those murders

121

when he was alive; punishing those he believed were sinners, mostly prostitutes.

The writing on the wall: *aren't you glad didn't turn on the light.*"

Actual Legend

Mid 1950's US.

A teen couple in lovers' lane, when the radio tells of a serial killer escaping from the local prison. The killer has a hook in place of a hand. The girl wants to return home. As they kiss, she stops him after she hears noises in the woods. They argue, he drives her home and opens the car door for her, then turns pale and faints. She runs out, hears a clunk and turns to see a bloody hook hanging on the door handle.

The teens suffer a lucky escape. If they had been in the woods, they wouldn't have been so lucky and also if he hadn't sped down the road. Lucky escape since the hook was left on the door, showing how close he's been to them.

Do you believe this urban legend exists? Writers state that there were murders in the 1940s in Lovers Lanes over the US but none were committed by anyone with a hook. One reason why this legend may have had added impact is that the 1950's saw a rise in the origins of rock'n'roll and parents and children, especially teenage girls had a growing rift between them, becoming more independent. An increase in loose morals. If the girl hadn't wanted to go home, they'd have been killed, but she wanted to return home because of the killer on the loose rather than having loose morals.

Another take on *the Hook* urban legend is *Knock, Knock, Knock,* originated around 1960's USA. In the first version, a teen couple is driving home at night when the car runs out of petrol. He pulls over and leaves her in the car – it won't take him long to return. She doesn't want to stay alone, of course taking her along would defeat the purpose, and there'd be no legend. He tells her to hide under his blanket in the back seat and only open the door when she hears three knocks on the roof, that'll be him.

Later she hears three knocks, as she is about to open the door, she hears another knock, more continue and finally she gets in the driver's seat, starts the engine and drives. The car stalls and she has to run out to save herself. Turning around she sees her boyfriend hanging from a tree branch, a noose around his neck. He was suspended above the car and making sounds on the roof was him trying to stay alive. When she drove the car forward, she killed him.

This part of the legend forms the opening scene to this episode, when Laurie gets out of the car, she sees Rick hanging.

The second version to the legend has all the above details, but as time passes and she finally hears three knocks on the roof, but she hears five knocks altogether and hides under the blanket. Falling asleep, she finally awakens to police sirens and lights (isn't it hard to fall asleep when you're petrified and afraid for your life?!) A policeman tells her to leave the car and not look back (how did they know she was inside?) On the roof she spots a man with scary eyes, she then notices he's holding her boyfriend's severed head.

This legend is also known as *The Boyfriend's Death* and bears some resemblance to *The Hook*. Other versions have the man on the roof with a hook instead of his hand. This legend has also become even more notoriously well known than *The Hook*. The earliest version of this legend was written by Daniel R Barnes in 1964, when he was a freshman at the University of Kansas.

Cunningly – this episode of *Supernatural* combines two urban legends into one episode. The other legend is known as *The Roommate's Death*. From around 1950's US again. A college girl comes home in the middle of the night and takes her things with her without turning on the light. Her roommate was sleeping in the same room. When she came back the next day, she finds the police outside where she discovers her roommate has been murdered. Entering the room she reads the message in blood on the wall: "Aren't you glad you didn't turn on the light?"

The other version: - two roommates in college were meant to study for an exam. One was studious and the other wanted to party and went out on a date. At the end of the date she returned to her room and heard sounds from her roommate's bed, thinking she was having a restless night, she chose not to turn on the light and wake her up. Next day, she awoke to find her still in bed. The covers were drenched in blood, pulling the covers away – she found her stabbed. Falling to the floor she saw the same message written in her friend's blood: "Aren't you glad you didn't turn on the light?" This is the title these legends are sometimes also known as. The fact that the murders took place when the surviving roommate was present is the scary element in these and if she'd turned on the light – she wouldn't be alive.

The source of this one seems to have been parents worried about their children's' safety on campus and that they should be weary – as the Reverend worries about Laurie here and (wants her to live at home; she says she's got her own life). The same message is on the mirror in blood. This seems to suggest her father's warning of worrying about her in her dorm should be heeded.

Music

Merry Go Round by Split Habit; *Bang Your Head (Metal Health)* by Quiet Riot; *At Rest* by APM; *Royal Bethlehem* by APM; *Noise* by Low Five; *U Do 2 Me* by Paul Richards; *Peace of Mind* by Boston

Ooh Bloops

When Sam paints the purple on the boy, he paints with his right hand, then left, then right again, as the camera switches too and fro.

When Laurie goes to bed, there are no lamps on the bed, when she awakes there's a lamp there.

When the policeman finds Sam and Dean in the woods, Sam puts the gun down, but when the camera shows Sam and Dean, Sam still has the gun.

This episode is set in Iowa, but as they drive into town, palm trees can be seen.

Locations

BCIT Library. Burrard Street Bridge. Lorne Mews.

1.8 Bugs

Written By Rachel Nave & Bill Coakley. Directed By Kim Manners
Original US Airdate 8 November 2005

Guest Stars: Andrew Airlie (Larry); Anne Marie Loder (Joanie); Tyler Johnston (Matt White); Michael Dangerfield (Dustin)

Oak Plains, Oklahoma.

(Almost burst out into song there, i.e. *Oklahoma* – the musical.)

Sam reads about a man dying from Creutzfeld-Jacob Disease (Human Mad Cow disease) where the brain of the man degenerated in a matter of hours, rather than years. Dean however wants to send his hard earned poker money! (On women and booze, no doubt.)

Notes

Dean will go anywhere for a free feed. Having said so much about being freaks in the previous episodes, Dean comments he hates normal and that he'd want their way of life no matter what.

Sam and Dean get mistaken for a gay couple (the first of many times). These people are quick to judge aren't they. Haven't they anything better to do in normal suburbia! (joke). Then get mistaken for a couple again which Dean acknowledges with "Okay Honey" to Sam.

Another chance for Sam and Dean to argue over Dad, his treatment of the two of them; Dean being the obvious favourite because he was the dutiful son and Sam being the outcast; the black sheep as he wanted to do other things.

Those spiders looked too CGI so weren't that menacing to look at. Also the spiders on the towel seemed too plastic and fake.

Best bit was Dean with his hair wrapped in a towel (now who's a girl?) He tries the steam shower and then has to go out in the rain – their perks of the job (as in **1.6 Skin**). They also have umbrellas like Mulder and Scully.

Seems Sam and Dean can't have a conversation now, at least Sam can't with someone else about their family; without it becoming an issue about Dad, their own family and Sam leaving. Dean's advice about sticking with his family – at least for now, is good – but how long can he do that for, especially since Matt's family is meant to be normal. Everything always boils down to them and Dad with Sam and Dean, or Dad and Dad or Sam and Dad, as Dad can't accept Sam didn't want to hunt and Sam calls himself a freak this time.

Again Dean gets the dirty job of putting his hand in the earth mound with the worms and pulling out the skull. Alas poor Yoric – ah Dean!

Dean can't resist calling Sam a girl as he describes him as the blonde one in *The Munsters*, i.e. the normal one in the TV show; but since the others were 'monsters', she was seen as the freak! So Sam is the freak here because he wanted college and not demons; creatures, spirits and ghosts...

Sam's choice phrases see episode **1.20** with vampires when Sam and Dad have their first big blue. Well, first for us as we actually get to see one. Dean finally tells him Dad was proud of Sam and used to go by and see him at Stanford; as for Dean saying Sam could've called, but didn't Dean want to see Sam there too and call him too. It does work both ways, this brother thing.

Joe knows they're not students and proceeds to tell Dean not to lie using the words, "truth is..." similar to season **2.2** when Dean puts his foot in it and can't say anything right to the carnie performers. Joe likes Sam, he's not a liar. Hang on what about all this stuff in **1.6 Skin** about Sam lying to his friends about being a hunter.

When Dean calls to warn them, Travis doesn't recognize Dean's voice.

Most Native American legends and curses have their roots in the various massacres carried out by the White man; in taking what rightfully belonged to the Native Americans.

Luckily it's daylight when the 'spray' runs out, otherwise what would they have done, get stung some more!

The scene where the swarm attacks was like the scene from Alfred Hitchcock's *The Birds*, where they came at the house from all directions, including the fireplace and the attic where Melanie (Tippi Hedren) went up and was attacked.

Sam wants to apologize to Dad when he finds him, but Dean knows better, they'll only fight again – which is true. (See **1.20 Dead Man's Blood**.)

Sam wants to find Dad to apologize for everything. He was doing the best he could. Dean tells him they'll find him, Sam will apologize and they'll fight again. Which is true again.

Willard is a reference to a 1973, 2003 film, where a man uses his friendship with a rat to seek revenge on his colleagues, who always put him down and were mean to him.

This was one of Eric's least favourite episodes, "It was my fault. I take full responsibility for it. I really wanted to do an episode about bugs [re *X Files* cockroach episode **War of the Coprophages**]. Bugs are creepy and there are a lot of great urban legends about bugs. But it had an inherent B movie, slightly campy feel to its concept. It was a very well executed episode, but the concept itself didn't resonate or wasn't as cool or scary as some of the other episodes. More like a B movie feel in the vein of *Arachnophobia* and the shower scene with the spiders in this film.

Jensen explained how they got stung by bees during filming of this episode, "The sound guys were in full head-to-toe bee suits but we were in normal clothes. I got stung, it was inevitable. But the bees didn't show up on camera so they had to add computerized bees afterwards, so we went through that for nothing."

Special effects and CGI are used though for most of the demons. These are more than just special effects, showing us just what these boys will go through and endure for their craft!

The article in the paper says it's written by Christopher Cooper who is the Property Master on the show.

There is no Oasis Plains in Oklahoma.

Quotes

Sam: "There's nothing wrong with normal."
Dean: "I'd pick our family over normal everyday."

Sam: "Dad never treated you like that. You were perfect; he was all over my case."

Dean: "He's too disappointed in his freak son."

Sam and Dean's Take on the Urban Legend/Lore

Sam comments hauntings sometimes include the manifestations of insects, bugs. There are cases of animals being controlled by someone. Like *Willard,* rats and cases of psychic connections between people and animals –elementals telepaths. Dean mentions the whole *Lassie*/Timmy thing.

The professor tells them about the 170 year-old Native American timescale when relocation was common. Joe's grandfather told him his ancestors lived here 200 years ago and the US cavalry came to relocate them. They resisted. The cavalry raided and kept coming for six nights and then one last time. In the morning everyone was dead in the village. On the 6th night, the chief whispered to the heavens, "No white man will ever tarnish his land again; nature will rise up and protect the valley." On the 6th night no one will survive. Friday 20th March was the Spring Equinox.

Film/TV References

The Oprah Winfrey Show, Lassie, The Munsters. Strangely, no mention of *Arachnophobia,* or *The Birds.*

X Files Connection

Creutzfeld-Jacob was mentioned in **Our Town**. Also numerous episodes with insects. Such as **War of the Coprophages**, Scully likens the outbreak of deaths associated with cockroaches to a disease, as Sam does in the start to Creutzfeld. The sheriff found a dead body in the bath with cockroaches over him, like the real estate agent in the shower with spiders all over her. Mentioning psychic connections of animals and people.

In **Shapes**, Mulder meets a tribal leader. In **Darkness Falls**, Mulder and Scully have to keep the mites away with their generator failing as morning approaches. Like Sam and Dean keeping the bees at bay, saved by dawn's early light.

4.21 Zero Sum, a mail sorter is killed by a swarm of bees.

Music

No One Like You by Scorpions; *Rock of Ages* by Def Leppard; *Poke in the Butt* by Extreme Music; *Medusa* by MasterSource; *I Got More Bills Than I Got Pay* by Black Toast Music

Ooh Bloops

Travis runs in, the shadows of the crew can be seen. Sam comes out of the hole clean.

After Sam has been in the hole, they drive by a truck. Dean speaks, then Sam again and they drive past the same truck again parked in the same place.

Locations

UBC Chemistry Building.

1.9 Home

Written By Eric Kripke. Directed By Ken Girotti.
Original US Airdate 15 October 2005

Guest Stars: Jeffrey Dean Morgan (John Winchester/Dad) Samantha Smith (Mary Winchester/Mom) Loreta Devine (Missouri); Kristen Richardson (Jenny)

Lawrence, Kansas

Sam and Dean return home, when Sam has visions about their family home.

Notes

This episode was formerly entitled *The Journey Home.*

Funny how the Winchester family photos are still in the cellar of their old house, wouldn't Dad have wanted to take these with him and no one cleared out the house during all this time and it was rebuilt too. For our purposes, the chest is still there, almost as if it was put there deliberately so that Sam and Dean are recognized when they return there. However, they were only little in the photos. Doubly odd since Sam says their old house was rebuilt after the fire. The 'Thing' in the girl's closet, is it just the Poltergeist or is their mother in there all along, as no harm has come to the little girl, perhaps Mom is protecting the girl from the Poltergeist.

Sam dreams about a fire and a woman in the window with a tree in front of their house, before it dawns on him that it's their old house. Sam finally opens up to Dean about dreaming of Jessica's death four days before it actually happened and he didn't know what it meant back then. Now he knows he has these visions and he needs to help the people he sees in them. The poor, unfortunate souls.

Dean is obviously upset since he promised himself he would never return there (another reason why he didn't want to visit Mom's grave when they return home again in Season **2.4 Children shouldn't Play with Dead Things**. So why didn't Sam visit her grave this time round too and did they even think of going back before this? Doubtful.) Dean was thinking of himself here, when usually he's the first to hunt and do the job. Didn't Dean want to pay his respects to Mom at her grave? Understandably he's apprehensive about returning to the place where all their troubles started.

Dean's line of "blowing up your skirt" to Sam was in reference to the Marilyn Monroe movie in her famous scene when the air blows up her white dress.

When Dean breaks the door down with the axe and his face can be seen through the hole; as in *The Shining* in the scene where Jack does the same thing and his face is seen in the door.

Well now Sam's secret is out – the one he was keeping from Dean in **1.5 Bloody Mary**.

Dean questions her about what she's seen/heard; something he does a lot and especially when he's being judgemental (Season **2.4, 2.9**) or feeling guilty sometimes. Like Sam, he opens up and tells Sam that he carried him out on the night of the fire. Sarah describes the woman as being on fire too. (See above.)

However at times of trouble, Dean turns to Dad with his heartfelt plea which seems to fall on deaf ears. Probably for the first time in his life he begs Dad for help and Dad just can't seem to face him or Sam.

He makes the entry in his journal of learning the truth from Missouri – whom Dad chooses to confide in once more, rather than his sons. Is it Sam and Dean Dad couldn't face or did he know Mom's spirit was still in the house. Was it her he couldn't face knowing he failed her and wasn't able to save her. What would they have said if he did see her once more, like she appeared to Sam and Dean. How was it possible for Mom to manifest herself in human form again?

Everyone seems to make fun of Dean here, just like he does of Sam when Missouri recalls he was "one goofy looking kid." Sam is always comforted by everyone! Also Sam was fat as he called him that in the pilot when he said, "Sammy was a fat kid."

Missouri could only tell Dad the 'Thing' she senses was evil". She says something's keeping an eye on the place – which could only be Mom. Just as Sam says he feels "something's starting", the little boy gets shut in the fridge.

As for Dean not wanting to return here, he's determined no one else will die here. All of Missouri's readings point to two spirits.

Dean tastes the pouches as if it's real food! Really Dean! Missouri mentions there's crossroad dirt in those pouches – any connection to **2.8 Crossroad Blues** I have to ask?

Sam seems to be taking his time digging the hole in the wall when sinister events are unfolding. Dean is forever being attacked by knives (like in **2.2 Everybody Loves A Clown.**)

Obviously it's not over as Sam hasn't seen his vision coming true yet. Dean has to help Missouri down the stairs which she managed by herself in the cellar. Also Dean is allotted cleaning duty too. It's Dean who gets the children out of the house just like he did with Sam and has to kick in yet another door – probably fast becoming one of his specialties by now.

Mom wears the usual white like all the other moms and Jessica too. She only calls out "Dean" but says "Sorry" to Sam. Why? (See Notes.) When Sam asks her why she doesn't answer much to this. Sorry for what happened; not there for him…Another big question, sorry because Sam's not Dad's son? Ooh the mystery, or because she knew she was going to destroy herself this time to save her sons and this family, taking the 'evil' in their house with her. She's still possessive as she tells it to leave her house. Looking back at this episode, it's now apparent why Mom fought the Poltergeist. If you watch this episode again after watching **4.2**, that's when we discover Mom was also a hunter, so she'd know exactly what to do.

Other questions why did Mom come back in the same form she died, as fire: why now and in that house. Did she ever leave? It was like she knew Sam and Dean would be back and almost waiting to see them before having to do what she did.

Again why couldn't Sam sense his own father? If he has visions (but usually they're of death) why did Sam say he senses 'It' was here? Was he referring to Yellow Eyes?

Dad's excuse for ignoring them and in particular, Dean's plea for help is that he can't face them until he knows the truth. Leading up to more questions here: truth about what? Mom's death, why it happened, why Sam, why their family? The truth about Sam and who he really is?

Almost halfway through Season 1, we're left with more questions than answers which is how it should be. Can't have simple answers just thrown at us for everything that's happened; will happen and is happening to them now; otherwise we'll lose interest if everything is solved in a nice, neat package. It's also better to question and to speculate about our fave show and characters too. Adding more mystery to a show about mysteries, legends, myths, spirits and family.

It wasn't Dad who came to their help, but Mom! What truth did Dad learn from Missouri as written in his journal and about what?

Missouri is a powerful medium and knows a lot about what happened to the Winchesters and what is happening, yet Yellow Eyes didn't kill her. Also in season 3, Ruby says all of Mom's friends were killed and her family too, but even though Missouri wasn't family, there was no mention of her, since she had connections with the Winchesters.

Missouri says in front of Dad that Sam has got such powerful strong abilities, so why does Dad act so surprised when Dean mentions Sam's visions in Season **1.20 Dead Man's Blood** and Dad asks why no one told him or called him. That was an annoying bit. Dean called him lots of times, but he never bothered to come or to call them back!

When Dad told Missouri he didn't want to see Sam and Dean, that he wanted to find out the truth before facing them, makes me wonder if this was because he found out Mom was really a hunter and everything that happened to their family was because of that. He had to have worked out, or found out she was a hunter since he met all those people along the way and fellow hunters too; who would have known of the Campbell's, if not knowing them in person.

Was this another reason why he wouldn't go into their house, when he said he's never been back there, not only because of what happened – but also since Mom was a hunter. He couldn't have known she was 'there' at this moment though.

This secret she kept from him and then he kept from Sam and Dean (if he knew about her hunting.) Mom kept it from him. So thinking about it, the Winchesters were a family adept in keeping secrets. So we can say we now know where Sam and Dean inherited their secret-keeping skills, especially Sam! It runs in the family. Also Dad kept Adam hidden from them too. (See **4.2, 4.19**.)

Missouri's poultice contains angelica root, Van Zandt oil, crossroad dirt and a few other odds and ends. If the house had such evil in it, why wasn't it purged until now, surely Missouri could've told Dad to do it when he met with her after Mom's death, or again did he not want to step foot in their house. Dean managed it, even after promising he wouldn't. It's not clear if he actually went back in there when Missouri says Dad took her to the house.

Eric Kripke: "I thought for my money the garbage disposal was the single creepiest scene we did last year... [This episode] was good and I really liked **Asylum**. Those are the ones we really nailed and that I was proud of."

Loretta Devine said, "Those guys are just so bad. You never knew what they're going to do, and you can't keep your eyes on both of them at once."

In a deleted scene, the garage owner tells them he called Social Services about Dad because he sold his share of the garage to buy weapons. Dean tells him Dad was always well in the head and he should've been loyal to his friend.

Zelda Rubenstein played Tangina in *Poltergeist*.

Quotes

Sam: "I have these nightmares and sometimes they come true, Dean. I dreamt about Jessica's death for days before it happened."

Dean: "First you tell me that you've got *The shining*, and then you tell me that I've gotta go back home especially when ...when I swore to myself that I would never go back."

Missouri: "Your Mom destroyed herself going after that thing."

Missouri: "The boy, he has such powerful abilities, why he couldn't sense his own father, I have no idea!"

Actual Legend

Angelica root is used in protection and removal of spells or a hex. (Angelica means 'uncrossing.') Earth such as crossroad dirt has a negative effect, so called, but particular forms of earth can "ground" spells.

Film/TV References

The Shining.

X Files Connection

In **The Calusari**, Romanian holy men attempt to cleanse house from an evil presence. Scully finds a boy's mother pinned to the ceiling. The holy man warns Mulder, the evil inside the boy knows him. Mulder believes a poltergeist may be involved, as well as Munchausen's By Proxy which is Scully's belief. Ash is found known as vibuti – holy ash, when spirits are present. A father is strangled on a garage door opener when his tie catches. Mugwort is a charm against evil, from European medieval folklore. See also **3.5 Bedtime Stories** in *Supernatural* for mention of Munchausen's Syndrome.

Home involves incest, dead babies and some deformed brothers, only loved by their mother, in the literal sense. Not that *Supernatural* involves anything like this, but just thought the title was the same and also they came across Mom for the first time as a 'spirit' in this episode.

Ooh Bloops

When Sam and Dean rescue Jenny, her door appears to be unlocked, so they don't have to break it down. When Dean runs to the house with the axe, the cameraman's shadow can be seen on the grass. When the boy climbs into the fridge, it closes and the safety latch locks. When the mother opens it, it's undone.

Locations

Keefer Street. West 57th.

1.10 Asylum

Written By Richard Hatem. Directed By Guy Bee
Original US Airdate 10 January 2006

Guest Stars: Brooke Nevin (Kat); Nicholas D'Agosto (Gavin); Norman Armour (Dr Sanford); James Purcell (Dr James Endicott)

Roosevelt Asylum. Rockford, Illinois.

Sam and Dean ponder the whereabouts of Dad when Dean receives a message on his phone with co-ordinates. They read about the asylum in the paper and Dean notices Dad marked this in his journal.

Notes

Just as Sam talks about their Dad and he may be dead. (Season **2.1**). Dean gets the text message with the co-ordinates. Sam saying he can hardly use a toaster was a bit harsh, a toaster isn't a phone and besides as Dean says there's a lot in his journal that they can't work out – not even Sam. So they understand some things Dad's written in the journal but not everything – like the information on Wendigos. Like this one, where they have an entry for the asylum. Why did Dad make an entry about this place, it didn't have that much of a significance.

In the wendigo episode, when the camera shows the wendigo drawing in the journal, there was a newspaper clipping there which disappears in this episode. The wendigo has disappeared here from that page too. When Dean opens up the journal to read about the asylum clipping and what happened to the children who broke in there, the wendigo picture is strangely missing.

As far as Dean's concerned, Dad told them to go and he's following his orders.

Dean tells Sam to let him know about dead people he may see, is exactly the premonitions that Sam does get - only Sam hasn't had any such visions yet (only Jessica), in the sense of premonitions, but only strange dreams – as Sam calls them. So this is a pre-emptive comment on Dean's part.

Dean's comment on who the hottest psychic is, well obviously it's Sam because the others are real actors names he mentions and not their character names; which implies for the sake of argument, that our show *Supernatural* is real and the others *aren't*! It's not nice when TV shows mention other shows where they imply what they're doing is really true to life and what others do is just imaginary. For example *Charmed*, when they talked about *Buffy*, only it's fine when our show does of course!

Dean's really into Jack Nicholson. (See also **2.11 Playthings**) when Sam and Dean stay at the possessed hotel.

Dean's reinforcement of Sam saying he's perfect (in episode **1.8 Bugs**) when Dean says he always got the extra cookie for doing what Dad said, which Sam hates doing. Shame we don't get to hear what Sam would've said to the doctor about Dean.

Dean saying the patients have taken over the asylum, paraphrasing, "the lunatics have taken over the asylum." Apparently demons and spirits always lurk in the boiler room. See also **2.1 In My Time Of Dying**. When Dad summons the Yellow-Eyed demon in the boiler room; Dad being chased by Meg and her brother in the penultimate episode of season 1 also looked like a boiler room, of sorts.

Though some critics didn't like the doctor lurking across the screen, I thought it was a good touch – made the scene more atmospheric (just like the Hookman in episode 7, when Dean turns around and there's nothing there.) The doctor lurks in the scene again, which was good because from that we learn he had an effect on Sam's state of mind.

ITV2 (in the UK) inserted an ad break where the doctor was attacking Sam – what a stupid place to cut the scene!

Dean's alias is the name of the lead singer from *Spinal Tap*.

Dean's quote of "Don't ask, don't tell" is the US military policy when referring to sexual orientation.

Another chance for them to explore their feelings about each other, but when they talk about following orders, being jealous; they are usually "taken over" by something or someone. So although we know they have issues between them – most of the time it takes someone else for such issues to re-surface again. Since Sam doesn't tell Dean anything he doesn't already know about not taking Dad's orders, blindly obeying them. Dean gives him the gun to shoot him and Sam does - probably to Dean's shock. But then again, he probably knew he would, since it wasn't loaded. They're usually more honest when they're not quite themselves. Sam does recall what he said to Dean. Something Dean didn't know about in **1.6** unless he was awake, when he was tied up by the shapeshifter in the same place as Sam. He says he didn't mean any of it, but he did because he's said it before – especially in the previous episode (**1.8**). Except for the shooting Dean part, of course.

Dean's not in the mood for a heart-to-heart talk right now. Dean asking Sam if he can really kill him, his own brother? Well, Sam's not himself right now, but that's exactly what Dad will make Dean promise to do, if Sam turns evil in Season 2 opener. The question is will Dean be able to kill his own brother if the table's were turned and the obvious answer to that would be no, of course not. Would you?

References to Patricia Arquette and Jennifer Love Hewitt were all shows about seeing dead people. Which Sam really can't do, but he did see Jessica after she dies. Sam only sees what happens to them, or the death they will face.

This episode Eric Kripke likes as it was scary.

Did you know, when Sam and Dean drove up to the asylum building, Tom Welling, *(Smallville)* was hiding out in the back seat of the Impala as an in-joke.

The tri-fecta of the Winchesters: destiny, hunting, family.

Brooke Nevin guested in *Charmed* and Nicholas D'Agosto was Zack in season 2 of *Heroes.*

Quotes

Dean: "Let me know if you see any dead people Hayley Joel."

Dean: "The freaks come out at night." (Like them Ha!).

Dean: "So who do you think is the hottest psychic? Trish Arquette, Jennifer love Hewitt, or you?"

Dean: "Kind of like my man Jack in *Cuckoo's Nest...* Kind of like my man Jack in *The Shining.*"

Film/TV References

Medium (as far as being Medium, it's not even mediocre. That was my bad joke!)
Ghost whisperer, Amityville Horror, One Flew over the Cuckoo's Nest, The Shining. Star Wars, The Sixth Sense.

Music

Hey You by Bachman Turner Overdrive

Ooh Bloops

Dean's lighter goes off, then works perfectly again. Dean throws the lighter towards the doctor's body; the lighter goes off as soon as he throws it.

Locations

Riverview Hospital. The Old Terminal Pub. 8th Ave Alley, New Westminister.

1.11 Scarecrow

Teleplay John Shiban. Story By Patrick Sean Smith.
Directed By Kim Manners
Original US Airdate 22 November 2005

Guest Stars: Tania Sauliner (Emily); Tom Butler (Harley); P Lynn
Johnson (Stacey Jorgeson); Brent Stait (Scotty); Nicki Lynn Aycox
(Meg Masters); William B Davis (College Professor)

Burkitsville, Indiana. One Year ago.

Dad calls Sam and Dean telling them to stay away form home, he's
on the hunt for a demon. Sam and Dean fall out over this as Sam wants
to find him but Dean wants to hunt.

Notes

This is the episode where the events of that night 22 years ago begin
to come together when Dad calls them to tell them the 'Thing' aka
Yellow Eyes is in truth a demon. He's also heard about Jessica and tells
Sam he's sorry – something Sam wouldn't expect him to do. Ha also
warns them that, "They're" everywhere... "They" being other demons;
others like Yellow Eyes, or that demon just possesses to use for its own
ends. It's not revealed who "they" are yet, but from other episodes to
come, we can judge they are other demons. Dad gives them an order
which Dean obeys like the dutiful son – even telling them to stop
looking for him. Also having nothing but praise for Dad, here it's with
regard to the journal and the information he put together on the three
missing couples. "The man's a master."

So Dean didn't find anything confusing in this section of the journal,
whereas in **Asylum** he couldn't make heads nor tails of Dad's research.
(In season 2, they'll need Ash's help to decipher the journal.) {Not
surprising those entries must've been confusing because it was all to do
with a mental hospital and insanity – sorry it's a bad pun I know!}

Sam wants to go to California in search of Dad (directly ignoring his
order!) Dean who pulls over to talk to Sam. Sam wants to interfere and
help Dad stop the demon. Would Dean do this if he was alone – go in
search of Dad to help him rather than do the job. He'd probably be
conflicted, but in the end he wouldn't really contravene an order or his
wishes, unless he knew Dad's life was at risk.

There was ample opportunity for them to have another argument involving Dad and Mom and Jessica, and what happened to them. Jessica died recently, it's understandable Sam was there when it happened (again) and old enough to comprehend it's full effect and the repercussions surrounding it – but by saying Dean was only four when Mom died and it happened so long ago, he's really belittling Dean's feelings and how he coped and felt after losing her. Which is unfair and wrong in a way too – even if losing Mom was 22 years ago, Dean knows exactly how Sam feels. The best scenes, or most of them are when Sam and Dean have their fights in and out of the car.

Sam once again questions Dean's "blind faith" to Dad, but sometimes you have to do what you're told or the consequences can be greater than you expected. Sam didn't listen; went out on his own all gung ho and trigger happy, not remembering or wanting to heed Dad's warning of demons being everywhere and the consequences: he ran smack, bang into Meg – who was just ready and waiting for him by the roadside to make her move. Entice him away from Dean and Dad, by turning him against his own family using the old sob story ploy about her own family and boy did Sam fall for it. Even to the point of interrupting him when he's about to call Dean, obviously deploying a strategy of divide and conquer. Sam being the more gullible one open to human emotions more and thus the easier target.

Dean was calling his bluff when he told Sam he'd leave and Sam did. Dean tells Sam he's selfish and just does what he wants – a conversation he'll repeat again towards the end of the season. Sam will also say this in season 2, 3 and 4.

Dean has photos of the people he knows on his mobile phone directory but decides against calling Sam in the end. Plus, lots and lots of women's names, including Carmella. Meg's favourite line of being "some kind of freak" which Sam and Dean call themselves plenty of times but she echoes the sentiments again later on.

When Dean comes across the scarecrow in the orchard, the EMF goes off in the backseat (which just happens to be there, because usually they keep their bags in the boot.)

Leatherface was the main character in *Texas Chainsaw Massacre* who made masks from his victim's faces. The *Wizard of Oz* references: Emily lives with her aunt and uncle. The scarecrow wanting a brain.

Everytime the scarecrow comes to collect on its sacrifice, does it then take on the persona of its victims as seen from the tattoo it now has on its arm of its latest kill. Maybe as a keepsake; or to number its kills.

Meg doesn't appear at all innocent. From the moment you see her hitchhiking, you know she's up to no good and just happened to be heading to California too, when she knows full well what Sam has been doing and who he's looking for. Lying to emulate everything Sam's been through with Dad and especially Sam wanting to be his own person, with a life of his own.

Dean is run out of town once more. Notice on the mile marker, they're almost always three miles out of town (like in Lawrence, next episode). But he's right about Sam's puppy dog look; more people do trust him – like the Native American Indian in **1.8 Bugs.**

They finally apologize, with Dean almost admitting he'd have liked to have had Sam's life; stand up to Dad (at times) and live his dream – but he can't resist calling Sam 'geek boy'.

They seem to be getting knocked out a lot in season 1. The first time Sam steals a car to save Dean. He'll be doing a lot more of that.

Seems the townspeople got off likely for taking part in cold blooded murder, just to reap the benefits and the town dying doesn't really appear to be justice.

Sam finally saying Dean's all he's got and that Jessica and Mom are gone which Dean says in 1.21, when Sam doesn't like what he says. There Dean goes again in his "I don't have to be serious when I don't need to be, so I'll just joke around" mode; when he tells Sam to hold him!

Finally it's revealed (what we knew all along) Meg is in league with Yellow Eyes and calls it "Father." They sure do have strange ways of communicating. She tells it she could've taken them both – yeah in her dreams or should that be, you and who's army? What's worse than a demon is a big headed demon; she couldn't take our heroes on and win! (See the season 1 finale.)

Dean uses John Bonham as an alias, the drummer in *Led Zeppelin.* Tania Sauliner and Jensen began dating after this episode. Jensen: "We both have girlfriends [at the time] which are probably a good thing because at the end of the day you want to hear a familiar voice and I am too old to be calling my Mom everyday." [Jensen still has a girlfriend who he doesn't talk about, but Jared is single.]

Jared: "Selfishly I'd like Sam and Dean to split up a little more like we did [in this episode] because it means more time for me and Jensen…we thought it [this episode] was a great show, one to be proud of and we had a great director, Kim who is one of our producers. The story introduces a character that's going to be in a couple more episodes [Meg] and you see Sam and Dean butting heads for several episodes. They finally say, 'This is enough' have some time apart and realize they love each other [course they do]. They will go back together because they're family. So I really like [this] episode. They're still looking for their Dad and it just overwhelmed Sam and he goes after him. It's real emotional stuff."

Jerry Wanek said that many people switched off this episode! Why? It has everything: fights, separation, vulnerability, that two are stronger than one, and making up!

In a deleted scene, Dean speaks to the couple in the diner for longer. The names on Dean's phone are the names of the crew. John Bonham is the drummer in Led Zeppelin. Scandinavians originally lived in Burkitsville first, hence the link to Norse legends.

The apple trees in this episode were actually hazelnut trees.

Quotes

Sam: "How old were you when Mom died? Four. Jess died 6 months ago. How the hell would you know how I feel?"

Dean: "Dude you fugly."

Dean: "you've always known what you want and you go after it. You stand up to Dad. I wish...I...I admire that about you. I'm proud of you Sammy."

Dean: "Hope your apple pie is freakin' worth it!"

Dean: "Hold me Sam, that was beautiful."

Sam and Dean's Take on the Urban Legend/Lore

The scarecrow is some kind of Pagan god. With an annual cycle of killings. Victims are always couples, like a fertility rite. Locals fattened them up. A sacrifice to appease pagan gods. The scarecrow takes the sacrifice for another year. The professor alludes to Pagan ideology. Ancestors from Scandinavia, lives in the orchard. A 'woods god.' Dean refers to it as 'Vanir.' Villagers built effigies, practice human sacrifices. Its energy comes from a sacred tree. If burnt then the god will be killed. The 7th night of the cycle, it's their last chance. The apple tree was brought over by the immigrants, "the first tree" in the orchard.

Actual Legend

The Norse goddess, Idun was the purveyor of the apples which gave the Norse gods their eternal youth. Idun means 'ever young'. Apples were connected to religious practices in Germanic Paganism, claim scholars. Buckets of apples were discovered in a burial site in Norway. There is also a link to apples and the 'Vanir': gods who were associated with fertility in Norse myth. Fruit and nuts were connected with symbolism and nuts can still be thought of as a symbol of fertility in Norse myth.

X Files Connection

Season 5 episode **Schizogeny,** is about trees (which were hazelnut trees) dying which Mulder attributes to the 'curse' of a bad man. A blight is caused by a man in town. The men worked in the orchards and their lives were connected to the hazelnut trees, which now bleed. Mulder claims nature defended the abused children, or someone controlling nature had their hand in it.

Mulder does some grave digging here, which Sam and Dean have done on many occasions. Also the orchard where this episode was filmed is the same one where *Supernatural* was also filmed.

Music

Lodi by Creedence Clearwater Revival; *Puppet* by Colepitz; *Bad Company* by Bad Company

Ooh Bloops

The edges of the cup Meg collected the man's blood in were rather clean.

Sam and Dean argue, Sam says it's been 6 months since Jessica dies, then it wouldn't have been April, but the first week of May, i.e. Sam's birthday.

When Dean talks to the professor about the scarecrow and the Pagan legend, when he approaches the door, a camera can be seen behind the lamp.

Rebecca Warren is the name of the character from **1.6 Skin**, i.e. Sam's friend.

Locations

Deer Lake. Burnaby Village Museum.

1.12 Faith

Written By Sera Gamble, Raelle Tucker. Directed By Allan Kroeker.
Original US Airdate 17 January 2006

Guest Stars: Julie Benz (Layla); Kevin McNulty (Roy Le Grange);
Rebecca Jenkins (Su Ann Le Grange);

Sam searches for a cure to save Dean after he electrocutes himself
on a hunt and needs a new heart.

Notes

Dean was having his 'up and down' moments in this episode. First
he was about to die, then miraculously healed by dark magic and he
didn't have any adverse side effects when he was cured. No dark
thoughts, evil urges – only regrets and finding it hard to come to terms
with being saved, when it should have been Layla instead of him.
Something he'll repeat again in the early episodes of Season 2, when
this time Dad makes the ultimate sacrifice for him. This Dean also
regrets, perhaps sounding a tad too ungrateful once again.

Dean then experiences euphoria, then guilt at finding out he lived
and someone else died in his place to save him. The 'ups and downs'
also include his faith – lack of – wanting to believe in God, good, in the
unknown, but only choosing to believe in what he can see and that's
just evil. Curiously though he mentioned God in almost every scene,
like God saving them from the do-gooders who believe in God and not
playing God. (See **2.13 House of the Holy** when he clearly says he
doesn't believe in angels or God and then saying he'll pray for Layla.

(Also jumping the gun here but in season 4 he'll find out all about
angels and even work on their side, so he kind of comes round full
circle in his beliefs. In contrast to Sam who begins to kill demons not
for the sake of it and uses his powers to do so. Not necessarily bad but
his intentions behind the killings are. More on that when Season 4 is
covered.)

Julie Benz was exceptional in this episode (and one of the more
nicer blonde guest stars they've had on the show) and yes Eric Kripke
did get another *Angel* cast member to guest. You really felt for her and
what she was going through and having no future – she was so
understanding and forgiving of Dean – so selfless.

The reaper they met in this episode, at least seen by Dean was so
different from the one Dean sees again in the season 2 opener. Though

'she' said 'she' took on a form that wouldn't scare Dean. None–the-less, he sees 'her' because he's not meant to survive.

Dean's line, "he's seen what evil does to people" neglecting to mention the evil that men do themselves! Sam telling Dean to have a little faith and he repeats the same to him later on, when he tells Sam he's going to need faith too because Sam hasn't or can't see it [the reaper.]

Dean having to face death twice in this episode, when after saving him, Su Ann changes her mind saying Dean is wicked and shouldn't live.

Well the old credit cards come in handy to pay for insurance, as they don't have any for Deans' hospital bill. Sam calls Dean 'Joe' since he's meant to be a dead body.

Another in-joke when Dean mentions, comments on daytime TV is terrible, that's where Jensen started out, as we know in the Daytime soap, *Days Of Our Lives*. This was actually shown in the UK by five, back in 2000.

In another one of Dean's "I don't have to be serious in a time of crisis" moments, he thinks of his beloved car and yes we do believe Dean would haunt Sam if anything happened to his baby. Which he says he can see right through. "I laugh in the face of death!" Comment by Sam sounds like straight out of *Buffy*. Something Xander would say. (Which he didn't do in Season 4! i.e. haunt Sam when he went to hell.)

Dean always seems to be drawing the short straw as he's the one facing death again in Season **2.1 In My Time Of Dying** and in the Season 3 finale. Though to be fair Sam did die once too in the Season 2 finale **All Hell Breaks Loose Parts 1 & 2.** (As well as being struck by lightning in season 4.) Everything's happening to Dean; he didn't want to go home but had to for Sam. He didn't want to die; it's as though fate is conspiring against him to keep him away or get him away from Sam and they're both stronger when they're together. Probably Sam would go to pieces without Dean. (See Seasons 2. 3 and 4.) Obviously this was written by me before Seasons 2 and 3 were made and screened here in the UK.)

The number on the phone message is the same as in the previous episode. Sam calling Dad, once again falls on deaf ears, in a dire matter of life and death. Presumably he can't listen to his voice mail or doesn't want to. Dad sure keeps up his promise of not being able to face them not even when he could be seeing Dean alive for the final time. He does come good in Season 2 when he saves Dean.

Sam sounds as though he's giving a Mulder speech about having more faith in the unknown and unexplainable rather than being skeptical and not believing, akin to Scully. Scully would believe in such an instance as it's a question of faith, not aliens and the intangible. Whereas Dean plays Scully here and contradicts Sam – he only believes in reality – what he can see, touch, feel etc. Well it's a well known fact you can't feel emotions or thoughts in the sense of grasping at them or putting your finger on them, but you know they're real because they're a part of you. Dean doesn't believe in faith nor has any faith since it can't be seen, especially with the things they both do see everyday. The vast majority of which is all evil. (See **2.13 Houses of the Holy.**)

Dean has seen first hand what evil does to people, then why can't he conversely see the good in people too and what good is capable of achieving. As he fights evil that doesn't make him evil too. It's just like someone who, unless they actually saw them fighting evil, wouldn't really believe it's what they do, in a way. Dean has faith in Dad.

Dean conversely tells Sam he needs some faith when he tells him he saw a dark figure as he was being healed since Sam couldn't see it for himself. The Reverend's reasons for Dean being saved, he saw Dean had a job to do and he needs to finish it – that of fighting evil and protecting people. (Season 2).

Layla's mother questioning why Dean was chosen to be saved instead of her is something Dean can't comprehend either. It was wrong (also see season 2 and especially **2.4 Children shouldn't Play With Dead Things** when he feels so much guilt over Dad's death.) Why should someone else die to save Dean? If not Dean then who else would be saved? Sam tries to justify it by telling him they didn't know this would happen. (As in **2.1 In My Time Of Dying** when Dad makes the deal and Sam tries to justify it by saying they don't know this happened until **2.8 Crossroad Blues**) but someone else would've been healed if not for Dean, most likely Layla.

In a way this episode could be seen as another forerunner to the events in Season 2 which seem to be repeated then all over again: Dean in a coma; about to die; the reaper after him; someone dying to save him (Dad). Maybe he thought this was his one and only way of making it up to Dean when he wasn't there for him (and Sam) in **1.9 Home** and here.

Dean wants to kill the reverend because he thinks he's controlling the reaper, playing God. Sam doesn't want to kill him, that makes them no better. There was no debate on morals or who has a right to give and take life here. Yet time and again it's always Dean who has to make that decision of taking lives, saving lives and actually carrying out the deed of killing. (See Season **1.21** and **1.22.**)

Dean refers to God saving them from people who think they're doing his work does he really believe or does he just use that as an excuse. Again see Season 2.

There are more references to crossing to the dark side to save Su Anne's husband, like Dad making the deal with Yellow Eyes to save Dean. The reverend cheated death just as did Dean here and again next season. The cross Su Anne used to control the reaper is a Coptic cross and represents the crucifixion and resurrection of Christ.

Would Sam have said it's not right for someone else to die to save Layla if Dean hadn't been healed. Now, in a way, Sam and Dean are playing God by choosing to stop what the reverend's wife is doing: who were they to interfere? On the one hand you could argue and on the other it could be said, they're right it is wrong to pick and choose like that and involve other innocent deaths, since dark magic is at work.

This is really what Su Anne is about to do again by taking away the 'life' she gave Dean, who is going to be sacrificed to save Layla. So in a way he could've saved her. Su Anne calls Dean wicked as he tries to stop her. A bit of a waste with Su Anne dying, if Sam hadn't broken the cross, Layla could've been saved. Cruel irony there. Su Anne's death would have been her punishment for taking all the lives of those she thought were immoral. Then again it would have been wrong to do what she did.

Dean does offer to pray for Layla, which must be a big turn around for him, or is it out of guilt?

Hasn't Sam found the faith to keep going, however, things may turn out without having to resort to asking Dean to kill him, anytime things go wrong remotely dark. If destiny is already written then why do anything about it, can you really change it. Great continuity from this episode title, to the next episode, about faith and 'angels.'

Dean choosing to end the conversation on Layla: a hot chick! Sam is eager for Dean to go forth and get healed. This episode was a little like giving your soul to the devil to be saved, i.e. what Dad did for Dean; and Dean for Sam, is also like Su Anne choosing people to be saved at the hands of those who are unworthy to live.

Julie Benz was Darla in *Buffy* and *Angel*. As well as playing the girlfriend in *Dexter*. She can also be seen in *Punisher: War Zone, Saw V*.

Robert Singer's favourite season 1 episode is this one; "I thought that said something. I thought that really was more of a look at the context of 'what is *Supernatural*.'"

Eric Kripke liked this episode "because of the depth of character and theme it reached. But I love the scary ones."

145

In a deleted scene, where Marshall swims, the pool scene is supposed to be longer, going back and forth between Dean being healed and the pool.

Quotes

Dean: "I'm not gonna die in a hospital where the nurses aren't' even hot."

Sam: "You know this whole, 'I laugh in the face of death thing', it's crap. I can see right through you."

Sam: "When people see something they can't explain, there's controversy…maybe it's time to have a little faith Dean."

Sam: "You said it yourself Dean, you can't play God."

Sam & Dean's Take on the Urban Legend/Lore

Sam asks whether Dean believes it's the grim reaper, like the Angel of Death collecting your soul. Dean corrects him, not *the* reaper, *a* reaper. A reaper lore in every culture and has over a hundred different names. Reapers have the ability to stop time and can only be seen when they come for the person who is meant to die. Dean saw him. Sam alludes to the cross on the tarot card. In early Christian era, Priests using magic crossed to the dark side. The art of necromancy: how to cause death.

X Files Connection

In Miracle Man a faith healer uses his powers for good and evil. Mulder comments: "I think people are looking for miracles so hard they make themselves see what they want to see."
Scully: "Don't discount the power of suggestion, Mulder. A healer's greatest magic lies in the patient's willingness to believe. Imagine a miracle and you're halfway there." More applicable to Layla than Dean.
Though Sam finds the dead body when the clock stopped to indicate his time of death at the moment Dean was saved, they could just call that a miracle, but as it's our show, *Supernatural,* more of it had to be made than just a miracle. Scully: "Apparently miracles don't come cheap."

Music:

Don't Fear The Reaper by Blue Oyster Cult.

Ooh Bloops

Sam couldn't have escaped from the narrow window in the basement or could he?

Locations

Fort Langely.

1.13 Route 666

Written By Eugenie Ross-Leming, Brad Bruckner.
Directed By Paul Shapiro
Original US Airdate 31 January 2006

Guest Stars: Megalyn Echikunwoke (Cassie Robinson); Kathleen Noone (Mrs Robinson); Alvin Sanders (Jimmy Anderson); Dee Jay Jackson (Cyrus Dorian)

Dean gets a call from an old girlfriend to help investigate her father's death.

Notes

Sam putting it nicely when he says Dean dated someone for more than one night, since Dean never really dates in that sense of the word. Also when Dean tells Sam he went out with Cassie a few times and told her their big family secret, which Sam didn't tell Jessica, the phrase 'so much for family loyalty' comes to mind. So Dean dated a college geek too, so much for making fun of Sam all the time for being a geek.

Cassie retells the story of what happened to her father and says he was driving a truck when in actual fact when we see him in the opening, he was driving a car. He was driving a truck years ago in the flashback scene.

They wear their *MIB* suits once more.

The rumour of Dean being dumped was that Cassie was probably too tough for Dean to handle!

Dean doesn't think he should've told her the truth about himself, but surprisingly she was the one who dumped him because she couldn't handle what he told her about who he is and what he does. Unless she just thought he was lying.

Dean and Cassie don't look at each other because they have unfinished business and feelings for each other still. It's true, whenever Dean doesn't want to get too close or open up about something, he either jokes or changes the subject, like he does with Sam on so many occasions whenever he's trying to get him to talk or ascertain his feelings or what he's thinking. It's easier that way.

Just a thought, but in **1.5 Bloody Mary** when Dean's eyes also bleed, and this happens when you're keeping a secret, might it be that Dean spilled the beans about the family business. We were never told why his eyes bled?

The Steven Spielberg movie, *Duel* comes to mind here with the truck driver after Dennis Weaver in the car, although no one found out who drove the truck, it wasn't a ghost.

There is salting and burning involved, the truck can't be destroyed in that way, only the driver. Notice the massive exchange of saliva between Dean and Cassie when they kiss at the end. Sam gets to drive again.

A routine episode for *Supernatural*. There's not much spooky stuff going on here, well scary goings-on, and aside from having the opportunity to delve into Dean's past and the one time he found true love, nothing else is added. It's the least one of my favourite episodes and believe me I love 'em all!!

Much to Sam's surprise, big brother was capable of a long term relationship, so maybe even commitment eventually, to which he doesn't really reply and this time instead of joking, settles back for a nap.

Dean without his shirt on again!

Don't really think Dean would somehow give all this hunting up for a chick though, not for a long time, maybe? Besides she should consider herself lucky, since he doesn't open up to anyone, especially not a chick and very rarely to Sam. (See Season 2 episodes.) Dean trusts Sam enough to drive to the exact co-ordinates of the church and stop the car there, hoping his plan will work and the truck won't ram into Dean.

Sam mentions ghost ships, see the Season 3 episode **Red Sky At Morning** where he talks of *The Flying Dutchman* again.

No matter how much our guys strive to bring us the best in the series, there are some things they just won't do, as Jared says, "…it originally had us drag a truck out of the water. It's November in

Vancouver and we were supposed to be knee-deep in water. We're thinking, 'It's snowing outside right now and they want us in the water'. They ended up changing it for us and then you do those killer physical episodes."

There used to be an actual Route 666 in the US. It had it's name changed to Route 491.

Quotes

Sam: "Our big family Rule Number One: we do what we do and we shut up about it... I do nothing but lie to Jessica and you go out with this chick in Ohio a couple of times and you tell her everything!"

Sam: "I miss boring and conversations that didn't start with this killer truck."

Sam & Dean's Take on the Urban Legend/Lore

Dean mentions *The Flying Dutchman*. Sam explains about the ghost ship imbued with the captain's evil spirit. Demolition can awaken spirits or disturb them so they seek revenge. Evil spirits can be destroyed in hallowed ground.

Film/TV References

Duel (though not stated.) *The Flying Dutchman* (an opera called *Die Fleigen Hollander* by Wagner.) Also see *Pandora and the Flying Dutchman* with Ava Gardner and James Mason.

Music

She brings Me Love by Bad Company; *Walk Away* by James Gang; *Can't Find My Way Home* by Steve Winwood

Ooh Bloops

Sam and Dean are dry when they attach the chain to the sunken truck.

In the flashback the truck is being pushed into the swamp, when it's pulled out, the front faces out. (They could've been raising the truck from the other side of the swamp.)

When Dean and Cassie kiss at the end, her hand's on his neck, then the camera moves in and it's no longer there.

Cassie's Mom tells the story whilst drinking from her cup; you can still hear her voice.

Dean has to drive the car 0.7 miles. The milometer reads 70098.3, then 70100.6. Is that more than 0.7 miles?

Locations
Cannery Row, Steveson.

1.14 Nightmare

Written By Sera Gamble & Raelle Tucker. Directed By Phil Sgriccia
Original US Airdate 7 February 2006

Guest Stars: Brenden Fletcher (Max Miller); Beth Broderick (Alice Miller); Avery Ruskin (Roger Miller); Cameron McDonald (Jim Miller)

Saganoff, Michigan

Sam has a vision and they must rush to prevent it coming true.

Notes

The episode where Sam's visions beg into take on a more sinister turn and begin to get more violent and painful for him. Continuing on from **1.9 Home**.

Simmons and Freely are from *Led Zeppelin*. Another chance for Dean to 'pig' out on cocktail sausages when the dress as priests. Dean partakes in his usual bout of questioning, asking about noises at night and so on. As he did in **1.9 Home** and other episodes. Sam sums up his feelings in one line: "It's tough losing a parent especially when you don't have all the answers." That's what they don't have (along with us). They're still nowhere nearer to finding out why Mom was killed by Yellow Eyes and why. As Sam also has yet to realize his destiny in season 2, if he does.

Sam's headache is another vision, this time the dead man's brother being killed and Dean, being the loving brother, can only think of protecting the upholstery in his car. Not only is Sam getting visions in his sleep, but during the day or when he's awake, so he's experiencing nightmares in the day, but he asks the question we all want answers to : why Sam and why now? (Partly answered since Sam is the only one who gets them, was he especially chosen for these visions because of when he was born; are they a result of good or evil. As we find in **2.21 & 2.22 All Hell Breaks Lose Parts 1&2** when Yellow Eyes shows him the flashback to that night in the nursery when it transpires Sam has demon blood in him. Dean of course isn't bothered by his visions; maybe he might be if he was the one who got them. (He got one vision in **2.21** which hurt like hell.)

As for Sam and his visions, he has to suffer headaches and nightmares too. He didn't ask for this responsibility or 'power', it was given to him, albeit, he was 'chosen' for this. It was an unwanted gift and a curse too. The *Angel* episode, **I've Got You Under My Skin**, was based on *The Exorcist* with lots of references to it as well.

For the first time in an episode, Dean actually thinks of wiping their prints at what is now a crime scene.

Sam puts it all down to being cursed, including their own family. That's not really the case since Sam was one of the chosen few and the leader for the demon army. (See season 2 finale once again. He could have a point though, as we'll discover in season 4, that Mom was a hunter and made a deal with yellow Eyes to save Dad, in return for letting him into the nursery in the future.) Dean puts this all down to being different and having "dark spots". He does think Sam is dark. Can entire families be cursed, it's a belief many people hold to be true.

Dean, going on personal experience, says that all families aren't happy or even normal. Different to **1.8 Bugs** where he said he doesn't want to be normal like those people living in suburbia and he's glad he and Sam are not normal either.

Sam has another vision and sees Max. They're connected as they both have psychic abilities. Sam and Dean have their usual argument once again about whether Dean's going to kill him. Dean wants to as he's nothing more than a monster, a murdering one at that. Whereas Sam wants to take it all in his stride – think about it and is against killing Max (as in **1.12 Faith** where he argued on the reverend's side.) To Sam, talking is easier and the better option than killing since he says Max is a person. Yes but a killer none-the-less.

Sam finally admits he was better off having Dad, they both were and if Dad had lost it after Mom died, who knows where they'd be now. Dean has to add, Sam's extra bonus is having Dean around too!

Sam wonders why the demon killed them; perhaps wanting their powers but Dean tells him it's not about Sam, only about Yellow Eyes: finding it and destroying it. Dean's wrong, it is about Sam and his abilities and all the others like him, as we'll find out next season. Dean's not worried since Sam's got Dean looking out for him, but Dean will worry over Sam turning out like Max and becoming a killer in seasons to come. So in some ways, this episode opens up that storyline: that Sam will, at some point go dark as Dean described him earlier, only out of fun of course. Then again, he doesn't know how his comments turn out to have a deeper meaning at times.

It's good the way some episodes set up nicely; or perhaps unintentionally, when they were written and conceived, snippets of what's to come later on into the series and into next season. As you don't think the show will head in a particular direction until you've watched all the episodes and think, 'So this is what the writers, producers intended after all'. Sometimes they will have developed the storylines afterwards, especially for later episodes and Season 2.

As for Dean wanting to go to Vegas because of Sam's premonitions so they can win big, as we know, Sam's visions are only ever about death. Still some light relief in what could easily be seen as one of the most violent episodes of Season 1 so far. As well as Dean giving Sam the spoon to bend at the end. All this bending leading onto the next episode; **The Benders.**

Sam and Dean looked so hot as priests! That'll be a thousand Hail Mary's for me then and everyone else who thought that!! The names of the Fathers are from the founding members of the band *KISS*.

There was a deleted scene in this episode similar to Sam's premonition when Dean is shot, in the deleted scene, Dean is shown actually being shot.

Sam's reference to the Illinois Theatre refers to the Lincoln Square Theatre Decatur, Illinois, where the ghost of a stagehand who was killed during a performance – known as *One Armed Red.* Spirits have reportedly been sighted there.

Quotes

Sam: "I know one thing I have in common with these people, both our families are cursed."
Dean: "Our family's not cursed. We just have our dark spots."
Sam: "Our dark spots are pretty dark."
Dean: "You're dark."

Sam and Dean's Take on the Urban Legend /Lore

Although no legend here per se, Dean does mention banshee attaching themselves to families or vengeful spirits. Banshee, *Bean-sidhe* in Irish – means *fairy woman*. Her wailing is also known as *keening*, which if *keen* is taken from the English means, lament in Irish. I.e. *caoineadh*.

If a banshee appears to someone and is crying, it's a terrible omen, as this is deadly. A banshee wails to let people know of the death of a human/mortal. She appears to only the most reknown families in Ireland as a warning to heed her. These families are those that have ancient Celtic lineages – or those whose name starts with the suffixes: *Mac/Mc/'O'*.

Appearing as a white figure with long, grey hair and a whitish cloak – pale face and with distinct red eyes due to her wailing for an eternity. Has also been seen with red hair and long green dress; or even in a dark cloak. Wailing is heard where Irish have made their home or even in US or England. Also known as *the woman of peace*, she is also seen in such a state, on occasions.

X Files Connection

The season 1 episode, **Shadows** where Mulder and Scully investigate murders committed by an unseen force, where Mulder thinks psychokinesis could be involved. Here Max used his ability too and in one scene in the *X* Files, a man is pinned to the wall and a knife shoots into the wall, seemingly suspended in mid-air of its own accord, like the scene where Max holds his stepmother hostage, before he stabs her in the eye, in Sam's premonition. In **Sleepers**, Mulder is shot by the use of psychic powers.

Clyde Bruckman's Final Repose, the main character can see when people will die.

5.9 Schizogeny a boy, Bobby, is accused of killing his step-father. He claims to have been abused by him. Mulder believes there is more than just a killer in the town – but something far more evil at work. This episode guest starred Chad Lindberg (Ash) as Bobby and also Katherine Isabelle (Ava.)

5.10 Chinga which had its title changed to **Bunghoney** in the UK airing and in re-runs in the US since this is offensive Spanish slang: 'chinga tu madre'. A woman has a vision of an employee with a knife protruding from his eye. Mulder suspects witchcraft is involved. Kim manners directed this episode.

9.18 sunshine Days a man claims to see *The Brady Bunch* house. When he's killed breaking in, investigations reveal another man to have psychokinetic powers. The boy can alter reality. (See also **2.20** of *Supernatural*.)

Music

Lucifer by Bob Seger; *2+2=* by Bob Seger

Ooh Bloops

When Sam and Dean talk to each other outside the Miller house, a man walks past them in a hat; when the camera moves, the man walks past again in the same scene and walks in the opposite way. When the camera angle changes, the man walks in the same direction again.

When Dean is shot, he falls in front of Alice. He then ends up facing away from her.

When Sam is given the coffee cup by Alice, it's a green cup with a leaf, the camera then shows her give him a white cup. Dean has the green cup with the leaf.

Locations

610 Jervis Street

1.15 The Benders

Written By John Shiban. Directed By Peter Ellis.
Original US Airdate 14 February 2006

Guest Stars: John Dennis Johnston (Pa Bender); Jessica Steen (Kathleen); Ken Kirzungen (Jared Bender); Shawn Reis (Lee Bender); Alexia Fast (Missy Bender)

Hibbing, Minnesota

Sam and Dean investigate a spate of disappearances and Sam ends up disappearing too. Coming across one of America's most twisted and dangerous families.

Notes

Sam says phantom gassers take people from anywhere at anytime, just like the Old *Martini* ads on TV, to the tune of "anytime, anyplace, anywhere..." Okay, I added that in for some entertainment.

Like episodes in seasons 2 and 3, Sam is on his own when he's abducted and pity, but they don't let him put up much of a fight since he is a brilliant fighter. Due to the missing people and "phantom attacker" should Dean really have let Sam venture outside on his own. As he says, he let them get Sam. Dean says Sam can't handle his beer as he bursts into karaoke (liked to have seen that!). See **2.11 Playthings** when Sam gets drunk and Dean doesn't let him live it down.

The Deputy Sheriff, Kathleen, describes Sam with brown eyes on his record but his eyes are more blue than brown. Dean calls 'Dean' the black sheep of the family and refers to himself as handsome again. For the second time, (so far!) First time was in **1.6 Skin** when he comments that the shapeshifter chose the handsome one to turn into.

Sam is shocked to discover his abductors are human.

Dean says he has Michael Jackson's skin disease, whereas in **1.5 Bloody Mary**, he was meant to be Japanese, in name only. Let's face it, no one checks out photos on an ID especially when they're meant to.

Dean's job is to keep Sam safe: he doesn't see it as a job, but it will become more of his responsibility when Dad tells him about Sam in season 2. This time Dean doesn't have a paperclip to undo his handcuffs as he did in the Pilot, to escape.

The scene where Dean sees the jar of teeth must be déjà vu since he used to collect the teeth of his victims when he was Ben in *Dark Angel*: **1.18 Pollo Loco.** Dean would prefer to fight demons than people; you know what you're up against. (See **4.11.**) So much for telling Sam he was taken by people, Dean couldn't even fight a girl, but he did put up a fight. Sam and Dean know about a hunt or two, only they don't usually hunt people for sport.

The house looked like the one in Season 2 vampire episode when the vampires were hiding out and Sam and Dean tied up Gordon there.

Dean has nothing but choice jokes for them.

Sam does go missing again in the Season 2 vampire episode and Dean doesn't look for him and also in the last 2 episodes of Season 2.

Kathleen shoots the father without a second thought which means she has more in common with Dean. Dean shoots like that too, but more often than not he has Sam to act as his conscience. (See **2.9 Croatoen.**) Then Sam has been protected by Dean and Dad when it comes to hunting and actually shooting and killing. In many episodes it's always Dean who does the killing to spare Sam from having to do it, for example, **1.20 Dead Man's Blood.** They don't let him kill any vampires and again in the season 2 vampire episode, it's Dean who beheads the vampire and contrary to how it may appear, it's apparent from the expression on his face that Dean doesn't like doing it. He just has to because someone has to take that step; so it might as well be him rather than Sam. That all changes in the coming episodes and seasons.

This episode was a bit of a time out from hunting demons and supernatural phenomena and turned into Sam and Dean being "hunted" by none other than humans. Demonstrating that even humans can be demons once they surrender to their dark sides, or some in general are just freaks of nature and know no better than senseless killing. Which is why Dean prefers demons, at least you know their motives, always evil, never chopping and changing.

Sam's record: Record Id: DF43034/9. Physical description: 6'4." Height. 180-190lbs.

Name: Sam Winchester   No distinguishing marks or tattoos.

Born: May 2 1983   Relevant UNK

Place of Birth: Lawrence, Kansas.   Dean Winchester (deceased) brother & subject.

Sam (Jared) does have a distinguishing feature, a mole on the left side of his cheek, by his nose! By season 3, he will also get a protection tattoo on his chest, along with Dean but that seems to come and go. Both Sam and Dean's height in the police database is stated as 6'4."

This episode and others, their investigating cases, usually means they meet up with people in similar situations they've been in, like events mirroring their own lives.

The notion of human monsters is as scary as any supernatural being and perhaps even scarier.

What an episode to air on Valentine's Day! Dean died on 7 March 2006 in **1.6**, so why are they still chasing Dean?

Dean's reference to the ashtray (again in **2.11**) is in reference to Ed Gein, a serial killer who used body parts as decorations or furniture and used human skulls as ash trays.

Quotes

Sam: "Don't call me Sammy!"

Sam: "Dude they're just people."
Dean: "And they jump you – you're getting rusty…people are just crazy."

Sam and Dean's Take on the Urban Legend/Lore

It's perhaps the hunting ground of the phantom attacker (sounds more like something out of *Scooby Doo!)* A local folklore of a dark figure at night abducting people and vanishing. Dean says phantom attackers take you from your bed. Sam says phantom gassers take people from anywhere. Turns out there are no spirits involved here, they're only people.

Actual Legend

Mass murderers in the US, called *The Bloody Benders* (hence the title of the this episode, rather than the UK critics going gung ho over the use of the name 'Bender' since it has a completely different meaning here. In England, 'benders' is an offensive term for someone who is gay.) This was a family of serial killers who ran a store in Labette Co, Kansas. Here they murdered about 24 people with a hammer to the skull at dinnertime. Scarily they evaded capture by the police and were never found.

FBI Agent Robert K Ressler came up with the phrase "serial killer" in the 1970's. The US has 76% of the world's serial killers. 84% of them are Caucasian. 90% are male. 65% of victims are female.

X Files Connection

Scary Monsters a boy claims his mother was killed by monsters. Here a boy witnesses the disappearance of a man when he hears noises and attributes it to a mysterious monster. Sam is also abducted.

4.3 Home Mulder and Scully come across the Peacock family – specializing in in-breeding, they have deformed their bodies and their souls. The three brothers kidnap a woman and force her to have their children – only the mother of their children turns out to be their own mother. Mulder comments: "What we're witnessing is undiluted animal behaviour. Mankind absent of its own creation, of civilization, technology and information. Regressed to an almost pre-historic state, obeying only the often savage laws of nature." This episode was directed by Kim Manners and guest starred Sebastian Spence (who was Yellow Eyes' son in season 1.)

Music

Sweet and Low Down by Composer; *Rocky Mountain Way* by Joe Walsh

Ooh Bloops

When Sam is caged and talks with Alvin, the boom mike can be seen above Alvin's head.

Sam's ID record on the database is DF-23094. Dean also has this number on his record which should have been different.

1.16 Shadow

Written By Eric Kripke. Directed By DK Man.
Original US Airdate 28 February 2006

Guest Stars: Nicki Aycox (Meg). Jeffrey Dean Morgan (Dad); Melanie Papalia (Meredith)

Chicago, Illinois

Sam and Dean investigate a bloody and violent killing. Sam meets Meg again.

Notes

Times have changed and so Sam and Dean need costumes and gimmicks to enable them to hunt. Sam was also in the school play. So they did go to school then (as mentioned in 2.9 and **4.13** which was actually set in one of their old high schools.) Sometimes you wonder if they did have a proper education being on the road so much. Sam's school play was *Our Town.*

Dean seems to be into star signs doesn't he – of the astrological variety. Everytime he gets information from a chick, he has to get the lowdown from them too or the 411 and this always includes their star sign, which he couldn't resist giving. His own sign that is, when he's arrested in season **2.7 The Usual Suspects.** He also likes to get barmaids' phone numbers on napkins. Sam spots Meg at the same bar they just happen to be at. So much for California (Ruby also turns up at the bar in **4.9** for Sam's help.)

Dean coughs because Sam so rudely forgets to introduce him to her (you're not missing anything not meeting her Dean!) and Meg puts her big foot in it like she's oblivious to who Dean really is. Then says, ironically, she'd kill Dean if she was being dragged around like Sam. Yes Sam did 'bitch' to some evil chick about Dean in **1.11 Scarecrow.**

Meg was into Dean but for all the wrong reasons thank God!) Then Dean reverses what Sam said about Dean, thinking too much without his 'upstairs' brain in the bar. Actually meaning: Sam <u>really</u> is thinking with the brain in his head – rather than lower down! He is right when he says there is something strange about her.

Meg deserved a right old bitch slapping especially when she tells Dean to stop coughing! (Not that I'm an advocator of violence!)

Meg mentions Chad Michael Murray and Dean asks who that is? Really Dean, to ask that question when he knows everyone. Chad was Jared's room mate at one time.

Dean shows he's just as much of a geek as Sam when it comes to carrying out research. In this case he called Caleb (Dad's friend) it's much easier, and advises Sam to get it on with her (Yuk!) Sam having more sense than to listen to him, (Yay Sam!) and no Dean, Sam doesn't have a "thing for the bad girl." (That doesn't develop until later!)

Did Sam think Meg didn't notice the car, she was watching Sam anyway.

Sam works out Meg's in league with Yellow Eyes, but just because all of the victims were taken from Lawrence, Kansas, it didn't really mean anything. If they thought about it because Max (**1.14 Nightmare**) also with powers wasn't from Kansas and both Max and Sam were connected.

Dean leaves another message for Dad, the third one they've left for him about Meg and Yellow Eyes. He then tells Sam he doesn't want him to return to his usual life if this all ends tonight. That he came to Stanford to get him because he wanted to find Dad first – and the demon too, but wanting to find the demon became Sam's objective from the point when Jessica died. They have another argument over family and what Sam wants to do – to leave. So having come this far together, nothing's really changed for them, or between them.

Perhaps Dean thought Sam would want to stay hunting after a while, it'd be in his blood and not return to school. In later episodes and seasons the situations change. Dean wants to quit hunting and Sam wants to carry on because he wants to find out about his destiny – what he may become and Dean would be justified in calling this selfish on Sam's part!

The banter between the three of them borders on the fun to a bit silly, when Dean tries to buy time to untie himself, but it's really Sam who does this and Meg can't sense what they're trying to do, not very clever is she. She tells them they're Dad's weakness and he's vulnerable when they're around him, which is what Dean also says and so they have to go their own way.

Dean's advice to Sam to find a normal girl, obviously he was thinking of Sarah in **1.19 Provenance**. Dad did turn up this time but only arrived when Meg fell out the window. Was he there already and just didn't want to take part in the fight. Like in **1.9** when they went back home, he left them to fend for themselves.

Dad looked just like the demon from behind (like in the Pilot) when he was standing in the dark – no wonder their Mom mistook him. So Sam and Dad hug this time round, too tired to argue.

Also poignant; ironic; what Dad said about Yellow Eyes trying to kill him once before because he knows Dad won't give up until he gets his revenge. Another early introduction to the events of the Season 2 opener, which is why if you think about it, Dean, was hurt so badly by Yellow Eyes in the Season 1 finale. It wouldn't be Sam because Yellow Eyes needs him; leaving him no choice but to see Dean die or to give himself in exchange. Getting Dad out of the way and killed was the demon's plan in this episode anyway and Dean asked him to help them out without thinking of the consequences for either or all of them. When Dean says random consequences happen and Sam replies random doesn't happen to them, Dean doesn't think of this before calling Dad for help and getting him involved.

Dean will get very familiar with demonic pit bulls in **2.8 Crossroad Blues** and even closer in the season 3 finale when they come to drag him to hell.

Since there are two of them and they're able to take care of themselves and each other, they have done so for years; did they really need Dad's help? –No. They only need him there for reassurance or to genuinely want him there as Dad and not as a hunter.

Sam said that about Dean in his suit in **1.4,** that Dean looks like he's at his prom.

Sam mentions werewolf again as a possible creature responsible for the killing. The second time he does this, so it was always Sam's calling to meet one and fall in love with one. (**2.17 Heart.**)

On this episode, Jared commented, "We see our Dad again and find out Meg is evil, was a challenging episode. I remember reading it and going, 'Wow!' This should be two episodes not one. How are they going to fit in 8 days? It was locations; prosthetics, lots of dialogue, lots of emotion and visual effects. It had everything in it and it wasn't all action."

As to getting injured in the episode Jared comments: "I get slashed across the face and the next episode I'm fine. I said, 'They just put some WB ointment on it. It clears it right up!'"

Dad drives a 1986 GMC Sierra Grande, CSG 8R3.

Jeffrey Dean Morgan commented, "I love that they're all based on real lore. Research has been done and done. Everything is so well thought-out. They just have such a great creature maker machine."

Quotes

Sam: "I think there's something strange going on here man."
Dean: "Tell me about it. She wasn't even that into me."
Sam: "No, our kind of strange."

Sam: "Dean we are a family. I'd do anything for you, but things will never be the way they were before."
Dean: "Could be Sam."

Dean: "Oh sweetheart you're dumber than you look."

Sam and Dean's Take on the Urban Legend/Lore

Sam doesn't think it's a werewolf, there are no lunar cycles. The blood stains form a symbol, a 'Z' shape. This is Zoroastrian. Two thousand years before Christ. It's a sidrel for a Deva, which means 'demon of darkness'. Zoroastrian demon is animalistic, like a demonic pit bull. They have to be summoned and bite the hand that feeds them. Not seen for millennia and no one knows what they look like.

Supernatural took on the divas as being essentially evil shadows, brought out to do Meg's evil bidding, turning on those that summon them.

Actual Legend

Zoroastrians were followers of scriptural religions, having Gnostic traditions in Iran.

Divas in the ancient eastern language of Sanskrit mean 'shining one'. They are also known as adhibautas and are similar to angels: "Opalescent beings who watch and direct the natural world." Devas undertake communication with humans by channelling or in the form of psychic communication.

Present day, devas are said to have evolved in Hinduism and Buddhism. They are thought to be more abstract beings and believed more good as opposed to bad.

Madame Helena Blvatsky, founder of the Theosophical Society, regarded devas in western civilization as angelic; that when human beings had reached a state of spiritual devotion, devas would communicate with them aiding them into more development.

Devas are believed to send out messages for peace and harmony. They are aware of human thought and can send messages to people who are sensitive and receive them through telepathic means, as well as clairaudient (heard within the mind.)

Some devas can take on the part of a sacred guardian at ancient sites and have been described as large, brown shadows seen at dusk. In ceremonial magic and Wicca, devas are said to be related to the four elements of earth, fire, air and water, known as "lords of the watchtower". They represent the "four quarters of the ritual circle". Archangels are also seen as taking on this role, such as Michael, seen as archangel of the sun; is associated with fire and Gabriel, as Archangel of the moon; associated with water.

In Hindi and Sanskrit, *Deva* is used broadly to cover all sorts of spirits, including angels, muses etc. These devas work with nature and also the "inner world" encompassing thoughts, such as devas of justices; religious ceremonies, as well as communication. In Eastern Asia and the Indian Subcontinent, people start their day by making an offering and acknowledge the existence of devas.

The Devas Song by Sir Edward Arnold (1832-1904):

"We are the voices of the wandering wind, which moan for rest and rest can never find;

Lo! As the wind is, so is mortal life,

A moan, a sigh, a sob, a storm, a strife."

The *Blue Oyster Cult Logo* is traditionally associated with Kronos. In Greek myth, he was King of the Titans. Also the alchemical symbol for lead, the chemical symbol of which is *pb*.

Music

You Got Your Hooks In Me by Little Charlie and the Nightcats; *Pictures of Me* by Vue; *The New World* by X

Ooh Bloops

How did Dean come up with the symbol on the floor when there were so many blood spatters? (He's very good at what he does!)

Locations

Century House. Malone's Bar and Grill. Victorian Hotel. Danny's Inn. Cambie Bar and Grill. The General Store and Bakery.

1.17. Hell House
Written By Trey Callaway. Directed By Chris Long
Original US Airdate 30 March 2006

Guest Stars: Travis Webster (Harry Spengler); AJ Buckley (Ed Zeddmore); Krista Bell (Dana); Shane Meier (Craig Thurston); Nicholas Harrison (Mordecai Murdoch)

Richardson, Texas. 2 Months Ago

Teens play pranks and one is hung.

Interstate 35.

Dean finds an ample opportunity to play a prank on Sam when he's sleeping, by placing a plastic spoon hanging out of his mouth.

Notes

Richardson, Texas is where Jensen was born.

The cellar in this episode looked just like the one in **1.15 the Benders** where Dean found the jars.

Dean's playing pranks on Sam to ease his boredom and reminds him of when he put *Nair* in Sam's shampoo. *Nair* is female hair remover.

The website Sam mentions i.e. hellhoundslair.com is an actual website. Hellhounds lair.com was begun by the producers of the show.

Each of the teen's accounts of what they saw in the house and description of the victim varies, including getting the correct terminology wrong, such as Pentecostal for Pentagram.

Dean calls Sam a geek once more, not in so many words, telling him that since he knows so much about everything, he never finds a girl. (Hey nothing wrong with being intelligent!)

The two amateurs who run the website get their names straight from the *Ghostbusters* movie, i.e. Zedmore and Spangler. Sam pretends to be impressed by their EMF and Dean asks if they've seen ghosts before, as if they really will have.

Sam, meanwhile gets Dean back for the 'spoon in mouth' prank and just think in **1.14 Nightmare**, Dean was asking Sam if he can bend spoons? Of the metal variety, not plastic. He also called Max a spoon bender in the same episode because of his psychic ability.

Some of this prank business goes a bit too far – like daring Sam to take a drink from the jar, why would he? Dean resorts to calling him a 'chick' again and that's why he was chased by Mordecai!

Another chance for Dean to get his own back and places itching powder in Sam's clothes. Best bit: Sam wet and in a towel!! Some would have preferred him to have lost the towel!

Dean doesn't believe in good spiritual things – yet he believes in Santa Claus and not getting any presents! Then again Father Christmas was created by Coca Cola…so…

Dean pulling the string on the laughing fisherman figure and then they proceed to take it to place outside the house so they can get by the police and wouldn't you know, the amateurs arrive too. So much for Dean's earlier comment about Mordecai coming after Sam, who now acts as bait to save them all.

Sam's words of wisdom or rather questions about how many things only exist because people imagine them to be real, or causing them to become real.

What was the point of putting a dead fish on the back seat, it'll only stink up! Should've put it in their luggage.

This episode shows Sam and Dean's real relationship as brothers: playing pranks on each other like they used to when little, though Dean seems to excel in taking the joke too far at times – like the itching powder and Sam follows suit with the glue on the beer bottle, considering it was already open, how long did it take Dean to drink from it again?! Dean saying Sam needs more laughter in his life, which he gets in the next shot of the scene. They even resort to playing tricks on the amateurs too.

This episode though having its dark, serious side about Mordecai and the legend, as well as the girl getting killed because of a dare; is just one big laugh fest. With one joke after another – this is welcome relief after the events of the previous episode. Boy haven't laughed this much in ages!

Dean saying they'll come back if the legend changes again at the end, but you do think those amateurs got everything they deserved – they were so annoying at times and thinking they could cash in on money, gained at the expense of Sam and Dean getting rid of Mordecai, was just too much. Just as well it was Sam's joke. They probably never came across a real spirit until now.

The *Blue Oyster Cult Logo* is traditionally associated with Kronos. In Greek myth, he was King of the Titans. Also the alchemical symbol for lead, the chemical symbol of which is *pb*.

Hey when are we going to get our own Sam and Dean action figures? Nothing against the amateur ghost hunters (Ghostfacers), sometimes they were just a bit irritating. AJ Buckley's great as Adam in *CSI:NY.*

Quotes

Dean: "What's the matter Sammy? You afraid you're gonna get a little *Nair* in your shampoo again."

Dean: "Bring it on Baldy!"

Dean: "…only goes after chicks."
Sam: "He does."
Dean: "That'explains why he went after you."
Sam: "Hilarious."

Sam and Dean's Take on the Urban Legend/Lore

A misogynistic legend who hangs girls from the rafters. Mordecai Murdoch lived in a farmhouse in the 1930's with his six daughters. During the Depression, he hung them and himself. Sam says the reverse cross symbol has been used by Satanists for centuries. The Sidual of sulphur didn't occur in San Francisco until the late 1960's, but he hasn't seen the 'upside down question' mark symbol before. Sam looks up Murdoch in the 1930's, had two boys, no record of killings. . Mordaci now use an axe. The legend keeps changing. A new posting on the website saying

Mordaci was a Satanist who chopped up his victims before slitting his wrists. Dean recalls the symbol doesn't mean anything; it's the logo of the *Blue Oyster Cult.*

Sam refers to the Tibetan thought form – the Tulpa from 1915. Monks visualized Gotham in their heads, meditated so strongly they brought it to life. They were only 20 monks. Thousands of web surfers would have a greater effect. There's a Tibetan spirit sidual on the wall which was used for centuries. Sam say it concentrated, "meditated thoughts like a magnifying glass." People on the website could have brought the Tulpa to life.

A Tulpa is an object or thing created through will power and exists because of people's thoughts or beliefs.

Actual Legend

The Legend of Hell House: a hell house is usually known as a "judgement" house. Normally by Christian churches and part-church groups. Such houses are meant to show to those who are "unsaved", who have not repented their sins; the effects of hell unless they convert to Christianity – giving their lives to Christ.

Within these houses are contained exhibits displaying various sins, including for example, adultery, satanic ritual abuse, alcohol, drugs, suicide, occultism, pre-marital sex, abortion, and homosexuality. The 1970's saw the creation of the first hell house by Jerry Fallwell. Also other churches have put together their own concepts of hell houses for their communities – these houses are usually 'put on' during Hallowe'en.

One of the first famous houses is known as *The Winchester House*. The legend of this house dates to September 1839 in New Haven, Connecticut. Sarah Pardee was born there – a woman famous for her musical talent, foreign languages. Also born at this time was William Wirt Winchester in New Haven. His parents became wealthy in 1857 and on September 30 1862, William married Sarah.

Their daughter Annie was born in July 1866. She was struck down by a fatal disease and died 9 days later on July 24. Ten years later, William died and Sarah inherited over $420 million.

After these traumatic events Sarah went to a medium and was informed a curse had been placed on her family – she was next in line; and was told to sell the house and move to San Diego, California – to follow her husband's spirit's request. She built a new house there, eventually reaching 7 stories. She was mesmerized by the number 13 and every furnishing, decoration in the house was related to 13. However, there were only 2 mirrors in the house as Sarah believed the ghosts were afraid of their reflection – those of her husband and a baby. She wanted to trap them inside that house. Sarah died aged 83 on September 1922. Legend has it her ghost haunts that house looking for revenge and it was said there was a hidden safe in the house filled with jewellery. The house is a historical landmark.

Some other haunted houses include: Whaley House Old Town, San Diego.

Anaheim Hills, California. Mohler St: an old house with old cars. With a sheep, alive for years. Still for sale.

In Richardson, Texas (Jensen's hometown). A spirit is said to haunt a local house, attacking girls and hanging them before the bodies strangely disappear. Some saw the body hanging in the cellar. Just like this episode.

Film/TV References

Ghostbusters, Buffy, Lord of the Rings
X Files Connection

In **6.13 Arcadia**, couples disappear from a community which has a number of rules. The president of the Homeowners Association is involved in a lot of travelling to Tibet. A man is attacked by a creature which Mulder believes has been developed by the President on his Tibetan trips, using Tibetan mystic practice and he can create a Tulpa. (The episode where Mulder and Scully went to the perfect community as a couple.)
6.8 How the Ghosts Stole Christmas. Mulder and Scully stake out a haunted house and end up shooting each other. (Though Sam and Dean didn't do this here or in **3.13** either.)

Ooh Bloops

Dean picks up an album called *Point of Know Return* by Kansas, who sing *Carry on Wayward Son* used in the show.

How come none of the police heard the shots fired from the guns in the cabin when they were nearby?

In the diner, the fish faces one way and then the other, when Dean has the bottle stuck to his hand. Superglue dries extra fast so the bottle couldn't have got stuck to Dean's hand (unless Sam just put it on) and also would've been tres difficult for him to remove!

When Sam and Dean go after Mordecai and he wields the axe and the amateurs see if they got the action on film, watch to the right of Ed and you see a cameraman on screen, dressed in a short sleeve shirt.

When the waiter gives Sam and Dean their drinks, after Dean puts itching powder in Sam's undies, the waiter says, "Jensen."

Music

Burning For You by Blue Oyster Cult; *Fire of Unknown Origin* by Blue Oyster Cult; *Anthem* by Extreme Music; *Slow Death* by Extreme

Music; *Fast Train Down* by Waco Brothers; *Point of No Return* by Rex Hobart and the Misery Boys

Locations

Rodeo Drive-In. Heritage Hall.

1.18 Something Wicked
Written By Daniel Knauf. Directed By Whitney Ransick.
Original US Airdate 6 April 2006

Guest Stars: Adrian Hough (Dr Hydecker); Venus Terzo (Joanna); Jeannie Epper (Shritga); Colby Paul (Michael); Alex Ferris (Young Sam); Ridge Canipe (Young Dean)

Fitchburg, Wisconsin

Dad sends Sam and Dean co-ordinates to this town. Dean says it's probably because there's something worth killing. He's right, it's the creature Dean let escape years ago when it came after Sam.

Notes

The opening of this episode was a bit scary, especially when the branches blew against the window, looking like fingers, even before actual fingers appeared lurking in the shadows. Similar to *Wuthering Heights* when Cathy's ghost appears to the lodger in the room at night (and the Kate Bush song of the same name, "…so cold…for me at your window…")

This time Dean doesn't say they have to follow Dad's orders when he sends them the co-ordinates to the town; he says it's because he's the eldest and he's always right. How does that go, the eldest is never wrong, or never right, well one of those sayings. In this instance Dean is right when he says there must be something worth killing; it's the one that got away from Dean, when he was younger.

Strange that woman in the playground didn't think Dean weird asking where all the children are - trusting a stranger – like why'd he want to know?

In a turn of events Dean notices an old woman for a change, instead of a young, nubile chick!

This mysterious disease affecting one child first and then the sibling the next night, was more than a bit suspicious, just spreading through the town in that way. Alarm bells also raised when it's the doctor at the hospital who says they all have pneumonia, even if they didn't call in the CDC himself, but accepts their help when Sam and Dean turn up pretending to be from the CDC.

Sam finds the handprint on the window which Dean instantly recognizes and in his flashback, now realizes why Dad sent them here. Dean's flashbacks prove to be very revealing too: like Dad laying the responsibility of looking after Sam on his shoulders, whilst he goes hunting and teaching him to shoot first and ask questions later, so that's why Dean still does that today. Dean doesn't, however, tell Sam what really happened, this time choosing to say he doesn't remember anything. Also the sacrifices Dean made for Sam, such as foregoing his share of the cereal so Sam can have it. Well, Dean could've had the Spaghetti Os; he didn't have to throw them away.

Another reference to people thinking Sam and Dean are a couple when Dean asks for "two queens" when checking into the motel. (See **1.8 Bugs, 2.11 Playthings.**)

Sam's comment that the Shtriga is invulnerable to all forms of human and spiritual weapons, is a direct reference to Yellow Eyes, nothing can kill or harm it, except for the colt. (See **1.19 Provenance.**) and here there is the consecrated rod of iron which can be used to kill the witch.

Best bit: the old woman telling Dean she sleeps with her eyes open and Sam getting to tease Dean about it this time.

Seeing the little boy get taken riles Dean up further since it almost happened to Sam too because of him and this time Dean means business. Sam commenting Dean's getting wise in his old age is true. This time he can't just shoot first and ask questions later since back then he hesitated and couldn't go through with pulling the trigger, another reason why he's so quick off the mark when he's hunting and doesn't think twice about wanting to end the hunt quickly. (See season **1.19, 2.3. 2.9** and this episode.)

The witch has to be killed when it's feeding.

Dean finally tells Sam the truth about what happened to him, that it was all his fault, as for Dean saying Dad didn't look at him the same after that, when we see them together you wouldn't think there was anything wrong between them; that it was always Sam who had all the problems with Dad and vice versa, which is why he probably never spoke of that night again.

Sam still objects to using Michael as bait, Dean saying it wouldn't work without a boy, and boy was he wrong since the Shtriga went after Sam, even after Dean shot him. He probably remembered Sam from when he was little, i.e. his one victim that got away. Dean admits to actually disobeying an order and on the first and only occasion he does, he could've got Sam killed. This was one insight into Dean's character and why he follows all of Dad's orders now to the letter and why he has Sam doing the same. He doesn't want a repeat of that night again, whereas in actual fact, events do repeat themselves and Sam realizes this too, apologizing for arguing over Dean blatantly following Dad's orders. Dean finally gets his prey and says he's a good shot (now!).

Dean telling Michael "sometimes nightmares are real" is true, take it from him and also Sam's nightmares are real too.

Sam wishing he didn't know of the dark things in the world and that they really exist and Dean being selfless and saying he wishes the same thing for him too. Dean really is a complex character (they both are). This episode was all about Dean and his failure to act when he had to as a child, but he wasn't to blame entirely for this. He was a kid too, like Sam and having to grow up so fast; having all this responsibility thrust onto him. Responsibility that even a lot of adults would shirk. Dad putting so much pressure and weight onto his shoulders and leaving them on their own so often to go hunt. Dad should carry some of the blame as well , he was right to be angry at Dean, but to never mention it again, not even when he sent them here, sending them co –ordinates and making Dean relive it all again, the hard way, was not the actions of a loving Dad.

Then after going through all this, Dean still wants to protect Sam, give him back his childhood and his life, if he could, as he says the same to Michael, he'd do anything for his little brother! (Including give up hunting **2.9**). If not to see Sam delve into his dark side.

Something Wicked This Way Comes, as in the title of this episode, partly, is a book written in 1962 by Ray Bradbury. His inspiration was the Shakespeare line from *Macbeth*, said by the three witches: "By the pricking of my thumbs, something wicked this way comes" – see something learned and recalled from English Literature after all!

The old lady's room number in the hospital is 237, as from *The Shining.* Also this room number was in **2.11**.

Quotes

Dean: "We're gonna kill this thing. I want it dead, you hear me!"

Dean: "Oh God, kill me now!"

Sam: "Sometimes I wish I could have that kind of innocence."
Dean: "If it means anything, sometimes I wish that you could too."

Sam and Deans' Take on the Urban Legend/Lore

Sam thinks it's a Shtriga, a witch. Dean tells him Dad hunted one in
Fort Douglas, Wisconsin, about 16/17 years ago. Albanian legends
dating back to ancient Rome, feeding on *spiritus vitae* meaning breath
of life, life force or essence. No known weapon of man or God can kill
them. Dean says they're vulnerable when they feed and so can be shot
with a consecrated rod of iron. They take on the form of a human when
hunting and are usually old women. Which is how the witches are old
women legends started. They feed every 15-20 years. Certain aspects
of this legend were retained by the show in this episode.

Actual Legend

Shtrigas are Albanian witches who suck out the life force of a person
whilst they sleep. Legends of these date back to Ancient Rome.
Children seem to be their method of feeding since they have a stronger
life force. Often seen as flying insects whilst hunting their prey.
Shtrigas are the only cure for their prey once they've been fed upon.
The children, if not cured, remain sick in a coma and finally die.
Shtrigas usually take on the appearance of an old woman. Here, it was
a male form.

To protect from a Shtriga: a cross made from bones in a church
entrance on Easter Sunday. If a Shtriga is inside, it can't get out. (Why
would it be in a church to begin with?) After the blood has been taken
from a child, it is said the Shtriga will vomit – based on Albanian belief,
if you put this blood on a silver coin and wrap it around your neck; this
gives permanent protection from it.

SIDS (Sudden Infant Death Syndrome, aka Cot Death), in early
twentieth century Albania was blamed on Strigas. See the lore on
vampires.

Music

Rock Bottom by UFO; *Road to Nowhere* by Ozzy Osbourne

Ooh Bloops

When Sam and Dean talk to the nurse and meet the doctor, the boom mike's reflection can be seen above the doctor's head in the glass wall.

When Dean shoots the Shtriga the blood spatters the camera.

When Sam looks at the empty playground, the Japanese restaurant that is really there, had its name changed to *Glasgow's Restaurant*, signs in the window still show Japanese writing. This was filmed in Port Coquitlam, BC.

In his research, Sam finds references to *Brockway, North Haverbrook and Ogdenville* these are places where the monorail appeared in *The Simpsons* episode **Marge Vs the Monorail.**

Locations

2400 Motel. Burnaby Hospital. Riverview, East Lawn. Port Coquitlam, BC.

1.19 Provenance

Written By David Ehrman. Directed By Phil Sgriccia
Original US Airdate 13 April 2006

Guest Stars: Taylor Cole (Sarah); Jay Brazeau (Researcher); Jody Thompson (Ann)

Upstate New York

Sam and Dean look into mysterious deaths which seem to be connected to an old painting. Sam meets a girl.

Notes

Dean looks into Dad's journal and finds three deaths over a number of years, 1912, 1945, 1970. All involving the same M.O (modus operandi.)

A provenance is a certificate depicting the origins of the object it belongs to, so the history of the object can be traced.

Dean gets another number from a girl in a bar, probably the only place he can meet women because of his line of work. Coincidentally, for this episode, Sam tells him he can get his own dates and he does! Sam beeping the horn when he knows Dean has a hangover (like Dean will torment him in **2.11 Playthings** when he finds Sam drunk with a hangover.)

An in-joke: the car number plate has *The Krip* personalized on it. Obviously after writer and creator Eric Kripke. It had to be an expensive Rolls Royce all nicely lined up and then we come across Dean's Impala, all dusty and dirty.

Another opportunity for Dean to pig out on fine food like he's been starved. Well, you don't get mini quiches and champagne when you're on the road. Then Dean is into the finer things in life: wine, women, good food, and um, demons!

Sam comments he's studying for an Arts History course. Dean's made several comments about Sam's artistic talents in **1.10 Hookman**, also in **1.3**: "chicks dig artists." That it's a good way of meeting girls.

Their motel room was rather funky – time stands still – from *Saturday Night Fever*. Dean had to tell Sam about Sarah checking him out, like Sam's oblivious to her and probably more shocked that she's not into him. Sam takes her to dinner, but only to get information out of her. Mind you, he wasn't too objectionable about this, so deep down he liked her after all.

Most definitely, Sam would know what a Provenance is (or not, as one TV Guide got the name of this episode wrong as *Providence*. Obviously they've never heard the word before!)

To show how awkward it was for Sam to talk to a girl and order, as he has a difficult time with the wine list. A skill he already should have acquired since he was already on his way to Law school, so that was an annoying bit. Not to say all lawyers are drinkers.

Sam shies away when she calls him reasonably attractive and wonders why he's not dated or taken. Don't let Dean hear her say that, it'd get him started on the whole, he's too brainy for girls to get him! Hey, Sam probably acts shy as she called him reasonably attractive and he's far from reasonable!!

Jared comments: "Sam did just get a girl, some action. It was due time for it. It's been a while since his girlfriend died and not that he's not an honourable, chivalrous kind of guy, but it was time for him to move on and accept what had happened. The best thing that the audience wants to see is this guy just whining and bitching and moaning and pining for his girlfriend who we knew nothing about." Sounds more like phraseology Dean would use! Besides Jessica was probably the first love of Sam's life so he could moan as much as he likes and he obviously knew her since he was at Stanford too.

It seemed too convenient Dean leaving his wallet behind, as if there had to be an excuse for them to return, just to find the painting intact again. So how did it become intact, well, paintings are often described as having a life of their own.

Dean's still waiting for the *Da Vinci Code* movie so he's not an expert and well, being Dean, he hasn't read the book! (So watch out for his comment in **4.14** when he tells Sam he reads, when he mentions The Odyssey.)

Sam not having fun is partly because of Jessica, but it's not like they'll be hanging around in one place for long to develop long lasting friendships, let alone relationships. As Dean knows from personal experience, re his ex in **1.13 Route 666**, when Sam asks if it's worth giving up everything to stay around for someone like her. Which strangely he doesn't ask himself, though Dean does say they could stay, but if they did for how long, before something from their past or their lives came into the picture once more, or even Dad turning up.

Dean's meaning of "fun" is Sarah, like 'fun' in **1.3 Dead In the Water**. Dean even tells Sam to marry her; he thinks she's that good for him, (like Sam thought Cassie was good for Dean.) Also since Sam is more of the marrying kind than Dean.

Sam tells Sarah he's cursed and everywhere he goes everyone dies. It's not death following him, but Yellow Eyes. She calls him sweet, which Dean called Sam in **1.11 Scarecrow**.

Dean turning on the radio to the timely tune of "I'm in love with a girl I can't do without…" referring to Sam of course. Sam doesn't want to hurt anyone or go through that pain himself again (but he will next season in **2.17 Heart**.)

Dean digging alone at night, once again.

Sam gives in to his feelings and kisses Sarah at the end, so another episode where Dean doesn't get the girl. (Good all the more Dean for us!)

Sam seems to know a lot about people being born tortured and their spirits remaining dark. Sam removes an eyelash from Sarah's face and tells her to make a wish, is something we do too.

Another episode showing how lonely and tough their lives are, being on the road, doing what they do, especially for Sam who doesn't open up to people, especially women, so easily.

Dean's reference to *Columbian neckties* being handed down by the father in the painting. See **3.16** where he uses the same reference, saying what, they should just perform a Columbian necktie on a girl who Lilith was possessing.

Dean paraphrases "mommie dearest' with "daddy dearest isn't here". *Mommie Dearest* was the film based on the life of Joan Crawford, on a book written by her daughter, Christina.

In one scene Jensen calls Sam, Jared, instead of Sam but there are disputes over whether he actually does this. I need to get around to watching this again.

9.9 of the *X Files* episode was also entitled **Provenance**.

The song playing in the bar is *Night Time* by Steve Carlson. Jensen sings background vocals on his other songs.

Quotes

Dean: "I'd like champagne please."
Sam: "He's not a waiter."

Sam: "Pick-ups are your thing."

Dean: "It wasn't my butt she was checking out." (See season 4, where Pamela checks out Sam's butt a lot!)

Sam: "...like that *Da Vinci Code* deal."
Dean: "I don't know, I'm still waiting for the movie on that thing."

Sam and Dean's Take on the Urban Legend/Lore

Sam says the lore on haunted paintings is that the subject of the painting is always the one doing the haunting. It's also a tradition that when a child dies, their favourite toy is put next to them in glass in the family crypt. Real hair was used to make the child's doll, her own hair.

Music

Nighttime by Steve Carlson Band & Darren Sher; *Romantic Pieces No 1* by Extreme; *Bad Time* by Grand Funk Railroad; *One More Once* by Black Toast Music

Ooh Bloops

How did Sam get Sarah's phone number, or was it Dean who got it, unless Sam called her at the gallery.

When the three of them enter the old woman's house, Sam tells Sarah not to touch her, but his mouth is shut.

Sam says the couple in the beginning, who had the painting died four days ago; he then says the painting was in storage until a month ago, when this couple bought it at a charity auction.

175

What happened to Dean's bullet when he shot at the glass inside the crypt?

When Dean has a photocopy of the painting in the old woman's house, with Sarah, the razor blade in the painting is open and in his copy, it's closed.

1.20 Dead Man's Blood

Written By Cathryn Humphris & John Shiban.
Directed By Tony Wharmby
Original US Airdate 20 April 2006

Guest Stars; Jeffrey Dean Morgan (Dad); Warren Christie(Luthor); Anne Openshaw (Kate); Brenda Campbell (Beth); Terence Kelly (Daniel Elkins)

Manning, Colorado. Present Day

A group of vampires attack an old man.

Notes

It's obvious the dinner plans the woman refers to is the old man when she looks at him. Continuing on from last week, Dean asks Sam if he wants to see Sarah, but Sam doesn't want to return there yet (and probably never will.) Yes Dean, you would spill popcorn salt near the exits of the house, wouldn't you. No, not really! Dad finally makes an appearance since **1.16 Shadow** and just to read the letter Elkins left him. Seems Dad has had a falling out with just about everyone he's met and not just his sons. (See also **2.2 Everybody Loves A Clown** when Sam and Dean come across other hunters like themselves, like Ellen and Dad fell out with her too.)

In their version of the lore, there's not much that will actually kill a vampire. Dean doesn't believe in vampires either, until he comes across them.

Sam is reluctant to blindly follow Dad's orders and doesn't waste any time in making his feelings known. It appears Dad told Sam not to come back once he leaves, which he didn't do until Dean came to get him the Pilot episode. Sam needs explanations and reasons for everything he does; for hunting, and needs to know the whys, hows and where fors…It's just his nature and he can't just do things for the sake of it, or because he's been told to, which causes friction and as always,

Dean gets caught in the middle. He has to play peacemaker even after Dad's silent treatment over the whole Shtriga fiasco in **1.18 Something Wicked**, but that's why Dean doesn't ask questions. Dean's happy with the way Dad's letting them run the vampire trap, but Sam isn't, he's still treating them like children. Dad became a drill sergeant to stop them from being so vulnerable, to protect them he taught them everything they know. Dad put away $100 every month into a college fund for them both. So Dad did want Sam to go to college and have his own life and Dean too, since he started college funds for them. Realistically would dean really have gone to college, what would he have done?

In ignoring his direct order, Sam and Dean save Dad.

Dean and Dad don't let Sam kill any vampires here either, since they still shield him from the killing side of hunting, but not for very much longer.

Dean being away gives Dad and Sam a chance to have an honest conversation for once, with Sam saying they've both lost someone they love to the demon, which should make them much closer than they are right now.

The colt is only one of its kind. The butt of the colt has a pentagram: the Pagan symbol of protection when it faces up; which was taken over by Satanists, in which case the fifth point of the star faces down. The actual original colt has an engraving of a quote from the Bible in Spanish from Psalm 23:4, which is *non time bo mala* i.e. *fear no evil*. "ye *though I walk through the valley of death, I will fear no evil*….The original bullets: one was used to shoot Luthor; one to shoot the demon in **1.21**; Dean shot Tom in **1.21**; Sam shot Dad in **1.22**; Dean shot at the demon in 2.22 that makes five bullets. (The new colt: Dean shot the vampire and Sam killed the crossroads demon. As well as Casey in later seasons.)

By the way, what become of Sam's camcorder, he never used it anymore, nor did he outgrow it. Since he found out his destiny. Remember they used to film their surroundings earlier on in the season.

Dean was being honest with the vampire when he told her he doesn't stay with a chick for long, no longer than one night, let alone eternity. That'd cramp his style.

There are lots of heartfelt moments in this episode, even with the arguing, as they make their true feelings known between each other, more so Dad and Sam who have an opportunity to make-up (whilst Dean's not around, curiously.) Then proceed to argue some more. You can't help but think there's something ominous coming right around the corner. (season **2.1 In My Time Of Dying** infact.) And if you watch this scene from this episode between the thereof them…and then watch 2.1 straight after (after having watched the series all the way through – watch it again like this! Then you'll understand the decision he makes: a momentous one where he bargains for Deans' life.)

Dad says it himself, that he doesn't expect to come out of this fight with Yellow Eyes, but he won't at any costs see his children die (underlying meaning: he won't let Dean die.) Dean asks the dreaded question himself: "What if you die?" This episode slowly, but surely becoming a reality next season. (Oh forget the fact Jeffrey had other work commitment! He could've been hunting somewhere else, not somewhere in the sky, as in heaven…of course!) What impact did losing Dad have on Sam and Dean anyway – nothing but guilt and Dean calling him an ass. (See later.) He then continues, "…and we could've done something about it…" which they couldn't.

There is nothing Sam and Dean could do, they didn't see it coming. Also what was strange is that Sam didn't have any visions and nightmares , even when he was awake about Dad's death and I know I keep harping on about it, but I'll harp on the bandwagon and say – that's what Missouri said in **1.9 Home**, why couldn't Sam sense Dad? What was preventing him from doing this? Okay I jumped the gun here four episodes forward, but the questions had to be asked and still remain unanswered.

After all that, Dad still says they disobeyed him and agree they're stronger as a family and should go after Yellow Eyes together. A big u-turn from the events of **1.16 Shadow** and what they said about being more vulnerable and really get beaten by Yellow Eyes and end up in trouble together, with Dean literally fighting for his life.

Dad isn't happy with the way Dean's been keeping the car and Dean should be ashamed too since she's his pride and joy. So Dad gave him the car, we know from Season **2.2 Everybody Loves a Clown** too and also in Season **3. Dream A Little Dream of Me**.

Daniel Elkins was Dad's mentor and a hunter and gave him the Colt.

An episode dedicated in the most part to vampires and their own take on vampire lore, setting up for next season's vampire episode.

Quotes

Dean: "Do you mean like demon protection salt or 'oops I spilled the popcorn' salt?"

Dean: "Vampires, gets funnier everytime I hear it."

Dad: "I don't expect t make it out of this fight in one piece. Your mother's dead. It almost killed me. I can't watch my children die too. I won't!"

Dean: "What happens if you die? What happens if you die and we could've done something about it...we're stronger as a family. You know we are."

Sam and Dean's Take on the Urban Legend/Lore

As far as vampire or vampire lore/legend goes, there are the usual number of ways to kill them. (See below.) *Supernatural* came up with its own lore: vampires can be weakened by cutting them with dead man's blood and can only be killed by decapitation (a la the immortals in *Highlander*) and Dad gives a pretty good potted history of the *Supernatural* version and yes they can walk by day too.

Dad says he thought vampires were extinct, but he was wrong. Dad: "Most vampire lore is crap. A cross won't repel them, sun won't kill them and neither will a stake to the heart. But the bloodlust that part's true. They need fresh human blood to survive. They were once people so you won't know until it's too late."

Dean: "Vampires travel in 8-10s –smallest packs hunt for food. Victims taken to nest, bleeding them for days or weeks." They aren't afraid of the sun, they sleep during the day.

Dad tells them about the colt: legend or story, Hayley's comet was overhead. Men died at the Alamo and Samuel Colt made a special gun for a hunter. He made 13 bullets and used 6 before he disappeared and so did the colt. Daniel found it, it can kill anything.

At least *Supernatural* stayed true to the lore in its own unique way, oh and also a shot through the head with the colt will also do the trick.

Actual Legend

Historically vampires originated in old wives tales, superstitions and folk lore, made famous by Bram Stoker's *Dracula*, (1897); Anne Rice books, particularly, *Interview With a Vampire*, including Carlotta Francis and her vampire *Lily*, as well as Tania Huff's Blood *Ties*. The list is endless like the legend itself.

When Bram stoker wrote *Dracula*, he gave the story a real feel by basing it on the fifteenth century Vlad Dracula (1431-1476) – Prince of Wallachia, now part of Romania. Vlad's father was Vlad Dracul, which

179

means 'devil' or 'dragon'. Vlad was known as Dracula, i.e. 'son of Dracul'. He was born in Sighisoara in Transylvania, meaning 'the land beyond the forest'. Vlad's home in Romania, could be *Bran Castle*, a castle at Hunadoara, or a castle north of Curtea de Arrges, built by Vlad.

This other genre of vampire encapsulated by Vlad Tepes, aka Vlad the Impaler, circa 1431-76 was nothing more than a butcher who delighted in impaling his enemies on wooden stakes. He became a Romanian hero, defeating the Ottoman Empire. I feel a *Supernatural* joke coming on, no one mentioned the Impala, Dean could've called it Vlad the Impala, but I don't think so.

The vampire myth was rampant with the gypsies in the 1400's and their name for vampire is 'mullo.' Many countries in Eastern Europe have 'vampiric' beliefs, especially Romania, for obvious reasons. There are many names for vampires, one in particular being, 'strigoi', i.e. "one who flies during the night and sucking the blood from sleeping children." Closely resembling the Shtriga legend of the witch in **1.18 Something Wicked**.

A shtriga (usually from ancient Greek) was a type of witch bale to transform into a bird at night and drink the blood of humans.

To repel vampires: Romanians believed garlic on the doors and windows. Also it was said the grave of a vampire could be found by holes around it, said to be where the vampire emerged as mist. Thus they poured water in the holes.

Also in Eastern Europe, St George's Day was on May 5. Today in the UK and parts of Europe it's 23 April. St George was reputed to protect against vampires. *Vrolok* means vampire or werewolf.

{cf *The Adventures of Sinbad* for their version of the vampire legend, along with every other show going from *Starsky and Hutch, Highlander, Relic Hunter*, which rigorously stuck to the common lore about vampires not having reflections, not able to come out in sunlight, crosses repelling them, etc. Also in numerous films, psychologically vampirism can be seen in mental patients. Vampirism known as the devouring of blood and gaining sexual pleasure whilst doing so. Such as the *X Files* episode.

Vampires are not just a western creation though the origins are most common in other cultures too, such as Eastern European history, Chinese and Indian.

Namia in many ancient legends was a beautiful woman and a danger to men and children. 'Lilith means *Queen of the night* from Hebrew and ancient Babylonian legends. Thought by certain legends she was created to be the wife of Adam, but became evil by her own choice.

(See season 3 when the demon holding Dean's contract turns out to be called Lilith. Again this was written even before Season 3 was had been filmed!).

Loogaroo from West Indian legends was a sort of witch vampire from the French, *loup garou*; meaning 'shape changer'. A widely-held belief, that if someone sleepwalked, there could be a tendency for the brother of that sleepwalker, usually, to become a vampire.

Nosferatu, *Greek for 'plague-carrier'*, later meant vampire or 'undead' in Romanian.

Other vampire legends include, the Indian Goddess *Kali* drinking blood, but gave life to those who believed in her. Vampires were believed to be able to change weather, storms and control night creatures.

Carfax (see Bram Stoker's *Dracula*) means 'crossroads' from the French word. People who committed suicide were buried here and it was thought they could turn into vampires. Silver was also believed to have been a deterrent against vampires. Transylvanians believed if a cat jumped over a dead body before buried, it would turn into a vampire, or become one if a person was born with teeth or was the seventh son of the seventh son. (There's the number seven again.)

Some legends also have Dracula being able to metamorphasize into a wolf as well as a bat.

During the sixteenth and seventeenth centuries in Hungary, Countess Elizabeth Bathory bit and drank the blood of her female victims.

There are many vampire legends, including from India, Greece, Rome, China and Egypt.

Film/TV References

Twlight Zone

X Files Connection

5.12 Bad Blood Mulder kills a man he believes to be a vampire.

Music

House is Rockin' by Stevie Ray Vaughan; *Searchin' for the Truth* by MasterSource; *Strange Face of Love* by Tito & Tarantula; *Trailer Trash* by MasterSource

Ooh Bloops

181

Why not use dead man's blood on the vampires in the nest to begin with, probably because they didn't want to alert them to their presence.

Sam doesn't have the machete when Sam and Dean run out of the nest and it wasn't in his hand inside the nest either.

The Battle of the Alamo was 1836. Dad says the colt was made the very same night in 1835.

When Dad stands outside the Impala, the window is closed, on the driver's side. When he gets in, it's open, partly, and then when he speaks to Dean outside, the window is fully open.

What happened to Daniel's journal?

1.21 Salvation

Written By Sera Gamble, Raelle Tucker. Directed By Robert singer
Original US Airdate 27 April 2006

Guest Stars: Jeffrey Dean Morgan (Dad); David Lorgren (Charlie Holt); Richard Sali (Pastor Jim); Josh Blackner (Caleb); Nicki Aycox (Meg); Sebastian Spence (Tom)

Sam has a vision of a mother being killed by Yellow Eyes, just like Mom. It's showdown with Yellow Eyes and Meg.

Notes

This episode was a dress rehearsal, of sorts, for what was to come in the season opener, looking forward to that episode and then back to this, talking about dying, staying together, how life should've been and more importantly, making sacrifices. What Dean says to Sam about never coming back, those they've lost, echoes in his sentiments. As in **2.4 Children Shouldn't Play with Dead Things.** Dean should never have come back; Dad should've been here and so on.

Sam pinning Dean up against the wall was a good scene showing Sam still has a lot of anger and grief over losing Jessica and Mom and what he says to Dean next season about opening up and sharing his feelings.

As they drive to Salvation, notice the town sign which at the bottom reads: *Are you ready for Judgement Day. JW 2:27.* Was this another sign of things to come, a foreboding of the future, i.e. when Eric Kripke said he was going to kill off Dad after all? JW, well that's John Winchester. Romans 2:27 in the Bible refers to Judgement Day. The

'2' could also refer to season 2. Though it's not so much Dad's day of judgement, rather his day of sacrifice (**2.1 In My Time Of Dying.**)

Rosie's mother telling Sam, ironically, "sometimes she looks at you and it's just like she's reading your mind." Since she's another one with special powers, otherwise Sam wouldn't have dreamt about saving her mother. She's also approaching her 6th month birthday, when the mother is usually killed off. At least, in the pattern of events so far, but all that changes in Season 2.

Sam also has a vision of Yellow Eyes and Rosie's mother being on fire like Mom.

Notice the camera pans in on the clown mobile hanging from her crib (see **2.2 Everybody Loves a Clown**, Sam hates clowns.

Dad says they should've called him about Sam's visions, now we know (from Season **2.1**) that he wasn't just having a go at them for not telling him about Sam's nightmares, but because they mean something more than that: leading up to Sam changing to fulfill his destiny, what he's supposed to become. Dean replies he called, but when they needed him, he wasn't available and he never answered their calls. After everything that went on with them, didn't Dad want to know Dean didn't die (**1.12 Faith**) in the end because he wouldn't have known this until **1.16 shadow**, unless they rang him to tell him Dean was okay, or he had other means of finding out.

Dad tells them he wants this all over and behind them, so they can have a normal life. Sam can return to school, Dean have a home. Who would hunt other demons and spirits then? (Seeing as we don't know there are other hunters out there until Season 2.) Also Dean keeps saying he doesn't want 'normal' (**1.8 Bugs**.) How long would it be before he just got restless again and he told Sam this in **1.16 Shadow**. Anyway, would this stop Sam from becoming what he's meant to. Dad sounds like he's given up when he wants this to be over, or to put an end to Sam's visions, which have only just begun, i.e. his powers. So it's easy looking at it this way to understand why Dad gave his soul to save Dean in **2.1** and didn't have to think twice about doing so.

Dean makes Dad promise he won't get himself killed and looking forward to Season 2, that's exactly what happens so he breaks his promise to Dean, irrespective of whether he does this to save Dean. Hence did Dean really have to keep his promise to Dad about Sam for so long. (See season 2.)

Did Dad carry the rosary around as he believes in God or for the specific purposes of blessing water, etc, making it holy. (See season 3 when Sam uses a rosary too and so does Dean in **2.14**.) Why doesn't Meg sense Dad when he's at the water tower.

Dean's speech about no one dying tonight is also a forerunner to the season 1 finale and the season 2 opener. (Something he says in later episodes too, when he's out saving people.) So Sam thinks he'd better say what he wants to Dean now before it's too late and thanks Dean for always being there. Sounds as though something's coming!

Meg saying Dad should be taller, like in **2.11** (and in other episodes too) Sam calls Dean short.

Yellow Eyes approaches, there's static on the radio and the lights flash inside. It looked as if the husband was waiting for them or someone to turn up with a gun, it didn't seem like a bad neighbourhood they were living in, so was he expecting something to happen and why did Yellow Eyes set the baby's crib on fire too, if he can't have the baby, then no one can; but he didn't do this to Sam when he was a baby. Yellow Eyes watching in the window taunting Sam to return and finish it off. Another question, he disappeared when Sam shot at him, so how did they even expect to kill him with the colt anyway, it wasn't as though it didn't know about the gun.

(See the season 2 finale when Yellow Eyes didn't vanish when faced with the colt, but stayed around long enough for Dean to finish the job.)

Sam and Dean argue some more about Dean preventing him from going back in, he saved him from getting himself killed and that's not worth it. He reminds Sam of what he said, that Jessica and Mom are gone and nothing will bring them back. Kind of what's to come in Season 2, when

Dean keeps saying "what's dead should stay dead" (and everyone else keeps repeating it too.) He says that here, but not in so many words and in season 2, he refers to himself. Sam's the willing sacrifice, something which Dean does in Season 2. Sam becomes reckless, Dean won't let anything happen to him as long as he's around and that's the main gist of Season 2. Dean needs to be around to save Sam, from Yellow Eyes, from himself even. Though they do go up and down in season 2, their feelings that is. Dean feels so much anger and guilt and Sam too, but once Sam finds out what his destiny is, he's the one who becomes agitated, feeling all sorts of emotions, wanting Dean around to protect him and worse.

Sam getting angry this time at Dean for telling the truth. He's only repeating what Sam said before but he gets defensive here. Dean telling him the two of them are all the family he's got, so of course he's going to be protective and play big brother and even admits he's barely keeping it together as it is, so without Sam he'll lose it altogether, which he does next season for a while. When Sam kept telling him everything he was keeping in, his feelings were all to do with Dad. Dean was already in a fragile state of mind, so losing Dad just pushed him over the edge. (See **2.8.**)

So Dean having said all this to Sam now, makes you wonder why Sam won't remember when the demon in the episode picks up on Dean needing Dad and Sam.)

Meg's call to them telling them they won't see their father again becomes a reality next season.

A straightforward episode, well as straightforward as a *Supernatural* episode can get. Picking up on Sam's visions, attempting to kill Yellow Eyes. Everything coming together in this penultimate episode for the season finale. Everything they've been throughout season 1, including a whole host of pent up emotions which simmer to the surface and boil over when they can't kill Yellow Eyes and Dad being in trouble too.

For a minute there, thought Sam wouldn't tell them about his visions, but then he had to. Liked the part where Dean told Dad he wasn't there for them when he needed a heart. Dad was possessed since he never lost his temper at Dean for wasting the bullet since he went through so much to get it. Thus Sam was right when he said they had to make sure, but pity he couldn't sense the demon. That was another clue when the demon, as Dad, told them water wouldn't work. In which case, the gun surely wouldn't work on the demon when he was possessing Dad, other than just killing Dad, the host body, or maybe not. Funny no one's come across Yellow Eyes before, or have they, since we never came across anyone else who may have tried to fight it. Only Mom seemed to know him. (See the penultimate episode of season 2 and season 4.)

Corner of Wabash and Lake used in *The Matrix*. On the radio, when Sam and Dean are waiting outside the house, Dean says he doesn't want to get mushy; you can hear, "This is your host Jack Killian on KJCM 98.3 FM. Goodnight America wherever you are." From the US series, *Midnight Caller* starring Gary Cole. (He was seen in **2.18.**)

In **1.20,** Dad says 13 bullets were made for the colt. 6 were used. 13 bullets were shown on screen, then 7. Dad says 4 are left. Where are the other 2? Didn't Sam and Dean still have them in the gun, since Dean used one to kill Yellow Eyes, that was from the original colt.

The dagger thrown at Meg says *God's Eye* on it, as well as other markings.

Dad had to have known of Sam's visions, as Missouri mentioned them in **1.9** when he was there. Also did Sam not sense Dad in that episode because he has demon blood in him, negating his senses useless when it came to family.

Salvation, Iowa does not exist.

Quotes

Dean: "Call you, me, you kiddin' me. Dad I called you from Lawrence, Sam called you when I was dying. Getting you on the phone, I've got a better chance of winning the lottery." (See Season 3)

Meg: "I can see where you boys get their good looks…considering what they say about you, I thought you'd be taller." (A line usually aimed at Dean!)

Dean: "You're just willing to sacrifice yourself, is that it?"
Sam: "You're damn right I am!"

Music

Carry On Wayward Son by Kansas

Ooh Bloops

According to Catholic teachings, only an ordained priest can bless water to make it holy.

Locations

St Andrew Wesley Church. Queensborough Bridge. Lulu Island Trestle Bridge.

1.22. Devil's Trap

Written By Eric Kripke. Directed By Kim Manners.
Original US Airdate 4 May 2006

Guest Stars: Nicki Ackoyx (Meg). Jeffrey Dean Morgan (Dad). Jim Beaver (Bobby). Sebastian Spence (Tom)

Blue Earth, Minnisota

Sam and Dean begin the search for Dad; encountering Meg along the way – with some home truths revealed by everyone; and come across more than they bargained for.

Notes

Dean says, "They've got Dad." As far as he knew he was only meeting Meg, and then says the demon's got Dad. If the penultimate Season 1 episode was a rehearsal for the Season 2 opener – then this episode had a lot more clues as to what was to follow next season. They're still talking about death and Dean was right in so many ways, it was uncanny – just like he could predict the future.

Dean's already willing to throw in the hunting gig as he says in this opening scene, so when he says the same thing in Season 2, it shouldn't come as a surprise to us or to Sam either. All he cares about now, is getting Dad back. In Season 2, all he cares about is living a different life, and he'll do just that if it means saving Sam from his destiny.

The same thing can be said about Sam when he tells us he's only doing what Dad would've wanted him to do: kill the demon, do their job. So again it shouldn't come as such a great shock to Dean when in Season 2, he keeps repeating that he wants to do what Dad would want, i.e. carry on hunting. Since Dean says it's "too little, too late, now that Dad's gone. It isn't too late as in the season finale, Dad is still very much alive and so Sam says all this when he's still around. In a way, it wasn't what Dean thought at all in Season 2; Dean thinks Sam is continuing hunting out of guilt.

Dean telling Sam to stop talking about him like he's dead already – well, it's only a matter of time, and another clue for us of what was really to come next season…

Bobby predicts something's on the horizon and rightly so, as the Winchesters are in the middle of it. Since the action's hotting up and there are more demonic possessions than is the norm. So how did Meg manage to find them at Bobby's (aside from being the first place any demon would look. Did she just go through Dad's little black book of contacts and look them up one by one. Okay, we know he doesn't have one, not that we know of) and could they have used her to find Yellow Eyes, as Sam thinks. They didn't need her as he probably found them at Bobby's and so sent Meg because they'd come looking for Dad. Also they were expecting Meg anyway.

Dean's reference to the spinning head, which he mentions in **2.7 The Usual Suspects**, which boasts a Special Agent guest star too in the form of Linda Blair.

Sam usually does all the Latin reading and chanting, but Dean chants too in **2.8 Crossroad Blues**. Sam sounds so seductive too! Dean threatens to march into hell to slaughter them all if they hurt Dad. In 2.8 (again) he thinks of doing exactly that when he finds out that's where Dad is and shouldn't be, before he threatens to send that particular demon there. (As for Hell, he'll get first hand experience of that too, in the Season 3 finale.)

The Devil's trap they draw for Meg and on the car boot (trunk) is the same one Dean also uses in **2.8 Crossroad Blues** to trap another demon.

Dean doesn't care if Meg is innocent or not, he's going to end it for her and so didn't think twice that he'd be killing off Meg, the real girl; but she was practically dead anyway after the fall from the window in **1.16 Shadow**. They couldn't really leave her in her possessed state.

As I said in the last episode, Sam says he wants to do Dad's work and Dean comes out and says it for the first time here, that since when did Sam care what Dad wants. (There's more of the same to follow in Season 2)

Sam recalls Dean brought him back into hunting and he's trying to finish it, but in the Pilot episode; Dean came for Sam to help him find Dad (which they're doing here now again. So they've come round full circle since the first episode, as far as Dad is concerned.) One nitpick, Dean didn't say he wanted Sam to find the demon or help him do that; he said they could continue on more hunts together. Sam only wanted to go after the demon after Jessica was killed, and that's more so because he blamed himself as he had visions about her death, but didn't tell her or try to save her. He went with Dean instead, in search of Dad. Funny Eric Kripke wrote this episode and the Pilot and changes what happened now… So you see in the end it was Sam's decision to return to hunting.

Dean calls Sam selfish, he and Dad not caring about Dean and how he'll be the one to bury them both. Well, he was right on both counts and Dad will sacrifice himself in Season 2, not for Yellow Eyes but for beloved Dean. Sam calls Dean selfish too in later episodes and they interchange between each other.

Sam uses holy water on Dad when they find him, it has no effect on him, so they think he's really Dad. Notice, the first thing Dad asks is, not how they are, or did they kill Yellow Eyes, (okay, granted he probably knew they didn't already) but no, he asks if they still have the colt? Dad wouldn't think of the gun first and his sons second; although we know he can be like that; not being there when they needed him.

Salting the doors and windows wouldn't work because Yellow Eyes was already in: inside Dad.

Sam tells Dean he didn't have a choice when he killed those things; he knew there were people inside their bodies still and he didn't think twice about it. This is something Sam will argue over with Dean in

Season 2 and we'll see Dean do that too, kill without hesitation, with Sam also telling him he couldn't do something like that in **2.9**, i.e. that they shouldn't just blatantly kill them. Even Dean regrets doing this because as he says now, he's scared by what he has to do sometimes; especially for him and Dad. It must be done, because Sam can't do it, without having to think beforehand and that explains why he and Dad have always done most of the killing.

Though Sam can kill evil spirits and doesn't have to think about that. This usually involves some sort of exorcism and not physical killing. (See later when all this changes for Sam.)

Dean pleading to Dad not to let the demon kill him echoes into **2.1 In My Time Of Dying**, sacrificing himself to save Dean, in response to Dean's pleas here.

Yellow Eyes telling Dean he needs them more than Dad and Sam need him, repeated again in **2.8 Crossroad Blues**. Well, practically every one and every demon will tell this to Dean. Truth is, they're family, they all need each other.

So Yellow Eyes tells Sam he killed Mom and Jess because they were in his way – of the plans he had for Sam and others like him, for the impending demonic war (see season 2.)

Yellow Eyes tells Dean he fights for Sam and Dad, but Dad's the one who needs them more than they do. That's why I said in **2.8** that the demon Dean had trapped knew so much about them and Dean, specifically, and Dean didn't wonder how or why because the same thing was said to him by the crossroads demon in **2.8**, i.e. that he needs Dad and Sam more than they need him. It also tells Dean that Sam is Dad's favourite; so in a way that explains why they always argue so much. Besides, the baby of the family is always the favourite, and I speak from experience.

Yes, but Dean and Sam said it so many times, demons lie, and so did Bobby. Dean killed Yellow Eyes' children so more than likely this was why the demon wanted Dad in the next episode, because he was so willing to save Dean and this was a chance to see Dean suffer when he lost Dad and also perhaps an attempt to draw Sam further into evil and realizing his demonic destiny without Dad around, thinking the grief would affect him in the wrong way. More so than to see

Sam suffer, since Sam was Yellow Eyes's favourite out of all the special children (**2.21.**) and again why the crossroads demon in **2.8** says Dean was in agony and wanted to give up on hunting. Not to mention Dean's plea to Dad to not let the demon kill him.

There's 1 bullet left in the colt at season's end. Also getting Sam to use his psychic abilities here to move the colt. Dean begging Sam not to shoot Dad and when he fires the colt into Dad's leg, Yellow Eyes escapes.

The Key Of Solomon incorporating protective circles to trap demons is used here for the first time. Dad's journal is used as it contains a depossession ritual, but with all the books Bobby has around, you'd think one of those would have something in there.

Dean's line about revenge rings true in the season 2 opener though it's Dad who ends up making the sacrifice to save Dean and Dean was the one to bury him, but along with Sam by his side, (it was more a cremation.) Again Sam wanted revenge for Mom, Jessica and now Dad too, eager to continue the family business.

Yellow Eyes reveals there are more like Sam out there and more demons too. Another teaser for us to meet the others like Sam, as so far in **1.14 Nightmare**, we've only met Max, a fellow psychic.

As for burying Sam, Dean didn't do this either, he couldn't in the Season 2 finale, instead he sold his soul to bring him back!

Still you knew it wasn't over, couldn't have them just drive away into the sunset to fight another day and still Sam didn't sense the inevitable at the end. Though he tried to use kinesis at the end to reach for the colt – you have to ask why Yellow Eyes let them go and left Dad's body too at the end.

Will they still have the fight left in them.

The annoying part, Sam not being able to telekinetically move that gun with Yellow Eyes telling him to go for it. Seems he only had that ability once and that was to save Dean. (**1.14 Nightmare**.)

What a blinding season 1 finale leaving the action on a cliffhanger with the truck crashing into them, as if they hadn't been through enough already this season and episode. Who saw that truck coming?

Meg and Tom are revealed as Yellow Eyes' children and it's only fitting he take revenge for them. The first time it's revealed that Yellow Eyes has big plans for Sam and for other children with special abilities. Meg was always involved from the outset, when she used to talk to her 'bowl of blood' she said "father" into it. It was so apparent in the penultimate episode they wouldn't get Yellow Eyes (otherwise season 2 would've been very different, for starters.) At least they got to say a few things to each other, though Dean didn't really want to hear them (as usual.) since he didn't want it to be the end (in more ways than one!!)

More importantly would Dean end up in the hell where Dad is now. How does he really know he's in hell or heaven or that place in between? Well, to answer, he didn't sacrifice himself here since he wouldn't then be able to save Sam later on. Is it the case that if you sell your soul you automatically end up in hell, aside from *Supernatural* lore.

Dean smudges the drawing of the Devil's trap on the boot of the car, rendering it useless.

So the ending had us on the edge of our seats for season 2. There was going to be a season 2, so we knew the boys would return; but not that Dean would be on the brink of death again and having to fight a reaper once more. With Dad going out on a swansong by saving Dean and the secret he tells Dean which plagues him through almost half of season 2. These were just some of my musings before season 2 was even filmed or screened.

As to this episode Jared comments, "It answered all my questions. I heard somebody say one time that your season finale is your pilot for the next season. Obviously with a pilot comes questions so there were a lot answered and a lot of new questions posed. At the end it is necessary for you to go, 'But what now?' You want the viewers to demand your show comes back so you can answer the questions they have. It was just a tremendous episode. It was 10 days of really long filming with intense acting. Again it was one of those shows where it is emotional, physical and all 125 people on the episode did their best work - it really all came together." How nice, some interviewers couldn't even be bothered to ask what sort of questions Jared thinks were answered in the season one finale!

Eric Kripke: "I was really, really pleased with how the season 1 finale turned out." He also wasn't certain if they would be back for a season at the time so in hindsight the thrilling cliffhanger in the season 1 finale with the car crash was a brave move on the part of Eric. "I wasn't 100% we'd get picked up another season but I was reasonably confident. We had, and continue to, have a very solid fan base and our numbers were pretty good. We thought there was a good chance. Besides you can't let the politics or the business affect the storytelling. We had known for a while that was how we wanted to end the season come hell or high water."

Quotes

Bobby: "Storm's coming and you boys, your daddy, you are smack in the middle of it."

Dean: "You're no girl."

Dean: "You both can't wait to sacrifice yourselves for this thing. I'm gonna be the one to bury you. You're selfish you know that. You don't care about anything but revenge!"

"Dean: "For you, Dad, the things I'm willing to do, to kill, scares me sometimes."

Sam and Dean's Take on the Urban Legend/Lore

There are two versions of the Devil's Trap in the show. One is the heptagram on the ceiling of Bobby's house. It is formed of two pentacles from the Lesser Key of Solomon, which make up a heptagram. The second is the pentagram – seen on the Impala's boot, drawn by Sam. It is also apparent in the following episodes: **2.8 Crossroads Blues, 2.14 Born Under a Bad sign, 2.22** in the giant Devil's Trap in Wyoming In **3.1** in the opening credits, the Devil's Trap becomes the shows title, *Supernatural*. Also on the boot of Bobby's car. Bobby traps sloth under one.

At Isaac and Tamara's house. Bobby traps Gluttony and Sam tries to trap pride and fails. In **3.3**, Dad's storage facility has one at the entrance. **3.4** Dean uses one under the rug to trap the barmaid, Casey. **3.16** Dean traps Ruby under one to get her knife. **4.2** In Bobby's panic room, in the roof and the floor.

Actual Legend

Sixth and seventh Books of Moses – compilation of black magic techniques. In these, the Sixth introduces seals and magical tables revealed to Moses on Mount Sinai and eventually to King Solomon, who used them to command spirits to collect his immense legendary books.

They didn't use the Book of Solomon again except for the circles in season 2. The Key of Solomon, mentioned by Sam is a form of protective circles used to trap demons. The Key of Solomon or *Clavis Salomonis* is a medieval book about magic attributed to King Solomon. Also used as a *Grimoire* occasionally. It is believed this led to the *Clavicula Salomonis*, i.e. *the Lesser Key of Solomon,* or *the Lemegeton* (as mentioned in *Buffy*.) These are probably rituals and conjuring in particular may have led to the development of this.

The Key of Solomon dated back to the sixteenth and seventeenth centuries and there was even one in Greek from the fifteenth century. The book doesn't contain anything on the 72 spirits which were held by King Solomon in a bronze vessel known as the *Pseudomonarchi Deamonum* from the sixteenth century) and the Lemegeton – seal of the demons. Solomon wrote this for his son, Roboam. Only those who are deemed worthy and God-fearing can use the book. There are two books. Book 1 has conjurations, curses and contains to 'contain' demons and dead spirits. Book II has purifications, i.e. what should be worn, instruments of magic needed… also informs how to perform necromancy. A reference to the *Lesser Key of Solomon,* a book of magic, aka *The Lemegeton.*

Devil's Trap is a mystic symbol used to control demons, from the Lesser Key of Solomon.

Music

Fight the Good Fight by Triumph; *Bad Moon Rising* by Creedence Clearwater Revival; *Turn to Stone* by Joe Walsh

Ooh Bloops

Bobby talks about the Key of Solomon to Sam, when Dean's in the background; you can see Jensen saying his lines.

Before the truck crashes into the car, Dean is sitting in the backseat, then he's against the car behind Dad; then he's behind Sam again.

Locations

Sunset Beach Road. Kensington Place.

"Their destiny will begin…" in season 2.

SEASON 2

Season 2 was advertised on US TV with Jo (Alona Tal) doing a voiceover: *"Let me tell you a story about a family of supernatural hunters - brothers destined to walk in the shadows. They travelled the land fighting evil and protect those who can't protect. Their journey is a lonely one, but they are not alone. There are more of us."*

193

(Me thinks, substitute hunks for hunters in the above line!) There are more of them, but they will still be alone, as they won't get on with or fit into the world of the other hunters they come across.

2.1 In My Time of Dying

Written By Eric Kripke. Directed By Kim Manners
Original US Air Date 28 September 2006

Guest Stars: Jeffrey Dean Morgan (John Winchester); Lindsey McKeon (Tessa/Reaper); Frederic Lane (Yellow-Eyes)

Dean and Dad are rushed to hospital, where Dean is in a coma. He finds no one can see him and a reaper is after him. Dad saves Dean the only way he knows how, by bargaining with the Yellow Eyes and losing the colt in the process.

Notes

When we see Sam with the colt – the only one who's still conscious – then next time we see him he's on the stretcher, when the helicopter arrives, what did he do with the gun? Did he hide it in the car – under the seat or somewhere else, since he later tells Dad it's in the car when he asks Sam to get it for him.

Notice the camera pan in on the exit sign when Dean's in the hospital, signifying his possible "exit" from this world into the afterlife. Dean walks into see himself in bed and Sam can't hear him either and at first doesn't even sense Dean's presence. As Dean tells Sam he should be able to hear him or sense him. Oddly though, or not, Sam repeats what Dean says about finding some hoodoo priest. This is something Dean is open to in this episode, whereas before in **1.12 Faith**, he was against this whole faith healing bit; as he didn't believe it and probably rightly so.

Sam can't believe all Dad can do is ask about the colt. (**See 1.22 Devil's Trap** where he never even got angry with Dean using up the bullets because it wasn't really him.) Instead he asks Sam for it. So the other things he says are for protection. Sam also tells him about the demon having plans for him and others like him but he denies any knowledge, which we later find out was a lie since he whispers it to

Dean, who definitely knows Dad's hiding something when he's walking around in the hospital.

Dean gives his whole "help me Dad" speech, pouring his heart out to him but thinks he can't or won't do anything for him. What can he do? Short of working miracles. But Dad's thinking about what he's going to do for Dean even before he begs for help; he worked that out when he asked Sam for the colt and the list he gave him. The list, which Bobby tells Sam, isn't used for protection. Sam tells Dad he knows he's going to summon the demon – but wrongly believes it's to kill it. Why couldn't he sense or feel what Dad was about to do for Dean?

Sam's speech echoes Dean in the season 1 finale when he tells Sam he's selfish; calls Dad selfish too and they only care about their obsession with finding the demon and exacting revenge.

Even when Dean's not around in the 'bodily' sense, he still has a way of stopping the two of them from arguing when he knocks the glass over; ah it's a demonic presence. How'd he manage that then? Some sort of telekinesis, but he's not meant to have any powers is he, though it's probably since he's in a coma.

Sam telling Dad to go to hell – he'll come to regret saying that and Dean heard it too. (See **2.8 Crossroad Blues**, when Dean finds out that's where Dad is now, or at least meant to be.) Sam now senses Dean when he's repelling the spirit away from his bedside (he doesn't know it's a reaper until later.) Why did it take Sam so long to sense Dean?

Dean gives the whole "what the spirit could be" to Tessa which was frankly wasted on her since she knew exactly what she was, playing Dean for a fool! He should've realized because unlike him, she was too readily willing to accept her fate. Dean telling her you always have a choice; to fight or not, proves he's come a long way in his thinking and acceptance of his fate; that you do have a choice; whereas in **1.12 Faith**, he was ready to do exactly that, roll over to die. Perhaps that was a different situation because when he needed a new heart and wasn't going to get one anytime soon, he made his peace; but here he's in a coma and there's nothing definite about that.

Only for him he didn't know death was already mapped out for him and there was no choice. So yes, he's right. Sometimes you do have a choice. Other times you don't – but Dad did and he chose to save Dean the only way he thought he could.

Can we change fate or does fate change us. Something Sam will contemplate later on in the season when he finds out about his own fate, destiny: at first saying no one can change it and then wanting to so badly.

Dean can't believe Sam resorting to the Ouija board – a last resort because it's the only way he can communicate with Dean. Also they haven't used it very much in their hunting. Dean can touch the board physically: perhaps explaining why he could knock the glass over before. Dean now knows it's a reaper and there's no way to stop it if it's here naturally (again another reference to **1.12 Faith** as they could stop that reaper as it was summoned by magical means) – but there was an unnatural way to stop it, which Dad does; using the demon.

It's so convincing the way the reaper prepares Dean to accept his fate; death. Otherwise he'll become a malevolent spirit himself, languishing in this state for eternity – but how do we know the demon wasn't behind Dean's fate (well it was since it physically attacked Dean in the season 1 finale, so he did have a hand in his 'death'.) If the reaper was there naturally then the way the demon just took it over was uncanny. Wasn't this a demonstration of good v evil and evil just came in and stole the show, taking over. Obviously the reaper was here to take Dean to a better place, it was his time, akin to the Angel of Death, but because of Dad's pact Dean was saved and Dad sent to the evil place instead, to hell?

Sam's convinced Dad will know what to do; but sadly he doesn't realize what that involves. The reaper's living on borrowed time again, another aside to **1.12 Faith**, when Dean was saved that time too, not once but twice, at the expense of another. That wasn't Dean's fault either and neither is this because he doesn't know what Dad will do. Sam opens up to Dean about not leaving him – only Dean's elsewhere fighting his own battle.

Tessa mentions the stages of grief – but in particular 'bargaining'. Dean still finds a moment to joke about prude chicks. The reaper thinking he's cute, just like the demon in **2.8 Crossroad Blues** so it appears all 'things' have a penchant for him! Demons and reapers are supposed to have a human side to them so one reason why they all seem to fancy Dean.

Dean's most likely right about his family dying if he's not around – Sam will need him and Dad, well Dad won't be around. The warrior's death could be a reference to Dad. (See **2.2 Everybody Loves a Clown** and the funeral pyre for him.) In the Pilot, Sam also says Dad raised them like warriors.

The reaper tells Dean he'll become what he's hunted; is likened to Sam saying in **2.9 Croatoen**, that Dean's becoming like the people affected with the virus, as all he wants to do is to shoot them without question or mercy. (Jumping forward to season 4, Dean will say the very same thing to Sam, about becoming what they hunt. As will Gordon in season 2 and 3.)

The lights flickering, another sign the demon's around, but Dean sees the demon smoke too so he had to have known at that point what was happening. Strange though when Dean wakes he can't recall, that'll haunt him for episodes to come: he'll have an idea of what happened to Dad but won't be certain until season 2 episodes **2.4** and **2.8** and as Dean was just about prepared to meet his destiny...being the season 2 opener we knew that would never happen.

Sam has his own doubts as he does not believe Dad didn't go after the demon and that's the only reason he believes Dad wanted the colt, until he starts to think otherwise, since Dean tells Sam in **2.8**, that Sam has thought of what happened to Dad, i.e. that he gave his soul for Dean.

Dad said Dean keeps the family together; what Dean's just said to the reaper, in contrast to the demon saying Dean needs them. (**2.8 Crossroad Blues**). Dad tells Dean he kept them together, even when they were little and he should've watched out more for them as a father should – this reminiscing on Dad's part is something he never does unless something's about to occur (as he made up with Sam **1.20 Dead Man's Blood**, when they were about to go after the vampires, telling Sam he was proud of him) and here now Dean should've suspected something was up, but conveniently he can't remember his coma events and Sam, well he's inconveniently sent away for coffee.

But it's a shame the writers didn't utilize Sam's abilities some more, being able to sense Dean eventually; but also that something was about to happen and something big involving Dad. All Dean could say to Sam when he emerged form the coma was "something's wrong."

Everything was wrong and went wrong from this episode onwards, including: morbid feelings about Dad; death; doing the right thing; drowning in guilt; realizing destiny; going downhill; resolving brotherly issues, to ending up slap bang in the middle of the FBI radar (and one agent in particular). This episode sets up efficiently the remaining episodes with immense character changes between Sam and Dean; to growing up even more, now that there's only the two of them (well as much growing up Dean can do with his joking around!) to overwhelming emotions and feelings in many of their conversations; roller coaster rides, highs to lows.

The final scene is one that captures loss and heartache completely (if you've been through something like this it's even more heart rendering). As Sam walked in to find Dad unconscious on the floor. The final moments of silence, Sam yelling "NO!" and calling for help;

everything silent except for the paddles – the doctor calling "time" (words no one wants to hear) and the look of sheer shock and horror on Sam and Dean's faces as the camera fades to black – appropriately.

In that time you can almost imagine, not the reaper, but the grim reaper hovering over Dad, life drained from him. But the scene is even more truly shocking for us as we know the real truth – not the reaper but the demon – ripping away life so cruelly. The scene with Dean in bed fighting for life was in stark contrast to the scene at the end, Dean having changed places with Dad who wasn't able to fight for his life and one instant which no one could have imagined.

Missed opportunities: what could have followed: five stages of grief for Sam and Dean: - Denial: this couldn't have happened – it isn't happening, after all this time how could Dad just be gone.

2) Anger: especially for Dean: it should have been him – he shouldn't be here. Why Dad? (Especially as they don't yet know what happened for sure, re the demon involvement, though Dean suspects). Anger at Sam: he was never the dutiful son and now he wants to do everything Dad would've wanted or done. Anger taken out on Dean's beloved Impala, also as Dad gave it to him. (See episodes such as **1.6 Skin**, **2.5 Simon Said**, where he's forced to lose his 'baby', i.e. his car, saying "I'll never leave you again."

3) Bargaining: what could Sam and Dean have done to make this not happen. Sam suspected what Dad wanted those things for, but not why he wanted them now, to save Dean.

4) Depression: maybe more appropriate for Sam's quandary at not being a good son; for leaving when he did – wanting his own life; defying Dad. How so for Dean? If he weren't in a coma this wouldn't have happened, things would've played out differently. Yet they both seemed to suffer bouts of guilt rather than depression.

5) Acceptance: understand what happened and why – are they still angry (see later episodes. Mostly **2.4 Children Shouldn't Play with Dead Things** and **2.8 Crossroad** Blues and perhaps Dean will come to accept, has he accepted already, that life goes on after Dad. No matter what he's feeling now, how much he's hurting and his world is falling apart (see episode **2.10 Hunted** Dean doesn't want to hunt anymore) that life very much does go on.

He has a continuing fight - to hunt the Yellow Eyes, other monsters for mankind, in preparation of the bigger fight of good v evil, somehow involving Sam; including monsters of his own and his mission now is to look out for Sam after what Dad told him. Though at this stage we don't really know what that was. Dean couldn't save Dad, even if he could…but he can save Sam and others too. He should find some sort of solace in that, that Dean came back for this purpose alone as no one else could do this job. Some words of comfort Sam may have said to him if he knew then what Dean has to do for him, in this episode.

As for Sam accepting, he seems to have when he wants to hunt and carry on the legacy, but he has yet to discover and accept his own fate.

The five stages of grief, for anyone who has studied Psychology 101 was reported by Elizabeth Kubler-Ross in 1969 in *On Death and Dying*. Though in the first stage, Denial she also included isolation which I haven't mentioned in this context, even though they are alone, Sam and Dean still have each other and yet Dean still chooses not to utilize this and open up to his brother, he wants to keep a brave face for Sam. (See **2.3 Blood Lust**.)

The doctor saying there must be an angel watching out for Dean, could it be Mom? However see season **2.13 Houses of the Holy** where Dean doesn't believe in angels even though he knows Mom did, ironically. Also season 4. This episode shows an insight into things to come then.

Dad, unfortunately, was going to have his number come up now, for a while, as decided by Eric Kripke. Dad makes a deal with the demon to save Dean, but it was never going to be a hard and fast business proposition. You see, the devil, or in this case the yellow-eyed demon, always demands satisfaction, and not only did he want the colt but also a soul for a soul! Hence Dad's Faustian deal.

Said Kripke, "There is an inherent flaw in season 1 and that Dad is off having more exciting adventures than the boys are. It is like they are always one step behind Dad and Dad is the one fighting the demon who dealt with their family [and Jess]. As much as I love the character, John, in a weird sort of way it kept the boys one step removed from the real fight, which is against this demon that killed their family and has these wicked plans for Sam. You sort of want to remove the person who is defending and shielding the boys from that so they can face it directly. Inevitably you have to kill the mentor. Take your pick of Obi-Wan Ken Obi, Gandalf, whoever the character is. So the boys have revenge and vengeance as motivations."

Yes, but the flaw with this line of thinking is that the boys already have revenge and vengeance to motivate them – losing not only their Mom in that way when they were so young – but Sam losing Jess too. So they were already on a quest to find the demon. Also Dad didn't so much as defend, shield or protect them from the demon – as in the demon had his own designs on them anyway, as in Meg. Having been in lots of scrapes, there were times when Dad just wasn't around to help them or to pick up the pieces. Examples include: when Dean was dying and needed a new heart. Even when the boys were 'meeting' Meg to have their showdown with her and the demons in **1.16 Shadows**, Dad only showed up at the last minute, and dare I say it, didn't do much!

This had a negative effect on the two obviously, leading to a reversal in their characters – Sam wanting to carry on the hunt and look for others like him. Dean wanting to leave it all behind and head to the Grand Canyon, or Hollywood with a penchant for bedding Lindsay Lohan (eewww or should that be no comment.)

In **2.16 Roadkill**, when Sam and Dean talk of what's out there for them; on the other side, only hope that it's good. Here Dean knows there's good out there for them, something more peaceful than this life. Tessa said he'd die a noble death; meaning he'd go on to a better place. (Or was she being cryptic.) Dean, however, couldn't recall all this as know, when he came out of the coma. Also the big finale with the lights when Molly finally leaves this world, should've answered their question, instead of just hoping, that is of course if they saw the lights.

As to the effects of the tragedy, continues Kripke, "It's been fun and interesting. Plus the actors are so damn good that we knew they could handle the heavy lifting that we wanted to give them this season. Having a loved one die as close to them as their father was just a lot of story communication, and underneath it all this has always been a story about family. [A bit like Buffy and Joyce.] Seeing how two siblings react to a death is always interesting and a way to reveal further dimensions of these characters. Jared is doing such a good job, but what I love about the brothers is how they are both taking very honest but opposite reactions to the death of their father." Which I mentioned above.

Kripke; "Sam is taking it and trying to do well by his father and as Dean rightfully pointed out, 'A man you hated while he was alive, and now, just because of guilt, you are trying to live up to some standard that you set.'" Sam did leave and went to find his own life but Sam didn't really hate Dad and it's a bit extreme for Dean to say that. (See **1.20 Dead Man's Blood** especially.)

They had their differences, but they made up to a point with Dad telling Sam he was proud. Rightly or wrongly Dean said this, but part of it was also his own guilt talking, his guilt, which he admits to in, **2.4 Children Shouldn't Play With Dead Things** by repeating, that he shouldn't be here. As for Dean's guilt, when he was wondering the hospital, Dean did ask Dad to do something for him, in all fairness to Dad, he did the only thing he knew how to, to give his life to save a life.

Jensen comments on Dean: he "is really screwed up and really messed up by what happens. He really kind of internalizes a lot of it and it comes across as anger and vengeance and wrath."

As for the season 1 pilot and season 2 opener, it was really a "rehash" of similar events –okay maybe I should use're-imagining' instead as that seems to be the word of the moment: losing a mother, losing a father – only this time they got to explore their feelings because the events were more real in the sense of being older, happening now. In season 1 Sam was just a baby and too young to appreciate what loss feels like.

This season kept up the high standards and was as good as last season, if not better. Some of the episode titles from season 2 are also the names of movies or rock songs, such as *Children Shouldn't Play with Dead Things; The Usual Suspects; In My Time of Dying; Born Under a Bad Sign; What is and What Should Never Be.*

Quick quips: Sam had the idea to use the Ouija board, not Dean, why do reviewers always get it wrong, don't they remember what they've just seen.

What Dad whispered to Dean really isn't that exciting. Sorry to have to keep harping on about it. Maybe if he'd have said how he may turn evil.

Now saying something like Sam will have to embrace his dark side before he can overcome it – would be more interesting – using everything he knows about Dean against him, i.e. weaknesses, guilt etc to turn him against Sam so he can help him revert to good.

Did you notice Dean had more stubble when he was in bed the first time and it became less when he was wondering around the hospital. The date on Dean's monitor is 12 August 2006. Also listen out for a page for 'Dr Bender' in the hospital. That 'reaper' wasn't too convincing either.

Dean was right when he said she accepted her fate too quickly – who would? He didn't since he was practically begging for his 'life' even if it meant wandering aimlessly forever and not all bad or malevolent spirits are all lost souls! (Look at Molly in **2.16 Roadkill**). However, see in season 3, where Dean puts on a brave face about his fate but then finally admits he doesn't want to die, which would've been obvious from this season 2 opener.

Sam should've suspected or known Dad would've wanted those things for 'other' purposes. He helped Dean with the faith healer, wouldn't Dad have wanted to try to help Dean too in his own way, regardless of what that way would've involved or entailed, surely he wouldn't be thinking of revenge or killing the demon at a time like this, since Dean would be his number one priority, even though he wasn't there for them when they needed him before.

Dad should've known Yellow Eyes wouldn't let him have Dean back in return for the colt, as there wasn't enough selling of souls involved and even demons exact revenge and expect an eye for an eye.

Don't suppose Dad could've substituted the colt for a fake again, for starters there wasn't enough time and he wouldn't tell Sam what he was doing.

It was unfair Dad didn't even get to say goodbye to Sam and vice versa, and Dean too. (I know how they felt!) and the scene where they couldn't revive Dad was so poignant and sad (especially for anyone who's been through something like that and only recently!)

In the UK ITV2 made a hash of the ad breaks in the middle of the dialogue when this episode was first aired. At least we get colour in our episodes, compared tot the US version where the episodes are practically all grey –ish with hints of primary colours and they have really deep voices too!

The part where Dean was flat lining was good (though I shouldn't say that) but you know what I mean and Sam was in tears and Dean came and stood behind. Dean wasn't "around" to hear Sam's heart-to-heart about only just finding each other again, as brothers. Dean should've known something was up when Dad was telling him about his hunting in the past and how he'd reassure him. That came out of the blue as they don't really do that. Sam had a feeling but he couldn't quite put his finger on it.

How did Sam know Dad was in his own hospital room when he found him after he brought back coffee. It didn't look like he'd stopped in to Dean's room first. What about how the coffee cup landed on the floor straight up. Usually they just roll over when they're dropped or fall.

Really like the way in this season how they've changed the way both think. In season 1, Dean wanted to continue hunting and when he said that to Sam in **1.16 Shadow**, Sam said he wants to get out after they've got the demon. Whereas here, especially the first half of the season, Dean wants to get out and Sam wants to continue hunting. No quest is too meager.

One critic commenting on this episode said that no one addressed the fact Sam was opening up all sorts of channels and spirits when he used the Ouija board and could've been attacked by anything. In response, Sam wouldn't really be thinking of something like that, when all he wanted was his brother back. Besides, nothing would've surprised him at this point and time. It was specifically a device to contact Dean the only way he knew how under the circumstances and not channel any evil spirits out there. As for calling up anything else, he would've known how to handle it, or hunt it. He's not exactly an amateur!

It would've been good if Dean could've been able to find out what Dad was up to and then tried to stop him, whilst having to deal with his own dilemma too.

If Dad could summon Yellow Eyes with that ritual, why didn't he use it before, or did he just find this out now. That was a niggling part and also how Yellow Eyes was the one who appeared to bargain for Dad's soul in person, rather than anyone else. That wasn't very clever on the part of the writers. In any case, there won't be a note in his journal on this.

It looks as though Dad was made to answer his own question when he asked, "how stupid do you think I am?" to Yellow Eyes because he didn't even think about the demon wanting his life in return for Dean as a sacrifice, or did he? Then, as said before, perhaps Dean would've found out what Dad was doing if he hadn't been so preoccupied with the reaper, understandably she appeared to be distracting him, and he couldn't have found a way to stop him and using the Ouija board device twice wouldn't have worked.

Even if Dad did sacrifice himself to save Dean, it wouldn't have kept Yellow Eyes away from them (and it didn't) since he's after Sam anyway.

Sam and Dean have yet more conflicts between them this season which is awesome and great to watch.

Season 2 about hunting, being hunted by death, those they loved, of guilt, new life, returning and being let down again, to where we started with the season 2 opener. Forgiving and perhaps moving on, at least attempting to, if only Dean didn't have that wretched one year death sentence hanging over his head at the end of this season and onto the next.

Dad is a legend. Now his sons carry on the legacy, as Sam said in **2.4**. Dean is the heart of the Winchester family, the one who keeps them going through all adversities. Eric Kripke says Bobby has less of "their father's borderline-psycho, cruel obsessions."

One of Kim Manners favourite episodes which he said was greatly acted by all three, i.e. Jensen, Jared and Jeffrey; they brought tears to his eyes.

Listen out for the doctor being paged as "Dr Kripke."

Re the 72 virgins, in Islam (though it's controversial) a martyr is promised 72 virgins if he dies a heroic death in battle. Number 72 is said in one of the Hadith – containing actions and statements from the Prophet Muhammad. Also the same thing Zachariah said to Dean in season 4 episodes, (**4.17** and **4.22**.)

Yanni: a Greek keyboard player. The title is a Led Zeppelin song from the album *Physical Graffiti*.

Quotes

Sam: "Dean is dying and you have a plan - you know what – you care more about killing this demon than saving your own son. How is revenge gonna help him, you're not thinking about anybody but yourself, it's the same selfish obsession!"

Dean: "There's no such thing as an honourable death – my corpse is gonna rot in the ground and my family's gonna die." [But his soul won't rot.]

Actual Legend

Crisis apparition is a vision of someone who appears after they are involved in a crisis, such as illness or death. Theoretically it was believed the person who is ill or gravely injured gives out a telepathic "image of themselves to someone who has a close relationship with them. It is thought that, the sender or agent is unconscious of sending any message."

Some apparitions seen after death are known as 'delayed' crisis apparitions. This is the most frequent reported form of hauntings. Only appears once and not seen again – has a form of comforting effect on loved ones. Only ever witnessed by the person to whom they appear and so they are impossible to prove or disprove. The account comes from a subjective perspective.

The use of a Ouija board to contact spirits is apparent in western cultures since the Biblical era. (*1 Samuel 14:37 – 42 + passion.*)

Its use arose in New York in the late 1840's, known as "spirit rapping", where sounds were used to make up messages using 'yes/no/ answers; or by saying the alphabet. It became known as "table-tapping", when the table rises up, the participants ask it questions in the form of 'once for yes', two for no.'

The Ouija board developed from the nineteenth century so messages could be received from spirits, dating back as far as 1867. Here the alphabet was printed onto a spirit board' to make to make this much easier to use. Most famous board was the *Oujia Mystifying Oracle*

Talking Board patented by William Fuld on 19 July 1892. After he had made the prototype he said he contacted a spirit and asked what he should call it, it said, 'o-u-i-j-a.' Others say he thought of the writer 'Ouida' (Louise de la Ramee 1839-1908) who wrote some novels in fantastic settings. The pen name 'Ouida' was made from the French and Russian words for 'yes' and 'Ouija' has the word 'yes and German 'ja'.

The board overtook the Bible and Prayer book in fraternity dorms. It was the most popular Parker Bros item after *Monopoly* and now a glow-in-the-dark letters board is also available.

Actual Legend

Bi-location is the appearance of someone in two places at once. One theory states it's the projected image of a double – either in a physical, solid form or in a ghostly form. The act of bi-location was familiar in ancient times, seen and practiced by saints, mystics, monks and even magicians. Saints included, St Ambrose of Milan, St Anthony of Padua. In 1774, St Alphonsus Maria de Ligouri was viewed at Pope Clement XIV's bedside, whilst he was still imprisoned in a cell which was four days away. Mostly, no one seems interested in such an event (of bi-location) these days.

'Fetch' is mostly a noun and mainly a British term, meaning an apparition or the appearance of a spirit of a living person, or a doppelganger.

TV/Film References

Ghost Whisperer, Ghost

X Files Connection

Dead Alive, Mulder wakes from his a coma – though not in the same way as Dean!

Audrey Pauley. After a car crash, Agent Reyes lies between life and death and needs to rely on a psychic woman, as she wakes to find herself in a 'floating' hospital in a void. She meets patients who believe they are dead – but she doesn't accept this. She's in a coma in a real hospital. Reyes notices a woman walk through a wall; she's a patient with the name Audrey, who tells Doggett, Reyes' soul hasn't left her body. Kim Manners directed this episode.

Beyond The Sea is an example of a crisis apparition was where Scully's father appears to her moments before she discovers he's dead.

Music

Bad Moon Rising by Creedence Clearwater Revival; *Strangehold* by Ted Nugent

Ooh Bloops

When Dean sees Tessa on the stairs for the first time, a man is being helped by a nurse. The he walks back into the shot unaided.

The machines Dean was connected to in his come disappear when he wakes up.

Locations

Riverview Hospital.

2.2 Everybody Loves A Clown

Written By John Shiban. Directed By Phil Sgriccia
Original US Airdate 5 October 2006

Guest Stars: Alona Tal (Jo Harvelle). Chad Lindberg (Ash). Samantha Ferris (Ellen Harvelle); Ken Kramer (Mr Cooper); Alec Willows (Clown)

Medford, Wisconsin

Parents are killed by a clown.

(How many times have they travelled to Wisconsin now?) Sam and Dean bid farewell to Dad.

One Week Later

Dean fixes his Impala and tells Sam to quit asking if he's okay. Sam traces a phone number to an address of a roadhouse run by Ellen, from Dad's journal. They go in search of the killer clown.

Notes

Aside from the comedic interjections and the several references to clowns and Dean's subsequent teasing of Sam for being afraid of them, this episode still has all the hallmarks of the season 1 finale and the season 1 opener. (In the penultimate episode of season 1 in Sam's vision of the nursery, watch out for the clown mobile hanging by the baby's crib! It's a prelude to this episode in a way.) Sam constantly strives to be the dutiful son (whereas he always questioned this about Dean.) With questioning why now, when it's too late – Dad'll never know.

The guilt they both still feel, but, so hard for Dean to show, brushing off Sam's attempts to get him to open up by saying he's handling it or dealing with it. Maybe he's attempting to put on a brave face on for Sam. Though it's clearly understandable when he says he's fine to Ellen (she's a stranger) he could open up to Sam since they are brothers and Sam only wants to help. This is all new to Dean; remember he doesn't need anyone's help.

Also they haven't come across a woman like Ellen before, i.e. a mother, friend of Dad's. She's a possible mother figure that they've never known their entire lives. (Aside form Dean having Mom for 4 years.) Dean even acts like she's a "mother" (see **2.5 No Exit**) he's afraid of her, as he tells Jo.

Guilt mentioned here, it's one of the stages of grief, but they'll be feeling guilty for a long time.

Dean is humiliated twice in this episode, not only does he have to drive a run down van with no good music on the radio! He gets hit by a chick! Not doing much for his macho image! Though for a second there, he thinks it may be a guy up close and personal behind him, hence his remark, "Oh God, please let that be a rifle!"

Sam asks Dean if Dad said anything to him before he died and for the sake of keeping his promise to him, Dean lies to Sam, until the lies keep on coming and eventually get to him. This is Dean's 'big' secret. (See how many secrets they keep from each other in the coming seasons!)

The title is in itself ironic, since everybody doesn't love a clown! Hey, my niece didn't play with her cuddly toy clown when she was a baby!

The ending in this episode was very déjà vu. (For those of you who remember *Charlie's Angels* and the circus episode when Sabrina was a clown and Kris had knives thrown at her.) Dean's still calling Sam a bitch and he calls Dean a freak. (Well, it was better than having 'dick' spouted all over the place in later episodes.)

Glad to see Dean restrained himself and didn't need to jump into bed with the first chick he came across. Sam should've said Dean's a clown too and why does Sam hate clowns?

Funny Dean didn't seem to like the song on the truck radio, "Do it to me one more time..." ahem. Highly appropriate for him.

Begging the question, why did they choose to cremate Dad and not bury him next to Mom. We know there's no body in there since Mom was killed by fire, but it's her memorial and wouldn't, or didn't Dad want that? This was their idea. Are hunters cremated so the evil demons out there can't do evil acts with their bodies, i.e. reanimating them etc and subjecting them to all sorts of black arts. (See **3.1** where they come across a hunting couple, Isaac is also burned after he is killed.)

What did they do with Dad's affects? Look more burning zone(s), okay, another bad joke. Dad's funeral was like a Viking's funeral, as befits a hero.

Dean was patronizing Sam as he always does this when he doesn't want to talk, open up, evade the issue; but we get the general idea from past episodes whenever there's a deep and meaningful conversation on the cards. His imagery is rather that of being on a date or sharing feelings with a girl instead of his brother, but then, he does call Sam a "girl" on many occasions!

To introduce new characters, Dean's back into that whole, "can't understand Dad's research" mode whereas from last season, there's a lot of chopping and changing going on. Sometimes they do understand the journal and other times (when the episode calls for it) they're stumped.

Whenever someone close to them dies, those anger and revenge traits pop up and uncharacteristically this time, it's Sam doing all the revenge talk, usually it's Dean. Besides the Pilot when Sam wanted to go after Yellow Eyes when he killed Jessica. More likely than not, he's trying to get Dean to talk – even if it's all about him being angry; anything's better than the silent treatment and keeping it all bottled up, especially where Dean's concerned. Dean gets humiliated quite a bit, as mentioned, a bit of a repeat of **1.15** when he kind of got waylaid by Missy.

Ellen mentions Dad was like family once. Ellen and Jo being the new friends and allies they come across before discovering there's a whole world out there of fellow hunters, which makes you wonder why Dad didn't tell Sam and Dean, particularly Dean, about all this and Ellen too, when conversely he's told Ellen about them. Jo also harbours a massive crush on Dean, (who wouldn't) but alas it's a case of unrequited love.

Dean once again demonstrates he doesn't need anyone or anyone's sympathy either, "Really lady, I'm fine." Proving his point when he doesn't even make a play for Jo, or come to think of it, for any other chick either! To find comfort in his time of grief and need, when normally he would. This is no ordinary time for him, he'd rather face solace in a beer and a case (no not of beer!) though he's almost about to suggest they could get together.

Also coming across Ash, the MIT geek who can make headway with Dad's journal. He's surprised anyone could track Yellow Eyes like Dad, using weather patterns; crop failures, which will help them out in **2.5 Simon Said**. Surprised they need someone to help with their research when usually they can manage that themselves! (Expect more of this trend in seasons to come.)

So Sam's fear of clowns stems from endless *Ronald McDonald* ads on TV (we don't get those anymore) and yes another episode for Dean to tease Sam about clowns, at every possible moment, as brothers do. Though really it's 1 for 1 when Sam says Dean's afraid of flying because Dean replies they crash and Sam's response, "Clowns kill!" (Another subtle reference to *Stephen King's IT*.)

Dean "I know what you're thinking – why'd it have it have to be clowns?" Paraphrasing "Why'd it have to be snakes?" from *Raiders of the Lost Ark*.

Best bits, Dean letting Sam sit on the clown chair, and saying Sam loves the bearded lady. Ah, me thinks that's you Dean – being quite the ladies' man!! Ha. Dean being chased by knives a lot this season. Sam asking if Dad and Ellen were an item and Dean replying Dad fought with everyone. Well, that'd explain Sam and Dad falling out.

You can feel another argument coming when Sam (in Dean's opinion) has the gall to tell him Dad would've wanted them to take this job and in true brotherly fashion, Dean has to mention Sam didn't want to do any of this hunting and now he does because of Dad dying. Dean maybe feels dejected, rejected, all the time he spent with Dad, hunting, doing everything he asked, no ordered, whilst Sam was off living the high life at college and now Sam comes in and takes over everything Dean's been doing and talking of Dad.

Dean doesn't feel he has a right to do that after fighting with Dad for so long. He wants to deal with his grief personally, thus his "these are your issues…" comment. Whereas to Sam, he probably feels the only way he can now move past this; come to terms with Dad's passing is by being the son he should've been all those years. On the other hand, he was the same son he, always was and will be, since they made up in **1.16 Shadow**. Dad was proud of his choices and going to college; it was in the end what he wanted for him, for them both.

Deep down, Dean is caring and sharing to the point where the secret he's promised to keep and the burden of it eats him up. He's ready to give it all up (not what Dad would've wanted, in contrast to Sam and the love he has for Sam is apparent: he'll do anything for him, protect him from his destiny (**2.10 Croatoan** and making another promise to Sam that perhaps Sam shouldn't ask him to keep in this episode.)

On the contrary, Sam didn't pick a fight with Dad last time he saw him (that was **1.20**). The last time he saw Dad was in **2.1 In My Time of dying**, when Dean was in a coma and Sam wanted Dad to do something for Dean. Yet they got beyond that when he told Sam he would help and promptly sent him for coffee. What was unfair on them is that Dad knew exactly what was coming and yet he didn't even try to say goodbye to them, most especially Sam. He sort of did to

Dean when he said he should've been there for him and no it shouldn't have been the other way around, i.e. Dean was always there for him. Oh and when he told Dean to look out for Sam and kill him if he becomes evil. (Still to be revealed to Sam by Dean.)

Sam in his own way is trying to make it up to Dad because in his own way, that's what he feels he should do – no matter if it is "too little, too late."

Dean put his foot into everything at the carnie just like **1.8 Bugs** when he was attempting to illicit information from the Native American and as payback for teasing Sam about clowns and the Bearded Lady, Sam doesn't come to his rescue.

In reply to Sam's question, Dean isn't dealing with Dad's death at all and dare I say it again, okay, his agonizing secret about Sam. He doesn't deal with Dad's death easily (who can?) when it comes to those he cares about and this can be seen in the season 2 finale when Dean just has to get Sam back any way he can. He obviously isn't dealing with death there either, does he want Sam back because he can't be alone more than anything else too. Having to go through the same emotions and feelings again that he kept to himself for a long time after losing Dad.

Notice when Sam breaks into the office, one of the first things the camera focuses on is the clown chair!

Sam didn't really need to apologize to Dean about what he said; re Dad (Dean didn't need to know he was right.) Perhaps making him feel this way so he can let out his emotions and begin to grieve properly. We know Sam wasn't fine at all, neither of them are, how could they be over Dad? Dean takes his anger out on his beloved car – the one Dad gave him, so in a way, he's taking his anger out on Dad too, for many reasons, but mostly for not being here (and in **2.4 Children Shouldn't**

Play With Dead Things) for doing what he did, i.e. his pact to save Dean.

First Dean says Sam spent half his life going against Dad's wishes and later he says, Sam spent his <u>entire</u> life fighting with him!

The funeral scene reminded me of *Beau Geste,* the book and the film when the surviving brother gave the others a proper send off by burning their bodies, like a Viking's send off in Norse mythology.

Alona Tal can be seen in *College; Kalamity. Veronica Mars.* She also guested on the **Crimson Casanova** episode of *The Mentalist.*

Quotes

Dean: "Come here, I wanna lay my head gently on your shoulders, maybe we can cry and hug and maybe even slow dance."

Sam: "Don't patronize me Dean! Dad is dead, the Colt is gone and it seems pretty damn likely the demon is behind it. Say something, say anything. Aren't you angry, don't you want revenge?!"

Dean: "...killer clown...Cooper clown...psycho carnie in clown suit...I know what you're thinking Sam, why does it have to be a clown...you still bust out crying whenever you see Ronald McDonald on television."

Dean: "What's the matter, you sound like you just saw a clown."
Sam: "Skeleton actually."

Dean: "I can't believe we keep talking about clowns." (Echoing Sam in **1.13 Route 666**, when he says he can't believe they keep talking about phantom trucks.)

Dean: "I hate fun houses." (Like Scully.)

Sam and Dean's Take on the Urban Legend/Lore

Sam and Dean ask if the rock salt hit it. So it's something dressing up as a clown. Ellen guesses it's a Raksasas, a race of ancient Hindu creatures, appear in human form and feed on human flesh. They're invisible but are invited in. They live in squalor, sleep on bed of dead insects and feed every 20-30 years. Legend says you need a dagger of pure brass to kill them.

Actual Legend

211

Raksasas: means to be guarded against, these are a class of demon. In Hindu religion, mythology, Lord Brahma took a body containing the quality of passion, this was known as the essence. In the darkness Brahma created vessels, or beings, emancipated with hunger. They were deformed, bearded and ran unto Brahma. "Those who said, 'No! Not Like that! Protect him" became known as the "Raksasas." Infesting Southern India and were controlled by the sage Agastya, who lived in a hermitage south of the Vindhya mountains and was the head sage in the South, he used his ascetic powers.

An urban legend tells of an intruder dressed as a clown, also known as *The Killer Clown Statue*; where a baby sitter looking after two girls, send them to bed. Telling her they can't sleep as a statue is watching them, they ask her to cover it. She finds a statue of a staring clown. Not wanting to damage it, she calls their mother about it; her reply is that they don't own such a statue. She tells them to leave the house and call the police.

The statue is found to be a midget dressed as a clown, who is a schizophrenic in a catatonic state, who had been hiding in the house for a week. (How understandable Dean's several comments of "clowns or midgets" sounds now!)

John Wayne Gacy used to don a clown's outfit to entertain at children's' parties and charity functions, but discarded the clown get up when torturing his victims.

Most people feel uneasy about clowns and many admit to having a morbid fear of them, mostly it's due to their make-up and its application; a sense of masking their true identity. (Easy to see why Sam hates clowns, not so much fearing them, with everything he's come across, he really feared what lurks beneath the painted face.)

The General Grant Center, a strip mall in St Louis, Missouri, has come to be named *Scary Clown Plaza*, due to a 15' clown statue. The local paper wrote, "…the sinister aura that seems to surround this supposedly jovial fellow, but too many folks from diverse backgrounds have commented on it to be just coincidence."

Did you know, in 1992, Noblesville, Indiana, a statue of *Ronald McDonald* (mentioned by Dean to tease Sam) fell onto a 6 year old girl, severing her fingertip. Damages were awarded. Perhaps one reason why he vanished from the *McDonald's* franchise for a while.

X Files Connection

In season 2 **Humbug** (also directed by Kim Manners) when Mulder and Scully check into the local motel, a trailer park, the proprietor is a midget. (Dean's encounter with the midget here.) Mulder and Scully also chase the "suspect" into a fun house. Kim Manners commented that casting "beat the bushes" and was also surprised on the show doing a comedy episode, which the fans clearly enjoyed.

Music

Shambala by Three Dog Night; *Do That To Me One More Time* by Captain and Tennille; *Time Has Come Today* by Chamber Brothers; *Mudd Walk* by Bad Poodle

Ooh Bloops

When Dean says to Jo, "Do you want to? At the end, it sounds like he says it in his Texan drawl.

Dean's hand holding the bottle at the end, the camera first shows him holding it from the top, then the bottom.

When they walk together and argue on the road, Sam doesn't hold a mobile phone.

Locations

Maple Ridge

2.3 Blood Lust

Written By Sera Gamble. Directed by Robert Singer.
Original US Airdate 12 October 2006

Guest Stars: Sterling K Brown (Gordon Walker); Amber Benson (Leonore); Samantha Ferris (Ellen); Ty Olsson (Eli)

Red Lodge. Montana

Sam and Dean come to the aid of some reformed vampires, whilst encountering another hunter, Gordon.

Notes

Oh finally! A woman is killed who turns out not to be a blonde! But a vamp! Seems lately, much pleases Dean, as Sam says, a pile of cow dung and a severed head make Dean happy. Dean's fixed his car finally, from last episode after giving it a beating. Now he's back on track with that relationship too! Dean wants Sam to look in the victim's mouth and notices the fangs.

Gordon calls Sam 'Chachi' from *Happy Days*. (In **4.15**, Pamela calls Dean Chachi.) He's come across their Dad too, who in hunting circles was probably a bit of a celeb then. He knew of their Dad's death, yet in **2.10**, he refers to him in the present tense rather than past, when he's holding Dean hostage.

Once more it's Sam and Dean who come to Gordon's rescue after saying he can handle the job himself. Also (once more) it's Dean and not Sam who has the grim task of decapitating and getting blood on his face and as Sam says and rightly so, decapitations aren't his idea of fun – as Dean and Gordon sit and celebrate their kill, or point in fact, Dean's kill. Dean's comment about knocking the 'buzz kill' out of Sam, which he does when he takes a swing at him after siding with Gordon instead of giving Sam the benefit of the doubt.

Dean seems to have found a "mentor" figure or kindred spirit or so he thinks, in Gordon. As he chooses to open up to him and talk about Dad and his own past, more so than he does with Sam. His excuse is he has to be brave for Sam's sake. The truth is he doesn't and Sam doesn't expect that of him either. Occasionally he'd like Dean to open up to him as that's what family is for in the end. Calling Dad indestructible – that nothing could kill him and you know what; nothing could, until he made that pact with Yellow Eyes. Gordon just appears to be feeding his own ego, as well as Dean's, by telling him everything he thinks Dean needs to hear; like his hole inside of him because of their respective losses (Gordon's sister and Dean's Dad.) which can only be there.

He's putting ideas into Dean's head that killing is everything and the only thing that'll keep him going when the simple truth is it is a crime to need the job. It won't keep you warm at night and it won't bring Dad back or help him through his grief either.

Sam meanwhile, confides in Ellen who gives him good advice in telling them they should stay away from Gordon. She does know him better than they do (and she's right about him too, when she tells Sam he's dangerous to everyone. As we find out in **2.10** in season 3.

Dean's right when he says Sam wouldn't agree with Gordon over his black and white analogy; that everything should be hunted and killed without question. Knowing Sam, we're sure that's something he always debates and encourages Dean to do too. Gordon's comment that Sam's different and he and Dean are born to hunt rings true, ironically even more in **2.10** when Gordon tries to kill Sam. Referring to chupracabras, and the cows being sucked by blood Dean not being able to recall the name of the paper and to easily be drawn in by Gordon, whereas Sam was more cautious, would've been the other way around as Sam is more 'worldly' than Dean, i.e. more experienced with talking with people. As for punching Sam, it felt as if he wanted to do that for a while, to settle an old score for leaving.

In this episode, it's Sam's turn to be knocked out and tied up – don't they appear to be letting their guard down lately, especially when they shouldn't with Yellow Eyes and his "disciples" out there. Also it's a shame Sam can't sense danger lurking right behind him – not like he could sense Ava in **2.10.**

Whilst Dean and Gordon are exchanging strategies on how to locate the vampires, Sam's already been found by them; taken and returned. Dean already thinks the same way as Gordon, i.e. if it's killable – kill it, which he reinforces here and Sam tells him what his job really is, i.e. hunting evil, not killing things that do no harm: here this particular group of vampires.

"Just like before, it's yesterday once more." Referring to Sam and Dean's constant bickering and lately over Dad, which will still continue until Dean talks about it and as I said before, Dean's filling up the place inside of him left by Dad with Gordon. Sam mentions the hole Dean's got and it hurts, just like Gordon did, but that Gordon's no substitute for Dad. Truth hurts and Sam gets punched for his troubles in trying to do the right thing by Dad and the vampires.

Gordon's story about his sister becoming a vampire is like that of Gunn in *Angel*.

Lenore, it seems, is living in a fantasy world where vampires and humans can live side by side.

That's far from the case, they can't. Maybe some vampires can adapt and change to survive without killing, but humans can't change, not all of them and especially not someone like Gordon; who didn't even think about killing his sister when she became a vampire. She was killed not for the sake of ending her misery because she was his sister, but because she was a vampire and that's all he saw: the hunt that needed to be destroyed. Just as he will with Sam in **2.10** which Sam works out again when he comments Gordon was killing these vampires anyway.

Even when he found out they weren't killing and feeding off humans. Gordon only sees Dean as a killer – just like himself, but Dean only answers him ambiguously in that he could be like Gordon or he couldn't.

Sam doesn't take the bait and to take a pot shot at Dean, and for his part wishes they didn't take this job. So what started out as a good day for Dean when he was all sunshine and smiles over this case, as well, turned out to be marred by meeting Gordon; slugging Sam and having to talk about Dad some more. Then Dean realizes they only hunted things which need to be hunted/killed and that was the best way Dad could raise them.

Dean even admits he enjoyed killing that vampire, probably because at that point he knew it was evil. They may have been raised to hate those things but it doesn't follow that everything they come across will need to be hunted. It's not surprising Dean says he was going to kill them all – judging from the last set of vampires they came across for the first time (**1.20 Dead Man's Blood**). They were evil and needed to be killed but his mistake was in following Gordon's lead thinking they're all like that.

When the Impala is shown fully repaired. AC/DC's *Back in Black* can be heard. Dean also played this in the Pilot when he meets up with Sam for the first time. The morgue attendant's badge says, 'J Manners', as in Manners, Kim.

Red Lodge is in South Montana.

Dean's quote of sleeping all day – was from the movie *Lost Boys*, i.e. "sleep all day. Party all night. Never grow old. Never die."

Dean: "Put the lotion in the basket" was a reference to Buffalo Bill in *Silence of the Lambs* where he'd shout to women he was holding captive, so they'd keep their skin moist; to kill and make suits from their skin later on.

Eric Kripke always wanted more actors to guest from similar genre shows like *Buffy, Angel*. "We made Amber the offer, sent her the script. She signed off on it. Hopefully, she was psyched about playing a vampire and that was a cool nod." So we're still waiting to see Eliza Dushku and Christian Kane guest star, for starters.

There are some scenes which are ad-libbed on the show, such as in this episode where Sam's afraid of clowns; they added some lines which weren't in the script and which were new to Jared as well since obviously he wouldn't have read or rehearsed them.

'86 them' means to 'get rid off'.

Eric said: "I think about doing an episode where the monster turns out not to be the bad guy and where the hunter turns out to be the bad guy." Sera Gamble: "Therefore characters Lenore and Gordon came about." Eric: "Lenore was a killer for a very long time but grew tired of all these hunters hunting her kind to death. She decided that the best way to survive would be to blend in so Sera said, 'We don't hunt monsters, we hunt evil.' There's a difference."

Sterling K Brown is in Army *Wives,* was in, *Starved, Third Watch.* He says, "I feel the atmosphere of any set is established by its leads, and Jared and Jensen create a wonderfully productive environment that is extremely playful at the same time. I learned a lot of what it means to be gracious by the example they put forth."

Amber Benson was working on a novel, entitled, *Death's Daughter.*

Quotes

Sam: "If you two wanna get a room."

Sam: "He's the only one who gets to call me that." (I.e. Sammy)

Dean: "We find 'em, we waste 'em. If it's supernatural we kill it. End of story. That's our job."
Sam: "No, it's not. Our job is hunting evil and if these things aren't killing people, they're not evil."

Gordon: "You're a killer like me."
Dean: "I might be like you and I might not…"

Actual Legend

Vampires' unanswered questions: at least questions you pose and ponder and don't find answers to. Most commonly: vampires don't have hearts; hence no heart beats or blood circulation. So where does the blood they suck head to, other than straight to their hips, I mean, stomach. More importantly why d they need this blood?: To survive but it's not helping with other bodily functions associated with blood, such as, breathing, brain function, clotting – so no ability to heal, or even the all important process of digestion; digesting the blood they drink and egesting, i.e. expelling the blood, or its by-products later on! If vampires can't carry out these functions, what happens to the beer they seemed to guzzle in episodes?

Dean says he's not into necrophilia, which for the purposes of *Supernatural* mythology implies when a vampire has sex with a human, that's exactly what they do.

Traditional ways to kill: stake through the heart of wood, the stake that is not a wooden heart! Holy water, fire; exposure to the sun; beheading. For *Supernatural* folklore, only the latter works. Though exposure to sunlight has some effect, it's not so deadly or definitive.

Oh and a bullet from the special colt made by Samuel Colt (for whom Sam is not named!).

Dead Man's Blood appears to make them weak, though why this is the case as opposed to live man's blood (does that mean women's blood too, sexist!) presumably living blood is warm and hasn't been exposed to the air; any contaminants and filters through a breathing heart. Dead Man's Blood, obviously lying stagnant in a dead body and no longer possessing the qualities of blood. (But it was fresh dead man's blood in this episode.) This still makes vampires cold blooded, immortal.

Repelled by holy water, crosses, garlic. Usually can't enter a home unless invited, but can frequent public places: of course in old movies, this wasn't the case since they'd always enter, usually through a window for a bite.

Have no souls; look human except for possessing fangs, pale looking or anemic looking. Usually invisible. Fangs here were found underneath the gums and so were retractable. If a vampire makes its victim drink its blood they will rise from the dead as a vampire. Vampires kill by draining the blood from its victim. A process known as exsanguination – the medical term, causing the victim to die from blood loss and if used to feed from several times can look pale and anemic (i.e. lacking iron in the blood.) Perhaps this is what vampires need from the blood to survive some cultures sew the mouth shut and douse holy water on the lips of the dead. The soul is believed to leave the body from the mouth and this is where evil can enter. In Greece, consecrated earth is placed on the lips of the dead.

Film/TV References

Silence of the Lambs

X Files Connection

Gordon mentions Sam and Dean should hunt chupacabra, which is Spanish for *goat sucker*. Livestocks are killed and marks are left behind on their necks and are drained of their blood. Originally thought to be half human and half vampire. The closest relative known to the chupacabra is the *Jersey Devil*. (See *X Files*). The creature has an arm and legs but can run on all four and is described as being like a kangaroo with such attributes.

Read lore and tales of this on the web, they're both amusing and fascinating at the same time.

Music

Back in Black by AC/DC; *Wheel in the Sky* by Journey; *Golden Rules* by Lil' Ed & the Blues Imperials; *Time and Time Again* by Long John Hunter; *Funny Car Graveyard* by Lee Rocker

Ooh Bloops

Lenore appears to choke when Gordon gives her blood, yet vampires aren't supposed to be able to breathe. So maybe it was meant to be more of a painful motion than choking.

When Gordon fights Dean, he breaks the table, which sticks up, broken in two. Part of the table then vanishes.

Locations

Pitt Meadows

2.4 Children Shouldn't Play With Dead Things

Written By Raelle Tucker. Directed By Kim Manners
US Airdate 19 October 2006

Guest Stars: Tamara Feldman (Angela Mason); Christopher Jacot (Neil); Jared Keeso (Matt)

Lawrence, Kansas

Sam wants to return home to visit Mom's grave. Dean stumbles upon a new case at the cemetery and finally reveals his true feelings about Dad and how he saved Dean.

Notes

The alternate title to this episode was **Afterlife.** The present title was the name of a 1972 zombie film, where actors perform black magic in a graveyard, making the dead bodies rise and kill them.

Dean doesn't really want to do much of anything at first in the opening of this episode and reluctantly agrees to take Sam because it's better than going to the roadhouse. The only thing Sam brings of Dad's is his dog tags and buries them. There's only a headstone for Mom, but he misses the point: that it's hers and that's something an uncle did,

Dad didn't even do that for her. He just let her go or did he say goodbye in his own way – something he must've done. Dad's dog tags carry information from his army days: he was AB blood type and he wasn't religious. Funny he then turned to religion (to fight demons using religious paraphernalia) and married Mary who was religious. A bit like Dean who also wasn't religious to begin with and still isn't. (See season 3 and 4.)

George A Romero was the director of the zombie films such as, *Night of the Living Dead, Dawn of the Dead.*

"Unrequited ducky love" is from the movie, *Pretty in Pink* where Ducky was in love with his best friend, but she didn't feel the same.

Mary Winchester 1954-1983 Beloved Mother.

Why did they go back to Mom's grave now and not when they went home the first time round?

Sam guesses something's going on with Dean but it's not about Mom – it's about Dad really. Only Sam believes Dean's looking for a hunt where there isn't one, only to avoid all sorts of, mostly personal issues.

In this episode, their characters are reversed too. Sam plays Scully to Dean's Mulder (not in that Dean keeps calling him Scully and a girl!) but he thinks there's nothing paranormal happening here, Dean just needs to believe there is – like Mulder – but of course Dean's right (he's older!) He does treat Angela's father disrespectfully, jumping to conclusions without proof when he thinks he's behind it all. Especially as he's taking his own frustrations out on him (just as he does to Ethan in **2.8 Crossroad Blues**). He needs to vent his anger but goes about it the wrong way.

Becoming grief counsellors as a cover, appropriate under the circumstances though Dean needs one of his own. I think deep down Dean really did want to pay his respects to Mom but couldn't. Perhaps if he wasn't in 'mourning' and having guilty feelings. Conversely that's probably what made Sam do it even more. Dean finally opening up and crying over Dad was welcome to see.

Even heroes cry and have their off days. Making him more human in our eyes than just being a cute killing machine, so to speak. Reinforcing his feeling that his coming back had something to do with Dad and that's why he was feeling guilty, alone. As I said before, he shouldn't have said 'what's dead should stay that way. He did sound ungrateful in a way, especially when he realized his being alive did have something to do with Dad.

Well for starters – it's true and Dad did "die" for Dean, making that small sacrifice for him, so he should stop saying he shouldn't be here because it sounds selfish and like what Dad did for him means nothing. Wouldn't any parent make any less of a sacrifice for their child?

You could tell how guilty Dean was feeling throughout this entire episode with the way he was keeping his real feelings from Sam. Did he not want to burden him or was it because Sam wouldn't understand, thinking he's wallowing in self pity. The way he kept saying "what's dead should stay dead'; when it was apparent he was talking about himself.

Secondly, to make him feel better he could have that group hug he wanted Neil to have with them, of course we'd all be in on that! No-seriously – now he's opened up and said what he's really thinking and feeling. It'd be a start for him to come to terms with losing Dad (which from my own personal experience – is easier said than done) and for still being here.

Cf the guilt part of the stages of grief – which will be familiar to anyone who's studied 'Psych 101' and to a few who haven't, so they were around in various stages and different episodes. (See **2.1**)

If Dean's got guilt – then Sam has guilt of his own for not being there all those years and now he feels he has to make it up in some small way. That's why this time round (Season 2) hunting is so important to him. Whereas Dean feels, "Oh Hang it!" Dad's not around – why or who are they doing this for anymore anyway. Though you can tell he's out for revenge as he puts so much more determination into his hunts, the kill factor, loose cannon – and why he's so easily swayed by Gordon in the previous episode.

Deep down is Sam punishing himself for not being around to help out, no matter how much he loved Dad, loves Dad – he can't forget what he's done and feels hurt for it. Dean won't let him forget either with his "too little too late" comment in **2.2 Everybody Loves A Clown**. Anyone else would've put their hunting on hold to grieve.

Dean, in any other show, would be deemed no better than a killer – able and willing to take a human life, Meg, Tom in season **1.22**; the infected woman in **2.9 Croatoan**. So much for worrying about Sam becoming a murderer. Perhaps circumstances necessitated such action make it justifiable. Yet when Sam says this about Andy in **2.5 Simon Says** when he shoots his brother

Dean calls him a hero for saving people. (Dean thinking of porn and sex at all the wrong moments in this episode or did he think of nothing else! Probably Sam setting it all off by the porn channel on TV!)

Dean's comment of "hell hath no fury like a woman scorned" is also appropriate or apt in this storyline. Again Dean calls Sam , 'lady' this time and jumps to conclusions for the second time when he finds

Ancient Greek writing in the coffin and accuses her father once more of dabbling in the dark art. He doesn't look the type to be doing all this.

When Dean refers to "what's dead is dead" he's talking about himself and just as in **1.12 Faith;** he says he shouldn't have been saved and brought back. (Saying it twice in the same episode – this time they (dead) should stay gone.) It wasn't meant to be – his destiny was already written for him and it changed twice. Firstly by Sam going to the faith healer and then in **2.1** by Dad giving his own life and more importantly his soul to save Dean. Compare to Sam saying they can't change his own destiny in **2.5** and in **2.11** where he wants to try to alter it.

Dean kept saying he shouldn't have come back but in the season 2 finale he does exactly the same thing for Sam, he goes and sells his soul and only for a year to bring Sam back. Sam never said he should've stayed in that state, i.e. dead.

Even at such times, Dean alludes to film analogies. Sam wants to help him, Dean won't let him in, he chooses to hunt; do exactly what Gordon said in **2.3** because it's the only thing that keeps him going.

Dean calling Sam's favourite the silver bullet as he'll use it in **2.17 Heart**, when he kills Madison the werewolf.

When Dean mentions about things staying dead, if he really knew the sacrifice made, the ultimate sacrifice to bring him back (and I know I keep going on about this) he wouldn't say that anymore, especially if he knew Dad gave his life to save one close to him, who he loves; I'm almost close to quoting Sidney Carton in Charles Dickens *A Tale of Two Cities*, hang on that would be appropriate here, 'I would make any sacrifice to save one dear to her (Lucy Manette, whom he loves) which can be paraphrased here, having said that, Dean does suspect Dad saved him.

Perhaps Sam should've told him to stop saying that and be grateful he's been given a third chance at life! See **1.12** Faith, where Dean also felt this way, i.e. regretting the way he was saved by someone else losing their life (this time Dad) but he seemed to accept it then, eventually. Maybe someone should say some things are out of our control. Let's lighten the mood with my joke, hey if possession is nine tenths of the law (or lore) how come we're not all walking around like evil zombies?!" Ha!! (Okay, I've said it before elsewhere, but it's better here, since this is a zombie episode.)

Angela is a zombie and they usually attack humans to devour their brains. However, Angela was a corpse who was reanimated for the purposes of unrequited love by her paramour. Also she's out for revenge, killing her ex, then going after his girlfriend, her best friend;

before finding out her 'lover' was going to betray her. This zombie, then, not portrays the usual characteristics. (Well it is *Supernatural* lore.)

All these sexual references by Dean. Has he really seen *Beaches?* Maybe with some chick! That's probably the only way you'd get Dean to watch a chick flick! Then again he does seem to watch everything.

Finally what we've been waiting for, we got to hear Dean's confession, of sorts. That Dad died to save Dean and it's his entire fault. That's only half of the truth he's told Sam, not the promise to Dad about Sam (yet). Also being back in Lawrence, (still home to strange goings-on) they didn't look in on Missouri (**1.9 Home.**)

Sam could possibly say a lot to make it right: life goes on; it was Dad's decision to make, no one else's; not Dean's fault, if he wants to blame anyone, then blame Yellow Eyes. No, what they could've said is that no one wanted to be hero of the hour or he didn't want his brother in that dangerous situation on his own.

Jared fell and broke his wrist, shown when the zombie, Angela's chasing him, he trips and says she broke his wrist. Hence, had to wear a cast on his right wrist for numerous episodes. "We're still fighting and holding guns so you can't really avoid seeing it, so they figured roll with the punches. We had an episode where a zombie [this one] is running after me and we're trying to trick her into going back into her own grave and she tackles me and I fall on my wrist, so that's how I did it. If I was still on *Gilmore Girls*, it would be hard to explain a broken hand. [Not really they could say he had a sports injury, or broke it stacking shelves, ha.] But Sam and Dean are running around causing a ruckus so it's much more believable that these guys would get hurt and also I'm happy because it frustrates me when we do a show and I'm cut up and bruised and my arm is in a sling, and then the next day I'm sparkly and clean. We call it Warner Bros ointment."

As for stunts, continues Jared, "maybe the fact I broke my wrist is the reason why they won't let me do any of my own stunts. It was actually not so much of a stunt but almost like an act of God that I fell in a fight scene. The camera had a close up of me and I hit the back of my head and fell out of the frame. As I was falling to brace myself there was still a stunt guy right in my way – so I sort of had to jut out my hand to catch myself and just snapped my wrist. I can't describe it other than a one in a million bizarre chance."

Kim Manners: "Zombies have been portrayed as walking stiff and that kind of thing. I always try to directionally give it real human emotion. Just put the pale make-up on her and give her a human spirit.

If you play her like a dead person walking around stiff it becomes a cartoon."

Dean's use of 'Alan Stanwick' was the name of a man in Chevy Chase's *Fletch*, where he played a reporter who could come up with 'instant aliases' for himself.

The title is from a Bob Clark zombie movie, *Children Shouldn't Play With Dead Things.*

Quotes

Sam: "…about her memory and after Dad, I just felt it's the right thing to do."
Dean: "It's irrational that's what it is."

Dean: "I get it, there are people that I would give anything to see again but what gives you the right. What's dead should stay dead!"

Sam: "Our lives are weird man."

Dean: "When someone's gone, they should stay gone. You don't mess with that kind of stuff."

Dean: "...I was dead and I should've stayed dead. You wanted to know how I was feeling, well that's it. So tell me what could you possibly say to make that all right?"

Sam and Deans' Take on the Urban Legend/Lore

The Ancient Greek Demonation Ritual used to bring back corpses to life: necromancy. They first think it could be a vengeful spirit but dismiss it when all the plants and flowers are dead, just like in the cemetery. Dean says zombies can't be shot in the head; Sam's favourite, silver bullet may work. Dean says there are over a hundred different legends on the walking dead. Kill them by setting fire to them, feeding their hearts to wild dogs. Sam mentions nailing the undead back into their grave beds and that's most likely where the staking vampires' lore originated. Notice in **1.20 Dead Man's Blood**, Dad says the whole staking a vampire lore doesn't work.

Actual Legend

Necromancy "actively seeks out the spirits of the dead" who have knowledge of information, not available to anyone else; or the conjuring the dead for divination, practiced by magicians, witches in Persia, Rome. It was outlawed in Elizabethan England under the Witchcraft Act 1604. (Perhaps something Parliament still needs today.) A practice commonly used in Voodoo. Where it involves either conjuring the spirit of the dead body; or summoning the corpse itself.

Zombies are present in cultures ranging in India, China, Japan, Native Americans. Are also associated with medieval Norse mythology where "dravgr" were the dead bodies of warriors brought back to wage war on the living.

Film/TV References

Stephen King's Pet Semetary. Beaches. Romero films.

X Files Connection

7.5 Millennium, Mulder believes necromancy is involved.

Music

Sad Girl by Supergrass

Locations

Van Dusen Botanical Gardens. Harbour Park. Barklay Manor. Strathcona.

2.5 Simon Said

Written By Ben Edlund. Directed By Tim Lacofano
Original US Airdate 26 October 2006

Guest Stars: Samantha Ferris (Ellen); Chad Lindberg (Ash); Elias Toufexis (Weber/Anson); Gabriel Tigerman (Andrew Gallagher); Blu Mankuma (Dr Jennings); Chiara Zanni (Tracy)

Sam has a disturbing vision of events and as they try to save the intended victims, Sam finds they can't be saved. Sam and Dean also encounter another with psychic abilities who has a deadlier twin.

Notes

Sam and Dean have another conversation about Sam's destiny of becoming a killer because it's so relevant to this episode, in particular, and Dean telling him the only things they kill are asking for it. Which reminds you that Dean also killed Meg, Tom; when they were possessed but still human inside? So yes there was a difference as he says, but not that much. See seasons 3 and 4.

Best bit was when Dean talked into giving up his car by Andy. He wouldn't let anyone drive it. Dean mentions there are no clown paintings on the walls, another reference to clowns, thought that was left behind.

Dean tells Andy the truth when he asks him and opens up admitting his own fears that Sam might be right and may become a killer after all. It doesn't work on Sam and it's not meant to since they're all connected in a way. It wouldn't suit Yellow Eyes' plans if their psychic mojo could work on each other. That'd defeat the purpose of this war that's on the horizon since those like Andy could just talk each other out of the killings. (However see the two part season finale, where the special ones are able to use their powers on each other.) Here Sam is immune to Andy's powers since he's meant to be the chosen one out of them all and has to lead the demon army. (Again see the 2 part finale.)

Sam's vision of the woman at the gas station comes too late for some reason and the woman turns out to have been Andy's birth mother, which if analyzed means Sam wasn't meant to save her and she should've been dead a long time ago, like Mom, but wasn't killed back then. So why now? Was it because she gave him up for adoption or was the weather pattern not appropriate for Yellow Eyes to make his move, though his adoptive mother died. More likely, it was Weber who killed her, under the influence of Yellow Eyes. Andy was born in 1983, like Sam. Did yellow Eyes make a mistake back then, hardly likely, but they explain the doctor dies because he was involved in the adoption and Andy was a twin. Sam has another vision of Tracy and this time they're not too late.

Dean calls Andy a hero for saving them – not a killer, his actions were inevitable. So will it be inevitable for Sam becoming a murderer too. Sam knows Dean's scared too now and Dean admits they don't know what Yellow Eyes wants and Sam shouldn't worry, that won't really help him. (Sam will use his abilities to kill in Season 4, only it'll be demons, at least for now.)

When Andy "mind controlled" Dean, he didn't blab about his promise to Dad which is always on Dean's mind. He just says he hopes Sam won't become a killer. That was annoying about this episode, that Andy got everything from Dean about who they are and what they do, except for that bit. Could Dean really subconsciously retain that piece of information to himself?

Dean telling Sam to stop worrying about his destiny, whereas Dean does far from that, he worries about Sam like hell. Here Sam says he was forced into this, back into hunting after Jessica's death. See **1.22** where Sam says Dean made him come back into this. When in actual fact, he was correct here, Sam went back to hunting because Jessica was killed.

Dean doesn't want to tell Ellen anything (well he already did enough talking, but Sam does all the talking and tells her everything, including about his psychic abilities.) Dean still wants to believe they're all dangerous because he doesn't want Sam becoming like that: an uncontrollable killer. (See seasons 3 and 4.)

Calling themselves freaks and non-freaks, they've done it so many times in jest that Sam seems surprised at Dean calling him a freak again, now that he's getting more premonitions. Yes, we know Dean was always the freaky one.

Jo's into *REO Speedwagon*. Dean admits to being afraid of Ellen (see next episode.) Dean sings some lines from the car radio and Sam can't believe it, but then Sam was there too, he must've heard the same song playing on the jukebox.

Dean mentions clown paintings, John Wayne Gacy Jr, serial killer, killed 32 men in 1970's Chicago. He used to visit children in hospital, dress as a clown for child parties. He collected clowns and also painted them.

Weber's quote of making people do what they want, referred to *Stephen King's Firestarter*, where telepathic hypnosis is known as 'push'.

Quotes

Sam: "So I'm a freak now."
Dean: "You've always been a freak."

Dean: "You're not a murderer Sam; you don't have it in your bones."
Sam: "No, last I checked, I killed all kinds of things."
Dean: "Those things were asking for it, there's a difference."

Actual Legend

Mind control or the concept of it, was seen in the fourteenth and fifteenth centuries when witches were burned at the stake since they could force people into committing sins for Satan.

Film/TV References

Star wars. Final Destination: Death still comes for its intended victims, only it's not death, but Weber, influenced by Yellow Eyes.

X Files Connection

This episode had some familiarities with the Season 2 episode **Ghost in the Machine** as fans of the show will recall. This episode was about a computer with artificial intelligence which kills, but unlike *Supernatural*, the killings are to preserve itself. (So was Yellow Eyes.) Can argue Andy's twin, Weber, was also doing this in some respects although he claimed to be killing only after he saw Yellow Eyes in his dreams, urging him to kill. As strangely some of the protagonists in *the X Files* used to get phonecalls telling them to commit the murderous deed.

At the end of the episode, the computer leaves a message, "Bye bye, all done." When it's completed its rampage. Here, Weber says "bye bye" to Dean just as he 'controls' him into putting the gun to his chin in order to shoot himself. Incidentally this episode also guest starred Blu Mankuma.

Also see the episode from Season 3: **Pusher**, where the 'Pusher' has the power to cause people to do what he wills. Note the scene where, under 'Pusher's' influence and suggestion, an FBI agent is told to douse himself in gas and set fire to himself, just as the twins mother was told to do in this episode. Here Weber says he can "push them" into doing what he wants. Dean also comments Andy was "pushed" into killing Weber. As does Sam, "Demon's pushing" us. Mulder echoes Scully, "He was always such a little man…was so finally something that made him feel big." Isn't Dean like Mulder anyway, like both having a penchant for porn?

In **Blood**, digital readouts in electrical appliances telling people to "Kill 'em all." Mulder said it was sending subliminal messages. He then got a call on his cell, with the message, "All Done. Bye Bye."

The episode, **Syzygy**, Mulder wonders if two people, here two girls born on the same date, could become the focus of unseen forces. As Sam here and some of the children born in the same year become the focus of Yellow Eyes; but later it's found other children don't fit this pattern.

The End, Mulder thinks a young boy; Gibson Praise can read minds and may possess alien genes. Similar to Sam and all the children like him who possess special powers, though more demonic than alien.

6.9 Tithonus. A man, who is a crime scene photographer, suspected of being involved in the murders he photographs. He points to a woman about to die and she is run over by a truck. Mulder finds his fingerprints on records as far back as 149 years. He claims to see people who are about to die in black and white. Notable for the psychic (psychotic?) vision episodes of *Supernatural.*

Music

Uncle John by Eric Lindell; *Can't Fight this Feeling* by REO Speedwagon; *Stonehenge* by Spinal Tap; *Fell on Black Days* by Soundgarden; *Tired of Crying* by Lil' Ed & The Blues Imperials; *Women's Wear* by MasterSource

Ooh Bloops

When the doctor walks to the store in Sam's vision, he talks to people, when he walks there for real, he doesn't speak to anyone. Andy's ear cuffs were on his left ear in this episode and then on his right ear in **2.21**.

Locations

Delta and Ladner. Delta Automotive. Massey's Marine Supply. Delta Museum and Archives. Cleveland Dam (also used in *Smallville* and *Dark Angel.*)

2.6 No Exit

Written By Matt Witten. Directed By Kim Manners
Original US Airdate 2 November 2006

Guest Stars: Alona Tal (Jo); Samantha Ferris (Ellen); Stephen Aberle (H H Holmes.)

Philadelphia, Pennsylvania

A woman disappears from her apartment. Ellen asks Sam and Dean to look into it, but Jo is already there.

Notes

Dean's jokes about Katie Holmes being kidnapped by a cult and Sam saying that's really bitchy coming from him, when usually it's Dean who calls Sam the bitchy one or "bitch." (See **2.11** where Sam suggests Dean comes across all butch, so this was an aberration for Dean, i.e. being bitchy.) The woman is abducted in the opening, just as Dean reads the newspaper about another 'abduction'.

Jo wanting to know what Sam and Dean think about her wanting to hunt, as if they're the right ones to ask – especially since Dean's afraid of Ellen and Sam respects her too much. Ellen doesn't want her to leave because she's already lost her father and hunting shouldn't be for her. Which Dean tries to tell her when he's away from Ellen – far away – in Philadelphia. Yet more <u>blondes</u> going missing here, in fact the killer's specialty is blondes and Jo just happens to be one too.

Dean's joke about dealing with the Marshmallow Man, who incidentally didn't ooze black slime (See *X Files*.) Black slime is ectoplasm.

Jo calls Dean, "Deano!" Hey she can't, I called him that ever since the Pilot episode! As for Jo saying she left behind a paper trail for Ellen after telling her she's going to Vegas, does she really think her mother's so dumb she'll fall for it. Especially since Ellen has MIT genius Ash on her side, who is also afraid of her.

Jo is being presumptuous when she tells Dean to untwist his boxers – does she even know he wears them, or has she been snooping through his stuff! (See **1.11 Hookman** when Dean tells Sam to stay out of Laurie's underwear drawer.) On a serious note, Dean tells her not lie to her mother because he lies to Sam and it's not okay! So he shouldn't do that either!

Just like Dean, Jo also got money to fund her trip, playing poker. Having just said what he did, Ellen calls Dean and what does he do, he lies to her and says Jo isn't here. After lying, he won't let Jo be alone (what Jo wants all along!) and has to keep her safe or feel the wrath of Ellen, even to the point where Jo tells Dean he sounds just like her mother when he gives her some good advice! What they do isn't a game and she could get hurt because she's an amateur; but she wants to prove herself and ignores his advice. He was not being sexist, he's all for equality.

Sam disappears most of this episode to allow Jo to hunt (darn!) and Dean still has notions of being able to do something different other than this 'job' and he admits he still loves it, but that's just him. On the other hand, we know he's really disillusioned and has doubts about wanting to continue. The first thought Dean has about Dad is when he took him shooting bottles. Coincidentally what he remembers about Dad happens to be about guns!

Jo wants to hunt so she can be close to her father. She wants to hunt for him, like Sam says he does. Isn't it strange how serial killers, killers, when they're caught, fear the same thing happening to them, i.e. what they did to their victims.

Dean's been caught out, he lied and promises to get Jo back, something Ellen's heard before, from Dad.

Was that one truck of cement enough to fill up that entire sewer entrance and yes the rock salt will wash away, that sewer was full of water?

Obviously Ellen has a big axe to grind – Dad got her husband killed, after trusting his life to him and now Jo did the same thing in trusting Sam and Dean. Jo tells them about Dad getting their father killed, though there are no details and tells them that's why he didn't come back to see Ellen. Ellen later tells Sam that she forgave their Dad a long time ago and by telling Jo this now, she was trying to discourage her from hunting; but has the opposite effect since she now goes off on her own. Whereas before, perhaps she would've hung around a bit longer. Hunting is in her blood.

"As cold as ice…" suitably plays on the radio at the end.

'Stay puff Marshmallow Man' was from *Ghostbusters*. Jensen and Jared like the shapeshifter episodes. Oh why did I mention that here.

Quotes.

Sam: "Funny and for you, so bitchy."
Dean: "On the other hand, cat fight."

Ellen: "That is why you don't have the sense to do this job right – you're trusting your life to them – like father, like son."

Sam and Dean's Take on the Urban Legend/Lore

Moyamensing built 1835, destroyed 1953, men were executed in the field where the building stands. Sam mentions Henry Webster Mudgett, real name HH Holmes a multi-murderer. He was America's first serial killer. All his victims were blondes. His body was in concrete. Built secret chambers in the walls.

Actual Legend

Henry H Holmes – actual name Herman M Mudgett went to medical school and had a great obsession with anatomy. At an early age he would dismember animals. Attending medical school at the University of Michigan, he stole cadavers from there and took out insurance policies on them beforehand. Later, expelled from university when his theft was found out. Bought a plot of land. The building he constructed came to be known as 'Murder Castle'. The guests, who stayed there, would never leave. The rooms were filled with traps, trapdoors, alarms, to alert him of any possible escapes, and he would watch his victims die.

The castle was rumoured to have been burned down in 1895, by an accomplice. Holmes admitted killing 27, men, women and children. He was hanged in 1896 and asked for the bottom of his coffin to be filled with ten foot of cement and then be buried. His coffin was filled with cement and nailed. Grave was buried ten feet deep and two feet of sand and cement were poured into the open grave before being covered with soil. The legend of Holmes known as the Holmes Curse, which said his restless spirit was seeking revenge on the people associated with him, as all met violent ends.

Hence Dean uses cement to pour down the sewer entrance and bury him forever.

Music

Mama by Godsmack; *Surrender* by Cheap Trick; *Cold as Ice* by Foreigner

Ooh Bloops

Jo says Moyamensing was built in 1835 until 1963. It was actually built 1832-1835 and demolished 1968.

When Sam and Dean open the drain, the camera shows them from below. Dean gives Sam the gun with his hand on it. When Sam and Dean are shown from above; Dean is holding the bottom of the gun and Sam takes it by the barrel.

When Sam, Dean and Jo talk of Holmes, there's a photo of Elizabeth Stude, who was actually meant to have been killed by Jack the Ripper!

2.7 The Usual Suspects

Written By Cathryn Humphris. Directed By Mike Rohl
Original US Airdate 9 November 2006

Guest Stars: Linda Blair (Det. Diane Ballard); Jason Gedrick (Det. Peter Sheridan); Shannon Powell (Claire); Keegan Connor Tracy (Karen Giles)

Baltimore, Maryland

Dean is arrested and held in custody for the St Louis murder. Sam is arrested too and they find a spirit is haunting people.

Notes

Mention Mulder and Scully all the way through practically – at least I have and now they actually mention them too, with Dean alluding to Sam as Scully, always the girl! This episode has Dean arrested for murder, once again being picked up for the outstanding St Louis murder too (**1.6 Skin**) the one committed by his shapeshifter. How come no one recalls the dead body they buried had Dean's face, so it had to have been Dean, he didn't exactly have a twin, but that's forgotten here. i.e. that it could've been a case of mistaken identity. Probably checked out his fingerprints. (Still no one would believe that now there'd not really be much of the dead body left to exhume anyway.). The St Louis police made a botch up of that case then. How could he have faked his death, wasn't he buried with Dean's face, since Dean said at the end of that episode he'll miss his own funeral.

This episode sets forward events – like another outstanding warrant for Dean, to add another dimension to the show (**2.12**) as Sam and Dean become the hunted, as well as having to carry **on hunting**; avoiding the law and with the two of them also having the burden of making sure Sam stays Sam and doesn't become a killer. Things seem to go from bad to worse for them since last season episodes and the season opener.

Reckon they're becoming a bit careless, though it's no fault of their own. They should be taking extra precautions. Maybe Dean was right when he said they should leave hunting for a while, at least. Perhaps they need to lay low and off the police radar. Yeah, that'll happen as **2.12** puts them right dab in the centre of yet more police involvement I was going to write brutality oops! This time from the FBI. It just doesn't get any easier for them. It appears the more they help, the deeper they get themselves into trouble (and we wouldn't have it any other way.)

Dean's questions again about hearing anything strange, as he always does. Sam lies to Diane when he tells her Karen gave them the key, actually they broke in.

Sam and Dean both working on the name and reach the conclusion: at the same time *Danaschulp* written everywhere, is an anagram for Ashland, a street name. Great minds (and bodies!)…

The policeman saying they have Dean's fingerprints from St Louis, as I said, the police there didn't do a very good job since they did find the killer, i.e. Dean's shapeshifter form, dead. So why was the warrant still out on him?

Matlock is mentioned once more (also in **1.5 Bloody Mary**, **2.10**.) by Sam and Dean. Dean's confession sounds more like he's making a video for a dating agency and yes he must be into his horoscopes as he mentions star signs in **1.16** too and his own this time in the show, Aquarius. (Jensen is actually Pieces.) and no, he doesn't look the type to enjoy walks on beaches and fishing! Well, depends on what he's fishing for.

Dean tells the truth; naturally no one's going to believe him. As for 'Redrum' that's another reference to *The Shining*. (Also see **2.11 Playthings**.) Surely everyone's heard of the movie classic, *The Great Escape*, starring Steve McQueen.

Spirits usually end up appearing in mirrors. Sam and Dean really are into their TV shows aren't they (as we are *Supernatural* is concerned.) since they thought of finding Jim Rockford in *Yellow Pages* when they're in trouble. Jim Rockford, the main character from the show *The Rockford Files*, had his private investigations business advert in the phonebook. (This method of finding each other didn't work in **2.10** when Sam left Dean to search his destiny.)

Sam telling Diane to use 'lojack', she's a cop why didn't she think of this when she found out Pete was driving a police van.

The in-joke at the end when Dean asks Sam if she looks familiar to him, i.e. from *The Exorcist* and his mention of pea soup, Yuk! Which he's said before.

The Nick Nolte reference by Dean was from when he was arrested for drink driving in California and his mug shot was used extensively in the press.

That St Louis part was niggling and as for her telling everyone they've escaped, which they did, she could've told them it was mistaken identity.

Dean under arrest like the *Dark Angel* episode, **Hello, Goodbye** when Alec was arrested for the murders carried out by Ben because of his face. (Alec was Ben's clone.)

They enjoyed working with Lind Blair in this episode. Jensen said, "She was a lot of fun to work with. She takes her work very seriously but she has a good sense of humour about it and it was interesting to talk about her experiences on *The Exorcist*. She said she got fan mail from devil worshippers because she played the devil. One said, 'Come marry me and we'll rule the world'."

Eric Kripke: "Linda took some more getting. We actually went to her first to play the preacher's wife in **Faith**. We made an offer to her in season 1 and she was a fan of the show but turned us down because she didn't want to play a supernatural bad guy. She had her fill of playing demonic evil. Then this other role came around for this female detective and that was right around the studio was calling and we pitched her part and she liked it. It's horror royalty. Now all I need is Bruce Campbell on the show and then I can die a happy man."

Quotes

Dean: "What'd think Scully, wanna check it out?"
Sam: "I'm not Scully, you're Scully!"
Dean: "No, I'm Mulder, you're a red-headed woman."

Sam and Dean's Take on the Urban Legend/Lore

Spirits normally end up appearing or being reflected in mirrors. Think it could be a vengeful spirit. The spirit is leaving a word behind and so "communicating across a veil". The words are coming out wrong but it's similar to 'Redrum'. Dean explains vengeful spirits are created by violent deaths, and come back for a reason, e.g., for revenge against those that caused it pain.

Sam says it's not a vengeful spirit but a death omen; she's trying to warn them. Occasionally spirits want justice and lead them to their killer. After Pete is killed the death omen should be at peace now. The 'P' in 'Danaschulp' was for Pete, her killer. Or for 'police' partially.

Actual Legend

Death omens are plentiful in cultures, which outline birds, cats, bats or black dogs. Folklore and superstitions mention ghosts as one and the appearance denotes the onset of something bad. These ghosts are either unknown, strangers or family members.   They appear before the occurrence, but cannot forewarn or foretell what this event will be and also cannot stop it from happening.

Danaschulps is an anagram from the Greek, ana meaning again and *graphin* meaning to write.   Letters are arranged in a word, phrase to make new word, but the letters from the first word can only be used once. Another example of an anagram was that of "All work and no play makes Jack a dull boy" Jack Nicholson's quote from *The Shining*, movie and book. Where he types it again and again.

Film/TV References

The Great Escape, ChiPs, Matlock, Rockford Files

X Files Connection

In **4.22 Elegy**, a spirit is encountered by a girl with the writing, "She is me," etched onto a bowling alley. Mulder holds the apparitions in the case are of importance. Scully sees the apparition of a woman when she's in the bathroom. Mulder believes only those who are close to death can see the apparition.

Ooh Bloops

In the hotel room with Diana, Sam puts on his jacket, in the next shot, he's holding his jacket.

When Diana reads Sam's file, he crosses his arms, then does this again in the next scene.

Locations

Point Grey. Granville Street at 41 Street.

2.8 Crossroad Blues

Written By Sera Gamble. Directed By Steve Boyum
Original US Airdate 16 November 2006

Guest Stars: La Monde Byrd (Robert Johnson); John Lafayette (George Darrow); Jeanette Sousa (Crossroads Demon)

Greenwood, Mississippi. August 1938

Musician in a bar is chased by dogs.
***Sam and Dean investigate a number of black dog sightings. Dean finally learns the truth about Dad's death. Or at least tries to come to terms with it.

Notes

Dean is now officially on the FBI database (relevant later) and thinks Sam is jealous because he's not on it.

Crossroads dirt is used to summon in rituals. When Missouri used it (**1.9 home**) it was summoning the Poltergeist to leave their old house, or at least it's good to think it could be used to summon Mom to fight the Poltergeist, but she was probably there all along.

Now Dean knows Dad died for him, all he wants to do is just give up (see next episode) that's his legacy.

Crossroads as the title suggests, makes a turning point, or crossroad in the show and their lives too. Dean, now certain Dad gave his soul to save him doesn't know how to handle it or how he's going to live with this knowledge. Sam telling him it's okay because Dad saved all those people – now he did the same for his son. Also reinforces Dean's laments from **2.4-2.8** that he wasn't meant to be here, the same thing the crossroads demon said to him.

Dean should've known he'd be dealing with more than just a lower level demon from hell/purgatory, or wherever it came from. The real demon wouldn't let him gct away so easily, without his pound of flesh, or at least having fun tormenting Dean on the whereabouts of Dad!

Who else would know except the real demon (Yellow Eyes) and about the bargain they struck together in **2.1**. It's common knowledge in the demon fraternity who the Winchesters are and what they do. Dean being fooled again into letting it escape, when he could've vanquished it with the Latin ritual or could he? Not to mention the fact, it was goading Dean into killing another human it was possessing, like Meg et al. The crossroads demon calling Dean handsome and just edible, well there's another good bough to eat line relating to Dean!

Dean finally got to chant some Latin and boy don't Sam and Dean sound seductive when they do that!!

Dean put his photo, black cat bones…into the box to summon the demon and placed it at the crossroads. In **1.9 Home**, Missouri mentioned her poultice (pouches) to place in the walls contained crossroad dirt, probably used to summon the demon or draw it away from their house.

It is believed leaving coins in the middle of a crossroads is good luck since it disperses in all four directions. A bad luck trick can also be removed here when cars drive over it. The innocent aren't harmed by this activity.

Dean asking if *myspace* is like a porn site. You can swear his character is just like Mulder's in many aspects, especially when it comes to porn and believing in the supernatural and paranormal.

Sam stepped into the circle pretty quickly didn't he to keep the hellhounds from getting them. In the scenes between Sam, Evan and the hound, it's almost as if Sam can hear or sense the dog, the way the scenes are played out, but we know only Evan can hear it and see it since he made the pact. So it'd only be after him, but Sam has the good sense to jump into the goofer dust circle, just in case.

Begging another question, why when the hounds came for Dean in the season 3 finale, didn't they draw one of these circles to keep them away from him? Interesting.

Dean's also up on his songs and blues music too when he tells Sam all of Robert Johnson's lyrics contain references to hell hounds and crossroads.

Dean doesn't want to help those people as they sealed their own fate and now should suffer the consequences, Ooh double standards: Dean when he seals his own fate in the season finale, for saving Sam and bringing him back. Then in season 3 they have to find a way of saving Dean from his bargain within a year and Dean finally admits he doesn't wanna die and go to hell!

Dean's not feeling particularly charitable here; but under the circumstances he'd just think of it as another hunt and go after the damn thing, as he called it. Problem is he's got Dad' on his mind and his deal to save Dean. So he can say the same thing about this Evan too, nobody forced him into the deal and yes about himself in the finale. It was Dad's decision, like it will be Dean's, to save Sam and not used to become some genius or famous, or make money either.

Dean is now thinking of chicks in Princess Leia garb.

Dean must ask if the bargain was worth it – would it be worth it to him if he could bring Dad back at his own expense – the cost of his own life. In effect, he'd just be doing what Dad did and reversing it because Dean didn't want to be like that – too great a cost. Then Dad wouldn't appreciate it after all the trouble he went to in saving Dean to begin with. Well, seems like I've answered my own question really about whether it'd be worth it to Dean if he could sacrifice his own life for

Dad, since he does just that at the end of this season, for Sam! That's what you get for writing this episode by episode and before I saw the season 2 finale!

Dean, kicking in yet another door but Sam doesn't let him kick in the second one. Once again Dean's being judgemental and jumping to conclusions as to why Evan made the deal (as he did in **2.4 Children Shouldn't Play with Dead Things** when he accused Angela's father of bringing her back from the dead.) He wanted to save his wife's life essentially doing what Dad did for Dean, which makes his situation different. Once more he asks the question of how she'd feel if she knew he sold his soul to save her; he was selfish because he did it for himself: he couldn't live without her and now she'll have to live without him. Dean probably saying the same thing about Dad, he did it to save Dean and didn't think of how Dean would feel once he found out: guilt, anger, rejection. Again see the season finale and Dean being in exactly the same predicament, he didn't give a second thought as to how Sam would be able to live without Dean, when Dean couldn't bear to be without Sam!

Dad didn't make his deal at the crossroads, but made it at the crossroads of his life when he realized he wasn't meant to go on; and couldn't, whilst Dean just lay there and died. Not when there was something he could do; anything, to save him.

Dean finally comes out and asks if he really did swap his soul for Dean's life. The demon comes out and answers his question, putting any doubts to rest. Also the demon appeared pretty soon after he buried the tin, almost as if it was ready and waiting and knew that's definitely what Dean would do? This episode was a mythology story, as was **2.4 Children Shouldn't Play With Dead Things,** as well as being a zombie story, which also entailed some aspects of the mythology, at least as far as losing Dad was concerned and Dean being saved.

Now Dean's willing to do the same thing, this time give his life to save a stranger, but he's got a trick up his sleeve. When Dean was attempting to save the writer and the crossroads demon possessed the body, she knew exactly what to say to Dean and what he wanted to hear, like Dad's in hell – which is the worst place for him to be and Dean sent him there. We find out he was there at the end of this season, but why was there no divine intervention for Dad, was he not worth it? (See season 4 and the revelation of what Dean did in hell, and the seals.) Also she had that "demon smoke" as Sam calls it.

When Dean was reading that Latin exorcism, he sounded so sexy in Latin, usually it's Sam who does that. Now all they had to do was read some Latin when they were dressed as Priests! Okay, another one hundred Hail Mary's for this thought too.) This means Dean wouldn't have been able to destroy that demon, other than sending it back to hell, since the demon takes pleasure in tormenting Dean about Dad and how Dean can think of nothing else. Though it is right, Dean does need Dad maybe even more than Sam, but Sam could've done with him around for what he may have to endure: his destiny. Sam wouldn't have wanted to hear being called 'Sammy' by it.

Dean doesn't like to be "violated with demon tongue", like he was by the vampire in **1.20.** Finally it torments Dean some more about Dad and his hell – in hell. A silly thing to do since he can still exorcise it.

Sam tells Dean demons lie, like Dean said to him in **1.4 Phantom Traveller** when the demon on the plane knew all about Jessica.

Dean chooses not to tell Sam if he intended to go through with the deal and bring Dad back. He went through with it to save Sam, so that would have answered his question.

Sam says they save people for Dad because that's his legacy. In **2.11 Playthings** when Sam's drunk, he tells Dean he has to save people, many people, so he can change his own destiny, at that moment he wasn't really thinking about his own legacy.

In **2.4 Children Shouldn't Play with Dead Things** (this means you Sam Winchester, another bad joke! But relevant for season 4 and what Sam does with Ruby!) When Dean asks Sam what he can say to make it all right, well, another thing is that Dad gave his soul to save Dean, it wasn't for Sam he did it, but for Dean. There's no comparison. His final mortal thought was to save Dean, give him back his life. Just for Dean. His final thought about Sam was to make Dean promise he'd kill Sam if he ever became a killer! Sam: "He did it for you!" As Dean will do for him!

Notice how the demon gives Dean 10 years if he makes the deal to bring back Dad, 10 years as a family. Whereas he only gets one for bringing Sam back. Dean has the opportunity to facilitate the return of Dad. If he went ahead with this, he would've been selfish not to mention the dangers involved of wanting this. He went through so much and it would've been so easy for him to make this bargain with the demon who clearly sees his anguish and taunts him, goading him into making this decision. Dad's in hell and what he's going through, but he doesn't fall for it.

Dangerous because he does realize the implications of this. It would be unnatural for one, as he says in **2.4 Children Shouldn't Play With Dead Things**, his being here is not natural when he finally confesses to Sam, it's with regret, he shouldn't be here, Dad should. If he went ahead, on the off chance, his heart ruling his head and asked for Dad back would this undo the entire process? The sacrifice Dad made – would it have been for nothing and more importantly would Dean end up in the hell where Dad is now. How does he really know he's in hell or heaven or that place in between? Well, to answer, he didn't sacrifice himself here since he wouldn't then be able to save Sam later on.

Jensen: "The crossroads demon is not someone with the utmost power. There's definitely a lot more – we use the term *celebrity demons* that have now been released."

Jared comments on this episode, "They sold their soul to the Devil for 10 years of fame and fortune and now it's 'How far are you willing to go to get what you want and what do you really want? Do you really want to save your brother or do you really want to not be evil? Do you really want to fight against what it is that you're terrified of becoming and which is more important to you – saving your brother or not becoming evil?' At first that's why Dean starts thinking, 'Hey, maybe that's why Sam is getting more careless because I only have a year to live and he's trying to save me' and Sam is really motivated to take action...whatever the reason he's motivated to save his brother and nothing will get in his way." (See season 3.)

Also Dean doesn't believe in God, the spiritual, does he then believe in hell because it's evil? (Or that he will actually end up there in the season 3 finale.)

In *The Shining*, Jack says he'd sell his soul for a drink. A bartender named Lloyd turns up. Lloyds bar is referred to here as the bar near the crossroads.

Questions about raising the dead, do they ever come back the same anyway? No, look at zombie Angela who went on murderous rampage and to steal Dean's line in this episode, "what's dead should stay dead." No matter how much we would want someone back.

Sam uses an apple 15 Powerbook/MacBook Pro.

The BEST episode of Season 2 so far!

My joke for this episode; okay it's not funny: re crossroad blues, the title of this episode, dromophobia is the fear of crossing the road. So maybe Dean felt this when he was at the crossroads and so couldn't go through with the deal to save Dad. In other words, he couldn't cross the road.

Does he cross-over to the other side of the road (the spiritual, paranormal) and save Dad by giving his soul, or does he stay on this side of the road?

Watching this episode, who'd have thought he writers were setting us up for a fall? That Dean does crossover and give his soul for Sam at season's end!

Quotes

Dean: "What have you got on the case then, you innocent, harmless, young man, you."

Dean: "Crossroads are where pacts are made. These people are actually making deals with the damn thing, 'cause that always ends good."

Dean: "We know a little about a lot of things, just enough to make it dangerous."

Sam: "…you never actually considered making that deal right?"

Sam and Dean's Take on the Urban Legend/Lore

Sam says the lore on Black Dogs is obscure. Spectre black dogs are known worldwide, some are animal spirits, some death omens.

Certain flowers in the middle of the crossroads are used for rituals, i.e. summoning rituals. The dogs are demonic pit bulls, hell hounds. Selling your soul for a deal is a legend. Dean says it isn't. He knows about Robert Johnson with occult references in his songs. He supposedly choked on his own blood after hallucinating and mentioning evil dogs.

Goofer dust is also used to keep evil out, like rock salt.

Actual Legend

Goofer dust (means graveyard dust) is used to inflict harm, to kill a foe. Derives from the Kikongo word, *Kifwa* meaning 'to die'. The word 'mojo' is a corruption of the West African, Yoruba word, *Mojuba* meaning, 'giving praise.' Rootwork' is not a religion, but spells referred to for healing. 'Rootwork', also known as Hoodoo in Southern US, derives from the African word, *juju*, meaning, 'magic' or 'voodoo'. Voodoo is also a corruption of the word 'vodirn', meaning 'spirit'. Rootwork is also the African-American version of *shamanism* using herbs, rocks or organic material as a way to heal the mind or body and to solve problems.

Due to African culture seen as having a negative effect and not being very dominant or inherent in the world, Hoodoo has been mistakenly seen as an evil practice associated with witch doctors, cannibalism. See the *Webster's Dictionary* definition of hoodoo as meaning voodoo. A person or thing that brings bad luck.

In the early twentieth century, rootwork focused in many rhythm and blues songs. Musicians felt they could sing about any topic thus performers did the same until the late 1970's...songs such Muddy waters', *I Got My Mojo Working.'* Robert Johnson's songs of mojos, curses, well known rootworkers and hot foot powder. This was a mix of red pepper, black pepper, sulphur and salt. It was sprinkled on the doorstep to make a foe move. Robert Johnson never shared his music with anyone, as he considered it to be his livelihood. Rumours abound that Johnson sold his soul and that explained his great talent as a musician. He was a strong believer in hoodoo and also used it. He didn't become a master guitarist by using the crossroads ritual. However, Tommy Johnson, a contemporary of his, is claimed to have used the ritual.

In Southern US states amongst African-Americans, it was common knowledge that souls could be sold at a crossroads. In African lore, the god, *Esy*, was believed the guardian of the crossroads, a gateway between humans and gods. Celts buried the dead who could not be buried in consecrated ground, near the crossroads. A crossroads in many cultures is a place which no one possesses and so can be used as a place to perform rituals and spells, where it is also the port of contact for spirits.

Crossroads date to ancient times, such as Rome. Mercury was considered the Guardian of the crossroads. In India, the god, Bhairava, guards the crossroads at the edge of some villages.

Black Dog is found mainly in English lore; a spectre and was regarded as a death omen. Bigger than an ordinary dog and having fiery glowing eyes. Seen at a crossroads or places of execution. Dogs always have a connection with death, such as Cerberus, guarding the underworld in Greek Mythology.

There is one such Black Dog rumoured to be known as the *Black Dog of Winchester.* (Sometimes you wonder why the name Winchester was chosen for the family, as there are so many references to it.) Black dogs are also known to inhabit Route 66.

On Hallowe'en, it is said if you go to a crossroads; the wind will speak your future; if you have the courage.

A purple candle means spirituality or humility. (Thought I'd just mention that since we're on the subject of myths etc.)

X- Files Connection

In **3.14 Grotesque**, evil spirits' possession makes a man kill. Mulder believes demonic possession may be involved. Agent Patterson comments: "So what is it Mulder, little green men! Evil spirits! Hounds of hell!"

Music

Cross Road Blues by Robert Johnson; *Key to the Highway* by Little Walter; *Chaos Surrounds You* by MasterSource; *Downhearted Blues* by Son House; *Hair of the Dog* by Nazareth

Ooh Bloops

When Sam and Dean visit George, Jensen appears to get his lines wrong, but quickly covers his mistake.

Did Johnson die 8 years later, instead of the usual 10, after selling his soul?

Locations

Boundary Bay.

2.9 Croatoan

Written By John Shiban. Directed By Robert Singer
Original US Airdate 7 December 2006

Guest Stars: Chilton Crane (Beverly Tanner); Bobby Hosea (Sarge); Kate Jennings Grant (Dr Lee); Diego Klattenhoff (Duane Tanner)

Rivergrove, Oregon

Sam has a vision about Dean killing someone and they go to the town to check it out. Dean finally tells Sam Dad revealed something about Sam.

Notes

Sam has another vision, this time about Dean shooting someone. There's another debate about whether Dean would shoot an innocent man which he says he wouldn't do and Sam tells him he knows that.

This is debatable in itself, see **1.21** when Dean wanted to exorcise Meg, even after Bobby told him she was a real person inside and wouldn't survive; Tom was another human and in this episode, he has to kill the mother, again because she was under the influence of the virus and inevitably the Yellow Eyed demon. So in some ways you can argue Dean only ever 'killed' them out of necessity and they were possessed at the time. It was the only split-second decision, spur of the moment choice he had. Although the virus was just a test; Dean wasn't to know, when the doctor tells them she didn't have any signs of the virus left in her. So no, he's never really killed an 'innocent' man before. So Sam's right, he wouldn't. (See also **3.12** when Dean strongly argues for saving Nancy.)

Sam asking Dean a silly question, if he paid attention in school. Nah, there were too many distractions around – girls! So we know from this episode, they did have a school education (well, okay I know Sam needed it to get to college, but they were on the road a lot. See **4.13**.)

The men seem to be controlling the town, at least the house Sam and Dean call on.

This time round (as there aren't any phone signals to contact the outside world) Dad's journal has become easy to read once more, so much for being confusing.

Dean shoots the father, Sam can't shoot the son, and well he hasn't shot at much yet, except if it's evil. There's that whole innocent argument again – you could say the entire town was innocent before the demon took it over. Dean berates Sam for not shooting the boy since this is no time to hesitate and decide if he could do it or not and reinforces this view when he shoots the mother; no one else was going to do it and they don't really know what they are dealing with. (Also see when Dean hesitated and the Shtriga got away, only to turn up again years later in **1.18 Something Wicked**.)

The annoying bit – no one asked about or questioned, was how Duane knew to come to the clinic, that it'd be safe there and he didn't just see Dean's car out there either! Another one of Dean's "awkward" quotes, which he seems to end up in – frequently, like when Sam was watching porn in **2.4** and he didn't want to wait for him at the roadhouse, making awkward conversation without Sam there.

Jeffrey Dean Morgan would've been right at home in this episode with viruses as per his role in *The Burning Zone* as a CDC doctor.

Sam's vision appears to be coming true.

Just as Sam says Dean wouldn't kill an innocent man, he now says he might kill an innocent man and Dean doesn't even care about that –

Dean's not himself anymore! Is the job meant to be tough as Sam says, is Dean really meant to struggle with his conscience – he didn't have to before. There was only one thing he had to struggle with, i.e. finding the evil SOBs and take care of them. There was no grey matter of whether it was innocent, or an innocent human. Dean can't shoot Duane until they know for certain. So Sam did have an impact on Dean, but he won't tell Sam why.

Funny Sam doesn't hear Pam lock the door and also he doesn't sense something may be wrong, or he's about to be attacked.

Now the tables are turned and Sam may be infected, Dean acts defensive and says no one's going to shoot him (not even Dean!) Now some would call that hypocritical Dean! No, Sam wants to shoot himself if he's infected. Dean confessed he's fed up with hunting and more importantly, this weight on his shoulders, meaning the promise he made to Dad about Sam. When Dean says it's nothing to do with Dad, as Sam's about to say, he's only partly telling the truth – it's also about Sam.

Dean's not going to sleep over the one that got away (and he says he'll lose sleep in **2.11 Playthings** too when Sam takes the initiative and agrees to take on a case.)

Dean wants to live life – some – after all Sam has, why can't he experience the Grand Canyon and other stuff.

This episode was the big one before the Christmas break in the US, so they had to wait a long time to watch it, I was lucky enough to have had it video taped. Thanks friend!

Dean wants to go to Hollywood and gets his wish in **2.18 Hollywood Babylon.** As for banging Lindsay Lohan, please…! No.

After all the times the Winchesters have been called gay etc, Dean says it this time round when he comments he doesn't swing that way!

What Dad told him – the entire burden was all about Sam – okay 50/50. The whole virus was a test to see if Sam was immune to the virus or not, which had those niggling bits – like why would the demon need to be sure of this; if it's so certain about everything else concerning Sam.

Also we now know that the town was wiped out probably due to Yellow Eyes testing this demonic virus until the time was right, or testing others like Sam, to ensure they were also immune, in preparation for the impending war. Perhaps rather glorifying it or simplifying the explanation; but for *Supernatural*'s purpose, this makes more sense than the Indian raid and the disease wiping out the colony, also it's a more appealing explanation.

Rivergrove is the demon's own virus testing ground, but why leave *Croatoan* carved on the tree: a clue or a red herring?

Crater Lake is in Oregon, there is no river Grove in Oregon, but there is one really, only not near Crater Lake.

Dean uses the names of two members of ZZ Top.

Schoolhouse Rock was a series of short education films in the US, utilizing songs to teach subjects like history, maths, and grammar.

"Shriner convention" refers to 'Shriners' aka, an ancient Arabic order of the Nobles of the Mystic Shrine, they wear fezzes and are akin to the Freemasons.

Mister Rogers' Neighbourhood was a US TV show.

This was Robert Singer's favourite episode, "It was psychological and very character driven. It had an underlying message to it – being afraid of what you can't understand."

Quotes

Dean: "A little too *Stepford*."
Sam: "Big time!"

Sam: "What the hell's happened to you? You might kill an innocent man and you don't even care – you don't act like yourself anymore Dean. Hell, you' reacting like one of those things out there!"

Dean: "I can't I promised Dad right before Dad died, he told me something. About you."
Sam: "What – Dean, what did he tell you?"

Sam and Dean's Take on the Urban Legend/Lore

'Croatoan' a lost colony by the name of Rowan Oak. The first English colony in America, late 1500's. It's been said there was an Indian raid and the entire colony was wiped out overnight. Dad's journal had a theory about Croatoans, was thought to be a demon's name, aka 'Reshef' (was thought to be an Egyptian god of war.) or 'Daeva': a demon of plague and pestilence. Sam calls it demonic germ warfare. Dean wonders if it's a Biblical plague.

Actual Legend

'Croatoan' or 'CRO' were letters found on a tree in 1590 on Roanoke island, off North Carolina, by Governor John White after he returned to the colony. It took White three years to return with supplies. The theory was the settlers were killed by a disease; but this was disproved since no bodies were found and the houses they built had also vanished. Most likely it was thought they deserted to live with the natives or were killed by them.

The colony was founded by Sir Walter Raleigh in the latter part of the sixteenth century as the base for a permanent English colony in Virginia. Between 1585-1587, a colony was attempted to be set up, but these people either disappeared or left. Those settlers, who were the last to disappear, were finally thought to have vanished when no provisions arrived from England. At the time, England was at war with Spain. They were believed to have assimilated into one of the local tribes.

Croatoan, was known as Roanoke was the name of an Indian tribe, as well as the oldest English colony in the US.

Reshef means 'lightning'. Can also be spelt, Reshpu, Rashshaf, Reshpa). Seen mostly in Syrian legend where the cult saw him as a god of war. In Egyptian writings, he's known as Lord of Eternity, Lord of Heaven. Description-wise he holds a shield and spear in his left hand and a club in his right.

Daeva (also the name of a vampire clan.) from Avestan language is a supernatural entity that has ugly characteristics. Also known as "warrior gods" sending out destructive forces, they only cared for their own name and prowess and are from Persian myth.

Film/TV References

Stepford Wives, The Omega Man.

X Files Connection

In **Ice**, Mulder and Scully are trapped in the Artic with a strange worm taking over people. Mulder tries to radio for help but can't because of the ice storm. There's a stand-off where the survivors wonder which one is infected. There's also a scene where they hold guns on each other; with Scully resorting to locking up Mulder for his own good. As Dean does to Sam here.

Medusa was all about a mysterious disease.

Zero Sum has a test involving small pox infested bees.

Nightfall where some extraterrestrial force is behind the disappearance of some loggers. Here the virus unleashed by the demon on a town where the folk have disappeared over the years on numerous occasions.

Ooh Bloops

When Dean promises Sam, the camera goes along the Impala revealing the dolly track.
Spatters on the edge of the bowl Duane holds, appear and disappear.

Locations

Fort Langley.

2.10 Hunted

Written By Raelle Tucker. Directed By Rachael Talalay
Original US Airdate 11 January 2007

Guest Stars: Sterling K Brown (Gordon); Samantha Ferris (Ellen); Katherine Isabelle (Ava); Chad Lindberg (Ash); Richard DeKlerk (Scott Carey)

Dean finally reveals Dad's big secret he's been harbouring all this time. Gordon takes Dean hostage to set a trap for Sam. Sam is saved by Ava who has visions of Sam being killed.

Notes

The Yellow-Eyed man in the dreams is almost an exact repetition of Weber's speech in **2.5 Simon Says** when he tells Andy of the plans 'It' has for him. He's killed before he can do any of it.
Finally the huge revelation we've all been waiting for, almost halfway through the season – all about Dean having to save Sam from becoming evil and if he can't, then having to kill him (and those were Dad's last thoughts – about Sam.) After it was revealed, it didn't sound like much of a shock nor had that great an impact, not as big as expected all this time. I don't know about anyone else but maybe if he'd said something along the lines of Sam having to face his darkside, and go through it before he emerges from it; would've been more interesting. Oh well, at least it's out in the open now, if a tad disappointing.

Dean, and especially Sam, shouldn't have been too shocked at this either. They've been talking about Sam's destiny and him becoming a killer, maybe, like forever, (particularly **2.5 Simon Said**). Perhaps the thing that shocked, was that Dad told Dean to kill Sam if he couldn't save him. This becomes moot point later on the episode, since Gordon turns up and is hell bent on doing all the killing for Dean anyway, irrespective of whether Sam turns evil or not. To him, it's safer than being sorry and we all know Gordon shoots first and asks no questions later.

Dean's line that he wished Dad never told him: he almost reiterates in the next episode, when he tells Sam, Dad shouldn't have asked him to promise such an absurd thing anyway. Besides, if Dean wouldn't shoot Sam in the previous episode, he wouldn't let anyone else either and he sure as hell wouldn't really go through with it if he did become a killer. He just couldn't shoot his own brother. Also in **2.11 Playthings**, Sam changes Dean's promise to Dad and makes it become Dean's promise to Sam instead – that he'll still have to kill him.

Dean calls Ellen, in a reverse of **2.6 No Exit**, where she calls them about Jo and he lies. She forgave Dad about Bill; but Dad didn't forgive himself, guess we won't know what happened there then. Ellen tells Dean where Sam is, unlike Dean. Didn't Sam think she'd tell Dean when he told her where she was going nor didn't Sam think Dean would call her?

Seems the three people like Sam are dead – but that'd be too convenient wouldn't it, (except Andy) since Sam meets Ava who's come to save him from the opening scene. Ava isn't like Sam, her mother's still alive, or so she tells us and she doesn't fit the same pattern, so it'd be hard to find out who's like them and who isn't. So the plot gets complicated now as they can no longer rely on the nursery fires and losing their mothers to find out about others like Sam, (the baby's Mom, would've also been killed in a nursery fire (in **1.21**) if Sam hadn't had his premonition and saved them. Sometimes there are still fires. Was that all a show for the Winchesters in that episode? Also Sam seems to get his premonitions when Yellow Eyes is involved, or there are others like Sam around.

When Sam walks along the window's ledge, Ava doesn't get his shadow across her body when she sits opposite the window.

Dean, meanwhile thinks Sam's found a girl, Yeah as if he would! Dean and Gordon fight again. Gordon is on a one-man crusade to save humanity by taking out all the psychics as they're on the demon's side and not "pure" humans because of their abilities. He was exorcising a demon and the girl didn't make it (like Dean with Meg). However, as for being tied to a chair, this time

Gordon gets the upper hand on Dean, who still has to make that reference to Sam surfing porn. Then Dean always manages to get himself tied to a chair! Oh, Sam does that now does he? Surf porn. After watching the porn channel in **2.4.**

Gordon makes an analogy with Hitler which really doesn't work in Sam's case. We already knew what Hitler would become, it was predetermined by history. With Sam it's not. He might become evil or he might not. So you can't see into the future as far as he's concerned. As for saying Dean's not the man his father is, shouldn't Gordon have said 'was' instead of 'is'. He uses present tense as if Dad's still alive. Well, Dean isn't like Dad, he's his own man and even if he was like Dad, he wouldn't kill Sam for the sake of it; for something that may never happen. Would Dad kill Sam? That's nice, he gave his soul to save one son, Dean, and if he was still alive, would he really kill another son, Sam? What makes Gordon think Dean wouldn't come after him for revenge.

When Sam looks through the front of the house – with Dean and Gordon sitting there, they looked kind of funny, like they were just waiting for Sam to burst through the door. Ok, maybe they just looked plain funny!

Gordon tells Sam he's no better than his hunts. Sam said a similar thing to Dean in the previous episode, when he said Dean's becoming like one of the infected people, when Dean wanted to kill Duane (and he'd have been right if he had killed him, he'd have released some demon smoke and then they'd know who was behind the virus for sure. Not that they didn't already, with the presence of the sulphur in the blood samples.)

Dean now wants to go to Amsterdam (hopefully not the Red Light District!) Dean thinks Ellen or Jo or Ash told Gordon about Sam. Dean's eager t jump to conclusions and besides, thought he was sweet on Jo, for all of 2 seconds. Anyway, didn't Gordon tell Dean that the demon he exorcised told him all about Sam, when he had Dean tied up. Also Gordon says he has his own connections and that's how he found Sam.

Dean doesn't believe in destiny (at this time, the phrase "screw destiny" comes to mind for obvious reasons.) but Sam says it's his destiny he doesn't believe in and he wants to change it (see next episode), but how can he change it if he doesn't even know for sure what his destiny is – oh which leads to another question I forgot to ask; how did Dad find out Sam's destiny, that he'd become a killer; was it through his meticulous research, that everyone with Sam's abilities becomes evil, or other means. Did he know more about Mom, Yellow Eyes than he was letting on?

Dean was meant to protect Sam, Dad told him to, but Sam tells Dean he can't do that, yet in **2.11** he wants Dean to help him. Sam finds Ava missing; the demon's been there, cue lots of guilt on his part in the next episode: she saved Sam, but he couldn't do the same for her.

In this episode, Sam the hunter becomes Sam the hunted.

Quotes

Sam: "Kill me….am I supposed to go dark side or something?"

Dean: "I wish to God he didn't open his mouth, so I wouldn't have to walk around with this screaming in my head all day!"

Dean: "The guy feels guilty surfing internet porn."

Gordon: "You're no better than the filthy things you hunt." (So what does that make Gordon?)

Dean: "I wasn't meant to do anything. I don't believe in that destiny crap."
Sam: "You mean you don't believe in my destiny."

Dean: "Bitch!"
Sam: "Jerk!"

Film/TV References

TJ Hooker.

Music

White Rabbit by Jefferson Airplane

Ooh Bloops

When Ash takes Sam's beer, there's more in the glass than when Sam was drinking from it. (Always the case in films and shows involving glasses.)

Sam uses his shoe as a decoy to lure Gordon. Then when they fight, Sam is wearing his shoe. Sam has no injuries in the Impala, when they go to see Ava, at the end, his injuries return.

In Ava's vision, the piece of paper with the address where Dean is being held is shown, then again towards the end of the episode, these notes are written in the same hand writing. However, when Gordon gives Sam the address, the writing is different to the other ones.

Locations

Skytrain Overpass, New Westminister. 148th Street at 64th Street, Surrey. 147th Street at 60th, Surrey. Langley.

2.11 Playthings

Written By Matt Witten. Directed By Charles Beeson
Original US Airdate 18 January 2007

Guest Stars: Matreya Fedor (Tyler); Brenda McDonald (Rose); Annie Wersching (Susan); Conchita Campbell (Maggie); John R Taylor (Sherwin)

Peoria, Illinois

Sam and Dean call Ellen who tells them about a serious of events at a hotel in

Cornwall, Connecticut

Sam makes Dean promise the impossible: to kill him if he turns bad.

Notes

When they come to the rescue, (like in **1.3** Dean kicks down the bathroom door and Sam rescues her from the bath, then Dean jumps into the lake to save Lucas) here Sam finally breaks open the door and dives in saving Tyler, whilst Dean kicks in the back door.

Lots of whiskey to drink in this episode, i.e. the entire cast had some! Sam feels sorry for himself or what he has to go through eventually. First he said it's his destiny and they can't change it, it's going to happen, or as Dean tells him in the last episode; now Sam says he wants to change his own destiny and Dean has to help him or hurt him if he turns evil. Why does Dean want or need to listen to Dad so badly now, when he never did when he was alive. Besides Dad could be wrong and Sam maybe won't turn evil.

Dean promised Sam he'd help him, if he does turn, why didn't he just say he crossed his fingers and never really promised him – childish, but works none-the-less and what's a promise to a dying man anyway or a man who's about to die worth? Even if it was Dad. As Dean says he shouldn't have made him promise. Something like a contract is null and void. Dean was hoping since Sam was drunk, he'd have forgotten what they talked about during the night, even when he teased him with the hangover remedy.

In this episode, it didn't appear to have been Maggie who was controlling events. As soon as Sherwin mentioned the nanny – I thought she was behind it. She wanted Rose now, especially since this was, or is, confirmed by the last scene with the doll that resembles Maggie. Someone else was controlling her and this was the nanny, she was the only one who could've effectively worked the voodoo. Maggie wouldn't have known about it since she was little when she drowned in the pool: could the nanny have drowned her? So in this episode, it wasn't the butler or Maggie, but the nanny did it.

Something which Sam and Dean missed and Dean asks if it's just over – wasn't it a bit too convenient! If Sam wasn't too caught up in his world, would he have spotted it and Dean too. No one saw her doll because it wasn't there before.

Dean can't believe Sam is actually taking the initiative and on cases without asking Dean, but then this isn't the first time he's done that. He did that in **1.10** when he wanted to go back home because of his visions; also **2.2**, the clown episode, although he hates clowns. As for thinking there'd be angst stuff, his imagery again is that of being dumped or getting over a broken heart, instead of being angry and sad over getting Ava taken and her fiancée killed. It was Ava who came to warn Sam so it's not his fault what happened.

Sam, on the other hand, sounds as if he's on a record to save people – in doing so, he believes he can change his own destiny of becoming a killer, or not, or evil. He can't. In the previous episode, he tells himself and Dean that he can't change it and neither can Dean, even if he wanted, he can only be there for Sam.

Dean's hangover cure: greasy pork sandwiches, served on an ashtray, all to make Sam feel even sicker.

Dean feels right at home in this hotel, if it wasn't for all those comments about them being gay (continued throughout the seasons.)

Sorry Dean, no sissy British accents in this episode (they're only sissy British accents when an American actor tries to fake one!)

This time they're asked if they want a king size bed and Dean doesn't get his answer of why they look the type". Dean has to part with money as a tip, he never does that either.

The dress on the wall in the room –is almost like the type to be bringing up bad memories for them, re Mom and Jessica on fire in white dresses. Dean thinks the butler could've done it. Well butler, cum porter, cum bartender... Sam's response to Dean's unanswered question, Dean acts too butch, whereas Dean could've answered this is probably because Sam acts too much like a girl or too girly, which he didn't. Rest my case. Dean's attempt to get into the room saying Sam plays with dolls and has a collection, now that's far from butch. I rest my case for a second time.

Also Dean warning Sam not to surf porn again! The room number is 237 (from *The Shining.*)

They come up with the deduction that voodoo is involved, being the black Creole version, but what spoils this episode is they do very 'shoddy' research; missing out large clues, big holes in this episode: the nanny's in the photo with Grandma Rose and because she has the quincunx on, they believe she's the one protecting Rose and probably the house too; and once they decide Rose can't do it anymore, due to her stroke, then her dead sister, Maggie must be behind it. As she's influencing Tyler and taken her over, even attempting to drown her. Susan tells them that (Margaret) Maggie was drowned as a girl – how then would she have known about voodoo? Sherwin only told Dean that Marie, the nanny, used to look after Rose, the younger sibling. They don't explore how Maggie drowned or what happened to her, or who could've really been behind the haunting.

To reiterate, of course it was the nanny: the obvious giveaway was the photo. I immediately knew she was behind it, though we don't know why she did it and why kill Maggie (the blonde one!)

This is revealed in the final scene when the girls are playing and on the shelf sits the doll of Maggie, an exact replica and she's being used to manipulate and deceive by Marie. That's who Rose actually promised to end her life, if she killed her. Also Marie was only Rose's nanny so how would Maggie have known about voodoo. (Oh just had another thought what if Marie was doing all this because Rose asked her to wanting to be reunited with Maggie?)

It's no wonder they do miss these clues, Sam gets drunk, he's feeling sorry for himself, though after his big 'saving many people' speech, how he does this now is anybody's guess. Personal issues between them have never led to them dropping the ball on cases, which they do here. Another reason why they think it's all over when it's not, is what the nanny wanted with the house; the daughters and Tyler. Also Dean says it to Sam in **1.15**, he's getting rusty.

Sam calling Dean "bossy and short". Yeah he's only 3" shorter. (Oh that sounds rude, height I'm talking about height here!) No wonder Dean gets him back with his hangover cure next morning! Sam getting drunk and dealing with the fallout of a hangover, does this denote Sam's stepping into more adult territory here, i.e. that of big brother Dean. Mind you Dean's portrayed as a drunk in **2.20**. As for Sam it's more a case of once bitten twice shy as he steers away from the demon drink and getting drunk, until season 3.

Sam gets drunk because he couldn't save the man from getting hung, well; it's not as if he had a vision about this. Oh and another thing, they should've realized he was the next victim, but only if they knew he was there, which they didn't. So this doesn't explain why Sam berates himself over this. Also they did work out the other two deaths were associated with the hotel and the sale, but as I said, they didn't know of the third man, so to speak.

The same reasoning applies to Ava, Sam had no premonition about her, so he couldn't have known what was coming and perhaps no visions of her mean she's probably still alive somewhere. Perhaps there's some other reason for her going missing.

(There I go jumping ahead of myself again, like I did with Dean saving Sam in the finale! Ava will end up surprising us in the final 2 episodes of the season. Here I was writing all this about her before even having watched those episodes! I have to write as soon as I watch the show, an episode; otherwise I'll lose my chain of thought.)

As Dean says, he can't save everyone – which is what Sam said in **1.3 Dead In the Water**. Is there logic in Sam's conclusion that the more people he saves, the more he can change the outcome. Thinking about it, it doesn't really work like that, it's only avoiding the inevitable, or prolonging the agony of his destiny.

Well, Dean's been watching out for him, for like forever, as they say. So he's not about to stop now. Another thing, why does Sam crave death so badly if he changes, there are other ways out of it, magic, more hoodoo; voodoo. Re Sam's destiny, **2.10**, what would've been more interesting is if they'd come up with something like Sam having to embrace his destiny, his dark said before he can overcome it, rather than just saying 'kill him if he turns bad'. As I already said many times over.

Sam reinforcing Dean's promise to Dad. Sam doesn't hear him when Dean says you don't have to do that to your children because Sam's laying the same crap on Dean too and yes, everyone around him dies because they're meant to, not because Sam has any influence over it (mostly it's Yellow Eyes) and when they hunt, people still die and so do their prey. So with all this, Dean is forced into promising again.

Sherwin says he wouldn't be happy leaving home (and Dean's right he wouldn't know about that because he only had one home for all of four years and never really had a real home). Sherwin mentions the hotel's got its blood like any other (most likely the one in *The Shining*.)

Rose is staring out of the rainy window, just like Sam seemed to be doing back then! Dean wants to poke her with a stick to make sure she's not pretending, he didn't do that to the old woman in **1.18**. So when Maggie says she doesn't like Susan, she's next on the victim's list, she's not really Maggie at all. The line Maggie says when she questions why she kept her away so long, isn't Maggie talking, it's Marie. Only thing that makes sense because the symbols must've been used by Rose to keep the nanny away and now she couldn't do that anymore since she had her stroke, so Sam was mostly right there, but for the wrong person and maybe the nanny having the symbols on the clothes was to keep her in check.

Dean asking where Maggie is and why she stopped? To answer: it was never Maggie to begin with so she didn't stop, the nanny stopped after she got Rose back and did she do all this to stop Rose from leaving here? The doll was just like Maggie, so Maggie wouldn't be using the doll, she'd come back as herself. Why would Maggie hurt Tyler and the others too? Since her sister Rose was old anyway and didn't have much time left. Also, if it was Maggie behind it all, why would she wait so long to come back for Rose?

Sam saves Tyler in the pool and he got his bandage wet too. Dean gives Sam the credit here, saying he could've saved her but let Sam do it.

Dean's opportunity to match make Sam again, she doesn't need Sam around and his hang ups, and anyway, she was a bit old for him anyway and had baggage too. Sam wasn't too drunk to recall Dean's promise to him

Susan calls Dean 'Mr Mahogoff', when she hands him back his credit card. This is a slang term and used with 'Jack' to describe when you want to be alone.

Dean's reference of "greasy pork sandwich in an ashtray" is quoted from the movie *Weird Science*. Both versions of *The Shining* have two evil sisters in it, but they didn't strike me as the ones being in control otherwise why show Marie's photo at the end. Also if Rose was really evil, why didn't she attack Tyler long before now?

Jared says, "Director Charles Beeson did a great job. I was really proud of that dull episode, because it could have been not scary, but the way it was shot was great."

Hey it wasn't that dull Jared!

Eric Kripke: "I'm never creeped out by any of this stuff and these dailies creeped the hell out of me. Racks and racks of old porcelain, black-eyed, dead-eyed dolls."

Agh! Does no one think the nanny did it! She was the only one who knew of hoodoo and was interested in it. Also who drowned Maggie in the pool? She couldn't have drowned on her own.

The name of the hotel *Pierpont* could be named for John Pierpont – a poet and who was born in Cornwall, Connecticut in 1785.

MILF = Mother I'd Like to F**k. I.e similar to a "yummy mummy" in the UK.

Quotes

Dean: "Not the patented Sam Winchester way...thought there'd be more angsty stuff, moody music and staring out of windows."

Sam: "No, 2 singles. We're brothers." You'd think after all this time someone would've noticed a little resemblance between them.

Dean: "Most troubling question is why do these people assume we're gay?"
Sam: "Well, you are kinda butch. They probably think you're over compensating."

Dean: "You can't save everyone."

Dean: "You were wasted."
Sam: "You weren't and you promised

Sam and Dean's Take on the Urban Legend/Lore

Sam notices the symbol on the urn is a quincunx: five spot. Dean says it's used in voodoo spells, Sam adds, with bloodweed it's a powerful charm to ward off enemies. Dolls are used in hoodoo spells, curses and binding. Sam says for the spell to work, you have to chant and use herbs.

Actual Legend

Quincunx is a five-spot, a "formation of five units in a pattern." like that on a domino, playing card or dies. It is used for "sealing and fixing spells in space."

A false crossroad in Hoodoo can be formed inside a house. Poppets were from European witchcraft, was a doll made in the form of a person so spells could be cast upon it, either for binding or sealing

Other haunted houses include, Myrtles Plantation – a bed and breakfast in St Francisville, Louisiana. Built over 200 years ago, over Tunica Indian Burial Mounds and was owned by Judge Clark Woodruffe and his wife Sarah. They had a slave Chloe, who he found listening in on his conversations and cut off her ear. As revenge, she poisoned his two daughters and his wife was also killed.

Chloe was hung and her body thrown in the river. Her ghost is said to haunt this house in search of exacting revenge on the judge. Sounds and strange sightings were noticed on the plantation after Chloe was killed, such as the blood in the pool, the grand piano being played – without a player seated in front and the spirits of two blonde girls and a voodoo priestess spirit were also seen, in the form of a young girl. Which sounds just like this episode.

Carolands Mansion. This is from hellhoundslair.com (website mentioned in **1.17 Hell House**.) These were based on people's own experiences/stories. Hillsborough, California, an abandoned mansion and the first house built there. Two girls wanted to enter it and the security guard took them to a vault where he raped and murdered them. Their spirits are thought to haunt the mansion.

Maribel, Wisconsin: where a hotel burned down three times on the same date. Sometimes a child is seen in the upstairs window that was meant to have died in one of the fires. Known as a portal to hell. Another legend states the presence of natural springs under it aka – the 'fountain of youth'.

Film/TV References

Though not mentioned, this episode alludes to *The Shining* and the car with a brain of its own, *Stephen King's Christine*. As well as *Scooby Doo*.

X Files Connection

Syzygy Mulder teases Scully about her little feet not being able to reach the pedal, that's why he always drives. Here Sam telling Dean he's short, after Sam's had a few too many. (Hmm the possibility of Dean always driving because his feet only reach the pedal and Sam's too tall comes to mind.)

In **Redrum**, a lawyer who's accused of murder discovers time is going backwards. But this episode is mainly because everyone mentions this title. A man has premonitions about the future and believes it's a chance to make amends, he's living time backwards.

Chinga (see earlier name change mentioned about this episode) was the Stephen King written episode where Mulder has to contend with an evil doll without Scully around. A bit like the doll here, where Maggie's doll was manipulated by the nanny.

7.14 Theef the words 'theef' in blood are found next to a dead body. Mulder and Scully believe the word 'thief' to be wrongly spelt. Mulder finds hex dirt and believes hex-craft to be at work and occult is being used to hurt a woman's family. The co-writer here was John Shiban, director

Kim Manners and guest starred Billy Drago (see **3.15** of Supernatural where he played Dr Benton.)

Ooh Bloops

When Sam is drunk, he has his cast on, when he's over the toilet, the cast is gone and he has his watch on. When he's dressed, the cast reappears on his wrist.

Music

Voodoo Spell by Michael Burks

Locations

Rosemary, Shaughnessy.

2.12 Nightshifter

Written By Ben Edlund. Directed By Phil Sgriccia
Original US Airdate 25 January 2007

Guest Stars: Charles Malik Whitfield (Special Agent Henricksen); Georgia Craig (Sherri); Christopher Gauthier (Ronald Resnick)

Milwaukee, Wisconsin

Sam and Dean look into a spate of jewellery store robberies, as FBI agents, when ironically, who should arrive later on, the FBI and their worst nightmare. They come across another shapeshifter.

Notes

Dean describing the life of an FBI agent, no more likely he's describing their life on the road together, hunting. Dean gets another number for his little black book, no he stores them on his phone doesn't he with little photos next to their names! (As in **1.11 Scarecrow.**)

The scene where Sam and Dean put their badges against Ronald's glass door is a classic, because they look like real FBI agents in that scene. Another film Dean's into, *T2*. Ronald thinks it's a mandroid – a funny part in this episode, but that name will keep popping up throughout the episode. He shows Sam and Dean a *Fortean Times* magazine with a photo of the Cybermen form the UK sci-fi series, *Doctor Who*. Ronald tells them he'll hunt the thing himself and they should've known that's what he'd do, as he was so determined. He's also correct about the thing living in the sewer, as that's where the other shapeshifter (**1.6 Skin**) had its lair.

Dean's badge reads 'Agent Jack Ryan' and Sam's reads, 'Agent Han Solo', both characters played by Harrison Ford, (whom Jensen admires.)

Sam and Dean recognize it's a shapeshifter as soon as they see the flashing glare the camera's picked up in its eyes. Sam's version of the "God's honest truth" isn't very honest or true. In fact it's the exact opposite.

Sam tries to keep Ronald out of trouble, it wouldn't do him any good to have his so-called theories proven a reality and in his own way he attempts to keep him away from the danger, as he later tells Dean, "It's better to stay in the dark and stay alive." They don't know how literal Sam's advice will become later on in the bank, when Dean also tells Ronald to stay out of the light and in the dark.

Dean can't believe how authentic an FBI agent Sam sounds and when other people are involved, he needs to be good and convincing. Unfortunately, in Ronald's case, it just made him more determined to prove what he believes. Sam's comment about Ronald staying alive if he doesn't get involved also rings true.

Dean hates shapeshifters more than Sam does because of the one in St Louis which stole his face. Don't think a gun would've helped Dean when Ronald was taking hostages and Ronald's gun would've been bigger than Dean's (Ha.) Dean feels naked without his weapons anyway. The last time Dean brought a gun where he shouldn't have, was in **1.14 Nightmare**, when he and Sam questioned Max about the killings and were taken hostage, when Sam sees Dean's impending death in a vision, so maybe it's just as well he didn't bring weapons. Besides the police had their weapons trained on them later on.

Ronald doesn't like Sam, he's too much of an FBI agent and he lies, the first person we've come across who doesn't like Sam and why he's happy to lock him up in the vault with the others. Dean volunteers as a hostage to get to the bottom of this and since Ronald likes him. Dean has a new fan in Sherry, the bank teller and probably one reason why the shapeshifter turned into her at the end!

Dean wasting time talking to Ronald when he should've been looking at the footage already, hey wouldn't photos on the cell/mobile phone worked just as well, has a flash too and a proper camera lens.

Sam is frustrated by Sherry being so enamored of Dean, he's a hero. (Actually they're both our heroes!) Um, where was I? Sam, a little ahead of himself, asks Dean how they'll get out of here when it's all over since Dean is wanted by the police.

Annoying bit: Dean's still wanted, again for the same reasons as in **2.7 The Usual Suspects** and **1.6 Skin**. Why didn't the police close the file again the shifter couldn't have changed his appearance back to Dean, after Dean had already killed him; so they had their killer in the form of Dean. It wasn't explained very well, but more likely to add more of a storyline to 2.7 and here, when Sam and Dean now get Agent Henricksen on their trail.

Apparently he knows all about the Winchesters, so what took him so long tracking them? Oh, they're so good! Also why and how does he know all about them? Obviously the cases in the above mentioned episodes wouldn't have been enough to have alerted him, well maybe 2.7 when Diane said she couldn't keep them out of St Louis, but Dean's on the FBI radar now. He was on the FBI radar before, when Dean says Sam is jealous since he's not. You'd think Agent Henricksen would be making meal out of Gordon (**2.9**) wouldn't you – especially since he was arrested by the police after Sam's tip off about them, with such an extensive array of weapons and also a murder charge. Perhaps Henricksen got his information about them from Gordon, his revenge for being arrested and more particularly for not being able to kill Sam, as he's evil. Oh the questions. So we can go round in circles talking about Dean's outstanding warrant.

Dean tells Ronald to stay out of the light. Also what a silly design for a bank, having to come in through the front door and down the stairs, there was no way of knowing what was happening on the street outside and the windows were so high up too. Not surprised then the shifter chose it for its next target.

Sam and Dean were a bit careless in this episode, the number of times they lost the shifter and then Dean fighting it before it escapes again as Sherry, when he finally stabs it. Also, when part of its skin peels away from its arm, Dean spent so long looking at it, as if he hasn't seen it shed its skin before, in St Louis and before in the office.

Sam and Dean are shocked when Ronald is shot in the back, he doesn't stay out of the light and alive – echoing Sam. Of course, Sam meant Ronald shouldn't know what's really happening when he says he should remain in the dark. Dean letting the security guard out and showing himself to the outside world when he's already 'wanted' wasn't such a good idea because now the FBI agent turns up. They now believe Dean's taken over from the original hostage taker. Dean says, "We're so screwed twice" because there's nothing else he can say! Whereas they could dodge the police wherever they went, they can't keep that up for very long with this agent, or can they; he's determined to get his hands on them.

But from what he says about there being a monster in the vault, he's not referring to the shifter but Dean. He doesn't know they hunt evil, he can't because he tells them about Dad; or at least what he thinks Dad is: some sort of gun-toting, crazy, white supremacist with a paramilitary/military background and training, who's into grave desecrations. Hendricksen's not the type to believe in monsters of the paranormal variety. (Not until season 3.)

Sam told Ronald not to talk on the phone to the police and yet Dean answers when it rings. Dean can still get a joke out in such a moment of crisis, only shows his resilience, when he agrees that

Dean's Clyde and Sam's Bonnie – the girl!

Dean defends Dad as a hero and that he doesn't know anything about them and what they do. (Last episode he called Dad an ass for making him keep that promise about Sam and next season he calls Dad, "an obsessed bastard!" (Excuse language.) He gives them an hour to come out, but we don't have an hour to kill, so it'll be the last 5 minutes then – just to add to the tension and whether they'll get the shifter and make it out before the bank's stormed.

Dean telling Sam earlier, that crazies the only game in town, which it is since the agent turns up and tells the police the same thing – that "crazy's in the bank", referring to Dean no doubt. Just what exactly does he think Dean will do when he says Dean's a bigger risk to those hostages. Shoot them all for no reason because he's painted as a glorified killer and was 'charged' with those murders in St Louis. He was suspected of them and he never got his day in court either.

Wasn't their evidence just circumstantial anyway, aside from his sightings, they didn't know for sure it was him and because he was caught red-handed in St Louis, didn't mean anything! (Here's a thought for an episode, Sam and Dean in a court overtaken by zombies and the like! Sam would be at home in a courtroom.)

The shifter made a huge mistake in choosing Sherry, as she faints at the sight of blood and seeing herself dead. Sam's about to kill her, but again it's not Sam who has to do the killing in this episode – it's Dean and there are no guns, so the killing is up close and personal too. Sam standing there with Sherry when she's just fainted, he's not going to kill it in front of her is he.

Can't help but think there was a lot of time wasting in this episode, when it came to tracking and killing it and they could've been out for there ages ago and not be in so much trouble. This wasn't to be since it's Sam and Dean! Let's blame Ronald for it.

When SWAT finds Sherry, why was Sam strolling back casually and why did they pull guns on him anyway, after listening to Sherry when she said she works there, they didn't know exactly who he is or was. Maybe Sam had the idea to take their clothes and dress up as Swat so they could escape.

Dean finally stabs and leaves the letter opener in the body – we know he's wanted for murder but he didn't have to leave the evidence behind with yet more fingerprints for them. Great scene when they escape right under Henricksen's nose, he must've kicked himself then. Did he really suppose they'd hang around waiting to be arrested!

As Max said in **2.2** of *Dark Angel*, "You must be the new bad guy in my life," to Agent White. So it can be said of the agent in Sam and Dean's life. Now hunting just got harder, will it make them look over their shoulder a lot more, or lay low. Don't think so.

They can't really say anything at the end because they don't know what's to come, or what they're going to do, but they're Sam and Dean Winchester, they're not going to give up so easily or hide away. The agent saying he knows all about them, he probably expects them to lay low, so they should do the exact opposite and not do that; just to show him he doesn't know anything about who they really are at all.

Not only do they have to keep hunting – wherever the job takes them, then Dean has to worry about Sam and what he may become and the promise he made to Sam to kill him, but now they have to concern themselves about this agent on their tail; proving Dean's comments, it's a dangerous and lonely life and all they have is each other!

Agent Johnson was named from *The Matrix Reloaded*.

During the helicopter scene, on one of the buildings in the background is a billboard of Sam and Dean (Jared and Jensen) for the promo of the Fall Campaign CW Launch.

Charles Malik Whitfield was a series regular in *The Guardian* with Simon Baker.

Quotes

Dean: "I just think it's creepy how good of a Fed you are."

Dean: "…one didn't turn into you and frame you for murder."

Sam: "Dean we're supposed to be looking for eyes." [Not chick's butts.]

Sam: "Fainting now won't help it survive."

Actual Legend

The famous witchcraft trial of Isobel Gowdie and Janet Breadheid, in Nairn, Scotland in 1662. Isobel claimed she could shapeshift into a cat, a crow or hare. Shapeshifting was described as early as this.

Film/TV References

Dr Who, Bonnie & Clyde, T2 (Terminator), Men In Black

Music

Renegade by Styx.

Ooh Bloops

Sam and Dean both hold badges in their left hands when visiting Ronald, then Dean holds it in his right hand.

In the jewellery store, Sam's hair is swept back, outside Ronald's it's forward on his face, and then it's swept back in the next scene.

Locations

Royal Bank of Canada.

2.13 Houses of the Holy

Written By Sera Gamble. Directed By Kim Manners
Original US Airdate 1 February 2007

Guest Stars: Dennis Arndt (Father Reynolds); Heather Doerksen (Gloria); David Monahan (Father Gregory)

Providence, Rhode Island

Sam and Dean investigate some possible angel sightings.

Notes

The alternate title for this episode was **Touched**, obviously as in *Touched By An Angel.*

This episode title is the name of a Guns'n'Roses album.

Eric Kripke called this "a cerebral episode where Sam and Dean start hunting this supernatural entity and soon realize they may be hunting an angel and what are the implications of that. Sam is questioning, 'Should we even be going after this thing? Is this an angel? Is this God's will?' Dean, who doesn't believe in God or angels says, 'c'mon it's a creature, let's find it and kill it'. You get to explore what the boys' religious and metaphysical views are." (Dad and the rosary in the penultimate episode of season 1.)

As this episode is all about angels, believing in God, faith, the unseen, it's set in Providence! Gloria, who's approached by the 'angel', believes she was chosen for redemption and to do God's work, by killing this man. Clearly you know something's not quite right since God wouldn't tell one person to kill another, it's not his will. Sam's convinced by her story.

Continued from last episode, since Dean was seen by millions on the news as a bank robber, he has to lie low, not literally of course; as he seems to be making the most of this vibrating bed in their less than stylish hotel room. Dean being bored, feels he has to get the most out of it, but for his quarters, he really isn't getting value for money.

Dean can't take Gloria seeing an angel very seriously and that's not hard to do when he doesn't believe at all. He mentions being 'touched by an angel', the long running CBS series about angels on earth helping people because it's God's will and "God loves them all, he hasn't forgotten his children." Clearly a bit clichéd, but then the complete opposite of this episode, as it's not God's work they're doing and they haven't seen any angel. Dean also mentions Roma Downey – the star of *Touched By An Angel,* again in the same way he spoke of Jennifer Love Hewitt and Patricia Arquette in **1.10 Asylum**. Sure the writers here were supposed to talk about the characters they played, rather than their actual names; since as I said before, it sounds as though their show's real and everyone else is just being acted off the screen by Sam and Dean! Or should that read Jensen and Jared! True in the case of *Supernatural.* Oh, I like Roma Downey. Her character, by the way was Monica.

Dean likens Gloria's actions to killing in the name of religion, but that's not what this episode is about and certainly has nothing to do with religion; to put some peoples' minds at rest. It's more about faith, choosing to believe in the unknown, what you can't see and your reasons for believing or abstaining. As Dean here demonstrates, he doesn't believe because he hasn't seen anything to convince him, which rules out the possibility of this 'angel' being real. (However see Season 4.) He's decided it's just a spirit and isn't open to any amount of persuasion on Sam's part. When Sam tells Dean they've seen things people can only imagine, mostly evil. Sam is open to all sorts of suggestions and possibilities because he believes there is good out there. It doesn't matter if they haven't seen it; they don't have to since they fight evil, it doesn't follow they would see any good or any signs of good existing in the world.

It's that age old tale of evil choosing to manifest itself in the world to fight the very good in people by challenging their faith. That's what makes believing such a powerful force as it can't be tested, proven; that good simply exists. The very nature of faith means you're tested everyday because it's your own decision and personal choice to believe. In Other words, "The evil that men do lives on after them." (*Shakespeare's Julius Caesar.*)

Dean has to be right in the end; it was a spirit, that of Father Gregory, which makes what he was doing doubly wrong. He's a priest; he should've known the nature of God's will. The fact he dies before Last Rites could be administered, has left his spirit, his soul in agony and he needs to be granted absolution? Would they have crossed paths with angels or met someone who has; probably not. They fight evil – as

Sam says evil and things most people don't know exist. By that very same fact, Dean shouldn't need any proof in good.

Funnily enough the church is called 'Our Lady of Angels' and Sam thinks an avenging angel could be involved, angels wouldn't need people to do their work. (Again see Season 4.) When Father Reynolds tells them the quote from Luke; he's expecting them to finish their sentence off by telling him where the quote's from – but they don't.

Dean is shocked when Sam tells them he prays everyday. He needs something to hold onto; Sam senses the 'angel' and then it appears to him because he believes already and he's willing to even now and some may call that being gullible.

Dean tells Sam something else about their past; about Mom, that he hasn't before – keeping all these things from Sam – that she believed in angels, doesn't make it wrong to do so. It was her faith; her decision. He can't say for certain she was wrong to do this. Dean tells Sam Mom believed angels were watching over him, last thing she said to him and it didn't help her, well, he doesn't have the right to question her beliefs, he does, but it just sounds like he was ridiculing them. He can't say what she should or shouldn't have believed in. Wasn't she right? Didn't the events of that night show someone was looking out for them. Mom prevented the demon from getting Sam (except for putting the blood in him), Dean got out alive (maybe since it wasn't after him, but that's another matter.) She was watching out for them; that girl in **1.9 Home**, and she saved them from the Poltergeist too.

Strangely their conversation here involves more believing and telling him about Mom, when Dean already has proof they're dealing with a spirit, as he already found the wormwood, whilst Sam was having his revelation (and not epiphany!) saying all this. He veers onto the subject of proof again, which is unfair to Sam.

Sam's reference to Whoopi (Goldberg) from the movie *Ghost*, where she played a medium who could communicate with the dead. Good to see Sam actually cracks a joke in such a moment which Dean acknowledges, since it's always Dean who does this.

Dean's line of defining 'stop', can only mean killing, considering what they do and once more Dean prevents Sam from having to kill someone or something. But this time Dean doesn't have to do any killing either, for once. He finds it very difficult explaining to Sam what he's just seen and having seen it for himself, still can't seem to grasp it and has to put it down to it being "God's will."

Again there's a reversal of their characters. Dean, always the skeptic when it comes to faith; now has his beliefs questioned, turned upside down, at least in this one instance. Sam, who began to doubt his faith, what he believes in, because he didn't really see an angel; says Dean's right after all: they need to believe in what they can perceive, see. Just as he doesn't think anyone's watching over him, Dean comes along and changes everything for him. Hopefully giving Sam back his faith, or at least, part of it. He needs it, as Dean said to him in church; if it makes it easier for him to deal with everything, then that's fine with him. The ending leaving them more skeptical than ever or still willing to believe. Sam has to ask if Dean killed the man in the truck?

Sam always the one to ask questions as to what it could be if not an angel. Well, he doesn't ask, he just says it has to be. Dean being the one doing all the thinking, he doesn't have to think much as he's certain it's a spirit.

Also in church when Sam is caught by Father Reynolds, he does a bit of a 'Dean', saying he can explain what he's doing, but maybe he can't. Father Gregory telling Sam he needs redemption. (See later.)

The woman Dean saves says, "Thank God" ironically (but hey, it's only Dean!)

Church, from *Dark Angel* will be familiar. **1.18 Pollo Loco**. A little déjà vu for Jensen, as Dean, as Ben, the one who was so open to believing in the spiritual, having faith – until this ultimately is his downfall, as he kills for the 'Blue Lady'(aka Virgin Mary): that no one was there for him – being let down by the very faith he believed in.

So Sam's willing to believe – recall *Abba*'s line from the song, "I believe in angels, something good in all I see…" and he does believe there's good out there. He says it in an episode, Dean says their job is to kill the supernatural and Dean says it's not, it's to hunt evil. Same difference?

Dean calls Sam a girl on almost every occasion he can since it's open season on his emotional side and isn't afraid to use that in their job, i.e. always to think about consequences and to empathize and understand what many victims go through. But in **2.14** he has to say that Sam had a girl in him for 7 days!

Sam's quoting of the Séance ritual from Dad's journal in Latin:

Amate spiritus obscure

Ee querimus te oramus

Nobiscum collequere apud nos circiter. Ooh shiver me timbers Sam!

Sam was disillusioned by the time he got to the end of this episode. All his faith, believing in angels, praying everyday – had been knocked for six. Adding more fuel to the fire of becoming evil since his very thoughts the spiritual, on good existing have been challenged. What good is out there to save him now from his pre-written fate?

269

It was good having Sam believe in angels, that you don't get to see, but find comfort in faith and believe in their existence. There was nothing wrong with Sam believing that to balance nature, of good v evil, and that good has every right to be, whether it is in God, angels or in good spirits. That there is a place for everything in the universe and because it's intangible, doesn't make it wrong to believe and unacceptable.

Dean not believing because he has to see it, kind of defeated the purpose in this episode at least, of everything that they do because evil chooses to manifest itself everyday in demons, vengeful spirits and even in people, doesn't necessarily follow good has to present itself in the same way. If you believe in your heart and you're open to the experience, it doesn't have to appear to you.

Like the spirit of Father Gregory appearing to Sam; you could argue it only did that because it was out for revenge, in the form of getting others to kill for it, granted they were criminals or wrongdoers themselves, again to Sam, it meant it was nothing more than an "evil" spirit, or rather more misguided in Father Gregory's case. So again you can say Sam only saw it because he was open to its presence and the fact it wasn't a "good" spirit in the usual sense of the word as it asked

Sam to kill and it ended up something they fight, in the same way Dean didn't see the spirit or was there when it appeared after Sam conducted the séance. Dean told Sam to hold the séance for the spirit to know for sure, so why did Sam use a Ouija board for Dean in **2.1** when it was the closest thing he had handy since Ouija boards are mostly used to summon evil spirits. What does that say about Dean. Fine, only joking! Sam probably used it as it was easier and Dean hadn't completely crossed over to the other side yet. He was still hanging on, barely, and so it was convenient.

Also playing God in this episode with the spirit appearing and commanding people to kill. It wasn't God's will; maybe it was with the second person. Appearing also to people who were down and out on their luck or prostitutes, what did that say about the spirit praying on the impoverished to kill, rather than anyone else: the rich, affluent. So why did it want Sam to do the killing too, was it because Sam was so open to believing it was an angel.

The faith issue allows Sam's character to evolve and to delve further into his true feelings, showing he's a more rounded person and there's more to him; he has other unique dimensions barely touched upon. He has faith – something he probably didn't yet tell Dean because of the reaction he'd get from him. This faith stems from Mom most likely. Also Dean believes in evil, demons and the devil even, and then surely he must also believe in the opposite, in the good, angels, God, a higher power.

So often episodes on TV steer away from issues of religion and faith for fear of offending and in particular, of alienating certain specific audiences, especially in the US and certain very conservative states, religious areas. This episode was different as it concerned faith, as opposed to religion. Faith in Sam's beliefs of what he saw; what those two people believed they saw; the ability to question these ideas; Dean's lack of faith and ability to believe because he hasn't seen good, it therefore follows it doesn't exist.

Dean doesn't believe in God – only that's funny since he believes in evil and demons. Is that because it's all tangible – corporeal and he can see them, but to have belief in good, spirituality, you need faith foremostly – in the intangible – things you can't see but need to feel and believe! In contrast to Dad, did he perhaps believe, or have faith?

Using the idea of beliefs; set in a supernatural show made this episode better from the norm; Dean believes in evil: wholly evil and no in-betweens – "…only chaos…" set against Sam (juxtaposed) who believes in the miracle he saw, even before he (thought) saw this as a miracle, but Dean shoots Sam down on every facet of his beliefs: when finally the twist at the end; what Dean sees makes him doubt his lack of belief for a moment. It seems, and gives Sam cause to think he was right to believe and his faith is still intact.

Dean saying he only believes in demons and things they've come across but nothing like angels.

Obviously he must believe in the devil, its existence to cause so much evil in the world, thus in a roundabout way isn't the devil himself a fallen angel. Proving the existence of angels.

The ending was left open in this episode for the viewer to make up their own mind on whether they believe or not so as not to cause offence.

700 Club is a news talk show of the Christian Broadcasting Network on cable in the US and Canada.

Quotes

Dean: "There really is magic in the 'magic fingers.'"
Sam: "Dean, you're enjoying that way too much. It's kind of making me uncomfortable."

Dean: "Gloria's just your standard issue wacko, I mean she wouldn't be the first nut job in history to kill in the name of religion, know what I mean."

Dean: "Odd, yes, supernatural, maybe, but angels, no."
Sam: "Why not?"
Dean: "Cause there's no such things. Sam."
Dean: "Because I've never seen one, so I believe in what I can see."

Sam: "Dude, I'm not enabling your sick habits. You're like one of those lab rats that push the pleasure button, instead of the food button."

Father Gregory: "Some people need redemption, don't they Sam?"

Sam and Dean's Take on the Urban Legend/Lore

As Sam says there is countless lore on angels.

Actual Legend

Dark angels are seen in angelic lore as those becoming demon-like, such as the devil; a fallen angel, not dark as in the true sense of the word. Then there are those that bring vengeance and are fierce, these are always empowering and compassionate and will never fail humans.

Angels encompass all faiths and religions from Christianity, Islam, Judaism and Zoroastrians. In religious circles angels are seen as stepping stones, or 'intermediaries' between God and humans.

Regarded as beings of light, they guide humans. Guardian angels are said to be near to people and so are seen as the most important on a personal level. Archangels rank higher than angels and so have less of a personal relationship with humans.

Some earlier views of angels in religion were seen as having 'fierce' or 'fighting' qualities. This stems from having to defend faiths, such as Islamic and Judaic, from nonbelievers. God is seen to be part of angels of light (sometimes mistakenly) and evil is seen to be part of angels of darkness, who have been associated with fallen angels. Demons must be angels who were too proud, refusing to praise God (as Lucifer did before being cast out of heaven, Lucifer, meaning 'light bringer.'

Theologians believe this led to a war in heaven and Lucifer, chief angel; Lord of Light and of the Seraphim (cf *X Files* episode **All Souls)** highest rank of angels became the devil. Angels who fought on his side were demons. The leader of the 'good' angels, Archangel Michael, defeated him. Lucifer was cast into hell and will remain there until Armageddon: when good defeats evil.

In *The Science of the Sacraments*, CW Leadbetter, has a scene-by-scene description of the angels that appear in Christian rituals. There is also a Christian invocation for 'Angels, Archangels; 'Seraphim' and 'Cherubim. During the festival of Holy Communion. In Islam, the Prophet Muhammad, was inspired by a divine angel.

Esoteric Hinduism, Gnostic Christianity, Qabalah; all have diagrams of angels. The sixth century Greek writer, Dionysus of Aeropagite, who wrote of an "angelic hierarchy" of: Seraphim, Cherubim, thrones, dominions, virtues, powers, principalities, Archangels and angels – being the highest.

Angels can be seen everywhere; statues of justice represent angels containing the notion of justice, equal before the law and so on. In the Chicago Commodity Market, there's a statue of the goddess, Ceres; the angel of grain and abundance.

As mentioned the folk lore on angels is many and too numerous to mention everything, but is an interesting area.

Film/TV References

Touched By An Angel, Ghost

X Files Connection

Revelations where a boy with stigmata is the chosen one and dark forces are out to slay him in the human form, part "of the great war between good and evil." The man hired as the gardener says, he's meant to protect the boy – his guardian angel; and has been asked to protect the boy by God, he asks Scully how she can help the boy if she doesn't believe. Mulder, in a role reversal is skeptical and tells Scully not to let her faith cloud her judgement [as Sam says here.] There's some great dialogue, as there is between Sam and Dean in the church. Scully: "…you go out on a limb whenever you see a light in the sky, but you're unwilling to accept the possibility of a miracle?"

Mulder; "I wait for a miracle everyday, but what I've seen here has only tested my patience not my faith." Mulder says Scully thinks she was chosen to protect the boy (as Sam thinks he was chosen by an angel to do God's work.)

A season 6 episode, **Patience**, where Scully essentially plays Mulder in a less skeptical way; she now believes, whereas Doggett takes on her role. Like Sam and Dean's role reversal in many episodes.

5.17 All Souls the priests name was also Father Gregory, who said: "Unless you accept the truth of God's teachings, that there is a struggle between good and evil for all souls, and we are losing that struggle. You are but fools rushing in." This episode was written by John Shiban.

5.12 Bad Blood, Scully also uses the *Magic Fingers* whilst in a motel room, Dean's vibrating bed, as does Mulder. She even remarked that she's just put money into it and won't get any use from it now, as Mulder wants her to conduct another autopsy. He says he'll use it instead and he does.

Music

There's A Good Times A Comin' by Doug Stebleton; *Down on Love* by Jamie Dunlap; *Knockin' on Heaven's Door* by Bob Dylan

Ooh Bloops

When the TV falls in Zach's room, the cable is unplugged and tied. Dean tells Sam, Zack stabbed the victim in the heart, but it wasn't in the heart.

When Sam and Dean enter the basement, there are three padlocks and when the camera shows them entering form the inside angle, the doors are just opened like they're not even locked.

Locations

St Andrew's Wesley Church.

Redemption

Why does Father Gregory say Sam needs redemption: the need to atone his past, unworthy acts. Sam hasn't done anything unworthy to atone for his entire life. It's been a quest for the truth; to find what happened to Mom, to Jessica; why, who he is and his destiny. Unless you return to Season 1, and the point where Sam says he knew what awaited Jessica, but did nothing. He hasn't killed for the sake or joy of killing, heck he hasn't done much killing, except evil and that's when he gets the chance.

What prays on his mind is the future that awaits him, an uncertain one. If he'll be become a killer? If he has to prematurely atone for what he could become and what he might do if this happens; then as rightly said, in **2.11 Playthings**, he needs to help as many people as he can; fight as much evil as he can without succumbing to 'madness'. There's so much going on in the world as they keep saying and nobody knows what's happening; the evil that's out there still. Not knowing what awaits them, as Dean said in **Pilot**, you need to be afraid of the dark. For this reason, Sam can't become evil and Dean can't let him because there'd be two important players lost in this crucial good fight. (We know there are other hunters out there, doing the same thing like them, but most of them don't have their consciences – even Dean has one. The ones we've come across – in Ellen's roadhouse, look nothing more than rednecks, only in the hunt for the love of killing. Another example was Gordon, he wasn't completely balanced either, especially when he came after Sam because of what he may become.)

If Father Gregory meant future redemption, then maybe he saw what Sam would become and that's why he said everyone needs redemption; or as Dean put it, he probably read Sam's mind, he was a spirit in the end and that's what many of them do.

Going back to what I said in **2.10,** that perhaps if Dad had revealed to Dean that Sam was going to go dark side, then he'd have to face his demons, before he could overcome them; then the theme of redemption would fit in well with this; however, it could also have been one theme which could have been explored further, particularly where Sam is concerned. Sam fears if he does become evil he'd no longer be able to fight and would do the very things he's opposed to.

Dean may also need his own redemption with what he's seen and done. He's endured pain, and suffering too and he never falters or fails to do good. But he's always helped people, even his own family. Does he need to be redeemed?

Also knowing what is out there; he repeats again, "there's…random, unpredictable evil that comes out of nowhere and rips you to shreds…" He's had the chance to do real good and this will forever continue for him. Even in **1.16 Shadow,** he tells Sam they'll always be something they need to hunt. Dean is redeemed by the loyalty he's shown and had towards his family; and when he promises to look out for Sam, it's no mean feat has to make such a dreadful promise to kill his own brother.

Sam's visions, premonitions, have an impact on him, they're helping people; saving them from their destinies, just like he wants to be saved from his. Hence his dejection when he realizes nothing may be watching over him, no saving graces. Would he want to be rid of his premonitions and abilities if he ever got the opportunity or has he been through too much; seen too much to do this. He's not the type to stop helping people and having a chance to be normal; as he could be; he was still drawn back into this life of hunting. He knows if he didn't have his abilities, the world would be an even grimmer place than it is. At least with his visions (for however long they last) he can attempt to outdo or undo some evil.

Did Dad get redemption? In the same way – he showed his loyalty to his sons; he never left them when they could have so easily become bad. As Sam says in **1.14 Nightmare**, he didn't realize how lucky they were having Dad until then. If he had been a weaker person he could've let his sons fall by the wayside into a darker spiral no one could've rescued them from.

He had the strength to carry on; even after Mom and even if it was for vengeance. Dad was redeemed since he loved his sons and he dies whilst sacrificing his own life and soul for Dean: his selfless act. Whom he found difficult to share his real feelings with until **1.20** with Sam and **2.1** with Dean.

They did more good and confronted evil because he trained them that way. As the two who were incited to commit those murders in this episode know, redemption for them came at a price: their personal freedom, which could be said made up for them by no longer carrying on as down and outs in their lives, but believing in some sort of inner peace. Is this the same peace Sam craved when he was willing to carry out the deed he'd been sent to complete.

2.14. Born Under a Bad Sign

Written By Cathryn Humphris. Directed By J Miller Tobin
Original US Airdate 8 February 2007

Guest Stars: Alona Tal (Jo); Jim Beaver (Bobby)

Twin Lakes

Dean searches for Sam who's been missing for a week. They come across Jo.

Notes

Though this episode was good in that it moved away from Sam constantly playing the good guy (we know he's good!) even if he had to get possessed to be evil and cruel! It allowed Jared to show far more of his acting abilities and boy does he do evil and mean, darn good! He got to take a break from playing doe-eyed Sam, whom everybody likes and we think he's loveable too; there's nothing wrong with his character, but occasionally it was great to have an insight into the Sam that he could be if he destiny was realized.

Also shocking for Dean, in that no matter how bad he appeared; how he taunted and beat him, Dean couldn't do the inevitable, what he was made to promise. Who could take their own brother's life, no matter how evil he became. Sam couldn't take Dad's life when he was possessed in the season 1 finale, so how could he turn around and make Dean promise the same thing; and here he was so eager to point the gun at himself by practically placing it in Dean's hand. You knew something wasn't quite right, what with Sam wanting to end it all; rather Dean ending it for him, for the one murder he thinks he's committed, but can't for the life of him (excuse pun) remember anything about.

Conveniently all clues and evidence led to Sam: the knife in the car, the video cameras catching the guilty act on tape and drinking and smoking, something he never does, well not smoke. Sam wants to be a lawyer, didn't really put up much of a defence on his own behalf; weighing up everything against him, playing judge and jury, passing sentence on himself and having Dean be the executioner!

Perhaps if he really was Sam, his true self, he would've examined it more rationally; instead of concluding he's turned after one incident. For example, why would he leave the knife lying around in the car for anyone to find and then wipe the prints off it now when Dean's around. Wouldn't he have thrown it away before, disposed of it elsewhere rather than carry it around with him – same goes for the cigarettes and didn't that motel have surveillance cameras of their own. He didn't bother wiping the bloodied print on the window handle, did Dean do this without us knowing, and also where did they dispose of his bloody shirt?

A niggling point about this episode, we didn't get to see how or when Sam was possessed; but from previous episodes (especially **1.21-22**) it's obvious a possession can occur from person to person, just by passing them; so that's probably how Meg possessed Sam. Also it's not properly explained why Sam left Dean, he probably doesn't know himself, as he tells Dean he can't recall everything, so the writer left that question unanswered, leaving a little mystery to some events in Sam's life, instead of wrapping up loose ends, as we know the show doesn't usually do, so in hindsight, this shouldn't look so strange.

Sam's use of the name 'Richard Sambora.' Again, warning bells, it's not a name Sam would've used, let alone thought of, he's not really into this sort of music.

Dean's shocked Sam's taste in stealing cars has dropped too since the last two occasions he stole in **1.11 Scarecrow** and **2.10 Hunted.** Funny Sam can't recall many past events but he can remember where the place on the gas receipt is and oh – he stole liquor, but paid for gas! That garage assistant didn't like his behaviour but gave him a receipt too. Dean accurately says Sam's behaviour is more like something he'd do – but wouldn't really, we haven't seen him throwing bottles for no reason. Wasn't Wedell being so obvious with the lights and cameras around his house, it was like a beacon saying 'hunter lives here!'

Again, why would Sam kill a hunter, he'd have no reason for this and he presumably didn't even know one (unless he was one of Gordon's fraternity, highly unlikely), but he kind of instinctively knows to look in his wardrobe and dragging him back to slit his throat on camera, should've had alarm bells ringing too. Sam wouldn't want his face on camera especially when he was out of sight when they fought. Also leaving behind so much evidence; blood, fingerprints, which Dean cleans up now. As for smashing the computer, Dean left the hard drive behind and Sam doesn't take it either, anything can be found on one of those.

Sam's reason for not telling Dean of his feelings of anger and rage over the past weeks and he didn't tell Dean because he didn't want to scare him, aren't convincing either. This from the Sam who made Dean promise to kill him; when he turns bad; was he asking for a reprieve now or thinking of one by not telling him and now that Dean's found out what Sam may have done; he completes a 360 and decides to come clean so Dean can end it all.

Dean misses the point entirely when he says, "no one can control you, but you," since they're so familiar with demonic possessions; of course that's not true. If you try hard enough you can still control your actions, like Dad in the season 1 finale when he told Sam to shoot him whilst still being possessed. Throwing the gun down Dean, dangerous since the demon possessing him may have influenced Sam to pick it up and use it on himself. Instead Meg wants to have fun!

Funny the manager wants extra money from Dean when he's just spent the night on the floor!

Dean gets beaten up a lot this episode and shot at and worst of all, it's by 'Sam'!

Sam looking at Jo in a particularly menacing way – like he has impure thoughts on his mind, but he was menacing the way he towered over her. Then saying Dean will never have romantic feelings for her. True because Dean just dismisses her really, whereas everyone else he would've been more 'gentle' with and he doesn't want her blood on his hands, like Dad had her father's on his. When Sam attacks her, why would Meg want Jo in that sort of a way? Me thinks a kinky demon there!

Meg tells Jo, Dad had to put her father out of his misery, makes you wonder if this is true and when Sam turns up at the bar where Jo works, ordinarily they wouldn't really have gone out of their way to track her down when she left and they weren't on speaking terms anyway; they'd have no reason to find her.

When Sam says Jo carries a torch for him, it almost sounds as if he's jealous in that demonic Meg sort of way. Then he goes into using third person speech and calling Dad, 'John' which he's never done and neither has Dean either, it's always 'Dad'. John would be too disrespectful anyway. You don't call your parents by their first names.

Sam was suitably evil when he says that line in a singy tone of voice, just like children taunt, "My Daddy shot your daddy in the head" reverting back to calling him 'Daddy' now, which they don't do either.

Yes Sam has many names and the most obvious one Dean would use is bitch" as he did in **1.21** and later. Also Sam didn't tell Dean not to call him Sammy this time, when he always does.

Meg saying all this was just a test to torment Dean, see if he'd actually go through with killing Sam and then at the end, Meg says she doesn't care about the demon's master plan, doesn't make sense – then why bother testing him anyway, if only to toy with them and then had all that time to get her revenge. So what if she learnt new tricks in hell, she didn't use them to any advantage here, when she could've done some serious damage to Sam and Dean and their relationship. Thereby helping her dear Daddy demon (Yellow Eyes) in the process! So that's what hell does, does it, teaches old dogs new tricks!

Also in **2.1**, Yellow Eyes tells Dad he wants revenge for them killing his children, well not quite if they're only in hell, they're still around. Meg crawled out. Besides Dean wouldn't kill Sam, it has nothing to do with courage or mettle, but it's about blood and love.

Dean's phone still works after being in the water and Dean should've jumped in, not got shot – he hesitated.

He won't call Jo later and she's right again, he doesn't need to. So demons lie and some tell the truth on occasion too and here Jo thinks it told the truth about her and Dean since Dean seems so indifferent towards her and probably would treat her like his sister. Hey he doesn't even treat her as a friend, but Dean having a girl as a friend, who's not his girlfriend would be very rare indeed! I won't go into the whole Sam's 'a girl' thing here either!

When did Jo get time to touch up her lipstick in between rescuing Dean and taking the bullet out of him?! Nobody called Ellen to tell her where Jo was.

Again Sam torments Dean about being alive whilst those he loves around him all seem to die. Uh- cockroaches don't come back from the dead, in some reincarnated form. (Ha) No they just don't die easily. Bobby seems to be on the ball from the get-go and has Sam pegged as possessed, but then he always does, like telling them Meg was a real girl (because it was so difficult to tell. Ha!) So this new trick Meg discovered was the binding link then. Didn't do much good and if this is was so clever why did she return to the scene of her demise first time round, finding itself in a déjà vu position again, so much for learning new tricks, recite a bit of exorcism ritual in Latin and hey presto – it only serves to prolong the agony of being expelled from Sam's body, a little later rather than sooner. Why didn't 'Sam' use the old telekinesis mojo on Jo, if he wanted to pin her down so badly on the bar, instead of being so physically hands on.

Dean gets hit again, this sounds a bit like the conversation Dean has with the demon at the crossroads, torturing him; being sent back to hell, telling him Dad's there and he couldn't save him because he's worthless. These demons know how to try to get Dean riled or pissed off, obviously he couldn't save Dad, and he was in a coma and didn't know Dad would sacrifice himself. Why would they have been better off without him anyway, also he hasn't even begun to save Sam yet.

Sam was priceless when he asked if he missed anything and Dean punches him back finally – only when he's really Sam though. So now, enemies they've got: Yellow Eyes and his following; Gordon; police on Dean's back, the FBI agent Henricksen and pretty soon some hunters are bound to find out that Sam did kill one of them.

After going through hell, not literally (yet), Dean still drives. Dean would comment, on the "dirty" comments - not once but twice, first Bobby; "stop it from getting back up in you." Then Dean tells Sam he had a girl inside him for a week. Strictly speaking it wasn't a girl and it would only be naughty if Sam was inside the girl! Oops.

So now Dean says Dad only told him to kill Sam if he couldn't save him, well he kept that pretty quiet until now, as far as we know, he may not have said that at all! But he says he'll save him even if he dies trying (oh prophetic words Dean, in light of the season finale and the season 3 finale.) Ooh Sam reciting more Latin here!

What's with those fish in the motel room? Plus the paintings in the manager's office. Twin Lakes, a fishy town, in more ways than one.

Lots of references to '2' for some reason, missing a week. Checked in 2 days ago. The garage where the car was numbered 2. It was pump number 2 at the filling station. (Being a hunter, Wendell has animal trophies on his wall.)

When Sam and Dean watch the video, notice Sam slits Wendell's throat right to left instead of left to right, which is the usual motion for right handed people. He holds the knife in his left hand, but neither Sam nor Dean noticed. Also when Sam holds Jo at knifepoint, the knife's in his right hand; but when Dean enters, he holds it to her throat in his left hand. When Sam shoots Dean – he holds the gun in his left hand. Also since when has Sam done any full-blown-hands-on throat slitting, no one gives him a chance to kill a spirit, (at times) let alone a man!

When Sam slugs Dean with the gun, Dean falls in front of the bed, yet when he comes too, from the manager knocking on the door, he seems to be in front of the table; nearer to the door.

What does Dean do with the flask when he's chasing Sam on the pier, he takes it out of his pocket and looks at it, then it's back in his pocket when he follows Sam. Dean loses the flask again at the end and why doesn't Meg break out of the ropes much sooner since she can, or was she having more fun. Well, enjoy it while it lasts, 'cause she ain't getting Sam again.'

Hey Sam and Dean could have their own version of *CSI*, especially when they piece the clues together in this episode and 'investigate' the car Sam is meant to have stolen – with blood, cigarettes and the bloody knife. Why didn't Sam just dispose of the knife instead of wiping his prints and throwing it back. Also they didn't wipe any prints from the car; garage door, lock etc, when they left. A bit dangerous for Dean since he's wanted several states over. (Ok so I exaggerate. See above.) No, but seriously they could have their own *Supernatural Investigations CSI* show, since they do that anyway, investigate strange goings on.

Whose car is Dean driving to South Dakota and to Duluth when Sam's taken his? Dean, shame on you, letting Meg drive your baby! Sam leaves his jacket behind at Jo's bar. As for cutting Bobby's phone wire, he's got a cell phone anyway (and in **4.14**, he had several phonelines too from the number of phones he had in his house.) Jo comes looking for Dean with nothing but a torch (she's carrying a torch for Dean. Ha!) When Sam's still on the prowl.

What if Dean does kill Sam, who'll pick up the pieces when Sam isn't around. Or deal with Dean's anger, rage, guilt and how will he live with himself. No one thought of that: better to fight than to die a coward. Selfish much Sam? Mind you, Dean did the same in this season finale. If it's the last thing Dean does, he will save Sam, cf season finale.

The exorcism:

Exorcisamus te, omnus in mundus spitirus omnus satanica potestas
Omnes incursion.
Humiliares sub potente magnu dei.
Sam: spiritus in mundum, glorum suarum.
Umitite. Palatum iram domine...

Hellspawn is a fictitious creation in the comic book, *Spawn*.

A binding link is a mark on a possessed human so the evil spirit or demon, can keep itself "locked" in the body; allowing exorcism rituals to have no effect. It can be 'unbound' by burning, thus providing a space in the link.

Richie Sambora from Bon Jovi. (Bon Jovi will also crop up in **3.16** when Dean chooses to sing to one of their songs, before his own swansong.)

Why didn't Dean track Sam's phone?

The scene at the end was originally meant to end when Sam asks if he missed anything, but Jensen and Jared came up with Dean punching Sam and the producers agreed to it.

The title is a song sung by Albert King and covered by Cream.

An alternate title for this episode was **Welcome To My Nightmare**.

The road was also used in **1.4** and **1.9**, where the sign reads 'Twin Lakes 100m.'

One of Jared's favourite episodes, "It was awesome to explore that different side of Sam, even if it was just because he was temporarily possessed. I've now played Sam for 40 different episodes, which is something like 320 days of shooting, and what is a long time to play a guy who has been a certain way for the majority of it. It was fun to have that little 'vacation' from Sam and to mess with Dean a bit. As a viewer, I love it when the brothers are at odds with each other. [So do I.]

They love each other and they are kidding around, but when you see them clash and go head-to-head, it brings a new, interesting dynamic...It was filmed right before the Christmas holiday.

After the first stretch of 5 months of shooting, you get to see the light at the end of the tunnel. It was fun to do the scenes with Alona [Tal – Jo] as you see Sam being a slime ball!" Jared also says this character was a lot of fun to film in this way. "This isn't as intense, but it's fun to flip around and play the bad guy so I'm excited about it. Viewers thought 'Why would your Dad say that about you?'" Definitely a Sam episode.

Jared: "I was possessed by a demon and that was one of my favourite shows. So I would love more of that."

Jared said at this point that Jo may be coming back, but only returned for this episode. But won't be so glad to see Sam, though he will be, since he doesn't know what he subjected her to. Though she probably won't be that happy to see Dean either since he 'bailed' on her after she patched him up and didn't want her going with him to find Sam, especially after what possessed 'Sam' told her about Dean thinking of her as a sister. Jared says, Jo'll probably have a knife with her, "She's a tough chick!" Just incase.

Sam's phone number is 1-785-555-2805.

J Michael Tobin said Jensen "had a wetsuit on – but that doesn't help much when the water's thirty degrees and you're lying half in the ocean. It was more than a little chilly." On the scene when Dean falls into the water when Sam shoots him, but he didn't go into the water. He also says he used a song from The Doors, who Eric Kripke hates, but he put his hate aside and actually went with the song as it worked for the episode.

Alona Tal is now in *Cane*. She was in *Half Past Dead 2* (as Ellie), *Taking 5* (Devon), *Split Decision* and *Veronica Mars*.

Quotes

Dean: "…God, this looks familiar déjà vu vibe?"

Dean: "It wasn't you, yeah, it might've been you, but it wasn't YOU!"

Dean: "I've tried so hard to keep you safe, I can't. I'd rather die."
Sam: "You'll live. "You'll live to regret this."

Sam: "Guess I'm full of surprises." (No, just full of girl demon!)

Dean "...dude, you, you full on had a girl inside you for a whole week. That's pretty naughty."

Music

The Crystal Ship by The Doors; *Ashes to Ashes* by Tarbox Ramblers; *Back on the Road Again* by REO Speedwagon

Ooh Bloops

When Dean talks to Ellen, he gets a call from Sam, and then he doesn't return back to Ellen after putting her on hold.

When Dean was hit by Sam, he had his right hand by his body; this changes and ends up by his head.

Jo sports a bruise on her forehead when she's tied, which becomes a cut when she helps Dean, and becomes a bruise again after that.

Locations

Canary Row, Steveston.

2.15 Tall Tales

Written By John Shiban. Directed By Bradford May
Original US Airdate 15 February 2007

Guest Stars: Richard Speight Jr (Trickster); Jim Beaver (Bobby); Barclay Hope (Professor Cox); Tara Wilson (co-ed)

Sam and Dean just seem to get into one argument after another, when investigating a death on campus.

Notes

The opening with 'Previously' had scenes when Sam and Dean played jokes on each other, (in **1.17 Hell House**) as a possible clue to this episode's story.

The professor didn't think it odd that one of his students was dressed in a skimpy dress when it's freezing outside and snowing! Dean isn't really acting that different than he normally does when he acts the slob all over Sam's bed eating that awful food and with his fingers, so you can't be sure anything wrong's with them, just them getting fed up with being in each other's pockets all the time. Sam tells him he didn't mess with his car and we don't know what's happened to his precious Impala until later on.

This episode is told in flashback to the three different stories involved with Sam and Dean not being around when the incidents occur, so they find out about each of the 'stories' as they normally would anyway, with investigation and listening to third hand accounts. A version of "he said, she said." So Bobby has to keep the peace between them. Anyway, why would Sam mess with Dean's car since it's the only form of transport he's got too? But you can understand Dean using Sam's computer and obviously it would be on such a website as bustyasianbeauties.com – though none of the Playboy models conjured in this episode were Asian, that busty or beautiful, for that matter! (Not that I'm into all this!) bustyasianbabes.com is a link to the WB site.

The student's professor was an author of *Modern Morality* and they had him for ethics and morals, so he didn't have any of his own, hence Dean's comment it was poetic justice what happened to him and the others. The anthropologist experimented on animals and was mauled by an alligator, whereas Curtis, who was into hazing was abducted by aliens and probed, what he'd do to others no doubt.

This episode flashes back and forth with Sam and Dean giving their own versions of events and the way they both exaggerate is apparent. Dean paints himself as the ladies man, of course and would never 'date' a slob, but an intelligent blonde (!) who can't see past Dean's good looks. Well, he's telling the story and no Dean wouldn't call chicks feisty or wildcats, rather a bitch! Than a cat – hey and Sam certainly doesn't "blah blah blah" at all. Whereas Dean portrays him as all serious and all mouth, and Dean's all about action! Dean calling Sam *Major Tom* from the David Bowie song *Space Oddity*, maybe appropriate as this was an odd episode, not in the *supernatural* mould we're used to. Sam doesn't overdo it when Dean stuffs his face because he tends to eat free food whenever he can. So was Dean using Sam's computer with that guilty look plastered on his face, as he walks away without answering, you think he did, but he hasn't.

Good to see they don't take all their 'jobs' too seriously, especially since Sam can't help and laugh at Curtis's abduction story being probed and slow dancing to *Lady In Red*. Best bit when Dean overdoes Sam's touchy-feely spiel with the other college boy – hugging him and comforting him, because we know that's not really what Sam does at all. He's just sensitive rather than "in yer face!"

Strange how Sam and Dean don't break into a morgue more often when they need to, instead of dressing up like doctors or paying off lab staff.

Weekly World News is a "mock" tabloid published in the US, using reports of 'extraordinary' news and in-house articles, all of which are works of fiction.

Bobby finally works out there's a Trickster at work here, who's been playing Sam and Dean off against one another, but he preferred not to resort to deadly measures with them; seeing as it was more fun to watch them argue with one another. If they hadn't been bickering, they would've noticed but then this would've defeated the entire object of what tricksters do and they would've realized what was happening. They didn't think it odd that they were fighting for no reason and

Dean was being more obnoxious instead of teasing Sam like usual. But for all of their fighting, they did come up with some valid points about each other. Dean's a bit of a slob compared to Sam, who isn't, but he isn't so perfect either as Dean says he is and he doesn't overdo the being 'too nice' bit, which isn't acting like a pansy.

So it was poetic justice for Dean to be beaten up by bimbos! Some might say this episode borrows a lot from the two *X Files* episodes, pray tell, was Dean open to belief then or did he just comment on the spaceship to contradict Sam. Since he said beforehand he doesn't believe in aliens. When he asked Dean for the magnifying glass in the morgue to closely examine the remains a la Scully. This episode was also meant to be a comedic departure from the usual episodes as bit like **1.17 Hell House**, when the brothers were playing all sorts of pranks on each other, whereas this time round, they were the objects of the pranks. Dean drinking 'Purple Nurples' in the bar, purple is widely associated with eroticism.

Also Dean wouldn't use language like that. i.e. 'dick.' (I spoke too soon here as 'dick' has been used endlessly in the later seasons.) The fight between them that was a long time coming, especially as it's what siblings do. Have you noticed whenever Sam and Dean are really honest with each other, it's always when they're under the influence of someone or something else.

The Trickster says he likes Dean here so why can't he just let him move onto the next town, from this episode it becomes clear why Dean was targeted by the Trickster again in Season 3's Groundhog Day episode. He didn't let him get away and was the one who staked him! Then again, that episode was mostly about Sam too and how alone he'd be without him around.

One qualm, when the Trickster conjured 'himself' for the brothers to stake, why didn't anyone realize he wouldn't let himself be killed so easily and would disappear, even the nature of his name suggests this; particularly if they can conjure anything and manipulate any scenarios. What made it even worse is that even Bobby didn't think of this either. So a bit lax of them in this episode, like in **2.11 Playthings**, when they thought the haunting of the hotel was over when Rose died.

Poindexter is also used to describe nerds.

There was also a Trickster in the series *The Adventures of Sinbad* episode **1.19 Trickster** where he prayed on each of the crew's fears by making them face up to their fears in reality. Sinbad's greatest fear being drowned.

Recipe for a *Purple Nurple: 1oz Malibu. 1oz triple Sec, ½ oz Blue Curacao liquer, 2oz Cranberry Juice. (Don't drink too much!)*

Quotes

Sam: "Dean what do you think you're doing?. Dean this is a very serious investigation,

Sam: "Dean were you on my computer? Oh really cause it's frozen on bustyasianbabes.com."

Dean: "Why don't you control your OCD."

Sam and Dean's Take on the Urban Legend/Lore

In this case, it was Bobby's take on the lore about Tricksters, "these things create chaos and mischief as easy as breathing." Tricksters are demi-gods. Known as Anasi in West Africa, Loki in Scandanavia. They can create things and make them vanish. Tricksters target people who are too big for their boots and put them down, (explains Sam and Dean then. Ha!) Using deadly pranks with humour.

Actual Legend

Tricksters are also known as Coyotes, but have different names in different languages. Since they are part gods – this means they couldn't just be staked or be killed in this episode and that's what they should have realized. Even Bobby says it when he mentions Loki, who is a Scandinavian god. Trickster was popular in Native American and Indian myths. One such mythological character was the Creator-Trickster Coyote. These myths scattered all across the South West and the Plains in the US. Some have likened him to being around even now – in the form of popular cartoon character *Wile E Coyote*.

In the North West he was known as 'Raven'. In the South East, 'Rabbit' and on the Plains, the Lakota tribe knew him as 'Spier'. Tricksters were seen as clever; but messed up their trickery by their own fool hardiness and usually wound up dead or injured themselves. But not for long. As they would rise again, (so maybe another name they should've been called was 'Phoenix' instead.) Sometimes

Trickster myths or stories were very distasteful and thus ensured the essential nature of having rules about morality.

Other Tricksters were seen as heroes for their culture allowing their tribe to be more civilized in the process of bestowing gifts to them, in the form of fire or banishing their monsters, demons. Stories about Tricksters became the stable diet of many tribes encompassing almost a tradition.

A famous story about the Trickster or coyote is one which involves a giant: told by the Navajo who used to say that giants walked the land and their favourite food was human children. The coyote attempted to find a solution to this. He asked a giant to engage in a sweat bath with him in a lodge. Coyote told him he would show the giant a miracle: he would break his own leg and then heal himself by putting it back together. After taking a rock he also took out the leg of a deer and broke it with the rock. After the giant felt his broken leg, the coyote spoke "leg become whole". His leg was now fixed. The coyote agreed to do the same for the giant who agreed. The coyote told him to find his leg; he would have to keep spitting on it. This giant did over and over allowing coyote to make his escape.

Others include Loki in Scandinavian myth and was seen in an episode of *Hercules The Legendary Journeys* being up to no good. In Viking or Norse mythology, Audumta, the primal cow or mother, licked a pillar of salt and bore Buri: the first of the gods. He married the Giantess Bestia, who had three sons – gods of the Aesir, the first was Odin (Spirit); second was Vili (Will) and Ve (Holiness). Other versions call the three gods; Odin, Hoenir (The Shining One) and Loki (Trickster, god of fire.)

The legend of alligators in the sewer originated in New York around 1980's. In one version, circa 1935, *The New York Times* wrote an article on some boys finding an alligator in the open manhole on E123rd St and dragged it out by lassoing its head. The alligator had to be killed as it became dangerous and measured around 7.5-8 feet.

The second version is from Florida in the 1930's, when New Yorkers on holiday took home baby alligators from the Everglades. Some disposed of them on the street, whilst others sought to flush them down the toilet, as Dean says here. The alligators grew by eating rats and the odd maintenance man. It's believed the alligators evolved into Albinos as they lived in the dark.

A former New York Commissioner of Sewers wrote a book where he stated that New York had a problem with alligators in the sewer by the mid 1930's. Another Commissioner said alligators were found in the sewers but were just 2 feet long. By 1937, it was stated all the alligators had been killed from the sewers. However, experts have said it's not possible for alligators to live long in sewers due to the toxic substances such as chemical waste, hydrogen sulphide.

Also from a biological point of view, alligators need the sun to reproduce – temperature from 86 or higher, meaning males will be born; anything under this will be female. Since sewer temperatures will be low, the ensuing off spring will be female and hence no others could be born. It is suggested alligators would become blind in the dark surroundings and only after generations would they evolve into albinos.

It is also believed this urban legend was the sequel to that of the Victorian legend of wild hogs in the Hampstead section of the London sewers. Rumour had it that a pregnant pig entered the sewer and had her offspring there, living off the waste. Seen as dangerous, they were rumoured to have emerged from the Fleet Street sewers. Thus the reference to journalists as "pigs". (Most of the London press was based in Fleet Street in the past, before it was taken over by lawyers.) That's another story.

December 1954, Chico, Cerro de las Tres Torres, Venezuela, small hairy beings were said to have touched down in an aircraft. 1955, Kentucky, USA, 5 small beings with dark, wrinkly skin and large eyes and ears were seen by a family at their farm. One touched a family member's head with a silver hand; these extra terrestrials were known as *Hopkinsville Goblins.*

Aboriginal cave drawings in Australia also show the presence of "celestial" beings possessing antennae. Alien abductions are said to be similar to fairy kidnappings – as they have to reproduce with human males. Alien Nordics, tall in stature and noble are said to look like "opalescent fairies" which are called "greys." These are extra-terrestrial, smaller than an adult with grey skin; large, almond-shaped eyes and oval-shaped heads. It is believed they want to mate with humans to ensure they own survival. Crop circles are also associated with aliens and are said to be lacking in morals and cruel.

Some argue that these extra terrestrials may be mistaken for fairies and the UFOs are the earth lights of fairy mounds beyond the bounds of human belief and perception.

Re alien abductions, a lawyer in Germany defends people who have been abducted by aliens. His first case was of a 23 year old chef who claims to have been abducted and has "never been the same since." He says he was sucked into space, manipulated and returned to Earth in the form of a shaman. He bathed nude in a public fountain and rode naked, then was arrested by police. The German lawyer, from Dresden began a lawsuit against Dresden saying, "The state is socially responsibility even for alien shamans if they cannot protect them from abduction." (From the Ananova website.)

Is the lawyer 'right' for taking on such a case/claim or is the so— called shaman in his right mind. Oh and where are Mulder and Scully when you need them. According to where your beliefs lie, you may believe of the alien abduction in this episode or not, as something that's a part of real life, as many people do make such claims.

Film/TV References

ET

X Files Connection

Bad Blood when Mulder and Scully give varying accounts of what happened in a town where vampires attacked; after Mulder kills a man he believes to be a vampire. Scully and Mulder retell their own version of events which greatly differ from each other, to Skinner. The sheriff is portrayed as either stupid or very good, depending on whose version is being relayed. Like Sam and Dean here. Dean is seen as a womanizer when Sam tells his story and Sam is seen as a do-gooder geek with a sensitive side, when Dean's telling it. **Josie Chung's From Outer Space**.

But you can say that was a bit in Scully mode in their flashbacks when Dean said he tended to talk a lot! (Though not since he calls him a girl and he called Sam, Scully last time.) When he says the marks on the ground were made by jet engines, that's similar to Scully's skepticism, compared to Mulder's belief in aliens when Dean says it was a 'saucer-shaped' engine.

In **Josie Chung's...** a novelist interviews Scully over the rumours two teens were abducted by aliens and it appears the account can be interpreted in various ways. Scully wants him to only tell the truth and he says, what happened is open to interpretations, "truth is as subjective as reality." The girl recalls being on an alien ship and Scully thinks it's, "too typical" seeing as there's so much about abduction lore out there. The boy admits to having sex; which Scully says is evidence that the girl wasn't probed by an alien. The funny part was where Scully is accused of threatening a witness not to talk and she's surprised, "He said I said what?" Just as Sam and Dean contradict each other now as to how each of them behave in their own scenarios and what they divulge.

Also in one scene, Mulder devours slices of pie, a la Dean with the sweets in the professor's office.

6.16 Alpha, Mulder and Scully come across a dog known as the *Wanshang Dhole*, a rare breed said to be extinct for 150 years, known as a trickster dog in legend.

Music

Next To You by Junkhood; *Lady in Red* by Chris De Burgh; *Walk Away* by James Gang; *Brenda and Me* by Rhythm Machine; *Can't Get Enough of Your Love, Baby* by Barry White

Ooh Bloops

At the end when they drive away, Bobby can't be seen in the back seat of the Impala.

Locations

University of British Columbia, School of Technology.

2.16 Roadkill

Written By Raelle Tucker. Directed By Charles Beeson
Original US Airdate 15 March 2007

Guest Stars: Tricia Helfer (Molly) Dan Gauthier (David); Winston Rekert (Jonah Greeley)

Couple in a car suffer a road accident, whilst Sam and Dean try to put the two ghosts haunting the highway to rest.

Notes

When Dean asks, or as soon he asks, if the man who's after Molly looks like he lost a fight with a lawnmower, you can tell they already know who he is and that they're probably on a hunt: after him. This is confirmed when Sam refers to him by name, i.e. Greely and when Dean asks Sam if he's gonna tell her the truth, which can only mean one of two things, either David's dead, or Molly is. Sam says he believes her story and they suggest taking her to the police, again confirming something's not quite right since they wouldn't think of going to the police to begin with.

Hey, they never need the police (re Dean's sarcastic comments in the Pilot about what a bang-up job they were doing investigating the disappearances.) Also the way he's been treated by the police, in **2.7 The Usual Suspects**, as well as the FBI.) His disdain for such authority figures, also they're wanted by the police. So Molly running into them is not just a coincidence, it never is with Sam and Dean. Strange Molly runs to Sam's side of the car. You know by the strange looks they give each other and when Dean drives straight at Greely and through him.

Molly wonders if calling David a jerk is the last thing she ever said to him, and you know she's right, it was.

Radio static and EMF plays a lot in their hunts, same thing in the pilot, with Constance saying she can never go home and in **1.4 Phantom Traveller**.

When Dean drives through Greely on the road and he disappears, he's dead, but he can physically take Dean hostage, but has to use his spirit powers to throw him against the wall and grab the knife. The same knife he's going to use to inflict pain on Dean. However, he's got Molly tied up and when he touches her; scratches her, she bleeds. Could be another potential clue that they're both in the same realm.

Sam repeats what Dean already says to Molly – that Greely won't let her leave the highway. He comes out every year on the night of his death looking for revenge and then she asks why her? She didn't do anything to him. Sam tells her spirits only see what they want, which basically forms the basis of this episode. Greely only sees Molly because she caused his death, leading to his wife's death by suicide; that's how strong their love was. Conversely, Molly sees what she wants, i.e. Greely because she contributed to his death. Even though she wants to find David, she doesn't see him.

A little repetitious here, mentioning *Ghostbusters* again (as in **1.17 Hell House**) and when Dean calls Sam Hayley Joel again at the end (as in **1.10 Asylum**) and Jennifer Love Hewitt.

Sam explaining things to Molly, like why they salt and burn bones; how spirits become evil etc. isn't a necessary indication that Molly's a spirit too, he could just be telling her what their job involves. In a roundabout way, perhaps if he told her about spirits not letting go, she'll find it easier to do this when the time comes for her to move on and that she's no longer part of this world. It's unfinished business keeping her here, as Sam tells her at the end – her need to find David, to know what happened to him. Dean, in contrast, seems rather harsh and abrupt when he tells Molly he just doesn't like any sprit – which presumably means Molly too.

If Mrs. Greely was meant to have hung herself, who closed the trap door and hung the carpet over it? Greely?

Sam and Dean look at each other in that way again; especially when Sam tells them they didn't know what happens when they're laid to rest (see **2.13 Houses of the Holy**.) They can only hope it's something better, but that wouldn't be the case for all spirits though, as they've touched upon the concept of hell before (**2.8 Crossroad Blues**) and where Dad may be. Sam should have said he believes there's something better – and not just hope, as he can't have lost all of his faith since **2.13 House of the Holy**, he must still hold on to some of it, after what Dean told him he saw at the end, i.e. probably "God's will" in action.

Again when Sam says it's cruel keeping her in the dark, it sounds like David is the one who was killed after all and they just don't think, well, Dean doesn't think it's the right thing to tell her. You feel he's more interested in the hunt, than in putting things right for Molly. But they're saved by the radio and yet none of them thought to get her away from the window, as Greely grabs her. Yes, Sam should've realized that trees can be used to mark graves. After the ordeal Dean is pleased to see his lovely Impala once more.

Sam finally breaks the sad news to her; she's the one who's dead. She drove the car into Greely and killed him and herself; which doesn't seem fair that David's alive and married and she's not, because from the beginning opening scene, it does appear he was partly to blame too, distracting her concentration off the road!

Supernatural lesson: that's what becomes of canoodling in a moving car!

The use of the flashbacks to put everything into perspective is a brilliant device especially here, since it tells you, if you hadn't already guessed or worked it out, that Sam and Dean knew of her when she came across them on the highway and as she recalls everything Sam told her, as though he was trying to break it to her gently.

They visit David (Dean looks like a proper schoolboy in his suit, jacket and trousers.) there's no bones to burn – she was cremated so they need a new approach to making Molly pass over. Hence Dean's comment about Plan A, is to get her away from Greely, which isn't working. The scene with David, when they go to ask about Molly's body should've been a bit longer, allowing Sam and Dean to perhaps ask when he got married, to let us know when he actually got over Molly and moved on because she was clearly stuck in the moment – and 1992! (Also Dan Gauthier was wasted in this episode in his little bit part!)

Sam saying he knows what it's like to argue in the car, yeah, 'cause they do it all the time! Dean kicking in yet another door!

An episode which made a change from Sam and Dean hunting purely evil spirits here, as they have one evil and one who refuses to accept her fate – a good spirit essentially and needs to have them help her come to terms with her death and leaving behind the real world. They haven't really done this before and Sam hasn't had such meaningful conversations with a spirit before either - moving on from the previous comedic episode, which also in a way reinforces Dean's view of Sam as being the sappy "pansy" who always wants to make it all better and make everyone feel okay, like wanting to bury Greely's wife in this episode – well it is the right thong to do. But at least it all comes together at the end – and yes Molly's right, they did 'use' her – but it was for her own good.

Sam's comment about spirits being trapped in the same loop over and over, a tad like Dean being trapped in his own groundhog day next season.

Sam's a bit pragmatic on the whole with the," not knowing" where you end up business. Why have Dean saying – they won't know until actually there? He's come across it twice now – in his time, **2.1 In My Time Of Dying** comments re the reaper. But Dean has to finish on his comment again – the last word on it. At least they didn't argue about it.

Reference to the movie *The Sixth Sense* here as Molly is dead and doesn't know it. Also, contrary to some opinions and critics, Dean wouldn't notice Molly was hot' because she's a ghost and he's not into such things; zombies, necrophilia and the like. So no, he wouldn't say it, although in one episode, he did comment on how good looking the chick was if she wasn't dead, but hey, Molly was a married woman/ghost.

Molly didn't get wet when it was pouring with rain and Sam and Dean were drenched. Greeley's house from the outside had square windows, with a circular one above the door, yet his wife was dead in a hidden 'room' behind some cupboard. What was the point of this when it had a large window and could be seen from the outside anyway? Suppose Molly could touch things and sit in the car since she didn't realize she was dead. But then most spirits appear to be corporeal in this show as they can touch humans, sit in cars etc.

Sam says he hopes they go to a better place, see season 4 where Dean says this a lot too.

The reporter in the newspaper article, re the accident with Jason Fischer, who is the first assistant co-coordinator on the show.

Tricia Helfer says, "Jared was fun to work with." Jared also said, when she was filming...how she and her husband were [watching *Supernatural*] and during some of the parts she audibly screamed. Her husband then jumped and they spilled Chinese takeout on themselves. It was so cool and I was flattered. I remember taking a doll and sneaking it in Jensen's trailer to try to freak him out. So it isn't scary for me because I'm familiar with the story, but it is creepy." Tricia was a champ, and so cool. She had one of the heaviest guest star roles that we've ever had. She worked, I think, [very late] which is usually just something Jensen and I do, while the lead guest star usually works 5 out of 8 days, or 6. Sometimes she was in before us and sometimes she was out after us. She was very professional and very fun to work with and very talented."

Tricia commented on the show as being: "wonderful...we shot in Vancouver in the middle of January. It was all night shoots in the pouring rain and freezing cold...we were wearing T-shirts and flimsy little jackets. I was in practically every scene, so the shoot itself was incredibly difficult and exhausting, but at the same time, it was fantastic. Everyone who works on the show was nothing but positive, and so was the CW Network in terms of thanking me afterwards and having me do some press. They really promoted this particular episode a lot, which they usually don't do for guest roles and were just terrific about it. I was really pleased with how the actual episode turned out and I'll definitely be using a scene or two from it on my demo reel."

Dan Gauthier is best known for his role as Lt Johnny McKay in *Tour of Duty*. Tricia Helfer, of course was in *Battlestar Galactica*.

Quotes

Dean: "We weren't cruising for chicks sis, we're hunting for ghosts."
Sam: "Don't sugarcoat it for her, Dean"

Dean: "Follow the creepy brick road."

Dean: "It smells like old ladies in here."

Sam: "After they let go of whatever's keeping them here, they - they just go, I hope some place better but we don't know. No one does."

Dean: "You're like a walking encyclopedia off weirdness."

Sam and Dean's Take on the Urban Legend/Lore

In certain cultures, Sam says, salt is a symbol of purity as it repels an unnatural thing, that's why you also throw it over your shoulder, because you don't want any bad luck when you spill any.

An old custom in the country, to plant a tree to mark a grave.

Dean says they're at an Interstate dead zone, a phantom hitcher. (See lore on this in Pilot episode.)

Actual Legend

Spirits with unfinished business are formed of the energy from a soul of a once living person who is not evil. A spirit that remains behind and refuses to move on is known as an 'intelligent' spirit. These maintain or reflect the qualities of the human soul. But if the person was bad or evil, the spirit will also retain such a character trait.

Trees used to mark graves. The willow tree motif symbolizes human life and that the tree also has to grow to reach heaven above. Willow means 'mourning', hence the name *weeping willow*.

Certain trees were carved into monuments from which they were made so as to resemble wood; e.g. chairs in cemeteries look like wood. Such markers show the tree is dead, similar to the person.

Music

House of the Rising Sun Eric Burden cover of The Animals.

Ooh Bloops

When Molly is being tortured by Greely, a lot of her stomach can be seen, when the camera shows her full view, only part is visible.

When Molly appears to Sam and Dean, in the next shot they're outside but you don't hear the doors open and close.

2.17 Heart

Written By Sera Gamble. Directed By Kim Manners
Original US Airdate 22 March 2007

Guest Stars: Emmanuelle Vaugier (Madison); Teryl Rotheray (Coroner)

San Francisco

296

Sam and Dean hunt a werewolf and Sam falls in love.

Notes

Another person wasted in their bit part in this episode was Teryl Rotheray, better known as Dr Janet Fraser in *Stargate: SG1*. (Not the name of the shopping catalogue either.) She played yet another doctor, agreeing with Sam that the findings on Nathan were strange, but wasn't willing to put her neck out and risk it! i.e. that the man was attacked by a wolf – that wouldn't be entirely strange, now if she said it was a werewolf, then yes, people would think her crazy.

All of the dead women had their hearts missing. This werewolf had a thing for hookers or where they just easy targets. Did Madison have a certain flare for missing hearts?

Sam calls Dean a geek in this episode, in a reversal – it's usually Dean who does this to Sam. Seems we've found another deep-rooted interest of Dean's – werewolves, as he's so trigger happy (as we know!) he can't wait to get out the silver bullets! Since all those critics and reviewers were being so pedantic about *Supernatural*, let me be the same, for a change (especially where this episode was concerned, I'd say it was easily one of my least favourites – not much hunting involved; or running around – a bit stagnant with Dean doing all the legwork and Sam choosing to baby-sit Madison, and no, she really wasn't Sam's type!)

Okay since silver bullets to kill werewolves are meant to be made of pure silver, but pure silver as it stands, is so malleable, it can't be moulded into a bullet and retain it's shape, so another metal alloy is added so it becomes hardwearing, hence the bullets can't be 100% silver. That's the science bit.

Dean's excited as they haven't seen a werewolf since they were little. (See **4.13**, where Sam writes about it in his high school class assignment.)

Sam calls Dean Sparky again, as he did before. Sam, sarcastically saying, they can go to Disneyland when they've killed it. Wonder if he regretted saying the "killing" part since it'll fall on his shoulders, well, he volunteers to do the killing. Also they could've ended up going to Disneyland as Sam says, as in the next episode they're in Hollywood!

You notice Dean is immediately attracted to Madison, whereas she only has eyes for Sam. If Dean wanted to baby-sit again, why'd he predictably choose 'scissors' again in their best of 3 of *Paper, Scissors, Stone*. Me thinks he quietly wanted Sam to win!

Dean's reference to Kurt being the "dogface" boy, (familiar to Jensen, since Joshua in *Dark Angel* was referred to as "dogface" and a dog.) Dean doesn't usually get to baby-sit the 'chicks', in **1.7 Hook Man**, it was Sam who stayed with Laurie and Sam who met cursed Meg in **1.11 Scarecrow**.

Funny Dean asks Sam what Madison's wearing when he calls, what did he expect Sam to reply, nothing! She probably was wearing no undies if that was her entire underwear collection she was folding from the laundry. All washed in one go! What she collects her dirty undies to wash in one go, eeww! Okay, let's veer away from the undies.

Sam and Madison watch the soap on TV, when the names Kendall and Ethan are heard; these are characters from ABC's *All My Children*.

Sam fumbles for the right words, his only experience with women being Jessica, so it's a repeat of **1.19 Provenance**, when Sam had the same trouble communicating with Sarah, at first (though Sarah was much more suited to Sam, she didn't have that wild pragmatic side!) Also he's not as confident as Dean around women, especially one's he likes because everyone else he's fine with. So it's not so difficult for Dean to anticipate Sam's on the couch, I was going to say on the prowl! Obviously Dean's eyes weren't solely glued to Kurt in the strip joint. (See **4.14** where Dean's ecstatic about being on a case actually involving strippers.)

So there's a whole lot of decibel noise at Kurt's apartment with the door wide open, but none of the neighbours heard a thing and no one finds Dean unconscious there all night either!

Madison's sheet placed strategically around her when she gets out of bed, minus her pajamas, which was silly because at the end, when she escapes, she's wearing Sam's shirt. No use Madison telling Sam monsters don't exist as he knows better! Lo and behold Sam mentions this to Dean again, twice. Maybe he does understand what she's going through, but he's not there yet, at that stage. Also notice Madison's cheek has tears, and then dries rapidly before becoming wet again all in the same scene.

Where did Sam get the notion Lycanthropy may have a cure? Perhaps a reference to *Supernatural* doing their own version of lores and stories, like their vampire lore. In which case, if they really wanted Madison to live, they could've changed the lore to suit, but glad they didn't!

Sam was right though, she'd never see him again and she never did! Annoying part was Sam and Dean not being able to work out Madison was the real werewolf all along (at least it seemed that way) and why did she growl/howl at Sam and then run, without attacking him, as she was ready to do this when he trapped her in the closet. She's a 'sleeper' as Dean calls her – a sleeper dog! (Bitch! Ha). There Sammy goes with his whole "I'm evil" routine once more when nothing is certain about him.

Madison lives in San Francisco but doesn't know where she's ended up this time and has to call Sam, whereas she's found her way back home on countless occasions after she's killed! Lots of holes/loose ends in this episode, you can't help but feel the writer could've done better!

Dean can't kill Sam, he's family and blood and his brother and unlike Madison, they haven't exhausted the possibilities that he may be or could be saved and the biggest thing of all is that, he's still Sam, for now at least! So how can Dean just end it for him already. (See **2.11** and **2.14** but that was possessed Sam talking.)

Dean can kill her because (we don't like her!) no since she's a killer and they've tried everything with her – to change or cure her, but there's nothing to do, as Dean says they could lock her up in a cage but who's going to be around for her – to baby-sit. Sam would volunteer no doubt. But we don't want this episode going the route of *Buffy's* Oz because that's what they did to him.

Madison begging Sam to end it for her is very reminiscent for Sam, as he's done the same to Dean on many an occasion – more recently, **2.9 Croatoan** – when he thought he had the virus.

Madison finally facing and accepting her fate that she's a monster when she denies they exist in the beginning and refuses to believe.

Dean takes the gun because he wants to do it and volunteers, but Sam does because she asked him to. One of the first times we've actually seen Sam take a life in this series (which isn't what he normally does – it's usually Dean.) and it just happens to be someone he cares about.

Another niggling bit: if Madison killed someone why wasn't she all covered in blood in Sam's shirt and now is, and when she returned after killing Kurt – he had been mauled! Why not finish Dean off too instead of just knocking him unconscious. Not only that, but she also finds loose change to call Sam on his cell and when or how did she get his number? Plus, when she turns and Sam shuts her in the closet, she managed to keep her clothes intact there too. Why not finish Dean off too instead of just knocking him unconscious.

Sam shooting Madison, showing Dean, in a way, that he can kill someone he loves, whereas Dean can't, once more because Dean doesn't even know if he has to yet! So who's more of the man?

There wasn't any mention of Madison recalling what she had done as a werewolf, aside from when she called Sam. According to werewolf legend even if the person doesn't know they're a werewolf, they will recall some event which will then cause them to remember everything they did. Hence having to live with what they did. How can you live with the knowledge you've killed and will carry on killing over and over during the cycle of the full moon.

Lots of man tears in this episode. Dean cries at the end too at the obvious pain Sam's enduring, so maybe now Sam will know or understand a little better what it's like for Dean too or how he feels everytime Sam throws the old "promise me you'll kill me Dean" line at him. It's not easy!

Dean leaving more prints behind in the apartment and Mason would've left hers too.

Oh, as I said in **1.3 Dead In the Water,** I could have done a six degrees of separation here with Sam and Dean and Daniel Hugh Kelly, who guested in **1.3**. Here Dean mentions *Stephen King's Cujo*, which coincidentally also starred Daniel Hugh Kelly.

Det John Landis and Joe Dante are named for werewolf movie producers.

On an insensitive note: Dean was actually crying because he didn't get to shoot her!!

As the title of this episode suggests, it's all about Sam's heart being ripped again by more heartache, but also the hearts Madison's taken from her victims, her prey, not as a woman, but as a werewolf and breaking our Sammy's heart too!

As for werewolf lore, these *Supernatural* werewolves had blue eyes irrespective of what their own eye colour was, Madison had brown eyes. Strangely, Phoebe in *Charmed* also became a werewolf and in San Francisco too, must be the Bay air and there happened to be a cure for her (well, naturally there would be.)

Eric comments, "Madison – she has the make-up effects of a vampire – the eyes, the teeth and the claws. The look of the werewolves was motivated by production and budget limitations. For me, the gold standard of werewolf movies is *An American Werewolf in London* and everything short of that level of credibility and brilliance in the creation of the werewolf world would be unsatisfying to me. So I never wanted to do it. Until Sera came up with this idea of 'What if Sam falls in love with a were creature?'[Yes but was it so much love as lust]. She wouldn't even say werewolf to me. That story justified the creature. I was like 'Ah I like that story but dammit I don't want to do a werewolf!' For a while we talked about making here a were cat or a

300

were we've never seen before [what about were, here befores?] Then in the middle of the script we said, 'Why aren't we just calling this a werewolf?' So I was dragged reluctantly into doing a werewolf story – kept it less subtle. We knew we didn't have the time and money to accomplish more."

Writer Sera Gamble said, "It was expensive to do a werewolf transformation that doesn't make you laugh." Like the one in British comedy *Carry On Screaming*.

Jared: "I had a love scene. I got the news 3 weeks before that I was basically going to be in my underwear, so I was like, 'All right, time for me to hit the gym and stop eating all this candy.' I started running with my dogs and doing push-ups and sit-ups, and eating my protein bars and drinking 10 glasses of water a day. It was so weird. I'd never done a scene like that. I was so nervous. But they were so nice and so professional. It was necessary for Sam and the show. I think I impressed Dean, <u>and</u> I got some." Hmm wonder what Jensen thought of his similar scene in **1.13 Route 666**? 'Hey dude', he'd probably say, 'I got some before you – and then kept on at it!" Though luckily, we didn't get to see this everytime he got a chick!

Jared: "Some should come Sam's way. Sam made his mark on society, now [girls] after all this time!"

Eric Kripke: "I'm excited that we are finally getting into our version of werewolf mythology…behind the scenes we laughed that [this] was *Supernatural's* version of *Old Yeller*. 'I love her! You have to take her out back and shoot her son!' Okay and then there's the gunshot. But I was very pleased with [this] episode.'"

Quotes

Dean: "She's a monster and you feel sorry for her."
Sam: "Maybe I understand it."

Sam: "That's what they say about me. Dean, me you won't kill but her you're just gonna blow away."

Sam and Dean's Take on the Urban Legend/Lore

Werewolves can only be killed by a silver bullet through the heart. Sam can now read Dad's journal again, where it states Lycanthropy can be cured, perhaps, by killing the werewolf that bit you, severing the bloodline. Which doesn't work.

301

Actual Legend

Werewolves known, as shapeshifters, were thought to be able to change into them by their own will, whilst some thought it was entirely voluntarily. Legends say a person is able to recall their actions whilst transfixed into a werewolf, even if they don't know they are a werewolf at the time.

Hence a person has to live with these painful memories. As Sam and Dean said, well, Dean did, they could put Madison in a cage, but this couldn't work out and would be against werewolf lore anyway. Also Madison couldn't recall her actions and/or didn't even possess the knowledge that she was a werewolf until Sam told her, well Dean told Sam first.

The werewolf legend, circa Europe 1520-1640's: France even staged its own wolf trials where the poor were accused of being these monsters (akin to witch trials) surprisingly there were never any vampire trials, at least if there were, these weren't reported.)

These werewolves were blamed for the cause of practically every human woe and suffering, for example failing harvests.

The common term for beliefs that a person is a werewolf is Lycanthropy (as Sam and Dean said) and was named for King Lycaon, turned into a wolf by the Greek god Zeus. See the *CSI* episode **Werewolves** where Grissom mentions 'hypertrichosis,' this is human werewolf syndrome, leading to an excessive amount of hair on the human body and face. Catherine calls hypertrichosis a "biogenetic" trait and nothing to be laughed at. *Wargwolf* is German for serial killer and was associated with werewolves.

[In a season 6 episode of *CSI:Miami*, a suspect actually took DNA from a wolf in the hopes of becoming one himself, at least to gain the prowess of a werewolf. He only succeeded in looking even more gruff and scruffy than he already was. Oh and he also had fleas.]

Lores suggest there are tell-tale signs to find whether someone may be a werewolf or not, including: sleeping due to excessive tiredness as a result of nightly wanderings. Madison used to turn after she had slept on the same night she killed. Sleeping with an open mouth (– which she didn't, but she did have big teeth!); hairy palms, and an extra long middle index finger, but then the *Supernatural* werewolves didn't possess excessive body hair!

A pentagram on a person's body was also a giveaway that someone was a werewolf which is said to occur on the body after the wolf has killed for the first time. Erm, Madison didn't have one of those either! Mind you: the title of Supernatural has a pentagram on the first 'A' in the opening credits!   Strange a pentagram should appear on a werewolf's body since these are meant to symbolize 'protection', when they're in a particular way.

Ways to become a werewolf: being bitten – the most obvious, though here, the story was a bit strange in that Madison said she was bitten when she was mugged, yet there was no other werewolf that appeared in the show, only her neighbour and she was supposed to have turned him; so apparently, she was meant to be the major werewolf protagonist.

Eating human or wolf flesh or brain. Only way to kill is by a silver bullet, also it is said a werewolf becomes a vampire when shot! Hey, that's one way they could write Madison back into the show, but we don't want her back. In *Van Helsing*, Van Helsing actually defeated Dracula after he became a werewolf and this movie played a lot on the vampire/werewolf lore.

As did others, such as the black and white movies, with Lon Chaney as the Wolfman. Also *I Was A Teenage Werewolf* (1957) with Michael Landon. *Teen Wolf* (1985) with Michael J Fox and *Teen Wolf Too* with Jason Bateman.

The wolf is seen as a messenger and guide to other realms, particularly when the full moon is out. A wise teacher in Native American culture. Cases in India where mother wolves raised abandoned babies. Lupa was the wolf goddess. Romulas and Remus raised by wolves and were the founders of Rome.

European folklore states that certain cycles or all cycles of the moon can lead to lunacy in people.

The Lunacy Act 1824, stated madness was a result of the full moon and it was more likely to happen during this period. The moon might not make men mad, literally but there have been experiments to show that the 28 day lunar cycle can have an effect on the male emotional side. Coining the phrase, "it's that time of the month" can apply equally to men. In 1998, a study of 1200 prisoners in a jail in Leeds (UK) found violence in men was on the rise days before and after the occurrence of the full moon. Leeds University also found that appointments with local GPs (doctors) increased 3.6% during the period of the full moon.

Michael Zimecki, from the Polish Academy of Sciences, wrote in his 2006 research paper entitled, *The Lunar Cycle* that the moon had an effect on criminal behaviour.

Danish scientist Allan Ersler in the 1950's examined urine samples to find the levels in hormone increased and decreased after a 30 day cycle; beard hair also did the same thing. Jed Diamond author of *The*

Irritable Male wrote, "It's assumed that women are hormonal and men are moved more by logic". However, men too have hormonal cycles. It's been said that a full moon leads to a drop in testosterone levels. The theories contend that since the human body is composed of 70% water, we are affected by the moon's tidal pull.

Mark Simpson, the author who invented the phrase "meterosexual," believes in the idea that men are now perceived as "moody, hormonal creatures". (See **2.15 Phases of the Moon** episode of *Buffy*, where Willow likened Oz's werewolf predicament as to that of female menstruation.)

Inspector Andy Parr of the Sussex Police Constabulary in the UK made the decision to utilize more police on one night of the month. He "compared a graph of full moons and a graph of violent crimes [in 2007] and there is a trend – the moon has a strong influence on tides and magnetic forces can influence peoples' Psyche."

Film/TV References

Cujo, Incredible Hulk.

X Files Connection

In the episode **Shapes** Mulder talks of how the 'members of the Lewis and Clark Expedition wrote of Indian men who could change their shape into that of a wolf'. In Native American lore, this is an evil spirit able to change a man into a beast. Similar to the shapeshifter lore. (**1.6 Skin** and **2.12 Nightshifter.**)

Traditionally shapeshifters cannot only travel across the 'physical' plane, but the spiritual too. Legend tells of how no shapeshifter will ever physically attack a human – unlike werewolves. These shapeshifters are known as *Manitou*; or *Ma' auitou* as Native Americans pronounce it. Comes from Ojibwe and means *god*. The Algonquin word for *mysterious*, i.e. commonly known as *the Great Spirit*.

Music

Smokin' Gun by Kip Winger; *Down on the Street* by The stooges; *Look At You* by The Screaming Trees; *Transformer* by Robert Kennedy; *Silent Lucidity* by Queensryche

Ooh Bloops

In the morgue with Sam, the corpse on the table can be seen to blink.

2.18 Hollywood Babylon

Written By Ben Edlund. Directed By Phil Sgriccia
Original US Airdate 19 April 2007

Guest Stars: Elizabeth Whitmere (Tara); Regan Burns (McG); Gary
Cole (Brad Redding); Don Stark (Jay Wiley); Benjamin Ratner (Walter)

Sam and Dean investigate a haunted movie set in Hollywood.

Notes

Just as Dean says in **2.9**, they should go to California and give it all
up. Round-about-ly, they end up in Hollywood.

Sam can't wait to run off the tour tram when he hears *Gilmore Girls*.
Seeing as he had a recurring role on the show. The tour guide says they
may get to see one of the show's stars, yeah, right there in the tour bus.

Sam's comment about the weather being Canadian as the show's
filmed in Canada, but it's also British weather, I might add, nothing but
rain.

Dean mentions Madison here, (**2.17**) which is the only time as she's
never mentioned again, even when Sam talks of werewolves in season
3! (But he mentions her in **4.14**.) Sam would rather hunt than think
about her. Then he gets mad at Dean for not wanting to share his
feelings – all the way through the first part of this season (and part of
next season too.)

Dean's a huge fan of Tara. As for the movie title, *Ghost Ship*, this
could've been the title given to **3.6 Red Sky at Morning.**

Dean gets his hand on plenty of free food and Sam even watches
him eat in revolting fashion. Dean missed his calling to be a PA you'd
think.

Of course the short, glasses guy, Walter who was in nearly every
scene, was the culprit staring us in the face.

Tara likes to take photos of the cast; this alludes to Jensen who takes
photos of the cast and crew on the show.

When Dean eats the mini Philly steak sandwiches and says how
good their food is, this was a snide reference to the food in season 1 of
the show and how bad it was. In season 2, a new catering company was
hired.

Supernatural's attempt at spoofing itself and other movies too, including making fun of its producers, directors, not many shows would dare to do this. Good to see the show can laugh at itself. Sam looks like he's going to be sick everytime he saw Dean with food in this episode [also in the finale with everything's that's going on, Dean still finds a chance to eat and watching him bite into his pizza slice when Sam asks what happened to him, is priceless.] Dean gets it on with his fave actress too. How many hunters could boast that they've been a part of their fave star's life and, ahem, trailer. Also in *The Amityville Horror* cameras found the image of a boy caught on camera too, but no one knew who he was. Lots of references and in jokes, as well as to McG, producer of the show.

They go digging and salt and burn again. This episode when Sam goes researching on his own, away from PA Dean, he doesn't get into trouble.

All the movie names are references to *Supernatural* episodes: *Cornfield Massacre* to **1.11 Scarecrow**, *Monster Truck* to **1.13 Route 666**.

Sam mentions the Latin incantation in the movie is real and so the spirits have been summoned or awakened using it, as in **1.17 Hell House**, where the Tulpa used by the students as a prank was real and had awakened the spirit of Mordecai, to kill in his house once more.

Sam talks about the crime scene says they probably wanted the movie closed because it was rubbish (something he should've repeated in **3.13 Ghostfacers**, that episode should've been canned!) Okay, but I wasn't alone in not liking it. Sam's camera phone idea is used in the movie, just like the amateurs were doing in **1.17**.

Dean running into a house on set with no wall on the other end! Was funny. Sam has to tell Dean to use the camera phone so the ghosts can be seen.

Dean's comment about there being an afterlife. (cf season 3 and Dean's journey to hell.)

There's Dean's use of 'God' again.

Sam and Dean walking into the sunset – only it's a backdrop and it's raining!

References to *Gilmore Girls* where Jared's character was named Dean!

Eric Kripke comments: "...the haunted movie set filming a crappy horror movie, cursed production in the *Poltergeist* vein; we really get to bite the hand that feeds us and make fun of the studio, the Network and the notes they give us."

The episode title is from *Hollywood Babylon* by Kenneth Anger about scandalous Hollywood celebrities from the 1900's to 1950's. Also the name for an *Angel* episode.

In one scene, McG – the real one – can be seen behind the actor who plays him.

The clapperboard reads, *Roll 6, Scene 6, take 6. (i.e.666)*

Johnny Ramone was lead singer of *The Ramones*.

Gary Cole, who played Brad, was in the TV series, *Crusade* – the dismal ratings for this show were blamed on the peculiar alterations the studio demanded of the show. Brought in Gary Cole because of having worked with him on *Midnight Caller*. Richard Speight did the Pilot with him, *Sam Givens* and worked with Jim Beaver. He would like Mark Harmon; Marlee Maitlin to be in the show at some point, but they're busy with other shows, Mark with *NCIS*. (Another great show.)

In *Three Men and A Baby*, it was rumoured a spirit of a dead boy and the gun he shot himself with can be seen in the film.

Quotes

Dean: "Like *Poltergeist*?"
Sam: "Could be a Poltergeist."
Dean: "No, like the movie. You know nothing of your cultural heritage do you?"

Dean: "What's a PA?"
Sam: "I think they're kinda like slaves."

Dean: "It's like *Three Men & A Baby* all over again – Selleck, Danson and Guttenburg and I don't know who was the baby."

Sam and Dean's Take on the Urban Legend/Lore

Three men and A Baby. The Latin incantation being used to awaken spirits.

Actual Legends

Universal Studios is believed to be haunted. Stage 28 built for the 1925 version of *Phantom of the Opera* starring Lon Chaney where a huge stage was built. Which still stands. Lon Chaney is thought to have become a "permanent fixture" too, just like the stage. People say it is haunted, seen is a man with a black cape and it is believed to be

Lon Chaney himself. Doors and lights open and close at night on the deserted stage, apparently all of their own accord.

Newspaper magnate, William Randolph Hearst, started a romance with Marion Davis and created *Cosmopolitan Prods* as a company for her. She was thought to be a lousy actress. He thought she was having an affair with Charlie Chaplin – Hearst saw them together – but shot the wrong man, Thomas Ince, in the head. Ince has been seen at Culver Studios which was also built by him; ghostly figures are seen at night there. For a further insight into the 'Thomas Ince affair', see the 2001 film, *The Cat's Meow*.

Film/TV References

Three Men and A Baby, Poltergeist, The Amityville Horror, Die Hard, Boogeyman; Creepshow; Critters; feardotcom; Ghost Rider; Ghost Ship; Gilmore Girls; Lois and Clark; Lord of the Dead; Metal Storm; The Destruction of Jared Syn; The Evil Dead Trilogy.

X Files Connection

7.18 Hollywood AD. A film is made about the FBI, leading Scully to tell Mulder about the Lazarus Bowl – made when Jesus raised Lazarus from the dead. This bowl has the power to raise the dead. Parts of this were similar to this *Supernatural* episode and also see season 4.

Music

I've got the World by James Darrin; *Green Peppers* by Herp Alpert

Ooh Bloops

Preview for *Hellhazers,* Tara holds a camera phone so the spirits will show in there, and another shoots at them. This shouldn't have been shown there, since Sam hasn't told Dean to do this yet in the episode. He says it near the end; and so this hasn't been incorporated into the *Hellhazers* script yet. Sam: "You find out there is an afterlife and this is what you do with it."

2.19 Fulsom Prison Blues

Written By John Shiban. Directed By Mike Rohl
Original US Airdate 26 April 2007

Guest Stars: Garwin Sandford (Deacon); Charles Malik Whitfield
(Special Agent Henricksen); Bridget Ann White (Mara Daniels); Jeff
Kober (Randall)

Green River County. Detention Centre

A man is killed in prison.

3 Months Later

Sam and Dean get thrown into jail on purpose to investigate a series
of prisoner and guard, killings to help out a friend of Dad's.

Notes

The light is flickering when the spirit enters the cell block in the
opening; it's almost like the signs indicating the presence of Yellow
Eyes. It's actually the nurse, usual run-of-the-mill, red eyed variety of
spirit. The clock ticks and then stops in this episode indicating she's
about to kill someone; occurs a few times though it doesn't stop ticking
when she first appears as a spirit to attack the prison guard. The nurse
happens to be a vengeance spirit (are there any other kind, well, yes)
getting her revenge on the prisoners since they killed her during a riot
and probably the prison guard gets it too, since Dean says, he was dirty.
Also because they did nothing to save or protect her. The Time of
Death is presumably between 8.30-8.45, which is when she appears.

A stand alone episode with no mythology except for the appearance
of Henricksen; which makes you wonder why Deacon didn't just let
Sam and Dean enter in the same way he let them out of prison, thus
saving on Henricksen homing in on them and Sam also getting a prison
record. Although he was still wanted for murder in Milwaukee,
alongside Dean, i.e.**2.12 Nightshifter**. But then that'd be too easy and
we wouldn't get to see how easily Dean fits in anywhere really, as Sam
comments.

Was Henricksen so gullible as to believe Mara would tell him the
exact location of the cemetery – which leads to the question of why ask
her, he had all the FBI resources at his disposal, so he could have
researched this for himself.

Dean also seems to come up with questions about whether he looks like someone or another, (Paris Hilton in **1.5 Bloody Mary,**) here's it's Nick Nolte. Jensen is 6'1", so why does he look 6'3" on the chart behind him?! Henricksen's "gameface" reference, the same thing Dean said to Gordon in **2.3 Blood Lust**, as he was trying to keep a brave face for Sam.

Three counts of first degree murder, Dean's charges are referred to in **1.6 Skin** and in **2.7 The Usual Suspects**, shouldn't that be four counts if they're including the lawyer and his wife in Baltimore and the shapeshifter in **2.12**, that's four altogether. Someone hasn't done their maths.

Even Henricksen can't be silly enough to believe they wouldn't know motion detectors were around to begin with, mind you, judging from **1.5**, when they broke into the antique store to smash Mary's mirror, they did trigger the silent alarm then.

On the police and the FBI, Jared says, "That will continue. I like that the police and the FBI are hot on these guy's trail. We know the demons are after Sam and Dean and they pose a major threat, but sometimes you forget 'aren't they doing illegal things?' Shouldn't the law be chasing after them knocking at their door a day too late or an hour too late?...we have a really intense run-in with the law and we end up in prison – or so I hear. The boys – what are they going to do?!!...someone's going to have to help us. We're going to have to call Bobby Singer and have him run a truck through the gate. Jim Beaver's awesome. He's fun." He got a SAG nomination for *Deadwood:* Best Ensemble Drama. He heard when filming and had to tell them. Jared: "I'm so happy for him because he's great and the whole cast of that show is great."

Of course, Sam and Dean have to share their cells with the stereotypical "butch, tattooed prisoners", accompanied by music which was almost akin to the theme of the 1970's series *The Odd Couple*.

Funny bit: one of many, the sign on the outside of the prison: "Attention. Inmate fighting will not be Tolerated" This means you Dean! which he ignores, although not deliberately. Dean isn't even inside yet and begins his comments to Sam about not trading Sam for smokes. Dean doesn't smoke. But it's prison money. Sam not liking his cellmate staring at him for obvious reasons.

Strange Dean didn't make any "bitch" remarks or jokes to Sam, this being a prison episode 'n' all, nor did he make any 'girl' remarks either.

But we know he has a plan to escape. Dean's reference asking if Sam's from Texas. A sort of in-joke, since Jared is and so is Jensen, sure Dean's said this before; but most importantly because

Texas has the death penalty for murder and because it executes the most prisoners, has the most prisoners on death row. Another reversal of their characters since Dean now says these people don't deserve to die even if they are prisoners. He clearly doesn't advocate the death penalty, when it comes to humans that is. You wouldn't think he'd be bothered either way and someone who would be affected by all this, Sam, doesn't really want to help them, even though they're hunting, even here. Shame on you Sam, you were going to become a lawyer: obviously Criminal Law wasn't his forte. (It is a bit of a turn around for Dean, since he hates human behaviour and prefers to deal with spirits and demons.) Normally Sam would be asking the questions and jumping right in to save people irrespective of who they are.

Dean still manages to eat prison food (not surprising considering most of the stuff we've seen him eat. Especially in **2.15 Trickster**.) Sam mentions they're doing this for Deacon, friend of Dad's, but we don't know who that is – yet. We assume it could be a fellow prisoner.

Did Sam and Dean carry out any research before they came in on who was doing the haunting and they assume it was Moody, a psycho killer into satanic rituals. Couldn't it have been anyone? If they did research, why didn't they come across Nurse Glockner and the prison riot?

A bit of a plot hole there. Also he died in jail, it would have stated his Cause of Death too and if he died of a heart attack, why would he need to execute his revenge in the same way and why on his fellow prisoners. He was also in a newly opened cell block.

Dean's comment of he's "really, pretty sure" it's Moody; Sam repeats the "really, pretty" sure line when Dean asks if Sam's plan will work or will he get beaten up for nothing.

Being a prison episode, Dean has to mention *The Great Escape* when he lands in solitary. Also mentioned in **2.7 The Usual Suspects**, when Dean passes the note to Sam about Steve McQueen and telling him to escape. Mind you, from that episode to prison! Dean notices the cold spot when the spirit passes him and kills Lucas in the next cell. Why didn't she not kill Dean then, or attempt to. Unless she kills one victim at a time.

Mara telling Henricksen she thinks they're more going on here because of the witnesses in Baltimore police, as in Diane and Milwaukee, as if he'd want to listen – why go to him anyway, he's not a judge and they're not on trial yet or even arraigned. It's not as if he'd drop any charges against them. Then she has second thoughts believing Dean when he asks her to do research for him and trust him, but she comes through in the end, just when you think she wouldn't. Hey, one chick Dean didn't make a pass at! She must be gutted! Well, she was a lawyer.

Randall's reference to *The Hilton*, hotel of the Hilton dynasty fame, can I add the London Hilton doesn't look too crash hot! Compared to other hotels. Without being sued! Well, it was compared to a jail cell here so...!) We can understand what Randall means when he says this cell's better than the old block and compares it to the hotel!

That's four actors' names Dean drops in this episode alone. Sam's definitely "really, pretty sure" Moody is who they're after and comes up with a plan, involving Dean in yet another fight. He likens Sam to Clint Eastwood and then himself to James Garner (who's 1970's PI show, *The Rockford Files* was mentioned in **2.7** and **2.10**.) Sam's plan being to slip away unnoticed to salt and burn Moody's blood when the guard's occupied by Dean, fighting. Why did Sam ask where they get the accelerant from, when all that most prisoners do is smoke and Dean's meant to be resourceful anyway. Dean answering back to the guard makes you think something's going on between them.

Tiny's story about him and his brother being beaten up by their father, until his brother shot him, could almost have been Sam and Dean's own story if Dad wasn't Dad! As Sam says this too in **1.14 Nightmare**. So you have to ask which one of them would have done the shooting? Well, you don't have to, but it does lead to a valid question.

Nurse Glockner appears at 8.45 and this time goes after Dean in the Infirmary (why'd she wait so long?) But he has salt handy. Dean clutches his heart as if he's about to have a relapse and his heart is very important to him, considering the trouble it took for him to get it. (See **1.12 Faith**.) Sam saying he called Deacon when he probably just got in touch with him – who we're not meant to know yet, since we don't find out until the very last moment (practically) that Deacon is the prison guard.

A lot of repetition in this episode of things they've already said and done and the line about Dean saying he earned those cigarettes is no exception, since he said the same thing to Sam about the money Dean earned from a poker game when Sam paid off the morgue attendant in **1.7 Hook Man**.

Apparently Glockner is not a vengeance spirit but a vigilante spirit as Dean points out, she's doing the same thing now as she did when she was alive, so she's not trying to get revenge for her death, but then Dean says at the end she is killing them because they killed her.

Sam wants out tonight and says they don't owe Deacon their lives, what happened to his wanting to continue hunting, with the proviso, 'only if it's not in a prison'. He's worried about Henricksen taking them back to face murder charges.

Don't think it'd bother Dean where he was since he was here to do a job and this coming from someone who wanted to give up hunting for good, at least for a while anyway. (See **2.10**.)

Dean tells Mara he's not guilty and then tries to make Sam feel guilty when he says they're leaving tonight, adds Dean, even if more people die. Did Sam not think about Deacon being one of those people and particularly since he saved Dad. Dean wants to stay and he'll do it on his own. Sam tells him not to walk away from him, do you get the feeling this fight between them wasn't staged? If it was, they make it look extremely convincing. Must be a first, none of them said "dude" in this episode either.

Said John Shiban, "...a really fun episode...and you can imagine the possibilities of that. We bring back FBI agent Victor Henricksen from **2.12 Nightshifter** because of the situation and the fact the boys find themselves in a country jail, he gets an opportunity to capture them and complete that. So it's really nice to see him back."

We finally get to see the guard, Deacon, if you hadn't worked out who he was already. The cerebral edema Glockner died from, that's what Dean suffered in **2.1** after the car "accident." The only thing Dean would miss in prison, even more than chicks, is his love, the Impala!

Sam does the digging this time, whilst you sit there thinking they're taking an awfully long time salting and burning, when the net's closing in around them- great climactic ending there as the FBI arrives – only to find the cemetery empty.

Sam mentioning going to Yemen – of all places, 'hey dude, you'd stick out there like sore thumbs!' Says Eric Kripke, "We don't resolve the Fed storyline this season. We wanted to but we sort of got too busy dealing with demons and wars and apocalyptic stuff. But we plan on getting back into it for season 3 and yes, you're right, the Feds cramp the boys' style for sure.

But don't forget Sam and Dean expertly trained, very clever and very cagey. They know how to drop off the grid when they need to. When they don't want to be found, they can't be found." Well, Bela keeps tracking them down, as if she's got one major voodoo mojo tracking spell for them in season 3. (Just thought of why that might be, since she's working for Lilith, so Lilith is probably keeping tabs on them, perhaps.)

A I said, Glockner finally comes after Deacon.

The Charles Bronson reference was from *Death Wish*. Dean's line about *Blue Steel* was from the movie *Zoolander* (2001) and is known as one of Ben Stiller's facial expressions. Dean doesn't wear his amulet and ring in this episode, also he didn't have it in **1.6** since the shapeshifter had stolen it from him to wear when he shapeshifted into Dean. You see Dean taking it back after he kills him.

When Dean plays poker and says the line, "Hey, fellas who wants to make a deal?" when the camera moves away from Sam, he can be saying this line with Dean.

Henriksen locked them up in this prison, but he later learned form his mistake in **3.12** when he was going to have them sent to a maximum security facility.

Since 9/11 and the Patriot Act, amongst other pieces of legislation, lawyers can no longer claim privilege between a lawyer/client if they know of any criminal activity on the client's part. Sam says Mara would have to talk, there's no privilege between her and them as her clients because she'd been seen as aiding and abetting in the commission of a crime – the research she provided Dean with, the subsequent info and desecration of another grave. So some real serious issues hinted at here, though we laughed along and had fun too.

Death Penalty in Texas: A Note.

Many of these cases are appealed by the Texas Defender Service, a non-profit organization which specializes in death penalty appeals. This was established after Federal funding for death penalty defence lawyers was no longer available in 1995. As well as these appeals, those cases where the prisoners have been allocated dates for their execution.

The sole method of execution in Texas is by lethal injection. Many cases where the defendants have received death penalties have resulted in such, due to inept representation by lawyers at their trial. Many are court appointed since statistically it's the poorest of defendants who end up on death row – after such negligent representation; there's also misconduct on the part of the prosecution. However, most judges have ruled, on appeal, that even if the lawyer doesn't pay attention in court, misses vital evidence, this does not constitute a violation of the right to adequate legal representation.

Some statistics: at present 38 of 50 states in the US has the death penalty. The New York and Kansas death penalty law was seen as unconstitutional in 2004. Texas has a wide and shocking entrenched belief in the death penalty. In 2004 there were 23 executions. Texas executed 351 prisoners – more than a third of the entire number of executions in the US. Harris County, includes Houston, and has the most number of executions. Altogether there are 254 counties in Texas.

So Dean's comment to Sam hailing from Texas is very understandable and disturbing too based on the above. A final note the death penalty is outlawed by the European Convention on Human Rights in Europe and it is regarded as a cruel and unusual punishment to be on death row for so many years.

Quotes

Henricksen calls their disappearance from Baltimore a "Houdini act." Which Dean says to him in **3.12**.

Dean: "I call this one the *Blue Steel*...who looks better me or Nick Nolte?"

Dean: "I think I'm adorable."

Sam: "He just keeps staring at me in a way that makes me uneasy."

Dean: "Are you from Texas all of a sudden just because these people are in jail, doesn't mean they deserve to die."

Film/TV References

Blue Stee from *Zoolanderl, Taxi Driver, The Great Escape, Escape From Alcatraz.*

X Files Connection

The Truth Parts 1&2, has Mulder in the customary prison issue uniform, like Sam and Dean.
4.6 Sanguinarium (meaning 'place of blood'. From Latin: sanguinarius =bloodthirsty, person feeding on blood.) A doctor claims demonic possession when he kills a patient. Mulder finds a pentagram on the floor of the operating theatre; indicating someone is attempting to protect the patients. The case leads to a nurse who was working at the hospital when there were other murders. She has occult objects at home. Mulder realizes she was protecting the patients and the doctor was the real murderer. Directed by Kim Manners. See also *Supernatural* episodes **1.10, 1.18, 3.15** all doctor episodes. Also the pilot.

Music

Rooster by Alice in Chains; *Green Onions* by Booker T and the MGs

Ooh Bloops

Jared mouths Jensen's lines when Dean plays poker.

When Dean collects the cigarettes they're in front of him, when the camera shows him from behind – the cigarettes are no longer in the same place.

When Sam and Dean are being processed inside the prison, there's a man with them in the queue who is already an inmate. He's seen inside when the camera shows the outside of the prison at the beginning.

Locations

Riverview.

2.20 What Is and What Should Never Be

Written by Raelle Tucker. Directed by Eric Kripke
Original US Airdate 3 May 2007

Guest Stars: Adrienne Palicki (Jessica); Samantha Smith (Mom); Michelle Borth (Carmen); Melanie Scrofans (Girl in White); Mackenzie Gray (Djinn)

Sam and Dean hunt a Djinn when Dean is transported to an alternate reality.

Notes

Dean's changed the number plate to the car, it changes twice in this episode from CNK 80Q3 to RMD 5HZ, in his "alternate" reality. In this episode, Sam and Dean are already on a case which makes a change from having to come across it in newspapers etc, or for someone asking for their help.

These three episodes in a row, **2.18-20**) seem to focus more on Dean than on Sam, leading up to the 2 part finale which is all about Sam and Yellow Eyes. At least the continuity from the previous episode hasn't been forgotten, as Sam tells Dean he's worried about the police car outside their motel. Also they keep using their "sure, pretty sure" dialogue form last episode too.

Dean's a big fan of Barbara Eden (Jeannie, in *I Dream of* Jeannie) and not so much of Elizabeth Montgomery (Samantha in *Bewitched*) and again Dean goes off on a tangent thinking about Barbara Eden, being hotter, obviously he's into 'older' chicks too! More likely she was a genie and this episode was about a Djinn. *Supernatural* nasties usually seem to have blue eyes. Here the Djinn has blue eyes like the werewolves in **2.17**.

The scene where Dean walks into the deserted building is similarly replayed again towards the end of the episode, but this time Sam accompanies him and he still has the knife in his hand too.

Dean wakes up next to a naked woman in bed, which ordinarily wouldn't be a shock to him or to us. Dean with no shirt! That makes him and Sam level at 2-2, when it comes to being shirtless: Dean in **1.13**, and Sam in **1.17** and **2.17**. A bit of a plus for us chicks and guys that "swing that way" to quote Dean! Another episode where neither of them said "dude."

Dean calls Sam when he finds photos of himself and the mysterious brunette; oddly (or not) she's not a blonde! At last a brunette! (See **3.2** where Dean meets another of his ex's another brunette. You know he's had more of a meaningful relationship with brunettes than he has with blondes, which must mean something! Score one for us brunettes for a change!) Sam thinks he's been drinking gin (add your own comments here about gin and Djinn.)

Then when you know something's not quite right – your belief is reinforced, confirmed by Sam closing his law book on *Criminal Law and Procedure.* Maybe you think you're mistaken since Sam could simply be brushing up on this or looking up something since they're fugitives. However, this line of thinking goes pear shaped too when Dean finds the photo frame and drops it in shock when Mom answers the door. We know for sure, at least pretty sure (ha!), Dean's in another 'reality' or dreaming. He and Carmen live at 53 Barker Avenue. There's a lot of '3's floating about here, also one in the licence plate of the car.

Other 'alternates' reversed in Dean's reality include; the house number, in **1.9 Home** it was 1841, here it's 1481.

Dean is watching TV at night when the logo reads '9am Central'. It's been one year since the plane crash in **1.4** date for which was 5th December 2005. Dean uses a lawnmower which has no blades.

Young Dean looked different in the photos; not the ones of Jensen and Jared actually used, but those of Dean in the show.

Sam being clueless about hunting was from the original Pilot draft – where Dean became a hunter since he believed a supernatural entity killed Dad and Sam was already estranged from the family years ago.

The Winchesters have a typically perfect white, picket fence house, something Dean's always wanted (see **1.16 Shadow**) and what Dad always wanted for Dean – a home. (See **1.20 Dead Man's Blood**.) Also in **3.10 Dream a Little Dream**, in Bobby's dream, he also had a house with white picket fence.)

Dean now wears a St Christopher around his neck rather than his usual talisman/amulet and the connotations for this are huge. St Christopher being the patron saint of travellers. Dean has that on since he's not only travelled to another realm/reality; kind of putting us and him on the real scent, that he hasn't gone anywhere at all! He's stuck in his own world/reality. (Notice Dean didn't think of a St Christopher when they went on the plane in **1.4 Phantom Traveller**, and Dean was afraid of flying (Okay, not enough time and they didn't know they'd end up on a plane. Also they should have one or 2 as they're on a never-ending road trip around the country. Constantly travelling!)

Dean has to ask a question we already know the answer to - what Mom told him when he was little – "angels watching over you." What Dean told Sam in **2.13**. Dean calls her beautiful, but he already knows what she looks like and has seen her in photos, but he never said this to her when she appeared to them in **1.9 Home,** but she didn't say anything to him. In that episode anyway. Dad died of a stroke and in **2.1** he died of cardiac arrest, at least that was the medical reason given, which is why Dean's relieved he didn't suffer. (Since he sold his soul for him and so could have suffered endlessly.) The photos of Sam and Dean are actually of Jensen and Jared when they were in their teens: Sam's graduation photo, Dean's in a tux **(see 3.6 Red Sky at Morning**, Dean wears a tux again in true James Bond style.)

Mom also makes the comment he's been drinking, just like Sam when Dean called, then when he turned up at Mom's birthday, Dean had a beer bottle in his hand; and again when he was with Carmen and she gave him a beer too. Even the professor asks if he's been boozing. There's got to be something up with that and there was. The beer bottle, all the drinking remarks – weren't suggesting to us that Dean was a worthless drunk – but rather that none of this was true or real.

Especially the number of times beer was mentioned and this holds true when you see Dean on the bed with the magazine in his hand – the photo of Carmen was from there and she was advertising beer – the same brand he was drinking. So when she gave him a bottle it was like "thrusting" upon Dean, this is not home or his life: stop drinking and look at the bigger picture! But when Dean opened the car boot (trunk), there were no empty beer bottles. What's funny is Dean suggests he and Sam have a drink to celebrate Sam's engagement to Jessica.

Strange Mom wanted Dean gone when he turned up telling him he should go back to Carmen's and do what? Have another beer?!

When Dean notices the girl in white across the road watching him, it's a scene reminiscent of Jessica watching Sam on the road as they drove past in **1.5 Bloody Mary**.

Dean's too eager to mow the lawn and he works at a garage too. You'd think he'd be doing something more exciting or different, instead of fixing cars. Especially when there's this whole wide world out there and he chose to stick around in Kansas. Fixing cars (not that there's anything wrong with that.) It's just it doesn't seem very ambitious for him and so out of character for Dean! Dean hugs Jessica like he's known her forever and he only met her once for a few minutes, seconds even. Dad used to work at the garage too, in **1.9 Home**, so here, he followed in Dad's footsteps.

In this reality, Sam and Dean don't get on and Sam's right when he says they have nothing in common, he wants out of Kansas, to be a lawyer and Dean appears to be stuck there in a job with no prospects. In this reality Sam comes across as a bit of a snob. He can write Dean off as a failure, but he's still his brother. This scene shows why they didn't really keep in touch when Sam went off to Stanford.

Luckily for us, Sam isn't a snob and doesn't look down on Dean, which would have people asking how Dean got to be dating a nurse? Fixed her car much? Reminds me of the scene between Madison and Sam in **2.17 heart**, when Sam asked how a girl of her intelligence, could date a loser like Kurt, who works at a body shop, isn't that a bit like Dean in this episode. (But our Deano's no loser!)

Dean then has flashes of his own reality and perhaps mortality – with the news report on the anniversary of the aircrash (**1.4 Phantom Traveller**, the ill children in **1.18 Something Wicked**), mutilated parents in **1.14 Nightmare**) and the drowned girl in the pool in **2.11 Playthings**.) The dead and the girl he keeps seeing are like an omen, he needs to save them but he hasn't realized that yet, or even that he has saved them already. He recalls his own work gone to waste: the people that he saved in the past- all turning out to be dead now because he wasn't around to save them. A little *It's A Wonderful Life*, when George (James Stewart) wishes he wasn't here, everything around him changes and his family, friends he knew, his town, aren't the same without him. The same as Dean's real world. That's what the Djinn did when he grants Dean's 'wish!'

Dean questions why he has to save everyone – be the hero – echoed many times throughout the series, sometimes Sam says it, "We can't save everyone." But then they can try and on other occasions Dean says it. Dean cries twice in this episode, there's plenty of 'man tears' being shed in season 2 by Sam and Dean.

The scene where Sam and Jessica are in bed asleep – is a repeat of the same scene in the pilot when Sam comes downstairs to find Dean and they fight until he realizes who it is. Only this time Dean gets one up on Sam as he can't fight, he hasn't been trained, he's not a hunter.

Dean stayed out in his car for ages, like he was waiting for Sam to come after him. Well, Sam had time to get dressed! A little like the scene from the Pilot again, when Dean comes back and breaks the door down for Sam, when Jessica burns; as though he knew something was wrong and he had to get back in. Eerily, it's almost like he's waiting in the car because he knows Sam will come after him.

Best bit: Dean calling Sam a "bitch" and Sam not knowing he has to call him a "jerk" back. He wonders why he called him a bitch to begin with.

The Impala has Kansas plates in reality: RMD 5H2. In Dean's reality: CNK 80Q3, (which are Ohio plates.) The date of the plane crash Dean prevented (with Sam) was 5th December 2006, but not in the real world. Telling Sam about things in the dark, again a repeat almost of the Pilot when they're at Sam's place and Dean tells him they are meant to be afraid of the dark since there are things out there – scary creatures, etc. Also in **1.18 Something Wicked**, Dean tells Sam he wishes he could give him back his innocence and reassure him there was nothing evil out there. Dean thinking it hilarious that Sam's going to protect him; he always does the big brotherly protection mojo! So more of his pranks displayed when Dean shines the torch on Sam to wake him up, Sam asleep in the car, how many times now?

Dean realizes he hasn't had any wish granted but is just fodder for the Djinn feeding off him and the girl in white, in his alternate reality.

Dean's old wive's tale is true when he says you wake up in a dream when you're about to die, well, it's more like when you're in a situation you can't get out of, for example, falling down a cliff, from the sky etc; you wake up with a jolt to find you'd been dreaming or having a nightmare. There's that "pretty sure" line, repeated from last episode, when Sam and Dean ask each other how sure they are and they reply they're "really, pretty sure." Sam had a girlfriend before Jessica, Rachael who Dean stole and he never came to his graduation, or kept in touch: again the same as in their real lives.

When they all appear at once to prevent Dean from stabbing himself, they all seem to be pretty selfish (and I'm "pretty sure" they were) in wanting him to stay and be a family. Sam's not at home, Mom was cold and seemed she didn't want him to be there from the outset, fobbing him off onto Carmen, who appeared to be plying him with beer! Now they want him to stay. Even if in Dean's reality he'll only live for a few days! How can that be better for him than anything he's ever had and it certainly can't be what he wants. Then what'll happen to Sam – Dean not being around to save him.

Mom telling Dean it'll be a lifetime for him – is reminiscent of the demon in **2.8 Crossroad Blues**, when Dean was told she can bring Dad back if Dean wants to trade places with him. Dad'll have his life back and Dean will have at least 10 years with him before he's taken away.

Sam asking why they have to save everyone, is similar to Dean saying over and over, especially in **2.8, 2.10**, that he wants to give up hunting for good. As well as them both telling each other that they can't save everyone. Can you hear the soppy violin music playing – tugging at Dean's heart strings. Oh it's more sad than soppy but one of the first times this has been done in the show.

At the end, with their attempts to stop Dean "leaving", it feels like a theatre production, when all the cast are on stage and the final curtain's about to come down – for the hero – Dean. (Wait there's no fat lady singing.)

Dean calling Aunty Em (a girl!) and that line from *The Wizard of Oz,* "there's no place like home." Their home was in Kansas just like Dorothy.

If Dean had really stabbed himself, then it'd no longer be sheep's blood on the knife, but Dean's. So technically wouldn't work on the Djinn! Dean is the one who kills the Djinn (again). So what do you think Sam's wish would've been – the same as Deans? But then Sam was never really into the whole family thing, as shown in **1.16 Shadow**. Sam wants his own life and there was no going back for him after all the hunting was over. Maybe he'd want Mom back: he never knew her or had her in his life. Then who would he pick with his one wish: to have back Mom, Dad or Jessica? How about asking not to become evil or even a hunter to begin with.

It was meant to be a perfect fantasy since Sam thinks Dean admits he wants to stay and never once come out of it. Something he doesn't own up to in **2.8** when Sam asks if he'd have wished Dad back, but as Sam says Dean was strong enough to return.

Dean makes the same comment about sacrifice as he did at Dad's grave, why do they have to be the ones. Answered by Sam, because no one else can. Putting some perspective into their lives: what they do is worth it!

Dean can't stay here in this idea of a 'perfect' reality, he doesn't belong here and needs to return to Sam, his family and not this "wish" of his – it's not his life. (It's not really his wish either.) Nor should he wish this life onto himself or anyone else.

Hence the title: 'what is': their lives as they are now; and 'what should never be': wishing for a perfect utopia because it can never be! 'Never' here meaning the past, wishing what has gone before, to be again! I like the way you can mess around with the title to come up with different variations all having the same meaning. Even though it is the title to a Led Zeppelin song.

This episode could be viewed a classic piece of postmodernism, in that Dean travels back into this alternate reality, or parallel universe, leaving us with the question of whether all this even really happened or not. Where all of their hunting, their sadness was a figment of someone else's imagination (or our imagination) but – here Dean's – as he's the only one who recalls the real world and that this is nothing more than an illusion, a bit of wishful thinking on his part. How perhaps, we ourselves, being transported to this utopia on Dean's part, is how their lives should really have been (and how very boring on Sam's part, as he portrays "Mr. American Dream.") Luckily Dean's world wouldn't involve him drinking at every hour of the day and practically being called a drunk, though not in so many words.

Would Sam have had the strength to come out of it? Alternate reality Sam saying they shouldn't have to sacrifice anymore and then real Sam saying he wants to save as many people as possible so he doesn't turn evil.

With everyone forcing him to stay in that fantasy world, Dean is the only one who can end his nightmare. Again another episode where Dean faces life and death decisions: if he sticks around in the alternate reality, he'll only be happy for a brief moment and only in his dreams, eventually he'll die from having his life force sucked dry, or maybe that should be bled dry. Jensen said this should be an episode of *The Twilight Zone*, "It [Djinn] gets its hands on me and basically sucks out what my innermost desires are. Dean's desire is that this life would have never happened for them, that they would have lived a normal life."

John Shiban described the episode as being, "a big twist in the whole genie idea."

In the season 4 episode of *Xena Warrior Princess*, **Crusader**, Njara and her concept of enlightenment, the calling she received from the

Djinn was a battle of light v dark, good v evil (as is always the case.) Also in *Angel*, the *Scrolls of Aberjian* depicting Angel's future and demise mentioned the Djinn.

Dean was watching the movie, *It Came From Hell* (1957) on TV. (A possible future reference to Dean in season 4!) Sam says Dean stole his prom date, Rachael Nave, she was the executive co-writer on the episode **1.8 Bugs**. The title is from a Led Zeppelin album called, Led Zeppelin II (1969).

Dad's gravestone reads: 'John E Winchester 1954-2000. Loving Husband and Father. Remembered Forever.. .' Yes, he will be.

To quote Alfred Lord Tennyson's *When the Blue Bird sings,* "…and over our heads float the Blue Bird – singing of beautiful and impossible things, things that are lovely, and that never happen. Of things that are and that should be…" A bit of a variation on this episode and the title. Summing up Sam and Dean's own world; "beautiful and impossible things" – such as their past world, a happy family. "Things that never happen" – no family, no constants in their lives, except one another and demons. "Things that are" – their own reality, a life of toil, not of their own choosing, but having to make do with it. "Things that should be" – happiness, a normal life like everyone else.

Okay, I quoted some poetry there, like Sam said to Dean in **3.14** when he asked him if he wants a poem?

In the children's' TV animated show, *Grisly Tales for Gruesome Kids,* in an episode entitled, **An Elephant Never Forgets**, the narrator at the ends says of what happens in the episode, "…which only goes to prove that, what's what is what for a reason and what might be, never should, for reasons too obvious to repeat…" (As in this episode of *Supernatural*.)

Jensen: "After 2 seasons of playing a character, you develop these comfort zones. I am able to fall into playing Dean very easily because I do it so often. It was different for me as a character and actor being taken out of the comfort zone and having to play in a world where I was completely unfamiliar with. When you see the episode, it doesn't even look like *Supernatural*. You think you're watching *Gilmore Girls*. It's a happy, lively looking show and putting in a character who is used to being in the dark, seedy environment really took me out of my element.

Quotes

Dean: "Chicks dig the danger vibe!"

Dean: "Great that he went peacefully, sure beats the alternative."

Sam: "Since when do you call me Sammy?"

Dean: "…Why do I have to be some kind of hero? What about us? Mom's not supposed to live her life – Sammy's not supposed to get married? Why do we have to sacrifice everything Dad?"

Dean: "Bitch!"
Sam: "What're you calling me a bitch for?"
Dean: "You're supposed to say 'jerk.'"

Sam: "…it doesn't matter, it's still better than anything you had, it's everything you want. We're a family again…why is it our job to save everyone? Haven't we done enough?"

Sam and Dean's Take on the Urban Legend/Lore

Sam says Djinns are centuries old and have been feeding off people for that long too. Some Muslims believe they're real, mentioned in the Qur'an. They're mythical. The professor doesn't believe they can grant wishes. Dean says in stories you never say the wish out loud, like a loved one didn't die, something bad didn't happen. Djins are said to have godlike power; can alter reality how they want and influence the past, present or future. Can't grant wishes but makes you think it has to feed off you. Dean: "Maybe he gives us some sort of supernatural asset and then feeds on us." To kill it, need knife dipped in sheep's blood and all the Biblical and Qur'anic (Koranic) connotations that go with sheep. (I.e. all the sacrifices, etc.)

Actual Legend

Ancient Arabs saw poets and *kahins* (soothsayers) as possessing magical or supernatural power; this was thought to have been developed from some sort of possession by a Djinn or *khalil* (a 'familial' friend.) The Qur'an states that Allah is the only one with supernatural power and the word of Muhammad was directly from God and not any Djinn or other spirit.

The poet al a'sha al-Akbar commented on such a relationship as, "Between us we are two intimate sincere friends: a Djinn and a human being who is naturally for him. If he only speaks [i.e. if he inspires me] then I will no longer be incapable of saying anything I would say. He suffers me so long as he is neither a tongue-tied now, nor an awkward stupid fellow." From this it follows the Djinns' inspiration was seen as coming from the poet.

However, Djinns can be seen either as evil, portrayed in this episode, and others are seen as good, embracing normal human traits, such as religion, but differing in still perceiving themselves as created from fire. These good Djinns live in their own parallel realm and do not fight or manipulate humans. Djinns originated in Arabian legend in the Middle East and are described as being invisible and able to shapeshift.

Djinns are mentioned in Sura 72, *Al-Jinn* of the Qur'an and Sura *Al-Naas*.

In Islamic tradition, they live on earth, but in a universe parallel to Earth and so can't be seen.

Another well known term for Djinn is a genie, synonymous with the most famous of all genies, that in *Aladdin*; fulfilling the wishes of those whose power they are under. As such the wish had to be phrased with great care as it would be granted in literal terms. (Cf *I Dream Of Jeannie* and *Charmed*, for a more humerous anecdotal portrayal of genies.) Powerful creatures as I based my fan fiction *Charmed* novel (entitled *Wicca Becomes You*, which I wrote back in 2001) on a Djinn.

Famously Djinns are kept in oil lamps, to be summoned and controlled by their master, who was oft times a magician.

Film/TV References

I Dream of Jeanie, Bewitched (the TV series) The Wizard of OZ.

X Files Connection

7.21 Je Souhaite (meaning "I wish" in French.) A man asks Mulder and Scully to investigate when his mouth disappears and believes his former employee was behind this when he told him to "shut up". A woman in black appears to catch Mulder's eye and he finds she always appears when men have found, firstly success, then failure. Mulder thinks she's a genie, but doesn't know if she's good or evil.

9.5 4-D. Scully recalls her crisis apparition of her father. The murderer is believed by Agent Reyes to be able to go between parallel worlds.

Music

Saturday Night Special by Lynyrd Skynyrd; *What A Wonderful World* by Joey Ramone

Locations

Deer Lake Park. West 57th Ave.

2.21 All Hell Breaks Lose Part 1

Written By Sera Gamble. Directed By Robert Singer
Original US Airdate 10 May 2007

Guest Stars: Jim Beaver (Bobby); Samantha Smith (Mom); Aldis Hodge (Jake); Fredric Lehne (Yellow Eyes); Katherine Isabelle (Ava); Jessica Harmon (Lily); Chad Lindberg (Ash); Gabriel Tigerman (Andy)

Sam is kidnapped, finding himself in a ghost town, literally and discovers the truth about that night in his nursery, before tragedy strikes for him and Dean...

Notes

Dean wastes his time attempting to deal with the static on the radio, when he knows it's a sign of Yellow Eyes. The episode opens with 'The Road So Far' containing clips of the special children and clues about Sam's possible destiny.

Sam has demon blood in him, now we know. One possible reason why he was immune to the virus the demon sent to test him (**2.9 Croatoan**.) Also the demon wants him alive because Sam didn't get infected by this virus, that makes him strong – can he come back from the dead (no see later.) At least the demon blood should have made him invincible at least, if not immortal, but it doesn't.

It's a pity the static on the radio came too late, i.e. after Sam had already gone in – but don't suppose it makes any difference as it can happen at any time, in other words, he could've been abducted anywhere. Dean asking for extra onions in his cheeseburger is almost a direct reference to the last episode, and his alternate reality, where Carmen said they can get one on the way home and as for pie, seems like Dean's been asking for pie since **1.11 Scarecrow** and beyond, but he just doesn't seem to get any!

What sort of a place was that diner in anyway – it looked as if it was screaming out 'demonic haunt'. The demon left behind its trademark of slashing peoples' throats, like Brady, Ava's fiancé (**2.10 Hunted**.) Although that was a big clue telling, or rather reminding us Ava would crop up, if you hadn't already guessed. She was the one who probably killed her fiancé.) Also the big tell tale sign of the presence of sulphur. Now Dean has to find Sam all over again – as in **1.15** and **2.10**, in the former he was kidnapped and in the latter he went off his own accord, but here Sam's been taken again and wakes up in a ghost town – literally – at least one devoid of human life, but full of ghosts, one for sure.

Ava's story doesn't sound convincing, how could she have woken up half an hour ago when she's been missing five months – what happened to all that unaccountable time - trying to convince Sam she only saw him two days ago. How did she survive five months without supplies. Obviously since Yellow Eyes was helping her. Andy mentions this, i.e. not having any food and so does she. On the missing poster for her, it says she's from Layfayette, Indiana, this is actually where her fiancé, Scott was from. Again Sam has to keep bad news from her until the last moment when he has to tell her – but she probably already knew anyway, since she's been homing in to her skills! As in **2.15**, there's more 'loose' language on *Supernatural* -with the use of "dick". Dean used it twice in **2.15 Trickster** – ohh slipping standards, no such uses in season 1!)

So just how many special children has Ava notched up on the body count? She's killed about three or four over the past five months; then another two already, then Andy and Lily. This means about four a day or a month, which adds up to plenty; hence answering the question in **2.5**, when they wondered how many special children there could be?

Dean looks to Bobby as he would, for help once more who tells him there's no unusual demonic activity, so the demon's obviously been keeping a low profile with the abductions coming out of the blue, so why did he wait so long to take Sam and notice Sam was abducted with two other people he knew - Andy and Ava. Seems pointless to introduce such characters only to have them killed off, still all adds to the impending storyline.

Ellen must be relieved Jo wasn't around at the roadhouse when it went up in flames.

Why did Ash make Dean come to him (obviously for the demon to strike and stop him from talking,) but he could've e-mailed or left a text on Dean's phone, at least some sort of a clue as to what was happening and about Sam too. Making us wait until the final moments to find out what's happening. Was 'I will not kill' on the board written over and over meant to be some sort of subliminal message – having to read between the lines, telling them to do exactly that. Or was someone desperately trying to fight their destiny of having to kill to survive, which is what this ghost town was all about. Weeding out all the special children, who weren't s special, but weak, in order for Sam to triumph as the victor.

Yellow Eyes was right about Sam when he said he needed a leader for his army. Since from this episode you can see how Sam can rally the troops around and assume command – by killing them. Telling them they need to find to protect themselves are things like iron, silver, salt etc, and also he'd make a good leader because he knows what's out there and what to expect and more importantly, how to stay in control and handle it. Sam finding the knife in the chest almost seemed too convenient, as though it was planted there for him (or was Ava hiding it there.) Maybe he should've left it there because it came to no good in the end.

Yellow Eyes comments Sam was to have a 'McMansion', alluding to *Grey's Anatomy* and Jeffrey Dean Morgan.

Sam wanted to be a tax lawyer (groan!) and was going shopping for a ring for Jessica, as Yellow Eyes tells him **1.22**.

This time round Dean happens to be D Hasselhoff, as in David. Funny he would've got more comments with that name rather than keeping low key, still suppose no one would think twice of suspecting the name usage. Dean realizes what it's like for Sam to get his headaches and go through the visions – wouldn't it have been interesting if in that moment Andy connected 'telepathically' with Dean, transferring some of his psychic power to Dean, unexpectedly. Why did he have a vision like that and no more consequently in season 3. Seems Bobby and Sam know where the town is, 'Cold Oak' but Dean is the only one who hasn't heard of it. We're back in South Dakota again. Dean experiences as much pain as Sam did in **1.14** when he got his vision here.

Sam's line to Jake about Dean always watching over him and how everything's going to be fine, kind of sounds almost prophetic, given the events to come at the end and in the finale. A bit like Dean knew everything would lead up to this moment and how he'd have to save Sam.

The demon says it's more than Dad got, i.e. a year to live in exchange for his soul, well, he wouldn't really have given him anymore time or any time at all to come to terms with what he was going through, but most importantly it's because he's getting his worst enemy out of his way.

Yellow Eyes, feeling charitable, as he outs it, telling Sam why he was chosen: not only for his skills but his intelligence and how he took care of people that got in his way – Jessica – because he would've married her, appears a little like Dean's version of the alternate reality last episode: Sam and Jessica were engaged and when Dean opened up to Dad about Sam not having a life and getting married. Tells Sam it was always about him and that Mom just happened to be a casualty of war, collateral damage, since she got in the way. Well, knew it was about Sam and children like him, but also why did Mom know him, which opens up more questions for the finale and Season 3. Where did Mom know him from, how, whose son is Sam? Sam has demon blood in him, presumably how he got his power or did he have it anyway. If that's the case, it would explain why Dean doesn't have any "gifts". If you can call it a gift.

Eric Kripke; "I think our story is larger than just the Yellow Eye demon. I don't want to give too much away; but I will say this: 'Our heroes confront and converse with Yellow Eyed demon in a way they never have before...and because of the demon feeling charitable he gives Sam some answers."

Which just gave us more questions to ask. Eric continues, "Our season 2 finale is a two parter and we've been busting our asses to give the fans something really climactic and special."

When Sam discovers it was Ava behind it all along, Jake breaks her neck – Sam doesn't have to kill anyone again. He can't do it even now and at the end when it came down to killing Jake, he didn't, couldn't do it. He's fighting so hard against fulfilling his destiny by not becoming a murderer, he hasn't had to kill before and you can't help but think if he'd done it, destiny wouldn't have played its ugly hand against him – but not only against Sam, but Dean too. (See next episode.)

Conveniently Bobby and Dean come across a tree in the road – which takes them getting to Sam even longer. Sam is too trusting of others for his own good, it's in his nature. He doesn't know Jake won't turn around and attack him – which is exactly what he does. Dad must've taught them not to turn their backs on anyone in such a volatile situation. There's that knife again and why did he put this down anyway, it's not as if Jake knew he had the knife, then to leave it there on the ground and walk away – see it's that damn knife come back to haunt him!. Why didn't Bobby or Dean just shoot Jake, surely it would've been quicker for Sam to have been saved in that way. Considering Dean must've watched that scene from *Raiders of the Lost Ark*, where Indy shot the man instead of fighting with him. But it was Sam's destiny to have died.

Dean, of course promises to take care of Sam and he'll make it all better. Why would the demon let Sam die anyway, when he needed him so much, or Dean making a deal to save Sam's life was just another way to get Dean out of the picture, he won't be around, what will Sam do without Dean to look out for him, turn evil, fulfill his destiny.

Before Part 2 was aired, writing about Part 1 in my notes, I've written, quote: "What sort of a deal will they make now to bring Sam back?!" This was definitely pre-empting on my part as to what Dean would do. It's been hanging over him most of this season anyway: the guilt over Dad saving him and now it's his turn to do the same. The question he never answered when Sam asked if he would have made the deal with the demon in **2.8 Crossroad Blues.**

This kind of all ties in full circle once more, or should that be, full circle – circle, since in season 2 we came in with Dad giving his soul to save Dean and now it's Dean doing the same to save Sam and he says it himself to Bobby, but it would have been the only thing left to do and what about Sam's demon blood, surely he couldn't have just been killed off by a knife, wouldn't it take it take something different or more powerful for him to be killed, okay, we know he's not immortal, but still…Herein lies the question, how will Sam feel when he finds out the price Dean's paid for his life and more importantly – did he want to be brought back at the expense of Dean's life and more especially, his soul. He would've wanted him to leave things alone – his life isn't worth anymore or less than Dean's.

Now Sam will feel everything Dean did throughout early season 2 and it was everything Dean didn't want Dad to have chosen for him and now he's done the same for Sam. (See all the episodes gone before in season 2 and Dean's comments, i.e. "I shouldn't be here" as that's how Sam will feel now.) He'd say it would've been better for him like this, what's done is done and then there wouldn't be any problem about him becoming evil and Dean having to make the choice of killing him because Dean would never do it.

But why did Dean have to be the hero here? He also said it in **2.20**, 'why do we have to save people, go on saving them and be the heroes?' As I said the positions have been changed between the two of them again, as Sam now finds himself in the same predicament as Dean in early season 2. For Dean to give his life to save a life dear to him – reminds me of *Charles Dickens A Tale of Two Cities*, (once again, I've mentioned it before when Dad gave his life for Dean) where Sidney Carton vows to Lucy, the love of his life, that he would do anything to save the life of someone she holds dear to her, and he does, ultimately making the sacrifice by giving his life to save her husband, Charles Darney. (I mentioned this earlier too.) It's not what Sam would've wanted, don't know about Dad, but don't think he would've wanted to see one son sacrifice his life for another either. What parent would?

Jake was the only one of the special children who was a non-psychic.

Frontierland is a themed land at Disney's Magic Kingdom Parks, globally. *Brave New World* is a novel of the same name by Aldus Huxley; which was originally inspired by William Shakespeare's *The Tempest* (i.e. storm.)

John Shiban said this episode, "Really expands the mythology. It answers a lot of questions. It answers a lot of questions about Sam and remember the demon said, 'I have plans for you and children like you'. It's a bold step for a second year, but we decided, 'Hey, we don't want to tease people for years and years'. The mythology is big enough to handle some revelations. So we'll learn some stuff at the end. Of course we'll open up numerous Pandora's boxes as we do that. But it's really cool, because I feel the whole season has successfully built towards this. All the threads you will see that we planned in episodes along the way are now going to pay off. I think the audience is really going to dig it."

Kim Manners commented this episode ended up being filmed on a soundstage since the cemetery was drenched. Jeffrey Dean Morgan's scene was filmed in February 2007 and the rest of the episode in April 2007. His scene was filmed against a blue screen with Jensen and Jared's part of the scene being filmed two months later, so they weren't actually together, all three of them at the same time. When Dad touches Dean on the shoulder, this was even more of an added effect. May also explain why he didn't appear to acknowledge Sam in the same way.

Jessica Harmon who played Lily was nominated for a Leo. She had to film the windmill scene for about two hours in the rain, which made her ill afterwards. After she watched the episode she was in, it got her hooked onto the show, though she doesn't want to sound big headed or anything, you know, after seeing herself on screen and everything. Her favourite genre is the whole vampire/zombie area. She starred in *Passions Web*, the director of which was her father, Alan Harmon. She was also in *Trust* which her mother produced.

Quotes

Dean: "…bring me some pie!"

Dean: "I'm not some psychic…that was about as fun as getting kicked in the jewels."

Yellow Eyes: "You're tough, you're smart, you're well trained, thanks to your Daddy, Sammy you're my favourite." (He called him Sammy and only Dean gets to do that)

"Dean: "I'm gonna take care of you – it's my job right, watch out for my pain in the ass little brother. Sammy! No!..."

Sam and Dean's Take on the Urban Legend/Lore

Achiri demon. Disguises itself as a little girl.

Actual Legend

Well, there is no reference to this that I found anyway. The name Achiri was mentioned in an episode of the cartoon, *Extreme Ghostbusters*, called *Darkness at Noon Parts 1& 2*. Achira was a disease spreading creature, who goes on to possess Kylie.

Ooh Bloops

When Dean and Bobby drive to the roadhouse, the Impala drives past a phonebox, when the camera shows a different angle, the car is behind the phonebox.

Does Ash's watch change wrists when Dean finds his remains?

Music

WrappedAaround Your Finger by APM; *Foreplay by Long Time* by Boston; *Opening* by Darker My love

Locations

Maple Ridge. Boundary Bay. Deer Lake Park.

2.22 All Hell Breaks Lose Part 2

Written By Michael T Moore, Eric Kripke. Directed by Kim Manners
Original US Airdate 17 May 2007

Guest Stars: Jeffrey Dean Morgan (Dad); Jim Beaver (Bobby); Samantha Ferris (Ellen); Fredric Lehne (Yellow Eyed Demon); Aldis Hodge (Jake); Ona Grauer (Crossroads Demon)

Dean makes a sacrifice for Sam. They try to prevent Yellow Eyes from opening Devil's Gate and releasing trapped demons.

Notes

Eric Kripke comments: "…the war definitely begins. We definitely tie up some major story threads. We climax the 'psychic children' storyline, for example, as well as deliver a few other surprises. But we're telling a multi-year story so in no way do we answer everything. Nor should we. We answer some questions, we leave some hanging. We ask new ones too." Also John Shiban said, "In the world of *Supernatural* you're not going to have a happy ending. The war is not going to be over, but we might win this battle. It will be a satisfying conclusion to season 2 but yet be a nice platform for season 3."

So Yellow Eyes had an ulterior motive for wanting the colt from Dad and not just to save his own sorry butt, but as now revealed, it was to open the gate to hell and silly demon, he brought it along with him to actually have it used on him, leaving the bullet in it too, unless the bullet was needed inside the colt to open the gate, don't think so.

Also Yellow Eyes saying he didn't think Jake would be the last one alive, to win the beauty pageant, a phrase reserved for Sam (a girl.)

Jared: "It's going to be interesting to see Sam, who we know is one of the 'chosen children', be the kid who finishes everybody off. The Yellow Eyed demon said he was betting on Sam before Jake killed him and now he's back, so we're starting to find out it could be either great for Humankind or terrible for Humankind, but either way I'm excited to find out."

So Dean was the one to finish off Yellow Eyes, at least he got some revenge for his "one year to live" deal, for Dad and his sacrifice for him, for Jessica, but most of all, for Mom. Sam missed Yellow Eyes telling Dean he did the same as Dad, selling his soul for Sam, when he was pinned against the tree. Understandably Dean didn't want to tell Sam, but you knew Sam would work it out anyway, how long could Dean keep it from him. (Sam didn't spend the entire season 3 feeling guilty, but instead trying to find an out for Dean, which will make a change.)

Then Sam not telling Dean what Yellow Eyes showed him in his dream – about Mom 'knowing' him – so that's another question left unanswered, for now and why didn't Sam tell Dean about all this too, hiding his demon blood from him. See later.)

Last episode Sam couldn't kill Jake when he had the chance, thus ending it all, but then they probably wouldn't have been able to get Yellow Eyes either since he never would've given Sam the colt to open the gateway to hell; knowing Sam would only use it on him. Sam finally gets to kill – in cold blood – and the look on his face, as if he was enjoying it. If looks could kill.

Maybe the 'old' Sam didn't come back; but something else or part of something else – so will he realize his destiny now, become evil and embrace it. Yellow Eyes said it to Dean and so did we: how do we know what came back in place of Sam or inside Sam and Dean said it throughout the opening half of Season 2, that "What's dead should stay dead" and he shouldn't be here. Though don't think Sam will say this too often, if at all, because he knows of the sacrifice Dean made for him and he only got a year out of it.

As for saying Sam came back evil, or what came back wasn't Sam, that's assuming Sam would've gone to hell since he didn't make any pacts or bargains with any demons, so he could've died a peaceful, warrior's death and been on his way to heaven; some place better!

Can't help but think Yellow Eyes was a little too cocky, thinking he could carry the colt around and that it wouldn't come back to haunt him, i.e. all his bad actions and deeds.

Sam repeating what he said in several episodes, about doing anything for him, including dying for him, which he just did, though not for Dean, per se. However, Dean will die for Sam.

Another question, if Samuel Colt knew of the demons; how to stop them, etc, he knew to build all those churches and railway lines to form a Devil's Trap, then why did he only make one colt with a limited number of bullets and no more.

When the car boot (trunk) is opened at the end, it's just like the end of the Pilot episode when Sam got back to hunting and now this time they're hunting the escaped demons as well as other things out there. Yellow Eyes couldn't save Sam, as he conveniently put 'I can't make deals'. But he made the deal with Dad and with Mom (in **4.2 In The Beginning**.)

Devil's Trap was the title of the Season 1 finale which kind of maps certain aspects of the mythology nicely, except for the unanswered questions.

A bit unfair Sam finding out Dean saved him already, still suppose that couldn't drag on like it did with Dean and Dad because Sam didn't tell Dean everything – via, that all this was because of him and Yellow

Eye's blood was in him too. Here's a thought: that's a volatile combination then isn't it. You know, Sam being killed and Dean 'selling' his soul to save and bring him back to life + demon blood = evil Sam; so if that's true how's he going to help Dean and get him out of this stalemate of his.

As for only getting a year, Dean should've remembered the demon in **2.8**, said her's was a one-time only offer to give him ten years.

Lots of man tears in this episode too and Dad got to crawl out of hell, as if he was waiting for this opportunity and touch Dean on his shoulder, as if to say he approved of Dean and his actions in killing Yellow Eyes and saving Sam, who knows? When Mom appeared in **1.9 Home**, she went to Sam and here, Dad acknowledges Dean. Looks like they were playing favourites there to the untrained eye, so to speak, but who knows if they had favourites or not.

The Pentagram on Devil's gate is facing up, i.e. as for protection when the gate is open and is facing down when the gate is closed (i.e. its opposite satanic meaning). Obviously to indicate it is a Devil's Gate and what it's holding in. So long as it's shut, the evil inside is being kept in.

Couldn't Jake just have broken the railway lines, thus no longer keeping evil out, allowing Yellow Eyes to enter and open the Gate for himself. Was that the plan all along, when Sam, Dean, Booby and Ellen just got in the way.

Sam wondering where Dad is now – similar to **2.16 Roadkill**, where they said they don't know what happens after you die, and Sam saying there's always hope, not to mention Dean adding they'd probably have to wait until it happens to them before they can find this out! So when Sam died, where did he go or end up, doesn't he recall? See earlier.

Also *Buffy* fans and aficionados will point to **5.22 The Gift** when Buffy was killed – well she gave her life to save her sister Dawn, as Buffy's gift was death and then in **6.1** was brought back by Willow. Here Dean's gift was sacrifice, to save a life he gave his own, for a year, but still, it's not something everyone would do. This definitely makes him Dad's son, in thinking the same thing – having to act upon it and not considering the consequences, especially for himself. His selfless act for Sam, always for his family, always for Sam. So yes, he was cheated in not being given more time: always the doer (sounds dirty! Unintentionally!) – the hero – the protector. Now Sam will have the situation reversed, again, this time he wants to protect Dean.

Still no one could see the sacrifice he was going to make except for Dean which is why he wanted to be alone. It was his ultimate decision to make and what brother wouldn't sacrifice himself to save his brother.

Like a father's for his son, it was the only option open for Dean, in his eyes.

If he hadn't done this, Dean probably may not have been able to continue the fight; "saving people, hunting things, the family business" as he put it in **1.2**, without Sam. Or maybe he'd become uncontrollable Dean blasting everything in his path, more dedicated to the job than normal with revenge in his eyes and a broken heart for Sam.

From last week's episode to the finale here, if this show hadn't been renewed for a third season, then this would've been the series finale. Would Dean still have brought Sam still back? Probably yes – only the ending would have left us with Dean having a year to live and wondering what if? What happens next? So no I don't think that would've been a fitting end to this fantastic series! Don't know about you...

Jensen: "It answers a lot of questions and wraps up some of the threads. It's really pretty big but it also does what you want a finale to do, and that's set up storylines for the next season."

Also Dean hasn't really mourned at all for Sam, let alone come to terms and accepted his death because he has other thoughts on his mind – of bringing him back the only way he can: defying the laws of nature and going against his own self-loathing and guilt when Dad brought him back.

The worrying and concerns for Sam, especially, haven't been all teary-eyed behaviour and okay, season 2 did have tears and a lot more besides from both; but the moralizing did add to the emotional content to the episodes, after the demoralizing they suffered from losing Dad, it wasn't going to be all rainbows and roses!

Why did Dean need Sam back, want him back? It was his job to protect him and look out for him, yes, but how did he know Sam wasn't in a better place, that be brought him back to - to this hell on earth once more – to his "destiny" (no one mentioned that, so is this still hanging over him.) When Sam was perhaps at peace, for saving all those people, he didn't die in vain, if prematurely.

Dean's own life was better with Sam in it, giving him purpose, meaning, so you can't call Dean selfish for wanting, should that be, needing him back. What will Sam's life be like without Dean, that's the greater question. Will Dean's hasty behaviour have a devastating outcome for them both and not just for Dean. Oh and Dean expects Sam to thank him for bringing him back. It's not something they'd do or want from each other. Who gave Dean the right to play devil's advocate in deciding to bring Sam back anyway?

Sam was chosen for his destiny since he was a baby and the fate of his own life was sealed, but which no one knew except maybe Mom. Since she recognized Yellow Eyes, but from where and how?

Then when finding this out in the penultimate episode he didn't tell Dean. So will Sam endure this revelation quietly – that it was always about him (putting a new slant on the expression "Me, me, me") that Mom may still be alive if not for him. (See season 4.) After everything they've been through, everything Dean's done for Sam, doesn't he deserve to know. More mysteries and you feel that part concerning Yellow Eyes is over, but still feel a little shortchanged too since the last two episodes opened up yet more unanswered suppositions, at least for us!

Kim Manners: "I thought what he did with the Yellow Eyed Demon was so controlled, so chilling. Fred was great, but we always kill the ones we love."

Eric Kripke on the finale," There's the beginning of a major Dean storyline…but I have to admit I've heard this comment before and I just don't get it. Not even a little. It's never been a show about family much more than it is about anything else. The mythology is only an engine to raise issues about family. A big brother watching out for a little brother, wondering if you have to kill the person you love the most, family loyalty v the greater good; family obligation v personal happiness…These are all issues that Dean faces, and in my opinion, they are just as rich, if not richer, than psychic children and demonic plans. Fans seem to worry unnecessarily at times and I'll say this; it's never going to be a show about just Sam or just Dean for that matter. It's always going to be a show about brothers. So quit worrying."

Dean's line, "We've got work to do" is the same line he says in the Pilot. Sam dies on his birthday May 2. Dean dies on this day too in season 3 after his deal with the demon and "rose" on this day too in **4.1 Lazarus Rising.**

John Shiban, "We've got some good twists and turns in there. We've obviously hinted at some big things from the top of the season involving Sam's destiny, involving Dean's mission and what the demon is doing. As usual in our *Supernatural* world, it's not going to be what everybody expects!"

Eric Kripke comments: "In a much more specific way, we are going to answer why Sam has these abilities and where they came from. We'll know much more about him, all the other children like him and we'll just have more insight into why the demon has been after the Winchesters in the first place, so a lot of it is demon origins."

Quotes

One of my fave speeches from Dean. Dean: "I just wanted you to be a kid. Just for a little while longer. Always tried to protect you, keep you safe. Dad didn't even have to tell me. It was always my responsibility, you know, like I had one job, one job and I screwed it up. I blew it and for that I'm sorry. I guess that's what I do. The people I love, they're dead now and now I guess I'm just supposed to let you down too, what am I supposed to do, what am I supposed to do? What am I supposed to do? What am I supposed to do?"

The above goes together nicely with this from Bobby. Bobby: "You stupid ass, what did you do. You made a deal for Sam didn't you? How long they give you?...damn it Dean!"

Bobby: "What is it with you Winchesters. You, your Dad, you're both just itching to throw yourselves down the pit."
Dean: "That's my point Dad brought me back Bobby. I'm not even supposed to be here. At least this way something good can come out of it, like that my life can mean something."
Bobby: "How's your brother gonna feel when he knows you're going to hell. How'd you feel when you knew your Dad went for you?!"

Also a great one from Sam. Sam: "What do you think my job is? You save my life over and over. I mean you sacrifice everything for me, don't you think I'd do the same for you. You're my big brother, there's nothing I wouldn't do for you and I don't care what it takes, I'm gonna get you outta this, cause I gotta save your ass for a change."

Music

Carry On Wayward Son by Kansas; *Don't Look Back* by Boston

Ooh Bloops

Sam appears to be breathing still when he's laid out on the bed.

Locations

Maple Ridge. Boundary Bay. Deer Lake Park.

338

Season 3

This season introduces new characters to enable Jensen and Jared to have a little less on-screen time as the show revolves entirely around them and they're almost in every scene. On paper, a good idea, it didn't transfer to the screen very well. Though Ruby (Katie Cassidy) was a welcome distraction to the stories. Bela (Lauren Cohan) wasn't. Her character seemed 'forced' and very excruciatingly out of place. Of course Sam and Dean can carry out their own research by now! (Always have, always will.) If they can't they can always turn to Bobby for help. Bela was always the archetypal British bitch and useless. She didn't add anything to the show, except for riling Dean and enticing Sam in an awkward moment, have to say, preferred the show, with only our Sam and Dean.

However, Season 3 proved to be as dramatic as the other 2, aside from the insertion of a certain Bela! Jared: "There have been comedy episodes and dramatic episodes. All genres in there. Sci-fi, horror, action. It's been testing my acting chops. I try my hand at comedy then action and then drama and crying over this and laughing over that, so it's almost been like acting class doing a bunch of different stuff every week."

3.1 Magnificent Seven

Written By Eric Kripke. Directed By Kim Manners
Original US Airdate 4 October 2007

Guest Stars: Jim Beaver (Bobby); Gardiner Miller (Wrath); Tiara Sorensen (Greed); Ben Cotton (Pride); C Ernest Harth (Sloth); Katya Virshilas (Lust); Michael Rogers (Gluttony); Peter Macon (Issac); Caroline Chikezie (Tamara)

Oak Park, Illinois.

Demons take over an entire town.

One Week Later.

Dean lives it up with only a year left to live. This episode reads one week later; however Dean says it's only been five days.

Just Outside Lincoln, Nebraska

Sam, Dean and Bobby chase the Seven Deadly Sins with the help of two hunters.

Notes

The Seven Deadly Sins as in *Se7en*, which Dean mentions to no ovations. Season 3 is different to other seasons, especially the opener, this time round Sam and Dean are being hunted by the demons as it's all out war, so the tables have been turned on them. They also need to find some way to help Dean exceed the one year life cycle ahead of him and now have to find a way to help Sam, since Dean told him if he finds a way to go back on the deal, break it, Welch on it, etc, then Sam will die too and that'll be the end of them both. (What happens if Sam dies anyway, i.e. killed in the line of hunting, saving Dean. That wasn't the case here and this season was about Dean, mostly. Does one of these women hold the key to helping them both out? Ooh pre-empted myself again, even before watching the entire season; yes Ruby does.)

Compared to seasons 1 and 2 before it, this season opens on a bit of a high, rather than sad scenes that we're normally subjected to and used to seeing – well, referring to the scenes with Sam and Dean of course. No, can't picture Dean drinking an Appletini either. Sam and Dean encounter more hunters – this time known to Bobby, but only for one of them to be expendable and used as the token extra when he's killed off. (Bobby knows several hunters too, just like Dad did.)

Makes you wonder why they didn't think about driving the car through the door before they attempted to physically break it down. Sam reminds us they let out the demons through the gate at the end of the season 2 finale. Also Dean's a bit reckless with his life sentence when he comes up with his plans to fight the Seven Deadly Sins. At least with everything he's going though he doesn't lose his sense of humour, whilst still retaining the objective in sight.

Sam gets an eyeful of Dean he'll never forget. With a year left to live, Dean's making the most of it with a threesome this time round no less! Didn't know he was into a manage-a-trois.

Sam's comment about being careful what Dean wishes for, a harkback to season **2.20** and his ideal reality, whereas in **3.11 Dream A Little Dream,** it'll be a case of 'be careful what you dream of'.

Bobby makes a reference to Dean and his cheeseburgers this time round; it's usually Sam who has to put up with his foody habits. One of their next moves being the old, holy water torture technique.

Demons can control humans, Dean was affected by 'Lust', it's just he wasn't completely taken over by it and could fight it. He knew what they were up against in the Seven Deadly Sins.

Ruby's knife will be much in demand too especially for the season finale. Jared on the knife, well, talking about the knife actually!: "It's an amazing discovery because it used to be that only through exorcism or trapping them under a Devil's Trap you can really get rid of a demon. Now, however, we're seeing that the knife can not only send one back to hell but full-on destroy it, which I'm thinking once again is going to be more integral toward the remainder of the series."

At this time, Jared had only read the script up to episode 12 of the season.

Bobby telling the man that being fat, dumb and stupid was no way to go through life was from the movie *Animal House*. Dean mentioning *Candygram* was a skit from *Saturday Night Live* with Chevvy Chase.

What if Sam becomes evil fulfills his destiny and then as evil Sam, finds a way to save Dean. Will he save himself too as he's no longer good guy Sam: "the hero next door." In the children's TV show, *Fireman Sam*, which UK viewers will know, the theme song has the lines: "Sam is the hero next door" which is why I wrote that line.) We know there's something going on with him, will Dean's predicament change him even more, speed up the process making him evil sooner than his destiny foretold for him, if it really was Sam who returned. Alas, more supposition on my part.

Now that Dean tells Sam that even if they can save Dean, it won't matter, Sam will die. Also why say this when he knows what Sam's like anyway – this won't prevent him from helping big brother anyway he can. He just won't give up, it's not in him. But if the worst came to the worst and he couldn't help him (or he could) then who's to stop him from sacrificing himself to save Dean.

Coming round full circle and making this a vicious circle too. Since it would've all been for nothing – all this "self-sacrificing" on Dean's part. Telling Sam he's tired and looking forward to dying may all be noble in theory – that he's done so much for this family and so – does that make him entitled to just lay down and die, to accept his fate without a fight and if he's so tired of fighting, why doesn't he just take a year out from it now and live his life the way he wants; or has always wanted to. How do we know he told Sam the truth – that Sam will die if Dean's saved? He could've just made it up to stop him from finding an 'out' for Dean and just get on with the war against demons. He was just going on what the crossroads demon told him, and they lie, so…

341

As for doing so much for the family and Sam calling him selfish, well, hasn't Sam done just as much, so wasn't he entitled to just stay where he was and not be brought back by Dean; something he didn't want to think about and didn't. He just wanted Sam back. Well, it wasn't that selfish too. Fate played its hand and that's what Sam was dealt. It was his time.

Conversely, it can be argued, it wasn't Dean's time then, or now, i.e. he entered the deal. Let's face it, it's nothing more then a contract which we know (and as a potential lawyer Sam should too!) All contrasts can be broken – there's always an 'out' clause somewhere for some reason, like there being no guarantee that Sam came back – whole –as Sam and not just a little bit different, altered. So that's not the 'bargain' Dean entered into: getting Sam back in return for his soul, meant just that: in other words, getting him back as he was! No ifs; buts or cheap, evil imitations!

'Pride' mentioned its open season on Sam, as he's the prodigal son" what did that mean? Other that what Yellow Eyes said about wanting Sam as the leader of his army. It's also open season as Yellow Eyes is no longer around. Does this mean as long as Yellow Eyes was around it was "hands-off" Sam and he was the only one who had any claims to him! (As we know he wanted him as the leader in the war – which has now begun.) Recall from the season 2 finale the demon made no mention of Sam returning to the 'dead' if Dean is "cured", saved. Also the first mention of Sam being the chosen one in this season, which will continue throughout the episodes. A case of Sam's reputation preceding him. 'Pride also makes a reference to "Here's Johnny, i.e. Jack Nicholson in *The Shining* as Dean mentions in **2.11** and **1.10 Asylum**. Trust Dean to end up with Lust!

Obviously Gluttony and Lust would be associated with Dean and would befall him, how about Sam? He had to contend with Pride. I couldn't wait for someone to say 'pride comes before a fall', oh well; I had to be the one to say it since no one else did – not even Dean!) Dean had to be the one to ask how a girl fought better than Sam. Also introducing the mysterious knife that kills demons, (see above) as well as the colt. So we're meeting new demons in their fight against evil – and the war in which they'll need all the help they can get!

The first heart-to-heart of the season with Sam questioning Dean about how he could make the deal. As if he needs to ask, they're brothers, man, just as Dean can't be without Sam, Sam can't be without Dean. They compliment each other, or complete each other, like two sides of the same coin. After everything they've endured, does Sam think Dean would've let his little brother go without doing anything for him? Maybe Dean should've just replied, "asked and answered" to that question, as they do in court when the same question is brought up again, that'd shock Sam, Dean knowing something legal, he'd probably say he got that out of *Matlock* too!

Hey, just out of curiosity, wonder what would happen if Sam had a voodoo spell performed on him.

The demon telling Dean if he welches on his deal then it's over for Sam, was an empty threat. How many would dare to take on Sam; like something said to keep Dean in line and making sure at least another Winchester was no longer around to give them grief.

(See later, when they come across a new threat and who really holds Dean's contract.)

Sam and Dean's argument revolves around Sam calling Dean selfish – again a reversal of season 1, where Dean called Sam this and Dad too when they both wanted to rush off after Yellow Eyes and Dean said he'd be left alone, having to bury them both. Then Dean saw Sam die in season 2 and had to save him and now Dean needs saving. It's like they can't do enough for each other and using Sam as a 'device' to stop Sam from doing the same for Dean, had to happen since they'd just go round in circles sacrificing themselves for each other.

Sam again reminds us of what Dad did, how Dean felt and what he went through in the early part of season 2, realizing the sacrifice he made for him, and Dean did for Sam, without thinking of himself and the consequences for Sam either. Suppose it was a neat way of explaining this to new viewers who were watching for the first time; or as a recap for those who have forgotten. Though how anyone could forget is beyond me!!

Dean admitting he sacrificed because he was tired - again so uncharacteristic of him just wanting to give up so easily. A repeat of **2.10** when Dean just wanted to give up hunting and go to Colorado and California; and yes, he was only thinking of himself there. How was Sam going to carry on without him – as Sam says himself in **3.9**, he's changed too because he'll have to do continue alone and live in this hell of a world. Imagine if they had gone to these places as Dean suggested, would Sam have still ended up in his predicament at the end of this season. Probably.

Jensen commenting on Dean's one year; "He'll keep going out and having fun, calling old flames to see if they want to go Round 2. But at the same time he knows there are people out there who need help. So he keeps in the reality of hunting…I have to stop Sam from doing that. But he's still trying." In each script he reads he has to prevent Sam trying to help him and doesn't know what will happen ahead of time, since the cast is kept in the dark.

Dean being called a walking billboard for gluttony and lust. Sam's comment of "Fun" isn't referring to Dean's idea of 'fun', i.e. having a good time with a chick or chicks.

At the crime scene outside the shoe shop, someone says, "Better call Grissom'. (From *CSI*.) It was probably meant to be a detective's name but alluding to the show which airs on CBS at the same time as this.

Sam reads an article which is taken directly from *Wikipedia* word for word.

Jim Beaver loves being on the *Supernatural* trading cards and was on one for *Star Trek: Enterprise*, but because he was in the Pilot episode, he said, "One card company used a terrible shot of me from that *Supernatural* episode where I wore a suit and pretended to be a lawyer. I hated that shot. I'm not sure how I feel about people making money off my photo on a card if they haven't checked with me, but basically it's flattering, I guess." He also said it was great to see Katie Cassidy on the set of *Harper's Island* on the first day of filming, after being in *Supernatural* together.

Quotes

Sam: "Let me see your knife...so I can gouge my eyes out – it's a part of you I never wanna see, Dean!"

Bobby: "So we're eating bacon cheeseburgers for breakfast."
Dean: "Well, sold my soul, got a year to live. I ain't sweatin' in cholesterol."

Sam: "And so I live and you die. You're a hypocrite Dean. How did you feel when Dad sold his soul for you. 'Cause I was there, you were twisted and broken and now you go and do the same thing to me. What you did was selfish."

Sam and Dean's Take on the Urban Legend/Lore

Bobby tells them in 1589, the Seven Sins were identified as actual devils.

Actual Legend

The Seven Deadly sins were Lust, Gluttony, Greed, Laziness, Anger, Envy and Pride. But are never actually mentioned in the Bible. Something interesting I came across in *The Picture Book of Devils, Demons and Witchcraft* by Ernst and Johanna Lehner, was that each sin corresponded with a punishment in hell. Also animals were used in sixteenth century engravings by George Pencz. Each sin also had an associated colour.

For Lust, the punishment in hell was being smothered in fire and brimstone. (Oh Dean!). The animal was a cow and the colour was blue. (A blue movie reference perchance?)

For Envy, the punishment was being placed into cold water. Animal was a dog and the colour was green (hence green being associated with envy.)

Anger, punishment was being dismembered alive. The animal was a bear and the colour was red, i.e. seeing red! when angry. Pride, punishment: being broken on the wheel. Animal was a horse and colour was violet. Greed: being thrown into boiling oil. Animal was a frog and the colour yellow. Sloth: thrown into snake pits. Animal was a goat and the colour was light blue. Goat has always had an association with the devil. Gluttony: made to feed on rats, snakes and the animal was a pig. Colour orange. Hence, the term greedy pig.

Talking of *Brimstone*, recall the show with this name when the Devil recruited a cop already in hell to find and return the 113 escaped souls or spirits back to hell. A pre-emptive Devil's Gate episode of *Supernatural*, perhaps.

Seven is again seen as a Biblical or significant number, hence the seven contrary virtues, the Seven Heavenly Virtues and the Seven Corporal Works of Mercy.

In contrast to these, the Seven Holy Virtues were, Chastity, Abstinence, Temperence, Diligence, Patience, Kindness, and Humility.

The line said by Envy, "Legion for we are many," was a reference to Mark 5:9 where a possessed man said this to Jesus after he questioned who the man was. Also see *The Classification of Demons* by Peter Binsfield in 1589 – a witch hunter and theologian. He put together a demon with each of the Seven Deadly Sins: Lucifer – Pride. Leviathan – Envy. Asmodeus – Lust. Beelzebub – Gluttony. Mammon – Greed. Belphegor – Sloth. Satan – Wrath

Film/TV References

Se7en, Scooby Doo

Music

Sealed With A Dying Kiss by Guns 'N' Roses; *Hells Bells* by AC/DC; *You Ain't Seen Nothing Yet* by Bachman Turner Overdrive; *Mean little Town* by Howling Diablos; *I Shall Not Be Moved* by JB Bornett.

Locations

Kirkland House. Old Terminal Pub. South Coast Casuals.

3.2 The Kids Are Alright

Written By Sera Gamble. Directed By Phil Sgriccia
Original US Airdate 11 October 2007

Guest Stars: Katie Cassidy (Ruby); Margot Berner (Katie); Nicholas Elia (Ben Braden); Cindy Sampson (Lisa); Kathleen Monroe (Diana)

Cicero, Indiana

Dean goes in search of an old flame and realizes she has a son. Sam meets Ruby and they find there is a case here after all, after some strange deaths in which a father is murdered.

Notes

Sam ordering pizza was funny, Sam hardly eats and when he does, we don't get to see him anyway that often.

Dean's ideal chick, Lisa, wasn't a blonde! (See **3.10 Dream A Little Dream** where she turns up again, thus his ideal.) Dean's line of Gumby girl and if he's Pokey, *Gumby Girl* was a children's show where the figure was made of plasticine. Best friend was Pokey, a red plasticine horse. They were meant to be very agile. Most people will recall the plasticene character, *Morph* and his friend *Chas* from *Take Hart* with the late Tony Hart, here in the UK.

Dean getting every last 'wish' of a 'dying' man being fulfilled. Again probably masking how he really feels deep down, but refuses to share it because somehow he refuses to accept and even believe his end will soon be upon him.

Beast bit when Dean notices Ben is practically the mirror image of him: thoughts; mannerisms; likes and dislikes and their love of chicks!

And food! It would have been great if he had been Dean's son – you know, that he would've been leaving behind a legacy of his own, someone to carry on his name – even if it wasn't Winchester. Not to carry on hunting though. In **3.10**, Dean still wishes he could be a family with Lisa, well dreams it at least. It wasn't to be. Still couldn't help hoping until the last minute that Lisa was lying and that he was really his son!

Another reference to Sam being tall, this time by Ruby and she calls him a girl too, she had to rescue him. Once again wearing suits this season. Notch that up as number 1. She tells Sam to look into Mom's friends and why they are all dead – wiping all record of her existence and we have to ask why this was? Why it's mentioned now and why Mom? Again she knew Azazel (Yellow Eyes) which leads back to Sam. Why Sam? Aside from being the special one, we already know from Yellow Eyes in **2.21**, but there must be more to it than that. There's something about Sam we still don't know. That's my impression anyway.

Dean teaching Ben to stand up for himself in typical Dean fashion. I was going to say typical Dad fashion (their own Dad.) He doesn't want Ben to go through life being called a girl.

Critics will be up in arms again, as fire is the only way to kill changelings. As in **1.8** where the town was a small suburb which had new developments being built - allowing evil to lurk beneath the boards.

Getting beaten up in this episode once more and a little slow on the reflexes with the lighter too.

Dean's words to remember or live by, he's not leaving behind anything except his car! More especially when he says it's not his life, we know – this wasn't meant for either of them, but again a look back to **2.20** where Dean was shown what could have been in his life. That wasn't his life back then either – but at that point in time, he did have a life to look forward to, for however many years that might have been and not just it being over in the space of one year.

Ruby answers Sam's question - it's all about him – and this theme will run in this season, with practically every demon they encounter saying this too. Okay, almost all the demons they come across. (Yellow Eyes told him it was all about him too, last season.) Seems Mom's friends were killed by Yellow Eyes to cover his tracks, which again brings up the question of the connection between Mom and Yellow Eyes and how she knew him? (Finally revealed in **4.3**)

Also **2.5 Simon Says**, all of the people who were connected to Andy and Weber were also killed and these twins also had special powers too – the chosen children who were killed off at season 2s end.

Ruby tells Sam she can help him save Dean. Sam ignoring Dean saying that demons lie and well, at this stage in proceedings, she did lie because she couldn't save Dean, but she wanted to help save Sam in a way, by helping him become a better (hunter) and fighter.

Sam checks records for 23rd November 2006 in Lawrence, Kansas, 19th July 2001.

Cicero was the name of a Roman lawyer and philosopher. Dean's used Siegfried Houdini on his fake credit card. Houdini gets quite a few mentions this season too.

Ruby saying Anthony Michael Hall, again referring to the actor rather than the character name, as they do in the show. Only since people will remember the actor instead of the character they played.

The title is a Pete Townsend song from *The Who's* My *Generation (1965). Also* an episode title to a *Dark Angel* episode.

Robert Campbell, friend of Mom's died on 19 July 2001; the month and day of Jared's birthday, but not the year, obviously! But since Campbell was Mom's maiden name, we're guessing this was a relative of Mom's, say her uncle.

The scene where Lisa kisses Dean wasn't in the original script and came as a surprise to Jensen. The reaction he gives is genuine, so then he had to kiss her again since the scene has to be filmed from different camera angles.

They wear suits again. That's number 2 so far.

On this episode Eric comments: "I was really interested in telling the changeling story because I'm a new father and the notion of what's just disturbing about children was at the forefront of my mind. It's such a classic subversion of what human relationships supposed to be because there's no stronger relationship than between a mother and her child and women are scorned by society if they don't show their child anything but the utmost devotion. So if you have a creature that preys and demands that much devotion…So if the mother tries to tell anyone the baby isn't hers, they're immediately vilified."

The women referring to Dean as the Dean, see **4.9** where Anna will call him that too

Quotes

The women: "The Dean, best night of my life, Dean!" Jealous much.

Ruby: "Sure comes in handy when you have to swoop in and save a damsel in distress…because you're tall and I like a tall man."

Sam and Dean's Take on the Urban Legend/Lore

Changelings. Sam says are: "creepy stare at you like you're lunch kids. They change children and feed on their mother's synovial fluid; bruises on the back of the neck are a sign. Only be killed by fire. The mother feeds on the human children.

Actual Legend

A changeling is a creature born to a troll, fairy, substituted for a human child; either be a slave to the fairies out of spite or for love of a human. As in *Supernatural* the changeling will feed on the children's' mothers until they are essentially fed 'dry', leaving a bruise on the back of the neck.

Anything standing in the changeling's way was killed. The best way to kill them was to make them laugh thus forcing its parents to take it back and give up the original child. Can't quite imagine a *Supernatural* ending where the creature is laughed to death.

Also a fairy changeling appears as a foul-mouthed, small man with a yellow face and when found in the cradle, a mother will know her son has been swapped for this ugly creature. They develop a set of teeth which grow around their entire mouths; have skinny legs and claw-like hands. However much they gorge themselves – they remain hungry.

Disposing of a changeling, seemingly human is to use a red hot shovel on the fairy and put him into a fire, make him drink foxglove tea and wait until it scorches his intestines.

The normal child returns in good health.

Films/TV References

Dead Zone.

Music

If It Ain't Easy (Instrumental) by Steve Carlson; *40.000 Miles* by Goodnight City.

Ooh Bloops

The man actually killed doesn't resemble the one with the photo in the paper.

3.3 Bad Day at Black Rock

Written By Ben Edlund. Directed By Robert Singer
Original US Airdate 18 October 2007

Guest Stars: Lauren Cohan (Bela) Jim Beaver (Bobby)

Sam and Dean find Dad's storage facility and investigate a stolen object from there; a rabbit's foot. Gordon breaks out of prison.

Notes

An oft used title, ranging from TV shows such as *The A Team*, to most famously the Spencer Tracy movie.

Dean asks Sam throughout most of the season if he's fine (e.g., **3.9** and so on.) and Sam always asks why he wants to know. He would ask if Sam's okay or not, considering Sam was meant to have come back differently, i.e. not Sam at all! But also when Dean tells Sam demons lie, strangely, it's also a demon who planted this thought in Dean's mind to begin with, well that we know of at least.

Sam is forever talking about using demons to try and help Dean – here Ruby- and then saying they need to be killed off without sparing a thought. Naturally Dean wouldn't want to be saved by a demon, would he?

Funny, well it strikes me as funny, every time a mobile/cell phone rings in a show, everyone rushes for their phone – do they all have the same ringtones? You'd think Dean at least would have some rock song or theme on his one! Here, Dean's been keeping Dad's phone charged, that's a new one on us. Also this is the first time Dad's phone has rung. They also didn't know he had a storage locker, but as I said before, **(1.10)** where did Dad put the rest of their belongings? Aside from that left behind in their 'home' in Lawrence. Dad's only kept a few memorabilia about Sam and Dean and mostly uses this storage to store demonic paraphernalia, weapons and a select collection of Pandora's boxes.

You just know things will go from bad to worse when curses are involved and the infallible, old rabbit's foot – an object of luck for many. However, in *Supernatural*'s case, the twist being the luck eventually runs out and backfires, resulting in the luckee (person who was lucky after touching and possessing the rabbit's paw) {in actual fact} becoming luckless and doomed to die! (A fate over shadowing them many times in *Supernatural*, since it's hanging over Dean now for the second time, well, third if you count his coma in the season 2 opener, from which he was never going to recover and yes, the Grim Reaper did rear 'her' ugly head for Dean and also for Sam since he was brought back from the dead by Dean and he can't have his beloved Sammy go through all that again, at any cost.)

Sam suffers the brunt of the bad luck here, from getting knocked out, falling over, losing his shoe (hey no biggie, he hardly wears trainers anyway! Still had to have a funny scene, or 2, or 3!

Again a bit of irony there – rabbit foot, losing his shoe from his foot! Oh well.) To getting abducted, set on fire and shot at! Great to see comedy's not wasted with Jensen and Jared!

Best bit: Sam whining over losing his shoe, not so much losing it, but the way he told Dean. Yes, it's the poor rabbit again, as Dean comments in **3.9**.

As for being the one millionth customers and having their faces plastered on the restaurant Internet site was just asking for trouble! If **3.11 Mystery Spot** was all about Dean getting killed and Sam having to learn to live without him, then this episode was all about Sam and his bad luck trip.

Bela (or Bella Donna as I call her, i.e. Deadly Nightshade!) using a name like Legosi after Bela, the famous Hollywood actor from the horror genre of the 1930's, most known for playing count Dracula with Hungarian accent 'n'all. We can also call her a man for using 'Legosi'. Since Sam's always being called a girl!

Enough digression! You just know Sam would bear the brunt of all the bad luck and Sam eyeing up the waitress chick! When he wouldn't give her a second thought, or look, ordinarily. Dude does not want to get lucky with a casual waitress!

Dean scoffing his face with banana sundaes.

Sam putting the foot away in his pocket, where it'd fall out, or get 'nicked', especially one of those type of pockets and she just happened to know where it was! Watching them from afar was she, or just had a grope of Sam without him feeling it! Also she knew where they were heading too, was she following them. Well, she couldn't have looked them up on the Net with their photo being taken so soon as the one millionth customers! Just what Dean needed, free food for a year!

Oh the connotations, or should I say irony! Only for one year, exactly how long he's got! Well, less than that now, the clock's ticking and aren't they meant to be under the radar!

You can bet as soon as you're told not to do something that's exactly what you do, you can't help it. So when Dean told Sam not to scratch his nose, that's what Sam would immediately do! This episode also shows the strife they get into (especially Sam) when they're apart from each other and of course Kubrick just happened to be passing by Sam's window. Talk about falling right into a hunter's lap. Cursed rabbit's paw!

Bela Donna would have a cat too, like her minion. Well, not like she'd have any friends.

Dean's right about her, when she knows everything that's happening out there she turns to stealing; to live off other peoples' misery, but then she's not really your caring, sharing type and another reason you can't really care about her and what's going to happen to her in **3.15** – that was her clue – when she says 'we're all going to hell'. Speak for yourself!

They got 2 up on her in this episode, stealing the rabbit's foot and then having her cursed with it; but then she comes along and gets 2 up on them with the scratch cards and shooting Sam. Somebody should've reminded her, 'what goes around comes around'.

Sam gets called a freak again. Dean as 'Batman'. In another movie, maybe.

Dean putting the winning lottery tickets – (in his pocket) when the light fingered pro would be lurking, didn't he learn from Sam and then taking his jacket off too, didn't need to do that either and yes, they could've disposed of the foot ages ago, but shooting Sam that was out of order.

Quick thinking on his part when he threw her the foot and she was daft enough to catch it!

C'est la vie, what would they have done with all that money anyway, at least they still get the free food! Judging form Dean's voracious appetite, he'd probably eat it all up in one go! Wasn't he a glutton for punishment (my bad joke aside), okay maybe it was Sam in this episode.

Sam's been through the wars and not just talking about the on-going demons v humans one either! Being kidnapped again, that makes three times. At least Sam can also do comedy without Dean around!

Dean had time to break in and write the 'post-it' and little Ms Bela (Donna) having the Ouija board shot at too! Which is probably how she located them, well you know what she's like.

Since Bela had a cat in her apartment, just thought I'd mention a few things about cats. An ancient creature of night globally. In Ancient Egypt Bast, the goddess of fertility was depicted with a cat's head or cat by the name of Bastet. Temples dedicated to her had sacred cats and when they died were mummified, placed with jewellery and buried as offerings by the rich. Cats also associated with Viking godess of love Freyja, her black cats pulled her chariot. Thought of as witches since their eyes glow in the dark, or seen as the spirits of dead witches. Maybe this would have been more appropriate for Ruby when she's revealed as a witch in **3.9**, however she just doesn't look the type to be having a cat cramp her style.

Dad's storage container, which no one knew anything about, still he would have had to store all his 'memories' somewhere, what little he had left; but wouldn't Bela have gone back there to steal some more "antiquities!, Also can't they find some answers to their questions there.

Those hunters didn't know what to make of them, over zealous? Somehow, knew Gordon would have his hand in somewhere, since he's obsessed with hunting Sam, even though he hasn't got his 'powers', not yet at least. Lo and behold he breaks out of jail and his last words are about Sam having to die, them there's words to live by, or die by. (see later.) The hunter, Kubrick, named for Stanley Kubrick, who directed *The Shining*, amongst other movies, oft referred to in the show.

Again why does everything go into their jacket pockets when they're so easy to pick, **3.6 Red Sky at Morning**, when Dean puts the 'Hand of Glory' into his tuxedo pocket! Also in **3.15**, this time Dean actually feels Bela's hand picking his pocket.

Bela lives in Queens New York, so much for calling Sam a drama queen.

The storage container Dad had under the name, Edgar Cayce is named after an American psychic.

Quotes

Sam: "I lost my shoe…"

Bela: "We're all going to hell Dean, might as well enjoy the ride there!" (She may sound cryptic but keep watching…to see her fate and why she says this.)

Dean: "It's lucky my lucky day…I'm amazing, I'm Batman."
Sam: "Yeah, you're Batman."

Dean: "Back off jinx...say goodbye wascailly wabbit."

Sam and Dean's Take on the Urban Legend/Lore

Bobby knew of the storage locker... a real voodoo Baton Rouge conjuring woman cursed the foot to kill people a hundred years ago. If you touch it, you own it and if you lose it, you die within the week. Sam says you have to bury it in a cemetery under the full moon on Friday the 13th.

Actual Legend

In American folklore, a rabbit's foot is akin to an amulet for good luck. Stemming from African-American Hoodoo, the foot has to be from a particular leg of a rabbit, i.e. it's left hind foot – the rabbit must be from a cemetery, or has to have been shot, either with a silver bullet or the foot must be taken whilst it is still alive. This must be done under the full moon or new moon. Variations of this: some believe it has to be done on Friday 13th, a Friday when it rains or just on a Friday.

Beware of imitations: not all rabbit's feet on the market are genuine!

A rabbit's foot is thought to be lucky, so were its body parts, but the foot was considered good luck and chosen because it dried fast, was small and looked good on a key chain.

Film/TV References

Batman, Rainman

X Files Connection

7.2. The Goldberg Variation where the survivor of a plane crash has been blessed with good luck ever since. It appears whenever he's lucky; someone else is unlucky as a result of this.

Music

Womens Wear by Daniel May; Vaya *Con Dios* by Les Paul and Mary Ford.

Ooh Bloops

When Dean says, 'son of a bitch,' when he's fuming at Bela, Jared turns away and laughs, unsure of what he should do. As told by Jared, at Chicago.con

The fork in Wayne's mouth appears to be longer.

Bela changes hands; first the coffee is in her left hand and the cloth in her right, which changes in the next shot.

The rabbit's foot is in the box when Wayne is being treated; later the foot is seen on the table. After Sam loses his shoe, he appears to have it again, but when he sits down, it's disappeared again.

Locations

Crescent Beach. Denny's on Maine. Powell and Raymur.

3.4 Sin City

Written By Jeremy Carver. Directed By Robert Singer
Original US Airdate 25 October 2007

Guest Stars: Jim Beaver (Bobby); Katie Cassidy (Ruby); Martin A Papazian (Richie); Sasha Barrese (Casey); Don S Davis (Trotter)

Dean gets trapped with a demon; Ruby helps Bobby with the colt.

Notes

Revelations in this episode: Dean pondering the idea of actually believing in God, now the time is almost nigh for him. But Casey could've told them a lot if Sam hadn't been so trigger happy and shot her. Even when Dean tried to stop him, obviously that wasn't to be. Probably just an episode to show us that demons can do damn well what they please and especially when it comes to humans and their vices. Dean was a tad slow off the mark when the walls became crumbling down, could've been out of there ages ago and called Sam since there was an open window-like grate for phone signals.

Ironically a demon would've possessed the priest, an obvious sign missed, at least Sam should've suspected. Dean having doubts about Sam being Sam whether he's evil. At least we know him not to be the same Sam anymore, those looks he gives to the camera, or when no one's watching look so 'evil'. Don't you just love them! It's almost as if you have to question it too, is he still the same or not? Clearly he's not, since he doesn't think twice about shooting anyone now, which in Seasons 1 and 2, he did. He gets to shoot, kill. The scenes with Ruby are way more interesting than Bela!

Dean is eager to carry out full-hands on research as opposed to the other type, i.e. computers/libraries. As for the red meat comment by Sam, could refer to the food (ha) not very likely, probably chicks. Sam wouldn't need to steer Dean in that direction. All these references to eating Dean and Sam up! Especially Dean, stemming from the crossroads demons.

Sam puts his foot in it again, also has nothing much to say to Trotter when nothing happens to him with the holy water, aside form getting wet. Already tried that on the other man too in the bar.

Dean's right, the town is full of scumbags, but most of them have been possessed to the point where the demons carry out the vices-provoking the townsfolk into following their lead. The expression 'den of inequity' comes to mind.

Dean has to read Latin from a book, unlike Sam who reads from memory. The number of times they've used the exorcism ritual, he should know it by now. No, he even had to read from a book when he encountered the crossroads demon in **2.8**. This demon calls Dean "bitch" back to his face.

Dean wants to believe in God, what's stopping him? (See **2.4** all the discussion in **2.13** between him and Sam about angels and believing in evil). Now the bartender calls Sam a "princess." Dean acting sarcastically surprised when he asks if Lucifer's real. Of course he believes in the bad, so he shouldn't really have to ask this. I mentioned Lucifer back in **2.13** (again before this season was filmed or filmed.) Dean had to ask what it's like down there before Ruby tells him what he'll become in **3.9**. [Also see **3.10** his encounter in his 'dream' with his demon self. I can't help but wonder if that was his subconscious acting on overtime; after Ruby told him he'll eventually become a demon. When you think of something before you fall asleep, it's a well known fact you always end up dreaming about it! Of course Dean's 'dream' wasn't naturally induced, but a result of the dreamroot. So that'd make it more realistic, or just that he was being guided in that direction.]

Sam mentions family business, but not <u>the</u> family business.

Dean putting on one of his game faces, he's not going to admit that he's scared of hell – he hasn't even spoken to Sam about it and won't until **3.10** and some of the later season 3 episodes.

As for the priest calling Sam "his brother's keeper", it's more a case of them looking out for each other and Sam gets into enough trouble all by himself, as seen form the episodes where he's abducted and has to be rescued by Dean, e.g., **1.15, 2.3, 3.13, 3.14**, let alone Dean being accused of leading him straight into trouble.

Dean's expression of "thank God" and everything I've said before about this – he wants to believe or doesn't know, but 'God' always comes to him when he's relieved and so on.

Yellow Eyes is mentioned as Azazel here by his name. Dad used the *Sigil of Azazel* in **2.1**, therefore he knew who he was all along and kept this hidden from everyone, why? Was it something to do with Mom? Casey calls Azazel a tyrant. She was prepared to follow Sam, so she could've been a help to them in terms of getting answers from her – but Sam shoots her without a second's hesitation, much to Dean's protestations. She could've proven useful in the way Sam says Ruby is to them. This is the first time he's been named and his name suggests something 'angel-like.') Another recap of his plans for Sam and how he was to lead the demon army (helping out new viewers)) Dean seems to know that's what his name was and who he was, whereas we didn't. Then Dean mentions yellow Eyes as Yellow Eyes and not his name and tells Bobby what he said about Sam coming back different and though we'd like to think this too, it wasn't to be!

Sam, in his conversation with Ruby, shows he's still the same Sam when he tells her he killed two humans possessed by the demons. (He doesn't show this when he shoots the crossroads demon in **3.5**. Sam calls her a 'bitch' – but she only tells Dean to stop calling her that in **3.9**.)

The title is from a Frank Miller comic and movie of the same name.

Robert Singer's favourite demon is Yellow Eyes.

Says Eric: "We try not to be formulaic and we try to keep people guessing."

Phil Sgriccia would like to do "the legend of Boggy Creek which is the Yeti thing."

Quotes

Dean: "Can fit that ass on a nickel."

Dean: "What're you laughing at bitch, you're still trapped."
Casey: "So are you bitch."

Dean: "…maybe when Sam came back from wherever that may be, he came back different. You think something's wrong with my brother?"

Ruby: "That's my boy. Have to do things against that genuine nature of yours...I'll be there with you, that little fallen angel on your shoulder."

Actual Legend

Azazel is from Hebrew scriptures and Apocrypha. Also found in Leviticus 16 and is said to mean *Angel of Death*. Azazel, in myth, from a fallen angel known as *Grigori* , i.e *watcher*. Was seen as corrupting humans and was banished from heaven.

Azazel is also found in the Old Testament of the Bible, lev 16:8, 10. 26 RV. It is the name of a spirit, which has its home in the wilderness. On the Day of Atonement, "the goat laden with the sins of the people was sent." (V20-22.) Mentioned once in the *Book of Enoch* in 2nd century BC: "As that of the leader of the evil angels who formed unions with the daughters of men." (Gen 6:2-4.) Due to his wicked sins on earth, the four Archangels: Gabriel, Michael, Raphael and Uriel (9:1) took him before God, who ordered Raphael to tie him up under rocks in a desert (called Dudael) until the Day of Judgement when he is thrown into the fire." Ironically, this is what he did to his victims, i.e. how he killed Mom and Jessica in the show.

In Arabic Azazel is known as Azazil. In Islam, Azazil is a Djinn who was cast out of heaven for not worshipping Adam and for his lust of mortal women. He had his name changed to *Eblis* i.e. *Despair*. He is mentioned in the Qur'an as being made from fire and he refused to bow down before a "son of clay": Adam.

Others claim Azazel to be a place near Jerusalem; or simply a demon living in the desert.

Music

Fool For Loving You by Whitesnake; *Run Through The Jungle* by Creedence Clearwater Revival; *Bad Seed* by Brimstone Howl; *Nikki* by Sasquatch; Did *You See It* by Mother Superior

Locations

Langley, Ulva Mexico. Choo Choo's.

3.5 Bedtime Stories

Written By Cathryn Humphris. Directed By Mike Rohl
Original US Airdate 1 November 2007

Guest Stars: Christopher Cousins (Dr Garrison); Tracy Spiridakos (Callie Garrison); Sandra McCoy (Crossroads Demon).

Sam and Dean investigate some maulings and find themselves in fairytale land. Sam crosses paths with a crossroads demon in an attempt to save Dean.

Notes

It could get confusing for newcomers not familiar with the show and mythology, since it's been said if Dean is saved then Sam will die and everything will revert back to how it was at season 2's end. Then they go on to say Dean can't be saved, period, Ruby says this too (**3.9**) so a bit pointless Dean telling Sam this to begin with.

The third brother hiding behind the bricks so he wouldn't be attacked. Dean almost drives over the frog in the road, um, the frog which gets around as a clue as to what they're dealing with; well if Dean knew his fairytales...

Sam and Dean having the conversation/ argument again about Sam wanting to summon the crossroads demon and use the colt to get answers, or more particularly, to get Dean out of the deal. Sam saying Dean's not Dad (**3.9** when he'll say this and plenty more about Dean being selfish). Dean doesn't really appear to want to help himself! Yet, again, Dean changes the subject or clams up when he wants to end the argument. Here he calls in the 'I'm the eldest' card so he knows better!

As to what they're dealing with here, Sam thinks it could be a werewolf – but no mention of Madison (**2.17 Heart**) here, which would've been a good time to see how Sam was handling it – or was it just a case of out of sight, out of mind.

Detectives, Plant and Paige members of Led Zeppelin.

Dean does recall Wile E Coyote. Sam's drawing turns out to be 'sausage' man, as opposed to a matchstick man, so he put some effort into it. Oh and they miss the frog again.

Harmless old ladies can wreak a lot of havoc (**1.18** when Dean saw the old woman in the hospital and thought she could be the Shtriga. Also in **3.8** the woman giving away the Christmas wreaths was nothing more than a Pagan god, and that's the moral of this tale.

Another *CSI* reference by Dean – about standing, watching by the crime scene and again, I will add – that's just what Sam and Dean do – investigate demonic and evil crime scenes!

Would've been funny if Dean asked if Sam thinks about fairies often and not fairytales.

Also Sam and Deans use the word 'crazy' interchangeably in the episodes, here Sam says crazy's what they do and later, Dean says nothing sounds crazy to him. *Q* What happened to carrying out research on a computer now, instead of trekking to the library? Answer: 'cause they wouldn't come across the frog now and the pumpkin on the doorstep. Who asked Dean to kiss a frog anyway? He'd only tell Sam to do it! We've heard every hotelier, motelier and lots of others tell them they're gay in one form or another and now Dean says it to Sam.

Good to see they start off on a serious note at the beginning of the episode, then it goes comedic in the middle, before returning to a sad one again at the end.

When Sam tells the doctor he can't understand what he's going through, shouldn't that have been he can understand. He saw Dean go through that in **1.12 Faith** – when he needed a new heart; in **2.1 In My Time of dying**, when he was in a coma and his chances were next to nothing and now he faces losing his life once more. So yes, he does know what he's going through now.

Yes, Dean knows movies, but also TV shows. There's that bit I've mentioned several times before, about saying the actual actor's name instead of the character name, well, okay, people will know the actor better than the character. Anyway, for someone who doesn't know fairytales – imagine Dean coming up with the 2 lines – first about the brothers being chubby and then going after the big, bad wolf.

In a scene reminiscent of several episodes, Dean has yet another fight on his hands. (That's why Jared and Jensen love their action scenes, more than the metrosexual, touchy feely stuff.)

Dean doesn't reply when Sam asks if he just wants him to let him go…into the night…well, it's not something Dean can let Sam do, or Dad to Dean, let them go so easily. So Dean is just a little fed up of hearing the same thing over and over. Oh the looks between them…

Every crossroads demon is just in awe of Sam and Dean. Sam being called 'Sammy' by them all. Dean calls himself the older brother here and the crossroads demon refers to Sam as the snot-nosed little brother. Charming! They really get to air their feelings about Sam and Dean. More references to Dean's broken psyche (as Jensen said too about his psyche being all shot to hell in season 1.) Notice how these crossroad demons not only wear the same clothes, are all brunettes (which is a good thing!) and hold their hands in the same way.

Sam's meeting with the demon where he said all deals can be broken, echoing my sentiments exactly, only this one will take longer and more work.

The crossroads demon's quote "Doth protest too much" is from *Hamlet*. Act III Scene II, "The lady doth protest too much, me thinks." Sam being called a girl again, well, the sentiments there.

Suddenly every demon seems to know Ruby's no longer on their side – why? Or did they already know. Sam clearly has changed and for the worst we can say; or is that his desperation showing, in wanting to save Dean? I'll say it again, those 'dirty' looks to the camera and when no one (but us) are meant to be looking, something's amiss and this trigger- happy scenario he finds himself in now, even more so that Dean, lately. Who just lets Sam keep a hold of the colt. (Which would have been just as well considering what's to come in **3.10 Dream A Little Dream**?)

The two demons he shot last week and the one now, not caring that they were possessing humans, as Bobby said to Dean in the season 1 finale about there being a real person inside Meg. No more hesitation or questioning on his part now.

So this "boss" who wants Dean's soul, why hasn't anyone heard of him/her before and not a peep out of Ruby either and who is she, what's she after, he could've got something out of her, especially since the demon brought up her name first. Clever of them to call the demon their boss and thereby hiding if it was male or female, throwing us off the scent until **3.12**.

Dean not wanting to save him, because, "you 'die' and "so do you," Sam telling him he's not Dad. Well, no, he already went and acted like Dad when he made the deal. No one mentioned when Dad made the deal to save Dean, he didn't even get a year like Dean did with Sam. So Dean's not heard of fairytales, not read any when younger, but he did mention not kissing the frog, so? Okay. He's heard of them but doesn't know any.

Dean saying he wouldn't kiss the frog, well that'd make him a princess then, just a butch macho comment on his part! So how did he know the tale about *The Frog Prince*.

Which one of them is the stronger brother then and which one's needier? Aren't they equal in both respects? Like the one doesn't function without the other. The demon doesn't tell Sam hell be dead if the deal is broken.

Sam was pleased with himself when he shot the demon and shooting Sandra McCoy too! His ex of late. At least Sam now realizes it'll now take plenty more to break the deal than crossing paths with a demon and maybe Dean can't be saved after all!

Fancy calling Dean a slob! He actually doesn't have food stains all over him and he's heard of personal hygiene too. Glad Sam shot her, another indication he's changed or changing, and though not necessarily becoming evil, but at least being more ruthless in his actions. That's it, more action, less thought. Maybe he's still Sam and fed up of Dean having to do all the slaying and thinks it's his time now, since he's in the war and Dean may not be around for much longer.

Then it'll be all up to him, if he carries on with hunting.

Perhaps Sam wants to save Dean so much, even if he has changed, as Dean will be the only will one who'll be able to save him, if he's becoming evil Sam, as well as brotherly love. He didn't hesitate and think of the demon possessing that body, so he'll be shooting a human, just like he did in the church!

When the demon said she doesn't have the contract and that she has a boss, for a second, Ruby came to mind, but only for a second. That'd be an easy way for her to get Sam to do whatever she wants and then either save Dean. If so, or not, why does she want to help them. To get ahead in 'demon-dom', is she in it for the fight? When she said she's his fallen angel on his shoulder and called him "my boy", were they possible references to Mom? Would explain how Mom knew Yellow Eyes and why he wanted Sam? What if Ruby was their Mom, had her soul (well I know I've mentioned this before, but it's something that could have been done if anyone thought about it.) Also how did she know all of Mom's friends, relatives were, dead when Sam and Dean didn't even know them, or think about contacting any of them. Why help with the Colt? We rather like Sam and Ruby's clandestine meetings when Dean'

Ruby knowing the colt wouldn't kill her, in contrast to Meg in Season 1 not knowing if it was the real colt or not when Dad took the fake one and she had to test it out. Is Ruby more of a 'higher-level' demon, hence the fallen angel reference perhaps, and is she only helping them to gain a better position in the demon hierarchy, when the war ends, potentially ends. Ruby isn't the "boss", part of his /her circle of friends, like Meg was to Yellow Eyes (his daughter.) Ruby doesn't mention who the boss is until **3.12** and all because the boss will appear on the scene.

In this episode, Dean commenting on the brothers being chubby, did they see the dead bodies then, otherwise how did he know, or just guess from the third brother's appearance? See, for someone who didn't know fairytales he knew about the *Three Little Pigs,* or did it have more to do with bacon and food. Fancy him not knowing about fairytales, surely Mom would've read him some; she was there until he was four.

Took five episodes to come up with the gay comments this season and Sam knowing the tales: - he's such a girl is what Dean should've said!

Mischa Barton played Kyra in *Sixth Sense* who was poisoned by her mother.

This episode took popular fairy tales and turned them around on their heads – or did it. You see there were all the famous characters around from the tales but one thing was missing: the popular girl, the heroine of the stories who always triumphed over evil and good won out in the end. Well, the twist was the little girl controlling the protagonists and turning peoples' lives into a living hell because that's what her life was like – and nobody listened. There was no one to listen to her and as in fairytale mode; the episode was played to the end.

Also in fairytale fashion, her stepmother poisoned her, *Snow White*- yes, but she didn't die, she too was in a deep sleep. Snow White was, as the name suggests, as pure and as white as the driven snow.

Also when Sam mentions Munchausen's By Proxy, that's why Callie's step mom poisoned her because she needed someone to notice her, be the centre of attention; the very crux of this syndrome, but that's what Callie was also doing, i.e. in killing those people off when she was being read to; she wanted her father to pay attention to her.

How do you get a 'spirit' or someone in a coma to pay for taking innocent lives? So you couldn't really feel sorry for her she did exactly the same thing as her step-mom.

There was a touch of hypocrisy in this episode, or was there, a grieving father failing to act when his daughter appeared to him, not questioning the 'why' and motives, but then how many of us would, rationally. He was asking Sam to leave for telling the truth. (In contrast, see **2.4** a grieving father unaware his daughter had been brought back from the dead, a zombie, and unable to act.)

A great episode showing us we can all become bad (evil) if there's no one to help us; guide us, when we need it the most. A moral for Sam: he would have embraced his destiny in season 2 – if not for Dean and for **3.9** when Ruby tells Dean he'll go to hell and become a demon. Whereas he could've had a peaceful 'death' in the season 2 opener, if fate hadn't intervened in the form of Dad selling his soul. How the reaper told Dean he'd be a restless spirit if he didn't accept his fate (death) and that's how demons are formed.

Her father reading Grimm's Fairytales was perhaps the ultimate irony. Instead of heeding how she was reaching out to him so she could let go – after he finds out the truth, now seeing she was a woman, albeit, in a coma and not a child, as he persisted in treating her like one in reading fairytales. Just as parents do anyway. But hey, aren't fairytales, just that – harmless, though they're violent. *Hansel and Gretel*: eating children, poisoning people. These sorts of violence aren't the norm of thuggery, assaults, but more the sort of thing you'd expect and do see in adult violence. They're just stories, so they're not censored but read without caution. Her father spent his time at work, whilst not really knowing her or his second wife, so not surprisingly he couldn't let her go, not knowing why she was there; why this happened to her.

Sam walked away, choosing not to be a hunter, whereas Dean stayed and chose not to be a normal teen. He had the choice to walk away from this at any moment. But Sam chose university because he could, since Dean and Dad were there to fight the battles and he no longer wanted to until he was dragged 'back by Dean; making him now chose the life of a hunter rather than a normal man. They were far from normal anyway! The bigger picture is what Sam would be like without Dean, he's showing us exactly what he would be like and what he would do alone.

Jared commented on the fairytales, "I actually went back and read some and was quite disturbed. I admit that I got a little spooked by them [Grimm's Tales.]"

Sandra McCoy commented that since she and Jared were so close, at the time, the producer wanted to find a role perfect for her, not something where they'd be close or all lovey, dovey. She auditioned for Jessica in the Pilot – but they actually wanted someone taller. Then she went for Sarah in **1.19** (all of Sam's love interests!) Some people would've labelled that bad luck, being cursed. Then she auditioned for Carmen in **2.18**. No one wanted to see her kiss Jared or Jensen, for that matter on screen.

She shot her scenes at 1am in the freezing cold of Vancouver and didn't put a jacket on in between takes in her skimpy number. Sandra comments that she and Jared weren't actually looking at each other directly when Sam pulled the trigger. It was one of her favourite scenes with him.

Sandra has watched every single episode of the show and doesn't believe Sam is like Jared and vice versa.

There were no bloops in their scene either since Jared wanted to be completely professional. She's a fan and absolutely adores the show (don't know how she feels now though that they're no longer together). She started watching the show because Jared was in it and watched it out of support for him. After the season 2 finale she became a fan and stopped reading Jared's scripts so she could just watch as a viewer/fan.

Her first impressions on Jared she recalls, Jared came onto the set of *Cry Wolf* when filming was already underway. She thought he was rude and he felt she was annoying. A case of *Pride and Prejudice* then, but not the fairytale ending to be for them, sadly.

Sandra wants to complete her Masters in Psychology and so is in a graduate programme. She prefers dancing to acting and is also a member of MENSA – like her mother. She's a big fan of logic puzzles and was in the video for Justin Timberlake's *Senorita*.

Quotes

Dean: "The things he can do with a pen."

Sam and Dean: "Got nothing."

Dean: "Who stood outside the crime scene and watched?"

Dean: "That's nice. You think about fairytales often?...

Dean: "Sam, could you be a little more gay? Don't answer that."

Dean: "Who knows maybe you'll find your fairy godmother?" [And maybe you'll find Snow White Dean!]

Dean: "I'm going to stop the big, bad wolf, which is the weirdest thing I've ever said."

Sam and Dean's Take on the Urban Legend/Lore

Sam: Grimm Bros folklore was violent, cannibalistic and had sex. Became sanitized over the centuries and turned into Disney films and bedtime stories.

Lillian Bailey a 1930's clairvoyant who believed thoughts and actions were caused by spirits. Fairytales included here were: *The Three Little Pigs, Hansel and Gretel, Snow White, Cinderella, Little Red Riding Hood.*

Actual Legends

365

Little Red Riding Hood: some versions had Little Red performing a striptease for the wolf, in order to distract him, whilst he's dressed as Grandma, then she escapes. (Though the mind boggles as to why a wolf would be interested in the sexual nature of the girl, considering all he wanted to do was to eat them.)

A few written versions, before the Brothers Grimm tales indicate the wolf cutting Grandmother to pieces and then feeding her to Little Red; obviously the cannibalistic version.

Cinderella: only turned up in the version written by Charles Perrault, he collated the *Mother Goose* stories. The pumpkin and the mice were in the Disney version. In the Chinese version from 850 AD, *yeh hsien* is given gold, pearls, food and dresses by a giant fish who can talk.

Stories differ to whether the Prince was walking the land with a glass or a fur slipper (the X–rated version!). In the Grimm's tale the sisters were so desperate to put their foot in the slipper that they cut off their toes and heels. When the Prince finds Cinderella, the step mother and sisters' eyes are pecked out by birds (which bring to mind Alfred Hitchcock's *The Birds*.) In the Disney adaptation, the stepmother falls from a cliff, which is pretty violent for Disney. In the Grimm's tale, the step-mother is forced into wearing iron shoes, which are red hot and made to dance until she drops dead, literally.

Snow White is meant to be 7 years old, so only a few years are meant to have passed when the Prince finds her! (Though in some cultures, girls do marry at an early age, even as young as 9.) When the stepmother asks for Snow White's heart, she wants to eat it literally. Other versions include her asking for all her vital organs, liver, kidneys, etc and one horrible one has her wanting a bottle of Snow White's blood, corked with her toe.

Lillian Bailey OBE was a deep trance British medium, providing advice to royalty throughout the twentieth century. Her gift let her "spirit self to leave its mortal shell and thus allow a communicator from the next world to take temporary control of it." The deceased loved ones were now able to communicate directly to their family.

She was instrumental in making 'spiritualism' being seen as a religion recognized by countries.

Film/TV References

Sixth Sense, The OC.

X Files Connection

Re Munchausen's Syndrome is associated with lying, faking an illness. Munchausen's By Proxy is where the parent produces an illness in the child to gain attention, not for the child, but for themselves. Mentioned in the episode, **The Calasuri**.

3.6 Red Sky At Morning

Written By Laurence Andries. Directed By Cliff Bole
Original US Airdate 8 November 2007

Guest Stars: Lauren Cohan (Bela); Tobias Slezak (Steve Warren); Ellen Geer (Gertrude Case); Samantha Simmonds (Sheila Case)

The episode is meant to take place in Massachusetts.

Sam and Dean look into the case of some dry land drowning.

Notes

Dean hasn't really met Ruby yet, in person.

Why Sam, didn't you replace the bullet in the colt after using it? Hmm, Dean eventually starts counting bullets now, or does he. Then he becomes a little hopeful that maybe Sam successfully got him out of the deal and Sam doesn't tell him the crossroads demon said there was no way out for Dean. He can't be saved and whoever holds his contract certainly doesn't want him out of it.

A case of divide and conquer the Winchesters and in the process, take care of 'its' own competition with Sam (See **3.9 Notes**.) Sam being the new leader 'n' all.

This episode was wasted on Bela. All about her, as if we really care about her and her past. Dean's probably right, she probably killed her father who was abusing her, or something, that's why she said no one, understands. As for saying Dean's damaged goods and "it takes one to know one", that was going a bit too far. He may be messed up, re family life, but when it comes to hunting and saving people, he doesn't think of what he'll get out if it first and as they've both said in the past: it's a lonely, unpaid job, but they have to do it. It's all they know, unlike her!

Calling them serial killers, yes, but only demons though and never people, except those who are possessed and when it's inevitable – collateral damage and then most of them really can't be saved!

Bela had to come crawling back to save her own skin, not fair she was saved by Sam and his "other way!" This puts a dampener on things, i.e. if he's changed or not. I mean, why bother saving her if he's not Sam. He does seem to be developing a bit of an attraction towards her. Eeww! The ship appearing to someone who's killed before was similar to **Bloody Mary (1.5.)**

No matter what's said about Bela, no sympathy for her whatsoever not, now or in the future.

Nothing much happened in this episode story wise but it had some great lines between Sam and Dean and Sam's new 'girlfriend'. (!) They can do their own research without having an excuse just to put her in the picture! Okay, the scene.

In **1.21** Meg tells Dad to watch out for his blood pressure, which Bela says to Dean here.

Dean in a tuxedo and Sam too! Spoilt for choice. Dean calling Gertrude, Sam's girlfriend, done before. Getting her paws all over Dean, that should read getting away with it! Double eeeww. Angry sex with her. No thanks!! The show will get boring pretty quickly if they have to keep running into her! Dean being fooled by her again. Of course she was only after the money!

Dean keeping the money since it was what she owed them and much more for the lotto tickets she stole. Glad to see they haven't stopped arguing – the best parts in the entire episode. Sam so convinced he can take care of himself and Dean's still worried about him. Dean saying he can understand Sam wanting to save him because he'd do the same, was good because hello, been there done that! Nice to know he wouldn't really think twice about making the sacrifice again for a second time. He says a lot but most especially in the season 3 finale during their heart-to-heart moment.

They haven't done much demon fighting so far, there's not much on the war, which is what season 3 is meant to be to be about, not Bela!

Sam's comments about Miss Haversham were wasted on anyone who doesn't know of, or has read Charles Dickens, *Great Expectations*. Like Dean, so he didn't see the movie version then. The difference here because the old woman was a widow but in the book, Miss Haversham was left at the altar on her wedding day and wore her wedding dress until she was old and died, just like the wedding banquet meal rotted on the table in her house and time appeared to stand still there, but not for her!

The ghost ship looked like something out of *Scooby Doo*.

Uncouthly, Sam's definitely turning into Dean – what with his use of 'smart ass'. Also not thinking twice about shooting even if it was a demon, she was still in a human body.

Suits again, that's number 4 and counting. Sam wanting to save Dean because he's his brother and because Dean's done the same for him so many times and this time it's for keeps.

Yet another 'killing' in the shower or just out of the shower.

Dean teasing about his new 'girlfriend' and their lines, what they said to each other in **1.16**

Shadow, when Sam was surveilling Meg, Sam told Dean to bite him and Dean said no, Sam should bite her.

More empty threats from Dean about shooting Bela. Oh get it over and done with and even Sam agrees this time. (In fact she's the one who'll be doing the entire shooting, first she shot Sam in **3.3** and then she shoots them both in **3.15**.) Why bother saving, her that's twice now (once in **3.3**) when she's already doomed! A bit of a waste of time, effort and energy. She calls them serial killers, and then grovels for help every time she needs it and in **3.15** too.

Dean has a panic attack when she steals his car.

If you kind of fast forward to **3.10**, Sam's question here asking Bela how she sleeps at night, is a bit funny since his dream sequence, when she turns up in her undies, almost getting it on with each other! She can't call Sam a drama queen, that's copyrighted to Dean! Et al who are more worthy! She can talk, she lives in Queens!

Since the brother told Sam he saw the ship when they went diving, with an angel figurehead that would've been enough for Sam to research, instead of having her show up.

Sam asks the important question of why they see ships before they die; see something good did turn up from hanging with his girl! Since they're all involved in someone else's death, a family member. Just like **1.5 Bloody Mary**, which pretty much answers our questions about Bela, she was responsible for deaths too of someone close to her. **(See** 3.15)

Dean's turn to tell Sam they can't save everybody, as in 1.3 where this all starts and continues on from there, when Sam said this to Dean, and in particular, Dean can't be saved at all either. Sam probably thinks this when he says he can't save anyone lately because he's too busy blowing away the bad guys!

Dean's line to Sam, not saying 'I told you so', which he also mouths in **3.9** to Sam about Ruby (but he was wrong about her, she was on their side.)

No, the 'Hand of Glory' is not a reference to Buffy. Bela now calls Sam a woman, after a drama queen. As for objectifying Dean, he does the same thing to chicks anyway.

Best Bits the 007 music when Dean walks down the stairs. Sam getting groped just about everywhere! Dean crossing his arms over his chest, as though Bela was undressing him with her eyes. No, only we can do that!!

As usual there's always a car accident in some *Supernatural* episode. Only in this episode it's people who 'spill' their own family's blood who see the ship. Hence Bela. Then Dean has it right all over again when he tells Bela to have a nice life – whatever little is left, don't know how right he was. Sam was taken aback by Bela saying she's got style. As if! (So it's an old phrase.) Sam reading more Latin.

As for Bela, takes one to know one, not really, Dean's never killed any of his 'family and Dad's decision to sacrifice himself was just that – his own decision.

Dean understanding Sam going after the crossroads demon because it's what he would do; yes go after it, but he means that's what he did to save Sam in **2.22**. The demon said it to Sam and now Dean says it (**3.5**) that Sam's stronger than Dean and he'll do just fine without Dean around. As for apologizing to Sam for his having to go through this, well, he doesn't want an apology, he wants his brother. Also in the previous episode, Sam tells Dean he doesn't need to apologize to Dean for trying to save him. Sam wants Dean to care about his life, that it means something and not to throw it away without a fight. Sam says he's a big boy now.

Dean's in this predicament because he couldn't quit caring about little Sammy. The way Dean clams up leaving Sam to wonder why he bothers to begin with, wasting his breath. Dean wants to play Craps, instead of replying, "Oh crap!"

Sam adding, "Nothing else to say for you," was funny since this sounded like Sam saying he's got nothing more to say on behalf of Dean, as if he was speaking for Dean. It would normally be said in England as, "Nothing else to say for yourself."

Bela mentioning Dean being a legend, that was said about Dad earlier on, think I said it in season 1.

Quotes

Sam: "You're my brother Dean and no matter what you do, I'm gonna try and save you and I'm sure as hell not gonna try and apologize for it."

Dean: "What a crazy old broad. Look at you sticking up for your girlfriend. You cougar hound."
Sam:" Bite me."
Dean: "Not if she bites you first."

Dean: "You can't save everybody Sam."
Sam: "It's just lately, I feel like I can't save anybody."

Bela: "Interesting how the legend is so much more than the man."

Sam and Dean's Take on the Urban Legend/Lore

There's plenty of lore on apparition ships, of old wrecks around the world; such as the Griffin, The Flying Dutchman. All these ship sightings were death omens. This ship was the Espirito Santo. A sailor in 1859 was charged with treason and hanged. Every 37 years a clipper is seen at sea. He was 37, which explains the 37 year old cycle. With a missing right hand, known as the 'Hand of Glory'. An occult object.

Actual Legend

Ghost ships are thought to be helmed by the dead. The most famous is *The Flying Dutchman*. Most stories relay this as a ship that is doomed to sail forever. Thought to have a light shining on it. The captain refused to put to port in a storm at sea near the Cape of Good Hope, and doomed his crew. It's said it would sail until Judgement day. Others believe the ship was stricken with a curse or plague.

Richard Wagner's play of the same name (*Die Fleigender Hollander* in German) where the Captain was allowed to return to shore every 7 years and find redemption when a woman is willing to sail with him. (The basis of the movie *Pandora and the Flying Dutchman* with James Mason and Ava Gardner. *The Flying Dutchman* was also mentioned in *Pirates of the Caribbean: Dead Man's Chest*. Great movie!)

The sighting of the ship is viewed as an omen of doom and is thought to be seen frequently during storms.

The Griffin: said to sail in the fog off Green Bay Harbour, North-West Wisconsin (*Supernatural* territory here) belonging to Robert Cavelier de la Salle – a French explorer. The biggest ship on the Great Lake, the Indians thought it to be an "affront" to the Great Spirit called *Metiome*: a prophet of the Iroquois tribe cursed the ship, which disappeared soon after and never seen again; except as a ghostly apparition in foggy weather. The legend says the ship "sailed through a crack in the ice."

The *Hand of Glory* must be the dried and preserved hand of a hanged man. It must be the left hand, or if not, then if the crime committed by the dead man was murder, then it must be the hand which did the killing. The hand was reputed to have been able to open any locked door.

The *Hand of Glory* was named for mandrake root, since the French word for this is *maindegloire* = hand of glory and *mandragore* = mandrake root. Mandrakes are known to grow under the bodies of hanged criminals. A hand pickled with the blood and fat of a hanged man, with a candle placed between the fingers. When a thief enters a house he would chant, "Hand of Glory, shining bright, lead us to our sports tonight." As the candle burns – the householders were said to be undisturbed by the thief.

Another version of the chant was, "Hand of glory, hand of glory, let those who are asleep remain asleep – in a sleep that is fast and deep. But those who are awake, be wide awake."

In the US TV series, *Poltergeist:The Legacy,* season 1 episode **The Substitute**, the Hand of Glory is also mentioned, here a variation of the chant was used; "Hand of glory, hand of power, conjured in the witching hour…"

Ooh Bloops

When the victim's in the shower, she doesn't have shampoo, then she does before she's strangled, which then vanishes from her hair again – presumably it was a bottle of *Wash 'n 'Go*!

Locations

Rosemary, Shaugnessy. (See **2.11**.) Coal Harbour Sea Wall.

There's a Winchester Station in Southern England, and another train station called Dean, not too far from it.

3.7 Fresh Blood

Written By Sera Gamble. Directed By Kim Manners
Original US Airdate 15 November 2007

Guest Stars: Lauren Cohan (Bela); Sterling K Brown (Gordon); Matthew Humphreys (Dixon); Michael Marsee (Kubrick); Mercedes McNab (Lucy)

Bela puts Gordon onto Sam and Dean's trail, as they chase after a vampire.

Notes

When Gordon told Bela he was going to shoot her, it was like she really didn't care. Bela taking Gordon's mojo bag said it all, taking his protection (sounds rude) that's when his luck started running out; that and going after Sam to begin with, on his Anti-Christ crusade.

Bela calls Dean, as if he'd really tell her where they are, or did she track him using GPS. Probably used some of her evil mojo. Crap, he wouldn't really fall for that from her another time!

Dean saying he tastes even better! Like the crossroads demons in when they called him delicious, edible and they could eat him up. As for a free lunch, well that's always something Dean's after! Dean's line of tasting good – also look back to **1.2** where he was goading the wendigo with his tasting good spiel. Great continuity for die hard fans; well at least those who remember what has gone before.

Did Dean really stay silent when Sam said he just wants him to be his brother again. To me, it seemed like he didn't want to hear anymore, to not argue more and just carry on with the hunt and find Gordon!

Bela's message of contacting a spirit and it told them to leave and not go after Gordon. There could be many reasons for such a cryptic message. Firstly, Gordon was a vampire now, so even more powerful, he said it himself. Secondly, she wanted help from Sam and Dean in future because of her own predicament (**3.15**); re hell hounds. Lilith wanted to deal with Sam herself, with Dean in hell; we didn't even meet her yet or know she held Dean's contract. Thirdly, she'd only consulted her Ouija board.

Bela had Gordon's mojo bag so she knew he wasn't protected anymore so he couldn't really do any harm towards them.

In **3.9**, Ruby says the same thing to them when Dean meets her the first time in the road. She tells them to leave town mainly because Tammy was more than a mere mortal, she was a demon and part of Lilith's army, gunning for the boys.

There's a lot to read into this, so whichever reason you think is the more plausible one or fits into the context.

You can see from Sam's expression he's lying when he tells Lucy they'll let her go. Lucy was straight out of *Dracula*. Dean's the one to end her life; again it falls on his shoulders to do the dirty deed. Sam actually feels sorry for her, for a change in this season!

Now it was Gordon's turn to wear a suit.

More *Supernatural* lore, this time having to ingest the blood of a vampire to turn onto one. The victim describing Sam and Dean, and Sam as that "real tall one." Well, that narrows it down! He's always referred to as the tall one and Dean the cute one. (see **3.12** when Lilith says this too.) This time all the female victims are blonde.

Oh Dean, more empty threats where Bela's concerned and in true Dean style, he stops off for pizza!

Irony in Gordon becoming the very thing he detests and hates – being turned into a vampire, just like his sister.

Sam showing his ruthless side again – of having to kill Gordon regardless of whether he can be saved or not and Dean telling him the old Sam would've paused for thought. Well, he tired getting him sent to prison and that didn't work. Sam uses nothing but strength or brute force to kill Gordon; obviously making Sam stronger than even a vampire (either that or he found the strength from somewhere.) See **2.21** where Jake was the only one of the special abilities children to have strength as a special power.

Also Lilith was afraid of Sam when her power didn't work on Sam. Have to wonder if Bela was really doing them a good turn in telling them of Gordon's location or whether she just wanted to get onto their good side so they help save her in the future. It's not as though they couldn't find him for themselves. Again, where the script let's us down in Sam and Dean suddenly becoming inept at both carrying out their own research and finding the bad guy!

Then there are some who'd say Gordon got his just desserts for what he wanted to do to Sam.

The vampire's speech was like he was preaching to Dean about being alone and helpless, knowing where you'll end up and not being able to do anything about it. Then Dean has to be the one to mention the same thing.

Sam and Dean have their argument in the middle of the episode. Again Dean being the one who's already dead or resigned himself to this fate. Dean writing poetry, that'd be something to behold. So what rhymes with "shut up?"

Sam pours his heart out to Dean once again and it's like Dean says before – all those episodes, he just doesn't want to hear it. He is scared but it takes a lot for him to admit this (**3.10**). Sam telling him he's always looked up to him because he's big brother and wants to be like him – and has to be like him when he's not around! (See **3.6**) and has nothing to say.

That's what Dean ends up doing, having to show little brother what to do (okay, even if it is in the context of looking after his beloved Impala!)

You could say Sam gets his taste of first real blood when he kills Gordon and not just with a proper weapon either, but it takes all his strength to kill him. Since they normally use guns. Yeah, well, why didn't Dean just use the colt on him after all! But Sam was like that even before he shot Jake, without a care in the world and his cruelty showed. Now it's explained away as

Sam needing to change to be like Dean, because Dean won't be around! A bit of a cop out since a lot more could be done with this storyline and Sam's character changes.

Sterling K Brown comments "When Gordon turns his aim toward Sam, it is not because he developed some sort of animosity from the way the brothers left him the last time they saw Gordon. He has information that leads him to believe Sam will become an instrument of evil in Satan's army, period." He wants to rid the world of evil, any evil, which is impossible for Dean to listen to since he's Sam's brother and he's deadly protective about him.

Jensen commented on Mercedes being great in the show. "She turned in a great performance. It's not easy playing those kinds of completely outlandish characters." She was Harmony in *Buffy* so is used to playing a vampire.

Quotes

Dean: "Really, just like that. I thought you would've been like, 'really, no we can't, he's a human, it's wrong!'"

Sam: "So you're the guy with nothing to lose now. Because wait, let me guess because you have nothing to lose now because you're already dead. I'm sick and tired of your old kamikaze tricks."

Sam and Dean's Take on the Urban Legend/Lore

According to the show, you only become a vampire if you ingest vampire blood.

Gordon's mojo bag.

Actual Legend

See the lore on vampires in previous episodes.

A 'mojo bag' is an African-American amulet, containing items of magic. The bag itself is considered to be a corruption of the English "magic" but is the West African word, 'mojiba'.

Locations

Lulu Island Trestle Bridge. Seymour Street Alley, Downtown.

3.8 A Very Supernatural Christmas

Written By Jeremy Carver. Directed By J Miller Tobin
Original US Airdate 13 December 2007

Guest Stars: Spence Garnet (Edward Carrigan); Colin Ford (Young Sam); Ridge Canipe (Young Dean); Merrilyn Gan (Madge Carrigan).

Ypsilanti, Michigan

Santa is dragged up the chimney as a boy watches and is killed.

Present Day

Sam and Dean investigate disappearances of men from their homes. Dean wants to celebrate Christmas.

Notes

Sam and Dean appear to have donned their suits in season 3 more times than they did in seasons 1 and 2 put together.

Dean not knowing who Dick Van Dyke is. Also mentioning *Mary Poppins* was wasted, now if there had been a porn version. Funny in **2.13** Dean said that how come Santa's not hooking him up with presents at Christmas, since he doesn't exist and here, he says exactly that. Which of course he was being sarcastic about. But he was the one to end Sam's fantasy about Santa when he told him there isn't one; but there are monsters under the bed.

Sam's mention of not having *Hallmark* memories about Christmas is a repeat of his phrase from **2.13** when he referred to angels not existing as they do in the *Hallmark* version'. Hallmark Channel is owned by Hallmark Cards.

Sam and Dean stay at the *Thomas Kincade Motel*, alluding to Jared's role in the movie as Thomas Kincaid.

All in all, an episode to give us some insight into Sam and Dean's childhood (once again, as in **1.18**) and how they spent their Christmas alone without Dad. From their flashbacks, you can see Dean was a bit of a pain in the proverbial and still horrible to little Sammy, when the mood suited him. Dean telling Sam not to talk about Mom and why not, she was his mom too. He didn't even get to know her, or see her in real life. Dean almost sounds like he holds some resentment against Sam for what happened to Mom, as if it was his fault she died. Also in **1.21**, Sam told Dean not to talk about Mom, when Dean said that she's gone and never coming back. So perhaps a little Sammy remembered what Dean told him here when he was big Sam.

Notice in their flashbacks, Sam and Dean's hair is always similar to how it is now, i.e. Sam has long hair and Dean's is cropped. It's fine, we can tell them apart when they're little. As always,

Dean feeding Sam nothing but junk, no wonder he hardly eats now!

Sam seemed to be stumbling a lot with his replies when placed on the spot and seemed to be putting his foot in it, something reserved for Dean (see **2.2**). Watching Dean make cranberry moulds, now there'd be a sight!

Sam hates Christmas because he's never had one to be happy about and get all into the season. You'd think they'd know the words to *Silent Night* especially Dean, not remembering the line, "Round yon virgin, mother and child..."

As in **1.18**, in this episode, Dean mistakenly took the old woman in the hospital to be the shtriga. Here, they got the wrong bad Santa.

An enjoyable episode none-the-less, since it was *Supernatural*'s first foray into Christmas. Good dashing of humour and the emotional, mushy stuff too, with Sam confessing he doesn't want to celebrate Christmas now because he'll be all alone next year at this time. Then he would've had the memories of this year instead! For that very same reason, that this was going to be Dean's last Christmas, is why Sam could've celebrated this one with him, which he comes to realize.

Curiously, the cookie devoured by the Pagan god had so much crunch to it. Loud or what...if he was supposed to be sweet smelling, then why didn't the boy say this when it was in his house.

Funny bit; Dean thinking Sam's reference to the wreath was because he liked it! So he'd want to ask about her shoes and handbag too.

Not believing in much, yet Dean still holds that Christmas is the birth of Jesus. As for Dean being Bing Crosby, he was probably dreaming of a white Christmas too, since they got snow at the end of the episode.

Sam discovering Dad's journal at Christmas and finding out what happened to Mom. Trust Dean to reach for the peanut brittle!

They seemed to be knocked out pretty quickly and not put up much of a fight against the Pagan gods.

End up being tied up again that makes this the third time this season for Sam alone. "Oh come all ye faithful..." plays as if it's just inviting Sam and Dean to their house.

It's okay to take Sam's fingernail, it'll grow back, but Dean's tooth gets saved by the bell. Hey, 'cause no chick would look at Dean twice with a missing tooth, or teeth.

Yeah, Dean, steal all the girlie presents for Sam. So that's how Dean got his amulet and how the whole calling Sam a girl business probably got started.

No *Supernatural* episode would be complete without the mention of porn, i.e. magazines this time.

Mr and Mrs God is from the book, *In The Creation Kitchen* by Nancy Wood (2006). Rather than creating, they were taking life here. *The Adventures of Ozzie and Harriet* was a US TV series.

Young Dean is played by the same actor from **1.18**.

Sam's reference to "ripple" which can also be a candy and ice-cream flavour, as well as being a cheap wine usually drunk by the poor and university students for their "get drunk quick" factor. Are they suggesting Sam was some sort of a secret-college drinker?! As Dean says he hardly drinks, aside from the odd beer or two. See **2.20**, where everyone implied Dean was a drunk in his alternate reality.

On this episode Eric commented, "We'll see a typically dysfunctional, screwed-to-hell snapshot of what Christmas was like for young Sam and Dean." Well, it wasn't that screwed to hell, at least they had each other.

J Michael Tobin comments, "The thing that's not said for the first three quarters of the episode is that this is Dean's last Christmas. That's the elephant in the room that nobody wants to talk about. It was interesting to watch the guys layer that into their performances in terms of having very different points of view on this holiday." On the scene where Sam and Dean are tortured he comments, "There's a wonderful mix of Christmas décor, like cookie cutters and candy – mixed in with all the Pagan stuff – the stone bowl, the blood, herbs and the big knife."

The amulet Sam gives Dean, originally intended for Dad, is a Mesopotamian Bull Man. It is known to be demon with a man's body above the waist and a bull below. Possessing the ears and horns of a bull. He is the fighter of evil; holding open the gates of dawn for the sun god *Shamash*. Seen in Mesopotamian artwork and also has wings at times. Statutes of this Bull Man were used as gatekeepers and finally became known as a good, friendly demon. In Akkadian it means 'The *Horned Bull*'.

Oh and do remember: A WINCHESTER IS FOR LIFE AND NOT JUST FOR CHRISTMAS.

Quotes

Dean: "Is it the serial killing chimney sweep?"
Sam: "Yep, it's actually Dick Van dyke."

Dean: "Looking for a Pimp Santa."
Dean: "My brother here, it's been a lifelong dream of his."
Sam: "He's just kiddin'. We only came here to watch. Thanks a lot Dean, thanks for that."

Sam: "It's just that Mr Gung Ho Christmas might have to blow away Santa."

Dean: "…sure you didn't wanna ask her about her shoes. I saw some nice handbags in the foyer."

Dean: "If you fudging touch me again, I'll fudging kill you!" (And he did.)

Dean: "Dad probably thinks you're a girl."

Sam and Dean's Take on the Urban Legend/Lore

Sam says there's an Anti –Clause version of Santa in every culture, such as, Belsnickel, Black Peter, Krampus; Santa's rogue brother. Meadowsweet is a plant in Pagan lore, used for sacrifices. Christmas is a Pagan festival (thought everyone knew that.) The Yule log, Santa suit were all cast offs from Pagan worship. The god of Winter Solstice,

Holnikar was sacrificed to him. Usually mild weather is a sign of the Anti-Clause, there's no snow here. Can be killed by a stake.

Actual Legend

Anti-Claus such as Belsnickel, Krampus and Black Peter. Belsnickel is of Pennsylvanian Dutch origins or myth, only leaves presents if children have been good. Was originally a frightening creature.

In Austria, there is *Krampusse,* children of poor families walked streets dressed in dark rags and masks, carrying charms and used to attach children with them. This tradition is still relevant today. Known as *Krampus,* wearing costumes and use switches to hit people, especially women. Black Peter was the opposite of Santa, stealing money from children.

The Wild Hunt: throughout specific times of the year, spirits ride in the sky along with witches, ghosts and fairies, said to be led by a Pagan god. Odin – the Viking was seen as one of the leaders of the Wild Hunt in North Eastern Europe, Germany and Scandinavia. In the Winter Solstice, Odin was said to leave presents at the bottom of his sacred pine tree, this was regarded as one of the tales of how Christmas presents were given Odin's 8-legged horse called Sleipnir, was the legend which gave pace to Santa's 8 reindeer. Santa was seen as Odin, and St Nicholas encapsulated one form. Odin was "demonized" and his huntsmen were known as the ungodly dead. They were barred from heaven and left out from hell to hunt souls. In the St Nicholas Day parades in Europe, Odin is seen in black, dressed like the devil – known as Black Peter or Black Rupert.

However, the concept of demonic riders looking for living souls was noted by monks who wrote of such ancient legends. This was seen as the reason why so many people disappeared in wild places such as woods, also wild animals roamed Merica, Europe and Scandinavia. In the nineteenth century; the abundance of werewolves, vampires and brigands who attacked travellers was seen as being real rather than just a myth.

Meadowsweet, a sacred herb for Druids and grows in ditches, wet meadows, ponds, riverbanks and found throughout Europe, US and Canada. Ritually, Meadowsweet is said to invoke happiness, peace and used in divination. Dried Meadowsweet is said to maintain peace in the house. Known to the Celtic moon goddess, Aine, who was thought to have given the herb its scent.

Balder was an Aesir god, son of Frigg and Odin. He was killed by mistletoe which his blind brother, Flod, threw at him. Loki, the Trickster, was believed to be responsible for Balder's death.

The evergreen as a symbol forms all parts of North European Winter Solstices. Evergreens were carried into houses to remind people their crops would begin to live (grow) again in Spring. Pieces of evergreen trees were used as good luck charms. Symbolizing fertility. Trees were also decorated with apples, symbolizing offerings of food to the tree (this is how placing gifts under the tree originated). Christmas trees refer all the way back to North myth , to *yggdrasil*, i.e. *the Great Tree of Life*. (Here stakes from the Christmas were used to kill the Pagan gods.)

Film/TV References

Mary Poppins, The Hardy Boys, Happy Days. Ozzie and Harriet.

Music

Have Yourself A Merry Little Christmas by Rosemary Clooney. *Silent Night* by Sam and Dean.

Ooh Bloops

Sam was cut on his right arm, the bandage is on his left arm and his right arm is clean. There's no cut on Dean's arm when the blood was pouring out.

When Sam and Dean burst into Santa's place, he's holding a bottle in his left hand and green pipe in his right. When he stands up this changes.

Locations

New Westminister. Maple Ridge.

3.9 Malleus Malificorum

Written By Ben Edlund. Directed By Robert Singer
Original US Airdate 31 January 2008

Guest Stars: Katie Cassidy (Ruby); Rebecca Reichert (Amanda); Marisa Ramirez (Tammie); Robinne Fanfair (Janet Dutton); Erin Cahill (Elizabeth); Kristen Booth (Renee Van Allan)

Sam and Dean investigate a witches coven. Ruby tells Dean some home truths, when he meets her for the first time.

Notes

Dean's obvious distaste for witches also extends to Ruby, but she's more of a demon than a witch. She saves his life. Dean's reference to the rabbit as "poor little guy" – have to wonder if he just might be talking about himself.

Sam and Dean in suits again. Isn't it always three witches: *Macbeth, Charmed*, etc.

Dean uses his own phone to call the police. Probably it's a disposable so the number can't be traced, or rather, it'll be in someone else's name anyway. They left their prints behind when Sam was searching for the hex bag. The women were using the black arts for personal gain and it wasn't even for anything big either. Still, again some would say they had it coming for meddling in things they shouldn't.

Obviously Bachmann Turner Overdrive refers to the group, more famous for the song, *You Ain't Seen Nothing Yet.* Dean also refers to Black Sabbath, not the band.

Dean mentions Mary Stewart; again, he also talked of her in the Christmas episode in reference to the Pagan gods.

Saying they all have secrets, yes Dean will have one at the end of this episode when he doesn't tell Sam he can't be saved, until later on in the season and Sam still hasn't told Dean about Mom's encounter with Yellow Eyes in the nursery and he was given demon blood.

Dean meets Ruby for the first time, nine episodes later in this season and he says nothing about her looks or anything, that must be a first for him. No wait, the first for him was with Bela where he just wanted to shoot her!

Dean can't believe Sam actually wants to kill them, without even thinking about it first and pondering the possibility of using other methods to stop them. Well, he was right about killing Tammy, she was the evil one, but Dean ended up doing the killing. Also Dean shouldn't be too surprised what Sam says about killing right about now, since he said it about Gordon in **3.7**, wanting to kill him or he'd kill them first. And he did too.

Where Sam finally admits he wants to be more like Dean, has to be like him to prepare himself for the inevitable – for life, hunting, without him. He can't afford to stop and take a moment. That's why he's been acting strangely – re the merciless killings! We thought that perhaps there was a tinge of darkness in him right about now. Sam wants to be more like Dean, does this mean obligatory leather jacket too.

Sam doesn't say Dean's going to die, he says he's leaving and the world is a better place for him with Dean around!

Sam sticking up for Ruby, she's useful. Dean said Casey (**3.5**) would've been useful too.

Sam and Deans' argument takes place in the middle of this episode instead of at the beginning; or more usually at the end. That's saved for Dean's encounter with Ruby and the reality of what he'll really become when he goes to hell. Ruby admitting she only wants to help Sam become stronger for when Dean's not around anymore. All talking about Dean in this episode, as if he's already gone to hell (so to speak.)

Another reference to Deans' height! Think they should just stick to calling him cute, but Ruby wouldn't say that to him! (Nor him to her!) "Short bus" is also a derogatory term for someone mentally ill. Such buses are used to take mentally ill children to school (similar to yellow US school buses but smaller). Thus Ruby uses it to insult Dean also about his height.

Wouldn't witches have had their own powers for whatever purpose, otherwise what is the whole point of witchcraft? So why the need to sell their souls to a 'higher' power, or more specifically, a 'lower' power.

Tammy calling Sam *Magnum*. Look, it's the ol' pin them against the wall ploy. Used several times and again in the season finale by Lilith. Eventfully all these demons get to call Sam 'Sammy' and he's always called 'little' too.

So if there's a new leader in the West, what about the other three points of the compass, or don't they count?

As for saying that Sam's no competition for this new leader, clearly that was an exaggeration; since the season finale showed Lilith was no match for Sam. She was even terrified of him, especially when she used her powers on him and they didn't work.

Everyone was a bit slow in getting to the knife to kill Tammy, but Dean took pleasure in killing a witch-cum-demon. Dean could've taken Ruby's knife now when he left it sticking inside Tammy.

That answers my question about Ruby being centuries old. Another question, why do demons bleed red blood; or is that their human host's blood.

Dean noticed the lights flickering before Ruby appeared but Sam, inside the room, didn't. When Ruby came to see Sam all these times there were no light flickering or radio static to indicate her presence. Or even when she appeared to save Dean. She says Winchesters are bigoted and in **3.3**, she told Sam to stop being a racist. Ruby tells Dean she's preparing Sam to fight alone and tells Sam this in **3.4**, but doesn't explain herself fully there.

Contrary to other demons Ruby recalls her humanity – being human, so what makes her think Dean won't recall it either. What was going through Dean's head when we fade to black?

That explains why Sam is all gung ho in season 4 culling demons with Ruby's help, especially in the introductory episodes because everything he's been through has been leading him to this moment!

The Secret is a self-help book and film. *Hellraiser* is a film based on Clive Barker's book of the same name.

Jared and Katie make a cute couple on screen and off, I think.

Quotes

Dean: "Freakin' witches…why does the rabbit always get screwed, poor little guy." (Maybe because his foot brought so much bad luck in **3.3**)

Dean: "I guess we all have secrets."

Dean: "Change into what?"
Sam: "Into you. I've gotta be more like you."

Dean: "The devil may care after all, is that what I'm supposed to believe."

Sam and Dean's Take on the Urban Legend/Lore

Hex bag containing bird bones, rabbit's teeth, Sam calls it old world black magic.

Actual Legend

Malleus Malificorum is Latin and means *the Hammer of Witches*: a handbook on witches written by Heinrich Kramer and Jacob Sprenger in 1486. They were associated with the Inquisition of the Catholic Church. The publication shed light on the existence of witches and to show the number of female witches outnumbered men. It laid down procedures whereby magistrates could help determine witches when on trial, thus finding them guilty of witchcraft and being a witch.

A note on The Blair Witch Project. In February 1785, Elly Kedward from Blair, Maryland, was branded a witch and exiled from her village, after being accused of luring children to her home to draw blood from them. Many of the other children and villagers disappeared, especially those who laid accusations of her being a witch. A fictional book, *The Blair Witch Cult* was published in November 1809 about how a woman accused of witchcraft had cursed the Blair village.

A town called Burkittsville was built over Blair in 1824 in the exact spot where the Blair village was located, called Fredrick County, Maryland. There were reports of child murders and other gruesome events carried out on the inhabitants. A murderer, in 1941, confessed to killing seven children and claimed he was forced to do this by the ghost of an old woman, who lived in the woods.

Hence, the arrival in 1994 of three filmmakers working on their class project, *The Blair Witch* legend. They disappeared and only their footage was found.

This was a remarkable feat as this urban legend was created for the singular purpose of marketing this movie, adding cult status to the movie, even before its release. The writers/directors used Netlore to market this movie.

Burkittsville, Indiana was the setting of **1.11 Scarecrow**.

Film/TV References

Blair Witch Project, Fatal Attraction, Magnum PI, Hellraiser

Music

Every House Has Its Thorn by Poison; *Put A Spell On You* by Screamin' Jay Hawkins.

Ooh Bloops

At the end of the episode when Tammy's killed by Ruby's knife, Ruby's fringe (bangs) keeps changing.

When Sam is pinned against the wall, his fringe keeps altering too from across his forehead.

Location

Izzard Street, Surrey. Crescent Beach Marina.

3.10 Dream A Little Dream

Written By Sera Gamble, Cathryn Humphris. Directed By Steve Boyum
Original US Airdate 7 February 2008

Guest Stars: Jim Beaver (Bobby); Cindy Sampson (Lisa); Damon Runyan (Henry Frost); G Michael Gray (Jeremy Frost)

Sam and Dean help Bobby when he's pursued by a killer in his dreams and Dean has a revelation in his dream.

Notes

Sam drinking again and on the verge of getting drunk; only for the third time in the entire three seasons. This isn't bad going for him per se and Dean's right for telling Sam he's not a drinker.

Obviously Sam's feeling sorry for himself because he can't save people and mostly he can't save Dean.

Question is, who told Sam that Dean can't be saved by Ruby or anyone else or anything else? Ruby only told Dean and he hasn't said anything to Sam yet. As for Sam telling Dean what'll become when he gets to hell, well, Ruby only told Dean that – he'll become a demon. Unless Sam is taking an educated guess, he can't know for sure that this is what Dean will become; remember he has to lose his humanity first and forget about his human life. With these demons around just wanting to and waiting to get their claws into Dean Winchester – that won't be easy for him to forget. Of course, he could just give up and join the demon brigade to get them off his back, so to speak, to become stronger by becoming evil. Hey. Anything to survive in hell.

Having said that, being evil doesn't necessarily mean stronger than being good. (Sorry, I did it again, talked about what Dean will do in hell, even before season 4 was made and aired!)

Sam however, emulates big brother by saying Dean's not the only one with a licence on getting chicks and drinking! Not that there were any chicks there for him, even Dean's picky that way.

That bit at the end with demon Dean telling Dean what he'll become was a repeat of what Sam says in the start of the episode – so not only will he recall that in his "dream stage" – but also what Ruby said to him in **3.9**, i.e. he can't be saved. Which was a wake-up call for Dean to

386

take a cold, hard look at what's really going to happen to him; to stop being flippant and act scared! Well, feel afraid at least. To share his feelings; try and help himself or any of the above.

Of course they believe the legends. Legends are the stuff of *Supernatural*!

Dean had to drink a beer. Sam can become Freddie Kreugar. (Jared is in a re-make of *Friday the 13th*)

See what I mean about Sam and Dean not being able to do things for themselves anymore – been hunting all this time and have to turn to Bela for the dreamroot. Oh crap! They're not that inept!

Ewww and triple ewww!! Sam dreaming about Bela. Why? He just said "crap" about her and he hasn't even taken any dreamroot yet either, so he's <u>actually</u> dreaming about her. Something wrong with his subconscious then, no seriously, having X-rated dreams about her, which he doesn't tell Dean about as he'll never let him live it down and neither will we! Either that, or

Dean will say he's seriously disturbed man! Pity Dean didn't get it when Sam stammers upon seeing Bela. Sam dreaming about Brad Pitt was funny and the denials from Sam too! His dreaming about Bela came out of nowhere. He was kind of attracted to her from **3.3** but this was going too far. She's not his type. Oh the drool Sam! Maybe Bela turning up in his dream is indicative of Sam getting his powers back (he 'repelled Lilith in the season 3 finale!) so his vision or psychic powers must be returning and his dream is a sign they are; because when he dreams of people – they're in trouble or impending death. So Sam and Dean have to save them; and that's exactly what happened to Bela in **3.15**. She was dying, or at death's door. Or perhaps what Sam's dream hinted at. (Also in season 4 he did get his psychic powers, though why they coincided with Dean's demise is another question.) Then Bobby asks Sam at the end if it could be his psychic powers and he says he hasn't got them.

Dean had to open the safe in front of Bela when she's taken everything else from them – did he really think the colt would be safe. Dean telling her to get a room and Sam (probably sweating profusely when Bela removes her coat, yeah like she had to!) Another funny bit, Dean asking Sam what he did in college and Sam asking why he's curious.

Everyone always dream of white picket fences – Dean did the same in **2.20** when in the alternate reality, okay I know I keep calling it alternate reality, well, it was in a way. Bobby wakes up in time to prevent Sam being clobbered. Dean telling Bobby he's a father to him and we get a little on Bobby's past life – having to kill his wife because she was possessed and he didn't know what to do. So he became a hunter after that. Leading to the question of why or how his wife came to be possessed – why her? If she wasn't then Dad probably wouldn't have met him and wouldn't be in this fight now.

Bela lying just to get her paws on the colt, when all Bobby did for her was to give her some amulet. Dean objecting to Sam digging around in his head, it's not like he had to, he didn't come across anything private or important (not that I'm saying there wasn't anything in his head!) Except for seeing Lisa, he obviously has deep-rooted feelings there; to become a family; wishful thinking on Dean's part to have a happy life and home with Lisa and Ben or he just wants to 'get it on'! No, he's really into her.

Speaking of Jared's pranks on set, in this episode he grabbed hold of Bobby's toe when he's in the hospital bed, but Bobby (Jim) never went out of character and said all his lines. Jared also likes to alter his lines when they're not being filmed and talk about other things so as to put people, like Jensen, off their lines. Jared is also a big fan of the Brit word "saucy" too, as Lauren (Bela) described her scene with Jared in this episode!

Dreams are an extension of our subconscious so when we dream it's about things, places, people, etc, that we've been thinking about.

Dean's reference to Edison and the phone, as in **3.14** where he's mentioned again. Also Dean doesn't recognize the back of himself when he's sitting at the desk. So did he mean literally dead inside or metaphorically? – He has had another heart; been brought back from his coma: the throes of death (and is heading that way again in **3.16**.) He can only be dead inside if he doesn't care for people, and has no heart (like Bela) and putting Sam, his family and everyone else first instead of thinking about himself, doesn't count as being dead in my book.

What can Dean do to save himself when he's been told he can't be saved? There's no easy way to handle this and a year sure isn't enough time to come to terms with being given a one year, uncommuted life sentence. Not like ten years that everyone else got for their bargaining. On the contrary, his life is worth saving as much as anyone else's. Dad didn't think this; yet Dean's "subconscious" is saying that Dad couldn't save his family, Mom or even Sam. But Dad isn't like that; he did save Dean, even if it took him his own life to do it. Also saving Sam, protecting him, isn't really Dad's 'crap'; Dean doesn't do it because Dad told him to, but because he's family, his brother and he loves him. (As I said before.) and Dean says it now: he was given a responsibility at so young an age, coming to terms with losing Mom, looking after Sam – where's Dean's childhood and everything he wanted to do?

Dean doesn't really resent doing everything he did; otherwise he wouldn't have sacrificed himself to bring Sam back! He doesn't deserve hell for his troubles. As for all the things demon Dean says, he is a demon and as everyone keeps saying, demons lie!

Here Dean says Dad was an "obsessive bastard" Dean's looking out for Sam now, he always has and says the same thing in **1.18**, Dean is the one who bears the responsibility and burden of looking after him, always has, always will. (For as long as he is around.)

Get the part about Dean not having an original thought in his head – true for where he saved Sam (**2.22**) would he have thought of doing this if Dad hadn't done it first. Anyway, that's for you to ponder. See, Dean dreams about becoming a demon, but as I said, only after the thought's been planted in his head by Ruby and Sam.

Dean takes the easy way out even in his dreams by shooting demon Dean. That'd help, so he doesn't have to listen to the truth.

Bobby asking Sam if it was his psychic powers, Sam doesn't think so but he will use these in the season finale and season 4 to save himself from Lilith. For some reason his psychic powers won't work now. Has he been suppressing them or does he genuinely not have them at this stage? Do they return as a result of seeing Dean in his anguish in the season finale.

When Sam mentions "Tim Leary" style, he is referring to Dr Timothy Leary, a psychologist and writer, he wrote about using psychedelic drugs and raved about the therapeutic benefits of LSD.

Dean talking to Sam about the *Wizard of OZ and the Dark Side of the Moon* is when you watch the movie and listen to the Pink Floyd album, both end up being in sync with each other. Most people watch and listen whilst being high (not encouraged at all!) especially at university.

Therefore Dean's asking Sam what he did at college and Sam being the innocent that he is, has no idea what he's talking about! Of course Sam worked hard at college!

This episode to tell us about Dean's impending fate and his resolve to not want to go to hell.

Perhaps he does harbour a little envy towards Sam for being able to life his own life, for a short while. Dean clicking his fingers at the end, another good touch: this is what he'll look like!

Just to be sure, Dean checks again what Sam saw in his head and doesn't tell him what he dreamt about and finally, he does tell Sam he doesn't want to die, which probably sounds a little too late. However, when Dean says he doesn't want this, it leads nicely onto the next episode where he does die and not just once, but over and over...

Some of the crew got their own back on Jared for his pranks, when he was tied to down, but we don't know what happened since that has been *bleeped!* out. Sorry censored. The part with demon Dean, they had to get a photo double for Jensen and had to film all the scenes completely in only one day.

Said Jim Beaver, "I'd like to know more about what Bobby was before he became a hunter, and how his wife came to be possessed. Maybe a little more about his relationship with John and the boys way back. Same stuff everybody wants to know."

Quotes

Sam: "I tried Dean...save people...where you're goin', what you're goin' become I can't stop it! No one can save you because you don't wanna be saved. I mean how can you care so little about yourself. What's wrong with you?" (Sam says this in most of the season 3 episodes.)

Dean: "I get it, I'm my own worse nightmare."

Demon Dean: "You can't escape me Dean. You're gonna die and this is what you're gonna become."

Sam and Dean's Take on the Urban Legend/Lore

Sam says African Dreamroot, *Selene Capensis* is used by African medicine men and shamen for dream walking. It's serious mojo and if enough is taken can even kill in dreams. Charcot Wilbrand Syndrome.

Actual Legend

Dream walking was akin to psychic and physical projection: the person is asleep. When an amateur takes part in dream walking and comes across some danger, this will lead to a much deeper sleep and dreaming subconsciously. "Lucid dreaming" inside your own mind. Others can dream into the minds of others. When the mind is open, it is open to all influences. Therefore Sam's encounter was violent and Dean's with his 'demonic' self.

African Dreamroot, also known as Xhosa. Is used in South African spiritual rituals – containing a "psychoactive" mixture leading to lucid dreams. In traditional terms, was used to make contact with ancestors. Xhosa shamen call the plant *silene, ubulau* meaning, white paths.

Charcot Wilbrand Syndrome is more usually associated with loss of dreaming in stroke patients. Named after the founder of modern neurology, Frenchman, Jean Martin Charcot and German neuro-opthalmologist, Herman Wilbrand. Defined as the "loss of ability to revisualize images". Came to light by a single case study by Charcot in 1883 and Wilbrand in 1887.

In modern times, it refers to any reduced dreaming or none at all – or where a certain part of the brain has been damaged. Dreaming is considered to be important to health.

X Files Connection

8.17 Via Negative (meaning negative theology. Latin for "negative way", i.e. describing God in terms of what he isn't.) Dead bodies of a religious cult are found. Skinner suggests that use of an Iboga hallucinogen maybe why no trace evidence is found at the crime scene; since the consciousness could leave the main suspect's body. The drug is reputed to reach "the depths of the soul". The Lone Gunmen suggest the drug enables peoples' dreams to be invaded, causing their worst nightmares to become reality.

Music

Long Train Runnin' by Doobie Brothers; *Dream A Little Dream Of Me* Mama Cass.

Locations

Eagle Ridge Hospital.

3.11 Mystery Spot

Written By Jeremy Carver, Emily McLaughlin.
Directed By Kim Manners.
Original US Airdate 14 February 2008

Guest Stars: Jim Beaver (Bobby); Richard Speight Jr (Trickster)

Sam and Dean investigate a mystery spot and the disappearance of a writer, where they face their own groundhog day.

Notes

Questions: why was the Trickster so interested in teaching Sam a lesson in pain and loss. It's not his job, he's a demi-god so he can manipulate and use people how he wants. Also as he said Sam was the butt of his joke – losing Dean over a hundred times. But it wasn't really his place to offer him advice as to why Dean's his weakness and vice versa, Sam is Dean's weakness. (See season 1 where Meg said Dad was their weakness (Sam and Dean say it to each other too) , now he's no longer around; they're each other's weakness and yes, blood ties do lead to such sacrifices , especially for them as losses run so deep in their family.

A repetition of Ruby in **3.9** when she told Dean she needs him to help Sam prepare for when Dean's gone. That's what the Trickster says he was doing here for Sam. A lesson in humanity, Sam goes over the rails when Dean's not around as though Sam keeps Dean in check to a certain extent.

A funny episode even though it dealt with Dean and the'd' word – dying. You couldn't help laughing at Dean's fate(s) in all those scenarios, though they weren't surprising, there were so many obstacles placed in Dean's way: dog, car, furniture, guns, shot with an arrow, even Sam axed Dean! (Perhaps a bit of an unintended pun there since the series was itself facing the axe after season 2!) Yes, after a few of Dean's 'deaths,' they just got hilarious to the point of ridiculous and so we just had to laugh out loud.

So after Dean's year is up, couldn't the Trickster bring him back, or does he only have control over situations and time loops of his own making. That'd be too easy, but it'd be good to see Dean as a demon and being *Supernatural* - maybe they would speed up Dean's 'demonizing' process and bring him back sooner – as a demon, if they go down that road.

Great acting, especially when speaking the synchronized dialogue. Like Sam uses a ruler every morning, to measure his 'manhood'! Ha. The look on Dean's face when the Trickster told them he can't be saved no matter what.

A quick gripe: the episode would've been even better if the Trickster wasn't shown in the 'previously' segment at the start, since these are always usually relevant to that particular episode.

Dean' referring to "clowns or midgets" harks back to **2.2 Everybody Loves A Clown** as Sam hates clowns, being afraid of them and Dean's reference to the midget when he couldn't get anything right and kept putting his foot in it.

Also Sam 'tiring' of seeing Dean killed, he can't take it anymore and to the other extent, wishing it'd all be over again! The final scene when he looks at Dean's unmade bed, as though that was the last time he'd see that; or the last time Dean would ever do that. Hey, Dean could've fallen down the stairs at the end! The dog looked so harmless, causing so much 'damage'. What was the big idea Dean petting a dog when he's never done that before.

Death comes to everyone but in their case, it's surfaced too many times.

Sam's final show of humanity, that he wouldn't just become a cold-blooded, unfeeling killer with Dean's demise (we hope), when he wouldn't kill Bobby, until he realized who it really was, i.e. the Trickster.

This episode also showed Sam could survive without Dean, venting all his anger and energy into killing demons. Actually got to see Sam eating too, for a change and he had the Impala all to himself!

The scene where the desk dropped onto Dean was straight out of a *Laurel & Hardy* sketch. Sam and Dean synchronizing their speech was a great scene, wonder how long that took to film and how many takes were involved, but knowing how great Jensen and Jared are, not too many.

It finally takes Dean to give Sam a clue about what was happening and it had to be a 'foody' reference too, i.e. just desserts. You'd think the Trickster would've noticed Sam would see he was now eating strawberry jam and not syrup; or did it look like the Trickster was getting tired of this prank and wanted to be found out. Dean also giving Sam another clue when they pass Hasselback's daughter handing out flyers, they passed her for a hundred Tuesdays and no one stopped to see who she was. Well, Dean would be the one to notice the chick, but a little late!

Dean eating once again and always wanting breakfast the next day! Dean asking Sam if the bra is his!

Asia playing over and over on the radio with *Heat of the moment...* relevant since Sam kinda woke up in such a state every day... also this song was sung by Cartman in *South Park* episode **Kenny Dies**, when Kenny died and didn't come back to life at once.

Dean's Deaths: Dean is shot. Run over. Desk squats him from above. Chokes on sausage. Falls in the shower. Poisoned by Tacos. Electrocutes himself. (Already suffered this one in **1.12 Faith**.) Sam kills him with an axe. Death by dog! Shot again and this time it's for keeps.

Dean has really been dead four months, so Sam actually had all that time to 'hunt' alone and experience life without him. (As in season 4.) So taking this into consideration, when Sam says he's changing, into Dean, and that Dean's going to become evil in hell, in **3.10**, it's because he's been through life without him, only this episode came after the dream one and not before.

Anyhoo, it'll still hold true for when Sam says he'll have to live in this crap world without him.

This episode was actually meant to be **3.12** but was changed around probably since **3.12** would've been a much better season 3 finale, had there not been another four episodes filmed after the writers' strike.

Sam has two plates of food on the table in the scene where he's without Dean, but that plate there could've been his dirty dishes, rather than setting a place for Dean, since they didn't set places for dinner for each other, Sam hardly ate.

The moral of this episode is that there is no out for Dean, whatever they do, or don't do, and they have to face the reality that Dean can't be saved from his destiny, all of his own doing. That Sam has to brace himself for life without him, even if it's for a short while. All in all an hilarious, side-splitting episode with its sad moments too.

Sam and Dean are meant to be dead now officially for the purposes of law enforcement as of this episode, but won't they find out they're not, with all these prints they're still leaving behind. It's not really something that's closed or ended when Henriksen told the FBI Sam and Dean were dead. (See **3.12**.)

Quotes

Dean: "My God, you're a freak!"

Sam & Dean: "Yeah, right. Nice guess."
Sam: "It wasn't a guess."
Sam & Dean: "Right, you're a mind reader. Cut it out…You think you're being funny, but you're being really, really childish. Sam Winchester wears make-up. Sam Winchester cries his way through sex. Sam Winchester keeps a ruler by the bed and every morning when he wakes up…!"

Sam: "Just had a really weird dream."
Dean: "Clowns or midgets." (Now we're even getting déjà vu dialogue too!)

Sam and Dean's Take on the Urban Legend/Lore

For Trickster lore, see **2.15**

Sam and Dean investigate mystery spots. Which Sam describes as "spots in the world where holes open up and swallow people, Bermuda Triangle, Oregan Vortex. Where strong magnetic fields can bend space and time.

Actual Legend

The mystery spot is an actual tourist attraction outside of Santa Cruz, California. The official website suggests aliens buried their spacecraft or unfamiliar metals under the spot; or perhaps there are carbon dioxide emissions from the Earth. This could be explained as a gravity hill' type of illusion."

Film/ TV References

X Files, Kojak, Taxi Driver, Groundhog Day, Dingoes Ate My Baby.

X Files Connection

6.15 Monday Morning. Mulder wakes on Monday morning to find his water bed sprung a leak and his alarm clock didn't work. He has to stop off at a bank. A bank robber enters, then Scully enters and Mulder is shot. Police trap the robber who detonates the bomb, causing the bank to explode...Mulder wakes on Monday morning...it's a time loop, events repeat themselves. The bank robber's friend knows of this time loop and has to warn Mulder and Scully of their fate. Mulder: "Scully, did you ever have one of those days you wish you could rewind and start all over again from the beginning."

Scully: "Yes, frequently, who's to say that if you did rewind it and start over again, it wouldn't end up exactly the same way?" This episode was written by Vince Gilligan and John Shiban; directed by Kim Manners.

Music

Heat of the Moment by Asia; *Back In Time* by Huey Lewis and the News.

Ooh Bloops

The first time Sam and Dean leave the diner, a woman in red leaves with a man from the store next door. They aren't seen again when time keeps looping.

Dean's hair is flat in the shower, then it's been moved back.

On the second Tuesday, a couple walk across the scene.

3.12 Jus In Bello

Written By Sera Gamble. Directed By Phil Sgriccia
Original US Airdate 21 February 2008

Guest Stars: Katie Cassidy (Ruby); Lauren Cohan (Bela); Charles Malik Whitfield (Agent Henricksen); Aimee Garcia (Nancy); Peter De Luise (Dep. Director Steven Groves); Rachel Pattee (Lilith).

Monument, Colorado

Bela lures Sam and Dean into a trap and they're caught by FBI Agent Henricksen. The new demon leader is finally revealed.

Notes

This episode has all the main cast and Bela and Ruby appear together for the first and only time.

Bela steals the colt, sells it, gets the boys trapped and then still expects them to help her in **3.15**. Again telling Dean he knows nothing about her. Sweetie, we don't really care either way! Dean gets to Colorado and misses out on seeing the Grand Canyon. (see **2.9**.)

As for calling Sam Dean's little half-wit brother, huh, Sam is the brains of the outfit! This time they're caught for real and there's no ploy by them to get into jail, as in **2.19**. So there'd be no escape for them either, conveniently the demons come a-calling in this episode, as the demonic version of the movie, *Assault On Precinct 13*. (Where a few police officers and prisoners, and a female worker, are under siege in a police station by gangs outside.)

Sam and Dean walking in chained and cuffed (yeah, we'd have 'em that way!) Dean's wanted poster pictures are the mug shots taken in **2.7**. Yet another gay reference with Dean having to say, yet again, they're not like that. (cf **2.9**.) Dean won't have anyone talk about Dad disrespectfully, unless he does it for himself, like calling him an obsessed bastard in **3.10**. He wouldn't even hear Sam say a horrible word against him throughout season 1 and part of season 2.

It's Dean's turn to get shot in the shoulder this time, last time it was Sam shot by Bela. (**3.3.**)

Sam and his Latin chanting and hey on the loud speaker, even better. Everyone still falling for Sam and his puppy dog eyes/looks, when he asks for a towel for Dean and takes the rosary from Nancy. See Sam's also adept at picking pockets and stealing.

Even in a time of dire crisis, Dean never forgets to think about food. Dean and his 'told you so'. That's the third time he's said it this season. He took a long time in the impound yard- which conveniently had to be near the police station and even longer watching the flickering lights. So nobody searched the Impala again for hidden booty.

Sam and Dean have a tattoo on their chests to prevent them being possessed. (Also see **3.16**, Ruby gave them amulets to prevent them from possession, why didn't she have one for herself when Lilith possessed her, or did they not work on her.

Dean has to get the line in about evil clowns eating people (*2.2*) lucky Sam wasn't around to hear him. Dean mentions all the monsters and creatures that they've come across in the show. He also believes the world will end in chaos and evil, so he'd rather go out fighting. He said this about Dad too earlier, that he should've gone down fighting – not sacrificing himself to save Dean.

Ruby can't believe they let the colt get stolen when it's needed more than ever. Also one of Sam's secrets is revealed to Dean – Sam knew of Lilith and yes there are more things he should know that Sam hasn't told him (re **2.21** and what Yellow Eyes told him.)

Dean is a person of virtue and can't believe Nancy's a virgin, his line about virgins form **2.1** comes to mind here and not being into prudish chicks. But he defends Nancy, not letting her get killed or sacrificed to save them. Sam's so ready and willing to go along with it. Again showing how their characters have changed. Dean would normally have all been for the no questions asked, no holes barred approach and Sam would be against it. But not even Dean would advocate killing an innocent. Where's your humanity Sam? Henicksen says it for Dean (to his surprise) if they kill humans, they're just like the demons they're fighting. Then Dean repeats it to Sam, that they don't kill humans as demons do. He'd rather lose the war than to lose sight of their humanity.

Ruby was prepared to sacrifice herself to save them which shows where her loyalties lie, but then she doesn't stick around to fight and saves herself at the first possible opportunity. They let one go who reports back, isn't she meant to be the all powerful, all seeing one. Lilith saying, one's tall and one's cute, i.e. Dean. Didn't anyone wonder why she was looking for older guys?

An episode showing how bloody the war will be with huge body counts and not many hunters around to fight them. The title, Jus In Bello means "justice in war". It is a guide for wars.

When at war, some believe it is all out war and morals do not exist. It's essentially every man for himself. 'Just war' theory doesn't apply to them. This theory embodies moral guidelines for war; that humanity must never be forgotten at all costs. Just as Dean and Henriksen argue here for saving Nancy.

Lilith didn't have an English accent here, contrary to what some critic said.

Cialis is a drug similar to Viagra.

Peter De Luise was in *21 Jump Street* before going on to star, produce, write, direct on *Stargate SG-1*.

Quotes

Henriksen; "...seeing you two in chains..."
Dean: "You kinky sonofabitch, we don't swing that way."

Henriksen: "Where's that smug smile Dean, I wanna see it?"

Dean: "I've got virtue."
Ruby: "Nice try, you're not a virgin."

Dean: "Since when did we throw away the rule book and stop acting like humans?...if that's how we win wars, then I don't wanna win."

Actual Legend

There is a myth that Lilith was Adam's first wife. One tale says that God created Adam and Lilith was his twin, they were joined at the back. Not getting the equality she demanded from Adam, stated by one Muslim legend, she left him and slept with the devil, thereby leading to the creation of the Djinn (made from fire.) The name is also found in the name of Sumero-Babylonian goddess Belit-ili. Lilith is also the name for a night demon in search of children to kill or kidnap (see **1.18.**)

Ooh Bloops!

Jensen's lips don't appear to move when he says the end of the line, "You don't poke a bear with a BB gun, it's just gonna make him mad."

When Henricksen calls Groves, he holds the phone in his right hand; removing the bullet proof vest with his left. When the camera pans in on him, the phone's in his left hand, then right and he uses his left hand to undo the same part of his vest.

3.13 Ghostfacers

Written By Ben Edlund. Directed By Phil Sgriccia
Original US Airdate 24 April 2008

Guest Stars: AJ Buckley (Ed Zedmoore); Travis Webster (Harry Spengler); Dustin Milligan (Alan J Corbett); Austin Basis (Kenny Bruce); Brittany Ishibashi (Maggie Zedmoore)

Sam and Dean investigate a haunted house, as it's what Dean wants to do and meet the amateur Ghostfacers on a reality TV shoot.

Notes

The opening scene is similar to *Masterpiece Theatre*. A 'real doll' is a life-size toy sex doll. In this episode the date is 28-29 February, indicating it's two months until Dean's time runs out, so he died in April as opposed to May 2 as was said before. There's some confusion with the dates here.

This episode was also a spoof of the sci-fi *Ghost Hunters* about real-life paranormal investigators who investigate hauntings at night.

See the CW website for links to an official Ghostfacers website.

Were Sam and Dean ever gonna turn up. Not much to say on this episode unless it was just to get our minds off Dean's impending doom. That it did – but has to be the least favourite episode of mine from this season. Then Sam reminds us he's got less than two months to live and he would prefer to go hunting in a haunted house, than find a way to save himself. Aside from also showing Sam and Dean have it in them to swear! Oh really and who wouldn't when faced with this episode! Well; prefer the show without the unnecessary foul language thank you. The bleeps were played for laughs, but that's not the point.

Sam being abducted once again and this time having to wear a party hat.

Ed comments on the "crippling writers' strike" referring to the strike that just ended.

Took a long time for them to recognize each other! Also a first for Sam saying, "Eeww."

They should've known what would happen to their movie is all I can say – not having learnt their lesson from **1.17**. I.e. never mess with Sam and Dean.

In my opinion a waste of an episode, yes, concurring with Sam when Dean only has a short while to live, anything else for them to hunt would've been more interesting!

Depending on what you read and who says what, and where, apparently it's been said Eric Kripke liked this episode, elsewhere it was stated that he didn't like it. So if a magazine tells you it's an exclusive story they have or an interview, don't be fooled because chances are you've read it before! Then as they say, don't believe everything you read – but that doesn't apply here with my stuff!

Jensen almost missed filming for this episode because it was Spring break and all the flights were booked out. He was almost an hour late for the flight from LA to Vancouver and the airline gave his seat away. He flew to Seattle with a woman and her yapper dog in the next seat (reminds me of when my sister and I flew from Houston to Kansas and she had a woman with a dog next to her – but luckily they got relegated to other seats. Hey, I'm not flying with a dog next to me!) Oh and he had a screaming child in the seat in front. (Wait 'til you're a Dad Jensen!) His driver picked him up from Seattle and drove him to Vancouver.

You see, the moral of the story – never mess with your flight since not being on set wastes thousands of dollars of production money costs, not something the production can afford.

AJ Buckley jokes that the Ghostfacers are the real deal – the tour guides of the spirit world. He says it's great how they bring it altogether. "Dean and Sam are sort of lost and when in doubt, who do you call? You can lean on Ed and Harry. The two most reliable ghosthunters in all of ghost-huntdom. We're there for what we think are the right reasons, but Ed and Harry and Sam and Dean never see eye to eye. Sera wrote a really great episode for us and then the director let us add *Ghostfacer flavour* to that, by riffing and improvising. Phil Sgriccia who directed the *Ghostfacer* video was crying with laughter so loudly that it ruined the scene. I'm pretty lucky to work on both *CSI:NY* and *Supernatural*. Not bad gigs."

400

Quotes

Dean: "You and Rambo need to get your girlfriends and get out of here."

Ed: "Chisel-chest." (To Dean.)

Sam: "…our experience, you know what you get when you show the world the truth."
Dean: "Straitjacket or punch in the face. Sometimes both"

Sam and Dean's Take on the Urban Legend/Lore

Sam explains a death echo: an echo is a trap in a loop that is played over and over in a place the person died. The echo isn't dangerous, but something else usually is. Dean says sometimes death echoes can be shocked out of the loop if they can get to the human part. Sam continues a death echo is a ghost haunting the place where it lived or died. Death echoes haunt the house since their bodies are still in the house.

Music

We're An American Band by Grand Funk Railroad; It's *My Party and I'll Cry If I Want To* by Leslie Gore.

Ooh Bloops

When Dean rescues Sam, he's wearing the party hat. When he unties Sam, the hat's not there anymore. (Could have gotten knocked off.)

3.14 Long Distance Call

Written By Sera Gamble. Directed By Charles Beeson
Original US Airdate 1 May 2008

Guest Stars: Jeffrey Dean Morgan (Dad's Voice); Ingrid Torrance (Mrs Waters); Tom O'Brian (Clark Adams); Cherilyn Wilson (Lanie Greenfield); Anjul Nigam (Stuwie Meyers)

Milan, Ohio

Sam and Dean investigate strange phone calls being made from an old phone number.

Notes

Sam and Dean once more don their suits. They fight in the beginning again this time when Sam tells him he's working to save Dean, and Dean finally tells Sam his secret, that he can't be saved. Ruby said as much. Sam retaliates by telling Dean he's keeping secrets and Dean says the same also. But Dean has told him everything now – only Sam still hasn't and he hasn't got very much time left either if he wants to spill. Didn't big brother deserve to know everything about Mom, Sam and if there was going to be as good a time as any to tell all, it would be now. Or maybe Sam thinks Dean's better off not knowing.

Sam and Dean use aliases of Campbell as in Bruce, actor, and Sam as in Raimi, writer, director, both part of the *Evil Dead* movies.

Dean still doesn't care what Ruby says, she's still a demon and Sam shouldn't either; even if she did save Dean's life in **3.9**. Dean mistakenly, threatening the widow by telling her it's a capital offence to withhold information from the police (only in some countries.)

Another tragedy, the result of a car accident – so that'd make how many now in all three seasons? Dean thinking of food yet again. Flies are a tell-tale sign of evil, demons, etc. (Also present in **3.9**.) Dean would notice bustyasianbabes.com, from **2.15** when the Trickster had Sam's computer frozen on the site.)

Sam drives a rental and is right when he says they're keeping secrets. Pray tell, we wonder if Sam will reveal his to Dean, so I keep mentioning it. Dean turning to get an eyeful of that chick on the street when he's saying the 'necrophilia' line to Sam. (This he also mentions in **1.20**.)

Again the only reason why Sam and Dean are separated is so that Dean can get the call from 'Dad'. Sam obviously didn't mean what Dad sounded like when he asked, but rather, how he sounded – you know – well. Why was Dean the one receiving the phonecall anyway? Why not Sam?

Best line: what Dean should say if he calls back? Sam: "Hello." Dean throwing Sam's university education and his averages score back in his face when Sam doesn't tell him what to say to 'Dad'. How about something like, 'Is that really you?' Where are you? What do you want?'

Sam didn't hear the phone ring (probably dreaming about Bela again! On another note about Sam dreaming of her in **3.10**, perhaps his psychic powers were cross connected and when he dreamed about her in her undies, he was actually meant to have seen what was really going to happen to her instead!)

Would Dad really question Dean selling his soul to save Sam, when he did exactly the same thing. He'd expect Dean to look out for Sam, he asked as much, or was keeping the promise to kill Sam if he becomes evil, more important than saving him for the sake of it, because he's Sam: his brother.

Also since Dad crawled out of hell, it could be him as Dean so desperately wants to believe. But he wouldn't say he can't watch Dean end up in hell, they don't know where he is.

Dean's reference to Sam meeting Chris Hansen, is from *Dateline NBC, To Catch A Predator with Chris Hansen*, he sets up child predators and pedophiles; relevant as Sam was going to meet the girl and help her.

Sam and Bobby don't believe the exorcism can kill Lilith. Dean, at this stage, is willing to believe it could be a way out for him and since Dad's been to hell, he would know. But who, what and why would anything/demon, tell a Winchester any demonic rituals and of anything to break the contract or kill Lilith. Ruby was there longer and she didn't come across anything. Or did she?

In a last ditched attempt to make Sam see things from Dean's side, he brings up Sam's age old "feud" between him and Dad. Like the early season 2 episodes. Sam shakes his head a lot at Dean a second time this episode, telling him Dean still trusts anything and everything Dad would tell him to without thinking about it first. (See **3.10** where demon Dean told him he was just his good soldier and not his son, following his orders.)

Yes, even toy phones can ring now! Sam finally tells Dean it's not Dad.

Sam in bondage (!) again. Like **3.13**, the other victim gets killed before him so Sam can be rescued or find a way out.

Dean was so ready to believe it was Dad and once again repeats (as in **3.10**) he's frightened and he doesn't want to go to hell. Sam once more tells him there's still has hope. What did Dean want – a poem? (Almost an echo of, dare I say it, Bela when she said in **3.6** that Dean didn't come back with some clever retort after her witty quip.)

Dean in season 2, didn't want Dad dying to save him, he'd prefer not to have been saved, saying he should've never come back, and now he really wanted it to be Dad on the phone, reaching out to save Dean on a second occasion, in some way. No Dean, he gave his life the first time, what could he possibly do now, when they don't even know where he went to after escaping hell.

Dean was being a wee bit selfish here, he wanted to be on this case and ordinarily he'd be the first to save people, but he berates Sam for doing this now, after Sam said they were on his case too. The situation was reversed. It's understandable he's apprehensive with so little time left.

Also Dean can only rely on himself and Sam, there is no out.

Quotes

Sam: "What did he sound like?"
Dean: "Like Oprah. He sounded like Dad?"

Dean: "Don't get too exited, you might pull something."

Sam:"Crocotta."
Dean: "What is that, a sandwich?"

Dean: "Deep revelation here, having a moment here and that's what you come back with."
Sam: "Do you want a poem?"
Dean: "Moment's gone…unbelievable."

Sam and Dean's Take on the Urban Legend/Lore

No exorcism can kill Lilith, even going back to the fifteenth century, or any demon, can only send it back to hell. Sam describes a Crocotta as a scavenger, luring people into the dark and swallowing their soul. So Dean would've been fine, he doesn't have a soul to be devoured, it's been sold already. Probably why Dean was picked here as the gullible one.

Edison's 'spirit phone' is an occultist object to communicate with the dead.

Actual Legend

A Crocotta is a mythical creature from India, Ethiopia. The Roman naturalist Pliny – described it as, "an animal which looks as though it had been produced by the coupling of a wolf and dog." Devouring anything with its teeth and immediately digest it upon swallowing.

Luring dogs to their demise by pretending to be a man in trouble. Said to hide in forests and listen to farmers utter their names, then called out to them, in the forest to eat. Also the description of this was said to be that of a hyena; the scientific name of which is (Crocuta Croarta), derived from 'crocotta'. Thought to dig up dead bodies for food. Deemed to have been behind the beginnings of the myth relating to the crocotta.

Ooh Bloops!

The blood on Sam's wrists from the ropes vanishes when he fights the Crocotta, which needs a phone line to call people; but at the beginning, he can still call the victim even after he's ripped the phone from the wires.

3.15 Time Is On My Side

Written By Sera Gamble. Directed By Charles Beeson
Original US Airdate 8 May 2008

Guest stars: Jim Beaver (Bobby); Lauren Cohan (Bela); Roan Curtis (Lilith); Billy Drago (Dr Benton); Steven Williams (Rufus Turner). Kavan Smith (First Victim)

Erie, Pennsylvania

Several victims are abducted and their organs removed.

Canaan, Vermont

Sam discovers a doctor who holds the key to eternal life and so may be able to help Dean.

Notes

More Latin from Sam. Yay! :
Omnis immundi pritus
Omnis incursion infernalis adversarii omnis legio

Dean's look to the camera said it all – he doesn't want to admit it but he's worried.

Another ironic title – time isn't on Dean's side, but it was on the doctor's.

Since Dean's so interested in hunting, Sam's giving him a helping hand. See **3.13**, when Dean wanted to hunt in the haunted house and **3.14**, when Dean said they were on a case. Was Sam thinking of turning Dean into a zombie. That'd be funny. Seriously though, after **2.4** and everything said in that episode comes to mind.

At least the maggots Sam mentioned didn't put Dean off his burger, like the man in **3.9** when he had maggots in his burger too. No Dean's got a strong stomach, he'll need one for the 'things' he's killed and methods used.

Sam and Dean arguing over immortality and if they found the secret to this, then Dean won't go to hell since he can't die and Sam will join him too, as an immortal. (Yes, we wish, then the show would never end. Ha.) But would immortality really keep the hell hounds at bay too, and then Sam and Dean would turn out to be nothing more than what they hunt. Becoming a Frankenstein himself, of sorts, well, Frankenstein's monster. (Jensen always manages to be a in a show or an episode where reference is made to Frankenstein, cf *Dark Angel*, **1.18 Pollo Loco**. When Max called him that.) Posing the question – 'who wants to live forever?' as in the song by *Queen*.

Dean meets Rufus, another hunter who keeps surveillance cameras on his property. (see **2.14**.)

In **3.13** Sam says Dean's got less than two weeks left and here Dean says he's got three weeks left. Even Rufus tells Dean he won't survive and if he does his future looks bleak, i.e. just like him, he'll grow to be a lonely old man. Well, rather that than hell.

Haven't Sam and Dean said the same thing before about knowing a lot of things. Yes, in **2.8** where Dean says, "We know a lot of things – just enough to make us dangerous." Bela is a stuck up sot. As for 'doing her ear'. EEww! Even if it sounds uncomfortable, Dean'll try anything once.

Sam getting into more mischief when he's alone and gets caught by the doctor. Dean was right in **3.6** about Bela's father when he abused her and no, Dean would never kill his parents, he wouldn't even kill Sam if he became evil, as Dad made him promise in **2.1**.

Dean doesn't want any of this immortal science mojo and would rather bide his time and face his fate than to turn into something like the doctor. As he says – it's black and white to him, good or bad and no shades of grey areas in between – that's not him. The grey areas are usually left to us geeky, thinking types instead, like Sam.

Oh Dean felt Bela's hand in his pocket this time round. He didn't in **3.6**, Sam didn't in **3.3**. Who else but Dean would come up with the idea of leaving the inflatable dolls in the bed; as opposed to pillows. Bela really thought she'd get out of her deal by killing off Sam and Dean, it wouldn't be that simple and Lilith would only want this done because she knows she has real competition in Sam; and with Dean helping him – they're unbeatable. That's why she has Dean's contract and refuses to give it up.

Strange Bela's ten years are up just when Dean's one year is about to end. Hearing the hounds at midnight, she got everything coming to her and no, didn't bat an eyelid or feel any sorrow for her either! Next episode is Dean's turn to face the hounds of hell! Oh woe is me.

From **3.10** it was obvious Bela was trying to get into their good books (and not Sam's bed, ha) to not only steal the colt, but so that they would help her save herself, cozying up to them, before she's finally taken by the hell hounds. Good to see Sam didn't go all starry eyed over her after his dream too. Don't think Sam and Dean would've got her out of this hole, no matter how much she begged from the way she treated them.

If they did find the magical' cure Sam wanted from the doctor and Dean agreed to it, they'd only end up doing the same thing as him, i.e. having to find innocent (or not so innocent) victims to steal their body parts, to survive. As Sam says, it may have bought Dean some time, but it's not something that could've been reversed.

An episode showing no one has the right to play God (and who would want to.) That when your time is up, it's up, regardless of where you are going to end up. You can't cheat death and even if you try, you only end up as some deranged monster having to keep on killing just to survive an eternity – who would want to live like that.

Benton mentions family reunion because he was already connected to the Winchesters through Dad. Dad was the one who 'killed' him – in cutting out his heart – being the only way to stop him, but no he couldn't be killed. Also in a way, it was Dad who could be said, started him out on his killing – serial killing spree. Since aside from his heart and his liver: two of the basic organs the human body needs to survive, everything else he took wouldn't necessarily mean the death of his victims. Then this gives rise to, or leads to the whole moral/ethical argument: killing is murder, is wrong and unethical and so is removing body parts without the rightful owner's consent. They're not exactly being voluntarily donated to the recipient, i.e. Benton.

407

This reminded me of **2.2 Some Assembly Required** of *Buffy*; where to bring his brother to life and in reconstructing a woman, the Dr Frankenstein-esque character needs the head from a living girl. (Who happens to be Cordy.) It was similar in the sense of Sam wanting to save Dean no matter what it takes. Even if this resulted in immortality – that in wanting revivication of his brother this would mean eventually having to become like Benton.

Although Frankenstein was alluded to here and Dean refers to being some kind of monster, it was more about saving people and how Dean would rather die than to become a mindless creature, needing to take more lives whenever a body part would be required. That no matter how much he wants to live and be saved, Dean will not become this monster and have to sacrifice people to keep himself alive. (A different Dean here than from his descent into hell and what he did there. See season 4.)

How did Benton survive without a heart and actually go out and find another victim to procure a heart from?

Dean alludes to *Dr Quinn Medicine Woman* when he says, "Doctor Quinn Medicine zombie."

Steven Williams was in *21 Jump Street*, *X Files* and was also in *LA Heat* as well as numerous other TV shows and movies.

Billy Drago is best known for appearing in *Charmed*. Kavan Smith, the victim in the beginning will be remembered by followers of Aussie soap, *Home and Away*, where he played Dodge, and more recently in *Stargate: Atlantis*.

Bela stayed in the Hotel Canaan Room 39, a Biblical reference as this was the home of Joseph and his family, i.e. of *Technicolour Dreamcoat* fame.

Sam and Dean talk to the doctor. He was the same playing Daniel Elkins in **1.20**.

Dad's encounter with Benton that Sam tells Dean about is in *Supernatural Origins No.4* comic.

Quotes

Dean: "Chasing some Frankenstein."
Sam: "Chasing immortality. Benton can't die so we have to find out what he did, so he can do it to you. If you can never die, you can never go to hell."

Dean: "Really now, demon's untrustworthy, shocker. Sweetheart we are weeks past help."

Sam and Dean's Take on the Urban Legend/Lore

Alchemy was used to live forever. Doctors used maggots to eat bad tissue, and still do that today.

Actual Legend

Devils Shoestring is a plant found in North America. Used in African-American mojo by hoodoo doctors. The species used is the Viburnam Alnifolium variety, from the Honeysuckle family. Used in protection to "trip up" the devil so he can't enter the house. (As Dean says.) Also used for good luck. In its ancient use, it was worn by people as an ankle bracelet; with nine pieces of shoestring and a silver dime. So they were not poisoned when they walked in Goofer Dust.

Most commonly put in a mojo bag and carried around. (Like Gordon in **3.7** when Bela took the bag from him.) So another reason why she wanted it for herself - to keep out the hell hounds or demons. That's why Gordon lost his mojo protection and was reluctant to give it up. Bela knew what it was for, obviously dealing in occult objects. Is this why she began this trade, to find some way out of her ten year bargain!

'Ear print' evidence, or more likely, latent ear print is used in the UK. A recent murder conviction was reversed when the evidence was based on such a print. A DNA analysis of the latent ear print, said to belong to the defendant in the case was definitely proven not to belong to him. On appeal. So much for relying on forensic science. Many photos will reveal dissimilarities in an impression of the ear taken from the actual person – not accounting for distortions, such as light and the fact the photo is more likely to be 2D than 3D in real life.

Ooh Bloops

Lilith has red eyes when Bela makes the pact with her. As Bela has made contact with her that's why Bela knows she holds all the contracts.

When Sam almost has his eye removed, it's his left one, Dean shoots and his hand is near his left eye which is red in colour; but then appears to be normal.

Sam drops his phone at the hotel; the screen on the phone is the one which indicates the phone is not in use.

409

3.16 No Rest for the Wicked

Written By Eric Kripke. Directed By Kim Manners
Original US Airdate 15 May 2008

Guest Stars: Jim Beaver (Bobby); Katie Cassidy (Ruby); Sierra McCormick
Sam, Dean and Bobby search for a way to save Dean from his deal.

New Harmony, Indiana.

Lilith terrorizes a family and takes over a community.

Notes

Fremont is named for Anthony Fremont from *The Twilight Zone* episode **It's A Good Life.** He has the power to alter reality.

The original title was **No Quarter.** No rest for the wicked, that's always a contradiction, seems the good do all the work and the wicked take all the credit.

Dean being chased in the woods was like the images of **2.8** when Robert Johnson was also dreaming about the hell hounds.

Sam usually ends up making promises he can't keep, not resigned to the fact that he has a few hours left and there is no 'out' for Dean.

Especially good to see was Dean seeing Sam in a 'jerky' head movement like the demons have in this show, since he's now beginning to see their "real" faces. Possibly wondering if Sam is a demon or will become one.

Dean doesn't want anyone else sacrificing themselves for him – there's been enough of that going on. Sam goes against Dean's wishes and summons Ruby anyway – which Dean, knowing Sam as he does, predicted already. So if they could summon Ruby anyway (as she's a demon) why not do this before when they needed help or information, but she's also available on the phone too, who got her number? No one. Ruby knew about Lilith all along, so at this point, you have to wonder if you can trust her after all. Also, if as she says, they weren't ready to fight her back then, what makes them ready now? The fact that Dean only has less than a day left by now; or that he can't really be saved. She also happens to know Sam's power would return to him – how? When he didn't even sense it himself, probably on the demon grapevine.

The hex bag were meant to keep Lilith from knowing their presence, but appears these didn't work since Lilith took over Ruby when she left the girl. Also was this because she sensed Ruby?

Sam and Ruby talking about Sam's "demon" given power when Dean's not around to hear! A case of Dean being the last to know.

Ruby's circus reference to Sam being a side-show freak, why would Sam care about how demons look at him, he's not one himself. How did Ruby get out of the Devil's Trap? Like to know what this exceptional 'bomb' is that Sam has inside him?

Dean's line of long walks on the beach, straight out of **2.7** when he said this whilst being interviewed in custody.

How would wiping out Lilith end Dean's deal – does this end when the demon holding the contract is killed.

Ooh language again! Seems like *Supernatural* lately has been instrumental in the'd' word – not demon – but 'dick'. We don't need it in our show! Language like that isn't needed when the writers have gotten by without having to swear or use profanities, especially as it signals running out of creative language. We hear such things everyday anyway; we don't need it creeping into our fave show either! End of rant!

Dean looking at Sam as if he really is evil or changed. Don't know if Sam can take out Lilith, she never hung around long enough for him to get the chance.

Sam and Dean speak again about how the Winchesters jump at the chance to save each other over and over, and you can only do that once. Then you run out of chances, of life and things go pear-shaped. They will always be each others' weakness because they're family and that's what families do – look out for each other. Sam is the one who can look out for the two of them especially when his powers return.

Summing up what they've been saying all season, "You do for me and I want to do for you" – give a life to save a life. Dean wants to have a fighting chance. He didn't need to have researched his *Eye of the Tiger* moment speech; he's practically said it enough times already.

Death comes to all and Dean must come to terms with his own mortality. Unlike others though, Dean is given a date and has the clock ticking to his final countdown. For him this was a reality. Of course Sam and Dean are faced with the possibility of death everyday, but to be given a life sentence puts a different stance on things. True to form and his nature, Dean lives for now and has to think with every echo of the clock, every second he's getting closer to the last death knell.

The danger is apparent but neither one of them realized how close they come to dying everyday whilst carrying on their hunting. The most horrific thing they, Dean, will ever face. (After losing everyone he loved that is.) Even with his denial, he did face it head on.

Dean's loss is extremely emotional and real to Sam (just as Sam's was to Dean) and in **4.9** we finally get to see how he carried on without Dean, but will we see him coming to terms with losing his brother and will he be reminded of it every time he drives the Impala, or goes on a hunt?

Dean's choice of song in a crisis moment and to think it was the last one he heard before facing his hero's death – or was it? See **2.1** with the reaper telling him that's what he deserves and what he'll get, only instead of the good place; he's going to the other. Dean called himself a ninja in **3.14**. Now Sam comes up with the line of "ninja past the guards."

Sam tells him it's not about Dean now, it's about saving everybody, he changes his tune very quickly – it was always about saving Dean, wasn't it. The entire third season that's all he talked about and now it's not just Dean anymore – would think Dean would come first, especially right about now as he's about to become "hell's bitch!" to quote Bobby. Couldn't saving everybody come later – especially since Lilith has to go first and then the other demons can be hunted. This was a niggling thing to have Sam say again. Okay more than a bit, a big niggle! Just like Sam said in **3.12** about saving 30 people with only Nancy being sacrificed (and Ruby). Lilith was involved in that episode and again now. Dean's hesitant again and Sam just wants to kill again!

Ruby's line of Dean's neck snapping like a chicken bone, déjà vu in *Dark Angel* **1.18 Pollo Loco**, i.e. 'chicken crazy,' when Max snapped Ben's neck like a chicken – that's how I described it when I wrote about that episode years ago.

The two girls (Sam and Ruby) having a cat fight. (Ha!)

Seems Lilith was all ready and waiting for Sam and Dean to appear. Why did Ruby disappear into the other room for so long, when it's clear the room's empty. But due credit to Sam , he did hesitate before taking out Lilith – so he could wait for Dean to arrive and tell him it's not Ruby, probably since maybe their hex bag didn't work and Lilith could sense Sam there.

Dean has to get the Impala in there! Once more the going round in circles speech about how saving Dean will kill Sam etc. Sam asking Dean what he's supposed to do, is what Dean said in **2.22** when he was sitting looking at Sam's dead body; asking Sam what he's meant to do.

Conveniently, all the demons look the same to Dean. Would've been better if somehow Lilith would've looked different to Dean, especially since he commented on Ruby's ugly face and well, that was a pointless comment, since he already said he can see their 'real' faces. Think that line could've been more significant. Eeww kissed by a demon Sam. Now he can say this too, kissed by Lilith and she didn't sense any of his power either. Wouldn't that have been dangerous for her to do because she's supposed to be his rival and from how everyone was raving about Sam being the Anti-Christ and powerful.

Think Lilith should've let Dean go, then she could not have underestimated him.

Sam cries now.

Now the screaming starts, so to speak. Dean's all alone and in hell – you can see how terrified he was all along and how scared; now he can shout all he wants because nobody can hear him.

There you have it, Dean's final descent into hell. What was coming all through season 3 finally happens.

How many thought there'd be a happy ending and Dean would get his last minute reprieve. A bit of a season 1 finale when all three of their fates were on the line. Season 2 was all about coming to terms with Dad's loss, his sacrifice for Dean, meeting other hunters and bringing back Sam. Then in season 3, it fell upon them to catch the escaped demons from hell. Ending with Dean in hell or purgatory and there's no way Sam can bring him back, otherwise his death would've been in vain and though he didn't really go out swinging – it wasn't a fair fight, at least he didn't sit around and take it like Bela.

Sam can't hear Dean shouting – paraphrase the *Alien* tag line "In hell, no one can hear you scream" (aside from demons) or can they? See season 4.

Antichrist superstar reference is to the Marilyn Mason album of the same name.

The policeman's car is number 54, so when the police dispatcher radios in to ask its whereabouts, they'll say, "Car 54 Where Are You?" A 1960's comedy of the same name with Fred Gwynn and Joe E Ross.

As for Dean ending up in hell and being attached rather painfully in chains. Jensen comments: "Hell, it was miserable. I spent about fours hours in prosthetics, because of all those hooks and pieces through the wrists and cuffs and everything, and once I was done, I walked on stage and they hooked me up. Cuffs around both wrists and both ankles and then just a belt harness around my waist, so I was wired up with five different wires. Five guys wrenched me up about 13 foot in the air. I had so much blood all over me, the harness slipped and the buckle was piercing into my hip and I hung there for what felt like ages and it got so bad that tears were rolling down my face and I was like, 'Let me down,' it was tough, but it turned out to be a really cool shot." So were some of those tears really Jensen's in the closing shots of the season? We all felt the agony and the pain along with you!

As for Dean's broken psyche – at least he has one. It's what keeps him going. He's not perfect but it never led to anything bad coming out of it, or Dean becoming evil.

As for *Supernatural*, it could be said, the series is all about Sam, in a way, and it is: Mom killed in the nursery, tending to Sam. Sam getting the demon blood, the latent powers: the visions, telekinesis. Sam getting to leave hunting; go to university – having a normal life. Meeting Jessica, losing Jessica, losing Dad.

Season 2: Sam being the one who needs to be watched incase he becomes evil. Sam then wanting to be like Dad – doing what he would've wanted. Sam getting the girl, Sam losing the girl (again). The crossroads demons, all references to Sam being needed by Dean. Sam being the demonic army leader; the chosen one; the one outliving the other children; Sam dying; Sam being brought back; Sam being evil when he comes back, maybe.

Season 3: Sam wanting Dean to open up to him; wanting to be the one to help Dean; Sam meeting Ruby first, Ruby saving Sam first; Sam killing demons. Sam killing Gordon. Sam having to be like Dean now to hunt and survive on his own, without Dean. The Trickster choosing to show Sam his life alone. Sam watching Dean die repeatedly. Sam being Lilith's competition; being better than her – her powers are nothing compared to his. Sam finally losing Dean again.

It does appear Dean was the ancillary character to Sam in the show and if it's plotted out like I've done – the bare basics, rudimentary; then it does look that way. But it was much more than that and just as much about Dean too.

Supernatural Easter eggs on the DVD. Disc 6 season 1 *Special Features*, if you highlight *A Day in the Life of Jensen and Jared* – a yellow bar in the right top right corner appears. Highlight this for a message from Eric Kripke.

Highlight *Stills Gallery* on this disc, Jensen's eyes become yellow on the left picture. Keep left and his eyes light up more. Press 'enter' and there are some episode titles not used in the show.

Season finales not different form any other. Still get speeches about going down fighting. Dean says he should go down swinging like Dad should've done, in **2.4**. Sam trying to tell Dean how much he means to him again, like in season 1 finale when Dean says he doesn't want to hear it. Instead they listen to Bon Jovi. Thought *Livin' on a Prayer* would've been more appropriate than *Dead or Alive,* since that's all about Dean and what this season was about too. Also Dean can now see demon faces, would've been good if he could've had a power of his own – instead of just being the 'freak' without powers. No, it's his destiny or deal coming true and also his dream in **3.10** when he dreams of himself as a demon: "this is what you're gonna become!"

To end, my quote which I think is quite apt here from *The Rubaiyat of Omar Khayyam.*

I sent my soul through the Invisible,
Some letter of the After-Life to Spell,
And after many days my soul return'd
And said, "behold, Myself am Heav'n and hell."

Quotes

Ruby: "Lilith would've pulled the meat from their pretty, pretty faces."

Ruby: "You can Sam…you've got some God-given talent. Well, not God-given, but you get the jist."

Dean: "…pattern here. Dad's deal, my deal, now this. I mean, everytime one of us is up the creek, the other is begging to sell their soul. That's all this is man."

Sam: "I think you totally should've been jamming *Eye of the Tiger* back there."
Dean: "Bite me. I totally rehearsed that speech too."

Dean: "Somebody help me. Sam…Sam…

Film/TV References

Star Wars, Carrie

Music

Carry On Wayward Son by Kansas. *Wanted Dead or Alive by* Bon Jovi and Sam and Dean.

Ooh Bloops

Dean's protection tattoo vanishes when the hell hounds attack at the end.

415

Dean holds the knife in his hand when he fights with ruby, but she doesn't seem to realize this. When Dean and Ruby fight, the same footage is used, as he falls when Ruby kicks him in the head, then when she head-butts him.

Season 4

The season 4 trailer, seen in the US and also on various internet sites. But we didn't get it on UK TV, Is as follows:

The Qur'an spoke of...great war and Buddha battled against Samsara. The Torah spoke of the End of Days and the Great book foretold the battle of good and evil. It's here. With Dean screaming out "Sam, Sam…" from the season 3 end scene.

4.1 Lazarus Rising

Written By Eric Kripke. Directed By Kim Manners.
Original US Airdate 18 September 2008

Guest Stars: Jim Beaver (Bobby). Genevieve Cortese (Kristy/Ruby).
Traci Dinnwiddie (Pamela Barnes). Misha Collins (Castiel).

Dean rises from the ashes and they search for who raised him from Hell.

Pointiac, Illinois

Dean tracks Sam here, not far from where he was buried.

Notes

Dean shouting for help and then for Sam to help him. He got his 'prayers' answered, at least his wishes, someone did hear him and came to help him. He was 'touched' by an angel – at least gripped by one and pulled out.

The CGI effects didn't add much to Dean having to crawl his way out of there, digging and clawing; looked rather false on the screen. As for the site looking nuked as he described it – it looked like his grave had been surrounded by iron spikes.

Why was Dean buried near Pontiac, Illinois? Since the paper he picked up at the garage had the name Pontiac. He was lucky to have been buried with his lighter otherwise he'd have been in complete darkness and not just in the dark about where he was and how he got there.

When Bobby took Pamela to hospital, weren't the staff surprised, or more likely suspicious as to what caused her injuries leaving her blind. No police were called in either.

Dean's nails were looking relatively clean for someone who just clawed out of the ground. Imprints of a hand were burned into his arm. Dean's supplies included candy, water and all his basic staples when there's no pie around! Or burgers and of course a copy of *Busty Asian Babes*, seeing as he's not on line. His first reaction to the static is to salt the windows and doors, but not effective in this case, since the high pitching, which we don't get to hear yet, broke the windows, glass.

Strange Bobby didn't recognize Dean's voice; at least he'd have thought some demon was playing games with him in which case he probably should've found out, that'd be one less walking around; if it was a real demon. Wouldn't he want to know who was tormenting him like that.

So instead of the sending demons back to hell storyline in season 3, we now get the Armageddon story; so it doesn't matter if they're still around, the ones who escaped from Devil's Gate since they'll all be going down one way or another; as well as taking sides against good like they've always done.

Bobby throwing holy water (or holy h2o as I call it) on Dean was reminiscent of him giving some to Ellen in **2.22** in the form of a drink before the whiskey chaser, to check she really was human after the fire at the roadhouse.

Sam took the only option of burying him and not salting and burning as per the hunter ritual, since he still had hopes of bringing him back. Dean believes Sam made a deal and 1) went against or crossed Lilith; and 2) brought back a mortal enemy of the demons: a famous Winchester brother! So he can hunt some more of them! But this time round it's more than just about hunting, it's about preventing the end of the world and Lucifer from coming out of hell. Dean's line of what he doesn't know about Sam, i.e. everything. Ironically there's plenty he doesn't know about him: demon blood, Ruby, using his powers after promising him he wouldn't and who knows what else. Whereas in the past four months, Bobby's been binge drinking; so did he get much hunting done.

Ruby, as Kristy, asking that stupid question of whether Sam and Dean are together, when she knows they're brothers anyway. Guess someone had to mention the first gay line of this season. No Sam doesn't have to pay girls, he's a got a demon gal! (Reminds me of what Aiden said in season 1 episode Tanglewood, of *CSI:NY* to Danny, when he says he had girls and he didn't have to pay, like Sam says to Dean here. Aiden then replies, he's paying in one way or another.) So true here, eventually, Sam will end up paying! One way or another. Dean again being ironic when he tells Sam he's some demon's bitch-boy, yes Ruby's! Although, well, he calls her a bitch, same difference. He always called her that.

Sam apologizes for not being the one who saved Dean but was he being sincere, especially the part at the beginning when it was hard to tell if he was glad to see Dean or in just plain shock; as he was trying to carry on as best he could. Also Ruby in season 3 said she wants to make Sam a strong hunter, the best he's ever been knowing full well he'd get his powers back, they were just dormant for the time being; hasn't been doing much of that it appears. Specially since that's all he's been using to kill demons: just his powers and he doesn't need to lay a finger on them.

Where Bobby says he hunted by himself, Sam still doesn't tell them about Ruby when he likes him to Dad. Which is exactly what Dad did, went out and hunted for Yellow Eyes on his own, after losing Mom. Only he wasn't alone, he had family responsibilities, which is where any similarity ends. Sam hunted for Lilith after losing Dean. So maybe he turned into or was becoming Dad, bringing him a long way from season 1 where he didn't want to hunt; to season 2 where he did and season 3 where he had to become like Dean, because he'd be alone eventually. (He wasn't, he still had Bobby, and Ruby, dare I say it. With hindsight, no I shouldn't have said it.)

Last season didn't like Bela much, didn't think be saying that about Ruby this season! Originally Eric wanted Ruby to change bodies every couple of episodes – which in this season is a very good idea! How many can she notch up on the ol' body count, would be fun to see! Body count as in possessing them rather than doing away with them.

Bobby asking Dean if he feels like himself; the same question we all pondered last season when Sam was brought back at the end of season 2: whether he really was Sam – or something else in his place; or came back different. Perhaps Dean is different too. Well, he is, not demonic different; but more attuned to who he really is. Also it wasn't Sam being brought back somehow different we have to worry about, but what he's become or will become this season and now Dean is back to keep him in check.

Dean doesn't recall hell or chooses not to recall it when Sam asked what it was like. A missed opportunity in season 2 finale and season 3 when Sam returned with no one asking where he was or what it was like wherever he was? Instead, everyone was asking what he felt like, still normal, still human. Dean claims not to remember, refuses to talk about it, then proceeds to have flashbacks about being ripped apart. Seems to sleep soundly too, doesn't he so nothing is changed there. Also Dean being 'plucked' from hell, was part of his redemption or atonement, at least setting him on the path of redemption for everything he was forced to do in hell. He endlessly says he doesn't deserve to be saved, but seems to have forgotten how he and Sam wanted to find some way out of his contract last season. (Remember he also said he shouldn't be here in season 2.)

Again Sam doesn't tell Dean about Ruby (know it was being saved for another episode) but Sam just ends up lying some more and tells Dean he was immune from Lilith. Once more bringing up questions about his destiny and his real purpose in regaining his powers again, which conveniently re-emerged when Dean wasn't around. Oh another lie Sam, about Dean's dying wish – clearly he did go there and now can't tell him Dean's last wish meant very little to him and that he couldn't do this little thing for him. No, he'll probably say it was because he was left alone and had to survive on his own, alluding to season 3, when he told Dean he'd have to stay behind in this worthless world without Dean around.

Pamela Barnes (not from *Dallas*.) Pam's imagery of Dean landing from the frying pan into the fire, and being rare; as he was some sort of flame grilled burger. So she too becomes another casualty to add to the notches on Sam and Dean's belt of those they harmed, even inadvertently and unintentionally: collateral damage. (See **4.3** where Dean contributes to his grandparent's death.)

Now, think Dean's bolder than ever going up against a demon like that in the diner, slapping her like that. Especially since they don't know how he came back, but just goes to show he won't take anything from a demon, just like before. Dean didn't get to eat pie! He likens himself to the smarter brother being back, whereas Sam thinks it's his duty to go back and finish off the demons which he does when he goes off in the night and leaves Dean as per usual. What if something happened to Dean?

We said in our *Supernatural* discussion that Sam and Dean should go off and do their own things eventually, and they finally do to a certain extent. Even perhaps ending up on opposing sides. Dean's on a mission from God and Sam is just killing demons or more? Maybe he's just doing the best he can with all the angst hanging over him and everyone watching him. But they still manage to come to each other's rescue.

Castiel turns up whenever Sam isn't around or can't see Dean talking (to himself?) The high-pitched noise, static, is due to Castiel attempting to communicate with Dean. So we have to see him in the flesh. This method of communication doesn't work since Dean doesn't believe in angels, so isn't open to the experience. Also an effective plot device at this stage since we're not meant to know he was saved by an angel, until later in the episode. Dean likens the noise to hearing church bells ringing outside of his head (!). Didn't he say the same thing in **2.21** when Andy communicated with him psychically?

Sam using the excuse of going for a burger – in the middle of the night; and besides since when did Sam used to crave burgers anyway; as Deans should know, he claims to know everything about Sam. Bobby saying they could use Sam here to summon what saved Dean. Obviously Sam isn't meant to be around right now to find this out or to see even, since Bobby isn't either. Sam's not worth in the angel's opinion. Besides Sam's too busy playing solo hero without telling anyone. Dean will know about Sam and Ruby being together when he sees her again and when he finds out she's really Ruby, so much for keeping secrets. Sam's look on his face was like he was thinking, 'Oh no Dean's back – that's put paid to all my evil plans' if he turns dark. You'd have thought he'd have been happier, no ecstatic, and excited than that when he greeted Dean!

Seems as if the season's (ending) is heading towards a showdown between the two brothers. One good, one evil and it shows with their respective destinies. Dean's good, rescued by an angel, sleeps with an angel to help fight Armageddon – to prevent it from happening. Sam loses Dean, goes off on his own and with Ruby – a demon (no matter how helpful), sleeps with a demon, uses his powers to kill demons without telling anyone. As if he's trying to fight his own destiny and what he may become in the future (continuing here and mentioned in previous seasons.) I could be wrong, since I'm writing this after watching only two episodes, but then I'm not usually wrong! Begging the question why didn't any angel come to save Sam when he was killed (aside from the fact Dean got there first and saved him before any intervention could take place. If any was going to happen.) Would he be rescued by an angel anyway, seeing as he's got demon blood in him.

Perhaps it's not the same but I thought of *Buffy* (again) when Angel was brought back from hell, in **3.10 amends**, like Dean's return from hell. Where angel realizes he was brought back because he was needed for a purpose. Just as though some greater power had intervened to make him <u>realize</u> this.

You just can't imagine Dean being so sadistic.

As for Sam. Maybe it's not the demon blood inside of him that should make Dean weary of him, but the man inside of Sam. Since it's not really the blood that makes him decide on his choices; or on using his powers, but the man that he is. (Yes Ruby has a hand in influencing him too.) Ultimately it'll be his choice when he uses his powers again.

You can understand Pam having her eyes burnt out when she saw Castiel's true form, but a demon having the some thing done to her, especially since they know he's really an angel, maybe it' was for the human body she was possessing as they remember everything that happens to them, whilst they're still possessed, but she was probably done for anyway, after Sam finished with her. So what does happen to the body she was possessing after Sam kills them.

The demon waitress was scared when she said it's the final battle, the end, anyway wouldn't it have been easier to smite, she was a demon after all, instead of leaving her alive to tell everyone (as they were all clueless as to what saved Dean to begin with.). No conveniently she was left for Sam to finish off and also for him to call Kristy, Ruby, by name just incase we didn't know who she was and to demonstrate Sam's new evolved powers, all he has to do now is to use a form of ESP. Her smoke goes down back to hell. So Sam's powers now enable him to send demons straight to hell; no Latin exorcisms, no spells, guns or knives.

Ruby says it's nothing she's seen before since she wasn't around 2,000 years ago, as Castiel says in **4.2**, that's how long angels have been not been roaming earth for.

Sam's happy for Dean to be kept in the dark for now, since he's not sure of what he's doing anyway, but he admits to enjoying it and that means he's come a long way from the Sam we used to know and love. Naïve, always wanting to do the right thing because it was the right thing to do; always questioning. Now he just enjoys killing demons. He wants to "keep going." But going which way – for good or for bad and won't this overwhelm him in the end and prove too much for him.

Bobby uses talisman from every faith which is good to see again (see **Seven Reasons About Supernatural**. Ruby saying Sam and Dean are brothers and she doesn't want to come between them. She's done that already, as for telling Dean, she could've done that herself in the motel room. "Hi Dean, I'm Ruby."

Sam says Dean's line from **1.2** of "saving people", well his phrase anyway, in the diner to Ruby.

Castiel appears and tells Dean his problem in a nutshell: his lack of faith, i.e. he does have faith but he believes too much in the wrong things. Dean must still punish himself for everything he's been through and seen and yet find he's back in the fight again.

The part where you can see his wings, which looks like they're just shadows of wings, was impressive and should've been overwhelming to Dean, but instead he still has his doubts and whereas Sam would question, now it's Dean who does all the questioning.

Also at the end of **4.2** Dean thought angels had fluffy wings and halos; how could he say this when he's been shown his wings and they were far from feathery and fluffy (or as in the name of the Cary Grant movie, *Only Angels Have Wings*. Not a religious movie but about flying.) Dean wasn't special enough to see/hear him, also since he has no faith, if that was the simple explanation.

Dean asking if he's an accountant, the way he's dressed. Far from looking like an accountant, I'd say he looked more like *Columbo* shabby raincoat and all. With the amount of movies and TV shows Dean's watched, you'd think he would've noticed the resemblance, especially where suit and shabby raincoat were concerned! Dean questions why they aren't there to help everyone,

Castiel replies that he's a soldier, recall from **2.13** (which Dean didn't) they discussed the entire concept of angels and it was agreed they were not the Hallmark version, as Sam called them, they were warriors and "fierce."

So angels also need to possess bodies to appear to humans, so as not to scare them, but they have to agree to the possession, do they have a choice really.

Dean asks why he burned out the woman's eyes, that woman had a name which he knows was Pam? He could've replied to him by saying, what woman's eyes. Since he did the same to the waitress, even if she was a demon possessing a human host.

Castiel should've said that Dean's taken the name of the Lord in vain on numerous occasions, for a non-believer!

When Castiel tells Dean he has no faith; the way he looks at Dean as if to say he can see his pain, his grief; what he s been through and that's why Dean finds it hard to believe, and just go on blind faith alone. It's easy to understand Dean's lack of faith too: he doesn't think he merits being chosen since all he's done is to rescue and save people. But there has to be more than this, besides the Apocalypse. Dean was saved for a purpose – something concerning Sam. As though he's the only one who can save him from what Sam is doing; or ends up becoming in the future on course for what he's meant to become. If not, he'll have to be the one to stop Sam.

Something echoing on from **2.1** when Dad told him to kill Sam if he becomes evil and he's fought it ever since. Dad must've known about Sam, if he specifically summoned Azazel. First Dad tells him to stop Sam and now pretty much an angel spells out the same thing. (See **4.3** where he tells Dean to stop Sam or they will. Meaning there are more angels on Castiel's side and their mission.

In this episode, Dean appeared to be wearing one of Sam's corduroy jackets, maybe something Sam left behind.

Dean's reference to the *Thriller* video (1983) from Michael Jackson's music video of the same name which had zombies in there. That is what Dean was meant to look like seeing as he was dead in hell. Funny no one said the same thing about Sam when he was brought back. Also Dean wouldn't look like a zombie because he was raised by an angel and not some spell or mojo.

Wedge Antilles is the name of *Red Two* in all three of the original *Star Wars* movies and books. An X-Wing pilot flying with Luke when they attempted to attack and destroy the Death Star.

The painting on the wall of the tiger appears to be the same one Andy had in his van in **2.5**.

For the first time, *The Road So Far* clips are featured at the beginning of the episode, rather than in a season finale. The date on the newspaper Dean looks at is the same date when this episode was aired in the US. In actual fact Dean was in hell for four earth months, as season 3 ended in May 2008 and the new season returned in September 2008 in the US.

Sam has Dean's amulet and he kept it to always have him close by, or to give it to him when he brings him back. Sam attempts to open Devil's Gate to "retrieve" Dean, didn't he learn from last time what happened and did he believe Dean would be waiting up there for this to happen, especially since he'd have problems of his own down there, not least of which being he's a Winchester and a hunter; and maybe Dean wouldn't even have thought of crawling his way up to the Gate (like Dad did) or be allowed to, if he knew where it was. He was too busy crawling out of his coffin instead.

Here's a question, why have Sam and Dean never attempted any form of communication with Dad, in some form or another. Maybe through a psychic – cue Missouri and a good way to bring her back. At least to find out where he is and what he's doing? Whether he's watching out for them? The same with Mom. If they can't find out about one then maybe they can do for the other.

Dean hasn't asked Castiel about his parents – where they are and Castiel hasn't said anything either. Especially since he knows the score and knows Dean's pain over their loss, more so since **4.3** and sending him back in time. Also when he was in Dean's car in that episode, Dean told him he'd do anything to save his family, even if this was selfish.

Bobby's full name is Robert Steven Singer.

Perdition is eternal damnation. The 'loss of the soul'.

Genevieve Cortese stated when she got the part as Ruby, it was for Sam's love interest as Kristy, not as Ruby. She was then given DVDs of Katie's brief stint in the part. She says, "If you look at Katie's last episode; you see that while Ruby's not responsible for Dean going to hell, she does have some guilt about it…I wanted to address questions like 'Why are the boys hanging out with her? Who do they need her for? It's not like she's kicking ass – she's asking Sam to kick ass for her. I almost feel deep down, she's really in love with Sam. One line in [an episode] I used to be human, and I still remember what it feels like." Maybe she was being manipulative, but maybe there's also truth to it." Ruby said this line to Dean in **3.9**. Actually it was just that she still remembers what it is like to be human and she didn't lose her humanity in hell, even though it strips you of it.

Genevieve says it's tough on fans to see a favourite character suddenly change, so she understands how people can be angry.

Eric Kripke told TVGuide.com that "If God is out there, he isn't sending angels to fight the battles [until this season 4] he's working through a very human, sweaty, outgunned and over whelmed group of hunters.

Tracey Dinwiddie writes her own screenplays. She believes in energy and its weird patterns and thinks she could be lightning or anything like that and believes that energy lives on. "Eric Kripke told me she [Pam] was created from the essence of the *Supernatural* fandom…I thought that was fascinating. Pamela Barnes loves a good laugh, but will lock it down when business needs tending. She's serious and cheeky." Tracey recently filmed the movie, *Seducing Spirits,* a thriller, where she plays a detective.

Quotes

Sam "…but what I do know is I'm saving people, stopping demons and that feels good. I wanna keep going."

Castiel: "I'm the one who gripped you tight and raised you from perdition."

Castiel: "This is your problem Dean. You have no faith."

Dean: "What visage are you in now, some holy accountant?"

Castiel: "What's the matter, you don't think you deserve to be saved...because God commanded it, because we have work for you."

Sam and Dean's Take on the Urban Legend/Lore

There isn't any specific lore mentioned here, but you could look up several tomes of angel lore if you like! Aside from Castiel being described as *the Angel of Thursday*. Seeing as the show is aired on a Thursday in the US. There is no angel with this name.

Samsara mentioned in the Trailer, is from Buddhism and Hinduism and means the eternal cycle of birth, suffering, death and rebirth.

Film/TV References

Star Wars.

X Files Connection

17.5 All Souls where a young, retarded girl has her eyes burnt out. A battle is ensuing between good and evil for all souls and a priest trying to protect four quadruplets from the devil, as they are an angel's offspring.

Lazarus Rising the title of an episode mentioning Lazarus of Bethany, from the Bible. He was raised from the dead by Jesus and this was retold as one of Christ's miracles.

Music

You Shook Me All Night Long by AC/DC. *Visions* by Jason Manns. *Fight Song* by Republic Tigers. *Wrapped Around Your Finger* by Martyn Laight.

Locations

Boundary Bay.

4.2 Are You There God, It's Me Dean Winchester?

Written By Sera Gamble. Directed By Phil Sgriccia.
Original US Airdate 18 September 2008

Guest Stars: Charles Malik Whitfield (Henricksen); Nicki Aycox
(Meg); Christopher Gauthier (Ronald); Genevieve Cortese (Ruby);
Misha Collins (Castiel); Andrea Ricketts (Olivia.)

Sam, Dean and Bobby attempt to banish ghosts from the past.
Castiel reveals a terrifying future to Dean.

Notes

So in season 4 we actually get to experience some proper cold spots
first hand, with mirrors icing over and cold breath too.

The title refers to a book by Judy Blume: *Are You There God? It's
Me Margaret*. About the discovery of spirituality by Margaret and
mentions life issues for teenage girls.

This episode is meant to take place three days after Dean is rescued.

No Dean you weren't groped by an angel (not yet anyway.) Dean
has to question why he's the only one who saw the angel. First, it was
why he was saved by an angel and now this. Okay they're both
questions he's still asking probably because no one is meant to see
angels. As Castiel says at the end, it's the first time in two thousand
years that they're walking the earth, therefore no one was meant to be
seeing one. No one that is except for Dean. Also not everyone will see
an angel.

So Dean should count himself lucky (at least for now,) but because
of his nature, he just can't help questioning their presence and his own
rescue since he doesn't believe, but at one point in **2.13 Houses of the
Holy**, he had that moment at the end of the episode when he witnessed
the rapist getting killed, when he thought he might really believe in God
(but that didn't last) when Sam was having his doubts. Then no one
believed, but Sam kept his faith and Dean went back to non-belief. He
didn't believe any of this or even when he told Sam Mom believed in
angels and said they were watching over them. Well, Dean had one
rescue him and you can't help but wonder or ask, what sort of angel is
watching out for or over Sam? A fallen angel.

Sam says Lilith is afraid of Castiel, how did he know this?

Also the writers seem to forget that in **2.13**, angels weren't described
as your average Hallmark version, even Sam said that they were fierce.

So here we get Dean telling Castiel he thought angels were meant to be all fluffy, with halos. Welcome to the real world Dean, and not make believe on TV!

Well, Dean can't use the excuse of not being able to recall anything now – of this time on earth, which he hasn't forgotten. It's only what he did in hell; of what happened there he doesn't appear to remember. As he still recalls Meg, Henriksen, Lilith, everything really.

Dean just carries on admonishing himself for actually being rescued, aside from moments when he is grateful, to see everyone, he needs to know why? Why him? Since he can't come to terms with believing there is a God after the years of skeptism. That even if there is a God why does he let his people suffer so. Deep down he's thinking – why did Mom suffer in that way, she was a believer, she had faith and why was his family put through all this suffering too.

When Dean asks Sam about whether Sam actually believes in God, the devil, he doesn't tell him why he's asking and again why does he do this.

Sam says the fact Dean's seen an angel goes to prove their existence rather than the main question of whether he believes in them or not; because they are, he's seen one, so he has   to have some sort of belief in them now.

Will Dean ever get his piece of pie? Sam always forgets the pie!

Ruby tells Sam everyone's heard of Dean's rescue by an angel – so who exactly is everyone, the forces of darkness no doubt, rather than anyone on the side of good. Aren't such things meant to be hush, hush anyway, their arrival is not meant to be announced, now the demons know the angels are on the warpath, everyone's gearing up for the final battle. All Ruby can do is think of herself (in typical demon fashion, and leave, which is just as well, as the less we see of her, the better!) which is one character trait about her that no one's changed and why pray tell would Ruby have ever meet an angel anyway?   There'd have no reason to 'visit' her, other than, as she says, to smite.

She also warns Sam to watch himself – again why? Since whatever Sam is doing, has done and will do in the future makes him in choppy waters so to speak. Even Castiel warns Dean to keep an eye out for Sam in the next episode. When he answers, he's not afraid of angels, did he mean this as a normal, general comment, as good Sam; or another part of him answering.

Yes, once again Dean catches up on forty winks and just happens to wake up in time to save Sam, as usual! (Whatever did he do without him and I don't mean with Ruby either!)

Sam thinks the spirits are out for revenge and Dean tells him it's in the here and now. Obviously they didn't know Lilith would return to the town in person in **2.12** and kill them all. Especially since she can and does do this to anyone, anywhere. They didn't know she'd show up in person as she's meant to be keeping off the radar.

Dean forever apologizing to Ronald and Meg. Again it wasn't his fault they were possessed by a demon, well, Meg was. Meg had no anger towards the demon she had inside of her, that made her go through all this. Though Bobby did tell Dean in **1.22** that there was a girl inside of her. Oh this is not meant to sound that way, that the demon was possessing a human. But they didn't know for sure how much of her was left, and also because her body was damaged beyond repair.

Being thrown out of the window was the demon's fault with the Devas coming after her, as they, as they tend to turn on those that summoned them.

On the contrary, Dean does know what it's like to be trapped and scream for help, he's been through hell and back; calling out for help and no help came. Not for four months anyway (in earth time) which is almost a lifetime of going through so much pain and anguish, so yes he knows exactly what it's like.

As for her fifty words of Latin sooner and she'd be saved, well, Dean doesn't do Latin, unless he has to with the aid of a book, Sam's the Latin expert. Also how would she still be alive, when as I said before, her body was so badly injured from the fall and everything else the demon probably put her through. What she's suddenly a medical expert now too.

Also funny how Meg and Henriksen can put a figure on how long he was tortured along with the others, since he really wouldn't have been timing how long it took for Nancy to be killed and how would Meg know fifty words of Latin sooner would've saved her.

Sam had seen the tattoo long enough to draw it (but he's not good as a sketch artist in **3.5 Bedtime Stories**.) Bobby's into the actress Bo Derek, her most famous film was *10* that's where the poster was from.

Bobby's *supernatural* panic room, would've been good to have this or at least known of it, everytime demons 'visited' the Winchesters at his place. Especially when Meg et al turned up. Also strange in **3.10** when he was being attacked by his dead wife, in his house, that he didn't think of locking himself in this panic room, unless of course he built it after Dean died. He was only dreaming too.

Well, Dean's ready for a road trip as soon as he hears "the end is nigh". Since when was he a Trekkie, wanting to do the entire *Star Trek Experience*.

As for Ronald blaming them for his death, Sam specifically warned him to stay away, but he didn't listen. He was shot by the FBI anyway and that had nothing to do with Sam and Dean not saving him. It was own fault and that of the shapeshifter. Yes, I'm apportioning blame where it lies.

What did Meg die from? Nothing really, no cause, a demon only wanted her physical appearance and used her as a vessel. She didn't serve any other purpose. But she is right when she says that about Ruby and Sam doing the dirty with a demon! That's just plain, erm, evil! How many has Ruby killed for a body to possess; even if she does want to help them, as she claims. Look how she's encouraged Sam to use his psychic powers and now Dean's back, she wants Sam to tell him about his powers. Though she wasn't too big on Sam telling Dean things last season.

Sam's right to say he doesn't even trust her, especially when even after she saved his life. (**4.9**). There could be something in it for her and she could also have an ulterior motive too. At the end of the day (or world) Ruby's a demon, always will be and in the final battle: the Apocalypse, there will only be one place for her and demons like her because she made her choice, sold her soul and got her comeuppance.

Besides she always leaves at signs of trouble, so where will she run to in the end (just thought I'd add that in.)

Oh and another thing Sam, as for getting it on with Ruby, all I can say is eeww, it's not even her own 'body' he's been sleeping with, but some other poor girl, since Ruby has no corporeal form, she's just demon smoke! The girl inside of her still knows what's happening!

Meg said what we were all thinking about Ruby – now she's back with new body (not as nice as her original body!) she obviously took over another host body so what will happen to it when she's finished with it; or tires of it. She is a demon, yes, the way she told Sam in **4.1** that she'd run a mile (or more from angels) regardless of what good she may have done. Ruby says she remembers her humanity (**3.9**) but fears angels, wouldn't what she's done for them, helping them bring her step closer to achieving her own redemption too, or maybe not.

So the witnesses are raised to ask Dean the question of why he gets to be saved. Henricksen asking Dean why he was given a second chance – why he was considered worthy, harking back to **1.12** and Layla's mother, when she asked Dean the same thing, why he was saved, why he deserved to be saved and not her daughter? (Another answer in a pedantic way, because it's the nature of the beast – substitute *Supernatural* for beast here!) But you can feel for them when Henricksen says they were tortured before they were killed. (Dean also knows a thing or two about that. See later.) His question of why him: probably part redemption for Dean and part of this involves helping with the seals now to make sure Lucifer doesn't walk free. Also Dean was chosen because it's more easier to 'convert' a non-believer than a believer – to challenge the faith that he never had in good, to begin with.

Another question of why Sam doesn't use his powers now, or do they only work on demons. Well, he could've used them, no one was really looking.

Oh boy, Dean calling an angel a 'dick'. Really *Supernatural* needs to improve its choice of words!

So Dean attended demon Sunday school. Castiel says angels are not here to "perch on your shoulder", in the next episode Yellow Eyes says that the angel on his shoulder can't help him when he has Dean ties up in the chair.

Dean doesn't believe in Lucifer now either. Yet he said he believes in evil, demons and so on, since he's encountered them and has seen them, fought them. Hell, he's even been to hell and seen such things (no pun meant). So now he has his doubts about Lucifer. Again in **2.13** Dean says he believes in evil because he's seen evil things, but not the good things; not angels and Castiel tells him he didn't believe in him either, three days ago. Three days back and they're already in the thick of things -"the rat race." Or rather the demon race. So if Dean doesn't even believe in the devil now, everything he said about believing in evil was all what, a lie (or forgetfulness on the part of writers, bad continuity.) Or does he simply not believe because

Lucifer was one of God's angels too before he disobeyed him and wouldn't bow down before Adam (man) and was cast out of heaven for this betrayal.

Castiel enlightens him about the bigger picture and that angels too are vulnerable themselves, as many of them have died in battles too. Castiel threatens Dean with hell if he doesn't show him some respect (just what I was talking about) but then can angels actually do this, since he says God commanded him to raise Dean from hell, so surely God is the only one who can send him back. They need Dean in the scheme of things anyway.

Also he demanding some respect after Dean called him a 'dick'. Seeing as he didn't say he should respect God and his ways everytime Dean said he didn't believe in him and why God lets bad things happen.

Bobby's line of shooting first is from the movie, *The Good, The Bad and the Ugly* with Clint Eastwood, Lee Van Cleef and Eli Wallach, where three go in search of gold. Here three go in search of angels and witnesses.

When the ball rolled down the stairs this scene was from *The Changeling*. Also twin ghosts were in the film *The Shining*. Alluded to in the show on many occasions.

This whole episode highlighted the ambiguity between Sam and Dean and their beliefs. Dean not believing in the good, God, angels and now he doesn't believe in the devil either. Not to mention the disparages between episodes gone before. Whereas Sam has convinced himself he's using his powers for good in banishing demons and saving people. Also in **2.13** Sam mentions there's tonnes of lore on angels and here, Bobby gives it to them to read! Whereupon he finds that only angels have the power to save people from hell, being able to bring them back.

Eric Kripke wanted to bring Adrienne Palicki back as Jess but she was busy filming her show *Friday Night Lights* and was unavailable, so he brought Meg back instead.

Quotes

Dean: "Proof that there's a God out there that actually gives a crap about me personally. I'm sorry but I'm not buying it because why me? If there is a God out there – I've saved some people but I'm just a regular guy."

Meg: "You think you're some kind of hero."
Dean: "No, I don't." After he's just finished saying he's a regular guy who's dissed on chicks.

Bobby: "So you thought our luck would start now all of a sudden."

Sam and Dean's Take on the Urban Legend/Lore

Bobby says only angels can save souls from hell. Their branding was the *Mark of the Witnesses* - the unnatural, Ghosts forced to rise on purpose. The spell used to raise them left a mark on their souls. The *Rising of the Witnesses* is from the Book of Revelations showing a sign of the Apocalypse. The Rising of the Witnesses is one of the 66 seals broken by Lilith. When the last opens, Lucifer walks free.

Actual Legend

Revelations, the last book of the Bible describes the Battle of Armageddon; the Four Horsemen of the Apocalypse (that Dean mentions here) and the Beast with the number 666. It was thought to have been written by John, but not one of Jesus Christ's disciples. Scholars consider the number of the Beast 666 as a reference to numerology. "The letters of the name were ascribed numerical value and added up to a given number." Here the name of Nero (Emperor of Rome) adds up to 666. As John had a vast dislike to Romans and their actions.

Armageddon is from *al-megiddo,* a place found on the Jazred Plain (in Israel). At the time of John, many battles were fought here and this seemed to him to be an appropriate place for the Final Battle.

There are seven seals in the Bible from the Book of Revelation 5:1.. The seven seals are meant to be opened by the lamb (Jesus). After one seal is opened, an event is meant to occur. The opening of the first four seals is known as the Four Horsemen of the Apocalypse. When the fifth seal is opened, there is a "vision of those that were slain for the word of God."(Revelation 6:9). Revelation 7 says when the sixth seal is opened, there's an earthquake. Signs appear in heaven manifested by how 144,000 of God's servants are "sealed...in their foreheads." After the seventh seal is opened, seven angels sound their trumpets. Rev 5.1 "And I saw in the right hand of him that sat on the throne a book written within and on the backside, sealed with seven seals."

Those who have studied the Bible, associate the seven seals with the "seven spirits of God" and other seven's found in the Bible. The seal has symbols referred to as death, famine, world wars, martyrdom, earthquakes, Anti-Christ. The Holy Bible, King James' version mentions 'six seals' in *The Revelation of St John the Divine.*

The Rising of the Witnesses is mentioned in the Book of Revelations Chapter 11: The two Witnesses and the seventh trumpet.

Bobby calls Dean a Ravana, or that he could be one. This is from a famous Indian legend. Ravana was the King of Demons from Hindu myth. Portrayed as having ten heads and twenty hands. He turned into a terrible monster due to his childhood, as people were afraid of anyone with such a demeanour. His real name was *Dasamuka,* i.e. *one who carries several heads.* , since 'das' means ten in Hindi or Urdu and 'mu' means face rather than head, so it should be 'ten faces'. [Oh just a thought, can you imagine what Dean could do with twenty hands? Okay, let's not!]

432

Ravana was also perceived as being a *Rakshasa* (one who hungers for human flesh and takes any chances to become human once more. As in **2.2**.) Ravana abducted Rama's wife, Sita.

Film/TV References

Paraphrasing of the TV series *Touched By An Angel* mentioned many times. Also *Highway to Heaven* where Michael Landon played an angel sent to earth to help people. You could call it the precursor to the former show.

X Files Connection

In the episode **All Souls**, Scully obviously believes in God; in evil and the devil, and yet she answered Mulder by saying "if demons exist…" surely she just contradicted herself, a bit like
Dean here when he's so skeptical as far as demons are concerned. Mulder said a similar thing Dean did in **2.13** about religion being responsible for wars and half of the troubles in the world. As Bobby here tells Sam and Dean to quit arguing about religion, about whether angels exist.

Music

Lonely is the Night by Billy Squires.

4.3 In The Beginning

Written By Jeremy Carver. Directed By Steve Boyum
Original US Airdate 2 October 2008

Guest Stars: Mitch Pileggi (Samuel Campbell). Matt Cohen (John Winchester). Amy Gumenick (Mary Campbell). Allison Hossack (Deanna Campbell). Misha Collins (Castiel). Christopher B Maccabe (Dr Brown, Yellow Eyes). Andy Nez (Daniel Elkins).

Sam goes off to hunt with Ruby.

Lawrence, Kansas.

Castiel sends Dean back to the past to help his parents.

Notes

Sam leaves Dean again in the night, in his only few second scene of the show and you know what, Dean is able to carry off the entire episode on his own, at least almost on his own. Sam is definitely ready to use his powers again and takes pleasure in sneaking off into the night, leaving Dean behind, who seems to be catching up on an awful lot of 'missed' sleep. Okay, I know I've said that before…well perhaps it's his guilty pleasure and as for Sam, I don't mean his guilty pleasure is getting it on with Ruby; I mean using his powers without telling Dean and then lying straight to his face. That's just not on and another way in which Sam has changed. Yet all we do is hear excuses about how he was alone, without Dean and had to do the best he could. Which is all fine and dandy, but did he stop to consider what Dean may be going through wherever he was, in purgatory, hell. He wouldn't exactly be having a picnic since all those demons they've exorcised, et al, were all looking for some revenge against the Winchesters – any one of them would have done.

Sam was having a reaction following in Dad's footsteps – he went off the scale, so to speak, after Mom was killed and all he could think of doing was finding what killed her. Here Sam was doing the same in looking for Lilith, to get her back for taking Dean and everything else too in the process. Was his action extreme – think of everyone else who has gone through some sort of loss, put it this way, the extreme hurt and pain can either make you or break you and if you can't deal and have no support you can veer off in all directions.

But Sam wasn't alone, Bobby was still here (Ellen too – though there's no mention of her! 'Gone and forgotten) but no he turned to Ruby. The one person who, with hindsight, on Sam's part, shouldn't have! All she wanted to do was to make Sam use his powers, was this making him stronger as she told Dean in **3.9**. No, far from it, Dean was right, it was like she was moulding and manipulating and living out her own vengeance fantasies through him; maybe for everything she went through after selling her soul and that makes her a better person how? Hence this deal was probably for her own selfish reasons anyway.

Dean always appears to, well he is, sleeping when Castiel appears, and almost as if he's just dreaming about him and all this hasn't happened or isn't happening at all. Castile asking Dean what he was dreaming about – oh a loaded question if ever there was one. As an angel he would know what Dean's dreams are about – they wouldn't involve any busty Asian babes either! At this point and from someone who can tell at a glance what Dean thinks, did he really have to ask?!

A bit cruel, in my opinion, sending Dean back to see his parents, only to witness his grandparent's death too at the hands of Yellow Eyes. Seeing as he not only wiped them out, but then proceeded to do the same with everyone else Mom knew. He must've thought them hunters too, in some way carrying on the family tradition of hunting as well. But sending Dean back under false pretences, convincing him he could "stop it" – whatever it was, when all he had to do was to tell Dean everything about his family and Sam, or didn't he think Dean would believe him again. Seemed a fruitless task, other than making Dean re-lives the pain all over again, or was it a case of what doesn't kill you makes you stronger!

As for Dean giving away his game plan, telling Yellow Eyes he'd be the one to kill him – seeing as Yellow Eyes saw he had the colt, why didn't he act on this in the future , if Dean had really gone back in time, and get rid of Dean completely when he came to "visit" and infect Sam. Writing it all up to not being able to change destiny was a bit of a cop-out. You change destiny everyday by the decisions you make. Yes, you are guided by a higher power – but they're your choices: should I wear this, do that, turn left or right. What of the destinies of the people they've saved and will save, it can't be written that all of them will be killed, possessed by demons etc and won't be saved.

In this way, Castiel is saying, that Sam can't change his destiny either no matter how hard he tries and he will be destined to have the evil inside of him consume him entirely, without having a chance to fight it. In which case, there's no point in him making his personal choice, as he calls it in **4.4** to stop using his powers again anyway because it's his fate.

Conversely, wasn't Dean's destiny changed. He was destined for hell, got there and then was saved which is what Dean should've said to Castiel, i.e. "My destiny changed." So everything's not written in stone!

Yellow Eyes confrontation with Dean in **2.22** when he was pointing the colt right at him, he didn't even flinch, as if he was invincible. In which case if that episode is watched with this one, then nothing makes sense or is at it should be. It all seems so clinical and tacked on as if this episode was an after thought (which it really was to everything gone before.) Thus I, at least, expected something a bit more than simply 'destiny can't be changed'!

Didn't anyone suspect something may have been wrong with Samuel when he said Lidy would be fine and he came out of the house alone. Especially since she was Mary's friend, shouldn't she have done the checking up on her. What made them believe she'd be safe now, since Dean knows demon smoke can inhabit anyone! As hunters they must have known that too. Samuel and Mary scoffing at Dean when he said he can kill a demon – what about exorcisms, oh they don't 'kill' in the usual sense, but they do stop. Sam can kill demons. What would they have made of Sam using his powers to <u>actually </u>kill demons! In the sense of sending them back to hell.

Conveniently Dean had to have Dad's journal with him (what he had it in his pocket) and you knew he was somewhere else after his phone had no signal, and when he got up from the bench since *Tab* – the sugar-free cola hasn't been available for decades now! Not many people will recall it either, unless you're from a specific generation, i.e. the 1970's.

In a homage to *Back to the Future* you get the diner scene. The date on the paper Dean picks up is 30 April 1973. When Mary made the deal with Yellow Eyes, they were well into May, at least the second, so Sam's birthday: the night of the nursery incident when she was killed was November 2nd 1983, six months after Sam was born.

Listen to the church bells ring as Dean walks out and Castiel crops up once again. Giving him no indication of what he's in for. Another *Back to the Future* reference with the De Loran which was the car Marty used to go back in time. Then also hearing the Winchester name being called out to find he's sitting next to Dad. So they didn't have any photos of their parents when they were younger – they must've seen one or two at least. Since they managed to find some belongings in the cellar of their old home; and didn't Dad keep any in his storage facility, as he kept some of their 'old' memorabilia and possessions.

So angels can 'bend' time to suit their own needs but can't alter destinies (see the whole discussion mentioned before).) It appears Dean does seem to have plenty of influence when it comes to altering their destinies or at least affecting them in some way: urging Dad to buy the Impala; perhaps getting to be called Dean after Deanna. (He didn't mention this to Sam next episode.) How come Sam and Dean knew absolutely nothing about their parents' ancestry, who they were and so on. Weren't they even a little curious to find out and to think Sam's really into his research too; to the point of not even knowing their paternal grandparents' names, except in **2.4** and also what of this uncle they mentioned in **2.4** and **3.2.**

When Dean says "something's after his Dad, you can hear tyres screech in the background, almost like in **3.11** when Dean got run over, but here it's as if to alert him that that's where he'll find Dad right about now – buying a VW camper van, all the rage of the 1960's and 1970's.

When Dean says Dad taught him everything he knows, he means not just about cars either, but hunting too and some harsh lessons in how cruel and unforgiving the real world and life really is.

This episode reminded me of Charles Dickens *A Christmas Carol*, I know it's not Christmas but it was like Dean was visiting (re-visiting the spirits of his family) that which had gone before, in some attempt to "stop it" from ever happening. Unlike Scrooge, he didn't return to find Christmas and time hadn't passed him by; that it wasn't too late to change, but found it wasn't too late to change Sam. There was still time to look out for him. Castiel says just as much when he tells Dean to stop Sam or they will. – ugh there he goes with the "stop it" from happening phrase once more! Then Dean has to question Dad about the cold spots etc, as if he may have been a hunter all his life. Nice twist when he learns it wasn't Dad, but Mom! The kick-ass beauty striking one for women and women's lib in the 1970's – the height of sexism. Dean also tells Dad to watch out for himself, like he'll tell Mom and they both didn't, at least not in the way he wanted. Dean can't fight back, because she's Mom!

Not much of a test asking how vampires can be killed, any vampire worth his salt would know the answer to that one and probably any demon too. Oh, clearly holy water didn't wash with them, (no pun!). Grandma can't believe Dad would ever get into the whole hunting gig – how wrong she was and she was always stuck in the kitchen too. Dean in priest attire once more (fine, I said my comments in **1.14**, read over!)

In *Supernatural* lore, Yellow Eyes has to be invited into the home before he can make deals, not in return for souls but to plant demon blood into their babies. A way of making the baby his own without actually having to breed, but it's not past him, as he says that to Dean about Mom.

If you now go back and watch **1.9 Home**, when Missouri tells Dad Sam can't even sense his own father was around, it now gives a bit of a clearer picture as to why. Far from Sam not being Dad's son (as we speculated for ages!) rather he had demon blood in him which is where his powers stem from obviously and are nothing hereditary in the normal sense of the word. Also when Mom appeared to them to defeat the Poltergeist and she apologizes to Sam, we now know that it was for making the deal and for Sam becoming what a he is, as well as probably apologizing for not being around for him.

Dean comments Charlie's pimped his soul to a demon, as he doesn't yet know it's not his soul he's after (like Lilith and other demons) but his offspring. What better way to get into peoples' homes than to pose as a doctor. Also a good cover for when the babies are born and he can feed them his demon blood.

Mom also says Dad wasn't a hunter, far from it and he became one because of her and so did her children, the very thing she wished against! Dean must have been surprised to hear how sweet Dad was, since they only knew him as a hunter: strict, militaristic, getting the job done rather than showing any emotions, if any. However, he did love them, even if he couldn't and didn't show it at times. Everything Sam said about Dad drawing him into this life and not wanting it was true, to a certain extent. It was because of Mom, though he didn't have much to say about this when Dean tells him in the next episode.

Dean is so emotionally overwhelmed when Mom tells him she doesn't want this happening to her family too. Ironic, of course, but also echoes Sam when he left for university and wanted out of hunting; to be normal. Wonder if looking back, Dean has any regrets now about going to get Sam and bringing him back into a life of hunting or whether he would've been into it anyway because of his blood and since Jessica got in the way and would've been killed by Yellow Eyes regardless, for the same reason. No, I won't go into pre-written destiny again, but food for thought none the less.

Castiel telling Dean to think of everyone he's saved, the same thing Sam tells him on occasions and Dean too at times. Again echoes of **2.18** when in Dean's alternate reality, everyone they had saved actually died as Sam and Dean weren't there: weren't hunters. Yes, Dean cares about them, but this is his family. When faced with the choice there really isn't one. Well, some may argue, he opted to save his parents, selfishly, and thus the events re-played themselves as before!

Castiel comments time is fluid -this can also mean Dean never went back to the past (future) however you want to look at it and Mom still made the deal anyway. In which case, he had no influence over the past or future and therefore didn't contribute to their deaths. No one knew of the colt or Elkins, until Dad found him and thus Elkins always had the colt. Mom and Dad would've named them after their maternal grandparents anyway (since Mom probably lost them both).

Dean never had that conversation with Mom, made her promise not to get out of bed and therefore she didn't recall it on that night and did get out of bed. Think she would've done this anyway, re all the static around, well flashing lights and why in Sam's flashback in **2.21** she knew Yellow Eyes, but how could she have forgotten the deal she made ten years ago? Thus Yellow Eyes wasn't afraid of Dean; he never met him before, which it appears how this episode was meant to have been viewed. (I think.) That Dean only went back now (or rather was sent back) in a last ditched attempt to find out about Sam and Yellow Eyes' true plan.

Dean misses his shot, like he couldn't kill the Shtriga in **1.18** and was berated for it by Dad, who never let him forget. Perhaps that's part of what made Dean such a good hunter too. He now punishes himself too at missing and duh if he had killed Yellow Eyes then there'd be no show. (Ha!)

Mom even tried to run from hunting, that's what she was doing with Dad when Yellow Eyes caught up with her. Again reminiscent of Sam's running away from this life too.

No doubt Dean had to put the colt on the table, not that he would have been able to take it out from his pocket since he was pinned down, but why didn't Yellow Eyes take it with him when he left to go after Mom and why not just finish Dean off when he had the chance so he wouldn't be a hindrance. Dean letting his guard down again and not thinking demons can possess anyone. Also what did Yellow Eyes mean when he said to Dean there was something about him – probably that he may have been one of his special children, that was before he proceeded to smell him.

Dean finally gets to hear Sam has demon blood in him (not from Sam) and that Yellow Eyes had more than just a demon army planned and pre-empts Dean by saying he knows there's an angel on his shoulder (not metaphorically) of course. So he's not giving anything away. Repeating what Castiel said in **4.2**, that he doesn't perch on his shoulder. Dean gives his own 'end game' away to Yellow Eyes about being the one to kill him, at least that was one promise he got to keep.

Also when Yellow Eyes says, 'like I'm gonna tell you' what the plan is, he echoes Meg in **1.16** when she meets Sam hitchhiking and says, 'like I'm gonna tell you, you could be some kind of freak' just like her father here. Using some sort of reverse psychology on Mom: if she doesn't promise then she'd be alone forever. It's not what she wants having just lost her parents (she doesn't know about her mother yet) and losing the man of her dreams too. Funny Dad didn't question what happened to Samuel with all that blood on him when he woke up.

Rather callous using Dean like that. As if he's some sort of servant to order around, to do as they please with him, just because he rescued him from hell. Again, showing him that Castiel can do anything he likes and Dean has to follow, otherwise it's hell for him.

Dean didn't get to her in time because the car he was driving was so slow (not his Impala) and misses his shot again. Yellow Eyes always taking the easy way out and disappearing already, jus as in **1.21** when

Sam tried to shoot him in the nursery and when he was possessing Dad in **1.22**. The real question is how Dean knew where to find Mom? Or was he just driving around and that's what took him so long, since he didn't know she was running away. It must have been the scent of the Impala he followed!

Dean wakes up once more, as though it was all a dream. Some way to learn the truth, when he could've just stood by and watched the past, be shown it like Sam was, instead of being an active participant. How come the angels know about Lilith and the seals but they don't know what Yellow Eyes had planned? Again he tells Dean to stop it, i.e. Sam's road or destiny he's on, but that can't be altered, he just said as much when telling him destiny can't be changed!

As for another Winchester in the mix, a long lost brother, what if this one has been fathered by Yellow Eyes, he said he'd like to breed with Mom. This Winchester becoming part of his end-game, pitting them all against each other. (I know we have yet to have this episode aired in the UK.) Well his goal can't be the same as Lilith's since she only came into the scene when he bit the dust, but was still behind the scenes as she held Dean's contract (**2.21**) for so long. Well, if I'm wrong which I probably will be, then I'll eat Dean's pie!!

This episode also all about cause and effect. Dean goes back in time because Castiel asked him to 'stop it'. All he witnesses are the death of his grandparents; he misses Dad being killed, and sees his mom making a deal with Yellow Eyes, which he cashes in on to the fullest extent, a decade later. After making the deal and promising not to interrupt him, she does exactly that, by going into the nursery, because of the deal or irrespective of agreeing to it, she wasn't going to stand by and see her family hurt. Even if it meant they would be the ones suffering the fall-out from her actions and that they would bear the brunt of everything, when she's gone.

If you watch the Pilot episode with this, when Mom goes into the nursery, she's oblivious as to what's happening. She either didn't remember the promise she made to Dean of not getting up on November 2nd 1983. Did she just forget, or did she really want to see what she promised Yellow Eyes: to see the price for bringing back Dad.

Mom was a hunter, so why was she so non-chalent in her life; so careless. No protection for her family; kept secrets from Dad, is it any wonder Sam keeps things from Dean and Dad did the same too – to begin with, like Mom. (So it was good that Dean didn't tell him everything too, in one go, not that they should have secrets between each other, but it gives Dean a few things to keep up his sleeve for once.) Therefore, Dad et al, would've been more protective of them too. Such as keeping Sam's crib in the nursery, wouldn't she have wanted him closer to hand. Also Dean too, though clearly, Sam was always the one in obvious danger, at first.

Still there must be something in the way she mistook Yellow Eyes for Dad in the nursery that night; fancy not being able to recognize your own husband. Again, all the static, light flashing, signs were missed, or could've been missed due to her being asleep. Dad wasn't, though if he had known he would've done something, or maybe not.

Also what Missouri said about Sam not sensing his own father – still and why not? Dad saying he didn't want to see them until he had all the answers. Once more showing he must have found out about Mom in his travels as a hunter, meeting others along the way who would've known her.

At least would've known who she married. As well as using Azazel's sigel to summon him, again, showing or proving he knew something.

Daniel Elkins was around too, so Dad must've known about Mom - eventually and kept that hidden from them too. Secrets much? I know I've said this before, but it seems right to bring it up again in the context of this episode.

Also, if all Yellow Eyes wanted was Sam as his psychic kid, he could've killed Dean back there and saved himself in the future.

Cause and effect again, a bit like the Butterfly effect. Dean went back and got his grandparents killed, at least it looked that way and what did he achieve in the end anyway? Castiel tells him he went back to witness it, that Sam would be given demon blood.

As for Sam not being chosen to go back, he had this chance with Yellow Eyes in **2.21** and he didn't tell Dean. Everything's that happened so far this season shows us that Sam isn't really deemed worthy of all this. There's still that whole debate of whether Sam <u>really</u> is good, regardless of what anyone else says, creeping in again, though very subtly.

In my opinion, it's all gearing up towards good vs evil. As opposed to what Sam said in season 2 about doing everything he can, saving lots of people so he doesn't turn evil, in an attempt to change his destiny. He's killing as many demons as possible now, so does he still believe he can stay on the side of good, since it can all become futile in the end. Castiel says it too, that if Dean doesn't prevent Sam from altering the course he's on, they will. Obviously he knows a lot more than he's letting on too. **Dean vs Sam**, even. Sam has so many secrets from Dean, how can **he think** this is a good thing; or that keeping them actually helps **either one** of them in the long-run.

Wonder if Yellow Eyes knew Dean came back or would be sent back. This kind of throws most things we've seen in previous episodes in the air. Yellow Eyes carried on with his ten year deals like he was selling cars. Sam and Dean were born. Can't say Yellow Eyes reference to the 'end game' was just something to throw him and the angels off the scent as to his true intention, i.e. wanting Sam, but then Dean already knew that. Could it possibly be something about Sam realizing his destiny after all, since Castiel spells out destiny can't be altered, so whatever happens to everyone in the future is still on track.

Now, see how you can write extra long essays in the guise of notes on every episode of *Supernatural* if you set your mind to it!

Mary Campbell was not the one from seventies sitcom *Soap*!

Mitch Pillage, of course played ADA Skinner in *X Files*. The Impala has the number plate C 45P4.

Why is it always Dean who gets to go back in time, in one form or another (not that I'm complaining!). Due to Dean's foray to the past, he's probably named for Dean, i.e. himself. The song *Ramblin' Man* was also used in the Pilot. Dad thinks Dean's phone resembles the *Star Trek communicator*.

The episode title refers to Genesis, the first book of the Bible. Here it refers to how Mom and Dad met and what happened to them, or what would happen to them.

God is my Co-Pilot is an autobiography by World War II pilot, Robert Lee Scott Jr, who flew in the US Airforce and it was also a 1945 movie.

Yellow Eyes calls Mom 'Little Orphan Mary,' a comic strip from 1924 called *Little Orphan Annie* by Harold Gray. Which was made into the musical *Annie*.

Quotes

Dean: "Sammy, wherever you are, Mom is a babe. I'm going to hell. Again"

Dean: "Even if this sounds really weird. Will you promise me you'll remember on November 2nd 1983 – don't get out of bed – no matter what you hear or what you see. Promise me you won't get out of bed."

Castiel: "You couldn't of stopped it. Destiny can't be changed Dean. All roads lead to the same destination."
Dean: "Then why the hell you send me back."
Castiel: "For the truth – now you know everything we do...we know

what Azazel did to your brother. What we don't know is what his end game is. He went to great lengths to cover that up.

Film/TV References

Back To the Future, God is my Co-Pilot.

Music

Ramblin' Man by The Altman Brothers. *Go ForSelf* by Kenny Smith and the Loveliters.

Ooh Bloops

When John is killed and Yellow Eyes tells Mary he'll being him back, the actor playing John, appears to be still breathing.

Locations

Delta Museum and Archives, Ladner. Lulu Island Trestle Bridge.

4.4 Metamorphosis

Written By Cathryn Humphris. Directed By Kim Manners.
Original US Airdate 9 October 2009

Guest Stars: Dameon Clark (Jack). Joanne Kelly (Michelle). Ron Lea (Travis). Genevieve Cortese (Ruby)

Carthage, Missouri

Sam and Dean try and help a man before he changes into a deadly animal.

Notes

Sam can also send Ruby straight to hell too, isn't she afraid of him or doesn't she believe he'll actually do something like that to her. What would 'evil' Sam do – if he went down this route? (Wish he would send her to hell, she's a bit of a waste of space this season and lacks any emotion.) Come on, Ruby must be afraid of Sam, since she did listen to him when he told her to take the victim to the hospital. Either that, or she's just not ready to show here true colours just yet – maybe she'll wait until she finds a weak spot in Sam or his powers (aside from Dean being one weakness, of course.)

Sam's power, its use, is nothing more than an addiction at times, like he uses it genuinely believing it's for the better, but can't seem to stay away from its draw – the pull it seems to have on him. Especially as we'll see further on into the season.

Dean was upset more than a little, at not being able to relate to Sam, re his power and how he uses it. He thinks of it as a curse, whereas anyone endowed with such psychic power, in the human use of the word, reveres it and calls it a gift.

Perhaps Dean is more frustrated at having been to hell and having Sam go through all this alone. Now that he's back he really wants to see Sam stay good and remain positive about who he is. Dean having the unenviable task of being stuck in the middle: Sam on one side, Castiel on the other. Pull for Sam, root for him, work for God with Castiel watching over his shoulder (not perched on his shoulder though) to ensure he keeps Sam in line or the angels will. Dean hoping somehow the two paths will meet, since they're all fighting the good fight in the end. Aren't they?...

Every demon knows Sam's been getting it on with Ruby, only Dean is in the dark again. Something the writers missed here is not having Dean put two and two together and recall she was the same girl who came out of Sam's room in **4.1**.

The way he greets her is good, i.e. straight to pistols at dawn, here knife at night! (Should've ended our misery Dean!). Ruby looked like she had a sinister expression on her face when she asks Sam how that felt. She seems to have so much influence over him – which could be his downfall, if he's not too careful.

Sam's forever explaining things – sometimes his attempts at explaining or explanations come a little too late!

The fishy motel room was a little like the one in **2.14** when Sam was possessed. Funnily enough, Sam didn't ask Dean how he found him?

Dean still using God in almost every sentence! Sam has managed to convince himself (or is it Ruby) that he's doing more good than bad when he sends demons to hell, as he can now save the possessed person. Is he doing this because of anything Meg said when she said they could've saved her and there was a human inside of her still. Or just for the sake of it. Most likely he's been doing this even before Meg was brought back.

Dean resorts to taking his anger out on the furniture now, seems Sam's face wasn't enough. Sam should've fought back or was he genuinely turning the other cheek thinking maybe Dean's allowed; perhaps it was his guilt playing on his mind. Dean spelling out to Sam in no uncertain terms that he'd hunt him if he wasn't his brother. That's what Sam's becoming – something to be hunted. Shades of what Gordon said in **2.10** and **3.7**, in Dean's speech, about being hunted by other hunters too if they knew about Sam. Dean didn't recall there may be some truth in what Gordon said about Sam after all.

Again the writers appear to have let that slip by, after repeating certain things over and over in episodes over the seasons, such as Sam becoming evil and wanting Dean to end it all if he does. Also like Sam's same old excuse, er, reason for being here alone, going on without him. Well it sounds a sorry excuse – since there are plenty of people who have to go on without their loved ones; as I said in **4.3** – ahead of myself! Was he really turning into Dad thinking this would be the only thing keeping him going – just hunting and nothing else.

Sam gave us the usual spiel about going on without Dean in season 3 and in **3.11** when he actually had to carry on when Dean was killed due to the Trickster's games. In that flash forward, of sorts, Sam was hunting using weapons and not his powers (we weren't meant to know he'd be getting them back yet) but also was without Ruby and he appeared to be doing just fine.

Dean finally tells him Castiel practically ordered him to stop Sam from what he's doing and mentions God – so **does** she believe now? God doesn't want Sam using his powers because they're demonic, or demon sent and so can't or shouldn't be used for good, in saving innocent people, as Sam believes to be the case, rightly or wrongly.

Also do you get the impression Dean needs to take orders from someone in his life, most of his life it was from Dad which he did without question and now it looks as if Castiel is doing the same thing to him, i.e. ordering him, in the name of God.

Oh and in Sam's defence, I'll say one thing: when he says he had to live without Dean, Dean couldn't live without Sam either in **2.22**. So he brought him back. Don't see Sam throwing that at him (not yet anyway). Their argument is cut short by the call.

Sam kind of falls into Dean's false sense of security, if Dean was suspicious of Sam, when he tells him about Mom and Dad, he goes on to add the only reason they were all wiped out was so he could have demon blood given to him. Telling Dean he knew about this all along – for over a year now (as I mentioned all those times before and sorry's not enough Sam, since Dean went to his death not knowing and if he didn't return, well…) it was his secret.. Dean hasn't told him about the seals yet, or anyone else either. As well as a few other secrets.

Dean going easy on him when he says Sam doesn't know about it as Castiel probably will.

The look of disgust on their faces watching Jack eat, even Dean must've thought he never pigs out like that! Dean stressing the only thing that matters is family, trying to convince Sam at least.

Sam was a mathelete.

You could say Travis could almost be relaying Sam's life story about changing and turning evil once and there'd be no going back for him. What Dean's been trying to hammer home to him too. Then Sam has to convince them they'll only kill Jack if it's the final straw – when all else fails. I.e. talking, bargaining, in Sam's case. He's desperately clutching, trying to justify not killing for the sake of it. So perhaps Dean will listen to what he's saying. Sam's come far (and so has the series) from season 2 when all he could do was to make Dean promise he'd kill him if he turned bad and realized his destiny. (Seems everyone's forgotten Dean's promise.)

Sam uses their real names when he introduces themselves to Jack. Not that it mattered since Jack wasn't going to be around for too long.

Sam even tries to convince Jack of this at the end, that he can only be bad or turn if he decides this is what he wants; if he gives in to his temptations (Sam's dark side.) It will always be his choice – but will it? Since Jack turned to protect his wife and unborn child from a hunter. What would make Sam change and push him over the edge, aside from Ruby,)see episodes later, when he begins to use his powers once more when the angels plan on wiping out a whole town of people. Sam believing this is the only way to save them: that it was all for good. Also he would do as much for Dean too.

Sam thinks being an idiot is worse than being a freak. But then Ruby said that Sam doesn't like the way demons look at him too, as if he's some sort of freak. (Dean said he's a freak too on plenty of occasions). The way he looks at Sam because he cares about him – he doesn't want him going all evil on him!)

Like the way everyone's being calling what Sam's doing a dark road all of a sudden, Castiel said it in **4.3** that Sam's on a dark road and Dean says it here too. But does Sam know the difference between right and wrong - wouldn't it be right to not use his powers because they are demon sent (or given). Isn't it wrong for him to use them because he can't get rid of them, or change the blood flowing within him (oh and it's also wrong to lie!).

Ruby says, last season, "Hello manipulation – I'm a demon; it's in the job description". So this is what Dean also tells Sam here, that she can't be trusted. As a viewer of the show, Jared sensed that Ruby was all good, but wasn't sure if Eric Kripke would have kept her that way. (See season 4 finale.)

As you'll recall Sam saying something in season 2, along the lines of the more people the saves, the less chance of him turning dark. Is this what he still thinks when he tells Dean he's saved more people in five months than they have in a year. Trying in some way, for the good to outweigh the bad. No wonder angels don't want to know Sam, because of his demon blood, don't know how he'll turn out or whether he can be trusted or not.

Sam and Dean break down the door of that girl's room – then Dean leaves his prints behind when he closes the door! Henriksen may have told his bosses at the FBI of Sam and Dean being killed in 3.12, before he died, but doesn't mean their prints won't still be on file.

Travis' comment she won't be around in 30 years. Will Sam and Dean be and if so, what's the bet they may not be hunting. Will there be a world in thirty years is the question that should be asked?

Sam and Dean are always overpowered so quickly and then both turn their backs away. It takes ages for Sam to ignite the gas tank (like in 3.2). Sam ends up in the closet (as in 1.14) could get a joke out here about going into the closet rather than coming out since they've had so many gay jokes on the show. Jack thinks Dean's the better choice to feed on. Actually it's so Sam can talk to him about understanding his predicament. But we don't actually see how Sam got out, surely the coat hanger wasn't working, which only leaves him resorting to the use of his psychic powers once more and save Dean this time round, which he couldn't use in 1.14. He had to use brute force to get out.

Sam forgets to ponder, or doesn't bother why Travis would want to kill his wife too, for someone who does an awful lot of thinking. It's not as though Travis was some crazed killer – he was a seasoned hunter and they couldn't discover it was because she may have been pregnant.

Sam trying to assure Jack and himself – you can only become evil if you decide to. (We shall wait and see!). Then another twisty turn around for the books, Sam doesn't want talk. The guy who always had an opinion on everything, even when Dean didn't want to know what he had to say; not wanting to talk was a shock! Dean's surprised. Sam makes his choice and tells Dean he won't use his powers anymore.

Sam can say to Dean the blood's not in him and everything when for weeks (episodes) he kept making Dean remember his promise to end it all for him. He really has become a different person and even more so after losing Dean. It was only four months, but what would the change in Sam have been if it was for longer. Also, appears not even big bro has much of an influence over Sam anymore. He wants to stay quiet now and wants to go through it all alone now. So much for wanting Dean back from hell and in his life! Has the younger Winchester come out from under the elder's shadow, whereas before he worshipped him!

This episode was more of a commentary on Sam's destiny, curse and life, instead of an episode about a Rugaru – or the "steps" to becoming one. Highlighted more so by Sam's struggle to come to terms with who he is and how he might also metamorphosize into the very evil that flows through him, preventing the inevitable from happening.

The Impala has the original number plates KAZ 2Y5, but new plates appear in the proceeding episodes.

Kobe Bryant is an NBA basketball player who gave his wife a $4 million diamond ring after he'd been accused of rape.

This episode was set in Carthage, the city of ancient Carthage was where their religious ritual consisted of human sacrifices, so they weren't far off the mark when they set this episode here.

Jared states he'd like to see Sam go dark (like I've been saying for yonks!). He says, "We've been toying with that now for a little while, and that's very un-Kripke like. Eric likes to get stuff done and not just toy with things. So I think he's going to make a decision one way or another, and we're either going to go a little darker with Sam or we're going to stay with good ol' boy Sam, who tries not to use his dark powers for the betterment of the world. But I hope Sam gets tougher and more dark-edged."

To have little Sammy stay like little Sammy could get tedious since he's always on the brink of being bad and then he gets drawn back and put into place by Dean telling him to stop using his powers. What if he can't?

Jared continues, "I want Sam to go dark. I want to find out what's going on with all these rumours about him. I want to know how bad he is or how bad he can be. I want to see the full potential of his supposed powers. We put the brunt of it off. If we had those extra in episodes [in season 3], without the strike, we might have been able to deal with that a bit more. But Eric figured that we waited this long to confront it, and he didn't want to slam it into four episodes. We want to approach it correctly and with the proper due diligence." As long as it is approached, since if Sam's always hanging on the corner of good and evil, then his character won't have progressed so much if he's not able to see first hand what bad comes from this blood. For him to want to fight and bring himself back, rather than being told by anyone else to prevent the inevitable from happening.

Eric finds it more interesting if Sam uses evil powers for the greater good, then if he turns evil himself. "Everyone's the hero of their own story, so even if he's doing something Dean doesn't like – Sam thinks he's doing it for the right reasons."

Quotes

Dean: "You don't need me, you and Ruby go fight demons…do you know how far off the reservation you've gone, far from normal, from human…"

Dean: "The way she tricked you into using your powers, slippery slope bro; just wait and see, cos it's gonna get darker and darker and God knows where it ends."

Dean: "Emotions aren't getting in the way here. You know, nice dude, but he's got something evil inside of him; something in his blood. Maybe you can relate."

Sam and Dean's Take on the Urban Legend/Lore

A creature that starts out being human, changing into a cannibal. Transforms when they can't stop the hunger for human flesh. Once they take a bite, they stay that way forever. It runs in the family. The only way they can be killed is by being burnt alive. Sam also finds that people can have the gene but they don't turn because they fight it and only eat raw meat.

Actual Legend

*Rugaru (*also *Roux-Ga-Roux* or *Rougarou*). A creature of legend close to the Laurentian French community. A cross between the Native American Wendigo (considered a cannibal) and the European werewolf. The name itself, *Rugaru* is thought to be a play on the French name for werewolf, i.e. *loup-garou*.

The legend has associations with the swamps of the US, more specifically, New Orleans; where it is known as *swamp ape*. Legend has it, if one sees a Rugaru, then you'll become one too and will roam the swamps as this monster. See the short story by Algernon Blackwood where the fictional legend held that when someone sees a Wendigo they will become a Wendigo too.

If spelt *Rugaroo*, then the creature is like a wolf. Believed to hunt Catholics who do not stick to Lent. Similar to the Quebec story of the loop-garou. To become a werewolf a person has to have not obeyed the rules of lent for seven years.

If spelt *Rougarou* then this forms part of Cajun legend about a werewolf who sucks blood; being formed by witches. Has a human body and the head of a wolf. One legend tells of the rougarou being under such a spell for one hundred and one days. This curse is passed from person to person everytime it sheds human blood. During the day, the rougarou is human.

Music

Phillips Theme by Hound Dog Taylor and the Housebreakers.

4.5 Monster Movie

Written By Ben Edlund. Directed By Robert Singer
Original US Airdate 16 October 2008

Guest Stars: Todd Stashwick (Dracula). Melinda S Ward (Jamie). Holly Dignard (Lucy).

Pennsylvannia

Sam and Dean pose as FBI agents to investigate reports of a vampire on the loose, committing murders.

Notes

The opening credits are like an old movie. When the lightning flashes on the 'Welcome to Pennsylvania' sign, it changes to read Transylvania. This episode was filmed entirely in black and white as an attribute to the old horror movies from the 1930's and '40's (and is still regarded as some of the best and better than their modern counterparts.)

Sam is more in the mood to save the world whereas Dean is glad of a break and back to a good old fashioned case, which he calls, "black and white". So were we, *Supernatural* back to its monster of the week', back to its best, when there's little or no mention of the story arc, as that's what the show does best most of the time; the stand-alone episodes, even if they do revert back to stories, plots, events already covered – such as the shapeshifter. It's good to have a break from the mythology arc.

They're back in suits again, for the first time this season. Since when did Sam watch movies, this hasn't been mentioned before; he did most of the reading etc. Dean was the movie/TV buff! Sam actually eats in this episode! Not once but twice, though it's more than a mouthful.

Sam's line of, "definitely the last thing Marissa Wright needed," sounded like something Stella or Mac would say in *CSI:NY*, seeing as they're always quipping about dead bodies?

So Dean's a rebel with a badge is he – well, he don't need no badge! chicks would be called wenches at Oktoberfest.

Sam notices the tissue with lipstick, picks it up, but doesn't put too much emphasis on it. Dean believes he's returned from hell, a fully fledged virgin (ahem!)

The sky is now clear so the full moon' is visible, whereas in the beginning, the moon was obscured by the clouds as it was raining and not, as some people have called it, a crescent moon and wonder how it become full the next night. It was full to begin with.

Dean getting a headache – but he can't he was meant to be meeting Jamie, this is no time for headaches!

Turning into a bat would be cool, just like Dean's beer moustache! How come for someone like Dean knows all the movies around and vampire lore, as well as Dracula and he hasn't heard of Mina and Harker. Has he not seen *Dracula*? Niggle, niggle, writers! Dracula made his getaway on a scooter! So much for the bat.

Dean pulls off his ear, like the scene from *Carry On Screaming* (British comedy where one of the hairy creatures loses his ear.)

Dean refers to the *X Files* as a show and what they do as real. When it's not, not in real life anyway. See my discussion in several episodes about this. Was expecting Dean to call Sam Scully again when Jamie said that, but thankfully it didn't happen – that'd be too much repetition.

Dean telling her there are monsters and what Sam and Dean really do, but he doesn't tell her Sam is his brother. This is what Sam said to Madison in **2.17** when he also told her about monsters being real and she happened to be one too. Again talking of their job being thankless and never paid for doing it. Jamie didn't freak out on Dean (like Cassie in **1.13**) when he told her what he does and not just because Jamie came face to face with a Dracula either. Not to mention; she was the one to pull the trigger without having second thoughts.

Dean is on a mission from God.

Why didn't Sam just call Dean when he found out Ed wasn't Dracula, well, then we wouldn't see Dean in Lederhosen! Sam calls him Hansel, who appears to be the only German/European character that appears in everything. Sam breaking in and then breaking down the fake door, oh and Sam was called Van Helsing, he was knocked out a bit quickly too wasn't he. Oh and the obligatory violin music accompanying the sob story/death at the end.

Sam saying he likes Jamie is what Dean said about Sarah in **1.19** and Sam said about Cassie in **1.13**.

Obviously Dean would want to appear in a raunchy movie. No episode would be complete without the obligatory reference to such.

When shapeshifters are mentioned in any episode of *Supernatural* (all the season had one, except season 3) the writers have to do a re-hash of everything that's been said about them before , which is fine for people or viewers who are new to the show - but for the rest – it's a bit tedious.) Not to mention they all have such low self-esteems of themselves and draw other people into their lives as though they're meant to feel sorry for them. They also all consider themselves different and freaks. Except for the one in **2.12** since no one spoke to him, but he was killer too, like the one in **1.6** and this one.

Far from being a letdown where Dean talks about his 'past', it was more of a chore for him since he doesn't talk about this to anyone. Also it was a kind of connection to the shapeshifter and his own woes! Well, his speech about being a freak, no one liking him and turning to monsters to instill fear in people and resorting to murder. Whereas Dean fights monsters (including his own inner demons and monsters) whilst keeping or attempting to keep Sam in check and fighting on the side of God now, building up to his revelation of what happened in hell. It was more of a commentary on the two's differing lives: one human, one shapeshifter. This one didn't read anyone's minds, suppose they have to be in the victim or shift into them to do this.

Agents Angus and Young, Angus Young was the co-founder of AC/DC. The Goethe Theatre where Ed worked, was named for German writer Johann Wolfgang Von Goethe who wrote *Faust*. Ann Rice, author of vampire books, such as *Interview With the Vampire*. *Dracula Meets Wolfman* was not an original movie (is a comic), but *Frankenstein Meets the Wolfman* (1943) with Bela Lugosi and Lon Chaney Jr is a movie.

Dean mentions 'monster mashing' as in the song, *Monster Mash* by Bobby 'Boris' Pickett (1960's).

Creature from the Black Lagoon (1954) starred Julie Adams and Richard Carlson.

Dean: "Dude will not abide" was from the *Big Lebowski* with Jeff Bridges, the title character was known as 'The Dude' and his phrase of 'the Dude abides' was to show he was in agreement.

Dracula says, "Beauty killed the beast," was the final lines of the *King Kong* movies said by Carl Denham in the 1933 original and 2005 re-make.

Todd Stashwick has guested in episodes of *Dark Angel, The Guardian* and *The Mentalist*.

Quotes

Sam: "Pretty sure women today don't react to the whole wench thing."

Dean: "Hey bar wench where's that beer?"

Dean: "Look at me – came back without scars, bullet wounds…which leads me to conclude sadly, that my virginity is intact. I have been re-hymenated."

Sam and Dean's Take on the Urban Legend/Lore

Dean says werewolves don't grow hair, it's a myth.

Actual Legend

In the form of a human, (werewolves) characteristically, have 'bushy' eyebrows, which extend over the nose bridge, with red nails, dry eyes and mouth and have rough, hairy skin.

Film/TV References

Dracula Meets the Wolfman, Raiders of the Lost Ark: The Crystal Skull, Creature from the Black Lagoon, Dracula, Frankenstein, King Kong, X-Files. Porkies 2.

X Files Connection

In the season 5 episode **Postmodern** Prometheus, Mulder and Scully go after a modern-day Frankenstein who exactly resembles a comic book character, known as *The Great Mutato*. Mulder meets a man who says the monster is his son. He's a scientist experimenting in genetic mutations. Mulder and Scully wonder who the real monsters are in the town as the townsfolk are overrun by mass hysteria.

See here, as Dracula/shapeshifter brought this question up too – in wanting to become a monster as everyone called him one, he looked to 'movie' monsters to enable him to fulfill this role in reality. This shapeshifter became a monster, a killer, only after his father beat him and others saw him as a freak. A destiny different to Sam, but in a way, not unlike his too. Sam sees himself as a freak because of the demon blood in him but he hasn't turned to killing yet (aside from hunting – but he only kills other monsters and demons). Dean referred to himself as being a freak also (**1.6**): "I'm right up there with you." But Sam's freak is much more scarier – as only someone he says, with this impure demon blood in him, can comprehend what he's going through: never being normal!

Something not made easy by Sam's run in with Meg's 'ghost' in **4.2** when she confronts him about sleeping with Ruby: "You don't send her back to hell-you're a monster." But this has little effect on Sam. Not until **4.4** when he seriously tries to justify to Dean why he does what he does, i.e. uses his psychic powers to kill demons (send them straight to hell).

Don't know about you but I got a slight sense of "the boy doth protest too much". Who was he trying to convince – Dean – or himself that what he's doing is for the greater good. As in **2.11** when he tells Dean the more people he saves the more chance he has of remaining good. Conversely, here the more demons he sends to hell using his powers, the more his powers can be seen as good and working on the side of good. Oh another question, was that really Meg "possessing Meg", could've been a demon or Lilith underneath all that? Perhaps she felt brave enough to confront Sam as someone else. Nah don't think so, she wouldn't tell Dean so much about Meg, she'd torment him some more! Sorry this was put here in the X *Files* bit, since it kind of slotted in here with the monster aspect.

Music

Toccata and Fugue in D Minor by JS Bach.

Ooh Bloops

When Dean says, "Pulled it off during a fight," when he shows the ribbon medal to Sam, it appears his lips aren't moving, but it's a bit too dark to tell for sure and it looks as if the line was added later.

Locations

Fantasy Gardens.

4.6 Yellow Fever

Written By Daniel Loflin & Andrew Dab. Directed By Phil Sgriccia
Original US Airdate 23 October 2008

Guest Stars: Siena McCormick (Lilith). Jack Conley (Sheriff). Stephen Duvall (Jack)

Rock Ridge, Colorado

Dean is chased by a dog, which turns out to be a Yorkie.

43 Hours Earlier

Sam and Bobby need to find a cure for Dean before he succumbs to scary 'ghost sickness.'

Notes

The part where Dean runs from the dog in the opening is merely a small teaser on what was to follow in the rest of the episode. Funnily, Dean knows what rib cutters look like – not that he's had occasion to use them, but because he's been in plenty of morgues. He hasn't been through any autopsies though; and just when he's about to pass out or puke, he's handed a heart! (Coincidentally it's always Dean's heart in major trouble, well either his heart or his soul!) Whilst Sam gets sprayed with "spleen juice." Ironically Sam's had blood on his face before (!) and his mouth: demon blood that is.

The medical examiner attributes the bruises on the victim's arms to being scraped across the floor as what usually happens to some dead bodies; or heart attack victims. He wasn't very thorough at his job. Even when Sam specifically pointed the injuries out to him so he could examine them in more detail – then maybe he might have found some woodchips in his bruises. (*CSI* wouldn't have him on the case!).

Dean acting – rather laughing - like a child when he mentions 'gamecocks'! Oh Dean, it's just what teens do when someone says a word they equate with being rude. (Like when we had a form to fill out in school, especially, where the question would ask to state sex, someone in class always managed a chuckle. Only these days, 'gender' has been substituted for sex.) Or as one of my friends used to write for sex': three times a week! I digress.

Dean's comment of Frank having a "big heart". Again ironically this is what the episode is about – being scared to death, literally. Big heart – scare easy! Poor Deano, he's always in the thick of it. Hey, stop picking on Dean; he's no 'dick'! All he ever does is try to help people and he does, besides if he was a 'dick' he'd never have been saved from hell! You can tell Dean's been infected as soon as he fears the wild animals – not to mention those teens by his car. He's not afraid of anything really (except dying and going to hell – season 3.) As for running from those teens, he told Ben to stand up for himself in **3.2**, so he'd hardly be afraid of them now, if he was normal Dean.

An episode like **3.11** when Dean had everything thrown at him, i.e. all sorts of ends he met: being shot, axed; even mauled by a puny dog! So it's understandable why he'd be afraid of such a dog here – even if he wasn't suffering with 'ghost sickness'. Hey the dog was a bitch too, with a pink bow! Since here, it's the pets, teens, speed limit, hotel room on the fourth floor; (again cf **3.11** he was shot) not turn onto incoming traffic; cat; jail. Dean was a prankster but you wouldn't really have seen him as a bully, and not necessarily a horrible teen. (See **4.13**.) How can people fear Pez dispensers, everyone loves those.

Another corny (excuse pun) name for a softball team: 'Cornjerkers.' (Probably thought here – since, the amount of times 'dick' was mentioned, they'd have come up with something along the lines of 'Corn dickers', or dickie birds, or something similar. Sam doesn't not exactly say Dean is not a 'dick', he actually says, "It's not just that..." see he doesn't really deny it!

As for scaring people as Sam says – that's not actually what they do – not the nature of the beast! They save people and only scare someone if they mention, not so much what they do; but what's after them – which isn't that often and only if they tell the person what's in store for them. Sometimes they're not scared at all. (For example, Jamie in the last episode (**4.5**). Didn't like how this was written since what they chase is what does all the scaring; not Sam and Dean per se. Though these days can't be too sure of Sam! (Ha!) He'd scare with his powers, but not lil' ol' harmless Dean!

As the words jump out the page at Dean, they sound like something Sam would say to him – in evil mode – like he did to Jo in **2.14** when he was possessed. Or what the crossroads demons would say to him as well.

Dean screaming like a girl when the cat jumped out of the locker was funny. One of the best moments in this episode. Who put the cat in the locker anyway? Obviously it had to be Luther since the same cat was the kitten in the flashback when his brother spoke about him. Dean drinks for Dutch courage, see **2.18** when he just drank and everyone practically had him pegged as a worthless drunk.

Sam missing an important clue when the deputy told him the sheriff was off sick, he should've fathomed something was up, since everyone was dying from the sickness. As he was the sheriff he would've done plenty to bully people and flout the law.

As soon as Dean mentions using the fake badges and ending up in jail, predictably they had to be closely inspected. Dean being scared obviously made him talkative, in **2.5** Andy made him do all the talking too.

Jessie seems to be a common name in the show. First there was Jessica, (Jess), then 'Jesse' tattoo on Pamela's back in **4.1** and now Frank's wife is called Jesse too. Also Luther was the name of the vampire in **1.20**.

Sam realizes what's really happening and Dean calls it a day and quits hunting, because what they do is crazy and normal people would just run, but they actually stay and fight. Or in a way, he's saying he's giving all this up too and doesn't want to fight to survive now. So a little pointless to be listening to *Eye of the Tiger* then if he was just going to give up, since that song's meant to inspire and encourage. Not the opposite! Then in a moment of further despair, rather fear, he describes himself in a nutshell: i.e. he listens to the same music, drives too fast and is stuck with Sam eight hours in the car, which is made worse by Sam's gaseous burritos! That's strange, because Sam hardly eats, even in the scenes with the food around!

The clock's ticking for Dean again in this episode, just as it was all through season 3 – only here he's got less time and he gets saved in the end!

Dean sees Sam as evil once more (in **3.16** he saw Sam with black eyes) here he's graduated onto more powerful yellow eyes, since Dean discovered he's got demon blood. Another teaser of sorts, since this is probably the only time we'll get to see Sam evil with yellow eyes too!

Sam saying he's going to become this – whereas Dean in **3.10** saw himself as a demon too, well demonic Dean was said he was going to become dark. But Dean denied it; he wouldn't accept such a fate for himself. Here Sam says he wants to become evil and uses his powers on Dean. Obviously here, it's Dean's hallucination, but it's what everyone's expecting from Sam – what we're hoping, yes some of us are waiting for Sam to turn evil.

Sam telling Dean he wants him to return to hell because he's been a pain in his ass, similar to what I said in **4.1** that when Sam saw Dean, he had this less than exuberant look of joy on his face! But I have to say Sam looked good with yellow eyes.

Also the point demon Dean made in **3.10** about Dean becoming evil and Ruby saying in **3.9** that it'd take centuries, practically a long time for Dean to become demonic, to lose his humanity. Then Lilith turns up telling him four months mean forty years, so in this time, he had a chance to become a demon, is relevant since we'll find out what he did in hell soon. That he did begin to lose his humanity because of what he was asked to do, just to stay "alive" and not be tortured himself.

This is what Dean keeps from Sam: what happened now and also that he saw Sam with yellow eyes when he was infected. Another secret on his part – which is good – he never told Sam he saw him with black eyes too in **3.16** just before the hell hounds struck. Looking at the clock, just as in **3.16** when the ominous clock struck midnight and Dean was no more; any wonder he didn't want to listen to its constant ticking.

Oh so Dean got yellow fever as he's a 'dick' for also keeping that secret about hell, what about Sam's secret with Ruby since only the demon fraternity know about that and obviously the angels.

Why didn't Sam use the EMF now to locate Luther since Dean wasn't around and it would've worked, would've saved a lot of time that way, so Dean wouldn't have to 'see' Lilith again and she didn't have to appear as a teaser to make us wonder what exactly Dean got up to in hell. She also tells us that Dean knows exactly what he did do in hell, whereas he told Sam in **4.1** he doesn't recall anything. Ooh another secret Dean! Probably another reason why Dean was also infected with the 'ghost sickness': i.e. for what he did in hell.

All this fighting other monsters and demons, when time's a ticking in another way; more seals being broken bringing the Apocalypse even closer.

Also when Dean saw Sam's eyes turn yellow at the end, he wasn't hallucinating now, or more rather imagining Sam like that: what's been hinted at, but perhaps won't happen and if it does I'll have to come back and edit this episode! The same as in **3.16** as I've just said when he saw

Sam as a demon. Makes you think what Sam's reaction would've been if Dean actually told him he's seen him in that way – when Sam finally came clean and told Dean he sees himself as unclean with demon blood in his veins, then Sam would say Dean sees him in that way too, so what's the point of fighting for good and fighting his destiny, if Dean's given up on him too, as he's also not using his powers now and he may as well be. So what if he could have used his powers on Luther, no one was looking, or wouldn't they have worked on him.

They actually come across someone who equates their name with a group. Sam and Dean in suits again this season.

Also nice to see Sam play the 'big' brother for a change, telling Dean to calm down and not to pick at his scratches. Dean spent all of season 3 trying to deny his fate, keep a brave face and refuse to share his feelings. When deep down he was terrified of what would happen to him and that he'd get to hell. In contrast here, those fears just manifest themselves and boil over so quickly and freely.

Tyler and Perry: Steven Tyler and Joe Perry from Aerosmith.

Dean's out-take at the end when he lip syncs, then proceeds to scratch his arm in the process, almost as if what he was doing was only a hallucination too, ha!

Another episode where *Supernatural* can combine the fun with the serious, since Dean being afraid was hilarious, the opposite to who he really is; along with serious moments interspersed with Sam as evil and Lilith reminding Dean of what he's done and how evil Dean can be too. So it's not just Sam actually doing terrible things in the future; compared to Dean who's already done such things in his past – even if he was dead and was coerced into doing them. Was Dean left with any other choice and as I said before, who knows what decision any one of us would make when faced with such a dilemma. But you've got to believe, at least Dean has to, that he made the right choice under such circumstances; or who can tell how he might have ended up.

Also remember he thought he'd be in hell forever, so maybe it was just easier to do what they wanted: a case of not being able to beat them, so he had to join them. Dean finally turns to the Bible here, voluntarily, or more particularly, it could be said, out of fright.

The title **Yellow Fever** is a disease, but yellow as a colour is also associated with cowardice, so it's literally 'yellow sickness'. Put another way, yellow fever can refer to yellow Eyes and what Sam's infected with. So Sam may not be a 'dick' for the purposes of this episode, but he's got a demon affliction instead.

Dean mentions "outbreak monkey" from the film *Outbreak* (1995), where the monkey was responsible for spreading the disease.

Rock Ridge Colorado was the fictional setting for the film *Blazing Saddles*.

It was Jim Beaver's idea to have Bobby speak Japanese since he just happens to be fluent in it.

The in-joke began when Jared wanted to pull one of his pranks on Jensen (hey they said they don't "prank" each other). When Jensen was air-drumming this in the episode, Jared had to bang on the roof of the car, Jensen's cue to stop, but Jared told everyone to keep rolling the cameras and he wouldn't give this cue to Jensen, to see what Jensen would do. Thus Jensen did the entire mime, or lip synch to the song and air guitar on his leg! Even though it was filmed from different angles, it's because Jared already told them to continue filming, and as we know, the show films using multiple camera angles.

In an interview, Jensen said his actions were spontaneous and he missed Jared's cue on purpose. Phil Sgriccia does the gag reel and he wanted something where people would respond. It was fun to do and even funnier on tape. Jared says some directors would just 'cut' on something that long, but Phil just rolled with it. Jensen said it was fun since the crew, being part of the family would have something fun to break the ice and have a good time. So they clown around as they film for such long hours.

Jensen likes comedy more than drama, to see the lighter side and have amusement between characters and the brothers on the show, instead of being one single [serious] note.

On the part where Jensen screamed at the cat, Jared comments it was fun to let the cameras roll. Jensen says his reaction was longer, Phil told him to scream as long as he wanted.

That sounded like Jared laughing in the background, Jensen's 'mime' was perfect so he must love this song and he knows it so well! (See **3.16** when Sam says to Dean, "I think you totally should've been jamming to *Eye of the Tiger* back there." (So perhaps Jared thought this an opportune moment to set up the prank for Jensen!)

Quotes

Dean: "Okay then, you're a dick too."
Sam: "Apparently I'm not."

Sam: "We've been ignoring the biggest clue we have."
Dean: "I don't wanna be a clue!"

Dean: "Those are real. Obviously I mean, who would pretend to be an FBI agent – that's just nutty."

Sam: "So what did you see in the end, I mean seriously?"
Dean: "..just the usual stuff Sammy. Nothing I couldn't handle."

Sam and Dean's Take on the Urban Legend/Lore

Ghost sickness, where as Sam explains certain cultures believe the dead can infect the living with a disease, so that's why bodies are no longer displayed in the house. With ghost sickness, you get scared, really scared and then the heart stops. It's not caught from a ghost but from person to person, and you have to be a 'dick'!

Bobby mentions the Buru Buru: born of fear. It is fear and you have to kill it with fear, or as Sam puts it, scare the ghost to death.

Actual Legend

Buruburu means 'the sound of shivering' and is a ghost from Japanese folklore. This ghost supposedly lurks in cemeteries and forests as an old person. At times, it possesses only one eye. Legend has it fixing onto a person's spine and causing them to feel a chill running down their spine. Worst case scenario, it leads to death.

Film/TV References

Wizard of OZ, Outbreak.

Music

Eye of the Tiger by Survivor

Ooh Bloops

The ME didn't record the autopsy but spoke to Sam and Dean about his findings and even handed them body parts, well Dean got the heart and Sam got spattered with blood.

Locations

Elgin Avenue, Port Coquitlam. Riverview Hospital – Peaceful Pines.

461

4.7 It's the Great Pumpkin, Sam Winchester

Written By Julie Siege. Directed By Charles Beeson
Original US Airdate 30 October 2009

Guest Stars: Misha Collins (Castiel). Robert Wisdom (Uriel) Don McManus (Don Harding) Ashley Benson (Tracy).

One Day Before Hallowe'en

A man eats candy and tries to remove a razor blade from his mouth. He is found dead.

Hallowe'en

Dean eats candy, whilst waiting to find the witch who intends to summon Samhain. Sam and Dean have to prevent this from happening as it constitutes one of the 66 seals being broken.

One Day After Hallowe'en

Uriel confronts Sam and threatens him in order to restrain him from his using his powers anymore. Castiel tells Dean his secret.

Notes

Dean was meant to be tested as a potential leader and see what decisions he'd make like 'saving people' to quote him from **1.2**, because that's what they do anyway, so naturally he'd speak up for the entire town now too just as he's always done. He also did this in **3.12** when he even went against Sam wanting to kill the hundreds to save the thousands and sacrifice Nancy in the process.

Dean being tested can be seen as another step on the road to redemption for him, for what he did in hell. Just like the secret he kept from Sam (and the rest of us) in most of season 2 about what Dad told him concerning Sam. This is how Dean's secret is being kept again until the final reveal and quite frankly I have to say again, it wasn't much of a revelation. He's only human - he'd have done anything to survive and to not endure the hell which wasn't really of his own making. Who knows what anyone would do in such a situation. He was having his own humanity being stripped away piece by piece, little by little. Must be a demonstration or explanation of how hell does this once you're damned.

Sam is scared of clowns and Dean doesn't like leprechauns and that's all that was said, Sam didn't draw the point out like Dean did in **2.2**.

This episode reminded me of **2.9** when Azazel infected the town with the demon virus just to test Sam's immunity to it. As well as his potential as the leader of his demon army.

Again all this smacks of building up as a showdown between Sam and Dean, eventually. Poor Sammy, having his faith and his patience tested from all corners; believing angels were merciful and then having his entire praying amount to nothing. With Dean attempting to reassure him that not everything or everyone in heaven is bad. Hoping Sam will not take this as a sign to change. That he should keep praying. Similar to **2.13** when Sam had his faith shaken and Dean said he shouldn't give up; even he was ready to believe in God back then from what he witnessed at the end of the episode.

Why was Sam so surprised when he saw what the angels were like, when he said in **2.13** that they weren't your average Hallmark variety: that they were fierce? So why then did he think they'd be merciful. Besides each angel has his duty, his place in the order of things. Then *Supernatural* also seemed to forget Mom believed – fully and unconditionally; otherwise she wouldn't have told Dean angels watch over them. Shame this couldn't have had more relevance for them, as if Mom was being literal and this was really one of the reasons why Dean was pulled from hell, would give Mom far more a meaning of belonging in their lives, than she already does, just to add that little twist in the story. That she actually stood for something a little more than just hunting.

As for the angels, Sam has to have an encounter with the belligerent Uriel – specialist in smiting – verging on blasphemy. It wasn't verging on; it was blasphemy when he referred to humans as "plumbing on two legs" and calling them "mud monkeys". This is exactly what Lucifer did when he disobeyed God by refusing to bow down before Adam because he was made of clay and Lucifer was made from fire. So his comment about not being a buddy of Lucifer was ironic (and loaded, see later.)

Since when can angels question God's will in such a way and behave in such a manner and then expect to command respect by making humans shudder in their boots. Uriel telling Sam he'll be stopped if he uses his powers once more is nothing more than goading him into doing just that. Also when Castiel tells Dean his secret about having doubts, not knowing what's right anymore, isn't something an angel is meant to think about, yet alone confess to others and being so descriptive about it too. He could've just said Dean's way of thinking and standing up is the right thing to do, since it is and nothing more. When he asks Dean about not questioning Dad's orders; Dean doesn't reply. Probably shocked to learn they know everything about him and yet waited so long to make an appearance, now that the Apocalypse is nigh.

Supernatural once again resorting to the use of 'dick' – twice. Get a grip and find another, less crude word. Sam picked the wrong angel to call it and then telling Dean he was right in calling them that.

Sam's line of everyday being Hallowe'en to them, hence all those monsters, demons and ghouls in the *THEN* segment. Since all of them shows how people dress and wear scary make-up and masks for Hallowe'en, only, what they hunt are real and their fancy dress is akin to evil spirits they encounter. Sam's line was similar to saying all they do is scare people in **4.6** – which is not all they do. They have an impact on people and are their watchers, like being their guardians.

Dean reminds us of his hatred of witches. Yeah, the one time Ruby could've helped them find a fellow witch; she disappears as the angels were in town! Not that they needed her help as they worked it out for themselves which is good.

Sam's reference of 'jail bait' to Dean is what Dean said to him in **3.15** when Sam helped the girl instead of hanging around waiting with Dean for Dad's phonecall. Sam saying everything they fight will all be in one place is like fighting when the Apocalypse happens.

Dean wanting to come back as a cheerleader – was funny – did he actually want to be with one (!) obviously, or be one himself – yeah, a girl! Oh which reminds me, all the references to Sam being a girl have suddenly vanished, now we get the 'dicks' instead!!

Me thinks Uriel believes Sam has far greater powers than him, and sees him as a greater threat to himself, more than even they possess and so it's easier to just stop Sam by killing him altogether.

Naturally, or unnaturally, the masks would remind Dean of hell, not just hell in general and the images he's seen on the computer whilst researching, but it happened to be the masks and then Sam comes in with his loaded question asking what Dean is talking about and Dean doesn't tell him. Bad timing and too early for us to know anything either. If I'm not mistaken, that scene was similar to the one in **4.4** in the car, when Dean mentions Mom as a hunter and Sam blurts out he was given demon blood. Dean didn't make the same mistake Sam did and tell him.

Also has it occurred to anyone that Dean didn't tell anyone of his time in hell because he's ashamed and because he's carrying around enormous guilt for what he had to do. That no one would understand unless they've been there and done the same thing; gone through it and come out of it unscathed at the other end. Thankfully he still has his humanity intact and still strives to do the right thing and forty years is a long time.

The same argument Sam made to Dean in **4.4** about having to suffer through having his powers alone, that he can't do anything about it or change anything and he's a freak; feels dirty because of that demon blood. In the same way, Dean has to go through this alone – if Dean was really so bad and enjoying what he did in hell, he'd never have been saved and brought back and even if it was for the purposes of the bigger picture.

As for the bigger picture, - that's another phrase Castiel also alludes to. He said something similar in **4.2** about there being other battles and being needed in other places, thus not everything revolves around Dean – well, apparently it does!

Sam's comments about being a teen, reference to **4.13** when they return to their former high school. Dean should've expected something bad from Astrokid – he got no candy and that look he gave Dean!

Another good scene with Castiel's first words to Sam being about the boy with demon blood, (like that was Sam's fault.) before being reluctant to shake his hand as if Sam would taint him or something worse. Also it sounded as though it was meant to send a shudder down Sam's spine and make sure he doesn't use his powers anymore. If Dean hadn't seen this himself in **4.2** , then Sam telling him in **4.4**, even if it was by accident, then don't think Dean would've believed what he was hearing right now. Which for the purposes of the arc, explains part of the purpose of episode **4.2**.

Does anyone think they believe Sam is using his powers more and more will send him over to the dark side – being completely consumed by them. Sam doesn't believe it; he wants to make something good out of the bad and believes he is doing that.

Strange the angels chose to reveal themselves to Sam on Hallowe'en of all days. If they knew about Samhain being set free as part of one of the seals being broken; then why didn't they appear to Dean earlier than on the actual day.

Uriel reveal in the killing of mud monkeys – I mean – humans, akin to the Angel of Death, but the Angel of Death removes souls rather than actually doing any killing. They're trying their best to question his goodness and if he turns, part of it will be their fault with their actions; especially Uriel.

Dean was right when he said the angels were compensating for something (so he can now read angels too) and that's needing him. Did they really need to test him when they've seen and know everything Dean's done in his life and what he stands for. How many times does he have to say if he "had to do it all again – he wouldn't change a single thing," oops, I've paraphrased one of Kylie Minogue's earlier songs (I wouldn't Change a thing.)

Why did Tracey's powers work on Sam?

When Castiel says there was no reason to save Dean and he has potential, to me it sounded as if he was saying Dean has potential to become an angel – eventually or something along those lines…maybe.

Why couldn't Sam have just used his powers on Tracey before she completed the summoning ritual? – well other than another seal being broken for the purposes of this episode. He over powered Samhain, she wouldn't have been any match for him. Also it seems strange the angels were not perturbed by another seal being broken since this was meant to be a test for Dean only and nothing more.

Yet in **4.2** Castiel was really angry that the seal then had been broken allowing Lucifer a further step nearer to being released, and after losing his brothers in battle. Yet here it's regarded as ancillary and merely trivial. What about what Sam and Dean used to say to each other about not being able to save everyone, which comes to mind here, but as long as you try is what counts.

Sam saying he gave the idea a shot as in **1.13** when he told Dean to drive up to the church on hallowed ground so the truck would vanish, then afterwards told him he wasn't sure if his plan would actually work or not.

The knife per se, is not enough as you have to be up close and personal to use it. Therefore need to have something else and Sam's powers have to be it. The amount of effort and what it took out of Sam to do the killing using his powers. Why didn't Dean just pick up the knife and stab Samhain in the back with it, he could see how Sam was struggling, but he could only watch, at least then, Sam wouldn't be using his powers for so long.

Uriel's comment about Sam only being alive because he's useful, how is he such, since he can't use his powers or because he can look after Dean and protect him. Sounds like Sam is to be some last final sacrifice or something. Also Sam must be useful as Dean would just about do anything for him (including dying for him) and so Sam has to be around otherwise Dean will refuse to do his part. Unless he means

466

useful for Uriel and his ulterior motive. Also notice how Uriel departs using his wings and the sound from them to intimidate, the way he flapped closer to Sam; whereas Castiel just disappears quietly. Didn't notice Dean being on a high-horse, he was just doing what he always does – and another question what took them so long to save Dean?

The decisions Dean has to make – of course, one will involve Sam and something in the order of taking sides. Once again the reference by Castiel to Dean knowing what hell is like and what happens there. This weight on Dean's shoulders is something he should be able to carry since he's dealt with so much, losing so much, living with the idea of death for as long as he can remember and then finally having to embrace it, even if it wasn't in the way he expected it should be. Unless it comes to Sam, that's one situation he doesn't want to deal with, but Sam isn't a burden to him.

Dean was under a test to see his reaction. In an all out war would Dean therefore have his own army to command in the upcoming battle. Would this have meant going up against Sam who was meant to be the demon army leader.

Let's see Castiel secret being revealed at some point further down in episodes. Castiel is, and all the other angels are, unequivocally supposed to carry out God's will. Castiel saying he doesn't know what is right and wrong. Does he also profess to not knowing what evil is now too.

Every now and then something comes along which gives you added joy, apart from *Supernatural* of course. *Popstar.com* wanted questions from fans and viewers to ask Misha in an interview and I was lucky enough to have one of mine asked and answered by him.

Q Why do you think Castiel has so many doubts and why do you think he revealed them to Dean?

A Misha:"Dean is Castiel's closest human confidant aand human beings wrestle with doubt all the time. Human beings are inherently conflicted and uncertain and angels aren't supposed to have doubt. They are supposed to have just pure conviction all the time and follow orders.

So I think that Castiel is going to doubt confession with Dean because I think Dean is someone who Castiel feels will understand doubt because of his exposure to Sam and Dean and I think he also has doubts because he has his orders that seem to go against his own moral compass. For example, he is given orders to smite an entire small town in order to kill a witch, however that doesn't resonate as conduct worthy of an angel."

That was insightful. It's great when stars of a show actually know what's happening in the show with the stories and their characters, rather then just coming in, saying their lines and going away. *Supernatural* is a show which thankfully has that in its regular cast, guest cast and crew!

Now we know why Ruby steered clear of the angels, smite a witch, should've smited her and saved everyone the trouble of having to put up with her!

Sam shows Dean a book in which the illustration is of Dante and Virgil in hell, conversing with the soul of the heretic Farinata Degli. From *Dante's Inferno Canto 10*. The illustration is by Gustave Dore (a reknown illustrator of Dante's *Divine Commedia*.)

Dean mentions Agent Geddy, Agent Lee, Geddy Lee is the lead singer of Rush. Also he introduces himself as Agent Seger as in Bob Seger of the Silver Bullet Band.

The title is a reference to *It's the Great Pumpkin, Charlie Brown*. Sam's allusion to the Pied Piper was from Grimms. Babe Ruth was the baseball player who had a far from perfect life.

The Tet Offensive was a military operation during the Vietnam War. *Betty Crocker* was the trade mark of *General Mills* in the US food industry.

Quotes

Dean: "Leprechauns – those little dudes are scary, small hands."
Sam: "Quit whining."

Dean: "No, I mean son of a bitch!"

Sam: "Bring back memories?"
Dean: "What do you mean?"
Sam: "Being a teenager, all that angst. What did you think I meant?"

Castiel: "And I you Sam. The boy with the demon blood. Glad to hear you've ceased your extra curricular activities." (Another school reference.)

Sam: "This is God and Heaven and this is what I've been praying to."

Sam and Dean's Take on the Urban Legend/Lore

Hexbag was filled with goldthread, a herb used by the Celts. Sam says three blood sacrifices have to be made, the last the day before the final harvest, i.e. Hallowe'en. The veil is thinnest between the living and the dead. Samhain was exorcised thousands of years ago, when people participated in blood orgies, demons. People hid behind masks, gave Samhain pumpkins to worship, and treats to appease him. The ritual is only performed 600 years. Once he is summoned, he can raise his own living dead: ghosts, zombies, leprechauns.. Hallowe'en lore states that Samhain will not notice anyone with a mask since he'll think it's part of his own dead company.

Actual Legend

The literal meaning of Samhain is *summer's end*. It is pronounced as *sow-in* or *sow-en*. (Couldn't someone have looked this up and have Sam say it in the correct way, he wasn't after all, saying his own name! With the advent of Christianity, Samhain was altered to *Hallowmas* or *All Saints' Day*. This was in commeration of the "souls of the blessed dead who had been canonized that year. So the night before became popularly known as *Hallowe'en, All Hallows Eve* or *Hollantide*. November 2nd is known as *All Soul's Day* and prayers are said for the souls of all those who were dead, and for those in purgatory, so they would enter heaven. (When in purgatory, a soul can go either way, so to speak: to heaven or to hell. So when in **4.1** Castiel says he's the one who rescued Dean from purgatory, Dean wasn't or couldn't have been in purgatory since he was sent straight to hell for his deal. He no longer was in possession of his soul.)
All Saints' Day is also believed to be when the souls walked the earth. Early Christian tradition dictated souls were released from Purgatory on *All Hallows Eve* for 48 hours.
To protect from any free roaming spirits, the Celts would offer then treats (hence the tradition of treats). Wearing costumes at Hallowe'en is believed to originate from the Celts disguising themselves at Samhain, so these evil spirits would see them as being fellow evil spirits. Samhain is a feast of life over death and for remembering the departed.

In Scotland, it is a widely held belief that a child born on October 31st (Samhain) had the gift of *an da sheallach : the two sights*; i.e.clairvoyance. Some believe Samhain was not the name of an ancient Celtic god of death and that Samhain is a reference to the holiday on November 1st, which occurs during the day part of Hallowe'en.

Like this Hallowe'en tradition: before midnight strikes sit before a mirror, lit by one candle or the moon. Ask a question, cut the apple into nine parts, eat eight without facing the mirror. Then throw the ninth piece over your shoulder. Look over the shoulder you threw the apple and you should see some sort of an image answering your question. For this you need to use your imagination to interpret whatever appears to you. Have to try this one, or not. It's a divination ritual. Oh and funny how Dean told Sam there are some bad apples out there, with it being Hallowe'en and apple bobbing.

Goldthread *(Coptis Trifola)* aka yellowroot, is a herb found in mossy woods in Canada, Maryland, Alaska and Minnesota. The plant looks similar to a strawberry plant. The root is the part which is used and is collected in Autumn.

In the first Book of Enoch, Uriel is the angel having dominion over thunder and terror. He has two characteristics: his eyes and his sharp mind, as well as his complete objective devotion and impersonal carrying out of God's will.

In the Apocalypse of St Peter, it was stated hell was not the exclusive place for demons and was controlled by some fearsome punishing angels. These angels were of wrath, vengeance and destruction. Uriel was their leader and was vehemently feared and dreaded.

The Apocalypse of St Peter also contains a description of how Uriel treated damned souls in hell, without mercy. Also as he was righteous, he was the angel God put into the Garden of Eden, to prevent entry into it. He was removed as an Archangel by the Christian church in 745 by Pope Zachary but was still honoured as St Uriel.

An interesting fact I discovered was that in one of the Dead Sea Scrolls entitled, *The Triumph of God* – where the *War of the Sons of Light and Sons of Darkness* is mentioned; Uriel is seen as one of these four leaders. Also in *The Triumph of God*, humans become warriors and are met with instructions telling them where to fight and which weapons to use. This was a bit familiar as the current plot of *Supernatural* about the Apocalypse and how Dean has been recruited to fight – and will probably be given instructions on who he has to fight, which will probably end up involving Sam too. Also the way Uriel has been created as a character in the show is very close to how he has been depicted in religion. He shows no mercy or pity and in *Supernatural* is rather self-righteous. In contrast to the show, Uriel was all in favour of obeying God, instead of making crass judgements about humans and their behaviour. Unless it was all an act.

In religion, Uriel is seen just as pitiless as any demon – so have to question why in *Supernatural* he has such contempt for Dean and what he did in hell. One answer would be since it is *Supernatural* and their own version of angels. Dean is tortured enough by his memories of what he did in hell without constant reminders of it.

X Files Connection

6.4 Sanguinarium, a nurse throws up needles before dying.

Music

Just As Through With You by Nine Days.

Ooh Bloops

Sam picks up goldthread when researching, when Dean gets back and talks about cheerleaders, Sam mentions the hex bag and he has the herb in his hand. In the next shot, he takes it from the bag, when he hasn't put it there. Well, he could just be taking more out of the bag.

Sam and Dean ask how many blades were discovered, his wife says 4, 2 on the floor, 1 in his throat and one in his stomach. When her husband is seen doing this, it's 3 he ejects, since one is heard falling to the floor. How is this a blooper since she says they found 4 altogether. Other than saying there were 3 on the floor, meaning there were 5 altogether.

When Sam and Dean leave the hotel the Impala is dirty and when they leave the house, it is miraculously (or not) clean.

4.8 Wishful Thinking

Written By Ben Edlund. Directed By Robert Singer
Original US Airdate 6 November 2008

Guest Stars: Ted Raimi (Wesley Mondale). Anita Brown (Hope). Nicole Leduc (Audrey). Barbara Kottmeier (Candace).

Concrete, Washington

Sam and Dean investigate when there's a series of sightings of a ghost in the women's showers. When they also chance upon a wishing well. Dean admits to Sam he does remember hell.

Notes

Take Sam's speech from **4.4** and turn it around for Dean to say in this episode. That he can only understand if you've been there. He can't explain it to him because he's the only one that went through it and it's something he'll never forget and will have to live with; exactly what Sam said. He's got powers, the blood, so he'll have to deal with it himself. So they've each got something the other one can't understand, or can he? It may not be the same thing – but they're similar – all connected to who they are and what they went through, demonic powers, demons in hell. Both will have to face this.

Supernatural's lesson in how not to talk about people whilst referring to them as 'dicks'. So Dean looks Sam straight in the eye and lies to him, which is what they've been doing a lot of late. First there were secrets; then some lies and still more secrets.

As soon as Dean hears naked women he's off, that's one way to get him to do something ASAP and can we really believe Dean hasn't been with a woman since he got out of hell, aside from Jamie in **4.4**. (And not mentioning Anna in **4.10**.)

Sam's reference to his book being called *Supernatural,* obviously and that he's collecting stories from around the world – which was originally Eric Kripke's idea, to have them be reporters covering supernatural events around the country, before that premise was changed to brothers. Just as well it was since being roving reporters has already been done – think *Nightstalker*. Sam would spot the couple in the corner, but then it was stereotypical in Sam wondering how such a nerdy looking guy with glasses snagged such a woman and Wes says the same thing to them in the car, about Sam and Dean having it easy – um – where it comes to chicks you have to agree with him, they can have their choice of any.

Those bear paw prints were too neat and perfect, especially the ones leading to the liquor store, to belong to a Bigfoot or a teddy bear, since when do teddy bears have paws that leave prints like that? Also when Sam found the piece of fur in the porn magazines section, the fur was too soft and cuddly to belong to that particular teddy, not to mention the fact teddy was black rather than brown. He wasn't shedding hair/fur.

Apt moments for Dean to pocket a bottle and have a copy of his favourite mag fall into his lap, so to speak. Yet another encounter with *BustyasianBeauties*. Dean's reference to David Duchovny who is a self-confessed sex addict and was recently in a clinic for this.

Why is Audrey talking to strangers – even if they are Sam and Dean and letting them in the house too! Steady on Sam: it's a giant teddy, not a demon, when he tells Dean he wants to burn it and shoot it too. First there was 'dick' disease in *Supernatural* and now Dean comes up with lollipop disease. What's next?

It was pointless Dean telling Sam he's not about to divulge what he wished for, since his wish comes walking through the door. Being Dean, he didn't wish for world peace (which is just as well, since it would've led to World War III!) but a sandwich, anything to satisfy his hunger. Which backfired on him, that was his own personal world war! With his stomach. Let's hope Jensen didn't have to retake too many scenes with the sandwich, having to eat it over and over.

Dean fumbling for the right badge (which he couldn't find in **4.12** when they were arrested.) Sam was right, for every wish granted, it just turns sour. A bit similar to the rabbit's foot in **3.2**. Thought they would've recalled that. Since the rabbit foot's was no longer in their possession and bad luck would follow.

Funny Sam should get the "deadly price tag" line though because he was the one who was struck by lightning and killed. Notice whenever something's meant to happen to Sam, involving his shoes, he always wears his trainers. Were they his lucky trainers because he had them on in **3.3** when he lost one in the drain.. (On another note, think someone up there's trying to tell him something, since he was the one who had that particular wish granted for him.) No Sam isn't that naïve –ish guy anymore after all he's been through now, he'll find it hard to live a normal life. Besides it's too late for normal anyway and he hasn't wanted to go their separate ways since season 2.

If only Sam and Dean could've ended it all with one wish: Lilith, the demons, the Apocalypse, but life is never that easy (and neither is death). Anyway, it wouldn't be Lilith's head on a platter; she has no corporeal body but inhabits all sorts of little girls! Yes what's with that, why does she only possess little girls?

Dean seems to come across children to help out lately and doesn't get anything for his troubles, no gratitude.

Teddy's message on the board. *Life is meaning less. Signed T. Bear.* Okay who pulled the trigger and shot teddy, Sam or Dean? (Joke) It looked like someone shot him from behind, rather than Teddy pulling the trigger. Teddy with a plaster at the back of his head.

First Sam suffered nightmares in season 1 when he saw Jessica and then when he had his visions. Now it's Dean's turn to suffer them, only in Dean's case they're more real and Dean is the last person you'd expect to just sit down and talk. Sam should know that by now – since he too got a serious case of clamming up in **4.4**. Be careful what you wish for has been said many times including in **2.18**. What Dean would wish for is his family and life to be perfect. But here you have him wishing for nothing more than a foot long Italian with jalapeños, a giant one at that, probably taking his cue from giant teddy.

Got the impression Dean wanted to work because he didn't want to face up to the guilt of what he did in hell and what he has to think about everyday, but drinking won't make it go away. The liquor store had no camera, even if it was a small town. Dean could've wished to forget the nightmares, but something bad would happen anyway, even before they found out about the wishing well and the coin. Sam said he couldn't trust it.

Again with the 'dick', a common occurrence. It has to be mentioned every week or it just wouldn't be *Supernatural*! So Dean looks Sam straight in the eyes and lies. Sam saying he's been down under as if Dean has been to Australia, since it's the name for Australia. (Well Jensen has been there, during the writers' strike and so has Jared.)

So the demons took a holiday. Just another routine episode and very slow to start. Not one of the best this season. Since wishes and how they don't come true, has been done many times on the show, not to mention the number of times, Sam and Dean have said the line of "be careful what you wish for".

Oddly enough Wes's dream girl had the name of Hope. Probably as in the saying, "hope springs eternal." i.e. people always want the best and wish for the best. There will always be hope, no matter how much adversity. The line is from Alexander Pope's 1732, *An Essay on Man*. Or if you really want to be picky, you might say Spring is associated more with water and not the season!

Dean mentioning when you get what you want you go crazy, like Michael Jackson and David Hasselhoff...

Dean running over the invisible boy was him getting his just desserts, even though it wasn't technically a hit and run, he couldn't see him in the road! Just what was he doing in the deep woods anyway?! Don't answer that.

"This house is clean," line is from *Poltergeist*. *Harry and the Hendersons* was a film about a Bigfoot living with a normal family and was made into a TV series too.

The line, "with great power comes great responsibility," is associated with superheroes but was actually said in the *Spiderman* comics by Spiderman's Uncle Ben.

"Kneel before Zod" is a reference from the *Superman* comics, said by Terence Stamp who played Zod in *Superman II* and was the voice of Jor El in *Smallville.*

George Neuman in the newspaper alludes to George Neuman, the set director on the show.

This episode was similar to the 1902 movie, *The Monkey's Paw.*

Quotes

Dean: "Damn right I wanted to save naked women."

Dean: "…he's a girl drink, drunk."

Sam: "Not what I'd wish for. It's too late to go back to our old lives Dean: " I'm not that guy anymore."

Dean: "What would Sammy wish for?"
Sam: "Lilith's head on a plate, bloody."

Sam and Dean's Take on the Urban Legend/ Lore

The coin is Babylonian. The legend serpent Tiamat, Babylonian god of primordial chaos. Priests into magic to sew seeds of chaos – whoever makes wish with coin, turns on the well and wishes get granted to everyone.

Actual Legend

Tiamat was a Babylonian goddess who is likened to the sea. She is often portrayed as a sea serpent or dragon and as the "embodiment of primordial chaos". The Baylonian Epic of Creation, known as the *Enuma elish*, where it's said she bares the first generation of gods and then wages war on them. *Water of Chaos.* Tiamat was defeated by the god Marduk who sliced her body in half. The lower part he made into the earth. The top half, the sky. Her water formed the clouds; and her tears were the source of the Rivers Euphrates and Tigris.

The connection between coins (fountains) and wishing wells and Tiamat, is water. She was the personification of water: the source of life and water is essential for life.

The concept of wishes being granted by wells, originated from the notion water was the home of the gods, or deities and water is viewed as a source of life. Celts and Germans thought wells and other places with water were sacred, as well as being associated with healing (such as baths and springs.) It was a common belief, if a wish was made at a well, it would come true in return for a gratuity (i.e throwing in a coin.) Coins were a gift for the wish being granted.

In Nordic myth, *mirmirs* well, aka, *the well of wisdom* had the power to grant wisdom in return for something close or important from the wisher. Odin gave his right eye and threw it in the well, in order to gain the wisdom of foreseeing the future.

Mirmir is the Nordic god of wisdom, whose well is located at *The World Tree*, i.e. *Yggdrasil*; which gets its water from the well. Disney's *Snow White and the Seven Dwarfs* had a wishing well.

Film/TV References

Poltergeist, Forrest Gump. Spiderman, Superman II, Harry and the Hendersons.

X Files Connection

Red Museum, where a boy who has been secretly tested with drugs, runs out of the woods in his underwear. Like the invisible boy here, who's naked.

Locations

Squamish – Town of Concrete, Washington. Dragon Terrace Chinese Restaurant. Rocky Point Park Pier.

4.9 I Know What You Did Last Summer

Written By Sera Gamble. Directed By Charles Beeson
Original US Airdate 13 November 2008.

Guest Stars: Genevieve Cortese (Ruby). Misha Collins (Castiel). Robert Wisdom (Uriel). Julie McNiven (Anna). Mark Ralston (Alaistair). Anna Williams (Ruby's first body). Drew Nelson (Crossroads demon.

Ruby tells Sam to rescue Anna who is being pursued by demons, as she's someone important.

Six Months Earlier

Sam attempts to make a deal by summoning a crossroads demon.

Six Months Earlier

Ruby returns in another body and saves Sam's life. Sam and Ruby get intimate.

Five Months Earlier

Ruby makes Sam realize Dean wouldn't want him to just throw his life away.

Five Months Earlier

Sam and Ruby walk into a trap as they attempt to kill Lilith. Sam uses his powers on a demon and sends him back to hell.

Notes

The opening of this episode felt like a recap with Anna summing up what was already said in **4.2** about the seals, Lucifer. As she was in a psychiatric ward, obviously her hearing voices was to indicate her schizophrenia rather than any angelic qualities. As Supernatural fans/viewers, we were meant to side with Anna, since we know this is what is about to happen or can happen, so she's not crazy, after all.

Sam and Dean in suits again. Anna saying the angels are fighting a losing battle because they need her back, since she's more powerful than Castiel and Uriel put together, at least we think so.

Never thought we'd see Sam take a leaf out of Dean's book and hustle pool! But then Sam goes and hands over all the money just because he spots Ruby. Oh come on Sammy she's not worth $500 of, probably, Dean's hard earned cash.

Yes Dean see what you've been missing when you were in hell. Lately, no one's been alluding to the place as hell, but rather it's referred to as 'the pit'.

Guess we should've known it was going to be one of those flashback episodes. (Well at least we didn't get any vivid flashbacks when Dean told Sam what he recalls! Or rather what he'd like to forget, for his forty years.)

Another reason why we know the Crossroads demon wasn't there to deal, as they sent a man demon and of course Sam wasn't going to kiss him to seal the bargain! Though he does mention Sam shooting his colleague (Sandra McCoy in **3.5**.) Also we see Sam's got out his jacket he mostly wore in season 1.

Again the demon was correct about the Winchesters not being able to resist jumping in and sacrificing one another – to save each other, though Sam was denied his chance. Pretty pointless if his deal had been struck, then Dean would've gone to hell all for nothing really. Then what would Sam expect Dean to do; just leave Sam down there and on and on it would continue. The never ending cycle of Winchester sacrifices. Dean said as much in **3.16**, about how all they ever do is sacrifice themselves and the demons are aware of this and love it. So that's why the demons know their weakness.

They want Dean in hell (where he doesn't belong I might add) because that's one less Winchester already and Sam would do just about anything to get him back. It's another way to torment Sam. Without really thinking Sam would be a formidable foe without Dean around since revenge would spur him on. However, perhaps they were thinking this after all, as it would mean Sam would dive head first into going after Lilith without any thoughts for his own safety and life; which is what he did and would have continued to do if Ruby hadn't shown him the error of his ways, along with some major seduction thrown in, preying on Sam's vulnerabilities like that!

The psychiatrist was forthcoming in giving out private doctor/client privileged information. Even going so far as to let them know Anna was suffering from schizophrenia and being, oh so very helpful! Quick sue her! In suits again.

Her comment about monsters and Anna believing they were all real was also a flash to Dean saying this in the Pilot episode and thereafter.

If Sam and Dean figured out Anna would go somewhere she felt safe, i.e. church, why the demons didn't, specifically Alastair work this out, as he professed to be one up on everyone and everything. Church is where one found sanctuary after all.

This church was one used quite a few frequently in the show and more recognizable to the one in **2.13**. Anna seems to be in awe of Dean! Just to hammer the message home to Sam even more, she tells him the angels don't like him! Dean has a rude awakening with Alastair.

After Sam said Dean wouldn't understand what he's going through because he doesn't have powers of his own in **4.4**, and Dean saying much the same to Sam in **4.10**, i.e. that he wasn't in hell torturing souls, so he won't understand either; good to know that here, Dean wants to understand now why Sam trusts Ruby so much. Well, she saved Dean once in **3.9**; she saved Sam too, so that generally makes them even, so why then does Dean say he owes Ruby one; when he attempts to apologize for misjudging her. Would've held out on that apology Dean, do we really trust her?

Lilith is big on getting other demons to do her bidding for her, especially in wanting Sam dead! Guess she had her bite at the cherry in **3.16** and misjudged it badly. If Sam was too powerful for her to defeat; to have her powers work on him, then why does she now think any other demon will be able to take him out? Especially Ruby. She had Bela try the same last season (though Bela wasn't a demon.)

We take it Dean had no encounter with Lilith in hell. She preferred to keep her distance and stick to her own corner of hell; and Ruby was too busy fending her off and convincing her she's on her side to even worry about where Dean may be and what probably might be happening to him. See saving her sorry ass once more, or perhaps thinking Alastair had control of the situation and Dean. Would've thought she'd loved to have taken part in torturing Dean somehow. Again, why did Lilith fall for Ruby's feigning and trust her? That she'd kill Sam for her. That's another reason why Ruby can't be trusted still. She's so manipulative and just is always in it for herself.

Interesting to see Ruby chose to come back as a blonde again. When Ruby says she took all those risks for Sam, it's almost like she's declaring her undying love for Sam (or as undying as she can get seeing as she already is dead and a demon).

Again, funny how Sam didn't question her about Dean: if she'd seen him down there, but proceeds to ask how he can be saved. Recall **3.9** when Ruby told Dean there was no hope for him and that he was heading straight for hell. Well; she tells Sam now that there's nothing powerful to save Dean (except for angels!) More could have been made of this moment I feel, since all through season 3 she was telling Sam she could save Dean or at least help to save him.

So it would've been interesting for Sam to say that to her. That maybe she was just stringing him along all last season, and that she lied just to get him to do things for her; to trust her and do everything she said, including using his powers. But no, this doesn't happen. Instead all Sam does is to want to throw her out of the car because she's of no use to him NOW! A bit hard to believe. It occurs to Sam to ask her whose body she's possessing, whereas all through season 3 it never really mattered to him. (See all the discussion about Ruby and her bodies.)

Even if Ruby takes the body of a coma patient who has been pronounced (dead), on her last legs, it still doesn't belong to Ruby. Even though it is a shell for her to inhabit and all my comments about her and Sam going at it with that body still apply! How gross!

First Ruby says she can help save Dean – season 3. Then she says to Dean she can't save him – but wants to help Sam fight and grow strong. Now she claims she can't bring Dean back – but can help Sam fight Lilith. Empty promises, she said that in **3.16** too!

When Sam shouldn't exorcise the demon from the possessed man and Ruby kills him, well that was just plain murder. Wasn't Sam perturbed there was a human still inside that body. (As Meg told them again in **4.2** and Bobby did in **1.22**.) It is what Sam and Dean used to do because at the time they weren't aware if the person was still inside the body and still alive; and they still do that. Ruby was the one saying Sam needs to be patient. What sort of pills was Sam taking and what were they for, his headaches or something stronger.

Ruby mentions she only wants two things form Sam: patience and sobriety, but casually forgets about the third thing she craves – his body!

Sam doesn't want to talk about Dean - once again for someone who never really stopped wanting to talk things out – that was another surprise, just like it was to Dean in **4.4**, when he was uncharacteristically quiet!

Ruby now tells Sam what she told Dean in **3.9**, about hell taking away the humanity from you but she remembers what it was like to be human: that she still has her humanity or so she claims. Well, it looks like she only told him this as a means of seduction, of course, poor, lonely; grieving Sam will fall for it. Did you wonder whether it was only a process of grief sex for Sam and nothing more. Then we'd have to know how many times after that they were together, and for some of us, as Dean rightly says, that's too much info! Dean doesn't want to hear the gory details about them even if he is into porn, that's his brother and a demon! Similar to the scene in **3.1** when Sam saw a part of Dean he didn't want to during his manage a trois!

As for the humanity aspect after being in hell, In which case, Sam might have said something to Dean about his time in hell, what he did there in **4.10/4.11**. That he held out on the torture for thirty years but through it all, he still held on to his humanity too and his sanity – even when he came back to 'earth' and to being himself. As much as he can be himself – he's now a different Dean to the one we know – covertly and on the surface he's the same, but inside he's hurt and damaged. He has no way to move on from the past, his past. For starters: no one will let him and he doesn't want to forget since he can't.

Ruby says again they need to be ready before they attack Lilith, she said this in **3.16** and look what happened! Did they really think Lilith would turn up for Sam to kill her, when she hasn't been showing her face around lately (except to Dean in **4.6** but the poor guy was having hallucinations.) Another question: why can't this Ruby fight like the old one?

Yes the moment was awkward Dean, because you didn't need to owe her one, knowing Ruby she'll probably collect on it too.

Mostly an episode to show us what Sam was up to without Dean – couldn't it have been less graphic! We got the picture; we didn't need to have it permanently imprinted on our minds. Building up to a showdown between good v evil in the next episode. But if this is how good battled evil – then boy are we in trouble, as Dean would say, well, no he'd say – we're screwed!

Sam and Dean leaving their prints behind everywhere, in Anna's parents' house. More evidence dude! So crossroads demons can be male too, just for the sake of setting the record straight.

Genevieve comments: "I was really excited for that episode Eric and I had a big discussion about it, to not have the attitude but show how she's coming from a lonely, desperate place. She has no one. All she has is Sam; she can't even go back to hell." No, but she can be sent back! She says it's a very physical love scene with her and Sam and she was nervous about it because Jared is so big and tough. Since Ruby was so emotional, "It was important to see that desperation. It's like *Monster's Ball*. It's about two people who are so broken and sad."

It could be said, Sam isn't really interested in Ruby; rather his ascent or descent towards her was purely and simply only grief sex, because he was now all alone and was mourning Dean. However, Jared comments that some parts of Sam are in love with Ruby.

Genevieve says, "It's the best way for the fans to accept that Ruby would have come back for him, he asked her to leave that body and she did…That's what I paid attention to: 'wow, she'd even jump into a new body for this guy. What's going on here?'"

Exactly – see my whole discussion previously about her taking over another human body, as she's nothing but a demon and the thought that her host body knows everything Ruby's doing whilst she's possessing her. How icky is that. So she's meant to be good, but her host body has no say in how their body is being utilized and that was the bodies she's taken over before and not the one in the coma, now deceased.

Since when can angels have thoughts, doubts and think and act for themselves. Answer: when they're part of *Supernatural* lore.

Quotes

Dean: "...the hell bitch is practically family. I came back and you're BFF with a demon."

Sam: "Dean, let's trade stories, you first. How was hell, don't spare the details."

Crossroads demon: "Round and round the Winchesters go."

Anna: "...and you're Dean – the Dean."
Dean: "Well, yeah, the Dean – I guess."

Ruby: "I'm a fugitive for you. I took all of these risks to get back to you."

Film/TV References

Girl Interrupted.

X Files Connection

3.11 Revelations, the father of a boy held in a mental hospital claims his son is the Son of God. The forces of darkness want him killed and he believes God will send someone to protect him. Scully believes that someone is her. Mulder thinks the man suffers from *Jerusalem Syndrome*, i.e. religious delusions.

Ooh Bloops

Sam holds a towel to his cut and his sleeve is bloody. When Sam finishes his flashback, he has a clean shirt and no towel on his arm and no blood either.

When Sam and Dean jump out the window, from the view inside, they both get to the window together, but when shown from the outside, Sam jumps out of the window first and Dean is behind him.

Locations

St Paul's Church. Riverview, East Lawn Building.

4.10 Heaven and Hell

Written By Eric Kripke. Directed By J Miller Tobin
Original US Airdate 20 November 2008

Guest Stars: Genevieve Cortese (Ruby). Misha Collins (Castiel).
Robert Wisdom (Uriel). Julie McNiven (Anna). Tracy Dinwidde
(Pamela Barnes).

Sam and Dean must save Anna from the demons and also from the
angels. Dean finally tells Sam what happened in hell.

Notes

Bet they weren't really all that surprised to hear Castiel come clean
and admit they are heartless – but then it shouldn't have been a shock
since Sam and Dean already realized this in **4.7** when they were ready
(at least Uriel was) to decimate an entire town. There was Sam thinking
they were merciful, whereas he knew from **2.13** they weren't.

Uriel hates Anna (well he pretty much abhors everyone) because
she's one of them and she chose to lose her grace and become human,
which to him is worse than being a demon – but for an angel he doesn't
come across as perfect either, calling humans mud monkeys, when
they're all made by God. Uriel was just itching for a fight with Dean, in
an attempt to knock him off his high horse, as he called it in **4.7**. There
was Ruby with her racist lines again which she also said in season 3.

Funny how Sam knows when Dean is confusing reality with porn!
Sam and Dean appear to get knocked around easily during their fights,
especially since season 3.

Another reference to *Godzilla and Mothra* (also in **1.15**) and yet
again Dean mentions Roma Downey.

Anna was Castiel and Uriel's boss which explains why she was so
much more powerful than them and did she really defeat Alastair,
another reason why she knew that spell to make the angels vanish, aside
from being an angel too. If Anna was born as a regular human mortal,

why didn't she suffer some greater fate or punishment than just being reborn, since she decided against being an angel.

Dean doesn't get to know why the angels want him and why he was saved, that'd be too easy. Strange Anna became human on the day Dean was pulled from hell, but she's been hearing angels talk all this time; so why didn't she hear what they said about Dean. Besides just saying Dean's been saved. Another niggling bit since even if she did fall, she can still hear them, which is why she ended up in a psych ward to begin with. So she must've heard them say something else about Dean, or was she just keeping this to herself?

Obviously Dean would stop at sex. He was right about humans, that's all they can do, be cruel to one another; fight, ridicule. He can also say this about himself too when he was in hell. All he did was torture and though he held out for thirty years, he still had some shred of his humanity intact (if not all) and so was also cruel.

Dean saying the angels are perfect and don't doubt themselves is exactly the opposite of what Castiel told him in **4.7** (he wasn't going to betray his confidence) but seems funny for him to make this comment especially since Anna is another one who must've doubted herself. Did she really just want to experience human emotions.

She mentions being on earth for 2,000 years. Castiel told him in **4.2** that angels haven't walked the earth for 2,000 years.

Dean can relate to Anna taking orders from her Father because he used to follow Dad's orders too – blindly, without question and thinking of the consequences. But Dean is human and had a choice; angels aren't human and don't have a choice, which is what makes them unique: they follow God's wishes, commands. Dad also seemed aloof and distant to him, many times; always putting hunting first and them second. Leaving them alone for days on end to fend for themselves, or rather for Dean to do the fending.

Sam with his porn comment again. Having two "girls" in the backseat of the Impala was hilarious. I recall a comment Eric Kripke made when Ruby and Bela were added to the cast in season 3, when fans were up in arms thinking they'd be love interests for Sam and Dean. He said it won't be the boys driving around with Bela and Ruby in the backseat. That's what this scene reminded me of; and that's what happened here. Though it wasn't Bela in the back, but Anna and Ruby: an angel and a demon! Whom they both were intimate with! Or rather me thinks it was a case of lust with Sam rather than anything else. As for Dean, let's see, he was probably thinking back to his comment in **4.2** about not being groped by an angel and lo and behold...

Again the angels threaten to send Dean back to hell: that's what Castiel said to him in **4.2** and Uriel in **4.7** and here. Seems there's no getting away from hell and its minions for Dean. In season 3 he had the threat of hell, well, it wasn't a threat, it was reality and he ended up there, or down there. Now, the angels threaten to send him back, but as Dean said in **4.7**, he was needed for something, so would they really disobey their orders. As Castiel said in **4.7**, they can't do that; Dean's important to their plans.

When Sam asks Anna if there's a weapon they can use on angels, she just replies, not anything they can find or get to in time, but she doesn't spell out what this weapon actually is, well for future reference. Wonder if she deliberately didn't tell him.

Now Anna's in denial, saying she doesn't deserve to be saved, just as Dean was earlier in the season, questioning why him and he didn't deserve to be saved.

Oh look, as I said in **4.7**, Anna says now, about Lucifer disobeying God and ending up being cast out of heaven.

Apparently Dean would say they've done things they have to answer for; specifically referring to what he did in hell, which we find out at the end of the episode. See my point about Anna not hearing what the angels said about Dean being saved; since they must still have talked about it after he came back. She now says it was only a week ago that she heard them talk about what he done in hell. The time-line for these events just doesn't seem to quite gel, especially since he's been out of hell for a while now, i.e. about six weeks or so, since it was recently Hallowe'en, so they're well into November now. Hence, why wouldn't they still mention plans for Dean. Also Castiel talked about it to Uriel in **4.7**. (Though not for our ears!)

Look it's *Titanic* in the Impala, i.e. steamy windows! Oh Dean, Dean, Dean, falling for an angel! Anna has to put her hand over the imprint on Dean's chest, okay, it's just an observation!

Dean explained where his tattoo went – the ones they got in season 3 – to protect against being possessed, i.e. in **4.5**, Dean said he came back without all his scars and old wounds; but what happened to Sam's tattoo, he didn't seem to have it when he was going at it with Ruby in **4.9**. It can't have been only temporary? Who knows.

Ruby telling Alastair she doesn't want to get in the middle of all this: of heaven and hell, is what she said to Sam earlier, when she told him to be careful and then proceeded to run away! Ruby summoning Alastair – in a scene where we were meant to believe she was betraying Sam and Dean by going back to her demonic past.

Uriel's comment about monkey's wearing clothes – well – here's news, so do angels! Which reminds me, Uriel wears dark clothes to portray his dark character and personality and what he actually does, i.e. a specialist in smiting. Which on one side may be a tad offensive to some in that, Uriel is dark-skinned; he's a darker angel, in the sense of what he does. Castiel is much more lighter, wearing cream/beige coat, having a completely different job to Uriel; and different character. Also how the colour black is associated with evil; whereas white is associated with good. Not that there were any such racist overtones here, it's just some people may take offence.

In the same way that Gordon was a hunter, who was black and messed up and how he had a racist attitude that all demons were evil and had to be killed. (We haven't come across many black hunters, aside from Tamara and Isaac in **3.1**) It's just also Ruby keeps mentioning the race card whenever someone says something bad against demons, so I just thought I'd mention this.

I haven't also said that Uriel's constant reference to monkeys (mud) could also be seen as racist. Monkey is often a term applied to ethnic minorities.

The angels didn't seem to think Dean could be replaced in **4.7** and who would they get to replace him – Sam? Okay, bad joke! Uriel's right about Dean being able to be broken – aside from his one weakness being Sam. In hell, Dean gave in to Alastair's demands – but not until 30 years. Dean attempting to drown his sorrows, when he knows it just won't help. The memories will still be there; always and that's what he said in **4.8**.

So if angels are everywhere; how come they weren't aware of Sam's plan to bring both sides together? So what sort of history do Anna and Castiel share together? Besides her being his boss; their history in battles and in following orders.

"Orders are orders," could be another tag line for this show!

Anna says Castiel doesn't know what it feels like to be sorry – yet he told Dean he does question what he does in **4.7**. She wasn't meant to know that; but if angels see and hear everything – why or how could Castiel confess his doubts to Dean to begin with?

Dean's comment of not believing Anna's happy wherever she is – how does he know this? I know she told him she doesn't like what she does etc, but she can't think like that now. Also where exactly did she take Alastair, or did he take her?

Sam says he wouldn't make Dean talk about hell – so now Dean decides to opens up anyway. Regretting what he had to do in order to survive: to carry out the torture of other souls en masse – the very torture he had to endure. He would feel guilty about that and now you can understand even more why he felt he shouldn't be saved. That there were others whom he would think more appropriate and worthy of being saved.

Dean was in hell for thirty years (four months earth time) in which time he confesses to torturing souls so he wouldn't be tortured himself. So it was so easy for him to forget his humanity – at least for the part when he was torturing these souls; weighing up his own suffering against that of those he had to torment. Obviously his was less, it was more important to look after himself. Why would he do this so easily, succumb so easily since he was all for good and saving people while he was alive. Did this mean so little to him when he found himself in a terrible place.

Not Sam or even, we, can imagine the sort of place hell is. (See **3.9.**)

However, with this hell/earth time difference, makes you wonder how long Dad was in hell for and what happened to him down there. Yet he was able to crawl up all the way to Devil's Gate, waiting for it to open. Whether he had similar experiences as Dean. But also whether he came across Alastair too, since maybe it would have been good for someone to mention this. Even Alastair says that Dad did the same thing as Dean or he didn't succumb. That would've made for an interesting discussion. Especially since Sam tries to reassure Dean that he held out for thirty years and no one even questioned what happened to Dad down there. No one even thought it, not even Dean as he's been to hell too.

The pain is too awful and unbearable for Dean; that he wishes he could just blank it out and forget; but he can't. That's part of his redemption too: to remember everything that he did and to atone for it in some way. To save people and see how he fits into the scheme of things now that he's been rescued. Why does Dean have these emotions now. At least this storyline about what he did in hell wasn't dragged out for long. But it will be mentioned in later episodes.

Dean's quote of it being 2 am somewhere, is a paraphrase of Jimmy Buffet's song *It's 7'O clock somewhere*.

NB writers please note: (oops that's you Eric! Okay, respectfully please note!) Roma Downey is the actor but Monica was her character name and hence Monica was the angel!

Do Castiel's powers not work on Alastair, aside from him being powerful because he doubts what he needs to do or is it his crisis of faith?

Quotes

Dean: "You're some heartless sons of bitches. You know that."
Castiel: "Yeah, and…"

Pamela: "That perky little ass of yours, can bounce a nickel off that thing." (Dean said in **3.3**, that you could fit Casey's ass on a nickel.**)**

Ruby: "Pretty buff for a nerd."

Films/TV References

Godzilla V Mothra. Touched By An Angel (Though only Roma Downey was mentioned and not the show.) *Power Rangers, the TV show as well as the movie.*

X Files Connection

In the episode **Deep Throat**, Mulder asks Scully, "Can I buy you a drink?"
Scully: "It's 2 in the afternoon Agent Mulder."
Mulder: "It's not stopping the rest of these people."

Music

Ready for Love by Bad Company.

Locations

Boundary Bay.

4.11 Family Remains

Written By Jeremy Carver. Directed By Kim Manners.
Original US Airdate 15 January 2009

Guest Stars: Helen Slater (Susan). David Newsome (Brian). Bradley Stryker (Uncle Ted). Alexa Nicholas (Kate).

Stratton, Nebraska.

Sam and Dean try to save a family from a ghost haunting their new home. Dean tells Sam about his time in hell.

Notes

Dean seems to be on a mission to find some sort of salvation for what he did in hell – like non-stop work will make him forget. Perhaps it's more of a case of, if he works, he won't fall asleep and has recurring nightmares. Also if he's not careful, he'll end up suffering burn out where nothing will mean anything to him anymore, not even hunting, and ultimately maybe not even saving people. Besides if he really wants more jobs or needs to find them, wouldn't it be better to find out about Lilith or where she probably might strike next as far as the seals are concerned. There must be some way to find this out. Yet not even the angels help him out on that score!

What makes Dean so positive that they'll actually sleep when they're dead. Dean would just prefer to pretend that none of this happened. Sam's right – he can't run forever since the past always catches up, as it has for Dean.

Well, the doll's head in the closet was a big clue for what else was lurking in the closet and indeed the entire wall space and basement of the house.

Sam and Dean have been coming across a lot of cremated dead bodies, which leaves them the problem of the thing they're hunting either being a ghost or someone else being behind it. (For example **2.16**.) Also Sam's right about telling them the truth – which is what they end up doing, but it's a case of seeing is believing otherwise they would never have believed it.

A prime example in this episode of what I didn't agree with, when Sam said in **4.6** about them always scaring people, it's what they do everyday, because obviously this episode shows they're not the ones who do the scaring. It's the ghouls etc, themselves; only in this instance they were scary humans. Again reinforcing what Dean has said on many an occasion of why he has a dislike of nasty humans: because they're even more wicked than the average evil spirit. See evil spirits and sons of bitches; don't have consciences to telling them what's right and wrong.

Think this is another reason as to why Dean eventually got a perverse and evil pleasure out of torturing souls on the rack. Well, if you're in hell – then you deserve to be there and need to be punished for your sins. As is the common thinking behind many religions. Okay, maybe this might be going a bit too far here, but something to ponder none-the-less. In Dean's defence, he really had no say in the decisions he had to made whilst in hell. Also since he did make the comment about hating what humans do in **1.15 The Benders**.

If Sam and Dean heard screaming, then how come they run to the house without guns blazing and weapons in tow, odd for them not to have a gun or too handy and very out of character, especially for Dean! They even knocked. Also Sam and Dean didn't get to hear about the licked hand business and didn't get to tell us about the urban legend relating to this because Kate didn't tell anyone what happened to her. Again that was strange for the writer to leave that out, especially since Danny talked about the girl in the wall. Thought she would've said something then, or did she just forget or not think it important. So that had to be her brother under the bed then. Well, obviously families usually consist of 2.4 children.

Dean's leather jacket is back. Sam must have kept it for him.

Best scene: Dean's face when he's asked if he touched the girl. Why pick on Dean as the one doing any inappropriate touching! So unfair! They wear suits again.

So the "wild twins" or should that be creatures, can actually write and presumably read too, a very un-character trait for feral animals!! Not that they would've been home schooled or anything. That was an annoying part. The type of ghost that messes with a man's wheels, is the type that isn't a ghost.

Don't you just love the way Dean takes charge of the situation! Ooh bossy Dean! Except probably when he was in hell. Of course they'd hunt ghosts better than Scooby Doo – they're not dogs and not cartoon characters either! Hey, we should get our own Sam and Dean cartoon show! (Not based on the comics, but on this.)

Dean is determined to make sure no one else dies due to making up for his hellish indiscretions. Dean also has trouble fighting the "twins" in this episode and ends up being the only one doing any actual physical fighting and shooting the boy. Dean would have to mention dinner! However, he can't hide his emotions or feelings and you can really see the hurt; anguish and his tiredness comes through, with everything he has to do and what he has to suffer everyday. Jensen is such a great actor that he has us feeling all Dean's pain right there with him!

Supernatural is back to having victims being killed in car accidents again, as in previous seasons. Also Dean didn't get to answer the question why he cares so much – saved by Sam, so to speak, but he should've had the chance to say something. For starters, he's always cared and then again he wants to strive to make it up somehow, even though he believes his efforts to be futile. Hell will always be hanging over him and overshadowing everything he does and who he is.

With everything Dean's been through, he cowers at the prospect of having his leg grabbed! There are far more interesting places you can think of grabbing Dean!

If nothing else, you can say *Supernatural* was topical with this episode, re the story from the Austrian headline, which has made all the papers, news shows. Especially in March 2009 with the case coming to trial. The Fritizi case, where Josef Fritzi held his daughter Elisebeth, captive for twenty four years. During which time he subjected her to physical abuse and rape. She had seven of his children. One died, three were raised by her and three by him and his wife. So his wife did nothing to stop the abuse.

Here Sam mentions the girl doesn't get to go free for murder, whereas they've never said that before. Which is what I said in **3.5** that Callie just gets to go free because they happen to be dead spirits who do the killing. Or in Callie's case she was in a coma. How's that justice?

Dean's being defensive (and or literal) when he replies that Sam really knows what it's like being in hell. When he doesn't know what hell is like and can't even imagine it, as he said to him in before.

Sam should've realized it was the dumb waiter that would lead them to her since he pointed out what it was to Dean, but again, trust Dean to think of food.

Dean rescuing Danny as he's got a lot to make up for, almost similar to what Sam said in **2.11**. As I've said over, that maybe if he saves enough people then he won't turn evil or in Dean's case, it's not a matter of saving a number of people since it won't make a difference to him: he can't forget what he did.

Why didn't the father come back into the shed the same way, instead of knocking at the door of the shed?

Sam and Dean wanting a head start on the police, whereas in the next episode they get arrested and nothing comes of it: sloppy police work! (That's why those episodes gone before about leaving their prints behind and nothing happening about them, don't make sense, especially since here, they don't want to be around when the police show up.)

Dean actually loses his appetite for once! The "twins" weren't really defending their territory as Dean says – weren't they also killing for food, who knows what else they had down in their "kitchen" and they did kill just for the sake of killing. Dean only tortured because the pain of refusing to take part was too unbearable. Yet he admits he actually enjoyed the torture.

How long was he meant to be sliced and diced and punished and tortured for 'sport' over and over. There was no possible end in sight for him and with thirty years gone, he didn't hope for a miracle. Since in his case the miracle took forty years in coming. So he tortured for ten years. At least Dean admits saving people won't change what he did (again Sam's speech in **2.11** was the opposite.) Which is what I've been saying. He'll always have the memories and that's not meant to sound like an old song. This confirms to an extent, he was losing his humanity and that was the effect hell was having on him. Dean can hope for redemption and try and aim for it.

Makes Dean forty years older doesn't it. So the time he was in hell, would make him in his sixties. So by all means he did reach his sixties. Of course someone will nit pick this suggestion! (See next episode.)

Question: when Dean was in hell, did he have a soul – humanity lasts if you can stomach not losing, but what happens to the soul. If he began torturing and enjoyed it then his soul had no emotions and he couldn't feel anything. Clinical point: but his soul was sold in the bargain to save Sam, so strictly speaking he was bound to hell and everything that happens in hell and also what hell stands for. A place of punishment, of torture.

Once more I make my point about souls in hell being far from innocent. The basic premise of most religions, if you are good and worthy, you'll go to heaven and if you're bad and sinful, your soul will be eternally damned in hell. Makes hell the bad place for bad people. Therefore, Dean was only punishing bad souls when he tortured them and it is to his credit that he, being the better person, and who he really is; that he remembers what he did. Even if he was cruel and heartless; he can't forget his actions because he was torturing human souls and not demons or evil spirits etc. It's Dean's own personal hell (if I can call it that) and as he finds out, there's no escape from it.

Dean and Sam are Agents Babar and Stanwyck, a play on the name of the Hollywood actress, Barbara Stanwyck. Dean quoting they'll sleep when they're dead in reference to the Bon Jovi song *I'll sleep when I'm dead*. (1993).

The movie *Juno* was about Ellen Page, a teen who had to decide whether to keep her baby or not.

Nell was raised in the remote woods of North Carolina. She did not know any proper English, only a "mangled" version. Here the two knew English. Perhaps their mother taught them, depending on when she committed suicide.

Quotes

492

Dean: "Yahtze!"

Dean: "It's not just a girl, it's psycho Nell. I'm telling you man, humans."

Sam: "I'm sure her life was hell Dean, but that doesn't get a free pass for a murder spree."
Dean: "Like you know what hell's like."

Film/TV References

Nell, Happy Days. Scooby Doo. Juno. Deliverance. Allusion to *Casper the Friendly Ghost.*

Actual Legend

The licked hand. A young girl left alone at home, locked all the windows in the house, bar one, in the basement, as she couldn't reach it. She took her dog into her bedroom and he lay under her bed. She let the dog lick her hand by hanging it over the edge of the bed as it was a way for her to fall asleep.

Waking to dripping noises from the bathroom, she was too afraid to get up and let her dog lick her hand again (what was the dog doing still awake and how can people actually fall asleep when they're afraid?) A few hours later she was woken by her parents returning home and could still hear the dripping sound. She found the dead and mutilated body of her dog. Running back to her room, she found a note where her dog used to lie. It read: "Humans can lick too, my dear." (So she wasn't afraid to go look in the bath when her parents were at home and then run back and look under her bed now; she could've been killed by now.)

There are other variations to this urban legend including one where there are two girls and a dog and one of them is killed along with the dog. Other times, the message is written in the dog's blood. Some versions have several girls at a slumber party and as the girl having the party refuses to sleep in the same room as her friends, her friends end up being killed too.

One variation of this legend can be found in a collection of modern fairytales entitled, *One Potato. Two Potato* (1976) by Mary and Herbert Knapp. This legend probably grew to make children aware; most people think it could've been made up by children to show how scared they are of being left alone. It also closely resembles the urban legend of *The Roommate's Death*. See **1.7 Hookman**.)

4.12 Criss Angel is a Douchbag

Written By Julie Siege. Directed By Robert singer
Original US Airdate 22 January 2009

Guest Stars: Barry Bostwick (Jay). John Rubenstein (Charlie). Richard Libertini (Vernon). Alex Zahara (Patrick.) Michael Rubenstein (Young Charlie)

Magic Week, Iowa

Sam and Dean investigate the death of a magician who seemingly died with ten stab wounds to his body but no holes in his clothes. Sam makes a huge decision.

Notes

Sam would have to be the one into magic when he was 13. Obviously Dean wouldn't be into anything so lame like that. No, he was more into conning – which is what magic is all about when you come to think of it.

Oh has *Supernatural* moved on from its over-used word 'dick' (probably not!). As we now get douchbag instead! Used no less than six times in this episode and one use of "douchbaggery" by Dean.

Actually, what Dean hates is how people know nothing about the real world: real magic, real demons and how you're not supposed to mess with it. Sam and Dean in suits again. (I don't have an obsession with their suits.)

When Charlie and Jay were having their moments together, it may sound funny to some, but it reminded me of Sam and Dean and one of (well many) of their conversations together; with Charlie saying he'd do anything for Jay, except watch him die. That's Sam and ultimately did see Dean die, as in **3.16**. Also Dean saw Sam die in **2.22**. Jay telling Charlie he's always there for him; like Sam and Dean are there for each other and would do anything for each other, as they've said so many times. Also when Charlie made use of the Grimoire and used the immortality spell – it was similar to what Sam wanted Dean to do in

3.15, to do whatever it took to save himself from hell, including reaching for immortality. With Dean refusing, he didn't want to play God and how many people would have to die for them to stay alive. That's also what Jay says to Charlie at the end. That he won't play God. Which is why this is reminiscent of Sam and Dean and that's why their speeches reminded me of them. Can you imagine Sam and Dean saying things like that to each other when they're 60: reminiscing about days gone by.

Strange here, Charlie is more like Sam, since he opted for immortality, again what Sam thought about for Dean and even told Dean he'd be willing to take the magic pill too if that's what it meant for Dean staying alive and out of hell. Charlie was the one who succumbed to using magic and wanting Jay to do the same. Sam is the one with the powers and he's going to revert back to using them. Precisely what Dean is against and what he always didn't want for Sam. So Jay is more like Dean, he rejects immortality – even if it results in him ending up being alone and old!

He's the one more attuned to reality rather than hedging his bets on the unknown and magic, real black arts magic that is.

Although Dean doesn't believe they'll get to 60 – Sam does and that's what he wants and needs to believe. Especially for himself and probably also for Dean too, when he tells Ruby at the end. He wants to grow old, even if this means being alone. (A reversal of Jay, he is old and alone and it's no picnic.)

Jay thought of Charlie as a brother (more so than he did of Vernon) and that is definitely a metaphor for Sam and Dean and their lives, and everything they've been through and will endure.

Jay kills Charlie at the end, which means he'll end up being alone. To him it was like killing his own brother Once more, substitute Sam and Dean and their lives and what may happen between them. Only question being will they really fight each other and resort to having to take each other's lives? When Dean tells Jay he did the right thing: that Charlie would've gone on doing what he did, the killing. That's another reference to Sam, though it wasn't intentional on Dean's part. Sam will continue using his powers, even if he believes it's for good and is the right thing to do.

When Dean says it's like crack and you get addicted to it, it almost feels as though he's talking about his time in hell and his torture of souls. As he told Sam in **4.11**, he actually enjoyed what he did and it became his addiction: all the killing and the torture. Even more so than hunting. Again, also alluding to Sam, who is addicted to using his powers. (I said previously.) He stopped for a while, for Dean and what the angels said, although he said in **4.4**, he was doing it for himself. It really must be hard for Sam to keep that promise – to himself – with Ruby on the scene. She tries to convince him to use his powers by convincing him he likes what he does with his powers and enjoys using them. Maybe like Dean in hell, but referring to what Dean was saying about addiction. This again shows how Dean may have been coming close to losing his humanity in hell because he enjoyed the torture.

That's why this episode has so many connotations to Sam and Dean's life and Jay and Charlie mirror them both so much. In which case, it really doesn't sound funny at all!

Once upon a time Sam would've had a beer with Dean, but now he's all fired up to go after Lilith.

How did Dean make his escape from the S&M place? Obviously he wouldn't have flashed his badge and the Chief was so much bigger than him?!

Ruby was also in this episode as a reminder that 34 seals have been broken – so whilst they're out hunting, everything's closer to going to hell! She really does know how to manipulate him and knew Sam would call on her, that's why she told him she'll be waiting for him.

Dean has to be cynical about life: what he's seen, and about hell: where he's been. There is no happy ending for him, for them, as he sees it. Sam doesn't want that. He'd prefer to fight, to actually get old, and to reach 60. He doesn't talk to Dean and ends up keeping another secret about what he wants to do and that Ruby came to see him. Talk about a bad influence. Even if he does mention they should go after Lilith, Dean is right when he tells him she could be anyone and anywhere.

Dean's reference to the VW must have been the ad where tonnes of people would fit into the VW, or was it an endless supply of people coming out of the car.

Dean doesn't want to be like Travis or Gordon, or even Bobby. Gordon wasn't old; he was just cynical and wanted to hunt anything and everything. Hey even Dean fell in with him at one point in **2.3**.

It was silly to tie Jay up, as Sam just said a second ago that he's a magician and they didn't even search for him in the room. Jay mentions his age again, as if 60 means something more. You're only as old as you feel (and not look, as some might say!).

How come the police took no fingerprints of Sam and Dean to run when they arrested them. Strange they didn't have their badges with them now, as Dean had quite a few in his pockets in **4.8**.

Charlie asking Jay if he believed Sam and Dean about real magic being involved since he was the one behind the killings and yes he does believe in it. Jay telling them how Charlie pulled him out of his mire, otherwise he would've been dead by twenty, or how Dean looked after Sam when he was little and how they still look out for each other.

Was there something to read into the comments Dean made about Sam liking magic, since he was the one who ended up with the demon blood; the powers: the "magic".

Jay mentions the price to pay for immortality. So Charlie came across the Grimoire with the immortality spell in it. Which means Charlie was even older than 60, since he said he got it from Barnum himself. How come Sam never found it, or thought about it in season 3, and if he did, could he have used it on Dean without him knowing? Charlie didn't want to come back and start life alone. He wanted his friends there with him, once more an allusion (as opposed to an illusion!) to Sam and Dean: each couldn't face life without the other. Thus Dean bringing Sam back by making the deal and Sam wanting Dean back at all costs, but he just couldn't bring Dean back.

It was compelling to think Sam would've been tempted to use his powers to get him out of the restraints and to save Dean (as he did in **4.4** to get out of the closet he was in.) But it was Jay who came to the rescue by killing his best friend and more importantly, his brother. Substitute Dean for Sam here...anyone? Especially when Dean says Charlie would never have stopped using magic and killing.

Summing up Sam and Dean's life: have to spend it alone, only with each other; it's all they have left. Dean would've been alone if he hadn't bought back Sam; and Sam was alone. He couldn't bring Dean back! So that wasn't right either.

Ruby got there quick smart. She probably never left because she knew Sam would come round. Which brings to mind the question of where Ruby disappears to when she's not around and more importantly what does she do?

Such a simplistic view for Sam to change his mind because he doesn't want to be doing this when he's old. Dean wants to die before 60 and doesn't think they'll live to see 60. Go figure! Noticeably rather selfish of Sam when he tells Ruby he wants to grow old – alone? Without Dean? For someone who was completely devastated by his brother's passing and wanted to help him in season 3 by foul means or fair, he now only thinks of himself at such a crucial moment. It's ultimately his decision to go after Lilith.

Sam could walk away from all this hunting to lead a normal life but he no longer wants it; even if Dean encourages him, since he's all for walking away and leaving it behind. Sam's come a long way and here instead of thinking about having a normal life now, he just wants to become an old man one day. (See **4.12**.) Well, for that to happen, the Apocalypse must be stopped and this breaking of the seals. There's still no certainty that he actually will live to a ripe old age. Just as Sam chooses to use his powers, he chooses he'd like to be around a bit longer. That's not really for him to decide, as in the end a higher power will make that decision for him (and I don't mean Eric Kripke!)

For the first time in *Supernatural* history, the Impala does not appear in this episode. No it was spirited away by a magic trick! Dean quotes that he hopes to die before getting old, from the song *My Generation* by The Who.

Dean is FBI Agent Ulrich, named for the drummer from *Metallica*.

Jeb was so much like Criss Angel and Jeb was alluding to Criss' show in Las Vegas called *Believe*.

Barry Bostwick is famous for many TV shows, especially *Scruples* and movies but is more famous for his role in *Little Shop Of Horrors*. John Rubenstein is also famous for TV shows and films, including the 1980's series *Crazy Like A Fox*. Younger Charlie was played by Michael Rubenstein, John's real son.

Jared: "They have a real magic trick with supposedly real swords of course. They're not real but they are hard and they could have cut me if it went wrong. I was tied up and it's still scary."

Quotes

Sam: "Do you think we'll still be chasing demons when we're 60?"
Dean: "No, I think we'll be dead for good."

Sam: "Wow, it's like a magic museum."
Dean: "You must be in heaven."

Jay: "Who else has to die so that we can live forever? What's the price tag for immortality?"

Sam: "I don't wanna be doing this when I'm an old man."

Sam and Dean's Take on the Urban Legend/Lore

Not so much Sam and Dean's versh of the Grimoire and the use of tarot cards, but rather Charlie's. Also Sam and Dean didn't mention any legends or lore in this episode.

Actual Legend

The Grimoire is a book of magic which has methods for summoning demons, angels and performing rites such as divination. It has been around since medieval times. A Grimoire is also a term given to a book containing magical spells. The name is from the old French word *grammaire* and from the Greek root word, *grammatikus* meaning *of letters*. From this was derived the word *grammar* and *glamour*. Grimoire became known as applying to books relating to the supernatural and to magic.

A Tarot is a set of cards having 21 trump cards. In countries where English was spoken, tarot cards were associated with the purposes of divining.

There is no evidence for the existence of tarot before those used by Italian nobles. However, some do associate the origin of these in ancient Egypt and India. Since tarots were used in dark magic, they were banned by many religions; which signalled their use in secret.

The *Hanged Man* in a deck of tarot cards is a desire to sacrifice, to get what you want; or the need to take a look at the situation you are in. Once the card is turned over, it may mean a refusal to accept reality. This is what Charlie was using to get what he wanted for jay, i.e. the fame and recognition he deserved and to remove those who stood in his way or were disrespectful to him. The Hanged Man: is not a card relating to life or death, but "suspension" – of selflessness: finding answers to problems or a time for things to stand still before they continue. Tarot cards were used to foretell future events and used by those who had an interest in the occult.

The *Magician card* is representative of power and knowledge that we all possess. It is the ability to tap into positive energy and means of success. This card is the reveal in the trick: i.e. Jay took the card from the pack without Charlie knowing and proceeded to 'fool' him with it, especially when Jay stabbed himself. The card has the ability to make things happen just be saying them (here Jay used action rather than speech). The magician is also seen to be represented by Mercury (the god of thieves.) He can be seen as a con-artist; a salesman and apt at sleight of hand. (See Mercury). Hence Jay stole the tarot from Charlie. Jay even admitted he was a con-artist before he became a magician. Therefore Jay used the *Magician* card instead of the *Justice* card and what more fitting than this since he was a magician too and turned out to be a better one than Charlie, as Charlie didn't see it coming.

Justice card is the balance between two forces in life; it can be physical, spiritual or mental. It is symbolic of fair treatment in all aspects of life, disputes tend to be resolved in your favour. *Justice* is all about obtaining balance, objectivity, cold facts. The card which tends to bring back into balance either socially, physically, emotionally or spiritually and natural order. Either signifying legal action – the end result will always be fair. Therefore not really a good card for Jay to have used since no one was really looking for balance or fairness, what Charlie did in killing those people wasn't fair and it certainly wasn't fair to have that card used for him. He would've gone on killing.

In 1949, Bertram Forer, a psychologist, published his study which showed the acceptance of people of general descriptions about their personalities, which could just as easily be applied to other people. Known as *The Barnum Effect* and attributed to PT Barnum, the circus impresario, who was known as a grand psychological manipulator. Hence Charlie saying he got the Grimoire from Barnum.

Film/TV References

Cocoon.

Music

She Makes Me Fall Down by Buva. *Douchebag Theme* by Christopher Lennertz & Steve Frangadakis.

4.13 After School Special

Written By Daniel Loflin & Andrew Dabb. Directed By Adam Kane. Original US Airdate 29 January 2009

Guest Stars: Colin Ford (Young Sam); Brock Kelly (Young Dean); Candice Accola (Amanda); Chad Willet (Mr Wyatt).

Truman High School, Fairfax, Indiana

Sam and Dean are left at school, longer than expected and have to fight ghosts and human bullies.

Notes

An episode to show no matter how things change; grow; go on, that some things don't and stay the same, i.e. school days and people don't really change either. Kids will be kids.

Always the ever present cliques at high school: popular v unpopular. Jocks v geeks. No matter how hard you try to fit in and to change yourself to this; you're either accepted or not.

You fit into one category or another, like Sam and Dean. Two opposites. Dean was the jock, if he took an interest in school (which he didn't) and Sam will forever be the nerdy geek. But school is hard on everyone and you have to be tough to survive, or blend into the background and hope the bullies don't notice you. Then get out, graduate and move onto bigger and better things. Like college/university: where it starts all over again, the societies, fraternities, and perhaps you realize that nothing has changed. You've just gotten older. Well, perhaps school in the UK, things isn't so bad. Since we don't have that whole US high school culture. Though bullies are omnipresent and will always be.

As Dean says, children are vicious and cruel.

Good to see a glimpse into Sam and Dean's school life; but as I said before, they were never really in one place long enough to get a proper education. Not that Dean wanted a proper education. This showed one of his more awkward teen phases of not fitting in here. So this was the longest they were in one place (at least for this episode) and, thus the action had to centre at this particular school for that reason.

Sam's chance to prove himself to be more of a hero than Dean. To take on the year bully and win. But even he regrets this when he finds out that both, bully and bullied ended up dead, through vicious circles and what life threw at them. That the bully became bullied after Sam beat him up. The label he gave of 'Dirk the jerk' stuck and had quite an impact on his life; leading him into a downward spiral. Also notice how Sam stuck to his phrase of 'jerk', same as what he called Dean, when Dean called him 'bitch'.

Again this was something that could have easily happened to Sam and Dean, but mostly Sam, since he was younger.

Notice how much taller Dean was to Sam – even though Sam wasn't fully grown yet, but when Sam grew, he sure sprouted, and ended up being taller than Dean! A subtle height in-joke there, and when Dirk calls Sam a midget.

Sam and Dean used their real name of Winchester here. Not that they would've had any reason to change it; but with the thing Dad was hunting on the loose, they'd expected to lie low (not that their name really mattered.)

Would've thought Dean would've been sent out of class for being disrespectful to the teacher, calling her "sugar" and "sweetheart". Well, if he was at school in the UK, he would've been.

Funny Dean says he hasn't got any books since they won't be there long enough, but in the next episode, he tells Sam, he reads too! No books, because he's already doing what he does best, eyeing the girls and being a womanizer – well, I would've said heartbreaker, but that won't apply until he's older. Also the way, in which Dean went from being popular, calling himself a hero at the end, having to justify who he is and how Sam, in contrast, became their hero without having to spell it out.

Dean in shorts again! Last time it was Lederhosen. (Jensen hated wearing those in **4.5**.) Okay, no comment! He definitely loved throwing his weight around as coach, since that's what coaches normally do. Didn't think Dean would want to hang around for a Sloppy Joe, after what went on with the food processor; I know it wasn't the canteen. (Schools meals, yuk!) A classic, Dean thinking of food yet again.

So things don't change when we still have the 'dick' word flying around, even back then!

Sam tries to control his fighting agility here when he was younger, just like now he's older, when he's attempting to abstain from using his powers, but just as he gives in here and can take the taunts no longer, he fights. Older Sam too succumbs to using his power, for what he perceives to be good again, for helping to rid demons.

Strange Dean mentions school being hell, since he's been there and wouldn't thought he'd equate the two, especially since in **4.11**, when Sam tells him the wild girl in the house was in hell, Dean says Sam doesn't know hell. First thought of teen Dean' is to beat Dirk up – all action and no thought and curiously (or not) that's older Dean's reaction too when he says he wants to rip the ghost's lungs out, later on. Nice to know not everything changes!

Have to emphasize with Sam, no one did ask him if he wanted to go into the family business. It was just expected he'd be a hunter too like Dad and Dean (and Mom) so that's another reason why he took his 'out' when he could and ran off to college. He wanted to pursue his dreams and maybe this is where he got his inspiration from. His teacher. One person who made a huge impression on his life and all because he took an interest in Sam, the boy and not Sam the man (hunter). He wanted to be ordinary and this was his chance. Being beaten up was normal for Sam because he was the nerd and this is what comes with the territory. Just as it's the jocks who are deemed popular and are always the bullies.

Dean was right about the hair though on the bus. Dean having to ask the awkward questions again because his whole life and 'work' revolves around awkward.

Sam was popular, more than Dean was and did know most people at the school, shown by the end of the episode when everyone got to know Sam. He stood up for himself, compared to Dean who tries to convince everyone he was worth something and was sneered and laughed at for his troubles.

Sam trying to convince himself he's not evil, not back then and especially not now. Yes he has seen real evil and it's not what he wants to become, or to be, though he might be heading that way.

It did get better not being in school and growing up, but it didn't really get better for them. Certainly not Sam with his whole demon destiny hanging over him.

When Dean said "I'm like *21 Jump Street*", I though it would've been better if he said, "I'm like Johnny Depp in *21 Jump Street.*" Then Jensen could've got to mention one of his idols.

Just thinking Dean could've had a photo of Sam being given the 'full cow girl' on his phone!

Dean hates being pitied. He didn't really think he'd get credit for doing nothing except appearing shallow and chasing chicks! Did he think he'd be seen as a hero for doing it? It wasn't like standing up to a bully and making some significant name for himself. (Not unless demons were involved.) Sam did make a name for himself, but after that he was gone. Wonder if he thought of the impact he had or whether he thought he'd done some good for the little guy. Also did none of the children remember little Sam Winchester, the kid who was there for a month and then left.

He stood up for himself because he could and he knew he could fight, not everyone has that sort of courage at that age. Teen Dean didn't like not being in the limelight. So would we have wanted to know teen Dean? He appeared to be more cocky and vain, than our Dean we love and know.

Sam doesn't answer if he's happy or not but we know he's not, so maybe he didn't need to for us. What happiness is there in store for him in his life and with what they do and what's he fighting so hard not to become.

Inevitably a Sam episode.

The number plate of the Impala is BNQ 9R3.

Jensen on those shorts: "I try and take it over the top. Like with the gym coach. I wasn't supposed to have the headband or such tight shorts. But I said, 'If we're going to do this, we're going all the way.'"

Teen Dean didn't look that hot. Everyone was raving about how he really looked like Jensen.

Dean's reference to the 'Captain, my Captain' was from *Dead Poet's Society* (1989) and the line was said by Ethan Hawkes at the end. Originally from a poem by Walt Whitman, written after the assassination of Abraham Lincoln.

Martha D Bump truck was from the movie, *Heathers* (1998).

Hello Kitty is a Japanese animation created by Yuko Shimizu. It's a cat without a mouth, as seen in all the associated merchandise.

David Lee Roth is of *Van Halen*. *21 Jump Street* (1987-1991) was a show about young police officers, who worked undercover in schools, etc.

Quotes

Dean: "Oh FYI, three of the cheerleaders are legal. Guess which one?"

Sam: "No."

Dean: "I don't do parents." No clearly he doesn't (okay that was my dirty mind thinking there.)

Dean: "Go have your Robin Williams 'Captain, my Captain' moment."

Sam: "I'm not evil. I'm not evil. Trust me I've seen real evil"

Sam and Dean's Take on the Legend/Lore

Dean says ghosts are tied to the places they haunt. Sam says the lore of spirit possession, and when it leaves the body it goes to the place where it haunts. The ghost can go wherever it wants.

Film/TV References

21 Jump Street, Heathers, Dead Poet's Society, Revenge of the Nerds. Hello Kitty.

Music

Long, Long Way From Home by Foreigner.

Locations

Riverview, Crease Unit. LuLu Island Trestle Bridge. Templeton High School.

4.14 Sex and Violence

Written By Cathryn Humphris. Directed By Charles Beeson.
US original Airdate 5 March 2009

Guest Stars: Jim Beaver (Bobby); Genevieve Cortese (Ruby); Maite Schwartz (Dr Kara Roberts); Jim Parrack (Nick); Fulvio Cecere (Wagon owner)

Bedford, Iowa.

Sam and Dean investigate after a man tells them a stripper drove him to murder his wife.

Notes

When home truths are revealed, Sam and Dean are always not themselves, i.e. they're , under the influence, not drink (though that hasn't stopped Sam in the past from speaking the truth see **2.**11) or possessed or not in their right minds, under a spell or a demon. Bobby giving them soda, hasn't stopped our boys from drinking and driving before. (Note: drinking and driving is bad for you and other drivers. So is excessive drinking.) Bobby could've saved them all the trouble by calling them too and telling them Vic wasn't a real agent.

Note 2: the strippers: Jasmine, Belle, Ariel were all named after Disney characters, but they weren't wholesome and pure here! (See below.)

The siren had to be a man. Surprised Dean didn't pick up on that (ha!). Something was wrong when he was in the strip club and Nick was telling Dean everything he wanted to hear and more particularly when he mentioned he drives an Impala.

Another opportunity for Sam to 'get it on'. The doctor was too obvious to have been a suspect/siren. Why would she become a stripper if she had been a real siren, as certain critics said. She had a lot more going for her than morphing into a siren. Also that's what all of the 'low-lifes' wanted their 'ideal' woman to be. Okay, their fantasy. Dean aside, he's no low-life. We all know Dean was enthralled to finally get to work a case close to his heart, i.e. one with strippers.

Dean overhears Sam calling Ruby and Sam still has the audacity to lie to Dean's face. As if Dean will forever remain oblivious to the real deal between him and Ruby. When Dean called Ruby and hung up, why didn't she call Sam back to see what he wanted. Then again she was into ignoring his calls, claiming she was looking for Lilith. Don't believe her!

Sam's reference to the greasy breakfast is a line from Dean in **2.11** when Sam got drunk and was having a rough time the next morning nursing a hangover.

Dean saying he reads. See the previous episode when he wasn't interested in school or schoolwork!

The twist in this episode: the siren wasn't a beautiful, enticing creature, but an ugly old thing and a man at that. So why pretend to be strippers and then not carry on this ruse with Dean (obvious connations aside of Dean not being like that, in other words he 's into chicks.) He didn't appear as a stripper for him, but rather as 'himself' because he felt what Dean needed was a real brother – unlike Sam! Who just keeps drawing further and further away and going towards the dark. Distancing himself from Dean with all his secrets and lies. So is it any wonder Dean would want to find someone altogether different to be his ideal brother.

As for seeing what people want – something Dean should've noticed when Nick took such a big interest in the Impala and his favourite type of music. Enticing him with everything he wanted to hear (as I said before) so in the end Sam and Dean would square off and only one would remain.

Dean is clearly not pleased about Sam and the Doc, as she only has eyes for Sammy (and a lot more besides). Sam lets go of his inhibitions easily now, whereas before, he was all shy and naïve, especially when it came to chicks.

As Bobby said, all it took was one phonecall to find out about him, but as in **2.11**, for example, they were both preoccupied with other things. (In **2.11** they missed big clues. All Sam could think about was wanting Dean to kill him if he became evil. So what happened with this storyline then?) They were also not curious about another FBI agent turning up on the scene, a same case like this; when it's hardly something that's happened before. It does happen, but the police/FBI, don't really ingratiate themselves on the case or with other agents. They just continue with their own investigation. Which usually involved chasing Sam and Dean. Also with so much publicity concerning Sam and Dean from previous episodes with Agent Henricksen, wouldn't their photos /wanted posters have been circulating around the Bureau in plentiful supply. So if Nick had been a proper agent, he'd have known who they were. Regardless of Henricksen having them being declared dead in **3.12**.

Obviously the blood would be missing because Nick was there and stole it. But that aspect was a bit of a red herring, so we'd think it was the party-loving Doc.

Just when you thought it was safe, another'd' comes out of Dean's mouth. (Er – that didn't come out right!) I meant Dean utters another 'dick'-ism.

Again with the flower because Dean happened to notice it at her office, once more pointing the finger at her, but didn't they read the reports of the other crime scenes, where any such flower would've been mentioned, if it had been found there. Then thinking she was going to drug Sam when she poured him the drink. Sam was right here when he told Dean she wasn't the one behind it. (But he's not right all the time, especially about Ruby.) Wonder if Dean had got the chick, whether he'd still have thought her guilty. But it couldn't have been the Doc as she didn't make Sam do what she would have wanted, killing a loved one, here Dean. As for Sam not picking up his phone, Dean could've been in serious trouble. The camera pans in on the flower again!

Dean has to get his rant in about Sam attracting the lowest of the low: Madison, Ruby, Kara. Judgemental much? Dean. As you'll recall, Dean also made a play for Madison, and would've for Kara, but she wasn't interested. However, Dean never liked Ruby like that (which is just as well!) So that's two out of three monsters he would've gone for, given half the chance. Only Kara isn't a monster! Oh and he never took that comment about her back either!

Ewww, Dean talking about STDs (Sexually Transmitted Diseases) one second and then taking another swig from the flask again (!)

Once again, *Supernatural* takes a myth and turns it on its head for the purposes of *Supernatural* lore. The siren becomes male. He can't trust Sam and so has to get him out of the way. Which is exactly what Dean wants to hear, as he doesn't trust Sam either. He can't – especially not with him keeping secrets, like being in contact with Ruby and not even admitting it, making Dean wonder what else he's been up to.

The way Sam looked in the mirror had me wondering what was really going though his head. That look in his eyes, making me think he's having evil thoughts...again the 'if looks could kill phrase' comes to mind.

The fight between Sam and Dean was along time coming, but they're always like this when they fight. See the home truths part above. As well as being a precursor to the penultimate episode.

When Sam finally says Dean's holding him back – that he's not strong enough to fight Lilith and he's too afraid, as he's the better hunter. (See **4.16** when Dean tells Castiel he's not strong enough to fight and to prevent the Apocalypse. Sam also tells this to Ruby about Dean! Yeah, she really needed to know Sam!)

Dean breaks out the axe to use on Sam – getting his own back for **3.11** when Sam axed Dean in one of the 'Groundhog Day' scenarios!

Sam not wanting to say goodbye to Kara and this time he doesn't, whereas he didn't want to say goodbye to Sarah in **1.19** but he did. Besides don't think Kara was interested in anything deep and meaningful here. Kara doesn't realize there are flowers in her office. So the siren has to trick Dean as Kara has something in her office which will give away her identity.

Have to say nothing much happened in this episode – just reinforcing what's gone before about Sam and Dean having real trust issues with each other and how far they seem to have drifted as brothers. Like Dean said, the little stuff between them is no longer there: the family stuff.

So they end up being 'estranged' from one another, with Sam having to ask if they're fine. When they both know, in reality, nothing is fine between them. Like they're just being polite to each other, another routine of just going through the motions like an old married couple who know the marriage is over, or should that be the love affair is over – but what can you do? They do refer to each other as a married couple, at least Dean has before, when he said there's no getting away from Sam, unlike real married couples.

Bobby saying the siren getting to them shouldn't make them feel bad, but it's much more than that. Their feelings towards one another go much deeper than a siren getting one over them, they just don't want to admit it for fear of making waves and yet more arguments.

Good continuity though in the start of the next episode when Sam has to mention it was the siren talking – everything that he said and Dean asking if it's okay for him to come along on the case and he's not slowing him down.

Ahh Sam and Dean - things just aren't the same between them anymore. Like they're doing all this together now because they have to and not because they want to. Especially when Sam goes off and does his own thing with Ruby! Big mistake!

The strippers: Belle from *Disney's Beauty and the Beast,* Jasmine from *Aladdin,* Aurora from *Sleeping Beauty* and Ariel from *The Little Mermaid.*

Maite Schwartz guested in an episode of *The Mentalist.*

Iowa doesn't have the death penalty.

Agent Stiles and Murdoch were from *Route 66*: Todd Stiles and Buzz Murdoch, travelled around in a Corvette as handymen.

The Adventures of Ozzie and Harriet (1952-1966) about real-life Ozzie and Harriet Nelson and their children David and Ricky. A TV series adapted from a radio show (1944-1954) dealing with issues surrounding an American family.

Mike Keyser is from the movie, *The Usual Suspects* – Keyser Soze: a criminal who is framed but his description is not known to law enforcement.

The Manchurian Candidate (1962 and 2004) based on a 1959 Richard London novel.

Quotes

Dean: "We're on an actual case involving strippers. Finally!"

Dean: "I read."

Dean: "Supernatural STD."

Sam: "You're one butt ugly stripper!"

Bobby: "Sirens are nasty things. That it got to you, that's no reason to feel bad."

Sam and Dean's Take on the Urban Legend/Lore

Sirens are beautiful creatures who prey on men by enticing them with their siren song. Which is a metaphor for their call, their allure. They live on an island and sailors chase their song and are dashed on the shore. They can read minds to see what men want most and cloak themselves into this allusion. Solitary. Bobby says the lore is from the Greek poem. A bronze dagger with the blood of a sailor, under the spell of the song and the toxin from the victim's blood will kill it. A dose of her own medicine will kill her. (Another red herring, mentioning 'medicine'.)

509

Actual Legend

Sirens from Greek myth. Had the head of a woman and body of a bird. With their songs they lured sailors to their death on the rocks around their island of *Sirenumscopuli*. The Argonauts (of Jason and the Argonauts fame) were saved since Orpheus knew of the danger awaiting them, once he heard them singing. He played his lyre to drown their voices.

Known as the daughters of *Phorcys*, or Achelous (the Storm god).

Ouid thought of them as the friends of Persephone: when she was kidnapped and didn't help her. Demeter transformed them into birds with the faces of women.

Sirens were also mentioned in an episode of *Charmed* and *The Adventures of Sinbad.*

Film/TV References

Basic Instinct. The Manchurian Candidate. The Shining.

Music

Thunder Kiss '65 by White Zombie. *Steal the World* by Brian Tichy.

Locations

St Viol. Patuilo Bridge.

4.15 Death Takes A Holiday

Written By Jeremy Carver. Directed By Steve Boyum
US Airdate 12 March 2009

Guest Stars: Misha Collins (Castiel); Tracey Dunwidde (Pam); Christopher Heyerdahl (Alastair); Lindsey McKeon (Tessa); Alexander Gould (Cole)

A man comes back to life after being fatally wounded.

Greyburl, Wyoming.

Sam and Dean try to find out how this man survived being killed and discovers 'Death' does not occur for residents in this small town.

Notes

Dean stuffing his face like he hasn't eaten for months – again and then getting annoyed, not so much at Sam telling him to get take out, but because if he goes with him then he'll be holding Sam back. Continued from the previous siren episode, when Sam, under the siren's spell, told Dean that he's better than Dean and stronger; that Dean's preventing him from doing everything he wants, which is defeating Lilith. Then what after that Sam?

The stronger theme of **4.14** and this, will also continue on in the next episode, when Sam kills Alastair after drinking more of Ruby's blood. Sam needs demon blood to grow stronger, which isn't exactly a statement on his strength, but rather he needs "superhuman" demonic powers to retain his strength. Whereas Dean is just plain human! That said, Sam again denies it was him talking; but the siren who told Sam everything he wanted to hear and vice versa. (See **4.21** where Sam tells this to Dean again, about being stronger and actually means it.)

Greyburl, Wyoming, where the "miracles" are happening: where death has taken a vacation. Curiously whenever something angelic or demonic takes place, it's always in Wyoming. Firstly the Devil's Gate in **2.21/22** and then that's where Dean "escaped" hell from too, Wyoming, where Sam was hiding out with Ruby, in search of Lilith in the season opener. Wyoming must be akin to a *Buffy* hellmouth.

Sam commenting miracles don't happen in their work or world: what about Dean being raised form hell, or that was probably put down as having a plan for him, at least at this stage still. See the end of this episode and what Tessa tells Dean.

So what did Huggy Bear have to do with reapers and carrying souls – bargaining – the middle man between departed souls and reapers. See *Starsky and Hutch* where Huggy Bear (Antonio Fargas) was their informant, carrying information too and fro, for them, hence he was like a reaper in some respects, since criminals were caught, or not, on the basis of the info he conveyed, sometimes.

Dean's hesitant at fixing this "case" as when the reapers return, good people will have to meet their maker. Not wanting them to die, but when reapers do return, they'll only be doing their jobs, carrying out peoples' fates. Oh – only Dean doesn't believe in destiny – funny that.

They are like the poster boys of the unnatural and they've both died and gone to…hell for Dean and who knows where for Sam? Since he doesn't mention this – whether he went towards the light or not, or perhaps he has no recollection of this after Dean brung him back.

Hate the way anytime Sam uses his powers on demons and here on Alastair, Dean is conveniently knocked out – unconscious. (Also see **4.16**.) It's getting to be like *Smallville,* where Lois and everyone else get knocked out whenever Clarkie has to use his superpowers as Superman.

Dean doesn't get to see the extent of Sam's powers (yet) and how freely he resorts to using them. The only time he has seen Sam use his 'demonic' power was in the early season 4 episode when Castiel sent him there. Also the extent to which Sam lies, denying using his powers, again the lies flow so easily. Sam saying he just tried to fling Alastair and he left! Would he really leave without a fight since he didn't in **4.9** and Sam and Dean were the ones who ended up flying through the church window to escape when Sam's power wouldn't work on him.

So Dean has time to watch TV then – this time he's been watching *House.* Whereas Dean catches on that Sam is lying, he wants the courtesy from Sam of not being treated like he's got no brains.

Question: where are angels in this episode – as if angels will always come to their rescue; as Castiel said in **4.2** – there are other battles and other places they're needed. Only this time, Alastair was keeping them out by using the script on the walls.

A little niggle: when San and Dean were wondering where Alastair/the black smoke would be – a little obvious – wherever death and reapers would be found and seems like a funeral home is a logical place to start.

Now Sam puts his foot in it, like Dean did in the past, of knowing just when to say the wrong thing – telling Pam she's a sight for sore eyes. (cf **1.8, 3.9, 2.2** etc.)

Why would Dean want to watch *Judge Judy,* brush up on his 'judging' skills. This episode had so many pop-culture references – like feeling up Demi Moore, Greasers etc.

A bit of a bloop, at least it looked that way: when Sam walks by the stop sign – he appears to move his right arm (left as we look at him) out of the way, so as not to hit the sign, yet they're meant to be spirits!

Dean putting his hand in Sam! Sam telling him to stop – like he hasn't been possessed before, by Meg in **2.14** for starters. In a reversal of **4.8**, Dean says he wants to peep into Victoria's Secret now he's an invisible spirit. Whereas the Invisible boy was told not to hang around and perve in the ladies' shower room.

Calls Sam, Haley Joel for the millionth time. Cf *1.11.*

Tessa's chance to full-on pash Dean! (oh pash is Aussie for kiss!) Seems crossroads demons need to seal their bargain with a kiss and reapers need to kiss to remind people of who they are – if they most especially happen to be Dean Winchester! (see **2.1.**) Where was Dean's line about not wanting to be tongued by 'dead' things. Oh well if I'm going to be pedantic, then Dean's a 'dead' thing too now! Or at least was.

Wanted to know how Sam would actually make sure Cole stayed here – haunting his mother or was he just lying? So Dean now says the hole he had inside of him was not from the guilt of losing Dad, but being here when he shouldn't and would've preferred to have gone with her – but he didn't have a say in that anyway; since Dad got in there and bargained for his life. Yet he seems to have forgotten all the protests he lodged at not wanting to be taken. He can't have it both ways.

As for Sam saying he'll make sure Cole stays – that's what Dean wanted in **2.1**, he wanted to stay here; even if this meant he'd become a restless spirit, a lost soul, even evil? Surely Sam wouldn't have wanted this for Cole. But don't suppose he'd know about this, Dean wouldn't have told him, since he didn't recall Tessa at all, or their conversations back then – so it's just as well, Pam brought Sam back to help her.

As I was saying, Dean's pain wasn't guilt; nor that he should have remained dead, but it was missing her – the reaper. Again, she was the one who was prevented from taking him. Thought his hole was guilt from Dad's sacrifice.

Tessa's line of the angel on Dean's shoulder, is just what Ruby said to Sam in **3.4**, when she tells him she's the fallen angel on his shoulder.

Again with the 'd' word Dean, with another reference to angels being 'dicks.'

Cole didn't know who Mr Myagi was – a film more appropriate for his age, but he didn't have to ask Dean what he meant by *Amityville*. Yes, clearly everyone's heard about that, even children. Sam's reference to *Fight Club* and then Dean with *New Jack City*.

Alastair trapping Sam and Dean now – see next episode when the chains on his feet, so to speak. *Three Amigos* . True to form, it's always the extra reaper here who is killed before Tessa. The chandelier falling to break the trap is similar to next episode with the water. But wait, another question, if Tessa is a reaper and death herself, then why was she afraid of dying – so much for telling Dean (in *2.1*) and countless others to accept their fate and not be scared. But she couldn't have known about the seal being broken, if she did.

Castiel tells Dean he saved a seal – small victory and lost Pam in the process! Didn't much like Castiel's explanation of being here the whole time; oh he couldn't get in because of the ritual writing on the building to keep them out and had to pretend to be Bobby to get them here, but why didn't he tell them where they'd find Alastair; instead of going through the sham of becoming spirits and getting Pam killed.

Dean says something similar to this in the next episode. Also they didn't heed what Bobby said in **4.14** about checking things out only takes a phonecall! So Bobby sure didn't call them here! Also Castiel's line of Dean doing the opposite of what he asks, sure he could've found another way to point them to the funeral home. Except, if in some roundabout way, Dean was also meant to help Cole accept his fate.

Dean's speech about staying here when his whole family will be gone is the same as Tessa said to him in **2.1**. There Tessa reinforces what Dean said in the opening about miracles not existing. Just as she tells Dean not to trust the angels, but only himself. (See next episode: the something dark being <u>told</u> to torture Alastair.) Then Pam tells Sam he's not using his powers for good, even if he thinks he is. So basically; he shouldn't trust his instincts when he thinks he's doing the right thing with his powers. (Also makes sense now if viewed with the season finale. Sam thinking he was using his powers to kill Lilith and prevent the Apocalypse, whereas he was doing the actual opposite and used his powers to do wrong.)

A funny moment, though it wasn't meant to be, Dean trying to convince Pam she's going to a better place. Perhaps he's convincing himself she is, just like Cole. (Also Dean says this about Adam in **4.19**.) Again Sam keeps Pam's last words to himself as does Dean about Tessa.

Strange Pam would've mentioned telling Bobby to go to hell (no it can't be his turn next!) Rather I thought what she meant was more ironic in the context of this episode; since Castiel tells Dean that he pretended to be Bobby to bring Sam and Dean here to save a seal; so when she tells Bobby to go to hell; she was in actual fact conveying this thought to Castiel! Who knows, sounded plausible to me at the time of writing! (Even though she told them Bobby should go to hell for introducing Sam and Dean to her – but in **4.2** – it was also Bobby who asked her to help. She wasn't rueful everytime she commented on Sam's cute ass!)

An episode to tell Sam and Dean that things aren't what they seem – all about deceptions:

Castiel deceiving them into helping by pretending to be Bobby.

Dean and his 'better place' argument. Is it really a better place?

Sam telling Cole he'll help him stay on earth.

Tessa telling Dean he's being used and to trust only himself.

Pam telling Sam he's in much the same boat as Dean concerning his powers.

So what this boils down to is that they can only rely on themselves and perhaps each other, when it finally comes down to the crunch! (see season finale.) So perhaps Sam and Dean won't have that showdown after all! At least not in the way we hoped.

Angels as shapeshifters – able to take on human form through human vessels and sound like other humans too.

When Cole's mother opens the book, there's a lock of hair which keeps Cole from leaving (see **4.13**) but was Cole cremated?

Pam being killed off – liked how Sam and Dean were both told what they were both doing wasn't for anyone's benefit. Knew there was a twist coming about Sam not really using his powers for good and Dean being used by the angels for their own ends, i.e. they've got each other and that's who they should really trust and rely on. (So if Dean hadn't been the one to break the seals – he would still be languishing in hell and would never have been rescued, just like Dad was still down there until Devil's Gate was opened.)

Pam's line of sick of "being hauled back into your angel/demon Social/Greaser crap" was from SE Hinton 1967 novel, *The Outsiders* about two groups of teens, the Socials and the Greasers, from different parts of town and this is reflected in their social status.

Mr Myagi is from *The Karate Kid* (1984).

Sam and Dean are in the form of spirits, their breath can be seen in the cold scenes filmed outside. But spirits do have breath because of cold spots and in **4.2** that was how they recognized the spirits in the case of the walking witnesses. Alastair is played by a different actor.

The title is from a 1934 movie *Death Takes a Holiday* with Fredric March who plays Death. He disguises himself in order to live as a mortal.

Chachi was Fonzie's cousin from *Happy Days* and was in spin-off series *Joanie Loves Chachi*.

Demi Moore's reference was to the movie *Ghost*.

The final credit had a dedication to Kim Manners:
Dedicate entire season to Kim Manners. We miss you Kim.

Quotes

Dean: "You are such a prude."

Tessa: "…I'm pretty sure deep down you know something nasty's coming down the road. Trust your instincts Dean. There's no such thing as a miracle."

Pam: "…if you think you have good intentions, then think again."

Sam and Dean's Take on the Urban Legend/Lore

Reapers being kidnapped: "any bloody death under the new born sky – sweet to taste but bitter when once devoured." Arcane version of Revelations: kill reaper under the solstice moon, maybe a prophecy which says demons might be able to kill reapers.

Actual Legend

The Book of Revelation Apocalypse: "Through the shedding of its blood it has opened the book with seven seals…when eaten by him it is found sweet to taste, but bitter when once devoured."

The Book of Revelations – The Last Book of the New Testament, also known as The Apocalypse. Referring to John 'sweet to taste' was God's words – but bitter in the stomach when he had to keep preaching his gospel over and over.

Astral projection: when the conscious mind leaves the body and enters into the 'astral' body. Known as an out of body experience. It is said that during astral projection, the person remains attached to their physical body by a "silver umbilical type cord" which can be seen by some. The person is still conscious of everything they come across during projection.

Film/TV References

House; Amityville; The Karate Kid, Joanie Loves Chachi.

Music

Perfect Situation for a Fool by George Highfill & Jai Josefs.

Locations

Union Street. Princess Avenue.

4.16 On The Head Of A Pin

Written By Ben Edlund. Directed By Mike Rohl
Original US Airdate 19 March 2009

Guest Stars: Mischa Collins (Castiel); Robert Wisdom (Uriel);
Christopher Heyerdahl (Alastair); Julie McNiven (Anna)

An angel is killed in an 'accident.' Castiel and Uriel 'kidnap' Dean
to force him into torturing Alastair.

Notes

The dead angel spread out on the ground with her wings, reminded
me of Jessica and Mom, who were also in white when they were killed.
The angel here even more so resembled Jessica as she was lying in the
same position with her leg bent to the side.

Sam telling Dean to get angry instead of being complacent like he
appears to have been in the past, everytime he says he's not strong
enough to defeat Lilith, prevent the Apocalypse. You can believe him,
not because he says it whilst defeated, lying in hospital with his battle
wounds and scars, but because he says it with such conviction. Dean is
different, changed. Hell has made him into something he never was;
and left him with a defeatist attitude (see next episode.)

The two "opposing" angels: Castiel tries to understand Dean and
what he's saying – again. He's not meant to have doubts and Uriel
using threats again; forever saying Dean should be grateful for being
rescued. Castiel does recall Pam. Small comfort. (**4.2).**

Although it's too much to ask Dean to torture Alastair – he needs to
do it (why angels can't torture, would've thought Uriel would have
been good at, but that'd defeat the purpose. The hell Dean's been
through, literally and metaphorically; seems he always ends up getting
dragged right back into it. There's no getting away from it for Dean.
Not to mention how torturing Alastair will affect his already damaged
psyche. Described as being "shot to hell" (!) having to torture here on
earth when he already <u>had</u> to do that in hell, may reek of poetic justice
to some. Karma gone wrong; or at the very least a case of what goes
around comes around. Not just for Dean but also for Alastair, getting
his "just desserts" of going through the torture himself. A form of
retribution for all the souls he tortured; and for bringing Dean into all of
it too. Though Alastair wasn't exactly tormented for 30 years; or one
hundred even – merely a meagre few hours.

This was Dean's first dilemma, having to torture Alastair to begin with, despite his protestations falling on deaf ears. The second dilemma: if that wasn't enough, Alastair reveals Dad didn't break in hell. He was tortured for almost a century (hell time) but he endured. Reinforcing him as being the stronger one; the better hunter; the martyr. That he didn't give in and become the very thing he hunted. All the torment Dean suffered at the hands of the crossroads demons (and others) telling him he was the needy one, he needed the others: Dad and Sam, rings true at this point.

His third dilemma: Alastair tells him because of his giving in, Dean broke the first seal and fell squarely into Lilith's plan: that a righteous man will break the first seal (and only a righteous man can save the world and prevent Armageddon.) All the questions about why Lilith wouldn't relent and give up Dean's contract are answered here. She needed him in hell but why not Dad. Bringing about the Apocalypse must have been part of Yellow Eyes' end game since Dad went to hell, to save Dean and Dean was going to a better place. (**2.1**). Is this what also made Dean a righteous man because when the reaper came to take him; he wasn't going to end up in hell.

Some small consolation for Dean, that he was even considered to be righteous, and small mercy that the hunting he did; the lives he saved, didn't go unnoticed and counted for something. At least it appears that way. Though it may seem like the angels and God only wanted to save him to save the world. But doesn't that seem right. Isn't it only fitting that he needs to be the one to prevent the end of the world.

The crossroads demons were right about Dean. Dean isn't so strong as an individual. At least as strong as he'd like to think he is. Also Alastair was right this time, in that as a demon, he wasn't lying on this occasion when he told him he broke the seal. Dad endured torture for a hundred years and Dean broke in just 30/40. Lilith's entire plan on wanting Dean in hell and why she wouldn't break the contract. Did have to do with Sam also, as we'll see in the season finale.

I asked the question if things would have played out differently if Yellow Eyes was still around (my question being answered in the season finale.)

Oh another thing crossed my mind, how Ruby doesn't mention anything about Yellow Eyes. Surely she'd have come across him in hell and his true intentions for Sam and his end game. (see season finale.) The seal being broken by, not father, but by son. That was a legacy Dean didn't see coming when he saved Sam.

Dean went to hell only to come out with this hanging over him. As for Sam, what's he doing to repay his brother's actions – he's using his demon given powers to kill demons. Only he appears oblivious that this makes no difference to them, but it has a hell of an effect on Dean to see his brother acting in this way. Being almost ungrateful and throwing it back in his face. For all the suffering, pain, heartache, violent torture, cruelty, Dean suffered, to find Sam thinking only of getting more powerful and killing Lilith.

As for the part about Lilith holding Dean's contract and everyone else's. Would've thought it would have been Yellow Eyes. He was still alive when Dean made the deal to bring Sam back (**2.21**) and wasn't dispatched with the colt until **2.22**. Surely Yellow Eyes held Dad's contract when they made the deal, he made it through Yellow Eyes, as did Mom. What I wanted to say is that it was ironic Yellow Eyes made the deal with Dad to sell his soul to save Dean, since it was Yellow Eyes who "saved" Dad to begin with after killing him and brought him back to the living; after striking a bargain with Mom. A case of demon's playing 'god' with peoples' lives. (See the season finale for this, as I wrote this before watching it.)

Pre-empting myself again. Okay, Dad was mentioned here, but once more, we get one episode of *Supernatural* here (rather than two in a month and then weeks missed out, as in the US, so I tend to write about the episode every week, instead of writing all the episodes at season's end. Not enough time to do it that way round.)

How does Dean feel? He broke in hell and Dad didn't. Dad is stronger in the sense he's dealt with hunting and far worse things than even Dean has come across yet (what could be worse than hell) or can begin to comprehend. So Dean sacrificed himself for Sam, as did Dad for him. Ended up in hell, like Dad, but couldn't stomach the endless torture. Yet you have to ask how long Dad was down there for. {Which we get answered here by Alastair.}

Dean must be contemplating if it was worth saving Sam sometimes. Specially since he was the one to save him to begin with, and was ripped apart by the hellhounds for his efforts. Suffering his fate. Then endless suffering in hell, only to discover he's the cause of the Apocalypse, whilst Sam just seems to be lording it up with his powers and using them without a second thought. The word dalliance comes to mind to describe his actions. Is this what all Dean's pain was for.

Dean saying he won't like what will walk out of the door when he's finished torturing doesn't seem much of a threat; with hindsight. Especially since he didn't emerge from there; stronger, but broken, bitter and weak. Dean having the tables turned on him when Alastair calls him "Daddy's little girl" – that was always Sam, as we recall from past episodes! When Dean said to find someone else, immediately Sam came to mind. (Which was the desired choice but not for the reasons we expected, see season finale.)

One way to redeem himself with all that demon blood and prove it was all 'hype'. Even if he has that blood in him – he's still good and can do the right thing – but probably – he's not righteous or considered as such; otherwise maybe he'd be in hell now instead! Also when Sam dies, where did he go? To hell, but that wasn't Yellow Eyes intention, or did he go to a better place, as everyone keeps saying. Would Sam have broken under torture?

Well, Sammy turned out to be a real demon-blood drinking, vampire. What doesn't kill, makes him strong. Speaking of Dean's strength, a sentence or two ago – then drinking her blood to make himself stronger doesn't make what he's doing right or better. Dean's human so naturally he'll be weak after what he's been through. He doesn't have the luxury of demonic aids to help him. Sam, on the other hand, only gets his strength from doing this, something unnatural. (Or does he. See season finale.)

Sam hasn't heeded anything Pam said to him in the previous episode, about what he thinks he's doing for the greater good; isn't. He's fooling himself, how long will he crave demon blood; clearly he's dependent on it now to increase his power. Opening up new questions of how he found this out. Did Ruby tell him to do this; or did he just figure out that since his powers stem from demon blood; a quick fix will increase them. Probably was Ruby with all the manipulating she's into.

Another secret he's been hiding – wonder what Dean would say to that when he finds out. Nothing he hasn't said already, about going so far out off the reservation and being a monster. (See later episodes.) To think in **4.4** Sam was going on about having demon blood flowing in him; that Dean won't understand because he doesn't and now he's voluntarily and readily ingesting it himself. That line he crossed Dean mentioned. Well, it's even worse now.

Is Sam just blurring the humanity within him because nothing good can come from the choices he's making. (Sam isn't aversive to being tongued by a demon, a dead thing, it's not even a thing; but just demon smoke and in someone else's body too – just a vessel. (See **4.9**). Whereas Dean needs a drink or several for Dutch courage; Sam needs demon blood for power and obviously the angels know what he's up to. Castiel calling him the boy with demon blood was an understatement in the Hallowe'en episode.

Sam drinking Ruby's blood so he'll become more powerful with it and we get to witness it for ourselves here. Good to see Sam kill

Alastair. Evil is as evil does, or demon is as demon blood does. It was also for Dean and for Dad. Castiel not knowing what to think, how to react when Sam did this.

Castiel tells Anna he still has orders to kill her. Also she was his 'boss' too. So it was only fitting she'd be the one to end it all and answering Sam's question in **4.9/4.10** about the weapon to kill an angel, as Uriel says, the weapon is another angel with a knife. From this episode, have to ask who did these orders really originate from? God or Uriel seeing as he's the one who always got revelations; who is to say he hasn't manipulated Castiel and everyone else for his true purpose; to allow Lucifer to be raised after all! I would say Lilith had an angel on her shoulder in the form of Uriel. Seems he was making it easier for her too. He only managed to kill seven angels. (There's that Biblical/numerological reference to the number seven again.)

Anna doesn't call what Dean has to do righteous – and knows Dean is the only one to save them; calling him the one weapon they have. So how will 'weapon' Dean be used?

See **4.15** when Tessa told Dean that he's been used – don't know what to make of that now, since Dean has to be the one to prevent the Apocalypse. This doesn't 'constitute' being used or manipulated - more of another one of those vicious circles, if he hadn't broken in hell; the seal wouldn't have been broken and he'd still be there! But since he did break the seal; he was "saved" to save the world in turn. So it can't really have been God's plan for him as everyone called it – since everything written about the seals was preordained, already written etc. The only thing that stands out here, is that if Dean hadn't begun the torture, he would not be seen as righteous and would've been abandoned to rot in hell forever!

Castiel was rather self-righteous here, saying Anna fell and he's not like her; convincing her or himself; as he's admitted to Dean already he's having doubts and now she's found this out too; he's defensive. She touches his hand to show him he is beginning to express emotions and doubts.

Anna in **4.10** says there's no weapon they could get to in time, to kill an angel and didn't let on what that weapon was. Here she had the weapon to kill Uriel. I.e. only an angel can kill another angel. (So if it wasn't a demon killing angels, then it could only be another angel. See above.) Demons can also kill angels and Alastair saying Lilith doesn't want to kill any angels, isn't that what she's doing anyway, in breaking the seals and wanting to set Lucifer free. As Castiel said in **4.2** so many of his brothers have died in battle; in preventing further seals from being broken.

Castiel can only watch Sam kill Alastair – with the help of Ruby's blood – his powers have increased from sending demons back to hell; but now he can kill them – begging the question – where do demons go when killed? Same as angels, where do angels go when they die or are killed? (Okay they already are dead in some cases.)

One demon killed: Alastair and one angel: Uriel.

Sam saves the day. Dean 'misses' Sam using his powers again as in the previous episode and doesn't hear Sam tell Alastair he can now kill demons. At this point, even if Dean did hear him, don't think he'd really care. So in Sam's opinion, everything Dean attempted to do was pointless, (probably thinking should've set Sam on him instead!) which leaves Dean worse off than he was before.

Castiel can't heal Dean – why not? Also Anna didn't either. She didn't even reveal herself to him – that she was "on his side". Though she's not meant to – at least she did want him to not torture. Dean had no flashes of hell this time. Then Anna doesn't help Castiel either in his moment of crisis (of faith?) she leaves him to his own devices and hence the water tap dripping providing him with a clue.

Anna and Castiel seem to have more than a brother/sister relationship, especially when she was all touchy/feely with him. Probably it was just meant to signify Castiel was now expressing his human emotions, i.e. feelings, particularly for Dean. He clearly hated having to make Dean torture Alastair when he shouldn't have been thinking about it at all and about how Dean would react to being told this. As for Uriel, there was always something dark about him – the way he acted – being self-righteous and indignant towards Sam. Threatening Dean and then refusing to bow before "mud monkeys". (Similar to Lucifer.) Uriel was the only one who received revelations, so he was using that position of his to manipulate everyone.

Knew Dean broke the first seal. That was awful, we really felt for him having that thrust upon him too, after everything, to discover Dad was stronger than him and he wasn't even the prodigal son. Neither is Sam. Dean went to hell for saving Sam, when Dad did the same for him. Dean didn't even think about the consequences of getting into a deal. It never crossed his mind what he'd have to endure, because probably deep down he hoped somehow he could be (would be) saved. But Dean has had it rubbed in his face a lot and on so many occasions he wanted to be just like Dad: hunter, saving Sam, in the way Dad saved him. Even suffering hell.

One thing he can also be compared with Dad and where he differs with Dad at the same time, is what happened to them in hell. Dad went through the agonizing torture and never gave in to the pain. Dean did succumb eventually. So how did he feel when he found out the first seal was supposed to have been broken by him. As Dean says on many occasions he wanted to be like Dad and thought he was, more recently in **4.19**.

Why do angels have to resort to using Devil's Traps anyway. Isn't that a more human form of, erm, entrapment, instead of "divine."

Castiel and Uriel have that whole argument about God, angels and Lucifer refusing to bow before humans, (see **4.7, 4.9, 4.10**.)

When angels are killed and they still remain in their host bodies, what happens to the host? Killed too presumably, see **4.20** for an explanation.

Dean was being reassured it wasn't his fault, but he was destined to break the first seal, so it's also up to him to finish it. But Castiel doesn't seem to know much, yet again. As he said before, no one was telling him because of his doubts. When Dean wants answers, he doesn't really have any to give him. So Sam misses this conversation between Castiel and Dean – hence another secret to add to Dean's corner. (He hasn't told Sam he broke the first seal; not yet at any rate.) Dean's reference to God as 'Dad' now – Castiel's dad, father. So he's not strong enough for what both Castiel and God wanted from him.

Supernatural maths: 30 hell years = 4 months earth time.
So 90 hell years = 12 months earth time
100 years = 13 months. Dad was in hell for his long, almost, as Alastair says. So Dad died in September and was out of hell by May the following year which is only 8 earth months in hell, hence he was there for roundabout 60 years.

Alastair: "It's your professionalism I respect" is from *Little Shop of Horrors* (1986) said when Arthur is being tortured. He enjoys the torture. The *Heaven* song is *Cheek to Cheek* by Irving Berlin, from the movie *Top Hat* (1935) with Fred Astaire.

Alastair's line of "grasshopper, you're going to have to get creative to impress me" is from the TV series *Kung Fu* (1972-1975) with David Carradine. He played a Shaolin priest and Grasshopper was his mentor.

Quotes

Dean: "I'm tired of burying friends."
Sam: "Get angry."

Castiel: "You're our best hope."

523

Dean: "…it's too big. Alastair was right. I'm not all here. I'm not strong enough. I guess I'm not the man either of our Dads wanted us to be. Find someone else. Just not me!"

Music

Cheek to Cheek sung by Christopher Heyerdahl

Locations

Riverview, Center Lawn.

4.17 It's A Terrible Life

Written By Sera Gamble. Directed By James L Conway
Original US Airdate 26 March 2009

Guest Stars: Kurt Fuller (Zachariah); Jack Plotnick (Ian); AJ Buckley (Ed Zedmoore); Travis Webster (Harry Spengler).

Sam and Dean end up in another alternate reality where they work at the same company, don't know each other, but end up hunting together.

Notes

As always, if you aren't familiar with the concept – but certain clips at the beginning of a *Supernatural* episode, in the *Then* segment, not only are there for the purposes of reminding people what has gone before; but at times, it provides a very big clue as to what the episode will be about; or what's going to happen in it. As was the case here, when the clips with the angels were shown, you knew they had to have their hand in somewhere. So when in their alternate reality, Dean and Sam weren't hunters and didn't know each other, there was more than having to find each other happening.

You wouldn't expect to see Dean in a flashy suit this time (and not his usual *MIB* attire) and think everything would be perfect.

This episode, I thought, was in complete contrast to **2.20** – the other "alternate reality" episode (more like Dean's 'perfect life' episode.) In that, Sam was the one destined for his dream career; wife and everything else that emcompassed; and not Dean. He was the one working at the garage.

Here, Sam's in tech support (he uses the computer a lot anyway) in a mundane job, behind his desk in a cubicle. Dean's the one who went to Stanford (Sam's university see Pilot.) Dean wouldn't even have thought about attending university, at least not the Dean we know and love. He calls Bobby his father, Ellen his mother and Jo his sister. (Ellen and Jo Harvelle from season 2.) Maybe deep down somewhere in his subconscience; this may have been his idea of the perfect family or his family life. He had to be Director of Sales and Marketing – seeing as he's such a smooth talker, or should that read smooth operator.

Another clue was Dean eating healthily and being on a detox diet too! When have we known Dean not to love his food and his beer. Then obviously there's Sam having his feeling of déjà vu – of thinking he knows Dean from before.

Dean's last name is Smith, Sam's is Wesson, as in the name of the gun, Smith & Wesson. Sam doesn't like his name, is it any wonder when he's a Winchester.

As for the CEO being named Adler, that's German for 'eagle', and they have wings. Eagles also being associated with heaven. As these episodes show, there's always a far more serious, underlying meaning or message than just the comical element. Here it was Dean needing to pull his finger out and pay attention to what's actually happening in the real world. He's essential and is needed and he can't go through life, this life – ignoring what's around the corner. He's the only one who can save the world; humanity, by doing what he's always done: hunting and saving. To stop wallowing and feeling sorry for himself; putting himself down and to take the initiative.

Sam's flashes in his dreams were from the vampire episodes **2.3**, **3.7**, from the episodes **3.5, 2.21. 4.15** when he saved Tessa.

In true *Supernatural* style Sam mentions the 'd' word twice. (i.e. dick.)

That yawn was so fake Sam! Dean warning Sam about over-sharing – which is what Sam does anyway, always having something to say, until at least this season, when he's, well they've both been, rather quiet on occasions, as well as keeping the obligatory secret or two. Another thing was Sam being able to draw now, whereas in **3.5** all he could sketch was a 'sausage' man, barely.

As for the message above the microwave, this episode should've come with a warning: 'don't try this at home.' "Don't heat up your fish here. It stinks!" to me, reverted back to **1.17** when Sam put the fish in the backseat of the Ghostchasers' car (who became known as Ghostfacers.) at the end of the episode, to get them back and play a prank on them. Though no one probably thought of it – it would've been a great piece of continuity (or was it?) very subtle, especially considering that the Ghostfacers were seen in this episode when Sam and Dean research how to hunt ghosts and banish them!

Dean seeing the ghost of the old man in the loo, and then the way he kept appearing reminded me of the doctor in the asylum episode **(1.9.)** How he would appear and disappear and the electricity running through his fingers.

Presume this episode took place in San Francisco (it could have been or was it Ohio) because of Sam's alluding to Madison (finally someone recalled her! That's twice in this season alone, as Dean mentions her in **4.14.**) Sam says he got the number of the animal shelter when he called. So she's alive and well and living in a cage – as a werewolf? Strange the angel should mention that in this alternate reality episode since it wasn't really necessary. Question: would Sam have gotten engaged to her if he hadn't killed her? Answer: nah, as they've both said, there's no room for putting down roots in their world.

Also at the end, when Zachariah reveals the ghost was real and everything really did happen; all those people died; then having Sam talk of Madison too, to say she's still around, or not. (Hey what if Sam never shot her and really let her go? Sam does have his secrets you know. Okay, that's wishful thinking on my part! Well, maybe not wishful, but lateral thinking.)

Sam's suspected of being psychic here by Dean and having his dreams too; visions. See how excited Sam was here about hunting and even Dean felt this too. Whereas Dean was a little reluctant at first to embrace this. Another reversal of season 1, when Dean was into hunting and Sam just wanted to be normal.

Another reference to Sam and something being in his blood, that he's destined for something, not so much greater, but more than what he's known. Something darker.

Dean calling him Sammy, that was Dean's "awkward much" moment.

You know something's not quite right when Sam and Dean have to reach out to the Ghostfacer's website to find hunting tips and techniques. Then mentioning Sam and Dean and not so much as a 'who could they be?" from either one of them. Suppose it was written that way since they were called the Winchesters, anything else and they would've guessed something was fishy (!) Sam saying he hates his last name, didn't he think Winchester was a cool sounding name! The

Ghostfacers of course, learned everything from Sam and Dean in reality.

Knew what was going to happen in the lift scene, as soon as it got stuck. Liked the 'iron baseball' scene with Sam and Dean taking turns to strike while the iron's hot! When Dean said they should be like the Ghostfacers and Sam said, no – they hunt for real and not what Ghostfacers do at all! Then of course Dean has to go into the whole stealing and living on the road scenario, since that's what they actually do. Sam has to the one who is on the right track, when he says the entire "what if" part. As that's their reality and they did have their brains scrambled.

Again, shades of **2.20** seeping in here when Dean was the enthusiastic 'hunter', whereas Sam wasn't aware of any of it. At least he knew there was more to life for him (them?) than just university. (See above.)

Dean on the defensive when he tells Sam he doesn't know him – and maybe he doesn't – what with everything that's happened to them and how they're changed in their own world: the secrets, the lies, they don't know each other. Not anymore.

Sam's life would have been Dean's in this episode, if he had quit hunting, he'd be in the office – the tax lawyer. One thing was missing from Dean's life in this reality: a chick! You know the whole meaningful relationship, but then he was such a workaholic, he didn't have the time – mirroring his real life. Always hunting, no time to cement meaningful, lasting bonds. Zachariah had to mention Dean had it good in his life with the chicks, fornication and Impala.

Dean calls his clothes 'monkey suits', harking back to Uriel and his mud monkeys reference. Yet again, every angel is a fashion critic too and isn't happy with wearing clothes! (Well, everyone except Castiel that is.)

Dean wants to know what he can stop and whether he can stop it at all: Apocalypse, Lucifer, but he didn't expect to get those answered, so he could just take up the cause knowing that he'd win in the end, without taking risks and not really having his heart in what he's meant to be doing. Everything Dean does is a gift and not a curse. He could be in Sam's shoes, where his 'gift' isn't a gift but a curse and a fully mapped out one too. (See **4.21** where Sam is told what he has isn't a curse.)

Zachariah tells Dean he can do everything he's destined to do and there Dean was telling Sam he doesn't believe in destiny, as he's also told us on several occasions.

Dean's pep talk episode. Or rather it should have served as a warning to us not to trust angels, at least some of them.

This episode was a cross between *It's A Wonderful Life* (with James Stewart about Clarence, the angel who appears to George to show him what life would be like without him. It's a better world for him being in it rather than not and George comes to realize this, and Clarence gets his wings.) In this episode it's an angel, Zachariah – showing Dean how much he loves hunting, it's in his blood – how saving people really matters to him and how now it's gone beyond the family business, even into something more religious.

That Dean is strong, if Dean won't be there to save them from the Apocalypse then who will. Hence the title, it would be a terrible life if he wasn't around: hunting, doing the right thing. That's what makes Dean righteous: fornication and the Impala aside!

The second part of the cross was between **2.20** with another alternate reality. Only in that episode, it was what Dean wished his life would've been like and there was no hunting involved. Also an allusion to this here; in that, if he wasn't a hunter, all those people on the plane etc (**1.4**) would never have been saved. Here it's a reality – the deaths really happened and the ghost did exist to show Dean he's needed. Again, if not Dean – then who? Not Sam, he appears to be too far gone in his thirst for demon blood. No good can come of it. Are we abandoning Sam just yet or is there hope for him still?

Also see **3.11** which was not so much an alternate reality, only Sam and Dean's lives aren't real here, but everything else is. Dean's comment of Sam not knowing him in this reality, echoed by Sam in **4.21** when in a moment of truth, he tells Dean he doesn't know him and he never did!

Why did Sam have a poker at his desk, besides it being made from iron. To repel ghosts, bit dangerous though, specially how he attacked his computer with it.

Our episode had no colours to fade in the scene – the end of the episode is just as bright as it was in the beginning, that's the beauty of a PAL system, as opposed to NTSC. Dean doesn't do much research unless he absolutely, positively must.

There were too many in-jokes not everyone would have noticed: using iron to repel ghosts, Dean calling him Sammy; research but having to use the Ghostfacer's website.

Also see **4.3** where Castiel tells Dean he can't change destiny. Here at the end, Zach tells him pretty much the same thing: that Dean's going to fulfill his destiny…That is destiny can't be changed, until you do change it. Didn't Castiel also say to Dean that he drives around in cars.

A topical reference to 1929 and the Wall Street Crash and now with 2009 and the credit crunch.

Decoupage is not a dirty word Dean! It's a crafting technique, involving adding layers of paper or card to form a 3D effect. From the French 'decouper': 'to cut up' or 'out'.

Hari Kari is a form of Japanese ritual suicide on the end of a sword. Mostly practiced by Samurai. Those who had shamed themselves, could redeem themselves – their honour, by dying at their own hands. Also known as *Sepuku.* Hence the Japanese were unfamiliar with POWs during wars and battles, as they believed a man should die in battle. Or if he survived and was caught by the enemy, then he should commit Hari Kari. This form of suicide was hastened by a friend, or someone decapitating the person who was engaging in this form of ritual to end their suffering, since it was such a slow death.

Quotes

Sam: "I feel like I should do something more than sit in a cubicle. There's just something in my blood, like I was destined for something different."
Dean: "I don't believe in destiny…we do what we do best Sammy, research."

Dean: "You don't know me pal."

Zachariah: "You should see my decoupage."
Dean: "Gross. No thank you."

Dean: "Ass clowns in monkey suits."

Zachariah: "Be everything you're destined to do, all of it."

Actual Legend

Zachariah is of Hebrew origin, meaning *the Lord Recalled.* In Judaism, Zechariah was a Jewish priest during the reign of King Herod. The angel Gabriel appeared to him to foretell of the birth of his son, John.

Zakariya also appears in the Qur'an as the Guardian of Mary, mother of Isa (Jesus). "Her Lord accepted her with gracious acceptance and caused her to grow an excellent growth and made Zakariya her guardian."

Film/TV References

Project Runway. Harry Potter

X Files Connection

Field Trip episode where Mulder and Scully end up in a various reality after some mushrooms have released spores that they inhale.

Music

A Well Respected Man by The Kinks. *Hollow* by Brian Tichy

Ooh Bloops!

When Paul is at the computer screen, it is white with black text. On a 'command run' programme, the programme is black with white text. It all depends on the type of computer it is.

4.18 The Monster At The End Of This Book

Written By Julie Siege. Directed By Mike Rohl
Original US Airdate 2 April 2009

Guest Stars: Misha Collins (Castiel); Rob Benedict (Chuck Shurley/Carver Edlund); Kurt Fuller (Zachariah); Katherine Boecher (Lilith)

Sam and Dean come across a series of novels chronicling every aspect of their lives thus far.

Notes

Good opening scene where the bookshop owner thinks Sam and Dean are LARPING: Live Action Role Playing, just carrying on like fans of the books. Sadly their series of books didn't sell many copies (whereas the real Sam and Dean *Supernatural* novels in our world are practically best-sellers, well to us fans they are and not just books either but a whole wad of memorabilia!) He describes the books as having a cult, underground following – in much the same way as *Supernatural* has a rare and select following of fans who can't mistake a *Supernatural* episode when they see one. Being so very unique! Also the show has a cult following even if it's not really on a major network in the US, but attracts a select group of viewers and fans nonetheless.

Sam wants copies of all the books. Greedy much! I know they're for research and since they are about them, but wonder whose credit card bill paid for them. Oh and Dean reading a book – as he says in previous episodes, such as **4.14**, he reads and doesn't just watch movies or read Penthouse Forums either! You'd have thought someone would've got movie rights to the books, or at least TV rights. Would've been a veritable hit me predicts!!

So who was the monster at the end of this book? Or rather at the end of this episode – Lilith making an appearance just to ensure Sam still has a stake in her demise. (See **4.22**.) Can tell you who the monster will be at the end of **4.20** and **4.21**. Sam.

Carver Edlund was obviously combining the last names of *Supernatural* writers, Jeremy Carver and Ben Edlund. The publisher of the books, Sera Seige, is named for Sera Gamble, writer and Supervising producer, Julie Siege is the Executive Story Editor. (She also wrote this episode.)

Funny Dean not knowing what slasher fiction is and says he reads!

The publisher referring to 'Dr Sexy MD' was a reference to 'Dr McDreamy' from *Grey's Anatomy*. Which is *Supernatural*'s rival in the Thursday night time slot.

Dean's line of "crying on the inside", similar to Sam and Dean's "laughing on the inside" spoken in several episodes. Though she's right, some of the best moments in *Supernatural* have been the ones where Sam and Dean reveal their innermost feelings and do cry. As well as the fighting scenes and their arguments. Which only serve to draw us further into their lives and the show.

Sam shows her their tattoos to reinforce how much dedicated fans they really are.

So who was Chuck Shurly named for? He's a real slob, so they can't believe he'd have real insight into their lives, write about them and also be a 'prophet' at the same time.

Another timely scene as Chuck writes what Sam and Dean will do now when they are in the process of doing exactly that. So if he foresaw Sam and Dean arriving, why wasn't he better prepared to receive them.

Sam and Dean trading soulful looks when he tells them he's a writer. He's into the whole *Misery* fan vibe.

The books about Lilith and the seals weren't published, why was that? In case Sam and Dean came across a copy and read them, then they'd know what was lying in wait for them – seeing as they did know about Lilith since season 3 and might, just might, get ahead of themselves...

Didn't like the way Sam and Dean just stumbled across the books when they were working a case in the beginning and just happened to end up at that bookshop. (what happened to that case?) Also why now after all these years and it's a bit hard to believe that they haven't come across them before, not to mention on the Net either. Someone surely they helped out, or knows of them, may have Googled their names, or even their own names. Considering the amount of time Sam spends on a computer. Probably made this difficult as their last name wasn't mentioned in the book; but still something should've emerged, as no two people could be called Sam and Dean and do what they do.

Will Chuck be used again as their "point of reference or research" in season 5, since last we see of him will be in the finale.

Or were they still not meant to have found out about the books, since Chuck didn't mention this. He was meant to have dreamt about that moment in the bookshop and written about it, especially since he's written about every facet of their lives. If indeed some of their lives have been glossed or embellished over.

Another great line from Dean about them having real 'fake' ids.

So they're only here and only found Chuck since he wrote himself into the book, which seems a plausible enough explanation. Even though, a little egotistical on his part. Again, why at this point in time and in their lives. Answer, it was willed by a higher power that he should dream about them now in this way.

There we go again with the 'd' word. Lately it seems that all they've been doing is calling each other and everyone else 'dicks'.

At the first sign of trouble and reading about everything in the books – well Chuck telling them about Lilith and Sam's clandestine rendezvous, Dean's first instinct is to run. To take Sam as far away from here as possible and wouldn't you know, the bridge is out. See previous episodes where Dean would always come back to town when he was driven out. Eg, **1.3, 1.11.**) Whereas here, his instinct tells him to get away from Lilith. Sam says it later in the episode – how he's frustrated when all Dean can do is run away.

Their speech in the launder mat and the diner was a bit like **3.11**. They talk of doing the opposite of whatever Chuck's written and told them about, so it doesn't happen. As in **3.11** where Sam thought if they did things differently, such as Dean not ordering the same breakfast, eating in etc, then he wouldn't keep dying over and over. But he did anyway so it was a fruitless task! Another example of Sam and Dean attempting to change fate (or should that be tempting fate) after Castiel keeps telling Dean, destiny can't be changed. (Hello, it can and does change for them at the end of this episode and the season finale.)

Then Dean chastises Sam for saying he and Lilith would, could, never get together, as if he hasn't done the dirty with Ruby previously and on many occasions after that.

As for Sam being reckless, well Dean was always the reckless one: the doer and Sam was the thinker – the cautious one out of the two.

Sam does have the right idea about confronting Lilith and then maybe things will be different but Dean just doesn't want to entertain the possibility, just incase Sam's wrong and he does succumb to his "firey passion" [for demon flesh.] Then again, Dean was right about many things, see **4.22**.)

The motel name changing to 'red' for danger perhaps. This motel was the same one as in **3.9** when Ruby told Dean about hell in the final scene. As for the hex bags, are we certain they even work against Lilith, especially since Ruby was the one who provided them in the first place.

Dean advising Sam to watch some porn again! Wouldn't this just make him think about Lilith even more. As for parking the Impala somewhere else, so Dean doesn't spend his whole time driving around, as Chuck tells them he will; what was wrong with the motel carpark, and also didn't he do just that, drive around in it. Only to end up getting his pink plaster (band-aid) and see stars in the form of the woman driver's earrings.

Chuck also knows about the demon blood, but didn't include it in the books since Sam would come across as "unsympathetic". Hands up who thought of Sam in this way. Yes we all thought he was doing the wrong thing – part it was part of the blood in him and what he was expected to do. Sam saying he wished (to God!) he could stop but he doesn't have a choice. Even when everyone's been telling him he's doing the wrong thing. He's mistaken about that, he does have a choice, but he doesn't realize it as he's taken everything Ruby's instilled into him as 'gospel'. That whatever she says he has to do – he can think for himself, even Dean's told him that Ruby is lying – but he just refuses to listen. Even Pam said it in **4.15**: that he thinks he's doing good with his powers, but his powers are demon-given and no good can ever stem from them. So he shouldn't use them.

If you think about it – how can demon blood make him stronger, he's not a demon. It made him immune from the virus in **2.9** but it

533

didn't prevent him from being killed in **2.21**. So he's not invincible. If drinking demon blood made him more powerful – why didn't he have any psychic visions too. Begging the question how would Yellow Eyes have got Sam to make his plan work (of killing Lilith). Sam wouldn't be drinking demon blood at that stage, i.e. if he hadn't been killed and Dean hadn't gone to hell; since Yellow Eyes was expecting Sam to come out the victor in **2.21/22**.

So Sam believes he's doing everything to help Dean and return the favour. Only he's deluding himself, since he's not helping Dean, but driving him away. Dean doesn't want his brother doing that and being dependent on demon blood, or want the favour returned. He's made his feelings crystal clear several episodes over, such as **4.4**. Dean doesn't expect the favour returned and certainly not in the way Sam thinks. Chuck foretells again by saying it all rests on Sam's shoulders – which it does (see **4.22**). Every sorry little, last piece of it!

Castiel admiring Chuck's work – paints Castiel in a very favourable light in his books, but then Chuck's a prophet and he has to write that about him. (If that's so, then Chuck also knows about Castiel's doubts, which means his superior's do as well. Did they find this out from Chuck here, see **4.20**.) Dean describes Chuck as more of a Penthouse Forum writer. He's into his forums, seeing as he mentioned Penthouse Forums in **4.8,** when Ruby and Anna were in the back seat of the Impala and Dean comments it's more like something out of a Penthouse Forum; an angel and a demon in the back of the car at the same time. Oh and more thing that comes to mind, Chuck also knows how Ruby is only using Sam!

Chuck's books will be known as the Winchester Gospel one day. He knows that for a fact? Castiel saying he's not kidding Dean and keeping a straight face too. Remember he's not the angel who jokes – Uriel was the one with the sense of humour, according to Castiel.

Castiel commenting that whatever Chuck's written is the "law" so to speak; thus everything he's seen will come true and he says destiny can't be changed all the time. See **4.2**, etc, but he always gets proven wrong and in some instances he is instrumental in helping to change that very destiny. Just as when Dean will ask him for help in saving Sam from Lilith in the end. That's another example of Castiel helping to bring about an alteration in their destinies.

Dean mistakenly believes Sam's using been using some sort of psychic 'mojo' to get stronger and kill demons – as he's only ever witnessed his psychic abilities and doesn't know he's been really devouring demon blood. Dean prays.

[When the time came and Dean was needed, as he says here, he didn't do anything really – seeing as he was held up alone in a "room". **4.22**.]

Dean's line about not asking Castiel for anything (and God) and he's asking now. Help in 'saving' Sam. See **4.20**. Castiel will say the same thing, rather Jimmy, Castiel's host body.

If only Sam hadn't burned those hex bags, they would have been a real indication as to whether or not they were protection against Lilith. Whether they could trust Ruby would've been answered then and there. Oh so much speculation on my part, at times I wish the writers would make things that simple, at least in an episode or two and actually write something along these lines.

Castiel helps Dean again – seemingly making his help appear inadvert, Whereas this is another reason why Castiel is taken away. (**4.20**.)

Chuck saying he didn't write the part of the story where he and Castiel turn up, and Dean telling him it's real because he's right in the middle of it – what, does that imply – everything else was a story, at least everything he's written so far, was just that, a story to him and yet he still believes this, that he has to be the one to write everything, even after meeting Sam and Dean in the flesh.

It wasn't so clear cut when Chuck prophesized this. As seen, Sam was meant to be sealing the bargain to sacrifice himself and Dean in order to save the world and prevent the Apocalypse. (I said this was why she wanted Dean out of the way and wouldn't release his contract in season 3. Then she'd only have Sam left to contend with in order for the final seal to be broken. Also wanting Dean in hell, meant he'd break the first seal, though there was no guarantee of this.) Again this showed that Chuck's prophecy wasn't so apparent as he envisaged . There must be some way to alter everything he sees about Sam and Dean in their lives. As shown here and later. Sam also changed his own destiny when he told Dean he wouldn't sleep with Lilith (no way in hell!) and he didn't, he was going to knife her. Ahh, just as bad.

Good to see Sam finally answer a question in this episode when at the end, Dean asks him if he'd go ahead and seal the deal to sacrifice himself (which included Dean). He replied he wouldn't and she'd only chicken out of it somehow. Coming all this way and having broken all those seals, she wouldn't really give up so easily, unless there was something in it for her. (See **4.22**.)

Funny part: when Lilith told Sam that sealing the bargain with her involves something more than just kissing – made me wonder how exactly she sealed the deal with Bela in season 3. Seeing as she was the one who appeared to her in the flashback in **3.15**. Oh mind out of gutter please because Lilith always appears in the form of a girl's body. Hence everyone thinks she's a girl.

A ruse on her part to make everyone believe she's so sickly sweet and innocent. Also Dean commented Lilith's a girl. Obviously taking over the body of the dental hygienist to get it on with Sam. Anyway, the whole thing smacked of ickyness to me. Lilith does have a predilection for babies, any wonder she takes over little girl's bodies. She only wanted Sam as her demon bitch, as did Ruby when she seduced him! Mind you, Ruby is a demon bitch anyway.

See **4.22** again when Chuck says the same thing again, i.e. that what happens wasn't meant to happen, without me giving anything away here!

Who is the faster draw? Dean, considering the archangel takes an awfully long time to arrive. Shouldn't he strike hard and fast, without the shaking sets and rumbling theatrics. As Castiel does call him fierce.

Lilith appears as a blonde, as usual. She must have a soriety of blondes in her demon entourage, well, our Ruby used to be a blonde too, when played so superbly by Katie Cassidy!

Shouldn't Sam have put the Devil's Trap under the bed – rather than under the rug, as Dean drew it under the Impala in **2.8**.

Looking back from **4.22** to this episode, Lilith appearing here, thought she was being clever; in telling Sam she'd be willing to forget about breaking the seals if Sam and Dean lay down and die. Specially since she knew he wouldn't agree to this, and yes, Sam was right at the end, she would've squirmed out of the deal. Also because she already knew she wasn't going to survive to see the Apocalypse and by offering up a deal now – knowing Sam and Dean would be even more determined to kill her then and there, instead of later. The part about not surviving to the end – was a massive clue for us, hint, hint. Her reference to all baby blood, all the time, see **4.21/22** – she fed on babies.

Again, Chuck must've written this. Okay he says he didn't publish what he wrote about Lilith, but he must've dreamt the part about Lilith not seeing the end; so again the part about the babies was another insight to where Lilith may hide out; especially if he had told Sam and Dean she's into babies. It would've seemed more convincing if Chuck would've been the one to have said this; instead of Ruby being the one to tell Sam. Before anyone says it, Dean and Castiel haven't arrived yet to change the ending, so Chuck has foreseen all this part.

Lilith calling Sam arrogant to put innocent lives before this deal (again see **4.22**) as she is just tricking him here, or did Sam just not get it, about her breaking the seal and getting killed. Again a prelude to events in **4.22** with Eric Kripke, leading us there. I was going to say, as the blind leading the blind, maybe that's not the right expression. Watching this and the season finale, we just did not think it would happen like it did. Even with the big clue here. Allowing us believe it could've all ended here with Lilith's demise, when that's exactly what we weren't meant to see coming.

Dean's reference to Lucifer rising here – was the title to the season finale, aptly and an even bigger hint that this may actually happen.

Sam's words will ring true in **4.22** of Lilith not surviving to see the Apocalypse, and truer words have never been uttered. As that's just what he ensured. Then as another teaser for us, Chuck actually dreams the finale and Zachariah prevents him telling Sam and Dean or anyone else.

Why must Chuck continue writing since events still happen irrespective of whether he writes about them or not. Sam and Dean come along and turn everything he's written upside down anyway. Whereas he thought he was writing fiction, he was writing reality. So they did change their destiny and it turned out completely different to how Chuck saw it and conveyed it, at least here.

What Sam and Dean said here is exactly what happened in the season finale. Pity we couldn't have foreseen this too – like Eric Kripke teasing us in this episode in the way he did – if only we knew, then the finale wouldn't have shocked.

I didn't know what to make of this episode; either verging on the ridiculous or the sublime. I don't know about you, but the books and everything just made it seem that Sam and Dean only existed, or wouldn't have existed and wouldn't have had their lives, if it wasn't for this 'prophet'. How he could have foreseen everything and then written about it; without knowing he was writing about real lives. Which is how they wanted it done in the show. Neatly planned lives falling into place. And their lives published in a collection of books, that they (and us) were oblivious about until now. I.e. everything that's gone before and we have to ask ourselves – why nothing could be done to help Sam and Dean realize what was happening with them or would that we could do this ourselves in reality. But it also shows that even if their fate was already written (no pun) for them they still were instrumental in changing their destinies on numerous occasions. Even with Dean saying he doesn't believe in destiny. He just accepts everything that's happened in their lives – see **4.19** where he says he gets they had to be hunters, but it doesn't mean Adam had to be like them too.

Again, why write about something Sam and Dean can change?

Makes you think how the teddy bear got to rear its head in **4.8**, aside from it being wished. If the case was their lives were foreseen; think of how all those destinies could be changed if they knew what was ahead.

Prophets are given God's word through angels which is presumably why Chuck used to dream and then write the books. Thereby creating the 'Gospel of Sam and Dean' – gory and full frontal nudey bits 'n' all.

When Zachariah tells Chuck not to tell Sam and Dean what he's seen about the Apocalypse: again Dean almost gets to change that final destiny too, the final scene of the season finale, but…he's too late – or is he? See season 5. Zachariah admits it all to Dean in **4.22** and so we see why he stopped Chuck here.

Chuck says they lived through the ghost ship. When in actual fact, the episode this alludes to, **Red Sky in the Morning** (season 3) is one of the episodes that wasn't published as a book. Dean comments the books cover everything: all aspects of their lives, yet not all of them were published. The Lilith ones weren't published either. That's explainable, as Sam and Dean weren't meant to know the real truth behind this.

The pilot episode book is called *Supernatural*. The *Then* segment has shots of the book covers.

Kripke's Hollow from where Chuck hails, is a reference to Eric Kripke.

Keegan Connor Tracy was also in **2.7** playing the wife of the lawyer Dean was meant to have murdered.

So Dean's got his tattoo back now, he didn't have that in **4.10**. Also Sam has too. Seeing as how Dean said in **4.5** he came back without any scarring etc.

The covers from the books appear to be from opening titles of the show.

References to Sam and Dean being Chuck's number one fans from *Misery*. As well as to JD Salinger, the writer of *Catcher in the Rye*, who was reclusive.

The line about "M Night-level douchiness" is in reference to M Night Shyamalan, the writer and director, who would write endings with twists, as well as writing himself into the movie as a character. Chuck writes himself into the book and so Sam and Dean meet him.

Agents De Young and Shaw; Dennis De Young is the lead singer from the rockband *Styx* and Tommy Shaw is the guitarist. Their song, *Renegade* was used in **2.12** shapeshifter episode.

The episode title is from *The Monster At The End Of This Book* starring loveable, funny old Grover, by Jon Stone, where Grover warns the reader not to read on as, there's a monster at the end.

This episode aired and then the show was on hiatus in the US, returning 23 April 2009. Whereas ITV 2 in the UK, went and did a similar thing, and aired **4.19**, after two weeks. They never take *Supernatural* off air here. We get a complete 22 episode run, week after week! I've got one word for making us wait so long, *WINCEST!*

Quotes

Dean: "Along a lonely California highway, a mysterious woman in white lures men to their deaths…" (from the Pilot episode.)

Dean: "I'm full frontal in here dude."

Dean: "I'm sitting in a launder mat, sitting in a launder mat reading about myself. My head hurts."

Dean: "I can't see your face but those are your brooding and tensive shoulders."

Dean: "No homework. Watch some porn."

Castiel: "I am not. Kidding you."

Actual Legend

A prophet is defined as someone used as a go-between with the divine and humanity; is blessed with exceptional moral insight and the unique ability to express this. In Islam Muslims believe the Qur'an was revealed to Muhammad, who was Allah's final prophet – through the angel Gabriel. Differing from Christianity and Judaism, as Islam defines a difference between a prophet and that who is a direct messenger from God. But both receive Allah's revelation.

Adam was the first prophet and Muhammad was the last. Jesus is also regarded as a prophet as he received revelation from God. Five are particularly recognized for unwavering commitment to God and in enduring immense suffering. These five being: Noah, Abraham, Moses, Jesus and Muhammad.

In the Bible, some prophets occur in groups.

Anna is a prophet named in the Bible, the Gospel of St Luke. She prophesized about Jesus at the Temple of Jerusalem. The Roman Catholic church views Anna as a saint.

Archangels are found in all three of the major religions. Christianity, Islam, Judaism and in Zoroastrianism. Michael is the only one named in the Bible. In Islam, Gabriel (Jibrail), Michael (Mikaaiyl), Raphael (Israfil) and Azrael, he is not mentioned in the Qur'an but is referred to as "Mal ak al-Mant in Arabic, i.e. 'the Angel Of Death. Jibrail is the angel who communicates with prophets. Mikaaiyl is the archangel of mercy, bringing rain and thunder to earth. Israfil signals Judgement Day by blowing his horn.

The Bible makes several references to angels, including those at the tomb of Christ after he had risen, as well as visiting Christ in his time of agony. (An angel bringing Dean back from hell. i.e. Castiel.) Only archangels mentioned are Michael and Gabriel. Uriel, also an archangel, is mentioned in Esdras. St Michael is shown in early Christianity as a "commander, who in his right hand holds a spear with which he attacks Lucifer, Satan."

Ooh Bloops!

Chuck doesn't seem to know Sam and Dean even after he's had visions about them.

The list of published *Supernatural* novels is incomplete. **1.3 Dead in the Water** is missing. After **1.16 Shadow**, there are more titles missing; such as three episodes from season 2 and five episodes from season 3.

4.19 Jump The Shark

Written By Andrew Dabb. Directed By Phil Sgriccia
Original US Airdate 23 April 2009

Guest Stars: Jake Abel (Adam Milligan); Dedee Pfeiffer (Kate Milligan); Heather Feeney (Lisa)

Sam and Dean receive a mysterious phonecall from someone claiming to be John Winchester's son.

Windom, Minnesota.

Sam and Dean find out if there could be a third Winchester son, as well as investigating the disappearance of his mother.

Notes

Dean would eat anything save for stale tuna. Dean finally getting another call on Dad's cell. That hasn't been used for a while. Glad to see they keep the phone charged. But have to ask the question of why Dad tore out the pages from the journal about Adam. Maybe not so much about Adam but the place where he'd been hunting and what he found there. Perchance Sam and Dean may stumble into that place on their road trip.

Dean's very flippant comment about Dad dying after the car fell on him. When you get to the end of the episode, notice that Adam is a ghoul and knows all about Dad and them. It makes the episode seem more or less pointless since the ghouls know all about the Winchesters. (Hence the title.) Just like all the demons know about them too and conversely, the Winchesters know hardly anything, if at all, about them. At least not until they've conducted research. Sam and Dean didn't even think about ghouls , though Sam does explain this at the end. It is something they've been doing plenty of, i.e. being lax and missing big clues in the cases they chase. (Starting from **2.11** and continuing...)

Know they've got Lilith and the Apocalypse to think about but the thing is – they haven't even been thinking about that much either. They appear to be caught up in their own little whirlpools... Sam with his "I need demon blood to grow strong" and Dean with his, "I'm not strong enough to take on Lilith." Then their defeatist attitude: Dean in saying he's just tired of everything and Sam and Dean not wanting to work out their differences and faults with one another to lay closure to it. But prefer to let things fester and boil to the surface – eventually. (See **4.21**.)

There was oodles of pie at that diner and Dean was having none of it.

My point about them not thinking about what was happening in the town and who, or what, was behind it, as they were thinking about Adam now and everything Dad did with him, that he didn't do with them. Those special father/son activities. Especially not with Dean, and taking Adam to a baseball match to boot, really was the kicker for Dean. Okay, my point was Dean using holy water and silver to check out the possibilities of what Adam could be, but there are so many to choose from, he could have been 'anything'.

With hindsight, everything Adam told them appeared to be just to rile Dean, mostly, and see their reactions. To have a bit of fun before the spoils of war, before they got down to the dirty and ate them too.

541

But Dean says it himself too, there were photos there and photos never lie, even if people and ghosties and ghoulies and demons do.

Also whenever they're distracted from conducting a proper hunt or investigation, the main distraction always centres around their personal life. Something that's eating them (no pun intended), like in season 2 it was Sam wanting Dean to finish him off if he turned evil or Dean wallowing in guilt over Dad's sacrifice.

Dad wanted Adam to be normal. Keep him away from hunting. Something he didn't and wouldn't do for Sam and Dean. Bringing them up as hunters and the life of hunters was their fate. Then ostracized Sam for walking out on them because he wanted to be normal and have a normal life. As seen for **4.13** this was something Sam always craved.

The looks on Adam's face give everything away – not that he was a ghoul, but that he was trying to keep a straight face whilst all the while knowing he's getting one over on them; just waiting for the moment his and his mother's plan comes together and they can get revenge on the entire Winchester family for what Dad did to his father.

Then Dad taught Adam everything too. Poker, pool and how to drive. Come to think of it, he'd probably have given him the Impala too, if Dean wasn't meant to have it. Then Dean must be thinking, Adam's been driving his precious car as Dad must have given him driving lessons in it! So yes, you can forgive Dean for having a pang of jealousy or two. There was plenty to envy here. Got the impression Dad was turning Adam into a mini-Dean, minus the hunting. But treating Adam like a real son, a normal son and doing normal things with him, without a hint of hunting.

Let's see, what did Dean do on his 14th birthday? Hunt a little, perhaps, look after Sam some more. Adam's Mom was another blonde, seems Dad had a penchant for blondes.

When they were searching the house Adam didn't convince at all with his sob story. Look at his body language, his eyes appeared to be all over the place. Dad in the photos clearly looked "Photo-shopped."

Sam and Dean play Paper/Scissors/Stone, haven't done that since **2.17** when they played to see who would "babysit" Madison.

Nice line from Dean of cops don't have his eyes. His hunter eyes that is. Or rather his green eyes you can just lose yourself in, oh where was I?

Dean being a mechanic – something he may have been, as he said at the end of the episode, he's got Dad's jacket, his car, likes his music and tried so hard to be Dad, but Sam actually is like him. So he'd have followed him into that line of work too. Also in **2.20** his alternate 'wish' reality, Dean was a mechanic.

Dean says it for us once more when he remarks Adam was too easily sold on what they do and their hunting. Whereas anyone else would've freaked out or just not believed what they were being told. As mentioned in season 1 and throughout by Dean and sometimes by Sam, if Sam's friends knew what he did, they'd freak. Another reason why he didn't tell Jessica, whereas Dean confided in Cassie (**1.13**) and she dumped him. So Adam was eager to fool them by feigning to fit in.

They also too readily and easily believed he was their brother, sure some people would have demanded more proof than missing journal entries, a time-line and some photos, especially when meeting complete strangers for the first time and taking everything on face value. If Dad wanted Adam to know about hunting he would've told him.

Sam knows what it's like to want revenge, so does Dean, since he wanted revenge for practically his entire family at some point, Dad, Mom, Jessica, Dean and even for what Yellow Eyes has turned him into. At least set the ball rolling into what he'd become.

Dean has thought about eternity and where he wants to spend it, he's been in hell for practically an eternity; he doesn't want to spend it there!

Where did Dean get his change of clothes from, viz the suit, since when he left the motel room he was in his casuals. He must obviously keep a change of suit in his car.

Demon blood makes Sam stronger, which is why he didn't need hospitalization after being drained of so much blood, whereas someone like Dean, more human would. (Not that I'm calling Sam inhuman.) It also takes forever for Sam to be killed whenever he's abducted by himself, so Dean can save him and the day, night. Sam almost being taken once more and being dragged under the truck, as he was in **1.15** when he was abducted by the Benders. Sam gets so easily knocked out again and doesn't seem to put up much of a fight anymore. Sam's 'mojo' only works on demons then.

Sam telling Adam he can only count on family, is what Dean used to tell him all the time. Then Dean would say they can only count on each other, but lately in season 4, ever since Dean returned from hell, that doesn't seem to apply to them anymore. Sam's speech is the one Dad gave him and he went to university anyway and now he's giving the spiel to Adam.

Dean's still adamant Dad had no choice but to raise them as hunters but he did have one with Adam. As Adam still had his mother and he chose for him to be normal. Adam's not meant to be cursed for the sake of being cursed. But is since he's a Winchester.

(It was the Campbell's who were 'cursed'. Mom's side of the family and this transferred onto the Winchesters after Mom married Dad, so in actual fact, it was the Campbell curse. Which is all moot point (I have lots of moot points.) So they were cursed because of Mom and Yellow Eyes wanted a child to carry out his true intentions, his 'endgame' and he latched onto Mom for that child, being enamored with her. Which is why Yellow Eyes went from town to town, making deals and giving his blood to babies. In search of that one special, elusive child, but he had already decided it would be Mary's child, Sam. Hence sniffing Dean in **4.2**, he could sense/sniff out his blood he'd fed to Sam et al. But even after he decided it was Sammy he desired, he still carried on "infecting" other babies. Maybe not the right place to mention this but since curse was on the table, I offered up my opinion too. Oh and apologies for all the 'foodie' references relating to this episode.)

When Sam asked Dean if he was jealous, Dean should've asked him the same thing, only Dean chooses not to answer him in typical Dean fashion. Before he would argue his point home and now he chooses to clam up. Sam did appear a bit eager in embracing Adam with open arms, welcoming him into the Winchester fold. He hardly knew him yet trusted him as he was one of them. Dean wanting Adam to be normal, when he's not. Too late. Oops.

Dean trapped again in a crypt as he was in **3.4**, he gets trapped very easily too, of late.

His mother finds the term 'ghoul' racist, as did Ruby when applied to her in the context of being a demon. Okay, well, she's just a demon bitch! So there was another piece of repetition in the script, being racist that is.

Adam tells Sam he uses the word 'monster' frequently, but doesn't know what it means because he's had it used to describe him and Dean will call him that a lot more towards season's end. Sam will become a monster, he's already halfway there with all his demon blood partaking.

So in this episode, the kills of the father come back to haunt the sons. Sam and Dean survived because they were trained by him; are hunters. Makes you think if Dad hadn't been so complacent about telling Adam who he really is and what he really does/did, that he and his mother would've been alive now. So he thought, like Dean, in that he too wanted Adam to remain normal. However, if you argue Sam's point of training him, it would've saved his life and he was right, there was no escaping being a Winchester for him either.

Dean has the dirty job of having to kill again. Oh another thing, Dad and Dean used to protect Sam from having to do any actual killing (seen in previous episodes, such as **1.20, 2.3** etc.) and Dean had to kill oft times too, but Sam seems to be making up with the shortfall now, as he's killing not only demons, but also ends up killing the humans they're possessing, in the process.

Dean's line again of Adam being in a better place and he takes comfort in saying this on many occasions. He also said this about Cole in **4.15** and Pam too. Perhaps more wishful thinking on his part, Dean would like to be in a better place now as well.

Sam would be the one to think about having Adam brought back, but how would this happen. Seeing as both Sam and Dean were also brought back and given second chances. He thinks Castiel would help, but how would Castiel achieve this. It's not in his power to bring people back. He hasn't been ordered to do this, like he was with Dean.

Dean acknowledging Sam's the one who's more like Dad, even if Dean was the one who emulated him. Why is Sam more like him – when in this episode they were the exact opposite and Dean was more like Dad, as he wanted Adam to be normal, as did Dad. And Sam just wanted him to be a hunter, which Dad didn't.

Sam thanks him for the compliment but Dean didn't appear to be giving it as such. Dean's just indifferent and he really did look as if he didn't care either way anymore. That he's way past caring about anything. So dejected and yet he still has to carry on. From Dean's expression, it was apparent he really is tired – of everything!

"Jump the shark": this scene was thought of nothing more than trying to increase flagging ratings of the show in which it was tried. I.e. when the shows writers come up with a surprise or plot etc, which is hard to take seriously or even believe. A show usually only jumps after several seasons of success, but even that doesn't necessarily mean it will be cancelled. See *Happy Days* which made another one hundred episodes after this 'Jump The Shark' episode, what of *Supernatural* you might well ask, we could do with another hundred episodes!!

Jump the shark also means a TV show airs for longer than it should have and has to lead into a new gimmick for the show, like the introduction of a new character, such as a sibling, here it was Adam. (That was short-lived and just as well.)

Jump the shark in-jokes, included Adam at Cousin Oliver's Diner. There's a *31ˢᵗ Annual Fonzarelli Ski-ing Championship* poster on the wall to signify the 1977 episode of *Happy Days* when Fonzi jumps the shark whilst on water skis, hence leading to the term, "jump the shark" being coined.

The shark was jumped in *The Brady Bunch.*

There's a *Sonny B* lounge ad in the motel where Sam and Dean are staying, Sonny jumped the shark when he left Cher in an attempt at a solo career. In this photo it's actually Kim Manners and not Sonny. They looked very similar. Also by way of a tribute to the late Kim Manners. The motel is called 'Kelsey Manor.'

Dean is agent Ted Nugent, a hard rock guitarist and singer from Detroit, Michigan.

In the *CSI* episode **8.16 One and a Half Deaths,** Captain Brass attempts to explain the meaning of 'jump the shark' to Gil Grissom, but Gil doesn't have a clue as to who Fonzie is. This episode was the crossover between *CSI* and *Three and a Half Men.*

Jared commented: "I'm tied up and when that happens you feel very vulnerable. I guess it makes you act better by default because you're already uncomfortable."

Quotes

Dean: "Now I'm thinking about Dad sex. Stop talking, dude."

Dean: "We are his sons."

Dean: "Should've gone for paper."

Sam: "Welcome to the family."

Sam: "It's never over."

Sam: "Being a hunter isn't a job…it's life."

Dean: "I think it's too late for us. This is our life, this is who we are. Fine I accept that."

Sam and Dean's Take on the Legend/Lore

Sam was thrown, as ghouls don't go after the living, they eat dead things, as they're scavengers. He says they rob graves of bodies and so can be considered body snatchers too, or more likely, corpse snatchers.

Actual Legend

Ghouls is from the Arabic ghul *or ghula*. From Muslim folklore, it refers to ghouls both in the male and female form, who have a hunger and feed on human flesh. They are found to live in graveyards, as in this episode, ruins and deserted places. Preying on stolen corpses (again like here) as well as those who travel alone, or even feeding off lone children.

In Muslim folklore, the *ghula* pronounced *gulah*, is seen as an ordinary woman who wants to ensnare a husband. Once achieved, she then feeds on him.

In the West, ghouls are seen as living creatures, feeding and forever hungry. Their attributes include, claws for nails; have extremely long limbs and their eyes look yellow and "jaundice". Ghouls in western myth, also inhabit the form of an "undead" human who lives in an unmarked grave, whilst feeding on those who visit the graveyard and on corpses.

The term ghoul was also used to describe body snatchers, also known as, "resurrectionists", especially in the nineteenth century. These so called 'ghouls' stole bodies from cemeteries and sold them for medical purposes; viz dissections for doctors' training, as soon as a newly buried body was discovered, it would be stolen. The most famous were William Burke and William Hare – Scottish body snatchers. As they weren't into "snatching" bodies from graves, they resorted to murder instead and were believed to have killed up to 16 people.

Film/TV References

Godzilla

X Files Connection

9.15 Jump The Shark was the last episode to include The Lone Gunmen, when they seal themselves up in a room to contain a virus, which ultimately "contains" them too, i.e. they meet their end. The title was a funny reference to shows which are no longer fresh and inventive and have reached their sell-by date. This episode was a series finale of the *X Files* spin-off The *Lone Gunmen* which had been axed.

In **9.14 Scary Monsters** the phrase "monsters under the bed" may prove to be real in this *Supernatural* episode and not just imagined by a boy as in the *X Files* episode.

Music

A Little Bitty Tear by Burl Ives.

Ooh Bloops!

The beer in Dean's glass at the bar changes in each shot.

4.20 The Rapture

Written By Jeremy Carver. Directed By Charles Beeson
Original US Airdate 30 April 2009

Guest Stars: Misha Collins (Jimmy Novak/Castiel); Wynn Everett (Amelia Novak); Sydney Imbeau (Claire)

Castiel attempts to tell Dean something before he's taken away. Castiel's human host returns to his own body.

Pontiac, Illinois

Castiel, i.e. Jimmy Novak returns home to his family, only for events to take a sinister turn. Dean witnesses first hand the extent of Sam's demon blood drinking and ultimate betrayal.

Notes

Pontiac, Illinois is where Dean found Sam hiding out in **4.1**.

An episode all about Castiel and how he came to take on Jimmy Novak's body. As for calling Castiel's human host, Jimmy, wonder if this was a silent nod to James Stewart in the film *It's A Wonderful Life* (not that James' character was called Jimmy or became an angel himself, but he was shown the error of his ways by an angel.)

Dean fishing in the opening scene, just sitting by the lake looking so calm and peaceful. Yes, it could only be a dream. So how often do you have these dreams about fishing Dean? Wouldn't think he'd have fish on his mind, especially not after the stale tuna sandwich Sam offered him in the previous episode! Oh fish again in **4.17** with the sign saying not to microwave fish and fish in **1.17** and **2.14** too.

Dean telling Castiel they're inside his head and Castiel replies it's not safe there as they can hear him inside Dean's head. So Dean's having all his thoughts monitored. But then angels and God are all seeing etc. Jimmy eats like Dean, but on this occasion, even Dean doesn't have an appetite.

Jimmy knows everything that's been happening to him whilst Castiel is in his body (just like the humans possessed by demons do too) so when Castiel was having his crisis of faith, his doubts about his emotions and everything he was being told to do; I kind of thought this may be due to his human host trying to take control of his body. So Castiel was experiencing human emotions in that way; and why he was taken away, before being returned after he was "cleansed" of such emotions. Unless of course, the host body is still there and can't take back its body until the angel leaves it. Just a thought.

Dean's brushing his teeth now in a reversal of the previous episode, where it was Sam. Sam can't wait for his demon blood fix and Dean asking if the Coke was refreshing. As in Coke fix, i.e. blood here, in true self-confessed addict mode. Anna also knows of Sam's secret 'activity' and isn't pleased about it. Yet Sam still doesn't get the hint and will continue with it. There's no stopping him, even when Dean and Bobby stage an intervention at the end of the episode and the next.

So they'll never get to know what Castiel was going to tell Dean, another reason why he's dragged away – after putting up a fight. Castiel seemed to be a part of that in **4.21**. Was this the same reason she was taken away for, that she found out the real truth about Lilith and the Apocalypse, as revealed in **4.22**.

Before Castiel takes over Jimmy's body, he's put through various tests to find out if he has real faith and truly believes. Jimmy believes he's chosen to do what he did and is told it's in his blood (a lot of mileage from that phrase of late) and says it's not his place to question God's will. This is what Castiel tells Dean on many occasions. That he can't question his orders and neither can Dean or anyone else.

Notice how Misha's voice deepens and sounds more gruff, when he's in Castiel mode, exerting the full authority of who he is in this way, "an angel of the Lord", in Castiel's words.

(Appears Ruby is staying away from Sam on purpose, so he becomes more dependent on blood drinking and in the belief that demon blood is the only thing that makes him strong; strong enough to defeat Lilith. Yet she reveals in **4.22** that Sam had it in him all along: he was strong enough without having to drink blood. But he chose to listen to Ruby without any doubts or hesitation. Showing to some degree the extent of his vulnerability and gullibility, especially when Dean was in hell. So instead of listening to Dean – he chose Ruby over his own brother. What's the line, "he ain't heavy, he's my brother.") Again doing everything she wanted. Including not telling Dean about Ruby to begin with in season 3.

[Ruby saving Dean's life in **3.9** was all a ploy to ensure Dean does get to hell and break the first seal. Though hedging their bets on whether Dean would actually break in hell, was one hell of a risk for them. What if he'd have been as strong as Dad and not succumbed. But then if Dean had died then and there in **3.9**, he would've still ended up in hell anyway. It was only to convince Sam she was on their side and would do anything to help them. Azazel in **4.22** had a knife similar to Ruby's so is this where she got it from or do all 'chosen' demons carry one.

Jimmy has been an 'angel' for a year or at least a host, so as Castiel was on earth for over 2,000 years, at least, he obviously has had different host bodies through the centuries. But the hosts have to be especially chosen and it must be in their blood.

Naturally, or unnaturally, it was apparent as soon as Jimmy got home that a demon would come-a-calling. Jimmy no longer saying Grace before a meal. Has his faith cowered now.

The demon woman saying Sam "Can't get it up now" when he's too weak to use his power. Talk about a double entendre! Demons have dirty minds. Like Ruby and her "grow a pesquiter" line in **4.22**, in place of telling him to grow a 'dick'. *Supernatural's* fave 'd' word. This wasn't used in this episode, for a change.

When Amelia came back – knew she had been possessed because the same thing happened to Gramps Campbell in **4.3.** He left the house last, after checking up on Mary's friend and had been possessed by Yellow Eyes. The same thing happened to Amelia here and we all know *Supernatural* loves its use of familiar plots and lines to do over.

Again, Sam declaring Jimmy can never go back to his family and that he has to leave them forever. An echo of what he told Adam in the previous episode: that he's a Winchester and he needs to become a hunter to stay alive. Well, so is being an angel and giving your human body over to one. In the same way, there's no going back for Jimmy as he's now in the real world of angels and demons and Castiel or anyone else can't really protect him. Advice from Sam about killing himself if he can't leave his family, that's a new one from him. Is there something we don't know Sammy? Has he thought about ending it all when Dean wasn't around? Aside from not caring whatever happened to him in **4.9**.

Sam asking Ruby what's left for him in this world in **4.22** and yet in **4.12** he tells her and Dean that he wants to grow old. Slim chance of that happening on his current chosen path.

Dean tells Sam he's not sugar-coating it. What Sam said to Dean in **2.16** when he told Molly about ghosts and spirits and what they do.

550

Molly was another one who was quick to accept what Sam and Dean do and believed in spirits and ghost, see **4.19**. When Sam was trying to explain things to her gently, instead of abruptly and to the point, like Dean.

Sam actually shown hot-wiring a car, for a change.

Dean telling Sam he fainted, whereas Sam puts it down to being dizzy – as in, hasn't eaten (or in his case – drank demon blood) dizzy. Also how did Amelia happen to have Sam's phone number when she called Jimmy. All demons have a hotline to his number, courtesy of Ruby.

Jimmy saying he's done everything Castiel's asked of him and yet he thanks him in this way, by staying away. Same thing Dean said to Castiel in **4.18** when he "begged" him for help whilst attempting to save Sam from sleeping with Lilith. Castiel did show up and told him how to help Sam, just as he turned up here in Claire's body. He was going to take her over now and use her as a host since it was in her blood and she too was destined for this. What was wrong with still using Jimmy, or did too many demons know and recognize him in that guise. (Jimmy's family was chosen to serve God in this way.) Lilith's specialty was to take over human, blonde girls and now Castiel was going to follow suit and use Claire as a host.

Sam finally showing his true colours, so to speak and drinking demon blood in front of everyone, including Dean who is completely disgusted at what he sees. Sam transforming into a monster (the very thing they hunt) right before his eyes. Then Sam had to drink the demon blood so he'd have the power to 'exorcise' the demon smoke from Amelia's body so, that Jimmy didn't die in vain and Claire had a mother to take care of her. (Unlike Sam and Dean.) Eeww, the blood around Sam's mouth akin to a vampire feeding frenzy. Dean was still in shock.

Castiel tells Jimmy he keeps his promises. Now Jimmy's in a better place. Well, thought I'd add that in since no one else said it.

Castiel returns a different angel, you know the phrase, a new person, well he's a new angel; the Castiel in **4.1**. He serves only God.

Sam and Dean not having an argument at the end in the car, so unlike them, we miss our Sam and Dean fights! Dean saying he's just plain tired. Another cop out! He's always tired, but Dean has called Bobby to let him know of Sam and he has the panic room all prepared for Sam's detox/drying out...

The episode title **The Rapture** is mentioned in Revelations. A prophecy foretelling of an event as in Christian eschatology, where devout Christians assemble to celebrate the second coming of Christ, including those who are dead, to be resurrected. *See Thessalonians 4:15-17.* So from the title and Castiel not being able to tell Dean what he wants, it appears the final curtain, Judgement Day is nigh and so he wasn't able to warn Dean about this. See the season finale.

Misha Collins spoke about how he, Jensen and Jared "have a lot of fun. We laugh a lot. That's the biggest challenge on set – not laughing during takes – which I think is a really good problem to have. I've been experimenting with different ways not to laugh. Biting my cheeks is actually very effective. There's a little tip.

Quotes

Dean: "…more private. We're inside my head."
Castiel: "Exactly, someone could be listening."

Dean: "Was it a refreshing Coke?"

Castiel: "I serve heaven. I don't serve man and I certainly don't serve you!"

Sam: "Let's hear it. You saw what I did…stop the car. Take a swing…then scream…chew me out. You're not mad."
Dean: "I don't care. What do you want me to say…I'm tired man. I'm done. I am just done."

4.21 When The Levee Breaks

Written By Sera Gamble. Directed By Robert Singer
Original US Airdate 7 May 2009

Guest Stars: Misha Collins (Castiel); Christopher Heyerdahl (Alastair); Genevieve Cortese (Ruby); Colin Ford (Young Sam); Juliana Wimbles (Demon nurse)

Dean and Bobby try to detox Sam, who during bouts of hallucinations, convinces himself he's on the right path to killing Lilith.

Notes

Another choice phrase from Dean's the writers like to use is, "I get it now…"

Sam is still deluding himself into thinking he can kill Lilith and he has to be the one to do it. When the "prophecy" states that only a righteous man can prevent the last seal from being broken; this righteous man is Dean. Of course it could be twisted round to read – 'only a self-righteous man can break the final seal'. In which case that'd be Sam! Dean's too weak to even try – in his opinion.

Akin to being in drug rehab; Sam goes through the process of hallucinations: of being tormented by Alastair and Sam begs not to be tortured. He can now only imagine how Dean felt in his place, all those years in hell. Okay, not so much imagine, as he believes it's really happening to him. So Sam is in a better position to understand why Dean feels he's not strong enough; which will probably only confound matters even further. Reinforcing Sam's claim he can defeat Lilith. Dean had to go through years of that torture which Sam isn't even enduring for real and yet Sam fears what's about to happen to him.

Hey, Sam even had the obligatory sick bucket. Appears the withdrawal symptoms from demon blood don't involve being physically sick; but suffering all sorts of hallucinations and being thrown around the room. Couldn't they just kind of 'exorcised' Sam. Nah, probably wouldn't have worked as Bobby says there's no demon detox manual. Also he wasn't possessed by a demon. How about getting him a complete blood transfusion – wouldn't that have speeded up the process to an extent. You know the process by which all the blood is removed from the body and filtered before being put back – or transfused. {Delving into **6.9** *X Files* episode **S.R.819**; where Scully believes she has found a way to remove the carbon from Skinner's blood. If only removing the demon blood in this way form Sam would work.}

Sam having hallucinations, about himself aged 14, saying he got away from Dad and he should've stayed away. He went off with Dean instead and got Jessica killed. Sam's still thinking about this four years on and still blames himself for her death. (See Pilot.) Sam running from what's inside of him. The hunter inside of him or the demon blood inside of him…he ran from his hunter destiny, only to return and embrace the demon blood part of his life and carry this on. So, no he couldn't escape from this.

As he also says, in **4.4**, he wishes he could stop this blood flowing inside of him but he can't. It's part of him and will always remain that way. He has no control over that; he didn't have to begin the blood fest

553

and add more to his system. Sam at 14, was a reference to **4.13** when we got an insight into Sam's school life and how he didn't want to be a hunter. Oh and another thing, Sam was talking about Dad's legacy to Dean in season 2 about being a hunter and continuing it on, well, Sam also had Yellow Eyes' legacy to contend with too. He was chosen by him to carry out his plan and that's exactly what he did in the season finale.

Bobby having doubts about locking Sam away at this time when he could be helpful and maybe can kill demons as he's strong enough. Dean just thinks it's a convenient way to sacrifice Sam in yet another battle and he doesn't want to lose Sam in that way (or any way.) He already did once – then we lost Dean and it'll be as though they sacrifice themselves for nothing again. If only Sam had remained in the panic room. Bobby says they love Sam too much and that's why they don't want him fighting. Besides, he's the baby of the family.

Sam's hallucinations of Mom again reinforce what Sam wants to do. That he's the correct choice. He should be the one to get "justice", as she calls it. But what he wants to do isn't justice. That's not the reason he's been told Lilith must die. It's to save the world – not justice for the family. That's too late and he did get justice or retribution or revenge; whatever you want to call it; when Dean killed Yellow Eyes. Who was the one who set the ball rolling for their family and set things in motion – like Sam's demon blood for starters.

Again Mom says Dean won't understand what Sam needs to do, Sam said this too in **4.4**. That Dean doesn't understand what Sam has in him because he doesn't have the same inside of him. What's not to understand? That even if Dean did have demon blood in him, he would leave it to lay dormant and wouldn't mess with it.

Everyone telling him he has to kill Lilith and to not let anyone get in the way; not even Dean – who is just too weak. But Dean hasn't even been tested or challenged yet. Dean says he's weak, yes – but is he really – he did after all have the courage to go in there and torture Alastair - of course that would've taken courage to face him again like that. Only for Dean to get beaten up by him too. Dean was ready to do whatever the angels asked him to. (See finale.) Also instead of doing the opposite; everyone Sam hallucinates about is telling him to kill Lilith! That he should be the one. So all that guff about a righteous man preventing the final seal from being broken, was just that, a pile of old guff.

Castiel tells Dean he has to be the one to stop Lilith – but in the end he lets Sam go because it's not Dean who is going to do this – but Sam. Otherwise why would Castiel even bother interfering and releasing Sam from the panic room. Anna discover this too and so she's dragged away so she can't interfere in any of it, and even attempt to warn Dean.

Dean has to stop the Apocalypse, yes – but not by killing Lilith. Where did it say Dean had to stop Lilith from breaking the final seal. This could have been achieved in any number of ways, without actually killing her. Preventing the final seal from being broken could've meant having to do anything. Also Ruby planted this thought into their minds – didn't she in season 3, when she said the time's right to kill her in the season 3 finale and then Dean would be saved. Whereas in actual fact, the opportunity would have happened regardless of what she told them as we'll see next episode. (Only if Lilith had been killed then the Apocalypse wouldn't have happened then since the first seal hadn't been broken.)

The angels, including Castiel only told them they had to prevent seals from being broken and Lilith was breaking the seals so she had to be stopped - not necessarily killed. Why does no one know about the breaking of the final seal in more detail – it had to have been "written" somewhere. (Aside from Chuck knowing and Zachariah) Ruby would know because she was in league with Lilith from the outset – for glory!

Dean, again with the'd' word (dick). Castiel sure must've got tired of hearing this! But gets Dean to swear to serve God and his angels. Only he is not really serving God. Dean believes Castiel now – when he can't really tell him anything – especially when he tried to warn him in **4.20** and was stopped.

Great special effects – Sam being thrown around the panic room. A case of – if having demon blood can do this to Sam – what cannot having any do! Drive him crazy and out of control.

Dean's limited this to two choices: he can trust angels or Sam can trust demons – meaning Ruby for starters. But it's not a question of trust. It's knowing what you have to do and believing it's the right thing to do that matters here.

Sam then hallucinates Dean, who appears to be telling him not to do this: again that Dean was picked to stop Lilith and not Sam. Which Sam probably took to mean Dean was being self-righteous. Dean calls it revenge and Mom called it justice.

Interesting how the scenes were filmed. Dean appears to Sam in a hallucination, telling him he's a monster and all the while, he's really telling Bobby how he actually feels about Sam. How he'd die for him over again, but won't let him turn himself into something unnatural. That's brotherly love. Then, uses the monster line here to Bobby, when "he's" just called Sam a monster in his hallucination. Again Dean uses the phrase, "I guess I've found my line. In Sam being a monster or turning into one. From freak to monster. Dean throughout past seasons saying the same thing. Sam demanding Dean doesn't call him a monster, he'll take it from anyone except Dean. Similar to what Sam said in **1.21** after Dean said Mom's dead and Sam tells him not to talk about Mom in that way.

Castiel lets Sam go. (For purposes in the next episode – so he gets to kill Lilith and set events in motion. But it's the wrong thing to do!) Anna must've known the truth about Lilith too, as she was Castiel's boss and that's why she's removed from the picture too. (As was Castiel in **4.20**.)

Sam doesn't take the Impala. He also sees Bobby in a hallucinatory state and Bobby tries to stop him, whereas he was telling Dean they should let Sam out earlier. Dean thinks Ruby could've let him out (no one heard Sam leaving now.) Dean wants Ruby dead. (See **4.22**.)

Ruby tells Sam – lies to Sam - that she's been busy and so hasn't been around, all the while she's been making Sam hunger for more of her blood, dangling the demon carrot in front of him and Sam falling for it. See **4.12** when he asks her where she goes or disappears to; at least Sam did ask.

Sam doesn't know Dean as well as he thinks; but Dean knows him better than that. See **4.1** when he tracked Sam down using Sam's *Star Wars* moniker, one of Sam's aliases and in **2.14** when he found him possessed by Meg. Dean knows that kid!

Ruby even tells Sam here that seal 66 can't be broken and only Lucifer's first can break it. Lucifer's first could only have been a demon. Hence it had to be Lilith. Besides everyone had been saying she was breaking the seals.

Dean didn't listen to Bobby when he told him to keep an eye on Sam (or Ruby) – they fight. Funny Sam wants to talk now! Yeah, all to save Ruby. Boy did Dean tell him she was TROUBLE!

Sam wants Dean to trust him because Dean's looked out for him his whole life and now he wants him to do the same for Dean. Sam doesn't realize this situation is different. It's not about whether they trust each other or not; it's about saving people, preventing the Apocalypse; irrespective of what they think of each other. It was never a competition about which one of them should do it – but about working together and mostly about Sam supporting Dean and helping him through it. Not about taking it upon himself to do Dean's work. If only they (Sam) had realized that. To have each other's back instead of going off solo. Sam was correct when he said Dean should understand Sam's the only one who can do this – he was - and all the demons expected it and wanted it that way. (As did Zachariah.)

So Dean finally calls Sam a monster to his face, reverting back to his hallucination: which became a reality.

Another showdown here between the two – but not as we expected between them. Sam getting the better of Dean and almost strangling him. If he wasn't his brother, he probably would've done it.

Dean saying he's not like Dad (most recently in **4.19**), yet he acts like him in this episode by telling Sam not to show his face anymore when he leaves and you know what? – Sam obliges and doesn't! It's Dean who will have a change of heart and will go to Sam – in the end – but it'll be too little too late, through no fault of his own.

The showdown between Sam and Dean, did come but it wasn't about Sam being dark and evil. It was about Sam trying to move past that and believe he was acting for the good of all!

Dean's reference to Planet Vulcan - from where Mr Spock hails in the original *Star Trek* series. It's been said Dean was actually referring to the portrayal of the Vulcans in *Star Trek: Enterprise,* the prequel series. Since they were more deceptive and cunning rather than their later "logical" selves.

The episode title is from a Led Zeppelin song, taken from an old Blues song dating back to the 1930's and here I was thinking it was a reference to the floodgates being opened, as it was every man for himself. Sam's demon blood intake representing his need for it and dependence. Hence the allusion to his being flooded, not only with hallucinations, but the demon blood in his system too.

On Sam's dark nature, Jared comments: "I like the dark side! Demons are more fun to play. Sam has grown and changed. He'll be redeemed I'm sure if something goes wrong, but I love the direction it's going in, I like the dynamic of brother v brother."

Quotes

Mom: "What you're doing is brave – not crazy. Being practical I am so proud of you." (In contrast to Dad, who wouldn't be proud.)

"Bobby: "Willingly signed up to be the angel's bitch excuse me, sucker."

"Dean: "I would die for him in a second, but I won't let him do this to himself. I guess I found my line. I won't let my brother turn into a monster."

Dean: "Killing's her next big thing on my 'to do' list."

Dean: "She's poison. Look what she did to you…That is French for manipulating your ass ten ways from Sunday."

Dean: "It means you're a monster!"

Sam: "You don't know me. You never did and you never will."

Dean: "You walk out that door - don't you ever come back!"

4.22 Lucifer Rising

Written & Directed By Eric Kripke
Original US Airdate 14 May 2009

Guest Stars: Kurt Fuller (Zachariah); Misha Collins (Castiel); Genevieve Cortese (Ruby); Katherine Boecher (Lilith); Rob Benedict (Chuck Shurley); Rob Labelle (Azazel/Father Lehne)

St Mary's Convent, Ilchester, Maryland
1972

A priest, possessed by Yellow Eyes slaughters nuns at a convent.

Present

Sam and Ruby set events in motion and Dean is transported to a "waiting" room for his final orders.

Notes

Yellow Eyes' "end game" is revealed here. The one Castiel sent Dean back to his parents home to find out about in **4.3**. This was Yellow Eyes' end game after he found Lucifer and where to open up his "cage" and release him. Only Sam could be the one to do it. Why he fed him demon blood as a baby and wanted him to be his army leader. He could feed him demon blood and "nurture" Sam into the one needed to kill Lilith. So it all makes sense now!

Father Lehne is named for the 'original' actor who played Yellow Eyes, Frederic Lehne.

Sam regrets what he did and said to Dean. He seems to be thinking this before Ruby opens her pie hole (!) and tells him Dean's the one in the wrong and shouldn't have said what he did to Sam. (More like Dean was right about her – all along – as was I.)

There's Sam's line about not having a future after all this is over. Probably thinking he can't ever make it up to Dean. So Sam's over wanting to grow old (**4.12**). Is there a future for anyone is the question Sam should be pondering here. Sam does appear to have changed, as he puts it, since he treated Dean like he did and after Dean was only trying to make him see the error of his ways, looking out for him. To show him he was turning into something he didn't like, what they hunt. Sam didn't want to hear it, and ends up saying it himself now.

Dean repeats what's gone before – that Sam didn't want this life; to be a hunter and wanted out of this family because of it. Since Eric Kripke wrote this episode, he had to squeeze that in again – as that's what the entire series is about. Sam leaving the hunting life behind and Dean bringing him back into it (the pilot episode) and how it all started for them. As for Dean being tired of chasing Sam, he didn't really – he just wanted to help him find Dad in season 1. Though Sam has gone off on his own on a number of occasions and Dean's had to go after him and help him out. Oh and Dean says he's tired once again!

Dean convincing Bobby he did the right thing in letting Sam leave, giving Sam an ultimatum and he went regardless. I.e it was Dad's ultimatum and not Dean's. He just tried to use it as a last resort; a last ditched effort to somehow make him see that what he was doing was wrong. Sam didn't listen to Dad, would he really expect him to listen to Dean? Dean will be forever defending Dad saying he wasn't a coward.

As if by magic, Dean disappears into the "green room" – didn't Bobby wonder where Dean had disappeared to so suddenly. Castiel informing Dean that its' almost time – when in actual fact – it'll be too late for him to do anything.

Another niggle: did nobody notice all those babies disappearing from hospitals. It didn't send alarm bells ringing or warning signs in any quarters – no newspaper reports – nothing. Not even from Rufus or anyone in the hunting community. Then upon investigation, it could've revealed some sort of connection to Lilith and of course, Ruby mentioned none of this either, until it was convenient for her.

Dean didn't notice all of the paintings around him and what they depicted. Castiel instructing Dean to have faith, after he's just 'lied' to him. Lilith has to be the one to break the seal – only Lilith is the final seal! As for reminding Dean who began all this – it was hardly his fault. Also double standards on Zachariah's part – since he wanted all this to begin with – he wanted the Apocalypse.

Sam's wasting his powers on torturing the demon nurse, as Ruby casually stands by and watches. Having Ruby be the one who was manipulating him all along, like I said throughout season 3 and 4. All her allusions to knowing what Sam really wants, searching him out in season 3 and that "fallen little angel on his shoulder" routine in season 3. A reference to Lucifer if ever there was one. Funny, perhaps no one thought of this when they wrote that; or maybe no one was meant to, as they probably weren't sure of where season 4 was heading. Glad I mentioned it then and now. Could Sam really be so naïve and expect Ruby to be just 'freed' from hell for helping them in season 3. Like the remark she made in **4.9** about Lilith torturing her and she had to deal to kill Sam and that's why she was let out of hell, and Sam fell for it.

How come no one knew what was written about the seals and seal 66 about the first demon being the one to break it. That was so *Buffy* with the First; the First Evil.

Another niggle: why didn't Sam think about Chuck to locate Lilith, instead of following Ruby's lead and going for the nurse, when Ruby was Lilith's right hand demon to begin with. Not to mention Ruby would've run a mile from the threat of Chuck's archangel. Also would he really expect our Deano to leave him a damning voicemail, when he's already had done with him and couldn't care less about Sam at that particular point in time. That was just the final nail in the coffin, so to speak, just to drive Sam forward. Dean's voice was a little too deep on there too. Sam not using his brain and getting sucked in majorly! (I won't go into the whole "thinking with your downstairs brain and not upstairs brain" from **1.16** here.)

Dean, the bigger man – showing he is better than Dad and calls Sam to apologize – going straight to voicemail and no matter, as Sam never gets to hear it anyhow. Not his message at least.

Ruby knows there's one final seal left to be broken; more subtle hints dropped by Ruby – but hey, Sam and no one else was listening: but Dean knew of her treachery and manipulation. Dean always knew and didn't trust her. So everything led to this and what Chuck dreamt in **4.18**. Now we know what the angels knew, what seal 66 was.

Yellow Eyes' orders to find a special child came from Lucifer who began everything, in a bid to rise. Yellow Eyes was feeding the babies his blood in search for that special child. Hey, if Lilith was out of the pit she'd be feeding on the babies! How did Lilith get out of said pit?

Ruby's joke: what's black and white and red all over – could be said about her too! Especially when Dean was finished with her and yes, he finally got to do what he always wanted: kill Ruby. Result!

The priest mentioned Azazel in the paper. So why did they never come across this before, whenever they researched something about him, even after they found out his name. A simple Google search (other search engines are available) would've resulted in this article. Curiously Dad made no note about it in his journal either! Especially as he knew all about Azazel and his name in **2.1**.

As Bobby said – in **4.14** a simple phonecall would've helped them out and here in much the same way, a simple Internet search would've revealed plenty and Sam was meant to be the brains of the outfit. (Oh I know I've said it before!)

Azazel was a demon too so only fitting he too would want Lucifer to rise even before Lucifer commanded this of him in 1972. Took him ten years to set his plans adrift, with Sam and some of the other babies.

Dean breaking the statue and then acting all sheepish when Castiel turned up. Castiel almost cracked a joke there and he didn't realize it – about which door Dean would use to leave. Tessa told Dean about the angels using him in **4.15**, which turns out to be true here, since all Zachariah did was "lock" him away and allowed the seals to be broken. (See also **2.1**.)

Ruby practically forcing Sam to listen to Dean's message because she knows it won't be what Dean really said and Dean claimed all along, as did Bobby, demons lie!

Zachariah and his howler monkeys line. Do all angels just think of monkeys. See **4.17** where Dean mentions monkey suits. As did Uriel. Zachariah finally tells Dean Lilith will break the final seal and it's already been decided – sans Dean. Zachariah knew all along and if the other angels knew, like Castiel, (but he did know) there'd be a rebellion in the ranks. Calling them "grunts," how arrogant of an angel and just like Uriel too. Which again makes me ask if he was in on it too – to get Lucifer out. Uriel mentioned in **4.16,** there are others like him who want the same thing, especially when he was getting Castiel to sign up to the cause too.

Sixty five seals wouldn't have been broken if this wasn't the "end game". They could've prevented it. Now this also explains why Zachariah stopped Chuck from telling them what he found out and definitely had to explain why Castiel was stopped from telling Dean in **4.20** and why Anna was taken. (To where though?)

Dean's still chosen – only he has to stop Lucifer. Kind of defeats the purpose of everything really. He rises, the world ends and Dean has

561

to stop him – for good. So what was the point of it all. Uriel wanted Lucifer back as he shouldn't have been stuck down there to begin with. So it's not God's plan or will after all, but the so-called bosses in the form of Zachariah. He did convey the impression he was one of those on Uriel's side and Zachariah's remark about telling Dean to quit hurling monkey stuff.

Again with Zachariah's language of 2 virgins and 70 sluts waiting for Dean in heaven. See **4.17** and his fornification line. Angels do not speak like that and should not. (See Castiel who has never uttered any profanities, he's had his doubts, but it's not the same thing.) Just because he's the boss doesn't give him the right to be crude and insulting.

Okay, you may think I went a little OTT in my line of thinking here, but it does all add up. Sam having Azazel's blood in him; but then Sam was killed in season 2. Afterwhich it worked out for the demons again since Lilith had Dean's contract and wouldn't give him to save the world (no pun.) The torture in hell and breaking the seal. Getting Ruby to work on Sam. Then season 1 with Dad sacrificing himself to save Dean, but not breaking the seal in hell. The demons then had to look for a new substitute, enter the son. Suppose I could go round in circles "like a wheel within a wheel," talking about this and ending up from whence I began!

But wait, I feel another niggle coming on, why all the fuss Lilith made over getting Bela to kill Sam and Dean in season 3? Just toying with her so she thinks she's doing something to save herself?

Castiel comes up with the destiny line again, all this has been foretold. Or as Dean would say, "enough with the destiny crap." He still doesn't believe in destiny and it's been proven that destiny isn't absolute and can be altered. It's not final. Dean prefers family to everything, to all the lies and this wasn't God's plan either.

Dean takes a swipe at Castiel! Funny scene even at such a time.

Was there anything in the burger then, as Castiel shows up just as Dean gave in to temptation and was about to take a bite?

Dean's speech is reminiscent of the one he had with Anna in **4.10**. When she tells him humans experience so much – so many emotions and that's what she wanted as well and why she fell. Whereas Dean thinks she's got it good as an angel and now Dean says it again; why should Castiel care about dying when he's already dead and doing the right thing is worth dying for! Dean is also, well, was also dead too and he died to bring back Sam and that was the right thing to do in his eyes.

Also in **3.12** Dean if to win a war you have to stop acting like humans then he'd rather not win. Here he says pretty much the same thing.

Castiel mentions here destiny can't be changed (again) but time and again he's seen it being altered and has taken part in it too.

Dean's message, the message Sam listens to, probably end up being fighting words for Sam. The final straw – there's nothing left for him to feel guilty about when his own brother disowns him twice over. Dean no longer has faith in Sam.

Zachariah using the "hell" word. Again not typical angelic behaviour. Chuck knows where Lilith is – so in between **4.18** and now someone could've found out from Chuck where Lilith was or at least attempted to! Pointless if he's there and they can't 'use' him! Especially now. Chuck once again comments what they're doing isn't in the story – as he did in **4.18**. Where Dean tells him he's part of it now and all this is real. Here Castiel tells him it's all being made up as they go.

Dean must stop Sam, so why wasn't he dropped off in the centre of it all. Dean casually strolling in as well! Ruby and her dirty looks! Yes Dean just watch her some more and for ages too! Still Sam didn't get it – that Lilith offered no resistance against being killed; that she didn't fight to save herself. It was all too easy. Dean calling out to Sam as he did in the season 3 finale to save him and now Dean has to stop Sam from killing Lilith but he's too late! Sam just assumed he'd kill her before any Apocalypse could be started.

The first demon is the last seal. They don't read any religious texts. Yes I've said it before, must be written somewhere. Sam doesn't have anymore strength left now, which is just as well. Couldn't they stop the blood circle from forming. Sam's sorry.

So Sam and Dean together, united at last. In a change to the final season finales in other other episodes. When someone would be killed.

I was right about Ruby leading Sam a merry dance, or not so merry. Good then Dean was right about her all along too. Don't know about you, but I got the feeling Zachariah didn't want Dean stopping the Apocalypse and that he was on Uriel' side. Especially with half the things coming out of his mouth in this episode and in **4.17** seemed devious in wanting Dean to 'carry on' (not as in their theme song, so no pun here) and stop the seals from being broken. Otherwise why reveal to Dean now that he wants the world to end since he knows Dean won't be going anywhere. At least Castiel saw sense and let Dean out!

Marsha was meant to be a reference to Marsha from *The Brady Bunch* and how Jan complained of Marsha always being the apple of everyone's eye. Sam is also the middle child, like Jan, if we take into account Adam; so in season 1, Dad gave Dean all his attention.

Ruby's "guess who's coming to dinner line, obviously was a reference to the Sidney Poitier movie of the same name. About a black doctor who's engaged to a white woman and is invited for dinner at her parents' house.

Ruby's Dumbo line alluding to *Disney's Dumbo* (1941) where Dumbo the elephant used a feather to direct his energy on, but Dumbo finally learns to fly on his own. Since he had it in him all the time to be able to do this. A great analogy, as Sam believes he needs demon blood to get stronger, firstly he's duped by Ruby and then she admits he had this ability to begin with, i.e. to kill demons.

Ruby's *Nurse Betty* is a reference to *Nurse Betty* (2000) with Renee Zellweger. Dean's line of the Holodeck is about the holodeck in *Star Trek: The Next Generation; Star Trek Deep Space Nine* and *Star Trek Voyager*. The holodeck was a virtual world created by the computer. Just like the 'green room' where Dean is being kept appears like a virtual world too.

"The Suite Life of Zach and Cas" is a reference to the Disney sitcom, *The Suite Life of Zack and Cody*, who were twins living at a hotel, where their mother was a singer. (It ran from 2005-2008).

Ruby's allusion to the Death Star was from *Star Wars Episode IV: A New Hope* (1977). Luke Skywalker had to fly his fighter in a suicide attack on the Death Star. Much in the same way Sam's attack on Lilith is almost a suicide bid, since there's no telling how he would have feared on his own against her. As his powers used to let him down at inopportune moments. Which is just how Ruby planned it and how she wanted it here by making sure Sam was fully tanked to the hilt, ensuring he managed to kill Lilith.

A year ago Dean went to hell and a year later, we're all in hell, viz, the Apocalypse! As well as the title, **Lazarus Rising** and **Lucifer Rising**, again coming round full circle to the first opening scene, Dean being raised to save the world and in the finale, he still has to save the world, but by destroying Lucifer to kingdom come!

Eric Kripke said the only problem with killing off Lilith, is the way in which Sam wants to kill her. Dean and Bobby, "just don't want to forfeit Sam's soul in the process…Sam lives for this one. We were getting a little tired with killing and resurrecting our guys – at least for now, they may die again sometime next season [5] who knows." Was that a big hint for us, as to how the season 5 finale and perhaps the last ever episode of the entire series may end. So we can't look forward to a happy-ever after for our heroes after they've done so much for the world!

Continues Eric, "There will be a huge confrontation, bridges burnt and a seemingly insurmountable chasm between the guys. But it will happen <u>before</u> the end of the finale. We'll deal with some of the repercussions of their split before the season's out just to torture our fans! Thanks!

Quotes

Sam: "You're talking like I've got an after. I can feel it inside me Ruby. I've changed for good. There's no going back now."

Dean: "He's my blood."

Dean: "Sweet life of Zac and Cas – it's a…never mind."
Dean: "It's me…still pissed and I owe you a serious beatdown but I shouldn't have said what I said – I'm not Dad. We're brothers, we're family and no matter how bad things get that doesn't change. Sammy I'm sorry."

Ruby: "You can't trust anyone these days." (Talking about herself again. Ruby has tickets on herself doesn't she. My favourite Aussie phrase, meaning she's vain; up herself.)

Castiel: "You're outside your coverage zone."

Castiel: "We're making it up as we go."

Ruby: "…and it is written that the first demon shall be the last seal."

Ruby: "Guess who's coming to dinner?"
Sam: "Oh my God…"
Ruby: "Guess again."

Film/TV References

Gilligan's Island, The Brady Bunch. Stepford Wives.

Music

Carry On Wayward Son by Kansas

Miscellaneous

Criticizing the Critics/ Reviewers: You Know Who You Are

So what do critics have against this show anyway and no comparing it to *Buffy* isn't a very good start either. They may be similar genres but that's about as far as any similarity goes or ends. *Buffy the Vampire Slayer* was meant to be all about vampires and then other monsters entered the furor as Sunnydale was situated on the actual Hell mouth – so comparing the two shows doesn't help.

It's been written, "*Supernatural* might not be quite super but it is often entertaining, witty..." On the contrary, *Supernatural* does put the super into this show. Always brilliant, aside from the odd aberration and odd episode, especially season's 3 **Ghostfacers** which deflected from the arc and the essential storylines. That and the addition of hopeless and worthless Bela, were my only gripes in an otherwise, always SUPERB series!!

Written in the spoiler Zone *of SFX* review for the pilot episode is the following, "It's nowhere near as good as Joss Whedon's show." [Well the best seasons of *Buffy* were 1-3,5 and 7, 4 and 6 were just mediocre and barely watchable chiefly with the introduction of the Initiative in season 4 and those nerds in season 6 ugh those nerds!] It continues; "A more useful comparison would be to the slew of horror movie remakes like *House of* Wax and *Texas Chainsaw Massacre*. It rigidly follows the template that's been established for a slick, shallow horror list that's guaranteed to rake in cash at the box office."

Speak for yourself but House of Wax the remake, wasn't really a sure-fire hit not with the likes of Paris Hilton. (Sorry Jared! who was in there too, but we'd watch him in anything!)

Referring to the inclusion of how Sam and Dean dress, the music and Dean's use of credit card fraud to garner instant cash (well not all the time, he does play poker too, as did Jo). SFX states: "It all makes for a pilot that's disappointingly predictable and over-familiar." *So why did he watch, other than the sake of having to review, not one episode but practically the entire first season! On the contrary it wasn't banal: the pilot was very good as far as certain other pilots go and set up the past history of the brothers, their family and what had transpired*

566

between them over the years and the present wonderfully; in the space of 40 minutes duration; considering they also had to find the spirit, follow their father's trail and get rid of said spirit too.

As for saying "It only takes them a few minutes browsing on the Internet to figure out that this is another 'woman in white' case because it's such a routine case for them, it seems equally routine and unremarkable for us." *Well, for starters: their Dad had done most of the legwork on the woman in white cases, as they found pinned on his motel room walls. Secondly, the use of the Internet was to set up the premise for the entire series, that's what they'll use 90% of the time because it's there, so get with the times. Also being an urban legend and that's what they mostly deal with, it's the best source for information. The finale and how they had to vanquish this woman in white wasn't on any database either, so that involved initiative on Sam's part – when he took her home! And no it wasn't routine for us, erm, unless you come up with such phenomena in your everyday life!*

The SFX reviewer obviously likes to contradict himself by stating "it doesn't help that the script has several failings, there's some horribly clunky expository dialogue" *referring to Dean's line when he mentioned Dad training them. Then at the end o f the review (if you know the layout for the magazine, there's a bit* at *the end where the best line from the episode is usually featured) for the pilot it happened to be Sam's line about Dad giving him a .45 for the thing in his closet. That's continuing on from Dean's dialogue so how can it be "clunky" on the one hand and not, and most especially when he then writes,* "The sparky dynamic between the two brothers is entertaining."

To end: "The makers of *Supernatural* have practically zero to offer in the way of new ideas. This sure ain't like *Buffy*…was witty…and was all about subverting the viewers' expectations. *Supernatural* on the other hand, fulfills your expectations every damn time."
Seems like he's stuck in Buffyville because as the series progresses you'll find there's plenty going on and not just between the brothers, but you get great continuity of plots and lots of cross-references between seasons 1 and 2, with added character development between the two leads and yes there are flashes of endless wit too.

The review of episode 2 isn't much better and you know what they say – if you want something done you have to do it yourself and do it even better! It appears the same reviewer is only into the Impala, the

567

special effects and the shows production values, *viz, the* "gorgeous desaturated colours" He *mentions the M&Ms that Dean had at the beginning of the episode when they went into the woods, but it wasn't the Wendigo dropping M&Ms from Dean's pocket because they'd probably all fall out in one go, wasn't it Dean leaving behind a trail for Sam to follow, which seems more logical. SFX wrote,* "This episode [2] is so formulaic…there isn't a single real surprise and the pilot episode was exactly the same. If they keep this up this show will get very tedious very quickly [*like some reviews.*] The weird thing is that the show is so coy about the paranormal content. It takes ages for the brothers to even bother explaining what a Wendigo is [*isn't it Piper from the episode of Charmed when she turned into one!*] Mulder was in love with paranormal lore – the Winchesters treat their Dad's journal like it's just an *I-Spy* book of murders!"

Oh boy here we go again. In the pilot episode finding out about the woman in white on the Internet came too soon in the sense that they just looked it up on there and hey presto: demon/spirit revealed. Now in episode 2, Sam and Dean talking about the Wendigo came too late. There's just no pleasing some people. Didn't Sam and Dean have to make sure they were dealing with a Wendigo and secondly they had to decide whether to tell Hayley and the et al that this is what they were hunting, they weren't exactly going to keep it a secret. Timing is everything and it's more interesting to build up to what is actually lurking in the woods that can open doors; you don't just blurt it out.

As for treating Dad's journal as being all about murders – that's not the case at all and as the show progressed we found that the journal doesn't hold all the answers and that there's plenty in there they can't interpret and decipher for themselves as Dean tells us. Someone should've mentioned that hasty reviewers do not good critics or criticism make. Well, okay I just did.
Mulder was in love with paranormal and alien conspiracies and the like but they never really came across many urban legends in the X-Files and if they did, they didn't really call them as such. Mulder only used them to make his point about what they were investigating and what the present case could mean for them. Also what makes Supernatural different and I reiterate yet again is that in Sam and Dean's realm, ghosties, ghoulies and demons are real. They exist!

There are yet more critical qualms for 1.6 Skin. You wish you didn't have to answer reviewers' posers and they'd work it out for themselves since they're supposed to be "informing" us! Here goes again: says SFX, "You can't help thinking the creature is seriously under-explained, it can 'download' mind and knowledge of others which still doesn't explain how it can perfectly mimic their voices."

Since it can shape shift into humans; it can take on their faces, appearances, it naturally or unnaturally follows that it will be able to mimic their voices too. Also shape shifter lore is meant to have evolved from werewolves, you wouldn't expect them to sound human, when a human is bitten and becomes a werewolf and besides Dean says it and shape shifter Dean does too when he says they're part human. Thus it takes on the characteristics and sounds of the human it transforms into. Otherwise it would leave itself pretty vulnerable and easily picked out from the crowd if it couldn't do this. Oh and another thing, Supernatural lore and creatures are different to the normal lore in books, etc, as demonstrated by the two vampire episodes they covered in both seasons.

Season **1.7 Hookman**. SFX says "…some pedantry. How would melting down the crucifix help? The hook was 'melted' down in the first place, and that didn't destroy its power. Isn't a large hook hand a bit bigger than a crucifix? What happened to the rest of the silver, presumably also imbued with evil mojo? And in the nineteenth century when someone lost a hand, would they really make a hook hand out of valuable silver?"

This is fast becoming a Q&A session for reviewers who don't do their homework. Firstly to the pedantry. Melting down the crucifix would help because back in 1862, it was given to the preacher – obviously when the hook was melted into a crucifix the evil within it carried on, this time feeding off Lori's moral indignation. But our reviewer forgot that this time round Dean salted and burned the bones which wasn't done when the preacher was buried and then the crucifix was also burned too. Well again obviously a hook hand would be bigger than a crucifix but we're probably talking in terms of weight here and not size (which isn't everything) so there'd really be no silver left over.

Yes they would make a hook hand out of silver in the nineteenth century since we're talking about a preacher here and not some common parishioner. The church had far more money than ordinary people.

569

This episode was likened to A Nightmare on Elm Street which can be said was a rip off of the Hookman urban legend so no use accusing Supernatural of doing the same!

Season 1.9 Home. *A blooper here in the review, it wasn't Sam who worked out the line in Dad's journal referring to Missouri as being the psychic, it was Dean!*

SFX: "You can't help the feeling that there's a missed opportunity too. What if all the evidence had suggested that their mother's spirit was the evil force?" *To begin with – there wasn't much evidence to suggest that anyway. As for missed opportunities – Mom would never be evil – not even after everything that she went through, she after all believed in God and angels as Dean tells us in* **2.13 Houses of the Holy**. *She dies to save Sam so she wouldn't have hurt the little girl but strived to protect her as she did and thereby she was in her closet. Oh and if evidence had pointed to Mom being evil, they'd have to do what they always do and put things right. Mom would be a spirit after all and they'd have to lay her to rest. That would appear difficult to do, she was Mom after all, but then she'd be at peace.*

Season **1.12 Faith.** SFX: "...if Sue Ann had been marking rapists and child abusers for death then you'd have an interesting moral debate about the ethics of playing God...as it is there is never any doubt she has to be stopped...once again it boils down to destroying a power source... *Don't Fear the Reaper:* such a fatuously obvious choice (not really!) that it makes you laugh out loud when you should be feeling creeped out." *No since you're meant to be feeling for the girl who's about to cark it and again it's another one of those "ironic" choices of music for a scene (see season* **2.6** *– when Dean plays you're as cold as ice on the radio with Ellen in the car and season* **2.14 Born Under A Bad Sign** *when Sam (in possessed mode) turns on the radio to 'before you lapse into unconsciousness' when he's got Jo tied up. Really sometimes you wonder if these critics watch the same episode let alone pay attention!*

Season **1.13 Route 666.** "The whole notion of a phantom truck is deeply silly and so is the realization with the truck revving up like a growing animal! And why doesn't it just materialize inside Cassie's living room...it's not a real truck walls can't stop it!" *Isn't the entire notion of a truck appearing inside a house a bit silly. For starters it wouldn't really fit – it menaces – but only kills on the road; besides the* *truck or Cyrus's spirit was probably after Cassie's mother rather than her. She didn't really have any part in Cyrus's death or the cover up. Anyway a vehicle in a house, already done in the pilot episode when Sam drove the woman in white into her house.*

As for salting and burning not working, well it wouldn't since Cyrus became a part of the truck when he was buried in the swamp still in the seat. It's mentioned in the episode that his spirit's become infused with it, this is a show about the supernatural, so a lot of ways to kill spirits and demons involve fire, what do some critics/reviewers want or expect BLOOD! Naturally fire cleanses so it's the first thing you think of, they're tried and tested methods, you wouldn't think of new ways to say, kill a vampire, when the usual methods work just as well!

The season 2 opener, some critics got it wrong when they wrote, "John's more concerned about retrieving the colt in case the demon returns...with livewire Dean confined to using a Ouija board..." *John wanted the colt for other reasons, as we know, to save Dean. But it wasn't Dean's idea to use the Ouija board but Sam's. So Dean didn't really have any other choice as it was the only quickest method of communication open to them.*

On Season 2 in SFX: **2.3 Blood Lust**, "The 'some monsters are good' thing has been done to death by Whedon and there's <u>a lot</u> of Gunn in Gordon [obvious much?] and while it's cool to see Amber Benson vamp out, she's rather dull. **Bloodlust** is let down by the fact its vampires are boring."

Here we go resorting to Buffy references again, well, this ain't Buffy and the some 'monsters are good' hasn't even been touched upon in this show until now. Does this mean there'll be a lot for critics to say when the big secret about Sam is revealed, well they didn't say much on that if anything because he's meant to be someone who's purely good becoming a monster (if he does.) As for boring vampires that's the nature of the beast, this beast at least and the only way to draw out Gordon's character is by making these vampires reform their evil ways. As for the later episode **2.10 Hunted***, it makes you see just how obsessed with hunting Gordon is and tries to influence Dean, encouraging him to be the same, something Dean doesn't need to hear at this time. There's more going on here than vampires who are just the back drop here to the real issues between Sam and Dean and reactions to Dad's death.*

On season **2.4 Children Shouldn't Play With Dead Things**: Xpose commented "...ripping-off of a *Ringu* scene with a dead girl seen on a TV screen (she even has long black hair and a white dress). More quarrelling between the Winchesters about living under their father's shadow, everything just drags..." *On the contrary, this was an episode, which opened up old wounds for the two of them, but more so for Dean, since the season 2 opener he's been harbouring so many feelings about Dad's death and he knows Dad did it. (Made the ultimate sacrifice for him.) Thus mentioning it over and over that he shouldn't be here. How would you deal with it?*

Season **2.5** *Xpose* wrote "...the lack of a rescue was quite unexpected given that the brothers had already failed to save one victim and thanks to Sam's continually growing power of second sight, they had a head start for this one." *Yes they did have a 'head start' for both the victim's concerned and on the contrary Sam did save the first victim – the doctor from shooting himself – so that was his premonition. Only he wasn't to know who at this point was 'pulling the strings' so to speak, hence it wasn't as if Sam knew he'd walk into a bus or was told to do this. None of them knew straightaway what was happening and their 'suspect' wasn't the one who was manipulating events.*

"...the mind control plot did cause me some confusion, why was the girl at the end aware (and naturally terrified) that she was being forced to kill herself when the previous two were blissfully ignorant?" *She wasn't aware she was going to kill herself – she was upset at what Webber was forcing her to do, i.e. he was going to rape her first. The bit where she was terrified was when Andy and Sam arrived to save her, then Webber didn't have any mind control over her and she saw Andy shoot his brother to stop him controlling Dean into killing himself. That's when Andy said he had to use mind control on her to make her forget those events.*

On **2.7 The Usual Suspect** *SFX says,* "The story is a little too similar to last season's **The Benders,** only this time Sam not Dean has to build rapport with the female cop who is more closely connected with the horror at large than is at first apparent. Still, highly entertaining and smoothly plotted." *One qualm, Sam has to make nicey with the female detective because Dean sends her to Sam so that he can help save her and she doesn't end up like the other victims.*

2.8 Crossroads Blues: "Dean doesn't make the deal – but we're left thinking that he was sorely tempted...which is pretty twisted, even for a

Winchester." *Even if Dean did make the deal – which he wouldn't for Sam's sake – it wouldn't be classed as twisted. He'd only want Dad back where he should be and to take his own place, where Dean should've rightly been. Besides Dad made the deal to begin with, Dean would've only been making it right in his own eyes. Put yourself in his position, after everything he's been through didn't he have the right to think like that, that's all he was doing, just pondering the possibility, 'what if'...*

Season **2.9 Croatoan**, SFX said, "Forget the fact we don't understand the ending. Instead let's focus on the fact that this is a ZOMBIE STORY WITH BUGGER-ALL ZOMBIES. We see a few infected people freak out, but that's it." *Clearly we can't have been watching the same episode, this episode was never about zombies (that was season **2.4 Children Shouldn't Play With Dead Things**.) The townsfolk were infected with the virus which made them attack everyone else and even Dean mentions The Omega Man because everyone was freaking out – violently. This ending was a cliffhanger for US viewers who had to wait until after Christmas for the conclusion. At least for what Dean had to tell Sam and as for not understanding the end, well it was a continuation from the season 2 opener when Dad whispered in Dean's ear about Sam. Also the ending was Yellow Eyes checking to see if Sam was immune from the virus and how strong he is, as he was sizing up his abilities to be a good demon army leader.*

Xpose wrote "who can blame Dean for having second thoughts about the 'norm' sacrifices he and his brother have made and wanting a taste of it? Winchester judgement isn't always so infallible." *'Norm' sacrifices, they did make them, yes, but didn't have to. Throughout, you can't forget they didn't choose their lives, but did have a choice to get out – Sam did -not for long. Dean wants to get out now, but Sam doesn't and won't let him. Once again fate conspires against them.*

Xpose: "There are enough well-timed 'boo' moments and double-bluffs as to identify the virus victims to make 'Croatoan' an episode of consistent substance."

Season **2.10 Hunted**, SFX comments, "The revelation that the lovely Ava might have killed her fiancé..." *This wasn't implied at all really, since it was either the yellow-eyed demon itself, or it made her do it. Which doesn't tally with the next episode because Sam feels* guilty at what might have happened to her as she disappeared after saving him, naturally he feels he's to blame.

"A decent example of how *Supernatural* can entertain well enough while doing away with the phantoms and vampires and just focusing on the two principal characters and their destiny…" *Yes an episode concentrating on moving forward the mythology of the show, but remember the show is also about hunting (not just being the hunted) and vampires, ghosts and evil spirits are also the backbone of the show and make it what it is.*

Season **2.11**. **Playthings**, "Overall though this episode doesn't quite hit the spot in its second half." *Is it just me or did no one (critics in particular) notice the nanny may have had a hand in what was happening more than Maggie, especially when at episode's close, the camera pans in on Maggie's doll which is her splitting image and has been used to manipulate her spirit!*

"The revelation lies with the two creepy sisters and the fact that we are tricked into thinking that both of them are real for half of the show…before the climactic swimming pool resolve banishes the source of the unrest." *Interesting title since Sam and Dean also become the focus of the 'real' culprit behind the killings. As well as playthings referring to toys, but also to how the dolls house and the dolls were manipulated to put Sam and Dean on the wrong track: missing the big clue as to who was really behind all the goings-on! No, the voodoo doll is not the secondary device in this episode, it's actually the first device, elusive to many viewers and critics, since the nanny, Marie, was the actual source of unrest and in pulling the strings and using Maggie, she was actually using the doll as a voodoo doll.*

Season **2.12**. **Night Shifter** Xpose: "…why show us the (near) ending when police surrounding the bank was so inevitable that it leaves us viewers with nothing to puzzle over en route to the conclusion?"
We knew the police would lay siege to the bank as soon as they knew a 'robbery/hold-up' was in progress and yes flashing back was putting the events into perspective and how they got there to begin with; showing Dean in yet another position where he's compromised and identified again with cameras around – which was inevitable.
There was so much to puzzle over: firstly the identity of the shape shifter kept changing and wasn't revealed straightaway; then there was

574

the dilemma of how they'd leave with the building surrounded – a bit of a teaser in that you did think Sam and Dean would resort to using hostages to leave and finally and most crucial of all was that you didn't know the FBI agent would turn up in hot pursuit of Sam and Dean and he'd know so much about them and be wrong, treating them as the bad guys.

Season **2.13 Houses of the Holy** Says SFX,"…a fitting precursor to the revelation that Sammy is some kind of angelic guardian." *This is something I pondered over too… (See later.)*

"…the revelation of Sam's ability to see bursts of light that Dean cannot might warrant a mental note." *Which it may – but not if taken into context – the "light" /spirit only appeared to the two people in the beginning because it wanted them to carry out its will and that's the only reason it also appeared to Sam, but because he believes in such things as angels; and when Father Gregory tells Sam he knows about redemption or that he needs it too. Sam was ready to believe this was an angel too. So it's doubtful it would've appeared to Dean.*

But a nice touch in this episode was that Sam was so willing to carry out the 'spirit's request' without questioning why, how, like he always does before they kill the bad things- but this was an interesting change to his character as well. I also said Sam was more religious (and more moral) than Dean. So one of them being religious was a good thing considering what they hunt. Dean could be seen as "fallen" or lost his religion and Sam could still pray (as he did) and that's a good theme.

*At least some aren't all negative reactions. Season **2.15 Trickster**,* SFX:"A quirky and twisted college-humour variant on the time-fragmented approach to recounting different versions…a rare laugh riot of an episode that fans will want to watch again." *Actually season **1.17 Hell House** was funnier since we had Sam and Dean playing pranks on each other as well as the nerdy ghostbusters, so watching them at play with their juvenile humour was more of a plus!*

Sci-Fi Now: "Some of the humour does work, the story doesn't make sense." *What's there to make sense in the story – there's nothing too difficult to comprehend. Sam and Dean investigate a series of deaths at a university campus but find it's a bit difficult than normal to figure out what's going on since a trickster is influencing their behaviour; making Sam and Dean focus more on each other's nuances, annoying habits, if you like, until it takes an objective eye – that of Bobby – to tell them what's really going on.*

*Season **2.16 Road Kill** SFX:* "What's sad, though is that from the moment she wakes after the crash you can't help but wonder if she's dead which makes the twist ending less impressive…is full of long speeches on the nature of ghosts too which also undermines the surprise…" *On first viewing you don't really wonder if she's dead just because her husband's not in the car, doesn't mean Molly's dead and there's no one else around and you don't think this especially when she comes upon the creepy guy in the road she's just avoided running over. But you begin to get suspicious when Sam and Dean give each other funny looks and also when they say they'll take her to the police, something they wouldn't do as Dean's wanted by everyone (including us!)*

The ending wasn't so impressive – but for the purposes of this episode it was, since Sam has been trying to tell her everything she's going through and been through, albeit in "third" person mode – he refers to spirits rather than her specifically, attempting to let her down gently. She needs to accept her fate before revealing what's going on; she doesn't and so they have to tell her abruptly.

As for the long speeches, well as said before, she's found out they hunt, it's what they do and looking at this from another angle Sam could just be telling her this, she's not exactly going to know about vengeful spirits and why they become like that, is something she won't know; so this doesn't undermine the surprise either seeing Molly is a very curious woman, um spirit! Only she doesn't know she's a spirit and needs to realize this before she can move on.

*Cf season **2.1** where Dean explains to Tessa what spirits are when she knows all about apparitions, ghosts. I.e. spirits of people close to death and asks her if she's okay with death – (yeah, she is death.) When Dean comments "you have a choice", not always the case. Seems familiar in the context of this episode when Sam explains to Molly about how spirits become bad; wanting revenge etc. It sounds similar to Dean in the season 2 opener. What's different is that Molly, here is in Dad's position, but she doesn't want to believe; hasn't accepted it, so she doesn't know of these things. In contrast, Sam is talking to a "novice" about death, when Dean isn't in the season 2 opener.*

Also Tessa tells Dean in **2.1** *he'll go mad wandering around in his 'body' – no closure for him and angry spirits are born in that way. Which is exactly what Sam tells Molly. Only she hasn't tread that path because she's motivated by love, not revenge and because she needs closure in the sense of finding David; accepting what happened to her and then moving on: closure for herself.*

Though it would be interesting to see if she learned her lesson here: - no canoodling in the car, it's dangerous! If she found out she was dead, she could have so easily become bad and exact her own retribution, maybe even on David. (It takes two to canoodle!) But Molly's character is in contrast to Greely: - he's become everything she didn't and he takes his revenge on her every year since she killed him.

On **2.16**, Xpose wrote: "this episode scores brownie points not for any particular scene involving the phantom enemy…but for its subtle cleverness while remaining a sad scene…" *To be honest you could tell what this episode was leading up to, as already mentioned in my notes to this episode. But it was superbly done*

Sci-Fi Now: "Molly delivers a perfect performance as a misguided spook who, like most ectoplasm echoes, doesn't realize she's ceased to be. Unfortunately there's too much exposition around her, while the plot does drag a little." See my comments above.

SFX wrote on **2.17 Heart**: "The sex scene is so blatantly aimed at female viewers, it's almost embarrassing – not that any female viewers are complaining – mind!" Well this reviewer definitely isn't! *The scene was a tad embarrassing wasn't it and not really necessary since it didn't add anything or take anything away from the episode, like it was just there for the sake of it. Since Dean got one in* **1.13** *so Sam had to get one too! Let's call it even and leave it at that. Such scenes really aren't needed in this show! As in* **4.9** *where Sam got a scene with demon Ruby and Dean had to have one with angel Anna in* **4.10**.

SFX continued: "Vaugier is a thousand times more interesting in one episode of *Supernatural* than she ever was in nine episodes of *Smallville*. *No – she wasn't really – she kind of droned on a lot in this episode! And you feel more for Sam than you do for her: - did she really not know she was infected, maybe she didn't, this was Supernatural's version of the lore after all.* SFX: "You might not fall in love with Madison – but you'll still care enough to feel for both her and Sam at the end." *Well only for Sam and poor Dean who had to watch his brother go through the pain of heartache.*

Continues SFX: "With the Feds chasing the brothers, you'd think Dean would think twice before leaving his prints all over the dead cop's crime scene. His Dad would whup his ass for that." *Dean didn't really leave his prints all over the cop's crime scene, there wasn't much of a crime scene to begin with! So what about his prints at Kevin's apartment then or were they conveniently forgotten by this reviewer. No worries though, since the Feds turn up in* **2.19** *anyway. Besides they didn't solve the hooker murders or Nathan's for that matter so they'll probably chalk it up to some wild animal anyway as the ME tells us at the beginning and since all the murders have similarities, they probably wouldn't go looking for prints. Well nothing's come from leaving prints thus far. Not everyone's as perfect as CSI.*

Xpose: "Despite this being at least the third *Supernatural* episode to date with a lycanthrope/wolf theme, it has quite a fresh feel to it." *This wasn't the third episode to date dealing with werewolves/lycanthrope themes – in fact this is the first episode dealing with this. Thus far werewolves have only been touched upon in passing! As part of a lore or in comparison to other creatures, eg,* **2.12 Nightshifter**, *when Dean explains that shape shifter lore extends from werewolves and they can also shape shift similar to wolves; and mentions lycanthropy one other time but not an entire episode has been devoted to it!*

Continues SFX: "The writer…allowing him [Sam] to sweetly drop the occasional awkward inhibitions that make Sam contrast so well with his horny brother…who couldn't feel sorry for Sam with those teary puppy dog eyes….casting a likeable female character as the, er bitch, in question" *Don't know about you but Madison didn't really come across as that likeable: in the scene with her undies, it feels like she's playing on Sam's uneasiness and using her feminine wiles , or should that be charm, to reel him in. Also judging from her ex- her taste in men varies dramatically (but werewolves don't pick and choose!) which makes you wonder what she sees in her ex when she's aching for Sam?! Even Sam comments on this. Being a werewolf clearly there's no accounting for taste, except when it came to our Sammy!*

Sci-Fi Now: - "…but with these two [Sam and Madison] the only things going bump in the night."

2.18 Hollywood Babylon: some good comments at last from SFX "great to see Dean having a blast as he takes a job as a PA on the movie set…good stuff if you fancy a chuckle…Some might say it's a little too 'silly'" *In the trailer for this episode in the US, on the CW Network when the writer is saved by Dean, towards the end, from being eviscerated into the wind fan and says, Dean's "one hell of a PA" Dean was given a sparkle on his teeth! (A bit like the old Colgate toothpaste ads! Or as Greg said in season 9 episode of CSI, "Ting.))*

"An amusing self-referential episode that dodges falling into the pure parody category and like all of this show's play-it-for-laughs episodes, it resists becoming too nudge-wink clever for its own good." *As long as you knew the references and in-jokes, this episode wasn't just played for laughs.*

2.19 SFX: "A Henricksen/Dean smackdown would be a dream come true. Instead we get the usual prison gubbins…the ghost is freaky but the biggest freak is Sam, freaking out about being in jail. Dean is having a ball; the second week in a row we've seen him fit in while Sam's the outsider." *Don't think they'd resort to a fight between Henricksen and Dean – not a physical one at any rate since Dean always plays his joker card when he's in those situations – well plays the joker, but still you get my meaning. Obviously Sam would be "freaked" about being in jail – it's not his kind of place is it. Dean's more used to such places, especially with most of the bars where he's hung out.. Sam is meant to be the outsider isn't he, perhaps his heart (no pun see* **2.17 Heart) really** *isn't in all this hunting right now, especially since Madison and even though in*

2.18 *he says he's fine. You have to wonder how much of a "game face" he was putting on for Dean since Dean's done the same for him after losing Dad!* **(2.2)**.

"…it's just a shame that after grabbing interest from the outset it turned out to be a rather mediocre episode with no particularly arresting images to speak of. We are back to tired old vengeful-spirit-appearing-to-off-bad 'uns." "Even the most hardened nutters are no match for Dean's ducking and iron fists." *At least there were a few revelations between the brothers and showing how you can get yourself put into prison, do the job and make your escape right under the nose of the law.*

2.20. "A fun what-if-episode- that develops Dean's connection to his mother, something that he has remained something of an icicle about. Sam is your completely boring lawyer in the making." *Well, it didn't develop that much of a connection, especially considering they all thought of Dean as just a bit of a drunk always with a bottle in his hand, someone who'd never really amount to anything.*

2.21. "*Supernatural* goes slightly *X-Men* for a while as a host of new faces with special dark powers are thrust together." *Not exactly, they were all thrown together to have a showdown with the winner helping Yellow Eyes in his cause. Have to wonder though, if Sam had come out the victor, there's no way Devil's Gate would've been opened and Dad wouldn't have gotten out. Also who knows if they'd have defeated Yellow Eyes.*

2.22 "The closing scenes between the brothers as Dean explains why he has a year to live – do pack enough of a punch to get one geared up for a third season with the double task of ridding the world of spirits they had to let escape and saving Dean in the next 365 days." *366 days actually, as 2008 was a leap year, hey look you get that '66' number in there, for starters.*

3.1 SFX wrote: "The seven sins gimmick is as much a handy device for letting the nastiness roll as it is relevant in turning a mirror on Dean's new pleasure – seeking 'dying man lifestyle'!

It may be Dean's pleasure in getting as many chicks as he can in a year, but the more real aspect of this season is finding how to get him out of the bargain.

3.3: SFX: "Because Bela and Dean BORN TO RIP EACH OTHER'S CLOTHES OFF!" *NOT bloomin' likely! She is not his type and not Sam's either. So much for Sam dreaming about her – in a way Dean is always accusing him of doing, i.e. when he tells him to stop surfing the porn sites! When Dean says he wants to shoot her he really wants to shoot her and no it's not a question of hate being a metaphor for love and all that. He really can't stand her. Hey Dean would so never resist a pretty chick or in Bela's case any old chick!*

3.4. "After a kick-ass triple bill *Supernatural* goes down a gear for an episode that holds the attention,...doesn't contain enough outstanding features to raise it higher than an average and rather generic episode it might seem odd to complain about proceedings being dulled by repetitive religious imagery or themes in a show like *Supernatural*, but they have made plenty of very good episodes without them dominating."

And the road to hell is paved with good intentions; relevant for Dean and his path to his demise. The significance of "religious imagery themes" being used was to show the hedonistic town activity, where everyone was out for a good time. Clearly the irony was in the priest being possessed by a powerful demon; demonstrating the evil in all things good and that, if not kept in check or ignored can cause havoc. To paraphrase a well-known quote about power: - 'absolute evil corrupts absolutely'..

Religion here also used to question Dean's beliefs once again, as he begins his circle downwards into hell. Whether he believes in God – even at this low point in his ever ebbing life slipping away from him and Sam. To show there still may be hope for him even now. In a show about demons and evil, there will always be a religious theme or plot running through it.

Also Ruby turning up, revealing her reasons for being here to Sam, and again; the all-important issue of whether Sam has turned to evil. Especially when he shoots Casey without pause, much to Dean's chagrin. She could've been a powerful info-wielding weapon in their quest to save Dean (and find who holds his contract for later episodes) since she was ready and willing to follow Sam.

3.8 TV Zone: "Wasn't it a cop out not showing us how the boys escaped their bonds, and why would both their captors leave them ungagged in the kitchen to call for help when people come to the door."

*Well in **3.14**, Sam escapes his bonds when he's tied up by the Crocotta. Also it'd be a little tiresome watching them undo the bonds. Remember hunters always carry secret weapons or find some around them. In the Pilot Dean used a paperclip and in **1.15**, he used a car aerial to get out of handcuffs. Perhaps Dean used his teeth, ha! Obviously if they shouted for help they wouldn't be the only ones ending up as sacrificed fodder.. Mmm fudge!. Not a mushy Xmassy feeling in sight- save for the Pagan god couple. Sickly sweet.*

3.9: SFX: "What does let this episode down, is the final scene with Ruby telling Dean what's waiting for him in hell: it's necessary but much too long."

*In a reversal to **3.4** when Sam shoots Casey with Dean protesting, here Sam comes to Ruby's rescue and stops Dean from shooting her to kingdom come.*

Anyhow, the end is not that long, but it has to be informative for us. This is Dean's second scene alone with Ruby without Sam around, and here she confides she can't save him which neither of them tell Sam for episodes to come. (Which is fine as Sam hasn't told Dean of his revelation of having demon blood in him.)

Also what Ruby tells him about him becoming a demon, is far from the reality of what his experiences will be down there; infact it's rather sugarcoated. I.e. every demon in hell will be gunning for a Winchester's blood. Becoming a demon in hell would've been the least of Dean's worries. At least as a demon he'd be on an equal footing with everyone (thing) else around him. But alas it'll take a lifetime for him to become one, or an eternity.

3.10:"Dean and Bobby discover that Bobby took part in a college experiment studying sleep disorders."
Actually the killer took part in the experiment. But only found out about him through his own research.

"An age-old idea artfully wrought, but with a barely adequate story."

The point was to show you inside Dean's head – for perhaps one last time before the end – for him – was perhaps a good plot device since he doesn't share his feelings with Sam (and not even with viewers) every so often – but we know what he's actually thinking none-the-less! Oh the point I was making was that, contrary to Sam saying Dean doesn't want to face his fate. Fact is that's all he does think about and he has thought about going to hell. Hell (oops) he even imagines what he'll become when he spends centuries in the fiery pit! Finally convincing himself to tell Sam he doesn't want to die.

3.10: SFX: "We already explored the inside of Dean's head in season 2 when he was spelled by a Djinn, so it seems a little redundant for us to see it again."

*When Dean's "head was explored" in **2.20 What Is and What Should Never be** – it was all about his ideal world and how he wanted things; his life to be like. But it wasn't real; it was the Djinn showing him this so called perfect world with Mom. Here Dean is actuall y dreaming – so everyone's inside his head, including Sam. This time round we get to see what Dean's really thinking – more so – dreaming and imaging himself becoming a demon. A rehash of what Ruby told him in **3.9** and now Dean finds out from his 'demon' self some home truths and he will be entering hell. Again what Ruby told him – he can't be saved and that's what made this episode different to the one in season 2.*

TV Zone: "Taking a break from battling ghouls and fixating about damnation, this highly amusing spin on the classic time loop torment of *Groundhog Day* is almost irrelevant to the continuing season 3 arc…but this only enhances its refreshing nature. It does seem slightly strange the writers would lighten the tone so drastically at this stage in the season after building up to Dean's death,…only to make a complete joke out of it…the Trickster shifts the tome into darker territory."

Far from being irrelevant to the season 3 arc – it rather enhances the dramatic nature of what fate awaits Dean. The parts where his 'death(s)' are speeded up to farcical point are funny by themselves; but shows how lost Sam will be without Dean. The Trickster reinforcing that everything comes back to Sam because it's all about him, shown by various demons they've met along the way, when they eventually all mention Sam in their conversations with Dean.

However, because of the writers' strike, the season was only going to go to 12 episodes and so would've ended with this episode showing us the only insight into Sam's loneliness without his brother, until season 4.

3.12 TV Zone: "after the fun of the previous episode, everything in *Jus Im Bello* feels tired and lacking in the spirit that usually sustains *supernatural* episodes to the end…the opening scenario of the episode too, seems to have had it's build-up bitten off retaining up at a point where the arrival and tracing of their destination was obviously considered to warrant no explanation…feels a little chaotic until the brothers are placed in cells."

*Far from feeling tired, the episode builds to a sure fire climax and you'd expect nothing less from this show. The brothers in jail -again- this time there from being arrested, rather than setting themselves up as in **2.19**. Not only have to deal with demons and Henricksen, but manage to include their usual arguments – especially Sam being so quick to sacrifice one to save the many (30). Something you'd expect from Dean – who can't believe what he's hearing from little Sammy.*

As said this episode would've been the last had the show not returned for four more episodes to round off season 3 and what an exciting finale preparing us for season 4 and Dean's fate..
If it was the final episode, it could've had Dean making a final sacrifice since he knew his fate was fast approaching and so ending up in hell, sooner rather than later, and in his words "taking down some sons of bitches with him."

3.13 TV Zone: "a brave experiment that doesn't look to be great one from the opening minutes, then ends up not only succeeding but for entertainment value alone, exceeding many of the 'regular' episodes."

A bit of a waste of an episode considering there were only four made after the writers' strike, so when it could've been used to add more or less to Dean's few meagre weeks left on earth. Was a ratings loser too when aired.

3.14 "The evil forces themselves are frequently too dull or derivative. The latest *Ghost In The Machine* story does not grip and you have likely seen scarier bills."

The story was gripping especially Dean needing to believe Dad could save him for a second time by procuring some miracle out of the hat, then realizing he needs to help himself; something Sam has done when he went off to live his life. Also the episode needs a setting, a convenient one in which the story has to take place and what better way to do this than have a Crocotta make phonecalls to his potential victims.

In a way, also showing monsters can be just as cunning as the human species and adept in manipulation when seeking out their prey. Then to hammer the point home – it plays on Dean's senses and insecurities – still. That he feels Dad could still come to the fore to offer him some kind of last minute rescue, salvation. Yet that hope is misplaced, as no rescue does come. The awe that every little boy has for his Dad; when things go wrong – dad – our hero – will always be there to offer us a speedy, guiding hand. To have it hammered into Dean that he has to rely on himself (maybe Sam too at times) and no one else. That Dad is gone and he finally works this out and accepts it: he couldn't expect Dad to just make it all easy for him. He made the sacrifice once and once is too much, as he knows too well.

4.11 SFX wrote: "The revelation that the girl is not alone and in fact has a brother in the house too is brilliant – you don't see it coming at all and it's perfectly executed."

Yes it was a brilliant concept but on the contrary, you do see it coming, since the daughter is human, which they figured out. She can't be in so many places so quickly: in the closet, under the bed to lick the girl's hand. She's not a spirit that can just materialize anywhere.

An answer for learning how to read and write, knowing how to slash tyres and steal (they took a leaf out of Dean's book and watched a lot of TV! Through the closet. Let's face it, Bill Gibson was watching it. Okay I know it sounds implausible.) As for taking their weapons: their basic instinct is to hunt, to survive, search for food, so they will steal and take anything they come across. Most animals hoard.

DVDs

There are Easter eggs, 2 commentaries, documentary on the season finale "from script to screen and the coolest feature where we've rounded up a bunch of history and folklore experts to give commentary on the urban legends used in the show. It kinda blows me away, having legitimate academic commentary about our little blood fest."

DVD Review: "But despite some decent ideas the first series never managed the same dramatic punch. The chemistry between Mulder and Scully as believer and skeptic became pop culture legend and buoyed the show through some interminable conspiracy theorizing. Sam and Dean lack that basic likeability. Wise-cracking and bickering but with an unconditional brotherly love that sapped the emotional drama. This meant that when the material was weak the episodes became less entertaining. *Supernatural* felt like a watered down version of something we'd seen before." Saved by the season 2 opener: From there it's largely back to the free-roaming narrative of the first series, but with an increase in intensity that glosses over the occasional silliness that once held it back."

Speaking of chemistry – how much can you expect between two male leads who are portraying brothers. There's a lot there between Sam and Dean (Jared and Jensen) – they instantly click and it's like they can finish off each other's sentences without having to think about what the other will say or do. The unconditional love has to be ever-present, they're a family and all they have in the world is each other. That's what this show is partly about and why the brotherly aspect works so well! Mulder and Scully (love them as we do/did) were partners, weren't related and their chemistry was more sexual, played to the viewers and fans, but which neither one would admit to.

The show wasn't written that way and rightly so since it would've spoiled the show if they got romantically involved (until season 9 and the movie) on screen together. So the two chemistry aspects can't be compared! Hey didn't Sam and Dean always get mistaken as a couple rather than brothers, what more can you ask for. There was drama, there was love, hate, regret, hope; never has a show given so much and expected so little, only for us to watch and enjoy, share the good times and the bad times with our heroes! Perhaps we had seen some plots/storylines before, yes, but they weren't in the same context.

Supernatural Season 1: More Questions Than Answers

In the penultimate episode it was obvious they wouldn't get the demon (otherwise no season 2!) At least they got to say a few home truths to each other, though Dean didn't really want to hear them, because he didn't want it to be the end for them (in more ways than one.) Don't really think they would have killed the demon though with the Colt because it disappeared when Sam fired at it, which means it definitely can't be killed by bullets and needs something more than a man-made weapon. Perhaps something spiritual and powerful and transcending time. Hey this means the gun wouldn't have killed it even when the demon was possessing Dad and was probably luring Sam into killing their Dad instead, one less hunter for the demon to face. Anyway, the gun, supposedly meant to kill anything, well, what if the demon isn't corporeal (not just a word in the realm of *Buffy* either. See **1.2 Wendigo**) as it can vanish so quickly and possess bodies. Also the demon is "other worldly" if it can appear in that way.

{So the bullet that Sam fired into the wall, missing the demon, pity it couldn't be retrieved and used again a la *CSI?*) Sorry but that demon still looks like Dad from all angles even when they showed its face with the fiery eyes in Sam's nursery for the first time in the Pilot; and when Dad was shown in the shadows and from behind in episode **1.16 Shadow**; when Dean saw him in their motel room. In the penultimate episode when it taunted them from the burning nursery. Though his face was revealed this time and lo and behold it no longer looked like Dad, unless someone decided let's get another actor.

So what does it want with those babies and what makes them so special – born under a certain sign/astrological projection or something, or are they just innocents waiting to be corrupted. Meg was always involved from the outset and she was possessed when she said "father" into her bowl of blood. Referring to her demon father as opposed to the devil. In the episode **1.11 Scarecrow** Dad warned Sam about demons being everywhere and what does Sam go and do, talk to strangers and fall for the sob story of an even stranger looking girl just because she told him what he wanted to hear.

Clearly it's going to take a lot more to kill the demon than holy water; special bullets (or bullet: there's only one left now) and rock salt. If the demon is also immune from fire then maybe it's made from fire or needs an old prayer or invocation.

Oh and why do these mothers have to wear the proverbial white gown like they're angelic or all pure in white, even Jess had one on when she was on fire in the Pilot and when Sam was dreaming of her in the next episode.

In the penultimate episode why did that woman's husband have a shotgun ready and say he's not going to let anything happen to them – like he was expecting something, since they didn't live in a bad neighbourhood. Oh and Dean had time to "eye" that nurse in hospital and his "God, yes!" sounded desperate when she asked if he needed help and we all know how desperate Dean can get! For a minute there did you think Sam wouldn't tell them about his vision, but then he had to. Liked the part where Dean told Dad he wasn't there for him when he needed a heart transplant in the faith healer episode.

Dad was possessed since he never lost his temper at Dean for wasting a bullet as he went through so much to get the Colt in the first place, well they all did. So Sam was right when he said they had to make sure by using holy water, but a shame he couldn't sense something was wrong. Oh that was another clue when the demon told them holy water wouldn't work; in which case the gun surely wouldn't; especially if no one's come across that demon before or we haven't discovered anyone else yet who may have confronted it, or tried to "fight" it years ago. Maybe something to consider in season 2.

Still you knew it wasn't over since you couldn't have our heroes drive into the sunset, wounds'n'all to fight another day and sadly Sam still didn't sense the inevitable at the end. Although he did try to use kinesis at the end to reach for the gun, you have to ask why that demon let them go and left Dad's body too. It couldn't have just been for that explosive and unexpected final scene.

Next season perhaps Dad may disappear again so Sam and Dean don't know if he's alive, missing or abducted since there's no trace of him anywhere, at least in the early episodes, asking the question do the brothers still have the fight left in them? Maybe Sam should get amnesia from the crash and perhaps he can attune himself a bit more to his powers. Getting a bit ahead of myself there, having written this before season 2 was aired and before Dad was killed off. But a lot of the questions and what I've written still holds true.

Okay the gun did work, but it could have gone the other way and not worked, or they could have used by the last bullet. It's missing now anyway, since Bela took the replacement Bobby made, with Ruby's help and sold it off in season 3.

Now for some bloopers and unanswered questions, a few at least.

In the final episode when Dean's car was at the auto yard the front was clean and when Sam drew those symbols on the boot it had layers of dust. They demolished it anyway. Also when they were arguing and Dean said he'd be the one to bury both Sam and their Dad, that Sam was being selfish, notice Eric Kripke got it wrong when he wrote this episode. He had Sam tell Dean he came to find him to search for the demon, when he actually should have said Dean came for Sam in search of Dad. (See Pilot where he said this.) Also in the Pilot why did Dean return to Sam after Jess was on fire? That's something that wasn't answered and bugs me! (See Pilot notes for answer.)

Always thought Dad was hiding more from them than he let on. See **1.9 Home**. Again when Dean poured his heart out to him on the phone begging for help and he chose to hide out. Why did he tell Missouri (the psychic) he can't face them until he finds out the truth. What truth?

It's early days yet and we won't be getting any answers anytime soon which is good that the show leaves open all these questions and allows us to speculate and think outside the pentagram and only answers a few questions, if any, much to many critics chagrin. Also what is it with these critics and their constant complaints about Sam and Dean using fire to kill. Fire is the most obvious choice – it purifies. You can't really have them using things like holy water etc because it only works for some things as does rock salt or have them chant spells every week – er there's no power of two here and that'd be bordering on just plain silly.

So it ended like it began with more questions than answers but that's one of the attractions since it's a show where you don't expect neatly tied loose ends all the time and especially not where the brothers are concerned.   Go forth season 2!

Other possible questions still to be answered or addressed from Season 2: did Sam come back wrong?. i.e. Dean should've realized Sam wouldn't be quite himself when he was bought back. Even Yellow Eyes pointed this out to Dean and we see it for ourselves when Sam ruthlessly finishes off Jake, almost with a glint in his eye and no feeling of remorse. Does this spell the end of Sam as we know him, refusing to take a life unless absolutely necessary and even then it was Dean who pulled the final trigger. If looks could kill comes to mind and the way he fired the gun and kept on firing. Then Dean didn't think of the final outcome when he wanted Sam back "consequences be damned" and he'll live to regret that phrase in his one year life sentence or death penalty, read it how you wish. Perhaps Sam will too, since if his destiny holds true and he turns evil, what hope of finding an 'out' for Dean that he so desperately wants.

Maybe if he turns evil, he can figure out some way of reversing Dean's bargain, but then would he want to and will he still recognize those feelings of brotherly love? Well, Sam is still keeping a secret, his personal demon, about Mom knowing yellow Eyes. Will season 3 become like Season 2 where Dean kept his feelings to himself for a while until he finally told Sam he knows Dad sacrificed himself to save him. The question being once again, why didn't Sam tell him? Didn't Dean need to know, would he completely misinterpret it, or as usual, will it come down to the demon lying, as they do.

So we also don't know the emotional extent of Sam's state of mind. Bringing up the question of where was Sam when he came back, in heaven, purgatory. Will we get to know this since that's the question Sam and Dean asked each other in **2.16 Roadkill**, where Molly would go and in the season 2 finale about where Dad might be now. Dean's past action will come to haunt him in season 3, hopefully with more references to his bargain, well, there has to be, if finding a way to move on from Season 2.

(As this was covered in season 3, this threw up more questions.)

2.20 What is and What Should Never Be, Dean's alternate reality may be fitting episode especially since the season 2 opener and episodes such as, **2.8, 9, 10**; Dean's been saying "let's get out". Forget hunting and do other things. So this episode does exactly that – giving Dean his "get out of jail" card (well, hunting in this context) and see what life would've been like with Mom and no demons. The thing is he doesn't forget his 'real' life and though he has his family there, it's not the same. He was given the chance to "live" this 'perfect' reality but it came at a price. It wasn't real and the way to live this reality would have ended up with Dean dying – eventually. Which he does anyway in season 3 finale.

Which leads to the penultimate episode of season 2 as Sam was the one who ended up dying with Dean being subjected to loss, facing their mortality (once again) especially Sam's and then having to face his own with only a year. So instead of dropping out of the hunt and doing something he wants, he embraces the idea of hunting even more and now there's about a few too many demons on the loose!

Why Sam and Dean are Pariahs.

Sam and Dean, two brothers on a quest to save humanity, but this goes beyond – they're almost like 'outsiders' to the modern world – almost living on the periphery - having to look in occasionally when the need rises, especially when they need to rescue someone in distress, perform a ritual or just plain hunt a demon.. Whereas Sam seemed to blend in, become one of the uni crowd, at least for a while and escape his destiny as long as he possibly could. Dean, on the other hand; was the complete opposite. Though you know Sam will be able to merge in whenever he has to and become just like any other human, be the ordinary dude on the street. For Dean this is harder and always will be. With Sam away he was always the loner; doesn't find it easy to interact with people on a one-to-one serious basis it's always a joke to him – well something is. Nothing is too emotional – except when it comes to family – his family.

In the late 1980's drama series, *Beauty and the Beast* in an episode entitled **The Outsiders** about how the comfort and safe haven of the tunnels below New York may be threatened by discovery from 'outsiders' i.e. those living above ground and who do not belong there, or know of the existence of the world below ground. In the same way

Sam and Dean: two brothers on a quest, but beyond that this goes further, they're almost like 'Outsiders' to the modern world – almost living on the periphery – having to look in occasionally when the need arises, especially when they need to rescue, perform a hunt or ritual.

Outsider - yes Dean didn't have much to look forward to growing up, the one who had to make all the sacrifices, follow orders. No aspirations of college; his dreams or dream career. He never had the chance.

Other issues which do not normally present themselves would be feelings of self-doubt, not where hunting is concerned but rather his personal self-doubt. Dean comes across cocky but what about the resentment he must feel towards Sam only touched upon in season **1.6 Skin**, **1.8 Bugs**, where Sam says, "There's nothing wrong with normal." Deep down that's the life Sam really longed for: - normal childhood with both parents. Something that Dean wants too and also wished for Sam. See **2.20 What Is and What Should Never Be** with the Djinn manipulating Dean which could be a case of wishful thinking on Dean's part! Sam the geek got to go to college and live his life his way. Dean tells Sam family is more important when Sam is encouraging others to go to college in two years and in the mean time he needs to put up with his father. Sam's comment, "I wanted to go to school and live my life!"

Then Dean being accused of always having to rely on his family, Dad and Sam, by the demon in **2.8 Crossroad Blues.** More than that, this is something he does not think about. How can he, he doesn't have the inclination or time. That is until Dad sacrifices himself to save Dean and he finally realizes this in **2.8**. It is a wake-up call for him; he has taken everything and everyone for granted so far, especially his family. So maybe he is the one who needs to get his priorities right.

Now he may find himself alone – once more. It is not the same sort of loneliness as before when he was on the road. Dad and Sam were still around but Dad's gone and Sam was too, until Dean brought him back revealing their vulnerabilities, that they are just human in the end with real fears; nothing lasts forever and they need to live every moment and do what needs to be done. To be bold, brave and have the courage to pursue their dreams, even if they cannot live them or they cannot come true. At least they would have tried.

Loneliness is a big issue, to be around people – have friends and never really be happy. Dean's attempts at finding happiness and his 'short-lived' relationship (he's only had one that we know of **1.13 Route 666** where Cassie told us she couldn't believe Dean, "…professionally pops ghosts".) Cassie has to take back what she thought of Dean and his demon hunting when needing his help now. Whereas Sam wonders if they meet someone special would they give all this up for lurve. More like one night stands are a sign of instant gratification than anything long term. There's really no room for love to begin with, since theirs is a dangerous trek. He has Sam – true but you get the impression this is not enough at times. His brother will be there for him through thick and thin but will not keep him warm at night.

Another factor to this is no one will believe what they really do: fight ghosties and ghoulies when Dean was honest with Cassie, she dumped him. He was some sort of a freak – this again making them "outsiders". As Dean says so many times (**1.6 Skin**) he is right there with Sam. They do not get to know people very much, if at all, which may work fine right now. Re - relationships; even if they did find anyone to settle with, hunting would get in the way, as it did with Sam and Jess, leaving her to help Dean find Dad meant he could never return to his college life but on the contrary, stepped backwards into his 'old' life.

The Pilot and other episodes demonstrate the series is not only about demons, fighting them, the mythology but also it is about family, brothers, parents and the need for family too. It is fighting your own inner demons, having to swallow your pride when you need to, like Dean when he came to Sam in the Pilot asking for his help, then realizing Sam did not want to do this forever in **1.16 Shadow.** That this is no way to live. Where Sam comments: "…things will never be the same as they were before." After Dean tells him he wants them all to be a proper family. There is a sense of Dean - more so than Sam – having to battle not only demons; but also preconceptions.

Perhaps a lot of preconceptions about how they feel about each other. Dean realizing Sam does not 'hate' him because he chose to stay with Dad and hunt and could not leave him. Sam finding out Dean did not want him at college – that Sam was the perfect son Dean would not be, even when he did everything Dad asked, wanted. More self-doubt there wondering why he was not regarded as perfect as Sam. However, Dean was perfect, it was Dad who made the sacrifice to save Dean in the end just as Dean did the same for Sam. Nothing more, nothing less. Wouldn't this have banished those misconceptions with paternal love and fraternal love finally conquering all.

Sam and Dean are 'outside' the normal fabric of everyday life because of what they've seen, endured and have to put up with, anything that would have driven those of a weaker predicament, sentiment; not having a strong mentality, to despair and sometimes this does happen, but not to the extent they find themselves drowning in a whirlpool with no way out: not only losing parents; but those they loved – Sam with Jess, then Madison, but somehow yet, managing to stay afloat.

These preconceptions are perhaps another way Dean copes. He's always the clown, having a joke or smart remark for all occasions or even a song or two. That's how he chooses to evade questions about his thoughts on a subject. There's no teenage angst here, no *Buffy* – the school years – fighting demons, vampires in between gym class, cheerleading and horrible adolescence; thank God we got past all that with Sam and Dean, but there is angst. The emotions, or about as emotional as a dude or two can get. Questions posed: 'Why am I doing this?' 'How long for?' 'What will I get out of it? 'Why us?' 'Why do we need to be the ones to save everybody?' As Sam asks Dean finally, pre-empting his own question with the answer "We can't save everybody."

Season **2.20 What Is and What Should Never Be** is a reversal for Dean and his characteristic "I don't show my feelings much" mode. Sam and Dean have lost so much and where Sam reassures him what they do isn't in vain and people are alive because of Dean, even if being a hero means enduring endless pain. In **2.8 Crossroad Blues,** Dean states, "…nobody put a gun to their head and forced them to play 'let's make a deal!" That's life and that's never fair!

Being abstract and abject from the world hasn't turned Dean towards the dark side though they may live in darkness a lot and deal with this too, it hasn't made him evil, although he has been tempted on a few occasions especially **2.8 Crossroad Blues** when he thinks of giving his soul to have Dad return but actually has succumbed to the demonic proliferation in his need to have Sam back in the season 2 finale. Where the demon challenges Dean's very existence and reason for being who he is, Demon: "…your first thought is 'I can't do this anymore.'" (I.e. be a hunter.)

Still it's only metaphorical until Sam does come back and he's changed. From having to battle his destiny of turning evil, perhaps Dean's thoughtless action, well he thought of it albeit for two seconds, but not the consequences, leading to a corollary no one expected – Sam becoming evil (maybe) and thus embracing his dark side because of Dean. It may have been Sam's eventual destiny but not in this way, who'd have thought it could be like this. To put it in perspective, a bit of an anti-climax to the rebellion both Sam and Dean wanted and fought against Sam's destiny; with Sam begging Dean to kill him if ever he did become iniquitous. If indeed that is the case with Sam in season 3 or 4. (Cf season 3 and 4.)

Their hunting puts them 'outside' of humanity. There's only a few like them who know of the seedier side of demons, true evil and its existence in the world and Sam and Dean are oblivious of other hunters until season **2.2 Everybody Loves A Clown** ,when they come across Ellen. Dad neglected to tell them they weren't alone. There were others out there doing the same thing, if, differently to them. For Sam and Dean it's not really black and white and so clear cut, at least not for

Sam. He doesn't go around killing everyone, well he hasn't done much of the killing anyway (thus far in seasons 1 and 2.) However, being on the 'outside' of society does come at a price with so much blood on their hands albeit demon, who are they going to tell if not each other. Or as one real-life police officer put it, about real *CSIs:* it's the same reason why forensic experts or CSIs don't have relationships with each other, you don't want to go home with each other and all you have to talk about is the work that you do or the DBs (dead bodies) you've just come across and all the goriness that entails.

Sam rebels against his so-called "double-life" when you think about it, he has been living such a life for a long time now and it only becomes apparent when the brothers are older. On the one hand, he's a hunter and the son of a hunter, (and in season 4 we find, Mom was the hunter to begin with and not Dad) and on the other he so wants to be a normal dude. Therefore his revolt against hunting, being with Dad and Dean manifested itself in "running" away to college. What Dean says to him time and again and in the Pilot for the first time, (Cf Pilot, **1.8 Bugs**, **1.20 Dead Mans Blood**). College is where Sam fits in perfectly and maintains this charade or sham – if you will- of a deception. He hasn't told anyone what he does, no one would believe him or accept it, not even Jess as Dean tells him about not being honest and keeping his true life to himself. Sam struggles here not to be an 'outsider' at college and if anyone knew what he did (does) he would be shunned. He longed for this life to be free of hunting and the burden of having to save others. As Dean comments, it's long hours, no pay and they're never thanked.

Being on the road allows them to intermingle in and interact with ordinary people for a while but at the end of the day, more usually night, they're both on the outside looking in, protecting the very society, the very world they are and should be a part of, and the very society that rejects them or would if they knew of their real work, since ghosts, restless spirits and demons don't really exist other aside from in the wildest imaginations; on TV; fiction or in the minds of those deemed crazy for believing. Those deemed outcasts and outsiders.

7 Things about *Supernatural*

The magic number seven again, so unintentional in my list, hence *Supernatural's Seven Wonders.*

7) Locations add to the atmosphere of the show – ranging from the musty old remnants of buildings; to that famous Vancouver stretch of highway from shows such as *X Files*, and *Dark Angel* familiar to US shows. Buildings such as the one used in **Asylum**, which actually was an asylum once.

The special effects are stunning too from devices such as having the doctor pass from scene to scene before the camera, only we can see him. That was eerie and so atmospheric. Also the Pilot episode with the terrifying scenes of first Mom and then Jessica burning on the ceiling – almost 'religious' in symbolism.

Not to mention Constance (the woman in white) roaming the bridge, appearing and disappearing in the back seat of the car.

6) SFX. The jerky head movements indicating the demonic possession or presence in the person. Especially stunning when Dean sees the same movement in Sam (**3.16**) when he can see the "faces" of demons and it ain't a pretty sight. Not to forget the hell hounds ripping into Dean.

Contrasted with the poignant scenes of the Winchester deaths: Dad in a cold, antiseptic hospital room; where Dean would've met his Maker – or the other fellow! Also Dean being electrocuted when chasing the monster in a freezing dark cellar. (**1.12**) Not a pleasant way to go.

The drab landscape when Sam is stabbed and dies, huddled by Dean in his arms. Laid out on the bed, again in less than picturesque – but dank surroundings. As with Dean, but this time the position is reversed and he's in Sam's arms. (**3.16**)

All this adding to the reality of the show and their lives – how bleak, empty and alone life is when you're one of the good guys chasing demons so humanity may survive longer. Ungrateful humans can rest at night and reap the rewards of their, sometimes, worthless existence.

5) Playing God an area only touched upon or hinted at. A show about evil; fighting demons will inevitably have its critics. Hinted at in **1.12 Faith** when the ritual saves Dean from certain death. Dean only believing in the bad because he's seen it and fought it.

Also not covered, or covered in depth, are the moral implications of taking one life to save another; as each one is just as sacred and special as another. Do people who condone this ritual killing have the right to deem one less worthy of living than another. When Dean was saved instead of Layla, he sees the injustice in this, it's unfair, with Sam telling him it would've happened to someone else, so why not him.

Just as Sam was willing to sacrifice Nancy in **3.12 Jus in Bello** – to save thirty, can he really defend killing one to save another few, if eventually they're all going to end up the same way: as demon fodder. Or that his way and Ruby's way would've been better since they wound up dead at the end anyway. Can this ever be justification for thinking and wanting to do such an act to begin with.

Dr Benton in **3.15 Time Is On My Side** taking human lives, killing to prolong his eternal life. The question why he did this to begin with wasn't asked, other than alchemy. Was he experimenting on himself. What good is eternal life if you end up in the state he was in – Dean said it perfectly when he said he didn't want to become him. Then needing to kill to survive like him.

These are stories and plotlines that make you want to think outside the box. Well, they did to me. That beneath every episode lies a sub-text relevant to life today. Other than the usual themes of family, friendship, kinship, fighting unimaginable horrors. Plots that show it isn't just black and white battling the unthinkable evil that exists. It's about making decisions, right, wrong; dealing with those consequences and yes, inevitably playing God. Such as Dean's split second decision to save Sam, resulting him being fuel for the deal now.

All showing the series is not just about eye-candy to many, but about challenging our perceptions of good, evil, family; about how we live our lives and make each moment count. *Supernatural* lives up to the spirit of the emotions contained within it and not just the spirit of the script - the written word. There's far more than spirits! (oops). **3.10 Dream a Little Dream, 2.20 What Is and What Should Never Be**, the alternate reality of these – adding elements of sci-fi (well they would be deemed this if the show was purely sci-fi) but making it appear like an everday occurrence.

It's more realistic because they fight entities people believe do exist, even if there aren't that many firm believers.

4) Non-Religious Affiliation What's great about *Supernatural* is that it doesn't distinguish, discriminate or is derogatory towards one religion or another. Each belief is treated equally and given the same amount of consideration as any other. Christianity, Islam, Hinduism, Zoroastrians, Buddhism, and so on, each has its own purpose in being mentioned in the way Sam and Dean encounter them or elements from each belief; in research; looking for possible answers; identifying the threat; which is good to see in a show instead of playing one religion or belief against the other. Which is extremely refreshing in this day and age. Even though you'd think that since it's about demons, spirits, monsters, religion would be alluded to in every episode, but it's not.

The only discrimination we encounter here is between demons; how to handle them and Dean forever calling everyone a bitch! – practically all and sundry to him.

Aside from the boy's and other characters' own personal beliefs, like Dean not believing at first and Sam praying. There's a balance which isn't too "in your face" or too non-chalent.

3) Unfriendly Demons

The ultimate evil – though they met many along the way; was Yellow Eyes at first. The grand master in the scheme of things with his plan to make the 'special children' special by adding his own blood into their chemistry, or should that be biology; conferring upon them their powers so he could find a leader; i.e. Sam. Someone he always intended to be the best possible.

His connection with Mom. But we don't discover his name was Azazel until later, but Dad obviously knew beforehand who he was. But as in season 3, we don't get an explanation as to who or what he was. (see season 4). His plan was put into disarray or went awry when Dean finally shot him with the colt. Leaving the way open for another to take his place, viz, Lilith. Hell bent on destroying the brothers, any and every way possible. Especially with Dean falling right into her hands when he bargains his soul to save Sam. Almost as if she had planned the entire scenario, but didn't. Taking care of one brother, she thought to make way for the next to be dealt with. Although not bargaining on her powers not working on Sam!

Demons were ruthless, cruel, scary and wanted to devour and destroy the whole of humankind (and anything that got in their way including other demons) with some classic demon salting and burning action to keep the boys hand in, making it more of a fairer fight than an outright large scale defeat.

2) Uneasy Ally Ruby (Katie Cassidy's portrayal)

Ruby is someone who wants to help Sam and Dean on their demon-hunting quest to find Lilith and end Dean's deal. She takes no prisoners, jumps straight to the point – telling it like it is. Often finding reason and sometimes truth, where Sam and Dean just won't listen or look. Though at times, she too was wrong. Like walking out on them during the siege in **3.12 Jus In Bello**, when they refused to implement her plan of sacrificing the virgin, which included sacrificing herself too, but then they didn't listen to her, so she did the same to them.

Ruby was a witch who sold her soul and escaped when Devil's Gate was opened. No telling how long she was waiting to get out, but as soon as she did, it was straight to the prodigal son, Sam, so to speak, pledging allegiance to him. Since as she told Dean, she remembers her humanity whereas the other demons don't. Thus she wants to train Sam to be the best at what he does and who he's meant to be. Seems like she had no other significant connections except for Sam and eventually Dean.

Ruby's a blend of fun humour and can give as good as she gets, especially from Dean and his bitch jibes. Best episodes, though she wasn't featured much include: **3.4 Sin City** when she helped with the colt; told Sam about mom's friends because Sam wasn't looking for the connection and probably **3.9 Malleus Malificorum** when she saved Dean and we found out she was a witch.

How can you fail to like someone who was on our Winchester's side and whose trusty knife came in so handy!

1) Sam and Dean

So cool watching Sam and Dean and their banter, jokes, family feuding – strong friendship, underlying their brotherly bond. They are so geeky together, at times, yes Dean, even you and watching them play off each other makes the show what it is.

Dean gets things done and Sam makes him think about his actions up until season 3 – that is when Sam was all hands-on and Dean had to restrain him. When Sam and Dean argue, we know it's because they care about one another more than anything else. They care about what the other thinks, does and the way they respond to each others character traits, keeping each other in check.

Meaning of *Supernatural* Names

Dean as a first name means *Valley* in Old English.

Sam in Hebrew, means *to hear; like the sun; heard God; asked God.*

John is Hebrew for *God's Grace.* In Greek, it means, *God is good.*

Mary in Hebrew, French and Irish means: *bitter.* In Latin it means: *Virgin, merciful, ransom.*

Jessica in Hebrew means *wealthy one.*

Ruby means a French gem.

Bela in Hungarian means *bright.* In Hawaiian means *pretty* and in Hebrew means *Destruction.* So it was apt for her.

Jared means *Strong* in English and in Hebrew means *Descending*. Jared was popular as a name in the late 1970's and early 1980's, Jared was born in 1982.

Jensen has no meaning as a first name, but as a last name in Norwegian, Danish and North German, is from the name *Jens* a shortened form of *Johannes* (akin to John.) It is the most popular surname in Denmark.

Some Supernatural Terms and Definitions

Myth: "Public dreams which, like private dreams, emerge from the unconscious mind." Freud.

Myth: "a fiction – something which is untrue." "A sacred story from the past" such as the origins of the universe. A myth is different to a legend or a folktale. Myths can be religious. Folktale is fiction: "a symbolic way of presenting the different means by which human beings cope with the world in which they live."

A legend is a past story or tale about a subject which has its origins in history. All about places, people and occurrences. A bit like a noun is a person, place or thing.

We Start With Family – We End With Family.

"We keep sacrificing ourselves" "We are family"

Family – the catch-all of this show. Hence my introductory line. What wouldn't families do for each other: including the ultimate sacrifice – the love of a father for his son, a brother for a brother. Even a mother for a son.

The opening of *Supernatural* was all about family too. A young family with their sons – one barely a baby setting the tone for the rest of the first season and for two and three to follow. What should have been a joyous time to cherish and raise and grow together as a loving family became an unthinkable nightmare. In seconds a mother cruelly taken because she knew too much and a family torn to pieces by demonic intervention.

Setting the scene for a lone father to raise his sons the only way he knew how – to become hunters, stand on their own two feet and drumming into them the importance of family. A sentiment not shared by Sam, at first. He had to leave for fear of drowning in family and not having his own life, but only hunting, which comes round full circle and nicely echoed by Sam, quite ironically even, in the season 3 finale, "We are family."

599

Along the way, the road travelled as a family, only having each other left. The last remaining Winchesters, carrying on family tradition and the family name. As Dean says, "family business." (**1.2 Wendigo.**)

In sharp contrast to other families and family units uncovered by along the way. Constance in the pilot episode, in comparison to their own Mom, a mother who killed her children out of jealousy and is now haunted by her children, to whom she can never return home. Children having revenge on their mother.

Sam and Dean are not normal, far from it, but they could've been so different and raised so different as Sam says in season 1, they were lucky, don't know how they'd survived and grown or become if Dad became a drunk and couldn't care less about them. Dean who recalls Dad as being perfect, until his promise leads him to call Dad an obsessive bastard who didn't know what he was doing laying so much on his shoulders.

The family in **1.2** Hayley ready to find her brother and going to any length to do so, who Dean is to echo Dean in season 2 and already has now in his search to find Dad, even recruiting Sam in the process.

Demon Dean in season 3 saying Dean wore Dad's jacket, has his car and everything else is Dean just trying to emulate Dad; even to the point of self-sacrifice when selling his soul to save Sam. Which can also be called a family looking out for one another. If not for Dad, would Dean have even thought of doing this. The unanswerable question put to him in **2.8**. Not something that can be shrugged off but finally shown by him to be true. Making him no lesser than Dad in his actions to save Sam.

Sam showing a strong affinity towards Max in **1.14** both sharing psychic abilities but their lives being different because of nurture as opposed to nature and becoming a cold-blooded killer cast adrift in separate ways.

1.3 an episode about family secrets and all families have these, when Sam hears Dean telling Lucas about Mom, feelings and thoughts he's never shared with him, not because he was keeping secrets, but just felt he couldn't. Dean, at this point, we find is not a caring, sharing sort of a person. He cares, yes, but about family and doing the right thing – hunting. But Dean bared his soul in more ways than one, in sacrifing for Sam, he shared. Or did this finally make him a man and give him the purpose and meaning he so desperately craved, spending a lifetime living in Dad's shadow, in Sam's shadow; finally stamping his mark and showing once and for all how much Sam really means to him.

But the Winchesters you could be forgiven for thinking and rightly so, have more than a skeleton or two in their family closet – no pun intended.

As far as families go, Sam and Dean were far from dysfunctional, out of the ordinary, strange, even freaky, but not homicidal to the point of hunting innocents for sport, as The Benders. **(1.15)**.

Though Dean went off half-cocked at times, he was always 'doing the right thing' and only killing demons for the greater good. He always had Sam as his safety valve; who always questioned whether a particular action or reaction was necessary, before an uncorrectable, irreversible mistake was made by either of them.

The Benders were the far from average family, but psychos. An example of parental upbringing gone wrong; or even as Dean puts it, in not so many words – as a result of in-breeding. Their hunting was for sport. Sam and Dean hunt evil and not humans. But an episode of Superatural, where this family wasn't possessed; but a crude example of evil. Again an example of nature and nurture gone bad, to the point of evolving in a cruel and sadistic way.

Another example of familial love, was that between husband and wife, a wife's devotion to her husband, to the extent where she hasn't realized she's no longer in the world of the living and can't pass over until she comes to terms with her fate, once more showing all actions have consequences that doing the right thing can sometimes come back to haunt, to bite you (like it did Dean).

The twins in **2.5** who don't know of each other's existence until the bad one kills off all the people who know they were brothers. Since their mother didn't tell them. Again showing how different or normal Sam and Dean's lives were in comparison to them and how easily their destinies could have been turned around.

Can this be any different from the father who protects his daughter, in refusing to let her go, now that she's a woman. **(3.5)** There for her now, when it's too late to be the dutiful and caring father, who wasn't there when she needed him as a child. When she reached out for him and he wasn't there. Grabbing his attention now, the only way she knows how by killing through the very stories he's mistakenly reading to her to keep her and her memory alive. Stories he should've read to her as a little girl. Trying to capture time when it's too far gone for both of them.

Not many family-orientated episodes in season 3, mostly about finding an 'out' for Dean wondering if Sam becomes evil, but that was long forgotten after **3.4 Sin City**. Less mythology of the arc and more concentration on introducing new characters.

In reality, though brothers, Sam and Dean are opposing points of a compass. Both hunters: Dean sees his hunting as probably not the best thing that happened to him – or was it (aside from Mom, Dad, dying, not being normal) but his hunting makes up for a lot of shortcomings in his life. He could see it as a blessing almost, people, (unwittingly and unknowingly count on them) to protect them from the presence of evil around them. He's their hero and yet no one hardly knows about him (just as well.) Sam wishes he could just have a normal life – especially in season 1; echoed in season 2 – until he convinces himself this is what Dad wanted from him too, after all.

Dean does things on the spur of the moment, gut reaction; instinct. Sam was more of the thinker, always questioning; demanding reasons for their actions and before killing. The turning point was season 3, notice now he's more of the reactionary – the action man. Eagerly wanting to play his part – that's the evolution in his character, perhaps some would say – where he becomes more of a man. (Some, but not Dean, to him, Sam's still a girl!) Sam feels the need to now become dangerous himself and be like Dean. Due to this change in Sam, we feel sorry for him even more than we did for them both when we first met up with them in the pilot and in season 2. When we learnt of their heartaches and tragedies haunting their young lives. Sorry because he has to take the lead now: the reins in the uncertainty of Dean's future; that he now will lose the very person who was always there for him, for that life force, his guiding light will be snuffed out so abruptly and cruelly. Everytime he kills a demon is he taking out his revenge on them for Dean's "fate". (Little realizing he is about to become the very thing they both abhor.)

As well as feeling sorry for ourselves as we agonize with Sam over Dean's future (or lack of) {as "one who dies so young"}. Sam wears a mask, disguising his true feelings and actions in season 3 (learnt from Dean most likely), especially the first half, until he finally tells Dean the real reason for his violent streak! Something I wrote about the episode was even aired in the UK.

They even dress differently: Dean and his leather jacket (so macho!) and Sam in his cotton, khaki, plaid shirts.

Sam is thrown back into Dean's world – something where Dean was always a part of. But Sam looked up to Dean because he was big brother and the only family he had growing up who was around 24/7, because he was different and had to be the one who was the more stabilizing influence in his life. The one, who never left him, though Sam eventually, did the walking out on Dean and Dad.

Foreshadowing in *Supernatural*

The concept of Foreshadowing. A literary term/device used by authors, writers, in books, plots and TV shows, as a way of dropping massive hints to enable the reader/viewer, to foretell what may happen at a later date in the tale, plot-line, such as future plot outcomes.

The most significant and apparent way in which this foreshadowing takes place, is to mention something by chance – which appears to be nothing more than a passing or throw-away comment – but crops up again in the plot/story later on.

The most famous literary example of this is the idea of *Chekov's Loaded Gun*: "When a certain setting is described, *it is mentioned that a loaded gun is hanging on the wall. Much later on, this is taken off the wall and fired.*" To make reference to the story/plot, such a device will be mentioned over and over. This was used by Anton Chekov in *Uncle Vanya*. Chekov was of the thought that anything mentioned in a story has to be utilized later on, otherwise there's no point in introducing it to begin with. "If in the first act you have hung a pistol on the wall, then in the following one it should be fired. Otherwise don't put it there." Preceding *Uncle Vanya* the device was found in the *Three Apples Story* of *One Thousand and One Nights*.

This device has also been used in many TV shows and movies, including *Babylon 5, What Lies Beneath, Harry Potter* books and all three *CSI* shows. In this, a witness, a do-gooder, will be introduced in the opening act, who ends up playing a crucial role at the end, most usually as a suspect or the one who committed the crime.

Supernatural is adept at this. Maybe the various themes were thought up in the show in advance. I'm going to write about foreshadowing and references to Sam and Dean's life in this context too; as there was a lot going on throughout the four seasons which was all related and we should have seen it coming. - eg, in **2.1** – Dad tells Dean that Sam will go darkside. Thereafter several references are made to this throughout season 2 and later seasons. It's not glaringly obvious but there are other subtle hints too.

4.10, Ruby tells Sam he's getting flabby and he says he's not doing that again. A subtle – if not obvious reference that Sam has been drinking demon blood – even before Dean returned from hell. Of course, if I had a one track mind, perhaps it could mean "getting it on " with her again. But don't think so! So this was Sam's way of carrying on after Dean. Ruby: "Yeah Sam, take a bite and suck, it'll help you diet! Make you big and strong too." So obviously she turned Sam as soon as Dean was out of the picture. So if she knew Dean was potentially the one going to break the first seal, why was Sam being 'force-fed' demon blood. Always the demons intention that Sam would break the final seal or aid Dean into doing it – by killing Lilith. Also throughout season 3 hints about her death, weren't merely referring to getting Dean out of his contract, but by not doing so, it would've meant he'd end up in hell anyway.

Plenty of food for thought here (no pun – again.) Dean always had a higher purpose in his life, a greater calling. Always clutched from Death's grip, literally, such as Tessa in **2.1**. In **1.12** Reverend Le Grange's comments about Dean having another purpose. Then in **2.1** (as said) Dean was going to be "saved" and sent to a better place. Ripped from Tessa by Dad's deal. Driving not only himself, but Dean also into something darker and a far from better place.

Then Tessa showing up again in **4.15** – warning Dean he's being used and not for the right reasons either, by the angels. (Again Tessa in **2.1**, foreshadowing, as a device used again later in **4.15**. Also here Dean telling everyone they're destined for a better place and going to one – after where he's just been. Not to mention, Tessa in **2.1**, once more telling him he was going somewhere better to find peace.)

In **2.13** Dean talks of angels/God – not believing again in either and angels turning up in season 4. Mom believing in them and he ends up rescued/saved by one. Castiel, Uriel, Anna and Zachariah, all introduced as angels, which were mentioned before. It was a show about demons, so angels had to crop up eventually. Dean being liked to the angel Michael. He is the one who has to stop him. (See above for my reference to St Michael in early Christianity, he holds a spear to attack Lucifer.)

Lilith in season 3, having Dean's contract and how it all became a part of Yellow Eyes' greater plan in the season 4 finale and the significance of why he wanted a special child, started in the pilot and concluded in the season 4 finale.

Another question: how could Dad have been the one to break the first seal – when Dad was never meant to have stayed in the picture (**4.3**) – other than fathering children for Yellow Eyes. Dad was the hunter by circumstance, by chance, in his quest to avenge Mom. Whereas Dean and Sam were true hunters by birth. It was always in their blood. Dean was the one destined for a more prolific and prophetic, almost, life than just hunting.

More foreshadowing in **3.10** when 'Demon' Dean practically predicted Dean was going to turn dark…"this is what you're gonna become…" Yes in 30/40 years he did become that. He turned "dark" and had to resort to torture to survive. Effectively, seeming to become inhuman, inhumane, losing his humanity and becoming 'demonesque' in the process – at least possessing demon-like qualities.

As Sam was never truly a 'demon'. Dean never truly lost his humanity as Ruby told him he would in **3.9**. So much for her stating she recalled her humanity and that's why she wanted to help them. Once a demon, always a demon. Also answering the question why she lay low from the angels and now come to think of it, Uriel's distaste of Ruby in **4.10** looked so false, since they both wanted the same thing. Begging the question, wasn't it more personal for Ruby, she wanted to prove her worth to Lilith! That she was the best. Egotistical much!

Alastair teaching Dean to torture, then the tables (torture table ha!) being turned on him. The student now using what he was taught on his teacher. Dean was always the one destined for bigger things. Though each time this was recanted by him, claiming not to believe in destiny/fate.

Sam's possession in **2.14** was just a forerunner of what was to occur to him in his destiny. Throughout season 2 was the theme of his becoming evil and Dean having to end it for him. Yet by the time season 3 entered, he was no longer thinking of that, but of saving Dean. Whereas having lost Dean in season 3's end was a turning point for him in his life. No longer around to "protect" Sam or save him, Sam was open to other influences – demonic; viz Ruby. Which led to his downward spiral. Deserting Bobby in favour of Ruby and his quest for avenging Dean, by chasing Lilith. Much in the same way as Dad (in season 1.) Which Dean nicely comments on in **4.19,** that Sam's more like Dad than he ever was. Also in the sense that Dad didn't break in hell, but Dean did. A loaded comment from Dean there!

Sam's "demon" potential from season 2 realized in season 4, but not in the way we envisaged. The foreshadowing came in the sense of, yes he became "dark" but this was a result of his demon blood – his addiction to it and grand deceit by Ruby. (Foreshadowed in season 3 when she says she's a demon and that means manipulator, as well as the fallen angel on his shoulder comment, a reference to Lucifer.) The difference being, he mistakenly believed he was genuinely helping to save the world. But in the way of not being overshadowed by big brother. Sam went about it in the wrong manner. Even though he's convinced he's doing it all for Dean.

Some Phrases Which Could Be Termed "Deanisms"

By "Deanisms" I mean as referring to him, or said by him, as made up by me.

Too many cooks spoil the broth – but then Dean Winchester will eat anything.

Great minds think alike, unless you're Dean Winchester.

A fool and his colt are soon parted: Dean Winchester.

Selling your soul should come with Caveat emptor (i.e. let the buyer beware) especially if the seller is Dean Winchester. (My favourite.)

All you can eat. Dean Winchester's motto.

All you can sleep with. Dean Winchester's motto.

All you can sleep with barring demons and dead things. Dean Winchester's motto.

When in doubt, play the joker: Dean Winchester.

Eat lots, party lots, hunt lots. Dean Winchester.

When avoiding a confrontation with Sam, claim the Fifth! Dean Winchester.

This was an idea I came up with for an episode written after season 1 began airing here in the UK in February 2006.

In Dreams

Seattle, Washington State

A reporter, Nadia, on a story finds clues to certain strange occurrences in small towns across the country, after first following up on a case of what she thinks is identity fraud/ theft, every time they use a 'stolen' credit card they leave behind a paper trail; which Sam and Dean don't really think about. (How easy they are to locate by demons etc.) This time Dean uses one of his 'fake' credit cards in one of her colleague's names. She finds the happenings in some way to be connected to Sam and Dean so she follows their trail hoping to get some insights and a big scoop but has also been chasing her own leads and stories on unexplained events and finds something leading or linking to the brothers, e.g., perhaps Dean's obit from the shape shifter episode, **Skin** (for continuity.)

Dean's suffers severe head trauma after an accident and ends up in a coma at the same hospital where her fiancé is a doctor.

When she finds out Dean's there, hoping to get some insight she sneaks into his room and touches his hand and has an episode or a vision (but she's not psychic.) She can see inside his head – everything he's seeing right now. Dean seems to know her, has feelings of familiarity when he was little – but her face isn't familiar – other than now they've never met. This is all taking place inside his head, or wherever coma patients tend "to be." But Dean appears to be running away from something or someone that's after him; an unknown, crazed figure who wants to possess him and/or his soul.

In one scene Dean walks into a bar and orders a Bloody Mary instead of his usual beer. That'd be a blast from the past! (and a bit of a joke.)

She doesn't really know Dean but sees his plight and fear and tells the 'person,' "You can't have him, he's mine!" The 'person' wants to take him over to the dark side now that he's in a vulnerable state and can't fight back, in the physical sense. Sometimes the only thing you can try to do is to discover evil before it takes hold and at some point the only thing you can do is just run and you can't fight it all the time. It's a sense of susceptibility, of human shortcomings in us all.

She thinks maybe Dean's ring is the mysterious link or portal to his mind – what's causing her to reach out to him as a sort of channel, she tells him to fight, which includes facing up to his own fears/feelings, resentment; why he didn't have a normal childhood, life, hatred. Who can he hate? Their mother for "leaving" them – not her fault what happened to her, or was it? Why their father isn't here? Why their family was targeted instead of anyone else? - Were their parents to blame – any pact with dark forces...? Always having to make sacrifices for the greater good, help others at the expense of their own lives.

But their mother didn't really abandon them/him; he's lucky in some ways since he actually knew her and had her for longer than Sam did.

Nadia tells Dean to resist – he's been fighting/battling forever, so maybe he feels tired now and has no fight left in him. Perhaps it's his turn now to do all the abandoning: the giving up and letting down. What does she care anyway; she's just a stranger. Maybe she's known about them too, all her life and been there all the time. Heard of reincarnation, believe in it? Just as many cultures and some religions have some sort of belief in it. Reincarnation of the body, soul and spirit.

Sam finds her in the room and breaks the connection – he doesn't know what she's doing. When she tells him about the ring he doesn't listen and when he tries to hold Dean's ring nothing happens and he doesn't feel the bond or has any visions or even ends up on the same "plane" as Dean.

A little on the mythology of jewellery as Sam discovers: well, certain jewellery does have religious connotations, like the cross, lucky charms, talisman like the St Christopher etc. As well as amulets and in different cultures it symbolizes different things, e.g. necklaces with an eye on them (I have one) which is meant to ward off evil and protect against the evil eye.

Also wearing a talisman is an old practice to protect and fulfill certain desires hailing from around the world. Ancients believed in the power of the living, sun and the evil eye and evil spirit. Anything silver sparkles and reflects the evil eye of the jealous. This is true in places around the world and cultures such as in Albania, Morocco, and Africa.

Nadia's fiancé, Dr E.Vale, is a surgeon and is responsible for organ donations and harvesting organs. Sam finds this out after running a search on her on the Net and sees them talking at the hospital, because he doesn't know if she's genuine or out to get them both. He cross-references her name and her husband's and finds the hospital records on patient's receiving donor organs outweighs the actual number of organs available – so where are they coming from, are they obtained/harvested illegally.

A bit on the ethics of harvesting organs: are the patients alive when they're removed – or are the organs "conjured up". What about the afterlife – when does the soul leave the body after death? Are the people really dead when this happens, do they feel anything, we don't know for certain. Some cultures believe the body must be intact for the soul to pass into heaven – needs to be buried whole in readiness of the afterlife – hence don't believe in donating organs. What price ethics as all morality goes out the window when you're trying to save someone you love, which is why the doctor is how he is. No conscience, perhaps she didn't know him after all or when he changed into what he is now. How many others did he purport to save or was she the only one?

Is he a version of the mad scientist – a case for creating Frankenstein's monster – the doctor is a modern day version of Dr Frankenstein. His channelling of souls to the dark side must be stopped. Why Dean's soul in particular as opposed to Sam's? Dean's purely good, strives to fight evil. Sam would've traded places with Dean in a heartbeat and especially if it also may have involved communication with their mother.

Monsters are an everyday part of their lives and have to deal with inner demons too. Humanity is one of the greatest monsters have to deal with – in trying to do good, end up creating the biggest demons in the process, as in Frankenstein's monster. "The road to hell is paved with good intentions" as Sam, mentions. As for Frankenstein, wasn't his creator the true monster?

Dean's really into his movies, therefore a reference to *Bride of Frankenstein*, alluding to Nadia, as a passing comment as she tries to help him in his dreams (doesn't know how right he is!) As well as *Arsenic & Old Lace* especially the reference to Raymond Massey looking like Boris Karloff all the time in the movie. Perhaps ironically since Dr E. Vale may have a basement lab too hidden away somewhere. Could be on some campus where he sometimes teaches. (Was watching movies a pre requisite for demon hunting.)

Sam also finds out that Nadia had a liver transplant from an unknown donor – but she knows things about them that only someone from their family would know, someone like their mother. Dean's special hopes, dreams, what he really wanted to do when he was older, like maybe calling him 'Deano' when he was little as only their mother did, or his favourite book being *Peter Pan* as a boy which only she would know and not even their father does. When Sam confronts Nadia, she recalls having an operation but not the details.

Humanity gone haywire, screwed up attempts to play God? No, maybe science has a far greater, evil purpose. Not so much playing God as in becoming god, believing human beings have more power than God. Science has its basis in fact not myth, whereas legends are based on fact. Human beings unleash the greatest monsters when striving for perfection, in the doctor's muddled up version or vision of love – he attempted to create life out of evil. Is he inherently bad for doing this?

Who is chasing Dean in his comatose state? Also question whether it's a state of dreams or nightmares – could he be fighting his inner demons? What of the evil inside of us all, knowing us and following us around, have inner conflicts and that's why we have a conscience but not everyone uses it or uses it for good.

The effect on Sam: feelings of guilt, helplessness, why he didn't see this coming (like he did with Jessica). He couldn't get through to Dean by touching his ring – perhaps because he can't; or Dean may be blocking him out. Maybe Sam has to face up to the truth/situation that this time he can't rescue his brother (like they save other people) and that task must fall on someone else, that sometimes you have to believe and trust in another person, a complete stranger, and that doing the right thing comes at a price.

Nadia begs Dean to come back to the world of the living – the world needs him and so does Sam. She tells him to "dare to dream" and it's not too late for him to at least make one of his dreams come true and do what he wants for once, that he can't be a soldier and blatantly follow orders forever: this anger will consume him, he has to let it go. He needs some 'me' time. She asks Dean about his innocence and childhood (perhaps some continuity from the season 1 episode **Something Wicked** when he said he wished Sam still had his innocence) what about Dean's innocence or doesn't he matter. He's been through more, seen more, remembers more and put up with more than Sam. Only he wasn't as lucky as Sam; he didn't get his way out so he didn't have a chance to live his dream, and needs to have the chance to do that now.

Sam notices she has a tattoo on her hand, the right palm she touched Dean's ring with. She tells him it's a henna tattoo she got when she found out she was sick, her fiancé suggested it to her and it also gave her hope back then, although it fades with time, she redoes it to remind her of fragility of life. [Henna brings new life to the sick when applied as a talisman of hope and love and can also be used to protect and for good luck. The henna plant heals and brings together the body's spirit and culture. If henna's used for healing why can't it be a gateway to the soul.]

Why does Dean feel strongly for her? Aside from her pretty face. A bit of a plot twist: - no donor was found but although her fiancé wasn't involved in her actual surgery, he was responsible for harvesting a donor organ for her. Dean sees Nadia as their mother or feels he does. Could the liver belong to their mother? But their mother was burned – only ashes, if any, so no organs could have been harvested. But not dealing with ordinary organ donation/harvesting. Beyond anything modern medicine or science can explain. If her fiancé cloned the liver, how did he get hold of a tissue sample to begin with? Does it involve more than a pact with the 'devil'? As a doctor, he's preying on despair, helplessness and lust for life – but he'd say he's just giving hope where there is none. The effect on her, re her fiancé, can she stand by him, he saved her life, ulterior motives: the price he's paying now for what he did, not evil man really or was he?

As Dean comes out of his coma, the doctor falls into one.

As for romantic gestures maybe Dean when he wakes, he tells Sam of this "hot chick" he dreamt about. He thinks he imagined her or were they destined to meet. Sam says even in his dreams/coma he still thinks of hotties! Before Dean actually sees her, Sam tells him about her motherly connection – kind of putting a dampener on things romantically. Although technically she's not even related or anything or is their mother. Maybe she and Dean can be future kindred spirits when he grows up a bit more re Peter Pan!

When they eventually meet, she tells Dean not to get the tattoo he's always wanted.

Song, couldn't decide between **Evanescence** *Bring Me To Life (a bit clichéd.) or My Immortal.* Well, *Bring Me To Life* is more appropriate for the context of what happens here.

The story explained or parts of it.

A bit of a cruel, ironic, sad episode, in that in a way it couldn't be their mother (or her organ) since in reality it just couldn't happen. There's no way to make sense of it by applying logic and common sense, the more you try, the more non-sensical it becomes. Also even though their mother was no more in episode 1.9, after fighting the Poltergeist – it's good to know she may be around in some form or another; still watching out for them. Perhaps there's a potential for pathos in Dean's dreams? Do coma patients dream? Also if you want the question of who was chasing Dean in his dreams answered, it was his own fears and emotions: anything ranging from pent up anger to jealousy, but I think it's better left unsaid so it could have been anything or even the doctor himself which would be more apt.

An episode where they don't have to work side-by-side leaving them more as individuals and where fire isn't used, as the blooming critics

611

keep harping on about! But we don't care fire cleanses after all!!! Not all questions will be answered. Have they gained an ally of sorts in Nadia and in their lone quest against evil.

A liver transplant was a good organ to use as it's essential for life and liver is from the Latin too.

Written 5 June 2006

References

The Physics of Angels Matthew Fox and Rupert Shadrake Harpercollins (1996)

The Many Faces of Angels Harvey Humann De Vorss (1988)

The Coming of Angels Geoffrey Hodson (1932)

Working With Angels. Fairies and Nature Spirts William Bloom Piatkus (1998)

Fallen Angels and Spirts of the Dark Robert Masello The Berkley Publishing Group.

health@Ukmetro.co.uk 9 July 2007

Rootwork: Using the Folk Magick of Black America for Love, Money and Success. Tayannah Lee McQuillan. (2003) Fireside.

Tales, Rumours, Gossip. Gail de Vos. Englewood Libraries Unltd (1996)

Urban Legends Jan Harold Brunvald *The San Diego Union Tribune* 28 April 1988

M Whales I Believe In You: Myth and Ritual Subdued Indiana Folklore. 11: 5-34

Illusions Induced By the Self-reflected Image. Luis A Schwartz & Stenton Pfjeld (1968). Journal of Neurons & Mental Disease. 146: 277-84.

A Complete Guide to Fairies and Magical Beings. Cassandra Eason Piatkus (2001).

Legends of America.com

Teachings Through the Mediumship of Lilian Bailey Complied by Marjorie Aarons. Regency Press Ltd.

Msnbc.com

BBC and Ethics

Handbook of Texas online

Cult Times March 2007

Tv Zone #224, 226, 227,

Starburst Issue 357

SFX 148 October 2006

Cult Times June 2006

Cult Times May 2006

TV Zone #206, 161

SFX April 2006 #142

The Works August 2006

Dreamwatch Issue 146

Shivers #126

SFX March 2009

Xpose 44. Issue 101
Cinescope 2005-10/08 *A Supernatural Number*
Digital Spy 2008
Starlog November 2008
TV Guide.com 29 May 2008
TVGuide.com 14 January 2009
TVGuide.com 24 March 2009
TVGuide.com November 19 2008
Zap2it.com 10th October 2007
Parade.com 14 January 2009
Post Gazette Now Pittsburg Post Gazette TV Editor Rob Owen.
October 22 2008.
The CW Source 30 December 2008
Zap2it.com
The Ledger.com
Buddy TV
Buddy TV 17 May 2007
TV Guide 19 November 2008
Eclipse Magazine Exclusive Jim Beaver Interview 3 May 2009
TV Guide 4 May 2009
TV Guide Magazine 4 May 2009
LA Times Hero Complex 13 May 2009
Coventry Telegraph.net June 2009
TV Guide Magazine 30 June 2006
http://www.prarieghosts.com/winchester.html
http://www.the shadowlands.net
www.myrtleplantation.com
Legends, Myths and Superstitions http://www.istranet.org/
www.chalicecentre.net/samhain.htm
Encyclopedia Mythica http://www.pantheon.org
http://www.bigfootmuseum.com/
http://www.supernaturaltv.com/
http://www.thefivepillars.org/
www.hell.houndslair.com
www.redbullsoapbox.ca/therace.php
purplesage.org.uk
E!Online. TV Guide.
mediaBlvd.magazine
Supernatural Anatomy. Christina Radish 8 May 2006.
Supernatural Creation Convention. Dallas 8 June 2008.
Jim Beaver: A Super Natural Guy Tania Hussain newsvine.com
ihateclowns.net.clown2.com

http://news.nationalgeographic.com/news/2005/10/103_051013_at
colony.html

Riverfront Times {Missouri] Best of St Louis 26 September 2001

The Legal Intelligencer: McDonald's Found Negligent in Statue Accident 27 October 1995

Aztec Motives in La Llorona. Southern Folklore Quarterly (1965)
Robert A Barakat

Natural History Book VIII Chapter 30 Pliny

Paranormality.com

Gurlyand's Reminiscences of AP Chekov in Teatr; iskusstvo 1904. No28 11 July P521

Myth From The Ice Age to Mickey Mouse by Robert W Brockway.

Folklore, Myth and Legends: A World Perspective by Donna Rosenberg.

About the Author

Writing – one of my first loves, though I studied something completely different: the law, as opposed to lore! Just like our Sammy.

I always wanted to write about something which had real people, real passion and super dudes! Supernatural has it all and a great theme of family underlying the entire series. Something that's so important to me and I'm sure to you, as well as to us all.

So here's my passion for the show realized. Hope you enjoy as much as I did writing...

Lightning Source UK Ltd.
Milton Keynes UK
05 December 2009

147114UK00001B/66/P